LOVE'S COMMAND

A fire was blazing brightly and there were fur rugs in front of the fireplace and he undressed me and I writhed naked on the fur, my body warmed by the heat of the flames and the heat inside. He stood over me, hands on hips, legs spread wide, looking down at me. He smiled slowly, his eyelids drooping slightly over eyes now filled with desire, dark, smouldering blue eyes that feasted on me as I stretched before the flames, sliding on soft fur. The smile grew taut on his lips and his handsome face was tense, the skin stretched tightly across broad cheek-bones. He kneeled over me, a knee on either side of my thighs, hands pinioning my wrists to the fur. He loomed there over me, his face inches from my own, lips parting. Slowly, slowly, he lowered his head, eyes shining brightly and telling me of his love, his need.

WHEN LOVE COMMANDS

JENNIFER WILDE

AVON
PUBLISHERS OF BARD, CAMELOT, DISCUS AND FLARE BOOKS

AVON BOOKS
A division of
The Hearst Corporation
1790 Broadway
New York, New York 10019

Copyright © 1984 by Tom Huff
Published by arrangement with the author
Library of Congress Catalog Card Number: 84-90907
ISBN: 0-380-89193-X

First Avon Printing, October, 1984

AVON TRADEMARK REG. U. S. PAT. OFF. AND IN OTHER COUNTRIES, MARCA REGISTRADA, HECHO EN U. S. A.

Printed in the U. S. A

WFH 10 9 8 7 6 5 4 3 2 1

To my agent,
JAY ACTON,
who makes it all
happen

WHEN LOVE COMMANDS

BOOK ONE

Chapter One

OGILVY CRACKED THE WHIP AND THE HORSES picked up speed and the coach rumbled noisily through the village, passing the inn, putting more and more distance between me and the man I had almost allowed to ruin my life. He hadn't wanted to marry me, no, for the illegitimate daughter of a barmaid and an English aristocrat wasn't good enough for him. He had found the perfect wife as soon as he returned to England, a lovely, gentle creature born to be mistress of a great estate like Hawkehouse, but he still wanted me. He wanted me desperately. I was in his blood, he assured me, would always be, and he couldn't live without me. He had instructed me to stay at the inn until he could make *other arrangements,* and he fully expected me to do just that. I could never be his wife, but I could be his mistress. He seemed to think that honor enough. How little he knew me.

The village was behind us now. The horses were moving at a brisk gallop. As the coach sped over the potted, uneven road, as the gorgeous English countryside seemed to flash past the windows in a kaleidoscope of shifting shapes and colors, I realized that he had never known me at all. I had been his obsession, as he had been mine, but it was over now. Derek Hawke was ensconced in his ancient manor house with his genteel new wife, awaiting the birth of his first child, and I felt no pain at all. I felt only relief. I was free at last, and a glorious elation stirred inside as I realized that the tormenting, all-consuming love I had had for

3

him had been dead a long time. I knew now that it had died the first moment I laid eyes on Jeremy Bond.

The elation swelled as I thought of him, and the love seemed to sing, filling me with music felt, not heard, a silent symphony of happiness so lovely I could scarcely endure it. Jeremy. Jeremy. He was waiting for me, and in a matter of hours I would be in London and in his arms and a new life would begin for both of us. What a fool I had been. What a bloody, blundering fool! I had almost cast this happiness aside. I had almost destroyed the best thing that had ever happened to me. "One day," he had informed me, "you will see what is in your own heart," but I had ignored him. Blindly I had turned away from him and come to join the man I stubbornly believed I still loved.

I knew at last what was in my own heart, and that knowledge filled me with a glow of happiness as radiant as sunlight, as inebriating as the finest wine. The music seemed to surge inside. Never, never had I known such elation. Never had I felt this way about any man, and how I had fought it. How I had struggled, spatting with him constantly, holding myself aloof, refusing to give in to those delicious sensations his mere presence caused within me. I denied them. I shut them off. I held back until that starblazing night in Texas when we finally . . . Horse hooves pounded, harness jangled, wheels spun in a noisy clatter, and I saw again that handsome, beloved face. I saw those vivid blue eyes so full of merriment and life, those broad, flat cheekbones, skin taut across them, that slightly twisted nose and the wide pink mouth with its amiable yet disturbingly sensual curve. I saw the rich, unruly brown hair, one glossy wave invariably flopping across his brow. How I longed to run my fingers through that hair and look into those eyes and trace the curve of that full lower lip with my fingertips.

Soon, I told myself. Soon! This very evening I would be with him and we would experience anew that shattering splendor we had known months ago in the wilds of Texas. Convinced that Derek Hawke was dead, I had finally given myself to Jeremy there under the Texas sky, and all the stars blazing above seemed to explode inside me as I experienced an ecstasy few women ever know. Jeremy Bond was a remarkable lover, and lover was the proper word. He had not taken me, as Derek had done. He had made love to me, expressing his love in the age-old way and with a tender fury that seemed to shred the senses. I remembered, and my body ached for him as the coach bowled along the road, as green trees and pale blue sky and low gray stone walls streaked past the windows.

There had been just the one time. Jeremy Bond had risked his life for me on more than one occasion, had rescued me from a fate indeed worse than death, yet for months I had denied him, denied the love I felt with ever-mounting intensity. After that night of splendor—the very next morning, in fact—I had learned that Derek Hawke was still alive. Jeremy Bond had known all along, had kept it from me, and I had been unable to forgive what I considered his base treachery. He had insisted on accompanying me to England, assuring me all the while that I loved him, not Derek, but that was something I had had to find out for myself.

I had left Jeremy in London. I had hired this private coach and journeyed to the country to be reunited with the man I still considered the great love of my life. I had seen him. I had met his gracious, pregnant wife. I had expected my world to come crashing down. It hadn't. A great feeling of relief swept over me as I realized that I no longer loved the man who had wooed me with promises he never intended to keep. Derek Hawke was the past. Jeremy Bond was the future, and that future was going to be wildly exhilarating. I could hardly wait to begin.

Moving to the opposite seat, getting on my knees, I opened the tiny window behind the driver's seat. I had already removed my elaborate black velvet hat with its spray of bronze, pale mauve and royal blue feathers, and thick waves of coppery red hair spilled across my cheek as I held the knob of the window and called to the driver.

"Can't you go any faster, Ogilvy!"

Ogilvy turned to peer down at my face, his strong hands firmly gripping the reins. "Can't push 'em much harder, Miss Danver!" he shouted. "They're in a fair sweat already!"

"Hurry," I pleaded. "Do hurry!"

"We'll reach London 'fore nightfall, don't you fret!"

I closed the window. We passed over a particularly nasty rut and the coach shook violently and I was thrown backward, landing on the opposite seat in a tangle of skirts, thoroughly crushing the hat with its wide black brim, its turquoise bow and spray of feathers. Pulling it from under me, I muttered an irritated *Damn!* and then smiled at myself. I wouldn't be needing fashionable hats in Texas, and the sumptuous wardrobe in the trunks strapped on top of the coach would be wasted, too. Silks, satins and velvets would have to be replaced by sturdier, more sensible garments.

Sitting up, I brushed the heavy waves from my face and adjusted the tight black velvet bodice of my gown, smoothing down the satin skirt with its narrow stripes of black, bronze, mauve, royal blue and turquoise. It was one of Lucille's finest creations, especially selected for my reunion with Derek Hawke. The gown was hopelessly rumpled now, but I would never wear it again. Another rueful smile played on my lips. Oh, yes, I had put on my finest raiment for Derek, expecting to be welcomed with open arms, leaving the man I really loved in the yard of the inn with an expression on his face that I would never forget. That sober composure, those eyes filled with tender emotions that belied the pain . . . How could I have hurt him so?

The horse hooves were pounding furiously now. The coach rocked alarmingly, threatening to fall apart. A whip cracked. We seemed to pick up even more speed, and I had to grip the edge of the seat to avoid being tossed about. I hardly noticed the discomfort, thinking of that sad departure. Had it been only this morning? It seemed an eternity ago that he had smiled that tender smile and touched my cheek.

"I hope you'll be happy, Jeremy," I had said.

"I haven't given up," he replied.

"What do you mean?"

"I still hope you'll come to your senses."

"And—see what is in my own heart?"

"That's right. I haven't given up. I'll be here at The White Hart for a week. I'll be hoping. I'll be waiting, Marietta."

He knew me so much better than I knew myself, and he wouldn't be at all surprised when the coach pulled into the yard of The White Hart and I climbed out. He would cock his head to one side and arch one of those slanting brows and make some jaunty quip. I would snap back at him and assume my haughtiest expression and we would have a rousing scrap as he followed me up to my room. The mood would be light. No sullen looks, no recriminations from Jeremy Bond, that wasn't his style. No tears of remorse, no plea of forgiveness from me. I would be cool and dignified, proud as ever, and he would tease and I would scold and he would finally crush me to him and we would tumble onto the bed for a rowdy celebration of joyous love.

I would never leave him again. Never. We would return to Texas together—that vast, wild, exciting land—and he would buy the spread of land adjacent to Randolph's property and build me a house like Em's with thick white adobe walls and red tile roof and patios with fountains. Randy had asked him to become his partner, and Jeremy was eager to settle down after years of adventure. They would breed horses and have the finest stables in Texas, and Em and I would sit on the shady veranda and sip cool drinks and gossip. We had been through so much together, Em and I. Marriage to Randolph had brought her happiness at last, and she adored her rough-hewn, good-natured husband, although they were undoubtedly still bickering and spatting with glee.

How I longed to see Em again, Randolph, too. Hurley

and Marshall and young Chris were at the rancho as well, working for Randy. I would be surrounded by friends, and I would be the wife of Mr. Jeremy Bond. Oh yes, the scamp was going to marry me before we left London. I intended to see to it. He loved me every bit as much as I loved him, I was certain of that, but with a man as mercurial, as jaunty and carefree as Mr. Bond, the ties had best be legal. He was altogether too attractive for his own good, irresistible to the ladies, and fidelity was not a notable male virtue. The rogue was going to marry me, yes, and if he even thought of straying he'd pay dearly.

The coach bounced, banging noisily. The landscape was flying past now, a blur of color. Horse hooves thundered on the road, pounding, pounding, pounding. Ogilvy had certainly taken my plea to heart, I thought as the whip cracked in the air again. Each passing moment brought me closer and closer to Jeremy Bond, and as I thought of our passionate reunion my elation grew. Was it possible to be drunk with joy? Indeed it was, and I gloried in the sensation. Soon. Soon. Those strong arms would crush me to him and those lips would fasten over mine and I would revel in his warmth, his weight, the virile smell of his body. I would catch my fingers up in that thick, silken brown hair and moan beneath him as . . .

The coach seemed to explode beneath me. I was thrown against the window as the shrill, shrieking noise of splintering wood filled the air. In that same instant I heard Ogilvy yell and the horses neigh in panic, and I was slammed onto the ceiling, banged to the floor, knocking my head against the side of the door just before it flew open and flew away and windows shattered and wood crumpled up like paper in the hand of a savage giant. The same giant picked the coach up and tossed it into the air and it rolled over and over and I was flung in every direction like a rag doll, banging, slamming, hurled finally into a black void pierced with pain.

Thick, heavy blackness, layers and layers smothering me but never smothering the pain. I struggled against it and firm hands held me down and I couldn't move. The black grew darker, darker, black so black it was a solid entity holding me captive, heavy, pressing down on me . . . I saw the slave block in Carolina and Derek Hawke and Jeff Rawlins, and Derek was driving me to his plantation and then I was on the Natchez Trace with Jeff, Derek had brutally cast me aside, and Jeff was tearing up my Article of Indenture and we were dancing together at Rawlins' Place in New Orleans, music swirling, chandeliers glittering in the candlelight . . . I was wearing a golden gown and Derek came in and then he and Jeff were holding pistols, firing at each other, and I moaned and shook my head violently . . . No, no, no, I couldn't go through that again, I couldn't endure the pain of Jeff's death . . . Those same firm hands continued to hold me down, and far, far away, on the other side of the void, I heard a gentle voice speaking to me, words I could barely hear, couldn't understand.

The blackness began to melt, liquid now, and I was floating and the sharp, savage pain had dissolved into a throbbing ache, my whole body aching as Helmut Schnieder laughed and locked me up in Roseclay as the flames leaped and I knew I was going to be burned alive . . . Helmut laughing, laughing, then crying out as Jack and Derek arrived . . . New Orleans again, Derek moody, sullen, telling me we would be married as soon as we reached England and Jeremy there in the courtyard with moonlight gilding the bougainvillaea and the fountain splashing quietly as he held me in his arms . . . "Love me, Marietta," he murmured and my lashes were wet with tears . . . "I do," I whispered. "I do. Oh, Jeremy, I do. You must know that."

I cringed as the pirate ship loomed on the horizon, sharp against the black as Em and Corrie and I were herded onto boats along with the other girls, moving over a black, black sea that engulfed us . . . I was drowning, drowning, desperately trying to swim to the surface, but something restrained me, held me down firmly, speaking to me again from the other side of the void . . . Nicholas Lyon, Red

Nick, holding me down, his harsh, handsome face over mine, those cold blue eyes ablaze with anger and love, that heavy copper red wave slanting across his brow . . . "I'll do anything you ask," I pleaded, "only don't kill Corrie. I will never try to escape again, I promise, I promise." . . . Corrie wielding a pair of scissors as his hands squeezed my throat, choking the life out of me as the island blazed . . . Nicholas on the floor, the scissors sticking out of him, blood pouring.

"Thank God!" I cried. "Oh, thank God!"

Jeremy holding me in his arms, soothing me, his hand stroking my brow and brushing the damp locks from my cheek. If only I could see him clearly through the mist . . . Misty black, no longer liquid, soft black clouds that swirled all around me, carrying me along with them, the ache dull now, no longer throbbing, not really unpleasant . . . Jeremy teasing me as we moved through the swampland and holding me tight after the Karankawa attack, Corrie dead, tears spilling over my lashes again, and then we were moving over the fields and the cottonwood trees rustled in the breeze and the Texas sky was filled with stars that blazed silver-blue . . . He loved me. How could I ever have doubted it? Oh, Jeremy, please forgive me, forgive me . . . He was in the courtyard of the inn and I was climbing into the coach to go back to Derek and that look in Jeremy's eyes was too painful to behold. How could I have hurt you so much? How could I? I love you. I love you. Forgive me, my darling Jeremy. Forgive me.

The pain returned, worse than ever, and I cried out as someone pressed and probed, moving my limbs . . . Demons in the darkness, tormenting me with hands strong and efficient . . . "Hold on, luv," Em said firmly. "You're coming to Texas to see me, remember? Any son of a bitch who tries to stop you has me to answer to." . . . I saw her pert face, a scattering of light golden tan freckles across her cheekbones, those greenish brown eyes full of wisdom beyond her years, her glossy chestnut curls burnished by firelight . . . I could see the firelight through the clouds, burning low there behind the screen, and Em was sitting beside my bed, a book in her hand. The clouds swirled anew, billowing away, a lighter black now, now ash gray, lighter still, evaporating completely as I moaned and lifted heavy lids to gaze at my friend.

Her hair was a rich golden brown, the color of dark honey, neatly brushed in long, sleek waves that fell to her shoulders. But Em . . . Em had chestnut locks that tumbled in wild disarray. Her eyes had changed, too, no longer hazel, violet-blue now, beautiful eyes full of secrets. They had an unusual new shape, slightly slanted, almost oriental, thick black lashes long and curling. She had high, sculpted cheekbones and a patrician nose and soft pink lips that curved sadly at the corners. Her violet velvet gown was adorned with delicate silver flowers in appliqué, a rich, exotic garment with exquisite gray fur at bodice and hem. A heavy cloak of the same fur was draped over the chair behind her in lavish folds that gleamed silver-gray in the light. I stared at her, frowning.

"Em?" I whispered.

The girl put her book aside and smiled at me, a gentle, demure smile, but the lips were still sad, the eyes still full of secrets. She couldn't be more than seventeen years old, and she certainly wasn't English. Italian, perhaps? French? Those high cheekbones and vaguely slanted eyes brought to mind savage Mongol hordes and barbaric splendor. Hair shining in the firelight, eyes dark and secretive, she was astonishingly beautiful in her exotic gown, and I wasn't at all sure she wasn't an apparition. I blinked my eyes and tried to sit up. The girl rose, velvet rustling, the fur cloak spilling to the floor in a silver-gray heap.

"You must stay still," she said gently.

She spoke in French, and while her voice was soft and mellifluous, there was an accent I couldn't identify. She sprinkled cologne onto a thin white linen handkerchief and began to bathe my temples and brow. My eyelids grew heavy again, and my body was one solid ache. The girl murmured something I couldn't understand, tenderly brushing a damp coppery red lock from my temple. The room filled with a softly diffused golden haze that gradually turned to gray, and I was floating again, slowly sinking into layers of gray that grew darker, darker, soft and black now, enveloping me.

"—better I think," the lovely voice said. "She's been sleeping."

"Has she said anything?"

The second voice was deep, guttural. They spoke in French, and the voices seemed to come from a great distance, muted, blurred.

"She keeps calling for someone named Jeremy."

"We've been here five days already. We must move on to London."

"The doctor said she must rest. There are no broken bones, but he isn't certain there are no internal injuries. We can't just aban—"

I moaned, swimming in darkness, fighting to reach the surface, and after a long, long while I saw a dazzling silver sunburst shimmering high above me. I struggled to reach it, moving up, up, up, sinking again, moaning as swirling black waves claimed me.

I opened my eyes. I sat up, wincing as I did. My head was clear. I was ravenously hungry. Cold silver rays of sunlight streamed through the windows, and I saw the whitewashed walls and the low, beamed ceiling and marble fireplace and realized I must be in an inn. Shabby but exquisite rugs were scattered over the polished hardwood floor, faded pink and blue flowers against a worn gray background, and a lovely bouquet of blue and purple flowers sat on the bedside table in a thick white bowl. The fire had gone out. The room was chilly. I was wearing a white silk nightgown inset with rows of fragile lace, the garment damp, clinging to my body. I had never seen it before.

The door opened. The girl I had dreamed about earlier came into the room, but she was no apparition now. She was quite real, as lovely and exotic as I had dreamed, now wearing a gown of golden brown brocade embroidered with flowers in shimmering gold thread. Bodice, hem and the wrists of the long, tight sleeves were trimmed with glossy golden brown fur. She was carrying a tray, and those lovely eyes widened with surprise when she saw me sitting up.

"Are you feeling better?" she inquired in careful English.

"I—I don't know—"

"I have very little English. Do you speak French?"

I nodded, shivering. The girl frowned.

"Oh, dear," she exclaimed in French. "The fire has gone out. The room is freezing. You'll catch a chill."

Setting the tray down on the table beside the bowl of flowers, she hurried over to the fireplace. Although she was clearly aristocratic and had undoubtedly been pampered by servants all her life, she lighted the fire with a brisk efficiency, poking the logs until the flames were crackling nicely. I shivered, pulling the linen sheets and heavy lilac counterpane around me, resting my shoulders against the soft pillows.

"Where—where am I?" I asked.

My voice sounded weak and faint. Although my French was fluent, it took a great effort to enunciate the words properly. The girl turned, putting the heavy iron poker aside.

"You're in an inn," she replied. "My uncle and I found you after—just after the accident. We heard the noise of the crash, heard the driver yell. There was a curve in the road, so we couldn't see, and by the time our coach got there the—your coach was demolished and the horses were running wild. They had broken free, and one—one of them—"

The girl hesitated, eyes dark as she remembered. "One of them was badly injured," she continued. "My uncle had to shoot it. The other three were unharmed."

"Ogilvy?" I whispered.

"The driver was apparently thrown clear of the wreckage. He—his neck was broken. He is dead. I—I'm very sorry, miss."

My eyes were damp. I could feel salty tears. The girl came over to me and took my hand, giving it a reassuring squeeze.

"You must try to—try not to be upset," she said quietly.

"It was my fault. I—I wanted him to hurry. I wanted to—"

I couldn't finish the sentence. The girl squeezed my hand again and then wiped my tears away. I sighed, trying to control the emotions welling up inside.

"You had been thrown out of the coach. You were crumpled up on the road, completely unconscious. Two of our servants put you into our coach, and then we brought you here and summoned a doctor. He examined you carefully and determined that there were no broken bones. He—he wasn't sure there weren't other injuries. He's been returning to check on you every day."

"How—how long have I been here?"

"A week and three days," she replied. "I've been taking care of you, giving you soup and water, changing your bedclothes. I—my uncle wanted to go on to London, but I felt responsible for you."

"A week—I've been here a week and three days?"

"You've been very, very ill, miss. The doctor made his last call yesterday. There are no internal injuries, he said, there would have been symptoms by this time, but he told us you would need several more days of rest before it would be safe for you to travel."

"I—"

Jeremy. Jeremy. I had to get to Jeremy. Panic rose and I tried to get out of bed. Scalding waves of pain swept over me. My whole body seemed to shriek in agony. The girl eased me back down onto the pillows, alarmed, and I sobbed as the black clouds enveloped me once more. I heard her speaking to me, her voice a distant murmur, and I felt something warm passing my lips, gliding down my throat. I knew nothing more for a very long time.

The pigeon was cooing loudly, a pleasant, peaceful sound that gradually penetrated the silent darkness. I stirred, and when I opened my eyes I could see him prancing on the window sill outside, pearl gray feathers silver in the early morning light. I knew that it was morning, but I had no idea how many days might have passed. My body felt stiff and ached all over, but the ache was dull and there was no real pain, not even when I sat up and swung my legs over the side of the bed. I stood up. A wave of dizziness besieged me. I gripped the headboard, closing my eyes as a million tiny needles seemed to jab my skin.

The sensation passed. My head cleared. I was weak, but all the clouds had gone and I was fully conscious for the first time. Catching sight of myself in the mirror across the room, I saw that I was wearing another unfamiliar night-gown, pale yellow satin. My face was drawn, my coppery red hair damp with perspiration, and the sapphire blue eyes that gazed back at me were dark and disturbed. Staggering across the room, I found a large white bowl and a pitcher of water behind a worn blue silk screen. I washed my face as the sunlight grew stronger. The pigeon had flown away, but geese were honking in the courtyard below and a cow was lowing in a nearby pasture. As I emptied the last of the water into a bowl, I heard a vehicle of some sort entering the courtyard, harness jangling, wheels crunching noisily over the cobbles.

"You're out of bed," the girl said.

I turned. I hadn't heard her come into the room. She was wearing white this morning, the thin, long-sleeved frock embroidered with delicate blue and violet flowers, a blue satin sash around her slender waist. Although exquisite, the garment was foreign in style, unlike any I had ever seen. Her golden brown hair was neatly brushed, her young face lovely yet disturbed.

"We must get you back into bed," she said. "You shouldn't be—"

"I'm fine," I told her. My voice was crisper than I had intended it to be.

"Perhaps—perhaps it's all right. The doctor said you should build your strength."

"Is this your nightgown?"

She nodded. "I'm smaller than you, not so tall, but the nightgowns are cut very full in Russia."

"You're Russian?"

"I'm Lucie Orlov. My uncle is Count Gregory Orlov."

"I'm Marietta Danver," I said.

" 'Marietta'—it is a beautiful name. It suits you."

"Why—thank you."

"Do you remember the conversation we had a few days ago, Miss Danver?"

"I—I vaguely remember you telling me about the—the accident. Ogilvy was killed and I was thrown clear and—" I paused, the horror sweeping over me again.

"You were very fortunate," Lucie said. "The coach was demolished. You could have been killed yourself. We were very concerned about you. I'm so relieved to see you feeling better. I imagine you would like something to eat."

"I would also like a bath and some proper clothes."

"Your trunks are downstairs," she told me. "My uncle sent two of the men back for them after we brought you here to the inn. I'll have them brought up. Would you like to eat before or after your bath?"

"I'll eat after."

The girl nodded again and left the room. A few minutes later the door was opened and two strapping men came in carrying my trunks. Both wore high black boots and odd-looking blue velvet livery with thick silver braid at shoulders and chest, and both were well over six feet tall, the towering black fur hats atop their heads making them seem even taller. Faces broad-boned and sullen, muscles bulging beneath the velvet, they set the trunks down beneath the window and left the room without so much as glancing at me. I put another log on the fire and jabbed at it with the poker, still weak but feeling more clear-headed by the minute.

The two men returned a short while later carrying a

large white porcelain tub adorned with strangely shaped
orange and blue flowers. The colors were extremely vivid,
each petal outlined in gold. The tub obviously did not belong to the innkeeper, I thought, watching them set it
down behind the shabby blue silk screen. Three more men,
identically attired, as powerfully built and sullen, came
with towels, soap, sponge and pails of water. None of them
looked at me as the tub was filled, as towels, soap and
sponge were arranged on the table. One of them said something in a rumbling, guttural voice, speaking in Russian,
and then they all trooped out, the last one shutting the
door.

Count Orlov must be extremely wealthy to have so
many servants, I mused as I removed the yellow satin
nightgown. The gold outlining the brilliant blue and
orange flowers on the tub was genuine, I noted, and as I
stepped into the water I was amazed to find that the inside
of the tub was completely covered with the same gold gilt.
The water was hot, steaming lightly as I sank down into it.
The pale lilac soap was scented with an elusive fragrance
vaguely suggestive of faded violets, and the lather it made
was thick and creamy, like liquid silk caressing my skin. I
reveled in the luxury of it, washing myself thoroughly,
washing my hair as well, relaxing as the warmth and wet-
ness soothed my body.

There were bruises on my arms and thighs, a rather bad
bruise on my right ankle, but they had all begun to fade,
pale tannish mauve, barely visible. I was fortunate indeed
to have survived the accident without sustaining any
major injuries, even more fortunate to have been discovered so soon by Orlov and his niece. Who were they? The
name *Orlov* seemed curiously familiar. I felt certain that I
had heard it before. I frowned, thinking hard. Orlov?
Orlov? It seemed to be linked in memory with some terrible act of political violence. A revolution? An assassina-
tion? It was all extremely vague. I might well be mistaken.

Running my fingers through my hair, creating a rich,
silky crown of lather, I concentrated on the present. I had

been here a week and three days when I first awakened and talked with Lucie Orlov, and I had no way of telling how many days had passed since. Jeremy had planned to remain in London for only a week, and then he was leaving for America. I faced that fact as calmly as possible. Something might have come up, of course. He might not have been able to book passage so soon. He might still be at The White Hart, but if he wasn't, if he had already departed, I would follow him on the next boat. There was no need to panic. All my money had been deposited in the Bank of England, Jeremy had gone to Threadneedle Street himself to open the account, and I was a wealthy woman. I would book passage and perhaps . . . perhaps I would even get to America before he did.

The sound of the door opening interrupted my thoughts. I was startled to see three of the Orlov servants entering, two of them carrying more water, the third with an embroidered blue silk robe over his arm. I cried out in protest as they came around the screen, great muscular giants, faces expressionless as they surrounded the tub. Arms folded over my bosom, I ordered them to leave in a trembling voice. They paid no attention. One of them took hold of my wrist and pulled me to my feet. I tried to pull free, terrified now, but the brute held me firmly as I slipped and splashed and almost fell back into the water. He had dark blond hair and sullen brown eyes and broad, flat cheekbones, and his wide mouth curled savagely as he spoke harshly in Russian, squeezing my wrist even tighter.

I cried out as the other two men doused me with the buckets of warm water, rinsing me thoroughly, and then the blond brute hauled me out of the tub and set me on my feet. Shivering, shaken, I stood there in horror as he took up one of the enormous towels and began to dry me off. His eyes were flat and expressionless as he massaged my back and buttocks with the fluffy cloth, moving around to dry my shoulders, bosom, and stomach. Kneeling, he dried my thighs and calves, lifting first one foot, then the other, bunching the towel up around my toes. Finished, he stood up and moved away as his companion handed me the gorgeous blue silk robe. I pulled it on, my hands trembling as I tied the sash around my waist.

The blond bellowed something in Russian. The other two men nodded and picked up the tub, one at each end. Filled as it was with water, it had to be tremendously heavy, but they showed no signs of strain, carrying it from the room without spilling a single drop. The blond gave me a surly look, picked up the damp towel and followed the others into the hall. I slammed the door behind him and locked it, outraged now, fuming as I found another towel and rubbed my hair briskly. I was still furious when, twenty minutes later, I unlocked the door to let Lucie in. My hair was dry, brushed to a gleaming coppery sheen, and I was wearing a bronze-and-cream-striped linen frock I had taken from one of the trunks, the full skirt belling over half a dozen thin cream linen underskirts. When she saw the expression on my face, the girl's eyes clouded with apprehension.

"You—your cheeks are terribly pink. Is something wrong?"

"Something certainly is! I was in the middle of my bath when three of your servants came barging in here. They jerked me out of the tub and poured water all over me and then—then one of them dried me off!"

Lucie saw no reason whatsoever for my alarm. "The job wasn't done satisfactorily?" she inquired.

"Satisfactorily!"

"Vladimir doesn't know his own strength. Sometimes he rubs too hard when he's using the towel. I've scolded him about it time and again. I fear my uncle will have to discipline him."

"You mean—" I was momentarily speechless. "You mean they—they attend you in the bath, too?"

"But of course," she replied, puzzled by my dismay, and then understanding dawned. "Oh, I see, your English customs are perhaps different. You are peculiarly—what is the word?—modest, I believe."

"You might say that!" I snapped.

"But there is no need to be," she explained. "They are merely servants."

That seemed to explain everything as far as she was concerned. These Russians were certainly different, I reflected, trying my best to see the humor of the situation. Lucie smiled a shy smile and stepped back to gaze admiringly at my frock, taking in the long, tight sleeves, the plunging neckline and form-fitting bodice and swelling skirt.

"It's lovely," she remarked. "So simple and yet so elegant. The clothes I have are so—so Russian."

"Your frock is beautiful."

"It is—how you say?—old-fashioned? I hope to buy a complete new wardrobe before I return to Russia. Perhaps you will help me select it."

"I'd be delighted to, if there's time."

"Please do not be embarrassed, but I must tell you—you are perhaps the most beautiful woman I have ever seen." She extended the compliment hesitantly, eyes lowered demurely, but I could tell it was completely sincere. "Your hair is like copper fire, so rich and lustrous, your features are those of a grand English lady without—without the haughty coldness, and your eyes are so blue, like sapphires."

"You're very kind, Lucie."

"I would so like to be beautiful myself," she confessed.

"But you are!" I protested.

Lucie shook her head sadly. "I have the features of my Mongolian ancestors who invaded Russia centuries ago, the slanted eyes, the too-high cheekbones. In Russia this is a sign of low caste. My father was a grand aristocrat, but my mother—"

She cut herself short and smiled another shy smile that begged me to forgive her for being so personal. At that moment the door opened and the blond giant entered, standing aside as four other servants trooped in bearing an ebony table inlaid with gold and mother-of-pearl, two chairs, a silver tray, linen cloth and napkins. I watched in some dismay as the table was set with gorgeous white porcelain china banded with rich royal blue and etched with gold, as silver tableware was placed and heavy silver lids removed to reveal a dazzling display of food. When the task was completed, the four men stood at attention and the blond, Vladimir, inspected their work with a savage expression. Satisfied, he growled an order in Russian and all five men marched out.

I stared at the plate of fluffy yellow eggs, the kippered herring and thick slices of juicy ham, the steamed mushrooms and crisp curls of bacon. There was a plate of scones, a rack of thin toast, jars of thick, clotted cream, strawberry preserves and marmalade, the *pièce de résistance* a mound of glistening pearl gray caviar surrounded by finely chopped onion and minced boiled egg. Lucie looked at the array with barely concealed disgust.

"Our chef prepared this meal for you," she explained. "He travels with us, of course. The English food is abominable, no?"

"Usually," I agreed.

"The innkeeper explained eggs and herring and that barbarous ham would be appropriate for an English lady. You really consume such fare?"

"I intend to eat every bite."

"I will have a bit of caviar to keep you company. Vladimir will bring the coffee in a short while."

We sat down at the table and Lucie sighed as I heaped my plate with eggs and bacon and ham. She watched me eat with disbelief, as though I were committing an act of defilement, but that didn't deter me. I had rarely been so hungry, and as Lucie indifferently nibbled a piece of toast spread with caviar, I ate heartily. Vladimir appeared with an ornate silver pot and filled two delicate cups with dark, aromatic coffee. I piled clotted cream and strawberry preserves on a scone as he left the room.

"How many servants do you *have?*" I asked.

"Only twenty with us," she confessed. "My uncle believes one should travel in simple style. There are just four coaches besides our carriage, carrying the barest minimum of necessities."

"Like the bath tub and this table and china," I said.

"And rugs and linens and such. When one travels one must expect—what is it my uncle says?—Spartan conditions. Are you feeling better, Miss Danver?"

"I'm feeling much better."

"Your color is good. You were so pale and drawn."

"You've been so terribly kind to me," I said. "I'm afraid I don't know how to thank you."

"It was my pleasure," Lucie replied. "It was so nice to—how you say?—to have an excuse to break our journey for a while. For months and months we travel, travel, travel. It is very wearying."

"Is your uncle on some sort of diplomatic mission?" I asked.

She shook her head, a faraway look in her eyes. "No, he travels to forget."

I longed to ask her what she meant by that, but instinct told me the question would not be welcomed. I took a sip of coffee. Lucie gazed into her cup as though it might contain the answer to some ever-elusive mystery.

"My uncle is a—a very restless man," she said. "We travel and travel and always he is eager to move on to the next place. We will stay in London a month, and then, at last, we will return to Russia. He feels it is time."

"You've been away long?"

"Two years," she said. "I was fifteen when we left."

"You must miss your country a great deal."

"I do not miss the old life," she said, lowering her eyes. "Sometimes I think of it, and—and I know it was a fortunate day indeed when my uncle took notice of me and decided to allow me to travel with him."

"He must love you very much."

"Yes," she said.

The word seemed to contain a multitude of meanings. As I finished my coffee, Lucie informed me that Count Orlov had departed for London three days ago in order to attend to some business and rent a fine mansion for them to occupy. He would be returning in two days' time.

"He—he was worried about leaving me behind, but I insisted he go on without me. I didn't want to leave you, you see. I couldn't leave and—and never know if you were really all right. I told my uncle I would be quite safe with Vladimir and the others to watch after me. He finally agreed, but he—he does not like to have me out of his sight."

Lucie fell silent as the muscular servants returned to remove table, chairs and dishes. She moved to the window, gazing pensively down at the courtyard. When the servants had gone, she turned to me with soulful eyes that made her seem painfully vulnerable and even younger than her seventeen years.

"When we return to London, you shall accompany us. We would be very pleased to have you as our guest."

"That would be nice, Lucie. Ordinarily I would love to, but—"

"I so long to have a friend, you see," she continued. "I have never had one before. I feel—I feel you are already a friend, Miss Danver."

"I feel the same way, Lucie," I said gently. "You have been wonderful to me, and I appreciate everything you've done. I—I'm afraid I will not be able to travel with you, though, nor will I be able to be your guest."

"No?" Her disappointment was moving indeed. "But why?" she asked.

"Because I'm leaving for London at once," I told her.

Chapter Two

VLADIMIR STOOD AT THE FOOT OF THE STAIRS, watching with sullen brown eyes as I made my descent. The ceiling was low, the hall narrow, and the Russian seemed even larger in the close confines. The high black boots and silver-trimmed blue livery had been augmented with a short, heavy blue cape trimmed with sleek black fur that matched the fur of his tall hat, and there was a pistol in his belt, a lethal-looking knife in a scabbard strapped to his thigh. He was an incongruous sight here in this peaceful country inn. His wide lips curled as I reached the lower steps. I might have been some despised animal, a creature scarcely worth his disdain. Muttering a guttural remark in Russian, he took hold of my arm and helped me down the final step.

"Let go of me," I said icily.

I tried to pull away. The hand tightened its grip on my arm, causing me to wince, and I was forced to totter along beside him as he marched briskly toward the front room. Flushed, angry, I could barely contain myself as he led me outside. Geese honked, scattering across the cobbles, and a flaxen-haired youth standing beside a wagon of hay gawked in open mouthed amazement as the enormous Russian let go of me and growled an order I could not understand. I rubbed my arm, certain there would be new bruises.

"Gemminy!" the youth cried. "Ain't never seen nothin' like *'im* a-fore! Whut is 'e, lady?"

"A brute!" I snapped.

"Look at that knife! An' ain't that a *gun* in 'is belt? 'E plannin' to go 'untin?"

"I've no idea."

Vladimir scowled, looking even more menacing in the brilliant midmorning sunlight that bathed the yard. He stood stiffly at attention, waiting for his mistress to appear. The hostler stepped from the stables. The youth grabbed his pitchfork and began to toss hay into the open stalls. A mud-splattered coach pulled into the yard and a solemn, gray-haired man in black climbed out, followed by two tittering young women in billowy muslin frocks. The man gave them a curt nod, and they scurried inside, tittering all the more as they moved past the immobile Russian in his exotic attire. A groom came to see to the horses as the driver removed the bags from the top of the coach under the suspicious eye of the dour gent in black.

The sun-washed cobbles, the honking geese, the smells of hay and manure and ancient wood—it was all very rustic and charming, but I was as out of place in these surroundings as Lucie and her entourage. Two days had passed since I had made my announcement to her after the lavish breakfast. I had been much weaker than I thought, so weak, in fact, that I had had to go back to bed almost immediately. Containing my impatience, I had realized that the only sensible thing for me to do was to wait for Lucie's uncle to return and drive to London with them, trying to build my strength in the meantime. I had rested and eaten solid, nourishing food and, accompanied by Lucie, had taken several short walks, Vladimir and Ivan following close behind.

Vladimir clicked his heels together as Lucie stepped outside, Ivan behind her. She looked much younger in a simple white frock with a yellow silk sash. Vladimir scowled and barked an order in Russian. Ivan hurried back into the inn, returning a few moments later with a heavy white cloak lined with yellow silk. Vladimir settled it over Lucie's shoulders and fastened it at her throat, and the girl scarcely noticed, accepting the ministrations of her servants as a matter of course.

"Is beautiful today, no?" she said. "So much sunlight. We take another walk."

"You don't have to come with me, Lucie."

"Oh no, you mustn't go alone. What if you felt faint?"

"I'm feeling much, much stronger," I told her.

"You have the lovely color. Such a beautiful English complexion. A soft pink flush to the cheeks. The English are a handsome race, I think, but they lack the fire."

We had left the yard and started down the tree-lined lane that led past open fields and pastures. Ivan and Vladimir walked ten paces behind us, two stalwart, scowling watchdogs. Lucie seemed unaware of them, but I was acutely conscious of those boots crunching heavily, those eyes boring into my back. Lucie's servants still did not trust me. Orlov had left her in their charge, and they were fiercely suspicious of anyone who came too close. I had the feeling any one of them would have slit my throat without giving it a second thought.

"The passion," she said. "The moods. The—how you say?—the temperament. The English men are—they lack the hot blood, the fire. They are cool and—everything is contained, held back."

"Not all of them are like that, I assure you."

"This man of yours, he is different?"

"He's very different."

"He has the temperament?" she inquired.

"Enough for ten men."

"Do you love him, Marietta?"

I nodded, brushing a speck of dry leaf from my full blue skirt. I loved Jeremy Bond, yes. The love was a lively, vital, mercurial force, contradictory and full of contrasts. It was elating and exasperating, gentle and furious, and frustrating. I longed to humble myself before him and beg his forgiveness, longed to stroke his cheek and kiss his eyelids and tenderly hold him to me. I longed, too, to pull his hair and kick his shin and pound his chest with my fists. I longed to fight with him, to be defeated, to savor the after math in his arms. Jeremy Bond inspired emotions I had never felt for any man, marvelous, conflicting emotions denied far too long.

"He is handsome?" Lucie asked.

"Yes and no. His nose is slightly twisted and his eyes are—so blue, so audacious. His hair is thick and brown and one wave flops over his brow, always unruly. He has a merry look, but there is ruthlessness, too, an undeniable hardness."

"The body?"

"The body is—superb," I replied.

"He makes love well?"

The question was utterly ingenuous, asked in that soft, mellifluous voice with its curious accent, yet I was taken aback nevertheless. What did this gentle, innocent young creature know of . . . of bodies and such?

"He—makes love very well," I said.

"You are most fortunate then, I think."

"I think so, too."

And the world's greatest fool to have almost lost him, I added to myself. Sunlight seeped through the canopy of limbs that met overhead, and bright golden flecks danced at our feet as we walked slowly down the peaceful country lane. I thought of Jeremy, impatient, so impatient to be off to London, to be with him. If he had left, as was likely, I would follow him. I would find him, and I would hold him fast and never, never let the scamp out of my sight again.

"One is enough?" Lucie asked.

"I don't understand."

"One man? One is enough?"

"This one is."

"Our Empress, she has many men. They are—the men are like bonbons, and she gobbles them up. She has the strong appetite, and she adores the variety. There is always one man beside her—Potemkin now—but there are always others to—how you say?—to fill in."

"Your Empress Catherine is a—remarkable woman."

"Yes. Very strong. Very forceful. Beautiful, too."

"You've met her?" I asked.

"I saw her once when she visited my—my father's estate. She was wearing the white velvet gown bejeweled with sapphires and pearls. There were pearls at her throat, too, and diamonds and sapphires. Her cloak was ermine with the glossy black tails gleaming in the white. Her hair was powdered. My father led her into the ballroom, and I stood outside in the darkness, gazing through the French windows for hours. I was six then, maybe eight."

Lucie sighed. She fell silent, gazing around her with pensive violet-blue eyes that seemed to be seeing other places, other times. Again I sensed that aura of mystery about her, sensed secrets that made those eyes far too sad and serious for one so young. She sighed again, peering at the wild flowers that grew in thick clusters between the tree trunks.

"So many flowers," she said. "So many trees, so much green—is not like Russia at all. England is a strange country, no?"

"I'm sure I would find Russia much stranger."

"We have the sweep, the grandeur, the vast spaces. In winter there is the snow and ice, everything white, the wolves howling. In summer there is the hot sun, the golden fields and the red, red poppies."

"It sounds lovely."

"It—is frequently depressing." Lucie sometimes found it difficult to express herself in proper French grammar. "The black moods come to all Russians and often there is violence. The Russian temperament is dark, brooding. There is little sunshine in the soul, much inner turmoil. The vodka makes one forget, makes one smile when there is no reason. Is not a happy country, Russia, but it is nevertheless the greatest country in the world."

"I know a few people who might disagree with you."

"They do not know Russia," she replied. "We have walked enough?"

Although perfectly willing to accompany me, Lucie

found the idea of walking for the sake of walking peculiar indeed, another bewildering English eccentricity impossible to comprehend. We had walked perhaps a mile and a half and, truth to tell, my leg muscles were beginning to feel the strain. I was ready to turn back. Leaves rustled overhead, heavy limbs groaning quietly in the breeze, and the pastures beyond were bathed in sunlight. As we neared the inn, a farmer approached us carrying bunches of vivid orange carrots and a string of beautiful silver-mauve onions.

"What lovely carrots," I said, "and those onions—I wonder if he grew them himself?"

Lucie showed not the slightest interest. The farmer grinned in anticipation of a sale, holding out the carrots so we could better observe their splendor as we came closer to him. He was tall and sturdy, dressed in ancient leather jerkin and patched brown breeches, his boots in deplorable shape. No older than thirty or so, he had a leathery face, friendly gray eyes and straw-colored hair that fell across his brow in a shaggy fringe. Lucie and I paused, and he came over to us in a loose-kneed shamble.

"Want-ta buy some fine carrots, lady?" he asked me. "I 'ave onions 'ere, too. Fine onions. Me 'an my wife growed 'em our—"

He never finished the sentence. I gave a gasp as Vladimir shoved me out of the way. Stunned, I saw a powerful fist swinging toward the farmer's face, saw it make contact, heard the hideous crunching noise as bone bruised bone. Vladimir growled as the farmer reeled backward several feet, tottering, finally falling to the ground with a thud, landing on his back. Vladimir unsheathed his knife and fell to his knees, seizing the unconscious man's hair, jerking his head up, ready to slice his throat from ear to ear.

"Vladimir!" Lucie cried.

She spoke to him quickly, harshly in Russian. Vladimir scowled, hesitating, eager to finish the job. She spoke again, even more harshly, and he released his hold and the farmer's head banged to the ground. Vladimir stood slowly and thrust his knife back into the scabbard with a violent plunge. Lucie spoke to the other servant then, and Ivan stepped forward and picked the still unconscious farmer up and slung him casually over his shoulder as though he were a bag of potatoes. Gripping the man's legs with one arm, adjusting his tall black fur hat with his free hand, he started toward the inn at a leisurely pace.

"My God," I whispered. "He—your man was going to *kill* him!"

"But of course," she said calmly. "In Russia, if a serf dares approach a young noblewoman he is—"

"This is *England.*"

"I know. You allow the serfs to be familiar. It is very strange."

"We don't call them serfs. We don't *have* serfs. That man is as free as you or I."

"Of course. That is why I stopped Vladimir. He does not understand, you see."

"Jesus."

"You are pale, Marietta. It is all right. Ivan will carry this free man to the house of the doctor and the doctor will tend to him and my uncle will see that the farmer receives much gold to—to"—Lucie struggled to find the right word in French—"to compensate for the damage Vladimir did to him," she finished.

Her manner was cool and patrician, those lovely eyes totally unperturbed. I was still shaken, but the incident hadn't disturbed Lucie in the least. She took my hand and gave it a reassuring squeeze, and I took a deep breath, trying to see the burst of violence from her viewpoint. We are all the products of our environment and upbringing, and Lucie was neither cruel nor unfeeling. Her attitude toward the farmer merely reflected that of her country and class. I shuddered to think that, had we been in Russia, she would not have intervened and the farmer would have been savagely dispatched. In Russia, though, a man of his class would never have approached a young noblewoman accompanied by two fierce bodyguards.

"It is over now," she said. "You feel better?"

"I'm all right."

We resumed our walk, the inn visible now at the end of the lane, pigeons cooing beneath the eaves of the steep thatched roof. Specks of sunlight continued to dart and dance on the shady lane, and birds frolicked in the trees, chirping pleasantly. Goats munched on the grass in a field nearby, the bells around their necks making a dull clatter. It was hard to believe that just a few minutes ago a man had almost been murdered right before my eyes. I was tired now, far more upset by the near-slaughter than I cared to admit. Lucie sensed this and took my hand again.

"I am sorry you were upset," she said quietly. "A fine, fragile Englishwoman like you—it must have been dreadful."

"I'm hardly fragile, Lucie. I've seen my share of violence."

"The violence is natural for the Russian," she explained. "The temperament is so brooding, you see. So much emotion held back, pent up, and turning inward— there must be an outlet, so there is the violence. The fierce fighting, the fierce lovemaking are part of the Russian character."

"I see."

"It is a fine race nevertheless. The heart is big, always, and there is always the generosity, the sentiment, the tears so easy to fall. Strong men cry as quickly as maidens."

"And then beat someone senseless."

"That is the Russian," she agreed, completely missing my irony.

The neighing of horses and jangle of harnesses filled the air as we passed the outbuildings that surrounded the main yard. Two more coaches had come and horses were being changed, a groom leading two beautiful blacks toward the stables. Lucie and I paused, gazed at the large, rambling inn with its soft rose-gray brick walls, heavily leaded windows and pale brown thatched roof. A weathered wooden sign hung in front, *The Wayfarer* black against a faded blue background, black coach and horses silhouetted beneath the lettering.

"My uncle will be returning soon," Lucie said. "He will be happy to see you well. He was most concerned."

"Was he?"

"As concerned as I. He did not want to leave when you were still—still in such poor condition, but it was necessary."

"There was no reason why he should have stayed."

"He felt responsible for you, as did I. He said—" She hesitated a moment, as though debating whether or not to continue. "He said you were the most beautiful woman he had ever seen."

"Your uncle must be extremely gallant."

"Oh no," she protested. "He meant it. He never makes the idle—how does one put it?—the idle words, the chit-chat. Is this correct? He gazed and gazed at you while you were sleeping. He brushed the damp locks from your brow. When you moaned, he frowned, deeply disturbed. He ordered the doctor to make you well, Marietta. He promised him much gold if he succeeded, promised him much pain if he failed. The doctor was most worried."

"I can see why."

"All turns out well, though," she continued. "You are restored to your health and the doctor will be much richer."

"And still able to walk," I added.

"You make the jest?"

"I make the jest," I replied lightly. "I think I'll go up to my room now, Lucie."

"We shall lunch?"

I shook my head. "I need rest far more than food. I will see you later, my dear."

Stepping inside the inn, I was enticed by the smells of strong ale and bacon, beeswax and herbs. The proprietor's wife was arranging pink roses in a glazed blue pot as I passed the front counter with its heavy leather registration book and tarnished brass bell. Much wearier than I felt I should be, I climbed the uneven wooden stairs to my floor, relieved when I shut the door of my room. The bed looked wonderfully inviting, though I had left it only a few hours ago.

You've overdone it, I scolded myself. You can't have a relapse now. Think of the poor doctor and what Count Orlov will do to him. Break both his arms and legs, probably, perhaps tear out his tongue as well. Use the knout on him at the very least. These Russians! I would be very glad to be rid of them, I thought as I unfastened the hooks of my pale blue dress, although Lucie was enchanting and Count Gregory sounded . . . most intriguing. There was still a mild, aggravating nag at the back of my mind that told me I should know the name Orlov, but I was unable to summon forth the knowledge, if knowledge it was. Removing the dress, I hung it in the immense, ornately carved wardrobe that almost reached the low, beamed ceiling.

So Count Gregory Orlov thought I was the most beautiful woman he had ever seen? I smiled a rueful smile as I closed the wardrobe door. I had been bruised, battered, feverish, soaked with perspiration and had probably been moaning like a madwoman, yet he had "gazed and gazed" at me, had brushed the damp locks from my brow. Had I been properly clothed at the time, or had I been wearing the white silk nightgown with the insets of fragile lace that had scarcely covered my bosom? I wondered if Count Orlov was one of Lucie's typical Russians, brooding, full of repressed emotion, given to bursts of violence and bouts of maudlin sentiment. It hardly mattered. He was obviously a very important person in Russia, incredibly wealthy, and after I rode to London with him I would never see him again.

Wearing only a thin white petticoat, I moved across the room to pull the curtains shut. The room grew deliciously dim, filled with hazy blue-gray shadows. The polished hardwood floor was cool to my bare feet as I walked over to the bed. What luxury to nap at this hour of the day, I mused, turning the covers back. I was feeling drowsy now, a bit dizzy as well, and it was lovely to climb between the crisp, fresh sheets, and sink into the softness. If I were to travel to London tomorrow, I would need all my strength, and a long nap was just the thing . . . London . . . Jeremy.

He moved toward me in that jaunty stride, the heavy chestnut wave flopping across his brow. The vivid blue eyes were full of mischief, and a teasing smile played on his lips. I scolded him—silent words I couldn't hear—and he tilted his head to one side and arched one eyebrow and pulled me into his arms and kissed me and I could feel the lovely fever stealing through me as he crushed me to him. We were walking across a large clearing with cottonwood trees in the distance and stars blazing above and I knew we were going to make love again and this time I would hold him forever. The grass was brushed with moonlight, a pale silver turning white, whiter, and wolves were howling, and ice encased the trees and the snow was so deep we could hardly walk. He was wearing tall boots and tight brown breeches and a loose beige satin tunic with very full sleeves. He spoke to me in Russian. I couldn't understand a word he said.

The wolves were howling, howling, coming nearer, and we were running toward a rustic wooden cabin half-covered with snow and then we were inside, safe, and the wind howled and the windows were covered with crystal patterns of frost. A fire was blazing brightly and there were fur rugs in front of the fireplace and he undressed me and I writhed naked on the fur, my body warmed by the heat of the flames and the heat inside. He stood over me, hands on hips, legs spread wide, looking down at me, the loose beige satin tunic gleaming in the haze. He spoke to me again, again in Russian, and I frowned and realized words were not important, there had been far too many words between us.

Jeremy smiled slowly, his eyelids drooping slightly over

eyes now filled with desire, dark, smoldering blue eyes
that feasted on me as I stretched before the flames, sliding
on soft fur. The smile grew taut on his lips and his handsome face was tense, the skin stretched tightly across
those broad cheekbones. He kneeled over me, a knee on
either side of my thighs, hands pinioning my wrists to the
fur. He loomed there over me, his face inches from my own,
lips parting. Slowly, slowly, he lowered his head, eyes
shining brightly and telling me of his love, his need. A
noise came from the distance, clattering, jangling, and Jer
emy turned his head and frowned, and I arched my body
under his and longed for those lips to cover mine, longed
for the pressure of muscle and bone bearing down on me.
Hooves clattered on the cobbles. A whip cracked and Jeremy disappeared, melting into mist, and I was alone and
lost in the snow. It was cold, so cold, and snow whirled
around me, white, yet whiter, blinding, and Jeremy was
gone and my arms were empty.

I sat up with a start, shaken, for a moment still caught
up in the toils of the dream. The skirts of my petticoat were
tangled around my legs, and the bedclothes were tangled,
too, and I was shivering because there was no fire in the
fireplace and the room was chilly. Loud noises were coming from the yard below. Harsh orders were being given.
Horses were stamping. Climbing from bed, I went over to
the window and held the curtains back. An enormous
coach, the largest I had ever seen, stood in front of the inn,
four perfectly matched grays in harness. The coach was a
gleaming white with sumptuous trim in gold leaf. An exotic crest of red and blue, surrounded by a gold sunburst,
adorned the side of the door visible to me, and blue velvet
curtains hung at the windows, concealing the interior.

Vladimir and three other servants were yelling at the
grooms and making furious gestures. A wagon of hay had
been overturned in front of the coach. Geese scattered in
panic. A black and white spotted dog barked at the Russians. The innkeeper's wife was wringing her hands, visibly upset by the commotion. The innkeeper stood stout and

happy in his thin black leather apron, smiling in anticipation of the showers of bright golden coins soon to come his
way. As I watched from the window, six horsemen came
charging into the yard on yet more grays. The men all
wore blue velvet livery and towering black fur hats and
short blue capes trimmed with black fur. All six were
heavily armed, sabres dangling at their sides, knives
strapped just above their boot tops, guns thrust into their
belts. The grays reared and neighed, kicking in the air as
reins were savagely jerked. The men dismounted and the
horses stamped and snorted and Vladimir and the three
other servants greeted their compatriots with lusty cries
and hearty embraces. Backs were pounded. Stomachs were
punched. Bodies swayed and stumbled in a joyous melee.
The Russians were indeed an emotional race, I reflected.

Miraculously, order was restored. The geese disappeared. The dog stopped barking. The wagon was turned
upright and dragged away, the loose hay scattered over
the cobbles. Nervous grooms led the skittish grays into the
stables, and the innkeeper's wife led the six outriders into
the tap room where, I assumed, they would drink themselves into an even more boisterous mood. In a matter of
minutes, the yard was empty of everyone but the innkeeper, Vladimir, and a now lethargic dog. It was then that
Vladimir opened the door of the coach and a tall, slender
man with brick red hair climbed out. He was wearing English attire—polished brown boots, tan kidskin breeches,
elegant rust velvet frock coat, gray silk waistcoat—and
carried a thin leather case that obviously contained papers. I couldn't see his features from where I stood, but I
was almost certain he wasn't Count Orlov.

I was right. Vladimir gave him a curt, clearly hostile
nod, and the innkeeper scarcely glanced at him. The Englishman turned, peering back into the interior of the magnificent coach. Vladimir nudged him aside and stood at
attention beside the open door. I saw a glossy gray leather
boot, a long, muscular leg tightly encased in pale gray
broadcloth and then thick folds of a dark gray cloak as the

man stepped out. The cloak swirled, and I saw flashes of its white satin lining before it settled into place, covering the man from shoulder to toe. The shoulders were extremely broad, I noted, and he was very tall, even taller than Vladimir. The innkeeper rushed over and began to fawn outrageously. Vladimir gave him a rough shove. The innkeeper stumbled, crashing against the side of the coach. Orlov appeared not to notice. Saying something to the Englishman, he strolled briskly toward the door of the inn. A sleek fur hat covered his head, and because of its tilt I could see nothing of his face.

Disappointed, I let the curtain fall back into place. Oh well, I told myself, I would soon have ample opportunity to observe more closely the mysterious Count Orlov. Not that it mattered, of course. He was merely a means of my getting back to London. Glancing at the clock, I was amazed to discover that it was already after six. No wonder I felt in such a stupor—I had slept the entire afternoon away. A hot bath was the only thing that would revive me, and I had considerable difficulty arranging that. The maid I located in the hall looked dubious, said it was terribly late for a bath and 'eaven knew they 'ad enough on their 'ands with all these mad foreigners chargin' all over th' place disruptin' things. I managed to persuade her to indulge me and to have a long, hot bath in front of a roaring fire in a plain, decidedly uncomfortable tin tub. I also managed to dry myself without any assistance.

Putting on a thin cream silk petticoat with half a dozen full skirts, I sat down at the dressing table and examined myself in the mirror in the glow of the candles the maid had begrudgingly lighted. Nature was going to need some help tonight, I decided, and after I had brushed my hair until it glistened a coppery red sheen, I took out my cosmetic case and began to apply pale brown powder to the lids, merely a suggestion of shadow, a touch of pink to the pale cheeks, carefully rubbed in to give a natural glow, pink lip rouge used sparingly. Better, I thought, studying my reflection, but I was not likely to launch a thousand ships. Not even one tiny skiff, I told myself. Despite the subtle use of cosmetics, I still had a wan, fatigued look.

I knew what gown I was going to wear tonight, one of the loveliest I owned. It was a heavy, cream silk completely overlaid with beige lace in floral patterns, lace as delicate as cobwebs, and it was worn with a narrow brown velvet sash that tied in a bow in back, the sash emphasizing the snug waistline and the lush swell of the skirts. The form-fitting bodice was cut low, and the large puffed sleeves were worn off-the-shoulder. As I put it on, I was honest enough with myself to acknowledge that I was dressing for Count Orlov. What he might think of me didn't matter, of course, but he had, after all, saved my life, and it was only natural that I would want to make a pleasing impression.

The gorgeous skirt rustled as I returned to the dressing table, the delicate lace whispering softly. Sitting down in front of the mirror, I began to put my hair up, arranging it in an artful pile of waves and letting a few curling wisps brush my temples and the nape of my neck. Finally satisfied, I stood up and adjusted the bodice that accentuated the full, rounded curves of my bosom. I might not launch a single skiff, but at least I looked far better than I had the last time Orlov had seen me.

Too restless to remain in my room, I decided to take a stroll in the gardens behind the inn, and as I stepped into the hall I could hear the rowdy merriment issuing from the taproom. There was gruff, hearty laughter, raucous shouting, the crash of breaking glass. The count's men were certainly enjoying themselves, tearing the place apart from the sound of it. Fortunately the inn had a private dining room for more affluent guests, so I needn't be exposed to the boisterous revelry. I assumed Orlov and his niece would be dining there and that I would be asked to join them. I was rather surprised, in fact, that Lucie hadn't come up to check on me.

Moving down the creaky back stairs that smelled of cabbage and soiled linen, I marveled at the curious twists and turns life held in store for us. Two weeks ago I had been in

London with the man I loved, convinced I loved another, and now here I was in a sprawling old country inn on the outskirts of a tiny village whose name I didn't even know, all through the kindness of an exotic, enigmatic young Russian girl and her mysterious, dazzlingly wealthy uncle. Had their coach not come down the road when it did, had they not acted so promptly, I might well have died. I owed them a great deal, and I intended to thank Count Orlov as best I could. Smiling at an untidy scullery maid who was busily polishing a pair of boots in the dusty back hall, I opened the door and stepped outside.

Twilight was just beginning to settle in, and the air was soft with a fine blue haze while, above, the sky was a pure pearl gray. I reveled in the marvelous smells of herbs, of bark and moss and rich, loamy soil. Completely enclosed by gray stone walls and surrounded by old oaks with low, groaning boughs, the gardens were quite extensive, extending at least half an acre, flagged walks winding throughout. Asparagus, carrots and lettuce grew in the kitchen garden, and there was a bed of peas and beans as well. The herb garden was a square of pink and purple and brown and a dozen shades of green from palest yellow-green to darkest emerald, the herbs cleverly planted to form an ornate pattern. A rake and a battered straw hat had been abandoned there. Walking past an old stone well dark with mossy stains, a rusty bucket hanging over it, I moved under the arched trellises and strolled slowly through the flower gardens, the lovely, deliberately unkempt beds ablaze with color.

How peaceful it was here, surrounded by the wild, riotous confusion of flowers. How serene it was with the oak boughs groaning quietly and a solitary bird warbling plaintively among the leaves. As the blue haze gradually deepened to soft violet, as the sky darkened to ashy gray tinged with amethyst, I smelled the heady fragrance of poppy and hollyhock and thought about the dream I had had this afternoon. A poignant sadness crept over me as I experienced anew the frustrations of that dream. I had lost

Jeremy in my dream. In my dream he had vanished just as we were about to experience the bliss we both craved. Had I lost him in real life? For the first time I faced the realization that he might no longer want me, and who could blame him?

Plucking a hollyhock blossom from one of the tall stalks, I lifted the luscious red bloom to my nostrils. Jeremy Bond had loved me from the first, and he had proved that love over and over again, only to be met by my disdain, my hauteur, my wicked, wounding tongue. He was a bounder, yes, a merry, mercurial scamp full of infuriating faults, but he had loved me as no man ever had or ever would. Did he love me still, or had that love finally been thwarted when I left him? Had he waited a week, still hoping I would return, finally giving up? Had he left London in despair or, even worse, had he found some woman to assuage his grief? Women would always flock around Jeremy Bond, drawn to him as moths to a flame, that virile beauty, that dazzling charm utterly irresistible, and, like moths, they would invariably be burned.

The hollyhock was a mass of bruised petals in my hand. I hadn't been aware that I was crushing it. Dropping the petals, I gazed at the flowers without seeing them, seeing, instead, that beloved face, that look in his eyes when I left him. The bird had stopped warbling. Leaves made a soft whispering sound in the breeze, and the first fireflies had begun to float among the shrubbery to dot the twilight with flickering golden glows. There was a tight feeling in my throat. I felt very frail, very vulnerable, for once unable to cope with these emotions inside.

"You must not be sad," he said.

I turned. I hadn't heard him approaching. He stood several feet away from me. He was dressed all in white. He was, without question, the most beautiful man I had ever seen.

Chapter Three

I WAS STARTLED, MOMENTARILY UNABLE TO speak, and I could only stare at him with disbelief. Standing there with legs spread wide, one hand resting lightly on his thigh, he seemed an apparition in the deepening violet haze. Six feet five if an inch, he had the superbly muscled body of an athlete in top condition, a body Michelangelo might have sculpted, I thought, seeing the broad shoulders and powerful chest, the slender waist and long, muscular legs. White leather boots came to mid-calf, and the legs were sheathed in supple white kidskin breeches that clung to every curve. He wore a loose, smocklike shirt of fine white silk, the full bell sleeves gathered at the wrist, the collar fitting around his neck in clerical fashion. A heavy white velvet cloak fell back from his shoulders, flaring behind him in sumptuous folds. He looked like . . . like a fallen archangel, for that face, while beautiful, was undeniably the face of an extremely sensual man.

His hair was a thick, luxuriant golden brown. His dark brows were perfectly arched, lids drooping heavily over eyes so deep a blue they seemed navy blue. His nose was Roman, a great prow of a nose, his cheekbones broad and slavic. He had a strong, square jaw with clefted chin, and his mouth was wide and pink, the lower lip generously curved. The near-feminine perfection of his features was offset by a stamp of rugged virility. He should smell of gunpowder and dust and sweaty flesh, I thought, and I sensed that he frequently had. He had the confident, near-arrogant stance of the soldier, a veteran of many battles, and the fine clothes merely emphasized the unquestionable toughness.

"Miss Danver, I presume," he said.

"Yes, I—I am Marietta Danver."

"Marietta—such a lovely name."

His voice was deep and guttural, yet there was a purring softness. He seemed to caress each word as it came from that broad chest. It was . . . it was an incredibly seductive voice, husky and persuasive. Few women would fail to succumb to it were it used to employ gentle entreaties and tender phrases.

"Count Gregory Orlov," he introduced himself. "At your service."

He gave me a polite nod and clicked his heels lightly together in a manner that made gentle mockery of the traditional military salute. He sauntered toward me, moving with lithe grace surprising in a man his size. Count Gregory Orlov was a magnificent male animal, his magnetism almost overwhelming. As he drew nearer I found myself growing more and more disconcerted. Never had I encountered a man who radiated such power, such presence. The very air around him seemed charged with energy.

"You looked so very sad," he said.

"I—I was just thinking about—something."

"You must not think this thing," he told me.

"Sometimes one can't help it."

"Ah, yes, the melancholy it comes, but we must vanquish it at once."

"And how does one do that, Count Orlov?"

"One thinks of pleasant things. One seeks pleasant company. One pampers oneself with the fine food, the fine wine—and other diversions."

That husky, caressing voice made the nature of those other diversions quite clear. He was standing close to me now, and I had to tilt my head back slightly in order to look into those deep blue eyes. I could smell his teak cologne and faintly moist silk and flesh, and his aura was so strong it seemed to envelop both of us like an invisible cloud. Count Orlov smiled, the full mouth curving, pink, the lower lip taut. The heavy eyelids drooped, half-shrouding those magnetic eyes. In love with Jeremy, I was immune to the charms of any other male, yet I was acutely aware of the sexuality he exuded through every pore, sexuality so potent it was almost palpable.

"You like these things?" he inquired.

"I—I enjoy a good meal."

"This is good sign. You like the wine?"

"On occasion."

"And the other—ah, it would be indiscreet of me to ask about that."

"Extremely indiscreet," I said stiffly.

He looked disturbed. "I offend?"

I shook my head and turned away from him, gazing at the hollyhocks, inhaling their strong fragrance. I could feel him there behind me, warm and big and solid. It was growing darker, the haze deep violet now, the sky turning black. The fireflies flickered a brighter yellow-gold. Soon the first stars would appear. The bird began to warble again, and the oak leaves made a soft rattling noise as the breeze stirred them.

"I do offend," he said, and his voice sounded pained. "In Russia we make light of these matters. We jest. We do not take them as—as seriously as you English. I am forgiven?"

I faced him. I nodded. He was visibly relieved.

"Good. We must not begin on—how do you put it?—we must not start on the wrong two feet."

"The wrong foot," I corrected.

"Right. We must not start on the wrong foot. You are sad and I attempt to bring the levity and step on the wrong foot immediately. I am the clumsy oaf on occasion, I fear. Too many years in the army barracks. The fine breeding is lacking."

"I—I guessed you had been a soldier."

"Oh, yes, in my youth I am the mighty Russian soldier. I ride like a demon and flash the sabre and put fear in the hearts of my enemy. I am more at ease in the thick of battle than in the drawing room with the gold gilt chairs and velvet hangings."

"I'm sure you exaggerate, Count Orlov."

"I am like the caged lion in those rooms. It is agony even now, many years after I leave the military and become a count. They try to civilize me, but always I long for the rowdy comrades and the brawls."

"You—you were not born a count?"

"Oh, no. My father he is a military man, a fierce soldier. My four brothers and I are ruffians. We terrorize the countryside. Many scrapes we get into, many pranks we play. The priest says we are spawn of the devil. My father thinks it is a compliment to him."

He chuckled, the navy blue eyes full of amusement as he recalled those days. I suspected there was still much of the little boy in Gregory Orlov, a simplicity of response the years had not diminished. He would be easily pleased, easily angered, and his responses would be as quick, as volatile and uncomplicated as a child's. Count Orlov, I felt, would ever be guided by instinct and emotion rather than intellect.

"It is good to find you well," he said. "I worry much."

"You—you and Lucie have been very kind."

"We find you on the road. We bring you here and bring the doctor. Is that not what anyone would do?"

"You saved my life."

"I suppose maybe. It brings responsibility, this, much duty. In Russia when you save the life, you are responsible for this person."

"I thought that was in China."

"In Russia, too," he assured me.

"I don't know how to thank you for—for all you've done."

"Is natural to do these things, no? We are cruel sometimes, we Russians, it is in our blood, but we are not savages. Only the savage would leave a beautiful woman broken on the road."

"Thank you all the same."

"Is heavy responsibility, this. Now I must see that you are not unhappy and do not have this sad look in your eyes I see when I first came into the gardens. I must make you to smile. My French, pardon me, is not the best. Always I find it agony to learn the languages. Even the proper Russian is hard for me to speak at times."

"Your French is more than adequate."

"In the court we speak nothing else. Always the French, never the Russian. The Empress admires everything French—the French manners, the French clothes, the French art and literature. She and this fellow Voltaire are always writing the letters. He is her mentor, she claims."

"Voltaire? I hear that he is extremely radical."

"Is true. He fills her head with the political nonsense, the hot ideas. She is a foolish woman in many ways, Catherine."

"Do—do you know her well?"

"I did once," he said.

There was a tenseness in his voice, the purr replaced by a growl, and I sensed that for some reason he was extremely touchy about the Empress of All the Russias. His eyes were sullen. His wide mouth turned down at both corners. For all his great size he looked like a surly little boy who longed to smash something with his fists. Count Orlov was hardly one to hide his feelings, I thought. A long moment passed while he brooded, and then he shook his head and sighed heavily and smiled.

"You must forgive me. I forget myself. I forget my task."

"Your task?"

"To make you smile. To make you forget sad thoughts."

"You mustn't bother about me, Count Orlov."

"Oh, but I have the responsibility, remember? I take this very seriously. Will you smile for me?"

It was such a boyish plea that I smiled in spite of myself. Orlov smiled, too, vastly relieved.

"This is much better. You are even more beautiful when this smile is on your lips. Your beauty makes the knees grow weak."

"What nonsense you speak."

"I speak only the truth. Never have I seen a woman as beautiful as you, and in my lifetime I know many women. It is a tragedy when my niece tells me you are already taken. This is correct?"

"I'm afraid it is."

"This man in London, he appreciates you?"

"I think so. I'm not sure I've ever fully appreciated him."

"You will marry him?" he asked.

"I fervently hope to."

"Then, alas, I must not try to seduce you. I must restrain myself and be just the good friend. I give offense once more?"

"Few women are offended to know a man would like to seduce them, Count Orlov. It is a compliment."

"I would like very much, but I have the code of honor. Only if the woman is willing do I use the seduction, the tender words, the touches that are soft and make them melt. I tell myself, though, that under other circumstances you would perhaps not be unwilling."

I smiled again, a wry, amused smile. All this was mere badinage, I realized, smooth words that meant nothing. A born sensualist, Orlov had probably started practicing his wiles on his plump old nurse as she fed him in her lap, and I felt sure that he used an identical approach with any woman under fifty. For a man like him, women were captivating creatures meant for bedding, and no doubt he bedded them by the score. One could hardly take offense at such obvious, simpleminded ploys. Handsome as a Roman god, charged with sexual allure, he undoubtedly found them successful nine times out of ten.

"We are friends, then?" he asked.

"Friends," I said.

"I settle for this with broken heart."

"I'm certain you'll find someone to mend it ere long."

Orlov grinned. One could not help but like him. His sexuality was potent, true, but there was genuine warmth and boyish charm as well. The scent of poppies was overwhelming here in the darkening garden. The leaves continued to rustle in the breeze. It was turning much cooler. I shivered, and Orlov was immediately distressed.

"I am the oaf!" he exclaimed. "Here I am so relieved to find you back in good health and I let you freeze and maybe catch the bad cold in that very lovely gown that leaves so much of the flesh bare."

He whipped off the heavy white velvet cloak and placed it over my shoulders with tender care, his huge hands arranging the folds, one of them gently touching the side of my neck as he did so. He let them rest of my shoulders for a moment, heavy and warm, the fingers squeezing ever so slightly, and then he sighed audibly and turned me around to face him. The cloak smelled of his musk, a male perfume that was as heady as the poppies.

"You feel better now?"

"I—I wasn't really cold."

"We must not take the chances. You are barely out of the bed. When I get here this afternoon I summon the doctor. He comes to see me with the pale face and the shaky knees. He stammers that you are recovered but still maybe a little weak. I pound him on the back and give him a sack of gold coins. I think he almost faints."

"Poor man, you probably frightened him to death."

Count Orlov looked incredulous, as though such a thing was utterly improbable. Me? his eyes seemed to say. Why, I am as gentle as a baby with a heart of purest gold. I couldn't help smiling again, and that pleased him. He took hold of my arms and squeezed them tightly indeed, so tightly that I winced, and then he slung a heavy arm around my shoulder and propelled me toward the trellises, a great, hearty animal full of exuberant spirits.

"We eat now," he told me. "I have my chef prepare a special meal for my English beauty."

"Really, Count Orlov, I—a very light meal is all I—"

He curled his arm closer about my shoulder, half dragging me through the arched trellises, past the herb garden. "We do not argue about it," he said sternly. "Orlov does not brook the insubordination."

"I am not one of—"

I stumbled, toppling forward. He swung a strong arm around my waist, supporting me. I could feel his hard muscle tighten as he pulled me upright, and I could feel his warmth and smell that musky male perfume as, for a moment, I rested against him.

"You twist the ankle?" he asked.

"I don't think so."

"Me, I forget myself. I am carried away. I am too rough. Always my old nurse she says, 'Too rough, Gregory, don't play so rough.' I bloody my brother's nose when I just mean to tap him and break the stableboy's arm when I mean only to tease him."

I pulled away from him, overwhelmed, feeling as though I had been caught up by a force of nature. Orlov looked disturbed and apologetic. I had lost a number of hair pins. My waves began to slide and tumble. Damn! I thought as I tried to push them back up.

"But no," he protested. "Let the hair down. It is like the liquid copper, so thick, so shiny."

"I don't seem to have much choice," I said as more pins fell to the ground.

I ran my fingers through the heavy waves and pushed them back from my temples while Orlov watched admiringly. We were standing by the kitchen gardens. It was almost dark. Pale silver stars had begun to glimmer lightly against a dark violet-gray sky. Orlov stood with his legs planted apart, hands resting on his thighs. His white garments gleamed dimly in the dust. His eyes were full of admiration, full of fondness.

"We go in now," he said. "I take your arm gently."

"You don't seem to know your own strength."

"My old nurse tells me that, too. 'Gregory,' she says when I knock Alexis to the ground, 'you do not know your own strength.' Alexis is big, too, taller than I am, but always I manage to make him submit when we wrestle as boys. He is better horseman than I am, though," he admitted reluctantly. "Feodor is a better shot than either of us."

"You must have had quite a rowdy childhood."

"Always my four brothers and I are rowdy and rough. We knock each other about and bash heads and such, but we stick together. We are poor, you see. We often are without shoes, often eat only thin soup and hard bread. It strengthens us though and makes us tough and sturdy."

He had certainly come a long way from his deprived, undernourished childhood, I thought, and I wondered how the son of a "fierce soldier" who couldn't always provide shoes for his family had become not only a count but also a man of such incredible wealth. Had a rich uncle died? Had Orlov inherited his title and estates? Was he, then, the oldest of five brothers? There were so many questions I would have liked to ask, but good manners forbade it. Gregory Orlov was definitely one of the most intriguing individuals I had ever met.

Carefully placing my arm in the crook of his, he led me into the back hall where old wax candles now burned in tarnished wall sconces. Sounds of revelry came from the taproom, louder than ever. Orlov looked very displeased, a deep furrow above the bridge of his nose. A liveried servant came into the hall and Orlov barked something to him in a very harsh voice, the Russian words unintelligible to me. Apprehensive, the servant hurried away and in a matter of moments the noise from the taproom ceased abruptly. Orlov gave a satisfied nod and led me to the small private dining room.

I had to repress a gasp. The snug, homey room had been transformed as if by magic. The dull brown oak walls were burnished gold from the glow of dozens of tall yellow candles in exquisite gold candelabra. The dark hardwood floor had been covered with sumptuous white rugs patterned in yellow and gold, and a glistening yellow satin cloth covered the table. It was set for two with gorgeous white china adorned with gold, gold cutlery and incredibly beautiful crystal glasses etched with delicate gold designs. A bowl of white and yellow roses sat in the center of the table, their fragrance scenting the air, and a golden samovar bubbled on a small side table, adding its own spicy aroma. The splendor was awesome, yet there was a feeling of snug intimacy as well. My host beamed proudly as I took it all in.

"You like?" he inquired.

"Thank God I dressed."

"I arrange. We celebrate your return to health."

"Apparently we celebrate alone."

"Lucie prefers to stay in her room and examine the gifts I bring her from London. Vladimir will take a tray to her. Sir Harry has the papers he wants to go over. He dines in his room, too."

"Sir Harry?"

"He is the English diplomat, Sir Harry Lyman. Many years he spends in Russia, doing the important work for his country. He handles the Empress with tact and does much good. He becomes my friend. Now he is retired, and he handles my affairs for me while I am in his country, makes the investments and such."

"I see."

"He is fine fellow, Sir Harry. I yell at him and give him the hard time, and he ignores me and goes about the proper business."

"Do you yell frequently, Count Orlov?"

"Frequently, yes. I am Russian."

Moving behind me, he reached around to unfasten the ties of the cloak, his fingers lightly pressing against my throat as he did so. He removed the cloak and tossed it aside, then, taking my hand, led me over to the table and helped me into my chair. He placed one heavy hand on my bare shoulder for the briefest of moments, rubbing his fingers lightly over the flesh. My skin seemed to respond of its own accord, tingling under that casual caress. Was Count Orlov merely being friendly and demonstrative, or was it very calculated, the first overture in a far-from-abandoned attempt at seduction? He was the kind of man for whom physical contact came naturally, I told myself, a man who would pound his comrades on the back and hug them heartily, who would kiss a woman's hand, squeeze her arm, lift her from her horse, touch her frequently and simply for the joy of contact. I had already had ample illustration of that. I had to admit that the contact was far from unpleasant.

"This candlelight, it enhances your beauty," he said in that husky purr. "It makes you even more beautiful."

"I wish you wouldn't say such things."

He arched a brow, the navy blue eyes full of surprise. "You do not like the compliments?"

"They make me—rather uncomfortable."

"When I see something beautiful—a painting, a work of art, a woman—I appreciate it."

"And try your best to acquire it," I said.

"Yes, I like to have the beautiful things around me. My houses in Russia they are filled with them. I bring some of them along to make the travel more pleasant. I transform this shabby room, make it a more fitting setting for the English beauty I find broken on the side of the road."

I fondled one of the gold-etched crystal glasses. "Everything is lovely," I told him. "I—I have the feeling I'm inside a golden jewel case."

"We start with the wine," he said.

He clapped his hands loudly and sat down across from me, the chair creaking beneath his weight. The door opened quietly and a slim, fair-haired youth in gold-trimmed white velvet livery entered with an ice-filled gold bucket containing an enormous bottle. Calmly, deftly, he set the bucket down on one of the side tables, removed the bottle and uncorked it, his brown eyes humbly lowered. He poured a small amount of the sparkling wine into Orlov's glass. The count took a sip, savored it inside his mouth and then swallowed and nodded his approval. The youth filled our glasses and left.

"The other servants wear blue," I remarked.

"Vladimir, the guards, they wear the blue and black. The footmen and house servants wear the white and gold."

"You certainly have a—a great many servants."

"Is fitting for a man of my station. In Russia I have thousands of serfs, I lose count. They come with the property."

Like cattle, I thought, taking a sip of the wine. It was delicious, light and dry, creating a warm glow inside. Orlov watched me drink, a pleased half-smile on those lips that were so pink, so wide, so very sensual. His eyelids drooped heavily, giving him a lazy, sleepy look, and the candlelight burnished his hair with a dark golden sheen. He really wasn't so extraordinarily handsome when you examined him closely, I observed. The mouth was too large, the nose too strong, the cheekbones too broad, but . . . but somehow these defects weren't defects at all. They merely strengthened that remarkable virile beauty. It was indeed a face that could be either tender or harsh, depending on mood. At the moment it was very tender.

"You like the wine?" he inquired.

"It's marvelous."

"Here, I pour you another glassful."

He got up, fetched the bottle and filled my glass, leaning over my shoulder to do so. I was almost painfully aware of his presence there behind me, of his smell, the warmth of his body. I noticed the way his large hand gripped the neck of the bottle, the fingers curled tightly. The wine made a soft splash as it fell and swirled in the glass, a hundred tiny bubbles exploding. I waited, breathless. Would he touch my shoulder again? Would his thighs *accidently* press against my back as he straightened up? I tensed for the contact. It didn't come. Orlov slid the bottle back into its nest of ice and returned to his seat.

"I have a sad duty in London," he told me.

"Oh?"

"This driver, this man Ogilvy, I take his body back, and I must see that he is properly buried. I visit his widow."

"That—that was wonderfully kind of you."

"I take care of everything. He has very fine burial, and his widow weeps when I give her a large sack of gold coins.

She kisses my hands. She goes to live with her sister in the country."

"Poor Ogilvy, I—I wept so. I didn't know him well, but I feel—I feel responsible for what happened."

I could feel my eyes growing moist. Orlov was immediately distressed.

"You must not weep again," he said sternly. "You are not to blame. The fates are responsible for these things. Tonight we celebrate. My chef prepares a fine Russian meal for you."

"I—"

"Tonight we enjoy," he informed me.

He clapped his hands again. The slim youth returned pushing a cart laden with chased gold dishes. So much gold. So much ceremony. I was beginning to feel slightly dizzy. The youth served bowls of thick red-orange soup, wonderfully hot and spicy. Orlov told me that it was borscht and made from beets. He took a loaf of coarse black bread and tore it apart with his hands, buttered a piece and passed it to me. It was marvelous, too, but not as marvelous as the next course of thin, thin pancakes folded around a filling of creamy cheese and topped with great scoops of red-gold caviar. Rarely had I tasted anything so delicious.

Orlov ate very little but, instead, spent most of his time watching me. Elbow propped on the table, chin in hand, he slowly rubbed his full lower lip with the ball of his thumb, navy blue eyes gleaming darkly, full of masculine appreciation. The candles flickered, their soft golden glow enhancing the intimate atmosphere. All my senses seemed to be soothed, and I basked in waves of subtle pleasure. The delicious taste of the food, the glorious smells, the beauty surrounding me, yellow and white and gold—all cast their spell, and a luxurious contentment spread through me, augmented by the wine and, yes, by the presence of this man who made a woman feel . . . so very appreciated.

"You—you're not eating," I said. The words seemed to

come from a distance, seemed to melt in air. Had I had too
much wine?

"This fare is too delicate for me," Orlov explained. "I
have the robust appetite. I rip the roasted fowl apart with
my hands and tear the flesh from the bone with my teeth. I
devour the great slabs of red meat and gulp down the stout
ale. Is carryover from the barracks, I fear."

I would love to see you tear the flesh of roasted fowl from
the bone with your teeth, I thought dreamily, and I was
immediately appalled, afraid I might have spoken the
words aloud. I had definitely had too much wine. Three
glasses? Four? I had lost track. Lethargic, lulled, I seemed
to be caught up in a silken web of contentment, and that
was dangerous. Dangerous indeed I realized as I looked
into those glowing navy blue eyes half-hidden by heavy,
drooping lids.

"Now we have the dessert," he murmured.

"No you don't," I said. "You most assuredly do not."

"You will enjoy it a great deal," he promised me.

"Per—perhaps I would, but—"

"Is very special. You never have anything like it before.
You must not deny yourself the pleasure."

"Despite what you might think, Count Orlov, I'm really
not—I—I have known a lot of men, it is true, but I have
never—I have always been faithful to the man I love and I
love Jeremy, and—"

"You speak the jibberish," he protested.

"The jibberish?"

"I speak of the dessert my chef especially prepares for
you. Is made of eggs and sugar and the special liquor,
beaten and baked, and served with sweet heavy cream
sauce."

"I—you must give your chef my—my apologies."

Orlov arched his brows, eyes dark with disappointment.
"I cannot tempt you?" he asked.

"You've tempted me quite enough for one night."

The count gave an amused chuckle and stood up, moving
over to the golden samovar that had been bubbling quietly

all this time. He really was magnificent, I thought, so tall, so superbly built, and he moved with that lazy, supple grace like . . . like a lion prowling in the jungle, the lord of all. I took the cup of strong black tea he handed to me and lowered my eyes.

"I—I think I had a bit too much wine," I said.

"It is very fine wine. It goes to the head."

"It certainly went to mine."

"The Russian tea is good for this. It will help."

He leaned against the wall with his arms folded across his chest, watching me as I drank. My head began to clear. The strands of the silken web began to loosen. I finished the tea and sighed and started to get up. Orlov hurried over to assist me, taking my hand, gently pulling me up, pushing my chair back with the toe of his boot. My limbs felt slightly leaden, but I was in complete control of my senses now, no longer lulled by flickering golden light and heavenly smells and the sight of a long, powerful thumb slowly rubbing a full pink lower lip.

"It was a wonderful meal, Count Orlov."

"I am glad you enjoy."

"I'd better go back up to my room now," I said quietly.

Orlov nodded, and I noticed for the first time the small roll of flesh beneath his chin, the merest suggestion of a double chin. That, too, merely added to the overall effect of sensuality. I judged him to be somewhere in his late thirties, no longer a terribly young man, but maturity had only added line and character to a face that, at eighteen, must have looked like the face of a pretty, surly choir boy.

"We leave for London tomorrow," he said as he led me out of that glowing womb of a room. "We leave at ten."

"I'll be ready."

"I will send a servant to your room with a breakfast tray."

"That won't be necessary."

"You must eat. He will also pack your bags."

"I can do my own packing, Count Orlov."

"Is work for servant," he told me. "I send him up."

His voice was firm. He would brook no argument. I wondered what he would think if I told him I had once been a servant myself, a convicted thief transported to America in chains, to be sold at public auction to the highest bidder and serve seven long years as an indentured servant. My accent might be cultured, my features patrician, but I was hardly the elegant lady he took me to be.

"It is very kind of you to drive me to London," I said. "You and Lucie have been wonderful."

"We of Russia have the heart," he replied. "Is well-known fact."

It was a flat statement, and I had to repress a smile at the manner in which it had been delivered. Although it really wasn't all that late, the inn was very quiet, the hallway dim. The Russian contingent had certainly settled down. Perhaps they had taken their revelry to one of the taverns in the village and were terrorizing the populace, I thought, or perhaps they were merely holding their breaths and creeping about on tiptoe after Orlov's servant had taken his message to the taproom. My skirts made a soft whispering sound as we moved down the hall toward the front of the inn.

"Lucie has grown very fond of you," Orlov remarked.

"And I have grown fond of her."

"She is a moody girl. Is good for her to have a friend."

The innkeeper's wife had already locked up. The front door was bolted. A candle burned beneath a glass globe on the counter. A fat calico cat was curled beside the heavy leather registration book. It stretched drowsily and waved its tail as we passed. Orlov cupped his hand about my elbow as we started up the steps, his palm warm, the fingers lightly squeezing my flesh. The contact sent pleasant vibrations through my whole body, and I felt a delicious languor. I loved Jeremy Bond with all my heart and soul, but I was human, after all, and I couldn't help but respond to this remarkable man on a purely physical level.

No candles burned on the second floor, but the window at the end of the hall was uncurtained and brilliant moonlight spilled through, making a pale silver pool on the floor and creating a soft silvery blue haze. There was a slight chill in the air. I shivered. Orlov's white garments gleamed in the semi-darkness. We stopped in front of my door. He stood before me. I tilted my chin, looking up at his face. He wore a thoughtful expression, and his eyes seemed sad.

"Is pity you have this man in London," he murmured. "I had hoped you would be our guest in the house I have rented."

Was he going to spoil it? Was he going to take me into his arms and try to use physical persuasion? Was I going to have to struggle and end the evening on an unpleasant note? Orlov looked deeply into my eyes for a long moment, and then he stepped back and took a deep breath, his chest heaving. I was relieved . . . at least that's what I told myself.

"Thank you for a lovely evening, Count Orlov," I said.

"I bring a few presents to you from London," he said, "just a few trinkets to amuse you. I have them placed in your room while we dine."

"Presents? But there was no reason for you to—"

"It is my great pleasure to give presents to a beautiful woman."

"Then—then I will simply say thank you again."

Orlov nodded and opened the door for me. The maid had left candles burning, and pale golden light washed over us. I told him good night. He hesitated just a moment, looking at me with sad eyes, then moved back. I stepped into the room and shut the door and leaned against it, closing my eyes. My head seemed to whirl, and my breathing was decidedly irregular, my bosom rising and falling, straining against its prison of silk and lace. The strong black tea had helped, yes, but I was still feeling the effects of the wine. How idiotic of me to consume so much. I had undoubtedly made a fool of myself. Count Orlov must think me a terrible ninny.

Orlov . . . Orlov . . . *Why* was that name so familiar? I

sighed and moved from the door, and it was then that I saw the presents on the table near the fireplace, three different-sized boxes wrapped in silver paper and tied with dark blue velvet ribbons, a tall crystal vase of magnificent red roses beside them. I really shouldn't open them. I knew that. I should send them back. There was no reason why he should have brought presents for me, and I certainly shouldn't accept them. "Just a few trinkets," he had said. The count would be offended if I returned them, I reasoned, and what woman doesn't like to open presents?

I opened the largest first, removing the ribbons, tearing away the paper, lifting out a large, oval box of satiny pale blue cardboard, a fashionable confectioner's name stamped in silver on the lid. I lifted the lid off to discover rows of beautiful chocolates, each in its own container of white paper lace. There was dark chocolate, light chocolate, each piece uniquely shaped. Much too beautiful to eat, I told myself, but I took a piece nevertheless. The rich chocolate shell contained a marvelous orange cream, sheer ambrosia. I licked my fingers and replaced the lid, still savoring the divine taste.

The second box contained a fan, the thin ivory stems opening to reveal delicate flowers in gold thread embroidered against white silk as fragile and translucent as butterfly wings. The narrow handle was made of gold. The fan was incredibly lovely, a work of art, and . . . and it must have been terribly expensive, I thought, examining the tiny, wonderfully detailed gold flowers on the thin silk. Just a trinket, the kind of trinket Madame de Pompadour might have used to conceal her lips as she whispered a choice bit of gossip to some courtier attired in satin and laces.

Putting the fan aside, I opened the final package and lifted out of its nest of tissue paper a small enameled metal box so dazzling that I could only stare as I held it in the palm of my hand. The deep blue enamel was partially overlaid with patterned swirls of silver filigree, and the center of the lid was set with a silver-mounted crest composed entirely of rubies and diamonds. It was the same crest I had seen on the side of Orlov's coach. Silver gleamed against the rich, dark blue. The gems glittered. Carefully, I opened the delicately hinged lid. The interior of the box was silver. On the back of the lid, surrounded by diamonds, was a beautifully executed miniature of Count Gregory Orlov at a considerably younger age, such a handsome face.

His hair was lighter then, more blond than brown. His mouth had a sullen curl, and his blue eyes were haughty and full of the arrogance of youth. The square-cut diamonds framing the miniature were flawless, flashing fiery rainbows of light. I would have to give the box back, of course. I couldn't possibly keep it. What an exquisite thing it was, though. If he gave presents like this to a woman he didn't even know, what kind of presents did he give to women who had done something to earn them? He must be rich as Croesus, yet . . . yet he and his brothers had had a miserably deprived childhood. I gazed at the miniature for a long time, frowning, trying to remember something, trying to call up scraps of information that had been filed away in my mind years ago.

Orlov. Count Gregory Orlov. Alexis. Feodor. *The Orlov Giants.* Where did that phrase come from? Yes, sometime or other I had heard the five brothers referred to as the Orlov Giants, but when, in what context? Slowly closing the lid, setting the box aside, I got up and began to undress, and it was not until I had blown the candles out and got into bed that the veils lifted from my mind and memory returned. I had been in school and we were studying Russia and I was very bored, longing to romp in the sunshine, longing to leave the dull, stuffy classroom that smelled of chalk dust and ink and old books. The schoolmistress, a flighty, breathless spinster with a penchant for court gossip had been chattering on and on about recent events in that sprawling, snowbound country none of us gave a hang about.

Russia had a new ruler. The bloated, sexually depraved

old Empress Elizabeth had died and her heir, Peter III, was quite, quite mad. With the help of the military, his young German bride, Catherine, had brought about a coup and usurped the throne. Peter had been spirited away and held prisoner, dying shortly thereafter. Some claimed he had been strangled by the Orlov Giants, who had been the first to leap to Catherine's support. She had rewarded all five of them most generously. On her coronation day she had made Gregory Orlov her Adjutant General and had given him the title of Count. She had installed him in a sumptuous apartment in the Winter Palace, which had a secret staircase leading up to her bedroom. He had been her first official lover, his influence over her the scandal of Europe.

For almost a decade Gregory Orlov had been the uncrowned Emperor of All the Russias and one of the most powerful men on earth.

Chapter Four

THERE HAD BEEN A BUSTLING COMMOTION IN the yard ever since dawn, and I was surprised to find it almost deserted when I stepped outside shortly before ten. A Russian in blue was giving stern instructions to the driver of the Orlov coach, which would shortly be brought around. The driver nodded a laconic nod, peering into space, then sauntered toward the stables. The other, one of Vladimir's cohorts, scowled and moved off in the other direction, and I found myself alone. The other carriages, those carrying all the baggage, all the candelabra and rugs and china and such, as well as most of the servants, had already left. My own bags had been brought down an hour ago. I assumed they were already on their way to London and would be left at The White Hart as I had instructed.

It was a mildly overcast morning, the sky light gray, the sun a pale white disk partially obscured by haze. There was a chill in the air, and I was glad I had put the hooded violet cloak over my blue silk with its narrow violet stripes. Orlov and Lucie were apparently still inside. I was relieved to have a few more minutes respite before facing them. I had returned the enameled box to him first thing this morning, sending it along with a brief, polite note explaining that I could not possibly keep it. I had given the box of chocolates to one of the maids, asking her to share it with the rest of the staff, and the lovely fan was packed away with my other belongings. I would keep it as a memento of an evening that now seemed dreamlike and unreal, a blur of flickering golden light made even vaguer by the alcohol I had unwisely consumed.

This morning, cool, clear-headed, I could view my attraction to Orlov with objectivity. I had felt a certain stirring, yes, but it had been purely physical and in no way a betrayal of my love for Jeremy. I had been in a sad, pensive mood, feeling very vulnerable, and he had been extremely amiable, extremely charming. Any woman would have responded to that potent, persuasive, sexual allure, but there had been no seduction and, all things considered, I had conducted myself in a blameless fashion. Orlov had shown me a great deal of consideration, had not pressed, had been a gentleman, however rough at the edges. I appreciated that. Another man might have turned the evening into a very unpleasant struggle of wills.

I pulled the heavy violet silk hood over my head and arranged the folds of the cloak more closely around me. Three more Russian guards came out of the inn, grumbling among themselves as they marched toward the stables. All three were heavily armed, I observed. I recognized Ivan and one of the others, but Vladimir wasn't with them. He was probably standing guard outside the door of Lucie's room, I thought, shuddering as I remembered the near-murder I had witnessed. Vladimir took his post very seriously, as, indeed, did all the guards. The villagers were certainly going to be pleased to see the last of them. One of the maids had told me this morning that "them 'orrible Ruskies" had almost demolished one of the village taverns last night after they left the taproom. There had been a bloody brawl, three villagers had been seriously injured and one of the serving wenches had been "brutally ravished" by six of the brutes, although "that Madie 'Awkins" wasn't any better than she should be and probably relished every minute of it.

Orlov had undoubtedly showered more gold coins around to pay for damages to persons and place, I reflected. The proprietor of the tavern was probably counting his profits at this very minute, and Madie Hawkins would be richer, too, in experience if nothing else. I stepped back as the magnificent white and gold carriage pulled into the yard, the handsome grays stamping restlessly.

"It seems we are going to have this splendid vehicle all to ourselves," a voice behind me said, "at least for the first lap."

I turned. Because of the noise of the carriage I hadn't heard Sir Harry Lyman come outside. Tall, lanky, with short-clipped brick red hair and weary brown eyes, he was elegantly attired in black with a splendid waistcoat of maroon satin patterned with black silk embroidery. In his late forties, he had the worn, slightly faded look of a man whose life has been harried by details and minor crises. The dashing clothes merely accentuated a complexion like old parchment, the fatigue in those friendly eyes.

"Sir Harry Lyman," he said, "and you must be the celebrated Miss Marietta Danver."

"Celebrated?"

"Count Orlov scarcely spoke of anything else on the ride back from London. Most aggravating," he added. "I had hoped to go over some very important papers with him."

"He told me you handled various business matters for him."

"And I rue the day I agreed to do so," Sir Harry said dryly. "Orlov is an interesting chap, but he has no head for business. The exasperation I endure is equaled only by the profits I make."

"I would imagine there are quite a lot of the latter."

"Quite a lot," he agreed. "My nervous system may collapse, my hair may turn white, but if he continues to turn over to me such generous sums for investment, I'll soon be a wealthy man."

Sir Harry removed a silver watch from his pocket and glanced at it distractedly, obviously preoccupied with the thousand and one things he needed to do in the city.

"You mentioned that we would have the carriage to ourselves," I said. "Lucie and the count won't be joining us?"

"Not this morning," he replied. "Lucie, it seems, was

eager to put on the English riding habit her uncle brought
her from London and decided to do the first lap on
horseback—she's an excellent rider, if a trifle headstrong
and reckless."

"And the count decided to join her?"

He nodded, putting away the watch he was still holding
in his palm. "He much prefers horseback, hates being
cooped up in a carriage. They've gone on ahead, and we'll
rendezvous at noon when, it appears, we will have a picnic
on the side of the road."

His dry, resigned tone indicated that he was less than
thrilled with the idea. Although I would have enjoyed
chatting with Lucie, I was relieved to have my next meeting with Orlov delayed. Why was I so apprehensive about
seeing him again? What did I fear?

There was a clatter of iron on cobbles as the four guards I
had seen earlier came riding into the yard, holding the
splendid grays to a slow walk. I had to admit that they
were an imposing sight as they took their places, two on
either side of the carriage. The driver settled back on his
perch, tightening his hold on the reins. A liveried groom
opened the door for us, and Sir Harry gave me his hand,
helping me into an interior that was all plush white velvet
and gold gilt. Sides and ceiling were covered with white
leather embossed with gold *fleurs-de-lis.*

"Modest little rig, isn't it?" Sir Harry said, sinking back
into the velvet cushions across from me.

"I've never been in a carriage so grand," I admitted.

"It's modest compared to some I've seen in St.
Petersburg," he told me. "Orlov himself used to have one
that put this to shame. When he was—ah—officially attached to the court, he owned a blue and silver rig that literally stopped traffic when he took it out."

The groom closed the door and took his place on the
standing platform on back of the carriage. The driver
cracked his whip, clicked the reins smartly. The carriage
began to move slowly out of the yard, the four guards keeping pace beside it. I looked through the window at the ram-

bling old inn with its mellow rose-gray brick walls and thatched roof. The faded blue sign swung gently on its hinges. The Wayfarer was a place I would not soon forget.

Sir Harry sighed, resigned to a long, unproductive journey. We passed through the brick portals and started down the road that led through the village. People came out to stare at the spectacle as we passed. Several of them booed, and I had the feeling that, had it not been for the guards, we would have been pelted with rocks and refuse.

"It would appear that Orlov's men have hardly endeared themselves to the local folk," Sir Harry observed.

"Hardly," I said. "Did you hear about last night?"

"In some detail. The good count severely reprimanded his men and scattered gold all over the village." He shook his head. "I'll never understand the Russian character. The same men who raised such hell last night will sob like infants at the sound of a native song played on a balalaika, tears pouring down their cheeks."

"You spent a great deal of time in Russia, didn't you?" I asked.

"Almost twenty years. Elizabeth was ruler when I took my first post—a very minor post, I might add. I was an attaché to an attaché to an attaché, little more than a clerk. Poor pay, very long hours, a great deal of youthful enthusiasm."

"It must have been terribly exciting."

"Exciting indeed for a youth of twenty-six. Elizabeth—now there was a figure for you, painted like a china doll, so bloated up she could hardly move without assistance, still—uh—lustily indulging in various pleasures. Her nephew and heir was a drooling, demented bully alternately drilling his private troops until they dropped or torturing his cocker spaniels—if he wasn't playing with toy soldiers, that is."

"And Catherine?" I asked.

Sir Harry hesitated a moment before answering, his weary brown eyes looking into the past. "A dull, colorless little nonentity back then," he said, "abused by her husband, ignored by the Empress and scorned by the rest of the court. She was marking time the whole while, ingratiating herself with the army, winning the respect of the people. Without a drop of Russian blood she became more Russian than the Russians, observing all the religious ceremonies, clinging to the old customs, making a great show of it. An exceedingly shrewd woman, this obscure German princess brought to Russia to wed the heir. Catherine was determined to take the throne. When the time came, she was ready."

"I find it incredible that she could just—just take over the country."

"Incredible, but not really surprising under the circumstances. Her husband was literally mad—it would have been disastrous if Peter had been permitted to reign—and she was, after all, the mother of the heir. Europe was scandalized, but the Russian people were happy with their new Empress."

"Is—is it true that she had Peter murdered?"

"The official word is that he died quite suddenly of colic," Sir Harry replied.

"I understand the Orlovs were holding him prisoner at the time."

"Peter was being—uh—detained, yes. For his own good, of course."

The irony in his voice was light, so subtle as to be almost indetectable, but I caught it nevertheless. As the carriage moved smoothly past open fields with the guards galloping protectively on either side, I saw that Sir Harry was still very much the diplomat. Although we were speaking of events that had taken place some fifteen years ago, he was not willing to divulge privileged information. I felt certain he knew the truth about Peter III's mysterious death, but he wasn't going to reveal any secrets that might tarnish the image of the man whose business he was handling.

"Count Orlov told me that you got along very well with Catherine," I remarked.

"I did indeed," he replied. "I was considerably younger

in those days and—uh—considerably more attractive to the ladies. The Empress didn't get along well with the British ambassador, a fusty type, and she preferred working with—uh—healthy young men, if possible. Our relationship was strictly a working one, but a certain amount of flattery and mild flirtation made it much easier to deal with her. Catherine was—is—a strong, shrewd, formidably intelligent ruler, but she is first and foremost a woman. Those clever enough to realize it have a distinct edge."

"You—you seem to admire her a great deal."

"Indeed I do. Catherine is the best thing that could possibly have happened to Russia at this particular time. Peter the Great brought the country out of the Dark Ages, and Catherine is striving to bring the Age of Enlightenment to a country still weighed down with medieval customs and superstitions. She has thrown open the windows, thrown open the doors, made Russia a part of the rest of the world."

Sir Harry paused as the carriage passed over a particularly bad rut. In the luxurious, velvet-cushioned interior, we barely felt the bump. He adjusted his neck cloth, his brown eyes thoughtful as he continued.

"When I knew Catherine, she got up at six o'clock in the morning, rubbed her face with ice and, after several cups of black coffee, set to work. She often worked ten hours without pause, surrounded by ministers who couldn't begin to keep up with her. I've never known a person with such discipline, such drive."

"Yet her private life is the scandal of Europe," I said.

Sir Harry allowed himself a thin smile. "It is traditional for kings to have their favorites—Charles II had Nell Gwynn, Barbara Castlemaine and a score of others, Louis XIV had Louise de la Vallière, Montespan, the straight-laced Madame de Maintenon—and they are admired for their virility. Is it so shocking, I wonder, for an Empress equally as powerful to have her male favorites?"

"I—I hadn't thought of it that way."

"Alas," he said, "the ladies I mentioned had far too

much power, far too great an influence over the sovereigns whose beds they warmed, and the same is true of the men who keep Catherine amused. Her—uh—extremely strong sexual proclivities render her quite vulnerable and are the one dent in an otherwise invincible suit of armor."

"Apparently Count Orlov kept her amused for quite some time."

"She loved him wildly, blindly, inordinately. His word was her command. She was, I fear, an abject slave to her passion for him. She heaped him with honors, lavished him with riches, built a marble palace for him and gave him more and more power."

"Yet she sent him away."

"Even the strongest passions begin to pale in time, and the good count was not always wise, not always discreet. A woman can tolerate just so many infidelities. She showered him with even more lavish gifts—another estate, six thousand serfs, an increased annual salary—and sent him packing. Orlov was desolate. All the wealth in the world—and he has a fair share of it—can't compensate for what he lost."

"Power, you mean?"

"Power," he said. "Orlov did his best to get her back. He gave her a solitaire diamond as large as a door knob, said to be the largest in the world. It is known as the Orlov Diamond, and it is indeed a wondrous thing, but it failed to bring her back. She accepted it graciously, had it set in the Russian Imperial Scepter under a jeweled eagle but sent him packing just the same."

"It must have been a terrible blow," I said.

"It was indeed. During the intervening years Count Orlov has spent most of his time traveling rather disconsolately from country to country, trying to forget. He loved her in his way, you see, although his way was a bit too casual for a woman as jealous and possessive as Catherine."

"He—he hasn't found another woman to replace her?"

"It would be a rare woman indeed who could replace Catherine of Russia," Sir Harry said.

I thought about all he had told me as we continued our journey in the luxurious coach that smelled of crushed vel vet and teak. All I had learned about him only imbued Count Orlov with more fascination, of course, vesting him with an even stronger aura of glamour. The man who had captivated Catherine of Russia, whom she had loved "wildly, blindly, inordinately," must have been splendid indeed, a lover beyond compare. Dazzling male beauty and a hard, superbly muscled body could account for only part of his success. He had to have other qualities as well to have sexually enslaved a woman like Catherine for so many years. I was intrigued, I admitted that, but my curiosity was . . . was merely curiosity. It would be a rare woman who could replace Catherine of Russia, yes, but there wasn't a man on earth who could replace Jeremy Bond in my heart.

It was well after noon when the carriage began to slow down. The countryside was lovely, grassy fields of pale jade green dotted with large boulders, trees spreading cool blue-gray shadows. The carriage stopped. The groom opened the door for us. Count Orlov himself took my hand and helped me down. Those strong fingers tightly pressing mine caused no emotional tremors inside. Those dark blue eyes peering so fondly into mine prompted no corresponding fondness, and the warm, gentle smile on his wide pink lips brought no matching smile to my own. Royal favorite he may have been, but I was immune to his allure. I was grateful to him for all he had done, yes, and I would be polite and friendly, but there would be no repetition of last night's cozy intimacy. Count Orlov was not going to have another opportunity to cast his spell over me.

"You have the comfortable journey?" he asked me.

"It was extremely comfortable."

"Ah, Sir Harry," he said, grasping the man's arm, half dragging him out of the carriage. "You kept the lady company. I suppose he bores you with tedious business talk?"

"Not at all," I replied.

"I'd like to bore *you*," Sir Harry said grumpily, straightening the lapels of his coat. "I've been trying for three days to talk to you about those coal mines, Orlov. If you want to invest in them we must—"

Orlov made a mock scowl and pounded Sir Harry on the back, almost toppling him. Sir Harry gave him a resentful, resigned look, and the count slung an arm around his shoulders in a hearty, affectionate hug.

"Always the boring details!" he exclaimed. "This man here drives me into the frenzy, Miss Danver. He has the clerk's mentality, always the numbers, always the papers. We discuss all this as soon as we settle in London, Sir Harry, I promise. Now we have the picnic. Is fine idea, no?"

"Positively inspired," Sir Harry said dryly.

Orlov curled his forearm around Sir Harry's throat and squeezed playfully, pretending to strangle him. Sir Harry coughed, freed himself and gave his robust employer another offended look as he stalked away. Count Orlov chuckled, planted his fists on his thighs and watched him depart. He was dressed in gray today, soft pearl gray velvet, although his sweeping cloak was lined with white silk. The invigorating horseback ride had given his cheeks a pink flush, and his golden brown hair was attractively windblown. His vitality charged the air.

"Is fine fellow, Sir Harry, but a fusspot, I fear. His head is full of the business matters, the facts and the figures. I tease him about it."

"I should say you're most fortunate to have him working for you."

"Ah, yes, he takes the money, makes it multiply. I will go and humor him a bit, let him tell me about these boring mines while the servants finish setting up our picnic. Here comes Lucie to greet you. You and I will talk later."

Lucie came hurrying to me as her uncle sauntered off to join Sir Harry. She, too, had a flushed, healthy glow, and her eyes were full of pride as she whirled around to show off her new blue velvet riding habit. It was very English, very smart, very flattering to her slim young figure. The hat had a black silk scarf tied around the crown, the ends floating free behind, lifting in the breeze. Neat black leather boots and a pair of supple black leather gloves complemented the outfit.

"Do I look English?" she asked.

"You look lovely," I told her.

"I was eager to wear it. This morning I felt carefree— sometimes I do, sometimes not. I wanted to ride my horse. It was rude of me not to share the carriage with you."

"Nonsense," I replied.

"My uncle and I had a race. Vladimir and the others were very perturbed because we flew on ahead and could not be properly guarded. My uncle was upset because I won. He pouted and said he was getting old, and then he laughed and said he would win next time."

"Sir Harry told me you are an excellent horsewoman."

"Yes, I ride much. I ride fast. It is good cure for melancholy, I find. It sets the heart free and drives away the sadness. It is good to feel the wind sting the face, to feel the great animal beneath you, under your control. Do you ride?"

"Not much," I admitted. "I once spent quite some time on a mule."

Lucie looked startled. "A mule? This long-eared animal that makes a hee-haw noise?"

I nodded, amused by her description. "It was several years ago, in America. I was riding through the wilderness on an overgrown trail called the Natchez Trace."

"This on a mule?"

"I grew very fond of her."

"There were Indians?" she asked.

"Savage Indians. They almost got me," I said quite truthfully. "I hid in a cave until they went away."

Lucie's violet-blue eyes were wide with dismay, then disbelief. She shook her head, smiling, convinced I was teasing. I smiled back, pleased to see the girl so lighthearted. A little way ahead of us four heavily laden coaches lined up at the side of the road, varnished golden brown wood

gleaming in the pale sunlight. Servants in white and gold
were opening doors, fetching various items, carrying them
to a shady spot beneath a spreading oak where carpets and
cushions had already been laid. Vladimir and the other
guards had selected a spot for themselves farther on behind more trees, where they were already noisily consuming roasted chickens and passing bottles of vodka.

"Come," Lucie said, taking my hand. "We will go sit under the tree. I am frightfully hungry after my ride. Our
chef prepared a special picnic lunch for us before we left
the inn."

The white rugs patterned in yellow and gold that were
spread out over the grass were the same from the night before in the private dining room. The cushions were plump
and white and soft. Lucie took off her hat and plopped
down, reclining with one elbow propped on a cushion and
looking very indolent and young. I sat down in a more dignified manner, spreading my blue and violet striped
skirts. Leaves rustled overhead. An acorn dropped into my
lap. Flecks of sunlight and shadow danced about us, and
the smells of grass and bark and root were mingled with
the marvelous smell of freshly baked pastry as one of the
servants placed a fancy white wicker hamper on the edge
of the rugs. I wondered idly if we were going to dine on gold
plate.

"My uncle tells me you had a lovely meal together last
night," Lucie remarked.

"It was very pleasant."

"I had the headache," she said. "I preferred to stay in
my room and see the lovely presents he brought me from
London. My uncle is very good to remember to bring presents. Is this grammar correct?"

"It will do nicely."

"All the time my French improves. One day I will learn
to speak English, too. My uncle likes you very much. He
says I am most fortunate to have so enchanting a friend."

"That was very kind of him."

"He makes you uneasy?" she asked.

The bluntness of the question startled me. "Why—not at all," I lied. "He was—he is very charming."

"He is overbearing sometimes," she said quietly. "So much energy he has, so much vitality—it is unsettling often to strangers. He is rough and loud like the swaggering soldier, but he has many tender sentiments as well."

The subject of our conversation marched over to us with long strides, his cloak flaring behind him like white-lined gray wings. In a jovial, mock-exasperated voice he informed us that in order to humor "this maddening clerk" he had agreed to talk about boring things while they ate. They would have chicken and stout fare with the men and leave the delicacies to us. He would pine for our company the whole time, he assured us, and then, with martyred expression, left to rejoin the persistent Sir Harry.

"Sir Harry has to badger my uncle much," Lucie said, smiling. "My uncle does not like the business matters."

"That's quite apparent."

"He gives in, though. He knows Sir Harry knows best."

We did not dine on gold plate but, instead, on beautiful china that might have graced the table of Louis XV. There was a cold, creamy asparagus soup and marvelous flakey pastries filled with liver pâté. The chicken wings baked in a honey glaze were delicious, as were the eggs in aspic and the enormous ripe olives. A bird scolded us from a leafy branch as we ate, and I was not surprised to see a parade of ants march across the rugs. We drank cold, sweetened tea served in glasses of ice, a most eccentric drink but quite refreshing, and for dessert there were small, square chocolate cakes iced with almond paste and filled with raspberry preserves.

"Your chef is incredible," I said, dipping my fingers into the crystal finger bowl thoughtfully provided. "I've never had such food."

"He studied many years in France," Lucie informed me. "Once he cooked for the Empress, but my uncle lured him away with much money. He grumbles at all this travel and the difficulty in getting ice."

"The cold tea—"

"He calls it *iced tea*. It is his invention. The Englishmen are sure he is mad, spoiling their national beverage this way. Would you care for another glass?"

"Oh, no. I'm far too full."

Lucie gave a languorous sigh and lolled back against the cushions. "Me, too. I am replete. This is a good word?"

"A perfect word."

Plucking a blade of grass, she toyed with it for a moment and then began to idly stroke her cheek with the slender green stalk. Her lovely face had a pensive expression, and her eyes seemed to be gazing at some vaguely disturbing memory. She sighed again and, tossing the grass away, sat up and folded her arms across her knees.

"I am sad that we get to London so soon," she said.

"But London is a very exciting city. Why should you be sad?"

"I will not be seeing you again. I make a wonderful new friend, and so soon I must give her up. Once again I will be alone."

"I am sure you will make many new friends, Lucie."

She did not reply. A long golden brown wave fell across her cheek. She lifted a graceful hand to brush it aside.

"I am happy for you, though," she said, gazing into the distance. "You have this man. You have someone who loves you."

"One day soon you will have someone, too."

Lucie shook her head, as though such a thing were unthinkable, and then, abruptly, she picked up her hat and stood. As she put it on I got to my feet, too. One of the servants came over to start gathering up the picnic things. I brushed my skirt, bewildered by these sudden shifts of mood. When she had adjusted the hat, Lucie turned to me with a bright smile, but her face seemed strangely hard despite the forced gaiety.

"I will see about my horse now," she said quickly. "We

will be sharing the carriage the rest of the way. We will talk nonsense and munch sugared almonds and be—and be very merry."

Lucie hurried across the grass to the area where the horses had been left, their reins tied loosely to an improvised post. What a strange, enigmatic creature she was, I thought, so young and vulnerable, and yet . . . yet there were times when those lovely, slanted eyes were full of wisdom, full of secrets I felt she would share with no one. The girl was charming and kind, and there was a poignant quality about her I found quite touching, yet it was as though an invisible cloud hung over her, obscuring the sunlight. I was convinced there had been some tragedy in her young life, one that had left deep scars.

As it would be some time before the servants had everything packed into the carriages, I decided to take a short stroll. Beyond the trees there was a narrow stream. I walked toward it. The thin sunlight bathed the boulders, flecks of mica glistening, and burnished the pale green grass with silver. Tiny purple wildflowers grew in scattered patches. Wild violets? Walking under the trees, I reached the river and stood on the mossy bank to watch the clear water rushing over the pebbled bed. It made a pleasant gurgling sound, soothing and serene.

Several minutes passed, and I was not aware of Count Orlov's presence until I noticed his shadow slanting long and black across the ground. I turned. He smiled a hesitant smile, the navy blue eyes humble. There was something on his mind, and he clearly didn't know how to go about expressing it. I was reminded of an awkward, overgrown boy as he stood there, undecided, his handsome face marked with adolescent torment.

"You wanted something, Count Orlov?" I asked.

"Is—it is not safe for you to wander off alone like this."

"This is England," I told him, "not Russia. There are no black bears roaming about, no wolves prowling."

"Nevertheless, you are under my protection. I would be desolate if anything happened to you."

He was quite sincere. I was touched by his protective-ness. He stepped closer, still hesitant. The boyish quality somehow emphasized his virility, augmented the potent sensuality. He was so very large, a golden colossus. Tall myself, I felt almost petite alongside him. He smelled of sweat and leather and dust, and his hair was slightly damp, gleaming like dark gold in the sunlight.

"Did—did you and Sir Harry have a profitable talk?" I asked.

"Oh, yes. I agree to make the investments, if only to get him to discontinue the—" He hesitated, frowning. "If only to have him stop the pestering. He is very pleased and I hope to enjoy my lunch then but he takes out the papers and goes on and on with the explanations. I long to grab him by the neck and choke him, but I listen with the patient expression and agree that it is a very wise thing to make these investments."

I smiled. "Poor Sir Harry."

"I—I wished to speak with you privately," he said.

He looked utterly miserable. I half expected to see him twist the toe of his boot in the ground.

"Yes?" I prompted.

"Is about the box," he began.

"I'm sure you realize why I couldn't accept so expensive a gift, Count Orlov."

"I—yes, I realize this when my servant returns it to me this morning. I fear maybe—maybe you misinterpret this gift. I fear maybe you take offense. This worries me."

"There's no reason why it should," I said.

"What you think is most important to me."

"You hardly know me, Count Orlov."

"This does not matter."

I waited. He apparently had some sort of explanation he wished to make, and it was very difficult for him to find the right words. We could hear the rattle of harness in the distance, the stamping of horses, the gruff shouts of men as they prepared to resume the journey. Thin, wavering yellow-white rays slanted through the trees, bathing the

scene with a softly diffused light. A bird swooped gracefully across the stream, perching on a rock on the opposite
bank. I was growing more and more uncomfortable as he
continued to hesitate. He seemed to be looking into the
past, and there was a deep furrow above the bridge of his
nose.

"I have this box made a—quite some time ago," he said.
"I commission the finest jeweler in St. Petersburg to fashion it for me. I intend to give it to a very special person,
but—but something happens and I do not give it to her. All
this time I keep it, waiting for someone else who is very
special to give it to."

"I'm flattered, Count Orlov, but—"

"I do not mean it to give the offense. I wish only for you
to have it as a token of my admiration. I do not expect the
favors in return. I fear maybe you think this."

His voice was a husky, guttural purr. Heavy lids
drooped over eyes full of concern. Standing there in the
softly diffused light, hands resting lightly on his thighs, he
exuded an appeal so strong it gave a true meaning to the
word *magnetism*. He actually seemed to draw one to him,
and one had to actively fight that forceful pull. I turned
away from him, gazing at the water, and when I spoke my
voice was much too crisp.

"I wasn't offended, Count Orlov, nor—nor did I misinterpret your gift. I simply felt it would be improper for me to
accept it."

"I wish only to please."

I turned around, cool, composed, safely behind the invisible wall I had managed to throw up. He sensed that wall.
It pained him.

"You are angry?" he asked.

"Of course not."

"I make the blunder. I realize this now."

"It's unimportant, Count Orlov. Please forget it. I really
think we should go back now."

"Yes, the carriage will be ready. I am glad we clear this

matter up between us. We shall have a pleasant journey to London."

It was going to be a damned uncomfortable journey for me, I thought as we started toward the road. The ground was rough, uneven. Orlov took hold of my arm to assist me, as though I were still an invalid. The skin of his fingers was like rough silk as they gripped my upper arm. I wanted to pull free, run ahead, but that would only have made matters worse. In a few hours I would be in London and free of these fascinating, bewildering Russians who had come into my life so bizarrely. In a few hours, if I were lucky, I would be in Jeremy's arms and nothing else would matter.

Chapter Five

LONDON WAS BROWN AND TAN AND DULL, pewter gray, spread with thickening violet shadows beneath a dreary, cloud-filled late afternoon sky. London was the stench of the river and rotting wood and fish, the squalor of the slums with masses of unwashed humanity jammed into incredibly filthy hovels, the cool elegance of majestic squares with lofty trees and formal flower beds and marble-porticoed mansions. It was vice and vitality, fever and furor, boisterous brawls, constant congestion, the most dangerous, the most exciting, the most stimulating city on earth. I felt that excitement in my bones as the plain private carriage took me through the labyrinth of narrow, twisting streets. Gin-soaked bawds yelled hoarsely, hawking baskets of rags. Thieves and harlots began to crawl out of the shadows as evening approached. Toffs in satin and velvet frock coats strutted like lords, lace handkerchiefs held to their nostrils, swords at the ready.

My bags had already been delivered to The White Hart. Count Orlov had insisted I spend the night at the imposing beige and white mansion he had leased—everything was prepared, it was late, I was weary—but I had firmly, politely refused his hospitality. I had to get to The White Hart as soon as possible. Very well, if I insisted, he would send me in the Orlov carriage with six of his men as bodyguards. I shook my head, adamant. We faced each other in the gorgeous white and gold drawing room, for the carriage had come directly to the mansion on London's most exclusive and aristocratic square. Frustrated, furious—Count Orlov wasn't accustomed to being defied—he had finally given an exasperated sigh and had one of the English servants who came with the mansion hire a common hackney and sent me off with great reluctance. Four of his men, in English attire and armed to the teeth, trotted alongside the carriage as runners, ready to slaughter any ruffian who threatened the precious cargo—me.

Count Orlov had given me no choice about this last detail. I would have the four bodyguards or I wouldn't be allowed to leave. He would tie me hand and foot. He would lock me up in a closet. I would have proper protection or I wouldn't set foot outside the house. I had given in. We had had wine in the drawing room as we waited for the hackney to arrive. Lucie, tearful, hadn't touched hers. I had given her an emotional hug before I left and promised to try and see her again before I left London. The girl had looked absolutely crestfallen as she stood there on the steps beside her uncle, waving forlornly as the rattling hackney pulled out of the drive. Poor Lucie. I would never learn the dark secrets that caused those violet-blue eyes to be so soulful. I would think of her and her uncle often, but I was mightily relieved to be out of their colorful, exotic, dazzlingly rich and emotionally charged orbit.

The shadows were growing thicker, black nests of shadows filling the alleys, gathering in corners, and the city took on a raw, raucous air as darkness fell. I was secretly relieved to have the stalwart, scowling runners as the hackney passed sordid gin shops and taverns, noisy brothels and gambling dens. The streets were so congested that our progress was slow, the runners moving at a lazy trot as the driver cracked his whip and fought his way through the tangle of carts and coaches, sedan chairs and wagons. Horses neighed, rearing. Drivers yelled obscenities at each other. The shrill, cacophonous din was as much a part of the city as the music of church bells and chimes. One quickly grew immune to it, and I hardly noticed as we continued on our way.

Another few minutes and I would be at The White Hart. We passed over an arching stone bridge. I smelled the Thames. More gin shops and brothels, a park, a slightly wider street lined with shops and stalls, lighter, slightly less traffic. Do hurry. Do hurry. Would he be there? Would he look up when I opened the door of the room he had taken? Would he make some jaunty quip as I moved toward him? Would we squabble playfully before he crushed me into his arms and made passionate love to me? Please let him be there. Please let him forgive me. We've been through so much together, and I love him so. I love him so. Almost there. Down a twisting, cobbled street with weathered signs hanging over shops. Torches beginning to burn as pitch black darkness shrouded the city. A thin white fog rising from the river. I love him with all my heart and soul, and I will never, never let him out of my sight again. If only he's there. If only he's there. Please let him be there.

After what seemed hours the battered old hackney pulled slowly into the yard of The White Hart. My nerves were ajangle. I was so excited, so apprehensive, I could hardly climb out. My knees threatened to give way beneath me as I stepped onto the uneven cobbles. The yard was a dark gray-brown, spoked with the yellow lights streaming from the windows of the inn. There was a strong odor of horses, hay and old leather. Chickens clucked. A dog barked loudly. Ivy clung to the worn brick walls, rattling quietly in the breeze, and the old sign hanging over the door creaked on its hinges. The front door opened. A servant appeared. I felt a wave of dizziness, and I realized that I was exhausted from the long trip to London.

Count Orlov had paid the hackney driver in advance. He was already turning the carriage around. Horse hooves clattered loudly on the cobbles. Wheels screeched. The four Russians in their ill-fitting English attire stood grumbling, waiting for me to go inside. Excitement and apprehension mounted as I followed the servant into the cozy, shabbily furnished foyer. Candles glowed softly. A worn, flowered rug covered the floor. The bald, bespectacled proprietor sat behind his counter, idly perusing a newspaper. Looking up, he hastily put aside the paper and got to his feet, smiling a broad, welcoming smile as he recognized me from my earlier stay.

"Miss Danver!" he exclaimed jovially. "We're so pleased to have you back with us."

"I—my bags—"

"All taken care of," he assured me. "I had them sent up to your room. I took the liberty of assigning you to the same room you had before. It's one of our most comfortable."

"Thank you. That was—that was very kind."

He frowned, examining me closely. Candlelight gleamed on his shiny dome. His spectacles had slipped down his nose. I smiled pleasantly, and I could feel the smile tight and forced on my lips. My legs seemed to tremble.

"You—I say, Miss Danver, you look a bit peaked."

"The trip. It was a—a bit exhausting."

"We'd best get you right up to your room. A nice long rest is what you'll be wanting."

"Mr. Bond—is—is he here?"

"Bond?" The innkeeper looked puzzled.

"Jeremy Bond. He took a room here."

"Oh! You mean that jaunty, good-looking chap who arrived when you did. Afraid he's already gone."

"He's gone?"

"Left three days after you did. Tipped everyone lavishly, he did, gave our Tibby five whole pounds. I say, Miss Danver, are you—"

The dizziness swept over me and the candlelight began to dance wildly as the room swayed. A dark cloud claimed me, shutting out the light, and I felt myself falling, floating. I drifted in a confused, chaotic void of misty darkness, yet I felt strong hands lifting me, felt myself sink against cushions. I could smell camphor and beeswax and an acrid odor I couldn't identify, and then yellow-orange lights be-

odor I couldn't identify, and then yellow-orange lights began to flash in front of my eyes and I heard the voices, one deep, worried, the other gruff but distinctly feminine.

"—never know what to do, you men! Get back, give her room, let the poor thing have some *air!*"

"She just fell into a swoon, right there in front of my counter. You could have knocked me over with a—"

"Fetch my cologne and a handkerchief! Do it *now,* you blockhead! Don't just stand there with your mouth hanging open. Move!"

The lights grew brighter, and I heard a low, moaning noise and realized I was making it. I tried to sit up. Firm, gentle hands restrained me. I murmured a protest. My eyelids fluttered, and I sank back into the misty darkness until something damp and cool bathed my temples. I could smell the strong, fragrant scent of flowers. I opened my eyes. The woman leaning over me was extremely plump with a round, bossy but amiable face dominated by a pair of vivid brown eyes. Her mouth was small, a bright cherry red, her cheeks powdered, and a black heart-shaped beauty mark rested coyly on her left temple. Girlish chestnut brown ringlets bobbed on either side of her face in thick profusion. The wig was slightly askew, I observed.

"I—" My voice seemed to come from a great distance. "I must have—"

"Now you just relax, lambie. Reckon you had a little faintin' spell, nothin' at all to be alarmed about."

She continued to dab at my temples with the scent-soaked handkerchief, and I frowned, my nostrils quivering at the overpowering fragrance. She stood back as I struggled into a sitting position, cushions shifting behind my back. I was on the sofa across from the counter. The candles seemed very bright. The proprietor was standing nearby, actually wringing his hands. Two guests moved down the staircase, pausing to stare. The plump woman snapped at them with a few choice phrases that sent them scurrying. She was wearing an old-fashioned gown of sky blue taffeta festooned with pink satin bows and rows of soiled white lace. The once sumptuous taffeta was shiny with age.

"I'm Mrs. Patterson, lambie, Mrs. Pat to the regulars. I run the place with precious little help from my husband here. Get on about your business, Benjamin! I have things well under control. Feel better, lamb?"

"I think I'm all right. I—I feel so foolish."

"Fah! We all get a mite faint sometimes, myself included. It's this world we're livin' in, so much noise, so much clatter, tries a person's nerves. Think you can stand now?"

I nodded. She took my hand. I got to my feet, still feeling rather shaky. Supporting me with an arm around my shoulders, Mrs. Patterson helped me climb the two flights of stairs and led me down the hall to the room I remembered so well. A fire was burning low in the fireplace. The bedcovers were turned down. A bowl of snapdragons sat on the low table beside the overstuffed, flowered blue chair. Less than three weeks had passed since I was last here, yet it seemed a lifetime ago. I thought of Jeremy. Tears sprang to my lashes. I brushed them away while the innkeeper's wife watched me with shrewd, compassionate eyes.

"I know it ain't none of my business, lambie, but you ain't expectin', are you?"

"No, it isn't that. I—it was a very long, weary trip, and I just felt a bit—"

"Reckon I know what you felt, lambie. I've been there before. You wouldn't think it to look at me now, but I've had my share of affairs of th' heart. 'Fore I met Benjamin an' nabbed him, I was quite a *co-kette*. He ran out on you, didn't he?"

I didn't answer. My lashes were still moist.

"I got eyes in my head, lambie, and I reckon I know what's what. I'd be in a slew-a trouble if I didn't, runnin' an inn an' all. I observed the two of you when you checked in last month—knew you were head over heels in love with him, even if you did take separate rooms."

I removed my cloak and dropped it across the back of the

chair and stared at the window. He was gone. He had promised to wait a week, yet he had left three days after I had. He hadn't even waited out the week. I couldn't blame him. It was all my fault. Mrs. Patterson fussed with one of the pink satin bows on her bodice.

"Them handsome, cocky devils are always the worst, all charm, all glib promises. Don't I know it! Had my poor heart broken more times than I care to remember. Charmin' scamps!" She shook her head, the ringlets bobbing. "Give me a clod every time. At least you know where you stand with 'em."

"He didn't run out on me, Mrs. Patterson. He just—just left."

"Sure he did. Don't they all? The fascinatin' ones, that is. Took me a long time to learn that lesson, then I grabbed myself a dull, steady, sweet-natured clod. Let me help you get undressed, lamb. You still look pale and weak as a kitten, shadows under your eyes."

"I'll be all right," I said.

"Sure you will, lamb. Sure you will. It hurts at first, don't I know it, but somehow we manage to get over it. No man's worth that kind of pain."

"I suppose you're right."

I was speaking by rote. My voice seemed to belong to someone else, someone completely detached with no emotions. Mrs. Patterson looked at me, deeply concerned, and then she took my hand and gave it a tight, reassuring squeeze that communicated compassion and age-old sisterhood.

"I'll leave you be now," she said gently, "reckon you'd like to be alone, but I'm havin' a bottle of my special remedy sent up. A glass or two before you go to bed'll work wonders. Never fails me when I'm feelin' glum."

She left with a rustle of old taffeta, closing the door quietly behind her, and I remained where I was, as though in a trance. The fire crackled pleasantly, filling the room with cozy warmth. Disappointment I could take—I had already faced the fact that he might well be gone—but the doubt was tormenting. Three days. He had left after only three days. He hadn't waited out the week. He had broken his word. He . . . he had every reason to do so, I admitted that. I had treated him wretchedly, wretchedly. I had rejected the love he offered so freely, so frankly, and yet . . . and yet all the while he had known I loved him. He had known long before I acknowledged it myself. Why had he left so soon? He must have known I would come back. "I'll be waiting," he had promised. Yet he hadn't waited even a week.

There was a knock on the door. A servant came in with a tray. He set it down, left silently. Several long moments passed. I forced myself to undress, put on a nightgown, brush my hair. The candles had burned down and were beginning to splutter. I poured a glass of Mrs. Patterson's special remedy and took a sip. It was straight gin. I detested it, but I drank it anyway, poured another glass. I blew out the candles and moved over to the window to stare out at the night, the room behind me illuminated only by the pale rose-orange glow of the dying fire.

The spires and steeples of London were silhouetted in stark black against a starless night sky. Heavy clouds roiled, gray tinged with purple, and there was a wind. The treetops in the park across the way trembled, limbs shaking nervously as though fearing the onslaught. It was going to rain. I could see the dome of St. Paul's, gleaming like polished jet in the darkness, and Tower Bridge was visible far to my right, an inky black sketch against the lighter sky. London, the city of so many dreams, a prison to me now that Jeremy was gone. I finished the second glass of gin, staring at the night, and I felt no warmth, no comfort, no easing of pain.

I couldn't sleep, I knew that, yet I set the glass down and climbed into bed and watched reflections of the firelight dancing on the ceiling, pale rose shadows skittering, skipping, growing paler. The crisp linen sheets were lavender scented. They were cool to my touch. I lay very still, watching the light disappear. The rain came. I heard it pattering heavily on the roof with a monotonous staccato. He was gone. I had lost him. I had lost my one chance for happiness. I closed my eyes, seeing his face before me, those vivid blue eyes full of merry mockery, the mouth curving in a half-smile beneath the slightly twisted nose. Desolate, I gazed at it until it, too, melted into the black.

The sound of bells awakened me. They were ringing all over the city, it seemed. A pigeon cooed, prancing on the windowsill outside. Bright rays of sunlight streamed into the room, making a warm yellow-white pool on the faded pink and blue rug spread in front of the fireplace. The bells chimed ten. I sat up, amazed that I had slept so long. Mrs. Patterson's remedy had done its job after all, I thought, climbing out of bed. My bones ached, but my head was surprisingly clear, and as I performed my ablutions and dressed I knew exactly what I had to do.

I would go down to the shipping office. I would find out what ship he had taken—they were bound to have a record of it—and I would book passage on the very next ship. I would follow him to America. I would follow him to the ends of the earth if necessary. My money had been deposited in the Bank of England, Jeremy had handled the transaction himself, so there would be no financial worries. Moving to the mirror, I adjusted my deep garnet silk skirt. My face was still drawn, thinner, it seemed, and there were blue-mauve shadows on my lids. My lips were a paler pink than usual, too, but I wasn't going to bother with cosmetics. There wasn't time.

Smoothing my hair back, I put on the garnet velvet hat with its cascade of curling black ostrich plumes that spilled over one side of the wide, slanting brim. I had never been one to cry, to mourn and bewail my fate. I had always been a fighter, and, by God, I was going to fight now for the man I loved. A steely determination had replaced the pain and disappointment that had tormented me last night. It was still there, locked tightly inside, but I wasn't going to let it deter me. I could stay in this room and grieve, I could make myself ill, or I could press on. Pulling on a pair of long black lace gloves, I went downstairs, asked one of the servants to hail a hackney for me and, less than ten minutes later, was on my way to the shipping office.

Splashed with sunlight, the air clean and clear after the rain, London had a sparkle this morning, everything brighter, colors sharper. As the hackney moved slowly through the traffic, I watched a muffin man selling cakes to neatly dressed matrons at the edge of the park, the trees bright green, the flower beds vivid patches of color. Shop windows gleamed. Majestic marble edifices looked stately in the sunlight, and a variety of spires reached above the multilevel rooftops to touch a pale indigo sky brushed lightly with wispy white puffs of cloud. A jaunty streetsweeper dashed in front of the horses to sweep a steamy mound out of the way. A baker's apprentice sauntered along the pavement with a tray of freshly baked rolls held aloft. The city had a lively air, the clamor a merry ring. Sun-bright days like this were rare, and everyone seemed to respond with a burst of good-humored energy.

The shipping office was a rather dreary gray brick building near the river. I could see the forest of masts as I neared it—traffic on the Thames was every bit as congested as it was on the streets—and as I alighted, asking the driver to wait, I could smell salt and hemp and rotting wood and that strong fishy odor that hung over this part of the city. A clerk leaped up to assist me when I entered the dimly lighted front office with its framed maritime prints on the paneled walls. A spruce young man in a cheaply made yet neat gray suit, he smoothed a thick wave of blond hair from his brow and gave me a polite, businesslike smile, my elegant attire informing him that I was a person of some means and entitled to every courtesy.

Did I wish to book passage to India, to Australia, to Canada? The office could provide the very best first-class accommodations. I shook my head, and his enthusiasm abated somewhat when he realized he was not going to sell passage and, no doubt, make a nice commission. He began to shuffle papers on his desk, his manner that of a very busy young bureaucrat who hadn't time to waste on idle inquiries. Very well, I would try another approach. I smiled a helpless smile and lowered my lashes, exuding an aura of feminine appeal that rarely failed to pierce the male ego. He gave me another look, his chest swelling. I touched his arm lightly with lace-gloved fingertips, my eyes telling him that I would be utterly lost without his help.

"I—I have a problem," I said. "You look so—so very strong and capable. I told myself a nice-looking young man like you would—would perhaps be able to help me."

My eyes were full of open admiration of his masculine charms, and the subtle compliment hadn't hurt, either. He was now willing to leap to the aid of a lady in distress who liked the way he looked and—who knows?—might even give him a special kind of reward. Spurred by visions of a clandestine rendezvous in some discreet waterfront room— for that is what my manner seemed to promise—he smiled a knowing smile and said he was at my service. As he helped me into a chair, his hand lingered for a moment on my arm. I looked up at him, totally overwhelmed by those clear gray eyes and that thick blond hair. Men can be such simpletons, I thought.

"I—I've just come up to London from Bath," I said, looking distressed. "I was to meet a cousin of mine, Mr. Jeremy Bond, but when I arrived at the inn I discovered that he was gone. The innkeeper told me that my cousin had booked passage on a ship."

He didn't for a moment believe the man I was looking for was my cousin. I couldn't fool him, oh, no. I wasn't a demure provincial come up to the city to see a relative. My clothes, my deep sapphire eyes, my slightly parted lips told him I was both worldly and experienced and looking for a lover who had abandoned me—precisely what I intended to convey. He smiled again, his gray eyes openly assessing my charms.

"Do you know the name of the ship?" he asked.

"I'm afraid not."

"Destination?"

"I—I don't know that either."

Feeling a fool, I gazed at him with admiring eyes that made him feel manly and superior. Like a peacock strutting before a peahen, he began to play the strong, capable male. If a Mr. Jeremy Bond had booked passage on a ship, any ship, during the past month, there would be a record of it, and he, George Randolph, would find it. I smiled my gratitude, my deep garnet skirt rustling as I crossed my legs. Young Mr. Randolph began to go through ledgers with admirable zeal. He frowned, closing the last ledger, left the room to consult another employee. When he returned, his gray eyes were puzzled and his brow was moist from his exertions, wisps of blond hair plastered to it.

"I can find nothing," he told me. "I've checked every possible source of information. No Mr. Jeremy Bond has booked passage on any ship during the past month."

"You're certain?" I asked.

"Positive. If he did book passage, it was under an assumed name."

"There—there would be no reason for him to do that," I said.

Puzzled, I stood up, a frown creasing my brow. Could Jeremy possibly still be in London? Perhaps . . . perhaps he had left The White Hart to go stay with a friend. I knew that he had a great many acquaintances in London, but how was I to locate him if . . . if he *was* still here? Moving toward the door, I forgot all about Randolph. He called to me. I turned. He looked absolutely crestfallen, his dreams of intimate coupling shattered. I took pity on the attractive youth whom I had so shamelessly used.

"You've been absolutely marvelous, Mr. Randolph," I said kindly. "Thank you so much for your time."

"I thought—"

"I may well be booking passage myself in the next two or three weeks. If so, I shall call upon your help again."

Frustrated, resentful, and rightfully so, he gave me a terse nod and returned to his desk. Outside, I hesitated on the steps for a moment, wondering what I should do next. London was so vast, so crowded. How did one go about locating someone who might or might not be here? It seemed utterly hopeless, but I refused to let go of that slim ray of hope. If he was here, I was going to find him. I would place notices in every newspaper and journal in the city. I would go to Bow Street and ply the constables and runners with lavish bribes and seek their assistance. First I would go to the bank. I was going to need quite a lot of money, and I had only a few pounds at the moment.

The hackney was still waiting. I gave him the address and climbed inside, my mind in a turmoil as we made our slow progress to Threadneedle Street. When I finally stepped inside the hushed, imposing main room of the Bank of England with its atmosphere of awesome wealth, I was due another surprise. I gave my name to the clerk who came to assist me and told him I wished to make a withdrawal. He looked perturbed when I told him I didn't know the account number but was extremely polite as I explained that the account had been opened by a Mr. Jeremy Bond last month. Asking me to wait, he left. I gazed at the marble columns and brass fixtures and paneled walls, the subdued elegance infused with an air of restrained excitement as clerks scribbled industriously in ledgers and scurried swiftly, silently hither and yon about the room like self-important bees in a golden hive.

Quite a long time elapsed before the clerk who had come to assist me returned. There was a worried look in his eyes as he asked me to follow him. I asked if there was a problem. He mumbled something deliberately unintelligible, leading the way down a long hall lined with windows looking out over the sunny, plant-filled central garden which, I knew, had once been the courtyard of the Church of St.

Christopher le Stocks. The clerk paused, knocked lightly
on a door and led me into a spacious office with honey-
colored wood paneling and patterned tan and salmon pink
rugs scattered over the parquet floor. The clerk nodded
nervously and left, closing the door behind him, and I stood
facing a handsome, friendly-looking man in his mid-fifties
who had risen from behind his desk when we entered.

"I'm Robert Bancroft, Miss Danver. I have the honor of
being one of the presidents of this establishment. Won't
you sit down?"

He had a pleasant voice and a relaxed manner that indicated he took neither himself nor his position too seriously,
yet there was an air of strength and capability about him
that immediately inspired confidence. His dark blond hair
was streaked with silver, his face attractively lined, his
deep brown eyes warm and amiable. Apprehensive, puzzled as to why I should have been shown into his office, I
took the seat he indicated.

"There seems to be a—uh—small problem, Miss Danver," he said kindly. He appeared to be choosing his words
very carefully.

"What sort of problem?" I inquired.

"It would—uh—it would appear the bank has no record
of any transaction made in your name, neither an account
opened nor deposit made."

"But—that's impossible!" I exclaimed. "The account was
opened less than a month ago, the money deposited by a
Mr. Jeremy Bond. I gave the clerk that information."

Bancroft nodded, joining his hands behind his back and
pacing slowly, his shoulders slightly hunched. My throat
went dry. I wanted to leap out of the chair, yet I was frozen
in place, an icy suspicion dawning. No, I told myself. No.
There—there's just been a misunderstanding. My money is
in here, safe and sound. It *has* to be.

"You authorized Mr. Bond to make this transaction for
you?"

The question seemed to come from the end of a long tunnel. The words didn't register. I gripped the arms of the chair so tightly I could feel my nails digging tiny grooves into the varnished wood. Bancroft repeated the question.

"Yes," I said. My voice sounded hollow. "I gave Mr. Bond the authority to make the transaction in my name. I signed papers, filled out some kind of form."

"I see."

He looked at me with pitying eyes. The world is full of confidence men, they seemed to say, and you, poor lass, have been taken by one of the cleverest. I could feel the color leaving my face.

"We have—uh—checked this out, of course," Bancroft said. "Mr. Bond did indeed open an account and make a substantial deposit a few weeks ago."

"In his own name," I said.

"I fear so, Miss Danver."

"The son of a bitch!"

Bancroft arched an eyebrow at my choice of words and straightened the lapels of his elegant plum-colored frock coat.

"He withdrew more than half of it a short while later, requesting cash. I am not, of course, at liberty to mention specific figures."

"There's no need to," I retorted, standing.

"If there's been some sort of criminal action involved here, Miss Danver, the bank will of course make a report to Bow Street and have an investigation made on your behalf."

"Don't bother," I said crisply.

"But—"

"He can keep the bloody money. He earned it!"

I have no memory of leaving the bank. One moment I was looking into Bancroft's warm, sympathetic brown eyes, and the next I was walking briskly down the street, a hard, cold, tight feeling inside. My heels rang on the pavement with a sharp clatter. My skirts crackled with the sound of dry leaves. People swarmed all around me, dirty

children chasing a spotted brown dog, dandies sauntering
in dapper attire, plump matrons scrutinizing the wares
displayed in dusty shop windows. I was scarcely aware of
them. I crossed a street. A collier's cart swerved violently,
the driver cursing me loudly as he yanked on the reins. A
barrel rolled off the cart, shattering on the cobbles. I
marched on, grateful for the anger that held all the other
emotions at bay.

A rather handsome rake in a burnt-orange suit and
brown velvet waistcoat was loitering in front of a clock-
maker's shop. Seeing me approach, he grinned and
stepped into the middle of the pavement to block my path—
any woman alone was prey for these audacious ne'er-do-
wells. I glared at him, daring him to make a remark, and
when he saw the murderous rage in my eyes he darted
quickly out of the way. I moved past wooden arcades full of
shops, the crowd greedily examining exotic green and turquoise birds in gilded cages, racks of colored ribbons and
beads, cheap pottery, paper windmills, honey cakes. The
odors of unwashed bodies mingled with those of dirt and
animal dung and rotting fruit, assailing my nostrils.

It took me almost an hour to reach The White Hart. I
stopped in the courtyard, so weary I wondered how I could
possibly find the strength to walk inside and climb the
stairs to my room. The anger had abated, and now it vanished entirely, leaving me numb, depleted. Standing under the shade of a plum tree, I watched an indolent calico
cat nursing three fat kittens in a pool of sunlight near the
stables. A horse snorted. Pigeons cooed under the eaves.
The bells of London began to chime again. It was one
o'clock, just one, and it seemed an eternity ago that I had
left for the shipping office.

I went inside and went to my room. I sat down in the
overstuffed chair and stared at the empty fireplace, and I
was still sitting there when, shortly after five, Mrs.
Patterson rapped sharply on my door and came in with a
tray of food. She clucked her tongue, set the tray down on

the table beside the chair and placed her hands on her hips, giving me her bossiest look.

"You didn't have dinner last night, lamb, and I know for a fact you didn't have breakfast or lunch today, either. I've brought you a bacon roll and some cheese and grapes and Cook's best popovers with a pot of strawberry jam. You're going to eat every bite."

"I'm not hungry, Mrs. Patterson."

"You're eatin' anyway," she told me.

Pouring a cup of hot coffee, she handed it to me and looked bossy and adamant until I finally took a sip. She was wearing an ancient, gray, watered silk gown adorned with light blue ruffles, the skirt hitched up in front to show off the ruffled blue petticoat beneath. I suspected that Mrs. Patterson got all of her wardrobe from the old clothes bin at Market or else from a musty old trunk in the attic, but the garment somehow suited her, as did the heavy makeup and girlish wig.

"It's very likely I won't be able to pay for this food," I said.

"Oh?"

"I went to the bank this morning. It seems I have no money there."

"Pulled a con job on you, didn't he? A woman in love's always a gullible dove. I've been swindled out of a few pounds myself in my day, and always by some charmer in tight breeches."

"I have only a few pounds left."

"We won't worry about that now. Eat your food."

"He didn't book passage to America. I went down to the shipping office to check."

"I could have told you that, lamb. Go on, eat that bacon roll. Starvin' yourself to death ain't gonna help anything."

"You know something, don't you? You're keeping something from me."

"Didn't feel it was my place to bring it up last night,"

she said, patting one of the ringlets at the side of her face. "I ain't tellin' you nothin' until you've had a proper meal."

I finished the cup of coffee, ate the bacon roll, some cheese, some grapes. Mrs. Patterson fussed about the room, tidying up, glancing at me every so often to make sure I was eating. Finally satisfied that I wasn't going to expire from hunger, she spread strawberry jam over one of the buttered popovers and plopped it into her mouth, licking her fingers when she had finished. I stood and moved over to the window to gaze out. The bright afternoon sunshine had started to fade, and the spires and rooftops of London were now brushed with pale silver light. The sky was white with just the faintest tinge of blue. My bones ached. I still felt numb.

"Have another cup of coffee, lamb," Mrs. Patterson said. "It will do you good."

I took it from her and crossed over to stand in front of the wardrobe, sipping the strong, hot brew as Mrs. Patterson perched on the arm of the chair and devoured another jam-spread popover.

"Well?" I said.

"He hung around for three days after you left, lamb, lookin' all dejected and broody, then *she* showed up. Oh, she was somethin', that one, dressed to the nines in pale lime green satin and silver lace. Her eyes were blue as the sea, her hair so blonde it looked like silver, spillin' in ringlets down her back."

"She *would* be a blonde," I said bitterly.

"She was a young thing, not more'n twenty, if that. He took her up to his room, and it was well over an hour 'fore they came down. He was all packed up, handin' tips around, said he was off to Scotland."

"Scotland?"

"That's what he said, lamb. They left together a few minutes later, fancy coach waitin' out in the yard. He had his arm around her, seemed to be comfortin' her."

"He's very good at that."

"Men're bastards, lamb. Every last one of 'em."

"I'm beginning to find that out."

I set my cup down, careful not to make a clatter. My face was beautifully composed, my manner one of cool indifference. I seemed to be made of steel and ice, sheathed in an unnatural calm that belied the emotions seething inside. A long time ago I had vowed I would never again give any man the power to hurt me like this, and if my world had just crumbled, if my life no longer seemed worth living, it was my own bloody fault. God *damn* Jeremy Bond. Damn him. Damn him. *Damn* him.

"I—I didn't want to tell you, lamb," Mrs. Patterson said.

"I'm glad you did. It makes everything so much easier."

Mrs. Patterson took my cup and set it on the tray. She looked far more upset than I did.

"What are you going to *do?*" she asked quietly.

I opened the wardrobe door and took down the garnet velvet cloak lined with black silk, slipping it over my shoulders and fastening it, pulling the hood up over my head.

"At the moment I'm going out. I need a breath of fresh air. I'm going to take a stroll in the park across the way."

There were very few people in the park for, although the day had been sunny, there was a distinct chill in the air, and it was growing late. Shadows were lengthening across the silver-brushed lawns, hazy violet-gray nests beneath the trees. Although crowded during the day with strolling couples, with nursemaids and their charges, with well-dressed gentry taking a turn, the city parks were deserted by respectable folk as evening drew near, for then they became the domain of pickpockets and whores, cutthroats and vicious ruffians who would cheerfully commit murder for a pocket watch or pair of shiny shoe buckles. As I strolled past the neat flower beds, past the fountains and the ponds where brown ducklings splashed, I felt a coldness that had nothing to do with the cool breeze that lifted the hem of my cloak.

What was I going to do? I would get some kind of work, for I was virtually moneyless, and even after I sold most of my fine clothes I would have barely enough to live on for more than a few weeks. I had worked before. I had worked like the slave I was in Carolina, cooking, keeping house, and I had run a gambling hall in New Orleans. I had worked here in London, too, serving as governess to the children of Sir Robert Mallory, another lovely specimen of mankind. I would find work—I would scrub floors if necessary—and eventually I would save enough money to pay my passage to America and I would make my way to Texas and my friend Em, dearer to me than any sister could have been, the one person on earth I could turn to and rely upon without question. Em would take me in. There would always be a place for me there on that spacious ranch with Em and Randolph and young Chris and the others who had shared our adventures.

I would start all over again. Dear God, dear God, once more I would start all over again. How many times had my life been turned upside down? How many times had I been left alone, bereft, forced to cope? Would it never end? Must I always have to be strong? Must I always be stoic? I longed for oblivion now. I longed for it all to end. I couldn't go on. I couldn't. It was too much to ask. For one black moment, as I stood staring at the trees, I actually wanted to die, and then that innate stubborn streak came to the fore. Oh, no, I told myself, you're not going to give way. You're not going to let that bastard destroy your life. You're going to be strong once more. Once more.

The shadows were growing longer, thickening. The light had taken on a dim pink-gold hue, and the sky was beginning to darken to deep indigo-gray. I held my arms folded about my waist, as though to hold back the pain, and I told myself that I would get over Jeremy Bond. Someday, somehow, I would get over him and the pain wouldn't be a live thing inside, tearing me asunder. My eyes felt hot and dry, but there were no tears. I was beyond tears.

I turned and started back, and I really wasn't surprised to see Count Gregory Orlov striding purposefully toward me, dressed all in tan, his cloak belling behind him. His face looked grave indeed, and I knew he must have gone to the inn, must have spoken to Mrs. Patterson. She would have told him everything. I stopped, waiting for him to come to me, and I felt no emotion at all as I watched him approach.

What was I going to do? I was going to survive. I had had quite a lot of practice during the past seven years.

Chapter Six

EVERYONE AGREED THAT MRS. PERDITA ROBIN-
son was an exquisite creature and a consummate actress
despite her youth. Only twenty years old, the protégée of
playwright Richard Brinsley Sheridan, she was enchanting as Jacintha in *The Suspicious Husband,* and the
audience at The Haymarket clearly adored her. Lucie, sitting beside me in the front of our box, was completely
enthralled by the bright colors, the dazzling footlights, the
movement and magic taking place on the wooden stage below. This was her very first time to attend any theater, and
she was like a child who has just spied a glittering Christ-
mas tree. Leaning forward in her chair, her folded hands
resting on the polished railing, she was all attention, relishing every word, every gesture, and she looked lovely in
the new gold-and-white-striped satin gown that had just
been delivered.

Perdita cavorted before the painted backdrop in blue
silk gown and powdered wig, a black beauty mark affixed
to one cheek, her eyes sparkling flirtatiously as she fluttered her white lace fan and exchanged bright repartee
with the handsome, bewigged hero. I tried to pay attention, but I was still too sick at heart to be diverted by the
mannered, artificial scenes. I had been the Orlovs' guest
for two weeks now, and although both of them had done
everything they could to make me comfortable and keep
me amused, I could not shake the dead feeling inside. All
joy, all light seemed to have gone out of my life, and the

profusion of pleasure jaunts, shopping expeditions and elaborate dinners I had endured primarily for Lucie's sake hadn't had any effect at all. The girl was so excited with the new wardrobe I had helped her select, so thrilled by the sights of the great city that I felt compelled to make an effort to be a pleasant companion, but the gloom continued to hang over me.

On chairs behind us, hidden by the darkness of the box, Count Orlov and Sir Harry Lyman sat quietly, neither of them enjoying the play. Sir Harry was too concerned with business affairs to be amused by the drama, and Orlov's command of the English language was too poor for him to understand much of what was going on. He sighed occasionally, shifting uncomfortably on the gilt chair that was too small for his size and weight. He had been a wonderful host these past two weeks, polite, attentive, restraining much of his natural exuberance out of respect for me. He knew I was desolate, knew the reasons why, and he had treated me with a quiet courtesy that showed the utmost tact. I appreciated it, and I felt guilty at being such a dull guest.

He had insisted I come to stay with them, of course, had refused to take no for an answer. When he learned the full extent of Jeremy Bond's perfidy, he was appalled, and he had promptly volunteered to give me enough money to get me to Texas. Naturally I had refused. Count Orlov informed me that I was stubborn and foolish and full of principles. I told him that I appreciated his offer but would earn the money somehow. I didn't intend to be obligated to any man ever again, and I had agreed to be their houseguest only because he assured me I would be doing him a great service by providing companionship for Lucie. I performed that service to the best of my ability, and most of the past two weeks had been spent gadding about with her. Count Orlov was occupied with his business affairs most of the day, closed up in the library with Sir Harry. We rarely saw him until the evening meal, though he was lavish with funds and showed keen interest in everything we did,

demanding details, beaming as Lucie described the glories
of the Tower, of St. James Park and the Exchange and the
plethora of exquisite shops where she spent vast sums.

The first act was drawing to a close. Having gotten
things into a complicated mess through flirtation and innocent coquetry, the effervescent Perdita waved her fan,
tossed her powdered curls and airily bewailed her fate as
the curtain came down. The applause from the pit was
thunderous, punctuated by cheers, that from the boxes
considerably more restrained. The houselights were
lighted and the ebullient crowd downstairs began to tromp
out noisily to gossip, flirt and drink during the interval.
Many of the gorgeously attired women sitting in front of
the exclusive boxes preferred to remain on display while
their escorts fetched champagne, ices and boxes of chocolates, but I was far too restless to remain sitting. Orlov and
Sir Harry were already standing. The count helped me to
my feet, Sir Harry performing the same service for Lucie,
and we left the private box with its velvet hangings and
plush appointments.

"You are enjoying the play?" Count Orlov inquired.

"It's quite amusing," I replied.

"I love it!" Lucie exclaimed. "I don't understand all the
words, but it's beautiful, like a jewel box come to life!"

"Mrs. Robinson is quite the rage," Sir Harry said dryly.
"All the beaux are mad for her. I wouldn't be surprised if
she landed herself a royal protector ere long."

The ladies who went on stage were, I knew, paid very
small salaries, and in order to keep themselves in velvets
and jewels, in coaches and fancy apartments and servants,
they had to rely on the generosity of admirers. Some of
them maintained virtue of sorts and relied on their talent
to get ahead, but the majority were glorified courtesans.
Sheridan's admiration and patronage had certainly helped
advance the extravagantly gifted Perdita.

Women in sumptuous gowns and men in full sartorial
splendor thronged in the hallway, moving toward the
stairs. Gems flashed. Skirts rustled. Plumes waved. The

air was close, filled with the scent of perfume, powder and sweat, and a merry din rose. Gentlemen took out their snuff boxes. Women chattered like magpies. Lucie took it all in, thrilled by the gaudy glamour of the scene, and I noticed a number of men casting appraising glances in her direction. Eyes sparkling, cheeks flushed pink with excitement, she was radiantly beautiful in her new satin gown.

Count Orlov took my arm as we moved down the wide, carpeted staircase to the crowded foyer below. He was wearing English-tailored black broadcloth breeches and coat, the lapels black velvet, and his white satin waistcoat was embroidered with white silk flowers. A lacy white jabot spilled from his throat. He was an impressive, imposing figure, half a head taller than any other man there, and if the men admired his niece, Count Orlov was the recipient of dozens of languishing looks from the women. Totally unaware of the stir he was causing, the count devoted his attention exclusively to me.

"You are not having the good time," he said quietly. "Your cheeks are too pale. There are the light blue-gray shadows on your eyelids. Your eyes have the sad, faraway look."

"I have a bit of a headache," I confessed.

"Is not good, this. The champagne will help."

"I really don't think I care for any, Count Orlov."

"You will have some," he said sternly.

Turning to Sir Harry, he instructed him to wait with Lucie and me beside the marble column and then sauntered off through the crowd to fetch our drinks. People moved aside to let him pass, the women whispering behind their fans and casting longing looks in his wake, the men sizing him up, wondering who he was. Still excited by what she had seen on stage, Lucie chattered with considerable animation, and I was pleased to see her so lighthearted. Sir Harry answered all her questions about the English theater, amused by the girl's vivacious manner.

"I would like to be like this Mrs. Robinson," she declared. "I would like to be on the stage and wear the lovely gowns and have everyone love me like they love her."

"The life of an actress is a hard one indeed," Sir Harry told her. "It isn't all adulation and applause."

"I wouldn't care. I would work very, very hard."

"I'm sure you would," Sir Harry said in his driest voice.

She sighed, and some of her animation vanished as she realized what an impossible dream it was. Her violet-blue eyes became wistful. She was an aristocrat, an Orlov, and the freedom and frivolity of the stage wasn't for the likes of her. I reached for her hand and gave it a squeeze. Lucie smiled, looking younger than her seventeen years. Her uncle returned a moment later, and she sipped her champagne quietly.

I made polite conversation with Count Orlov and Sir Harry, my mind elsewhere. Yes, it was a nice crowd and yes, the theater was beautiful and no, I had never been to the Drury Lane. I saw a man across the room, his back to me. He was wearing a splendid blue suit. His chestnut hair was rich and glossy. My heart seemed to stop beating. He turned to speak to a woman in violet satin and black lace, and I saw his face. He was quite attractive, but he wasn't Jeremy. How many times during the past two weeks had I caught a glimpse of someone who reminded me of him? How many times had I felt this same, stabbing sensation in my chest?

"—wish you would reconsider, Sir Harry," Count Orlov was saying.

"It's out of the question. Much as I enjoy your stimulating company, much as I admire your country, I've no intention of returning. I've put in my service, I've done my bit, and I've earned a spell of peace and quiet. No disrespect, my dear Orlov, but being with you is like being on the edge of a volcano. One always fears another eruption."

"This is unfair, Sir Harry!" Orlov protested. "Me, I am the most amiable, the most generous of men. If you come to Russia with me as my personal financial manager, I pay you a fortune."

"And I would be an old man within a year. No, Orlov, you must do without my services once you leave this fair isle."

Orlov scowled. It was apparently an argument they had had many times before. He looked like a big, petulant child, and Sir Harry looked weary and wryly amused. The crowd was beginning to thin as people returned to their seats. We finished our champagne and a waiter took the glasses. As we were moving toward the elegant staircase, Orlov saw the woman in red. He froze. He seized Sir Harry's arm, squeezing it so tightly Sir Harry winced. The woman stared at Orlov with dark green eyes that seemed to glitter with malicious pleasure.

"This woman!" Orlov exclaimed. "She haunts me!"

"I had no idea the princess was in England," Sir Harry remarked. "Prowling through the libraries and galleries, no doubt, conferring with our leading intellectuals and politicians."

"She is a meddlesome fool!"

"Meddlesome she might be, fool she isn't. Diderot called her the most intelligent woman in Europe, and he knows whereof he speaks."

"Damn! She is my fellow countryman. I must make the courtesies."

"It would seem so," Sir Harry replied.

Orlov looked vastly uncomfortable as the woman continued to stare, a smile now curving on her wide, thin lips. Accompanied by two attractive blond youths in black-and-white formal attire, she was thin and bony with a sallow complexion and an undernourished look. Her face was painted, her black hair swept up and worn atop her head in a stack of curls. Diamonds flashed at her throat and ears. Her deep red velvet gown left her bony shoulders bare and emphasized her flat bosom, the skirt spreading in layered flounces like the petals of a rose. Undeniably ugly, she nevertheless had a commanding presence and a bearing that could only be called regal. One sensed abounding energy and formidable intelligence and suspected a venomous wit.

"Might as well get it over with, Orlov," Sir Harry said lightly. "I doubt seriously that she will bite you, though she's rumored to have fangs."

Reluctantly, Orlov moved forward, stopped in front of the woman and clicked his heels. The woman nodded and lifted her hand. Orlov took it and brushed it with his lips, all gallantry.

"Princess Dashkova! It is a surprise to see you here."

"It is a surprise to see you, too, Gregory darling. I heard that you were doing quite a bit of traveling, but I never expected to see you in London. You are as handsome as ever."

"You look the same, too," he told her.

The princess laughed a dry laugh. "Knowing you, Gregory, I'm certain that isn't meant to be a compliment."

Her voice was brittle, laced with cynicism, but her French was flawless and without the faintest trace of a Russian accent. The handsome blond youths standing on either side of her, though fetching, were so overshadowed by her presence as to be almost invisible. In her way, Princess Dashkova had almost as much magnetism as Orlov, though hers was totally asexual.

"What do you do here?" Orlov asked.

"Your French hasn't improved any, I see. You really must learn verbs, darling. To answer your question, I've been at Oxford, brushing up my Greek and Latin and making a few friends."

She indicated her companions with a nod. Orlov curled his lip.

"Women are not allowed to attend this college," he said.

"I didn't attend, darling. I merely stayed."

Orlov scowled, finding it difficult to hide his animosity. That these two were long-standing enemies would have been obvious to even the most casual observer. Princess Dashkova seemed to delight in his discomfort, the cynical smile never leaving her lips as he shuffled uneasily and clearly wished he were anywhere but in her presence. When Sir Harry brought Lucie and me to be introduced, she gave him a nod, arching a thin black brow as her glittering dark green eyes swept over us.

"I see you still travel with an entourage, Gregory," she observed. "Who are your pretty companions?"

"This is Miss Marietta Danver. She is a friend. This is my niece, Lucie. Sir Harry Lyman you know."

"It's been a long time, Harry," she said.

She gave him her hand to kiss, pointedly ignoring Lucie and me. I was too disinterested to be insulted, but a soft pink blush tinted Lucie's cheeks. One of the young men eyed her with considerable interest, and, aware of it, she lowered her eyes demurely. Princess Dashkova apparently deemed her companions too insignificant to bother introducing them, but I guessed that they were students. I could guess, too, the services they performed, for her ugly, fascinating face had an undeniable stamp of depravity.

Sir Harry kissed her hand. "How are you, Princess Dashkova?"

"Restless as ever, Harry. You know me. I never change."

"Enjoying your banishment?" he asked.

"Finding it profitable. Travel is always broadening, and I've met some extremely interesting people."

"One hears you've become thick with the French Encyclopedists."

"I find them most stimulating," she replied. "Intelligent men are all too uncommon nowadays."

"Any plans of returning to Russia?"

"I've written to Catherine. I've no doubt she'll relent in a year or so. Considering the state the country's in now, she may well want me to return. She hasn't forgotten the services I rendered in the past. And you, Gregory?" she asked, turning to him. "When do *you* plan to return to the homeland?"

"I leave in two and a half weeks," he grumbled.

"Oh?" She arched her brow again. "But then you were

never officially banished, were you, darling? Just deposed."

"The play is about to resume," Sir Harry pointed out. "We really should get back to our boxes."

"Quite true," the princess replied. "I wouldn't want to miss a moment of this heady, intellectual fare. We must get together and talk over old times before you depart, Gregory."

"I will give a dinner at the house I have rented," he told her. "One of my servants will call on you."

"I'm staying at The Golden Swan, darling, on the Strand. I look forward to seeing you again."

Gathering up her two young men, Princess Dashkova turned and moved up the staircase with back straight and head held high, every inch a regal personage. The youth who had shown such interest in Lucie turned to give her a final glance, his brown eyes full of speculation. Lucie did not lower her eyes this time but, instead, looked back at him boldly. Neither of the men noticed it. I was startled by that frankly sensual challenge I had seen in her eyes but, a moment later, felt certain I had imagined it. Orlov scowled as he watched Princess Dashkova disappear around a curve in the staircase. He looked as though he longed to commit murder. Sir Harry smiled his dry smile.

"The princess always did know how to needle you, Orlov. You really shouldn't let her bother you so."

"This woman is poisonous!"

"Yet you plan to give a dinner for her."

"She is a fellow countryman," Orlov said glumly. "It is a necessary courtesy. I would prefer to be shot."

The play had already resumed when we returned to our box. Lucie seemed to be lost in thought, no longer enraptured by the stage, and I could feel her uncle sulking behind me. The charming Perdita fluttered and flitted and radiated an effervescent charm, now in pink satin, now in white, and the play eventually reached its climax and ended in a thunder of deafening applause causing the chandeliers to shake. Crystal pendants tinkled overhead as Mrs. Robinson took half a dozen curtain calls and accepted bouquets of roses. Orlov was still in a grumpy mood as we left the box, and Lucie looked overstimulated, like a little girl who has stayed at a party too long. Orlov went outside to summon the carriage, and Lucie went with him, holding wearily on to his arm. I waited in the foyer with Sir Harry, weary myself as brilliantly dressed, chattering people streamed past us on their way out.

"A most interesting evening," Sir Harry remarked. "Orlov never could abide La Dashkova, nor she him."

"I take it they've known each other quite some time."

"From the beginning. Dashkova was almost as important to Catherine's *coup d'état* as Orlov himself. She was only seventeen years old at the time but prodigiously intelligent, with a head full of the most astounding knowledge. She and Catherine held marathon discussions about art and politics and science, staying up half the night as they argued every point. Catherine felt, perhaps rightly, that the volatile, effusive girl was her only intellectual equal in Russia."

"Remarkable," I said.

"When the palace plots began to brew, Dashkova was in the thick of things. Impudent, courageous, fiercely loyal, she ardently recruited the support of officers and brought dozens into Catherine's camp. Later, when Catherine had secured the throne and rode herself at the head of the Semeonovsky regiment in full uniform to show her people that she intended to rule like a man, Dashkova rode beside her, also in plumed helmet and full military garb. I fancy it was her greatest moment."

"It must have been an intoxicating experience for a seventeen-year-old girl."

"Far too intoxicating, alas," Sir Harry replied.

He paused as Dashkova moved past, an ermine-lined red velvet cloak wrapped about her, diamond pendants dangling from her earlobes. The black curls artfully piled on top of her head made her seem taller than she actually was. One of the young men carried her red feather fan. The other held her arm, guiding her through the crowd. The princess's dark green eyes glittered maliciously when she caught sight of us. A wry smile played on her lips as she gave Sir Harry the curtest of nods.

"She's certainly—striking," I conceded.

"Striking is the word," Sir Harry agreed. "Dashkova was never a pretty woman, and her energy, intellect, and demolishing wit have always terrified men. Her husband was little more than a cipher, though he was named Chamberlain after the coup. Dashkova had to—uh—provide financial remuneration for masculine companionship even in her twenties. Catherine showered her with riches, of course, made her a lady-in-waiting, but Dashkova was far too restless to be satisfied with that. She felt she deserved more."

"I suppose that led to a rift," I said.

"Eventually. Dashkova wasn't happy if she wasn't plotting and scheming. Feeling the Empress hadn't treated her fairly, she grew even more restless, more resentful. Catherine adored her and found her amusing for a while, but the day finally arrived when she could no longer smile at the girl's meddling. Dashkova was packed up and packed off, and the court was considerably quieter."

"I can see why Count Orlov wouldn't take to her."

"He detested her, and the feeling was mutual. She considered him a boastful, boorish lout and was appalled by the influence he had over Catherine. She plotted against him and tried to get the Empress to replace him with someone more suitable."

"Her own candidate, I suppose."

"Very perceptive of you, my dear. She paraded a whole platoon of handsome young studs before the Empress, men who could be easily manipulated once they had won favor. Orlov's hold on Catherine was too strong, though, and the princess was doomed to failure."

"And this is the woman he's giving a dinner for." I shook my head. "Russians!"

"Never try to figure them out. That way lies madness."

Only a few stragglers remained in the plush lobby, and a moment later Orlov came for us, having already placed Lucie in the carriage. A snarl of carriages jammed the street outside, horses snorting and stamping, drivers yelling angrily as they tried to make their way through the melee. Passengers leaned anxiously out of coach windows, adding to the confusion with their cries, and link boys dashed about, their torches illuminating the garish scene with flickering orange light. Orlov helped me into the sumptuous interior, shoved Sir Harry inside and, slamming the door, took it upon himself to direct our driver out of the tangle. In a matter of minutes we were free, moving down the street at a slow jog. Orlov flung the door open and jumped inside, a wide grin on his lips.

"Dashkova's carriage is in the middle of this jumble," he cried merrily. "I see it myself. It will take her driver an hour to move a foot!"

Impatient she might be, but I doubted the princess would be bored with the two strapping young students to keep her company. She was indeed fascinating, as colorful and exotic as Orlov himself. The darling of the Encyclopedists, a Greek and Latin scholar who had chatted with Catherine about science and politics yet had to pay for male companionship—yes, she was colorful. As Sir Harry began to bore Orlov with details about Dutch shipping and the German mark, I wondered if Russia ever produced any normal people. Were they all larger than life?

A full moon hung like a swollen silver-gold ball in the sky, bathing the city with a pale, milky glow that intensified the black shapes of buildings and the masses of purple-blue shadow that filled doorways and alleys. The carriage moved slowly, horse hooves clop-clop-clopping on the uneven cobblestones. Link boys trotted along beside us, torches waving like ragged orange banners in the dark, and in the shifting light I saw that Lucie looked pale and worn, a pensive look in her eyes. She idly smoothed a graceful hand over her satin skirt, then bunched the cloth nervously between her fingers. Earlier on she had been bright and vivacious, and now she looked as though she had never known a moment's joy. What had caused this sudden darkness?

We dropped Sir Harry at his lodgings and, a short while later, drove through the brick portals and up the circular drive of Orlov's rented mansion. Lights burned in the windows, elongated yellow shafts of light on the drive. A bird was singing plaintively in the garden. Claiming she had a headache, Lucie said good night and went up to her rooms, slowly climbing the gracious spiral staircase with one hand trailing along the smooth banister, a lovely, lethargic figure in her gold-and-white-striped satin. Orlov asked me if I would like a glass of brandy. I shook my head and thanked him for a pleasant evening, then followed Lucie upstairs. Her door was closed when I passed, an indication that she didn't feel up to one of the late evening chats that had become our habit.

Half an hour later, I was sitting in my bedroom staring at the fire burning low in the marble fireplace. Although I had taken down my hair and brushed it, I was still wearing the blue silk gown I had worn to the theater. Only a few candles burned, casting soft light over the creamy white walls with their sky blue panels patterned with gilt, over the pale violet rugs and exquisite furniture. When it was late and I was alone, the memories returned to haunt me, and I felt a deep melancholy as I watched the thin golden-orange flames leap and lick at the wood. Though surprised, I welcomed the interruption when I heard someone knock on the door of the adjoining sitting room. Lucie probably isn't able to sleep either, I thought, getting to my feet. She probably wants to have our chat after all.

It wasn't Lucie. It was her uncle. He stood there in the doorway looking apologetic, as though he feared a rebuff. He had taken off his coat and waistcoat and, over the tight black breeches and thin white lawn shirt, wore a heavy navy blue satin dressing robe that gleamed richly. His golden brown locks were tousled, and he ran his fingers through them now, clearly uneasy. I suspected that be-

neath all the swagger and braggadocio Count Orlov was
quite insecure, if not actually shy.

"I do not disturb you?" he asked.

"Not at all, Count Orlov."

"I do not mean to bother you."

"You aren't bothering me, I assure you. I hadn't even
made preparations for bed. Do come in."

He entered the sitting room so hesitantly I had to smile.
The former paramour of Catherine of Russia and the veteran of hundreds of sexual conquests acted as though he
were breaking some cardinal rule of propriety by coming
into my chambers at this hour of the night. It was not hy-
pocrisy. It was, rather, respect for me that caused him to be
so circumspect. I was a guest in his house. There had been
no lazy, seductive glances, no lingering touches. Count
Orlov knew that I had been hurt, knew I had been reluctant to come here to stay with them, and he intended to do
nothing that might disturb the delicate balance of polite
friendship between us.

"You cannot sleep?" he asked.

"I haven't tried."

He looked concerned. "The headache still bothers you?"

"A little," I confessed.

"You should have had some brandy."

"There's a bottle in the cabinet here. Would you care for
another glass?"

"Will you join me?"

I nodded and went over to the black lacquer cabinet inlaid with brass and mother-of-pearl. The sitting room was
done in a Chinese style. The walls were hung with pale
yellow-tan paper vivid with multicolored peonies and chry-
santhemums and birds, and wheat-colored bamboo mat-
ting covered the floor. I took out the brandy, poured it,
handed Count Orlov a glass. He thanked me with a nod
and glanced curiously about the room. It was the first time
he had seen it, and he seemed a bit puzzled by the lacquered screens, the cloisonné vases, and the turquoise temple dogs guarding the fireplace.

"Is strange taste you English have," he observed.

"The furniture is Chippendale. His Chinese pieces were very popular a few years ago."

"You have been comfortable here?"

"I've been very comfortable, Count Orlov."

"I am glad. Is good for you to be with friends at this time."

I sipped my brandy. He drank his quickly, as though it were vodka, tilting the glass to his lips, throwing his head back, swallowing it in great gulps. Although I had put out most of the candles in the bedroom, some still burned brightly. Orlov gazed fixedly at his empty glass. I could tell that he had something to say to me, something he didn't quite know how to say. He finally set the glass down and turned to me.

"It has been most good for Lucie, too," he said. "She has had a proper companion to do these things with while I take care of the business matters. She is most fond of you."

"I am fond of her, too."

"I appreciate the interest you take in her. She is a strange girl, Lucie. I am much concerned. These moods are not healthy."

"She is very young," I said quietly.

"With you, she is better," he told me. His deep voice was melodious, a guttural caress. "She opens up. She smiles."

"Girls her age need a companion."

"This is my point. She needs a companion, and you are the perfect one. Already she trusts you, feels at ease with you. The arrangement would be most satisfactory."

"I—I'm not sure I understand what you're saying."

Orlov looked at me with eyes that seemed to be an even deeper navy blue because of the dark blue dressing robe. His handsome face was thoughtful. He had been so very kind to me, so gentle and considerate. I could not help but respond to his warmth.

"In two and a half weeks I shall be finished with all these tedious business affairs. Lucie and I shall be leaving for Russia. You will come with us."

"I'm afraid that's impossible, Count Orlov."

He seemed surprised. "But why?"

"I have other plans," I said, putting down my brandy glass. "I'm going to find work. Eventually I'm going to earn enough money to pay my passage to America."

"What is this work you plan to do?" he asked.

"I'm not sure. I may seek a post as a governess. I'm a very good seamstress. I may seek work in a dress shop—I once owned a dress shop myself in Natchez, a city in America. If—if necessary, I could become a housekeeper."

Count Orlov shook his head. "This is nonsense," he said gently. "Sewing, housekeeping—this is not proper work for you."

"I haven't led a pampered life, Count Orlov. It's been anything but that. I'm willing to do any kind of work to earn the money I need."

"Yet you are not willing to come to Russia."

"It was very kind of you to ask, but I have imposed on your hospitality far too long as it is, and—"

I let the sentence fade on my lips. Orlov stepped nearer, the skirt of his dressing robe making a soft, silken rustle. I could smell his teak shaving cologne and the musky scent of his body.

"But I do not speak of hospitality," he said. "I speak of the respectable employment."

"You want to *pay* me to go to Russia with you?"

Orlov nodded, amused at my surprise. A gentle smile curved on his lips as he explained.

"I know you wish to go to America," he said, "and I wish to help you. I offer to give you the money. You refuse. I think to myself, how shall I solve this problem? I see how Lucie admires you, see how happy she is to be with you, and I realize how long the journey to Russia is, how bored and unhappy she will be during the trip. I decide to offer you this employment as paid companion to my niece."

He was very pleased with this solution. I had to appreciate the offer, but I could think of any number of reasons why it wouldn't work. Sensing my reservations, Orlov lifted an eyebrow.

"You do not like this idea?" he asked.

I picked up the empty glasses and carried them over to the cabinet. Count Orlov tilted his head slightly, watching me, heavy lids drooping over his eyes. I set the glasses down, put the brandy bottle back into the cabinet, deliberately delaying my answer.

"Russia is—it's very far away," I said.

"This is true," he admitted. "The journey is long and very tedious. This is one of the reasons I wish you to keep Lucie company. I would give you a most generous salary, more than enough to pay your way to America."

"I see," I said quietly.

"Once we get to Russia, I would ask you to remain three more months in order that Lucie might have time to adjust and make new friends, and then I would arrange your passage to America. One can get there from Russia as easily as from England," he added.

"I realize that, but—" I hesitated, shaking my head.

"I do not see your objections," he said.

"I—I just don't think it would work."

Orlov seemed puzzled, and then he sighed and smiled warmly.

"You are tired," he said. "You have the headache. I propose this idea too quickly, I think. I choose the wrong time. I will not ask you to give me an answer now, Miss Danver."

"I'm grateful."

"I ask only that you promise to think about it."

"I'll think about it," I said.

"Good! Now I will leave you and let you go to bed. It has been an exhausting evening for you."

"I fear it has."

I followed him to the door. He lifted my hand and brushed it lightly with his lips, and then, nodding politely, he left. I closed the door and leaned against it for a moment, thinking of his offer. Count Orlov was generous, too generous. He was kind and thoughtful, could be gentle and very, very persuasive. If I accepted his offer, it would solve my predicament, yes, but every instinct told me it would present a whole new set of problems, problems of an entirely different nature. I could still see the warmth in his dark eyes as he gazed at me. I could still feel the touch of his lips on the back of my hand. I would turn him down. Of course I would. Going to Russia with Count Gregory Orlov was entirely out of the question.

Chapter Seven

SIGHING HEAVILY, I MADE A FINAL INSPECTION in the full-length mirror in my bedroom. The leaf brown satin gown had short, narrow sleeves, a very low neckline and snug waist, the skirt spreading out in scalloped flounces that parted to reveal the underskirt of alternating rows of sky blue and sapphire lace. The diminutive, chattering French hairdresser Orlov had brought in had parted my hair in the center, pulled it back, and arranged it in a mass of long sausage ringlets that cascaded down my back. I had applied pale bluish gray shadow to my lids, had smoothed pale pink rouge lightly over my cheekbones and used a deeper pink on my lips, but my face was still drawn, my eyes dark and disillusioned. I wasn't going to dazzle any of Orlov's guests tonight, I reflected, but at least I was presentable.

Leaving the bedroom, passing through the Chinese sitting room, I moved down the hall toward Lucie's room, dreading the evening ahead. Count Orlov's dinner for Princess Dashkova had grown into a major social event with over fifty guests invited. The house had been in an uproar all day, florists arriving with potted plants and great baskets of roses, musicians setting up their instruments in the ballroom, the household staff in a frenzy as special decorations were hung, Orlov's chef rebelling and throwing a tantrum when he discovered his culinary masterpieces would be augmented with food brought from London's finest eating house. Guests were already beginning to arrive—English diplomats, Russian émigrés, various society figures Orlov had met in years past when they were visiting his country—and Lucie and I should have been downstairs already. She was dreading the evening almost as much as I was, I knew, and had been depressed ever since morning.

Tapping lightly on the opened door, I called her name and passed through her sitting room to the bedroom. She was sitting at the dressing table, staring glumly into the mirror. Opening a bottle of perfume, she wearily dabbed the crystal stopper behind her earlobes, between her breasts, touched it to the backs of her wrists. It was an exquisite, subtle scent that evoked fields of sun-drenched poppies, but I wondered if it weren't a bit too provocative for her. Lucie replaced the stopper, glanced at me in the mirror and then stood up, moving across the room to pick up a topaz silk fan embroidered with gold and yellow flowers.

"Well," she said, "here I am. I feel like a fool. I know they're all going to whisper about me."

I stared at her, amazed, so amazed I was unable to speak. The buttercup yellow satin gown that had been delivered this morning was cut extremely low, leaving her shoulders bare, her breasts half-exposed. The bodice was form-fitting, emphasizing her slender waist, and the great skirt belled out in gleaming folds. I had helped her select the gown. I hadn't realized it was going to be quite so revealing, nor had I realized so keenly what a slender, voluptuous body she had. A diamond and topaz necklace hung around her throat, diamond and topaz earrings dangling from her lobes. Her hair had been pulled back severely from her face and twisted into an elaborate French roll on the back of her head, a diamond and topaz spray affixed to one side. Her lids were brushed with mauve shadows, her cheeks skillfully rouged to emphasize the unusual cheekbones, and her lips were a luscious pink.

I realized with some dismay that I was not looking at a girl. I was looking at a full-blown woman, gorgeous and

extremely sensual. Her poise was incredible, and the
violet-blue eyes that gazed at me were undeniably world-
weary. It was more than just the gown, the hairstyle, the
makeup. I was seeing a Lucie heretofore carefully
concealed, although there had been occasional small
glimpses.

"You just stare," she said. "You do not like?"

"You look—you look absolutely beautiful, Lucie."

"This silly man makes me sit for almost two hours, chattering all the time. I do not like what he does to my hair,
but it is too late to change it now. The gown I do not like.
The color is all wrong. I have trouble selecting the right
jewelry to go with it."

"It's a lovely color."

"Your gown I like," she said, eyeing it critically. "The
color goes with your hair. The sky blue and sapphire ruffles showing beneath the flounces make the brown seem
richer. Something is missing, though."

"Oh?"

"The jewelry. You need something to set everything off
just so."

"I no longer have any jewelry. I don't really think I
need—"

"Is easily taken care of," she said, interrupting me.

She moved over to the dressing table, opened an embossed white leather box and idly began to pull out a dazzling array of jewelry—diamond and ruby bracelets,
strings of pearls, emerald necklaces—tossing them carelessly onto the table as though they were the cheapest trinkets.

"Ah, yes," she said, "sapphires. The color of your eyes.
Here, try these. I think they will do very nicely."

The necklace she handed to me consisted of a dozen pear-
shaped sapphire pendants caught up in a diamond web and
suspended from a strand of large square-cut diamonds. It
must have cost a fortune, I thought, gazing at the flashing
jewels that dangled from my fingers. Dark blue flames
burned vividly, enhanced by the blinding silver-violet glit-

ter of the diamonds. When I hesitated to put it on, Lucie gave an impatient sigh and took it from me and fastened it around my neck herself, then handed me the matching pendant earrings.

"I'm not sure I should," I said, fastening one of the earrings.

"Nonsense. They are perfect. Now the other one. There. The picture is complete."

I had to admit that the jewelry was enhancing and added glamour, but I was still apprehensive about wearing it. What if something happened? What if the clasp broke on the necklace or one of the earrings slipped off without my knowing it? Lucie waved these objections aside and told me she rarely wore the sapphires anyway.

"You shall be the most beautiful woman here tonight," she declared.

"I think not, Lucie. That honor will unquestionably belong to you."

"You humor me. It is polite of you, but I know I look a fright. No one will notice me, and it is just as well. I do not like crowds. My uncle feels he must make the big splash to impress this woman he hates."

"I suppose we'd better go on down," I said.

"Yes, it is an unpleasant duty."

She might have been on her way to a firing squad as we moved slowly down the grand staircase, side by side, our full skirts spreading, rustling. The foyer was already full of guests, more arriving by the moment, and all eyes were upon us as we made our descent. Count Orlov hurried foward to greet us, taking my hand as we reached the bottom step.

"Here you are," he said. "You are a vision tonight, Miss Danver. All of my guests will wonder who this lovely creature is."

"Thank you, Count Orlov. You look resplendent yourself."

He grinned, preening a bit. His tall white leather boots were gleaming. His white breeches fit like a second skin.

The short white tunic was adorned with gold braid, and the waist-length white cape casually draping his broad shoulders was lined with cloth of gold.

"I wear this old uniform to aggravate the princess," he confided. "It fits perfectly even after all these years."

He was still holding my hand, clasping it strongly, as excited and aglow as a small boy with delicious mischief in store. Lucie stood beside me with a bored expression. Her uncle gave her a small nod, barely acknowledging her presence. If he noticed her remarkable transformation, he gave no indication of it. Music from the ballroom lilted quietly throughout the house, and servants were leading guests into the adjacent drawing room where food was being served.

"Is exciting evening, this," Orlov said. "I show them all that Orlov still gives the grandest parties. Is like the old days."

Releasing my hand, he beamed, went to give a hearty bear hug to a doddering, silver-haired ex-diplomat with a plethora of ribbons and decorations on the breast of his shiny black coat. Carriage wheels crunched on the drive outside, and within a matter of minutes all the other guests had arrived save the guest of honor. She would, of course, be late, I thought. The foyer was filled now, guests chattering in small groups before moving into the drawing room, servants passing among them with trays of champagne. Lucie and I were the recipients of many a curious glance, I noticed, everyone clearly wondering who we were and speculating about our relationship to the count.

"Ah, here is the princess!" Orlov exclaimed as a carriage was heard coming up the drive. "Is necessary for her to make the Grand Entrance."

A grand entrance it was, Princess Dashkova sweeping regally through the door with a handsome blond student on either side, one of them holding her black velvet cloak, the other her spangled black lace fan. A hush fell over the crowd as Orlov clicked his heels together and greeted her with great ceremony. She gave him her hand. He lifted it to his lips. Her old-fashioned black gown was completely overlaid with shimmering black spangles. A stunning diamond and emerald necklace rested against her flat collarbone. Matching earrings dangled from her lobes. A spray of emerald and black egret feathers was affixed to one side of her coiffure with a diamond and emerald clasp. Her lips were painted a vivid red, and they formed a condescending smile as she took in Orlov's uniform. She was clearly Not Impressed.

"I see she's brought her students with her," I remarked.

"Perhaps she hires them by the season," Lucie replied.

I turned, surprised by the bitchiness. Her expression was still bored. She raised her fan, unfolding it, waving it gently to and fro. Orlov motioned to us, and we went over to pay our respects to the princess, Lucie casually plucking a glass of champagne from the tray of a passing servant as we approached. It was still difficult for me to associate this gorgeous, worldly creature with the nervous young girl I knew, but young people love to assume all sorts of roles.

We greeted the princess. She swept her eyes over us, nodded, dismissed us. A huge square-cut emerald surrounded by diamonds flashed on her left hand. Her perfume was too strong, her makeup too thick and poorly applied, but she was an impressive figure nevertheless, with those glittering, imperious green eyes and that imposing carriage. Orlov told her how delighted he was that she had been able to come and added that there were many old friends eager to see her. Dashkova took her fan from the blond retainer, clicked it open and looked excruciatingly tolerant as Orlov led her away. Lucie and I were left standing with her two youthful companions.

The blond with brown eyes grinned. Not very tall, he was sturdily built and glowing with ruddy health. His hair was thick, the color of wheat, his cheekbones broad, his mouth full and pink and sensual. Perhaps twenty-one, he wore his formal attire with flair but looked as though he would be much more comfortable kicking a ball on a playing field than escorting an aging Russian princess to a grand soirée.

"John Hart," he said, introducing himself.

"How do you do, Mr. Hart. I'm Marietta Danver."

"I know. I remember you from the theater. And you are Lucie Orlov."

He turned to her, a grin curling on his lips. Lucie gave him a cold look and the briefest of nods. The other youth, taller, with pale blond hair and thin, rather cruel features, looked at us with icy blue eyes and introduced himself as Reginal Burton. A servant took the cloak he still held over his arm. Princess Dashkova called to them from across the room, and the two students strode over to join her, John Hart turning to give us a parting look. Lucie finished her glass of champagne and wandered off to find another, the skirt of her lustrous buttercup yellow gown swaying like a satin bell. I was relieved when, a few moments later, Sir Harry came over and asked if I would care for some food.

"I'm famished," I admitted.

"Quite a party, this," he said. "Orlov has really put on a lavish affair."

"It's been frantic around here all day. The servants have been rushing around in a frenzy. I didn't realize the party was going to be so grand."

"The good count believes in doing everything on a grand scale. I see we're to dine buffet style, in the French manner. I wondered how he was going to seat everyone."

"He certainly seems to know a lot of people," I remarked.

"Orlov made a lot of friends when he was—uh—shall we say, in power? He was most accommodating to visitors to St. Petersburg, always ready to do a little favor, grant a little concession, help promote a private interest. He was extremely popular with the English and French, if not with the populace."

"There are an unusual number of Russian guests, too."

"Aristocrats who, like Orlov and Dashkova, are no longer in Catherine's good graces and deemed it wise to move to more pleasant climes. We have a whole contingent of Russian émigrés here in London, a querulous, quarrelsome lot living on pawned jewelry and dreams of vanished glory."

"Is Catherine really so severe?"

"Only when she's crossed. She's basically a warmhearted woman and quite forgiving. Orlov was never officially banished, he can return to Russia anytime, and I've no doubt Dashkova will be welcomed back soon enough."

The enormous drawing room, which took up almost half of the right side of the ground floor, had been wonderfully transformed with brightly colored Russian flags and banners and potted green plants. A huge golden replica of the Imperial Eagle hung on the wall above the buffet tables, swaths of crimson silk draped on either side, and smaller replicas, on the ends of tall staffs, were held aloft by Russian guardsmen stationed against the walls in full military regalia, their gold-trimmed white, black and blue uniforms quite ornamental. Golden epaulettes shimmering, they stood immobile as statues, staring straight ahead and seemingly oblivious to the people swarming about the room.

Russian servants in white velvet livery trimmed in gold stood behind the buffet tables, helping the guests to a rich array of food dominated by a gigantic ice sculpture of an eagle, the center scooped out and heaped with glistening caviar. Luscious arrangements of meat filled golden platters—pink ham, orange smoked salmon, chicken and duck roasted golden brown—and there were pâtés and aspics and steaming soups and vegetables. The dessert table was a wonder to behold with cakes and pastries of every variety.

"I've never *seen* so much food," a stout, bejeweled woman exclaimed. "I must have one of those rum cakes, one of those cream-filled pastries, too!"

"I'll settle for more of this caviar," her companion replied. "I've never had better."

"The count always did have a bountiful table. When we

were in St. Petersburg eight years ago we dined at his marble palace, and, my dear, you wouldn't *believe* the food. Have you tried the chocolate cake? There's chocolate cream and almond paste between the layers and, yes, I do believe strawberry jam as well!"

Sir Harry filled plates for us, and we strolled over to sit at one of the small gilt tables scattered around the room in front of the plants. Sir Harry nodded to various acquaintances, waved to a woman across the room, then concentrated on his food. I spread goose liver pâté on a soft roll, ate a buttered artichoke heart, nibbled on smoked salmon. The noise level grew higher, merrier as dozens of bottles of the finest champagne were consumed and party manners gave way to high spirits. I looked around for Lucie but could see her nowhere. I assumed she had already moved on to the ballroom where dancing had begun.

Finishing his food, Sir Harry patted his lips with a snowy white linen napkin and poured champagne from the bottle a servant had placed on our table along with two sparkling crystal glasses.

"Care for some?" he inquired.

"A little," I replied. "I've a feeling I'm going to need it before the evening is over."

"Count Orlov tells me he's asked you to accompany them to Russia as Lucie's companion."

"He's asked me. I haven't given him an answer yet."

Sir Harry took a sip of champagne, his face expressionless. "Will you go?"

"I—I don't think so, Sir Harry. I need employment, true, but I have certain reservations."

"It's an extremely rugged trip. Even traveling in luxury as you would be, surrounded by every comfort, there would be innumerable hardships. Once you reach the Russian border the conditions are—uh—exceedingly primitive, and the trip to St. Petersburg is more than half the journey."

"I'm not afraid of a little discomfort," I told him. "I've endured my share of hardships, believe me. I—I'm just not sure it would be wise."

"It's a vast, barbaric country, full of dark superstitions and seething violence. There's a thin crust of civilization and culture in St. Petersburg, a few other places, but beneath that crust—" He shook his head. "Russia for the most part is still in the Dark Ages, despite the efforts of Peter the Great and Catherine."

"Were I thinking of going, your remarks would hardly be encouraging."

"Russia is no place for an Englishwoman alone," he said bluntly, "particularly one as lovely as you, if you'll forgive my saying so. I have quite a few connections here in London, Miss Danver. I would be delighted to help you find suitable employment."

"Why—thank you," I said, touched by his offer. "I'll very likely call on you in a day or so."

Sir Harry nodded and stood up, placing his napkin beside the plate. "It will be my pleasure to be of service. And now, if you're finished, I'll introduce you to some of these people. They're all quite curious about you."

"I've noticed that."

During the next hour I chatted with an aged Russian countess in dowdy brown lace and yellowed diamonds, a stout ex-ambassador who bellowed in bullish tones and half a dozen others. Sir Harry and I were soon separated, and I was left to fend for myself as Orlov was fully occupied. I saw Princess Dashkova a number of times as the crowd parted, the tall, thin blond always at her side. She seemed to have lost John Hart. I still hadn't spotted Lucie. I suspected that she had slipped up to her room after making an initial appearance, and I longed to do the same as yet another guest engaged me in conversation and subtly plied me for information about Orlov, assuming I was his mistress.

Little by little the guests abandoned the drawing room and moved into the huge ballroom with its pale ivory walls and blue ceiling spangled with gold stars. Half a dozen chandeliers hung suspended, crystal pendants shining in the blaze of candles. Silver cloth draped the walls, and baskets of pink roses filled the air with heady fragrance that couldn't quite cloak the odor of sweat and damp powder. Orlov was dancing with an attractive brunette in blue, the wife of a retired aide, and he cut a dashing figure indeed in his white and gold uniform. He moved with exuberance and lithe animal grace, executing the steps of the dance with polished skill.

There was polite applause when the music stopped. Orlov thanked his partner profusely and then, seeing me standing in front of the great white wicker basket of roses, he strode over to join me, the short white cape swinging from his shoulders, gold lining flashing.

"Is a great success, isn't it?" he said, smiling a happy smile.

"Everyone seems to be having a lovely time."

"Even Dashkova is impressed, though she tries to hide it. Is like the parties I give in St. Petersburg, everything lavish, everyone happy. You are having the good time, too?"

"A splendid time," I lied.

The music started again, a lovely, lilting piece. Before I could protest, Orlov took my hand and led me onto the floor, grinning at my surprise. We began to dance, and after a moment I was caught up by the music. His eyes held mine as we moved, smiling eyes, full of warmth and affection, and I smiled back, enjoying myself for the first time. The chandeliers glittered, flashing rainbow spokes, and the room seemed to swirl, a blur of pink and silver and ivory as we whirled on the polished parquet floor. When the music finally ceased, I was startled to find that Orlov and I were alone on the floor, the other couples having stopped one by one in order to watch us. They applauded now. Orlov bowed, grinning anew, and I tried hard to hide my embarrassment.

"We show them, eh? All the men envy me, dancing with the most beautiful woman in the room."

I was the target for quite a bit of envy myself, several of the women watching resentfully as Orlov lifted my hand

and brushed it with his lips. The musicians began to play
again. Couples moved onto the floor. I begged off when
Orlov asked for another dance, saying I would much prefer
a glass of champagne. He led me off the floor and went for
it himself. A thin, horse-faced Englishwoman in pale
green squinted her eyes to get a better look at me, the tattered white and green plumes atop her steel gray coiffure
waving as she turned to whisper something to a plump
woman in plum-colored velvet.

Orlov returned with two glasses of champagne, and we
talked pleasantly for a while, watching the dancers. He
was enjoying himself immensely, and I was pleased that
his party was going so well. It obviously meant a great
deal to him. After we had finished our champagne, he reluctantly took leave of me in order to dance with the ex-
ambassador's wife, and, feeling one of my hairpins coming
loose, I left the ballroom and went to the elegant powder
room at the end of the foyer. The two women I had noticed
earlier were standing in front of the long mirror that covered one wall, the woman in plum velvet opening various
bottles of perfume and sniffing them as the one in pale
green adjusted her plumes.

". . . who she is," she was saying. "She's dreadfully common, of course, probably one of his expensive trollops."

"Orlov always *did* have exquisite taste in women, and
you'll have to admit she is gorgeous, Bessie."

"That hair can't be natural, no one has hair that rich a
red, like molten copper. I happen to know that dress came
from Paris. She's probably a French whore he picked up
in—"

Catching sight of me in the mirror, the plump woman
blushed and gave her companion a violent nudge. The
other looked up and, when she saw me, gave me a frozen
stare. I smiled politely. There was a moment of awkward
silence, and then the two women bustled out of the room,
the one still blushing, the other with her nose in the air.
Immune to such comments and not the least perturbed, I
sat down at the glass and adjusted the loose hairpin,

smoothing back a wave, fluffing a long ringlet. I looked up as the door opened and was not at all surprised to see Dashkova in the glass.

"Miss Danver!" she exclaimed, pretending surprise. I knew full well she had followed me to the powder room. "I was hoping we would have the opportunity for a little chat."

Her thin red lips smiled, but her eyes remained hostile. Her spangled black gown shimmered as she moved over to stand beside me, opening a box of powder, dabbing a bit on her cheeks. I continued to toy with my ringlets, waiting, my expression cool. Dashkova put the powder puff down, examined her face and then pretended to notice my necklace for the first time.

"I see Gregory is still as generous as ever," she remarked. "That's a lovely necklace, my dear. The stones are perfect with your eyes."

"Thank you," I replied, not bothering to tell her the necklace was borrowed.

"Have you known him long?" she inquired.

"Not terribly long."

"Then I suppose the enchantment is still in effect. Gregory can be wonderfully enchanting in the beginning, simply sweeping a woman off her feet. The bruises come later."

"Are you speaking from experience, Princess Dashkova?"

"Heavens no!" She was appalled. "I have far too much good sense to ever get involved with a man like Orlov—I prefer my men less stupid, more polished—but I know a number of women who *have* been involved with him, including Empress Catherine of Russia."

"You were her friend, weren't you?"

"Until that man came between us! The way he used her! If you could have seen him—lounging in her private rooms, casually opening official documents and deciding which ones she should read, ordering her about as though she were his own personal slave, demanding this, demanding that. It still makes my blood boil!"

"That's quite apparent."

"He beat her, too. Did you know that? Slapped her about whenever he took the notion, once almost strangled her when she refused to have his apartment redecorated. There were bruises on her throat for a week—no amount of makeup could cover them."

She picked up a pot of rouge, examined it, put it down, very close to losing that haughty control. I didn't believe a word she said, but I was fairly sure of her motives. After all these years she still hated Orlov, and she would make trouble for him any way she could. Thinking I was his mistress, she hoped to turn me against him. I gave my hair a final pat and and stood up, amused by the transparency of her ploy.

"I find it rather surprising the Empress would tolerate such treatment," I said.

"Catherine always did need to be dominated by her men. It's a perversity not at all uncommon to very strong women. She rules the country with an iron hand, painfully aware of her awesome responsibility. In her private life—in the bedroom—she prefers to let someone else wield the power. It's an unfortunate weakness, often undermining the public good. The new man, Potemkin, is even worse than Orlov in that respect, though at least he has a brain and, so far as I know, doesn't batter her about."

Dashkova touched the side of her head, causing the emerald and black feathers to tremble. Turning away from the mirror, she looked at me and opened her spangled black fan.

"He was shockingly unfaithful to her, you know. Orlov is incapable of fidelity. He paraded his sluts before her, threatening to leave her if she didn't buy him another carriage, give him another estate, sign another document granting concessions to one of his wretched brothers or political cronies. Catherine put up with it because, inexplicably, she loved him and because his skills as a lover were—undoubtedly still are—nothing short of phenomenal."

I made no reply, maintaining a cool silence that left the princess to think anything she chose. She snapped her fan shut, and her green eyes glittered with malice as she continued.

"He has an incredible technique, I'm told, and a staying power that is not to be believed. Half the women at court slept with him. To be bedded by the great Orlov was a matter of pride. Catherine could overlook casual animal coupling, but when she discovered he was having a serious affair with Princess Colitsyna she finally had enough. Colitsyna was sent away in disgrace, and the randy stallion was dismissed."

"Generously rewarded for past services, I understand."

Dashkova arched one dark brow, her eyes widening. "So *that's* what interests you? I can't say I'm surprised. You look a bit more intelligent than most of his doxies, and he *is* almost forty. Perhaps he's losing some of his skills after all. If I were you, I'd take that lovely necklace and whatever other trinkets he may have given you and get out before the bloom wears off and your aging provider turns vicious. You'll be sparing yourself a lot of grief."

I smiled politely. "Thank you for your advice."

"Don't mention it, my dear," she said, equally polite.

We exchanged nods and left the powder room together as though the conversation had never taken place. Dashkova made some idle comments about the party as we moved down the hall, and I answered in kind, relieved when we reached the ballroom and Reginald Burton stepped foward to claim her, his thin, cruel young face petulant at the long delay. As he led her away I suspected that much of her malice might be due to the fact that she was one of the women at court with whom the great Orlov had *not* indulged. She had placed a bit too much emphasis on his skills and had obviously given them a great deal of thought. Had she perhaps offered herself to him years ago and been scorned? As I watched her disappear into the crowd, I thought it likely.

Putting Dashkova out of my mind, I resolved to be as pleasant as possible for the count's sake. I danced several times with various dignitaries and talked with their wives and had champagne with a boring, withered old Russian nobleman who had silver hair and a cracked voice that droned on and on about the glories of St. Petersburg under Empress Elizabeth. I watched the Russian folk dances Orlov had organized as entertainment, applauding politely when the dancers in their colorful native costumes finished their turn. More refreshments were brought, marvelous ices, chilled fruit and cheeses, and there was more dancing, more talk, and it was well after one o'clock when a few people finally began to leave. I told Orlov I had had a wonderful time and, pleading a mild headache, gratefully went upstairs.

Only a few candles were burning in the hallway, and it was dim, thick shadows flickering over the walls. I could hear the music playing as I walked to my room, for many of the guests were staying for the breakfast that would be served at five o'clock and there would be dancing all night long. As I passed, I noticed that Lucie's door was closed. She had the right idea, I thought, and I wished that I had had the good sense to come on up three or four hours ago. I hadn't been lying to Orlov about the headache. My temples were throbbing as I stepped into my bedroom and I was bone weary from all the dancing, the smiling, the strain; yet, tired as I was, I felt overstimulated as well and knew it was not going to be easy to get to sleep.

Removing the earrings and necklace, I placed them on the dressing table and sat down to brush my hair. What an evening, I mused, shaking out the long ringlets. The conversation with Sir Harry had been most interesting. He certainly hadn't minced words about the unsuitability of my going to Russia, though the reasons he had given were not my own. I was no stranger to hardship and discomfort, far from it, and the trek to Russia couldn't possibly be as harrowing as those I had made along the Natchez Trace with Jeff Rawlins and up the Gulf Coast with Jeremy and Em. Russia might be a barbaric country, but it could scarcely be more barbaric than parts of America I had known. No, those weren't the reasons why I intended to turn Orlov down.

I put the brush down and lifted my hair up in back, letting it fall in a rich tumble of natural waves. I was very grateful to Sir Harry for offering to help me find employment. I was eager to start working, eager to start earning the money that would take me to Texas and Em. I had delayed too long already, enfolded snugly in the luxury of these past two weeks. I would miss Lucie, for I was genuinely fond of her. She had a touching quality that moved me deeply, and I felt strangely maternal and protective toward her, though I was not yet ten years her senior. I would miss Orlov, too. I had to admit that. His warmth and good humor, his thoughtfulness and courtesy had made a very favorable impression, and I liked him a great deal, even though I knew there was another side to the coin and that he was undoubtedly amoral and could probably be utterly ruthless as well.

Not that I believed Dashkova. She might well be the most intellectual woman in Europe, but so far as Orlov was concerned her venomous tirade had given every indication of a woman scorned. She had been completely wrong about Orlov and me, but then she was hardly the only one tonight to make the same assumption. Standing, I caught sight of the jewelry and, on impulse, decided to take it back to Lucie. I doubted that she would be asleep, and I was a bit concerned about her.

Several candles had gone out, and the hallway was even dimmer than before, a long, shadowed corridor broken here and there by faint yellow-orange circles of light. Music still played, muted by distance, and there was a barely audible murmur of voices. An occasional burst of laughter rose, floated in the air, died away. The rustle of my satin skirt was unusually loud as I moved down the hall toward

Lucie's door, the jewelry in my hand. I was perhaps five yards away when the door opened and a flood of light spilled onto the carpet. I froze as a man stepped out.

Although his back was to me, I recognized those broad shoulders, that dark blond hair immediately. John Hart turned, giving me a three-quarter's profile, and I saw the smile on his lips, the triumphant look in his brown eyes. Swaggering, he straightened the lapels of his coat and cocked his head. The smile turned into a leering grin.

"Enjoyed it, luv," he said heartily. "We'll have to do this again one day soon."

"It's not likely," Lucie said coldly.

"No? Well, it's been lovely. I'm mightily obliged."

He turned then and swaggered on down the hall with shoulders rolling, hands thrust into his coat pockets. Lucie stepped into the hall in time to see him turn and start down the staircase, and when she turned to go back into the room she saw me standing there a few yards away. Her face was expressionless. I could feel her pain. I wanted to rush to her, take her in my arms, comfort her. Neither of us spoke for a long moment.

"I—I wanted to return this jewelry," I finally said.

"You saw."

"I could hardly help seeing, Lucie."

"Come in," she said.

I followed her into the sitting room. She closed the door. The room was done in shades of pale blue and gray and ivory. A fire crackled quietly in the marble fireplace. Candles burned low in silver sconces, filling the room with a softly diffused light. Lucie looked at me with the violet-blue eyes of a lost soul. Her hair was down, streaming heavily between her shoulder blades. She had removed her jewelry. Her gown was rumpled, the gleaming buttercup yellow satin sadly creased. Her lips looked bruised. There were faint smudges under her eyes.

"You disapprove," she said.

"It's not my place to pass judgment, Lucie."

"You are shocked. I can see it."

"Surprised, perhaps."

"Now you will hate me, too."

"Hate you? Darling, of course I don't hate you."

Her lips trembled. I thought she was going to cry. She didn't. She pulled herself together, straightened her back, assuming a cool dignity that was pitiful to see. I was still holding the jewelry. I placed it on a low table in front of the fireplace. Lucie brushed a damp golden brown wisp of hair from her temple. The hard-won composure threatened to slip at any moment.

"He is not the first," she told me.

"I—didn't think he was."

"There have been many. Many," she repeated, turning to stare at the fire. "Now you know. Now you will hate me."

"You mustn't use that word, Lucie. I could never hate you. I'm your friend and friends—friends try to understand."

"No one could understand."

"I think perhaps I do," I said gently. "You want to be loved, and—this is your way of seeking that love. It's the wrong way, I believe, and it can only lead to more pain, but—I think I do understand, darling."

Lucie was silent a moment, and then she moved to sink down into the pale gray velvet sofa. I sat down beside her. She didn't look at me but gazed down at the soft sky blue rug patterned with faded pink flowers. After a time she lifted her eyes and looked into mine.

"Since I was thirteen," she said. "The first took me by force in a pile of hay on my—my father's estate. None of the others have had to use force. I do not enjoy it. Please do not think that."

"I—I'm sure you're aware of the dangers."

She smiled a deprecatory little smile that looked strangely out of place on those bruised pink lips. "There are certain precautions," she said. Her voice was flat. "I carry a box of sheaths with me. Men never think of these things. They think only of their pleasure."

That did shock me. I tried hard not to show it. I idly examined the rows of sky blue and sapphire lace ruffles showing beneath the leaf brown flounces of my spreading skirt.

"Does your uncle know?" I asked quietly.

"I think not. I have been—how you say?—most discreet. My uncle is too involved with his own interests to pay much attention to me."

"I see."

"He is very good to me. You must not think bad of him. He sees that I have all the comforts, all the fine things, but my uncle is not able to—to look into the heart."

I could look into her heart, and I saw the pain, the confusion, the sadness. There were tears in her eyes now. They streamed down her cheeks in tiny, glistening rivulets. I took her hand. She bit her lower lip, trying not to sob. I pulled her gently into my arms and held her and murmured comforting words while she cried and cried and cried, and after a long while she sat up and brushed the tears from her eyes. The worldly woman was gone. In her place was a thin, frightened child.

"It is wrong, I know," she said.

"Yes, Lucie, it's wrong, because"—I hesitated, choosing my words very carefully—"because the love you have inside of you is something very precious, far too precious to squander on—on those who are unworthy to receive it. One day you will meet a fine young man who will be worthy of the gift of your love, who will love you in return. You will not want to give him a gift that is—that has been tarnished."

"Who could ever love *me*?" she asked.

"Darling—"

"No one ever has. They laughed at me. They mocked me. Everyone on the estate knew about me. I never belonged. I did not belong in the servants' hall because my father was the mighty Count Alexis. I did not belong in the great house because my mother was a gypsy woman of pure Tartar blood who died giving birth to me. My father should

never have taken me in. He should have left me with the
gypsies. He eventually sent me off to a fine school for aristocratic young ladies. I was tall and skinny and had
slanting eyes. The girls there all knew. They shunned me.
The teachers disliked me. They resented having the bastard child of a gypsy woman in their midst, even if her father was a count."

Lucie fell silent, remembering. The fire crackled, the log
a glowing pink now, beginning to flake away. Candles
spluttered. I looked at the girl sitting beside me, and I was
beginning to understand so much. How desperately she
needed a friend, someone to help heal her wounds. She finally looked up at me, her tear-stained cheeks wan.

"Until my uncle took pity on me and made me his traveling companion, I had nothing, no one. You are the only
friend I have ever had, and now—" She hesitated. A tear
spilled over her lashes, slid slowly down her cheek. She
wasn't even aware of it. "Now I will lose you, too."

I couldn't turn my back on her. I knew that already. The
child needed me, and I realized that helping her would
help me forget my own pain. I didn't want to go to Russia,
but my decision had finally been made. I couldn't accept
charity from Count Orlov, but I could conscientiously accept a salary. By agreeing to accompany them as Lucie's
companion and to remain in Russia for three more months
I would ultimately get to America much sooner.

"I know that my uncle asked you to come to Russia with
us," Lucie said. "I know that you haven't given him an answer yet."

"That's right."

"Russia is very far away and—and I can understand why
you wouldn't want to come. It is asking too much."

Lucie stood up. Wan, wounded, she brushed heavy
golden brown waves from her temples and smoothed down
the rumpled satin skirt. Moving over to one of the windows, she held the curtain back and gazed out at the night
for a long while, and when she turned back around to look
at me her face was carefully composed.

"I will be all right, Marietta."

"I'm sure you will, darling."

"This—this student, he was the first since I met you. I was feeling sad, and—and I was pitying myself because soon I would be leaving and never see you again, and—"

"I understand, Lucie."

One of the candles spluttered, went out. Pale golden shadows leaped nimbly over the walls. We could hear the music playing downstairs, the sound barely audible through the closed door. Lucie looked at me, her violet-blue eyes dark and defeated, inexpressibly sad.

"I am sorry this has happened," she said.

"But it's brought us closer together, and—and that's good, darling. We're going to be spending a lot of time together in the months to come."

She looked startled. "Does—does that mean—"

She couldn't finish the sentence. She was on the verge of tears again, her composure crumbling. I stood up and smiled and crossed the room, taking both of her hands in mine.

"It means I'm coming to Russia with you," I told her. "It will be exciting. It—it will be an adventure, and God knows I can use one."

BOOK TWO

Chapter Eight

I HAD SEEN SNOW BEFORE, OF COURSE, BUT never anything like this. It was a solid, shifting, swirling mass of blinding whiteness that came plummeting from a sky as black as night though it was not yet four o'clock in the afternoon. Huge flakes pelted and pounded the window through which I gazed, and the window itself had a glittering coat of rime, the icy turfs forming intricate patterns on the glass. I could see nothing but snow, snow spiraling in the air, snow forming fantastic mounds on the side of the road. How could the horses possibly move through this fury of snow, I wondered, yet the bells jangled merrily and hooves clopped noisily on the icy road and the broad runners of the troika glided smoothly over the hard, glassy surface.

"You mustn't stare at it too long," Lucie said in English. "It can cause blindness."

"I'm not surprised. It—it has a bizarre kind of beauty, doesn't it?"

"It can be lovely, particularly in the moonlight when everything is silver and blue. Shall we speak Russian?"

I let the heavy velvet curtain fall back into place and settled against the cushions, sighing.

"I'd rather not. I don't think I could concentrate on the words, much less the pronunciation."

"Your pronunciation *is* a bit eccentric," she informed me, "but your command of the language is already superb."

"Not nearly as good as your command of English. Your French has improved, too. You have a wonderful gift for languages, Lucie. It's a pity you never developed it before."

"It has been interesting—learning all this, teaching you my own language. It helps to pass the time."

"And we've had *lots* of time to pass," I added.

Lucie smiled, pulling the enormous sable lap robe closer about her, looking at me with a fresh young face framed by the dark golden brown sable hood covering her head. I wore a hooded ermine cloak and had my own lap robe, silver-gray mink, as large as a blanket. A silver brazier filled with hot coals rested at my feet, spreading warmth up my legs, and though I wore long kidskin gloves, I still placed my hands inside the large white ermine muff with glossy black tails trimming the sides. Despite all these comforts, it was still icy cold, and our breaths caused condensation in the air when we spoke.

"A cup of hot tea?" Lucie inquired.

"It might help," I replied. "Let me pour it."

"No, no," she protested. "Keep your hands inside the muff. Warm yourself for a while."

She opened the gilded, built-in cabinet and took out the tall silver container and poured hot, sweet tea into two delicate rose pink cups with silver handles. I took mine, sighing again, and sipped it gratefully, feeling warmer at once. Although I knew the container was lined with a special metal, I was still amazed the tea could be so hot. Lucie asked if I would like some chocolates, a piece of almond cake, perhaps some goat cheese or cold roasted duck. I shook my head. Settling back against the tufted violet and blue velvet cushions, she smiled again, looking all of fifteen, looking wonderfully content as the bells jangled and the enormous troika sped along with scarcely a jolt.

We had abandoned the carriages over a week ago, exchanging them for these elaborate vehicles designed to travel over the icy roads of Russia. Orlov's fine horses had been left behind, too—they would be sent to his country es-

tate along with the carriages when weather permitted,
months from now. The horses pulling the troikas were
sturdy, muscular animals with short, thick legs and extremely broad shoulders. Though shorter than the chest-
nuts, not much larger than ponies, really, they pulled the
huge troikas with ease and seemed immune to blasts of icy
wind and snow.

There were twelve troikas in our caravan, eight of them
to carry various supplies that would not be available
henceforth, and each vehicle was as large as a small room.
Orlov had his own, though he spent much of his time galloping along with Vladimir and the other guards, and ours
was equipped with every conceivable luxury. Lined with
padded, pale violet velvet embroidered with silver, with
blue velvet curtains and cushions, it had built-in cabinets
and shelves and a special curtained cubicle with porcelain
chamber pot and ewer. Candles glowed warmly inside
crystal globes affixed to either side, between the windows,
and in addition to those at our feet there was another,
larger silver brazier filled with glowing coals. Furs were
piled everywhere, glossy, gorgeous robes and cloaks, and
there were books galore and games and puzzles and an
endless supply of wonderful things to eat and drink.

The luxury was all very nice, but it was still cold. Lucie
assured me that I would get used to it and, truth to tell, it
didn't bother me nearly as much as it had in the beginning. She hardly seemed to notice, but then she had grown
up in this clime. Her uncle actually seemed to prefer to be
out in the open, galloping on his horse, claimed it was brac-
ing, and I had never seen him as vigorous and hearty as he
had been since we crossed the Russian border. I would personally take the sultry warmth of Texas any day, or even
the English spring. Still, if one had to travel through Russia, it was nice to do so bundled in ermine and mink and
sable and surrounded by all these niceties.

I finished my tea and handed the cup to Lucie. She put it
away and selected a chocolate, peeling away the silver paper and plopping it into her mouth. Was it really only six

weeks ago that we had sat there in her sitting room, talking until dawn? London seemed like a distant dream now, something vaguely imagined that had never really taken place. We had left a week after the party for Princess Dashkova, crossing the channel at Dover, watching the great white cliffs recede slowly in the distance. In Paris there had been dinners with aristocratic friends, a visit to Versailles, a flurry of buying at the exquisite shops. In Berlin there had been crisp apple strudel and stodgy German barons, dark beer and leather goods and a cuckoo clock for Lucie. Across Europe there had been accommodations ranging from the luxurious to the barely adequate. Since we crossed the border, there had been only dismal posthouses, each more squalid than the last.

The first lap of the journey had been interesting, full of variety—rustic French villages where one bought delicious homemade bread, dark German forests and plush spas where one avoided the sulphur water, mountain ranges covered with vivid green pine trees under a cloudless indigo sky—but in Russia there was only snow and ice and howling wind, with an occasional collection of hovels to break the monotony. Lucie assured me it was lovely in the spring and positively lush in summer, but I hoped to be on my way to Texas by then. I would cheer up when we got to St. Petersburg, she added. It was a magical city, created in the middle of a former swampland and one of the wonders of the modern world with its hundreds of bridges and huge, majestic buildings. It rivaled Paris in theater and music, its shops considerably better, with goods from all over the world, and Versailles couldn't compare with the Winter Palace.

I watched as she contentedly reached for another chocolate. The tormented child I had held in my arms six weeks ago seemed to have vanished, replaced by a vivacious creature with sparkling violet-blue eyes and a ready smile. She had never had a friend. She had never been able to laugh and share her enthusiasm and gossip cheerfully for hours on end. As the darkness in her soul melted away, a radiant personality came to the surface, the personality I had glimpsed so briefly that night at the theater when she had been enthralled by the play. There was surprising sophistication as well and a voracious new thirst for learning languages.

"I may—I just may go on the stage one day," she had confided, "and I will need to speak flawless French, flawless English, too. You should learn Russian, Marietta—I will help you. It will be fun."

And so we passed the hours away with grammar books purchased in a fine shop in Paris and I learned Russian and taught her English and helped her improve her French and we both laughed at our mistakes and stumbled on, hour after hour. Lucie had purchased dozens of books of plays, and she read them avidly. Molière was delightful, Racine a bit stuffy, Shakespeare exciting but hard to understand. Her favorite plays were those written during the Restoration, scandalous farces penned by Mrs. Aphra Behn, even more scandalous dramas by John Dryden. Reading them aloud helped her greatly with English, while I corrected her pronunciation and explained the meanings of unfamiliar words. My own progress in Russian was considerably slower, but I had a working knowledge of the language now, could understand it if it weren't spoken too rapidly and was able to speak it myself, if in a highly ungrammatical fashion. My Russian was every bit as good as her uncle's French, Lucie informed me.

Orlov was delighted with our projects, enchanted when I spoke my first Russian sentence to him. The grin on his face and the wicked twinkle in his eyes led me to believe I had been less than word perfect when I informed him that the horses were sturdy creatures and the weather was foul. The count had been a delightful and attentive companion in France and Germany, showing off his knowledge of the places we went, buying us little surprises, treating me with a courteous and disarming warmth. I might be an employee, but I was treated like a guest, my comfort of paramount importance to the count. I had had my reservations about coming along, true, but most of them had vanished. I knew that Orlov found me attractive, but he had shown me the greatest respect and had never once indicated he would like to go to bed with me.

There had been a woman in Paris, I knew, a woman in Berlin, a peasant girl at the last posthouse. Women were as necessary to him as the air he breathed, but as long as that husky, caressing voice and those seductive looks were used on others, I had no complaint.

Was there, perhaps, just a faint touch of disappointment? It was something I didn't care to examine too closely. I was human, flesh and blood, and Count Gregory Orlov was a magnificent animal, the most magnetic man I had ever met. I would be less than human were I not to find him physically appealing, but I was perfectly content with the *status quo.* I had no intentions of becoming involved with any man, however magnetic, after Jeremy Bond. Orlov knew, and he respected my decision, content to be a genial host and jolly companion.

"It is gone," Lucie said, peering at me. "Finally it is gone."

I snapped out of my revery. "I—I'm afraid I was lost in thought. What is gone? What are you talking about?"

"That lost, betrayed look in your eyes. It was there in London all the time. It was there in France, too, even when you were smiling. It is gone now. I think perhaps you have gotten over this man at last, Marietta."

"I haven't gotten over him," I said, "but I—I think perhaps I have made a great deal of headway. Being with you has helped. Traveling, seeing new things, all these experiences—all of it has helped."

"You love him still?"

"I detest the son of a bitch, not to put too fine a point on it. And, yes, I love him still. Damn his soul."

"It is strange, love. All these plays I read, so much to do with love, everyone in a muddle, laughing, lying, plotting, wrecking their lives for love. So much talk of splendid bliss. *Is* it blissful, Marietta?"

"It can be, darling. It can also be hell."

"Will you—do you think you will ever fall in love again?" she asked.

"Not if I can help it. I've had quite enough of the divine madness, more than enough to last me a lifetime."

"That is just talk, I think," she said sagely. "You are young and beautiful and men will always fall in love with you. You will love one of them back, it is inevitable. Is this the right word?"

"The word is right. The statement is wrong."

"I think not. Perhaps you will even meet this Jeremy again."

"I fervently hope so," I said.

"What would you do?"

"First I would slap his face so hard his ears would ring. After that I would think of something more painful."

Lucie nodded. "You do still love him. It is like in the plays. You want to hurt the one you love because of the hurt he gives you. When love is gone, there is indifference only."

"I think perhaps you have read too many plays."

"These things a woman knows instinctively," she replied, "even if she has never been in love herself."

"You will be, darling," I promised.

"I do not know that I care to be. There is too much suffering. I would rather be loved and admired by—" she hesitated, dreamy eyed, "by the people sitting out there in the darkness," she continued. "They would love me and I would feel their love, but it would not be able to hurt me."

"You were impressed by Perdita, weren't you?"

"I wish to be like her. I know my uncle will object, but I think—I think when I am eighteen I will go to the school in Moscow and learn to act. My father no longer has any interest in me, so that doesn't matter. My uncle will yell and throw things, but I think I can be stubborn and have my way."

"It is a difficult life, Lucie. Acting is a—a very precarious way to make a living."

"My uncle will disown me, true, but I will sell my jewelry. Is it wrong to have a dream, Marietta?"

"Everyone should have a dream, darling."

"You do not think I am foolish?"

I shook my head. "Of course not," I said gently.

"Do you—do you think this dream could possibly come true?"

"Dreams do come true, Lucie, if you are willing to work. If you are willing to sacrifice and persevere and keep going. If you can do this, there is no reason why you couldn't become anything you wanted to be."

"This I will do," she told me.

Both of us were startled a few minutes later by the sounds of hoarse shouting and whips cracking. The troika lurched, skidded, slid to a halt, causing dishes to rattle in the cabinets and books to spill to the floor. I lifted the curtain. Pandemonium reigned outside, wild-eyed men in peculiar costumes galloping on fiery steeds, waving their sabres in the air. One of them saw me staring through the window, jerked his steed to a halt beside the troika and yelled savagely, whirling his sabre over his head.

"My God!" I cried. "We're under attack!"

Lucie peered out, utterly calm. "My uncle's cossacks," she told me. "There is no cause for alarm."

"Cossacks?"

"Almost every great nobleman has his own small private army. My uncle has only twenty," she added, "but then there are also Vladimir and the others who are personal guards, not cossacks."

I stared, fascinated, as the men charged around like a band of marauding red Indians. They wore high black boots and full blue breeches that belled over boot tops. Their long-sleeved blue coats were belted at the waist, the flaring skirts hemmed with thick gray fur, and their squat gray fur hats were squashed down low over their brows. Most of them had beards and long, drooping mustaches that gave an added, devilish look to their tan, weathered faces. They yelled and cavorted, their horses kicking up great clouds of snow. Several of them fired pistols into the air. Never had I seen such wild abandon, such fierce exuberance.

"They—they do carry on, don't they?" I said.

"They are excited to see my uncle again. It has been a long time. They know he is returning, of course, but I wonder why they ride all this way to join us? I am puzzled by this."

Lucie frowned. The soft sable hood fell away from her face, revealing golden brown waves. I let go of the curtain and sat back, listening to the din that surrounded us. Horses neighed. Guns fired. Shouts rose, mingling with loud, diabolical laughter. All the demons of hell seemed to be unloosed out there in the snow, and I gave a start when the door of the troika flew open. Count Orlov peered in at us. He smiled, looking like a rowdy schoolboy who has just been joined by his chums.

"Is all right," he said. "No cause for alarm. My men join us. Is a surprise to me."

Flakes of snow blew into the troika, along with freezing gusts of wind. Orlov climbed inside and closed the door, brushing snow from his shoulders. He was able to stand without stooping, although his head almost touched the ceiling, and in the close confines of the troika he seemed larger than ever. His bulky gray fur coat completely enveloped him from shoulder to mid-thigh. His gray kidskin breeches clung snugly to his legs, outlining the strong muscles, and his gray leather boots were crusted with snow. A pair of supple gray leather gloves protected his hands.

"Why have they come?" Lucie asked.

"They are eager to see me. They cannot wait for me to arrive."

His tone was humoring, his manner off hand, but both of us could tell he was hiding something. Lucie adjusted her hood and looked at her uncle with cool eyes.

"They are so eager to see you that they ride hundreds of miles through stormy winter weather? This I do not believe. They could be snug in their warm barracks with their vodka and their whores. They do not leave that merely because they are eager to see your smiling face."

Orlov scowled, highly displeased. Lucie gave him a defiant look, waiting for his reply. The scowl vanished. He looked extremely uncomfortable. He brushed at the snow clinging to gray fur, took off his hat, brushed it as well, deliberately delaying.

"Well?" Lucie demanded.

"Is nothing to worry about," he said, petulant.

"What is this we are not to worry about?"

"There has been some unrest among the peasants," he confessed. "Some madman has been stirring them up, filling them with seditious ideas. Is nothing new. It happens all the time. Damn! You are much too impudent, Lucie. I do not wish to tell you this. I do not wish you to worry needlessly."

"How serious is this unrest?"

"Not serious at all. He—this madman has gathered together a few followers who believe he is some kind of saint. He preaches revolt against the landowners. Some serfs have run away. One or two troikas have been stoned and the passengers roughed up. These are isolated incidents, nothing to cause alarm. This madman will be put down quickly enough."

Lucie looked unconvinced. Orlov put his hat back on.

"My men are restless," he said in a conciliatory voice. "This gives them a reason to leave the barracks where they grow bored and flabby. When they hear I am coming, they take it upon themselves to ride out and act as protective escort for the rest of the trip, though there is no need."

Lucie made no reply. Orlov grinned again.

"Mostly they wish to ride and yell and carry on like men of action. For too long they have been cooped up. I am happy to see them, though this means twenty more stomachs to fill. We will have to buy provisions at the next village."

He adjusted his cap and shifted restlessly, eager to join his playmates.

"We will continue on our way now. You make me tell you these things against my will. You are not to worry for a moment. No handful of peasants with pitchforks will dare to throw stones at our troikas. There will be a celebration tonight when we get to the posthouse."

He left then, moving out of the troika like a great gray bear, icy flurries of snow blowing in before he slammed the door. The din continued, as riotous as before, and it was several minutes before the troika began to move again, gliding easily over the ice. The cossacks rode up and down the line on either side, making a terrible racket, thoroughly enjoying themselves. Orlov and his other men were no doubt having a jolly time, too, I reflected, placing my feet on the brazier. I wrapped the fur lap robe more closely around me and shook my head in dismay.

"They will wear down after a while," Lucie said. "Now they indulge in high spirits."

She picked up the books that had tumbled to the floor, replaced them on the seat beside her and then, selecting one, settled back to read. I tried to concentrate on a Russian grammar book, but it was extremely difficult. After a while I put the book aside and resigned myself, wondering what on earth I was doing in this luxurious but bizarre vehicle, riding through a snow storm in a strange country with seemingly crazed ruffians charging about outside. It was utterly improbable. Only three months ago Russia had been merely a name on a map to me, a country I had absolutely no interest in, and now here I was, swathed in fur, my feet on a brazier, heading deeper into the snowy wasteland. Somehow it all seemed unreal, so unreal that I could hardly believe it was happening.

It had stopped snowing when, three hours later, we finally reached the posthouse. The sky, black before, was now a dark pewter gray smeared with orange and pink blotches that gradually blurred. There was a deepening blue haze in the air and the dazzlingly white snow was spread with long blue-gray shadows, glistening in the fading light. The posthouse was a dilapidated two-story structure of weathered brown wood, the slanting roof threatening to collapse under the weight of snow. Great mounds of snow surrounded it, reaching the ice-glazed windows. Lucie and I stayed inside the troika until Vladimir and his men had cleared a pathway to the front door. While they did so, the cossacks busily set up heavy tents in the courtyard beside the stables.

"It looks as bad as the last one," Lucie said, pulling her fur cloak closely about her. "I only hope there are no fleas and ticks."

Orlov himself helped us out of the troika, holding the door open, giving us his hand. His cheeks were flushed, his dark blue eyes gleaming in anticipation of the celebration. Vladimir gave Lucie his arm and helped her up the wet, already icing path just cleared to the door, and Orlov gripped my right arm just above the elbow. Wrapping his free arm around my waist, he guided me slowly up the path. I slipped. He supported me, pulling me closer, tightening his grip.

"We must get you some fur-lined boots," he told me. "These silly shoes you wear are no good for walking on ice."

"I'll try to do as little walking as possible," I said wryly.

"Me, I will be here to see that you do not fall."

He gave my waist a friendly squeeze, and his strong fingers curled more tightly around my arm, squeezing the flesh with bruising power meant to be reassuring. I winced. Orlov chuckled, clutching me as I slipped again. The physical contact was disconcerting, and I was acutely aware of his nearness. Lucie was already inside now, and Vladimir held the door open for us. Orlov led me inside, released me. I was surprised to find myself a bit unsteady on my feet. My knees seemed curiously weak.

"It's heaven," Lucie said, leading me over to the huge black iron stove that stood in the middle of the large, incredibly squalid room. "The worst yet. Brace yourself, Marietta."

Filthy straw littered the bare wooden floor. Chickens squawked angrily, running freely about the room, and a loud, nasty snorting proclaimed the presence of a pig. He burrowed in a pile of rags in one corner, not at all pleased with this invasion. Oil lamps burned smokily, casting pools of ugly yellow light, intensifying shadows. The few pieces of furniture were utterly decrepit, coated with dirt and grime, and there was dust everywhere. Orlov was speaking sharply to the man in charge, an emaciated-looking fellow with thin brown hair and sunken gray eyes filled with alarm. He wore cracked black boots, baggy blue breeches and a loose gray smock that had once been white, and he was clearly terrified as Orlov vented his displeasure at the conditions confronting us.

The man's wife came trudging slowly into the room with a heavy tin pan filled with peeled potatoes. Her broad, peasant face was pasty-looking and etched with a pitiful hopelessness, her brown eyes blank, like the eyes of a dumb animal. Heavy and big-boned, she had oily black hair pulled severely away from her face and worn in a bun in back. Her white blouse and long green skirt had been darned in a dozen places. Her gray apron was ragged. Oblivious to Lucie and me, oblivious to everything but the job in hand, she set the pan of potatoes down on top of the stove and filled it with water from a tarnished copper kettle. She reeked of garlic and sweat. When the pan was full of water, she trudged back into the kitchen, chickens squawking in her wake.

Disgusted with the caretaker's stammering, monosyllabic replies, Orlov finally shoved the man aside with surprising brutality. The pig snorted and thrashed about in its pile of rags. The caretaker cringed against a wall, even more terrified as Orlov began to snap orders to Vladimir. Vladimir nodded and went back outside, and Orlov came over to join us by the stove, his handsome face dark with anger.

"The place is a pigsty!" he declared. "Worse than a pigsty! Give these people the least responsibility and they let
everything go to ruin! The servants will clean the rooms
upstairs and make them ready before I allow you ladies to
see them. The chef will prepare your food on a stove the
men will bring in."

He scowled, an angry blond giant in gray fur, and then
he shook his head. The caretaker sidled out of the room,
keeping against the wall. His wife trudged back in,
dropped two whole garlics into the pan of boiling potatoes,
added salt and left. Orlov pulled two rickety chairs over to
the stove, dusted them off and told us to sit down. Servants
began to pour into the posthouse, heavily laden, rushing
upstairs. Orlov went out back to join the cossacks. A few
minutes later four cossacks burst into the room and,
shouting gleefully, began to chase the chickens and brutally wring their necks. The caretaker's wife hurried in,
protesting vehemently in a strange dialect, her bovine face
showing emotion for the first time. The cossacks ignored
her, merrily slaughtering the rest of the chickens. When
she attempted to stop them, she was knocked against the
wall. Chickens all slaughtered, three of the cossacks left,
taking the corpses with them, and the fourth, a brawny
ruffian with long black mustache, seized the pig, hoisted it
up in his arms and carried it off, laughing as it squealed in
outrage.

The chef appeared next. When he saw the condition of
the room he turned pale and began to rant, throwing his
hands in the air. Vladimir ordered the men to set the huge
porcelain stove down and fill it with kindling, told the chef
to shut up. Somehow, amidst the chaos, a meal was cooked
and served to us on the wooden table that had been covered
with a snowy linen cloth. I found it wildly incongruous to
be eating magnificent stew with a silver spoon from a Sèvres bowl in a squalid room that smelled of rancid grease
and chicken dung, but at that point I was too weary to give
it much thought. After the stew there were thin potato
pancakes folded over savory rarebit cooked in sherry and

cream sauce, accompanied by a wonderful white wine. Vladimir hovered over us throughout the meal.

"Are our rooms ready?" Lucie inquired when we had finished.

Vladimir nodded. He led us upstairs. He showed Lucie into her room and then took me to mine, opening the door, giving me a little shove. In Russian I fervently hoped he understood, I told him to keep his bloody hands to himself. His face was inscrutable as he pulled the door shut, leaving me alone. The room was small with a rough hardwood floor and bare wooden walls. The bed had been covered with fine linen and satin counterpane and piled with fur rugs. A large silver brazier glowed warmly, filling the room with heat, and on the rickety wooden table beside the bed there was a carafe of hot tea, a pink porcelain cup, a plate of date bars and, surprisingly enough, my Russian grammar and a French novel. Tall yellow candles burned in silver candelabra. We might be in a squalid posthouse in the middle of a frozen wilderness, but all the comforts were provided.

I removed my fur cloak, warm at last, poured myself a cup of tea and picked up the novel. Madame de Scudéry kept me entertained for an hour or so, but the flowery, affected style finally began to pall and the shouting and raucous laughter rising from the courtyard was altogether too distracting. I wandered to the window, peering down at the tents and blazing orange campfires. The cossacks were enormous black silhouettes against the glow, lurching about, staggering, already much the worse from the vodka Orlov had provided. Several waved their sabres overhead. Others wrestled and roisted about. Orlov was probably among them, relishing the rowdy horseplay as much as they, but I couldn't pick him out in the shadowy crowd.

I was still wearing my heavy, sapphire blue velvet gown with its long, tight sleeves and low-cut bodice when, ten minutes later, someone pounded on the door. Startled, I hesitated a moment, then opened it. Count Orlov grinned at me, a decidedly lopsided grin. A lock of thick golden brown hair had tumbled down across his brow. His navy blue eyes were merry, his cheeks pink from the cold. He completely filled the doorway, weaving just a little. Not really drunk, he was certainly tipsy. Attractively so, I thought.

"Ah, you are still dressed," he said in Russian. "I intrude?"

"You do not intrude, but I wish you would speak French. Your voice is rather slurred and I can barely make out the words."

"My voice is slurred?"

"Definitely."

"This I find hard to believe, Miss Danver."

"Believe me."

"I will speak the French. You must study Russian. Is boring, speaking always the French. We are in Russia now."

"I would never have guessed it," I said.

Orlov looked perplexed, confused, and then realization dawned. "Ah, you make the jest. Me, I am dense."

"Your brain might be just the tiniest bit foggy at the moment," I told him. "You've obviously been enjoying the celebration in the courtyard."

"Yes, this is true. I enjoy being with my men. Is a very long time since I see them. We have roast chickens and pig and drink much vodka. They challenge me to drink a whole bottle in one swoop, without the bottle ever leaving my lips."

"You obviously accepted the challenge."

"I pass it with ease. I put the bottle to my lips, I throw my head back and drink it all in less than a minute. My knees do not even wobble."

"They're wobbling now," I observed.

"This is your imagination," Orlov replied, offended.

"Well—"

"I do not come here to argue. I come to bring you a surprise."

"Indeed?"

He nodded, grinning again. He had been holding one hand behind his back as we talked, and now he brought it into view, showing me a pair of beautiful beige leather boots lined with soft beige fur. Clutching them by the tops, he lifted them up so that I might better appreciate the soft, pliant leather, the elegant style.

"Why—they're lovely," I said. "Wherever did you find them out here in the wilderness?"

"One of my cossacks has them. He brings them along as an extra pair. He is very tough soldier, fierce and fearless as they come, but he has the small, delicate feet. When the other men tease him about these dainty feet, he bangs them on the side of the head with the butt of his sabre. I think maybe these boots fit you."

"I couldn't possibly take them."

"They are brand-new," he said. "He has not even had them on yet. He is honored to give them up for a good cause. I do not even have to twist his arm a little."

"That's reassuring."

"Maybe just a little," he confessed, grinning.

"I wouldn't want him to be without an extra pair," I said. "I appreciate your thoughtfulness, Count Orlov, but—"

"Do I have to twist your arm, too?"

"I'd rather you didn't."

"You will take the boots."

"I don't seem to have much choice."

"Is correct," he informed me.

I didn't want to smile, but I couldn't help it. Orlov tilted to the left, righted himself, grinned again.

"You smile. You make the jest. Is good to see you in this mood. I think you are not sorry you come to Russia with us. The hall is very cold," he added.

We were still standing in the doorway. I stepped back now, and Orlov came into the room. I closed the door behind him to keep in the heat, and he stood in the middle of the floor, looking at the bed, the furs, the flickering candle flames. The gray fur hat was gone, but he was still wearing the bulky gray fur coat that made him look so enormous. He seemed to fill the room with his vitality, as though the air itself were charged with a new energy. His magnetism was almost overwhelming in these close quarters, and I wasn't at all sure this was a good idea. He was so very, very attractive, exuding sexual allure, and I wasn't nearly as strong, nor as immune, as I would have liked to be.

"I think perhaps you'd better leave the boots," I said.

"We try them on."

"In the morning."

"Now."

He was tipsy. He would probably have only the vaguest memory of this tomorrow. If there was any sexual tension, it was all on my part. Count Orlov was intent only on presenting me with the boots and, in truth, was undoubtedly much too foggy with vodka to have given seduction a thought. He is just being friendly, I told myself. He is like a great big, frisky puppy. I am being absurd.

"You sit," he said.

I hesitated. He gave me a little shove that was much more forceful than he had intended. The mattress sagged and bounced as my derrière landed on the bed. A fur robe spilled to the floor. I sat up, slightly dazed. Orlov squatted down and, before I could protest, reached under my skirts, wrapped his hand around my calf and lifted my right leg, propping it over his knee. His powerful fingers dug into the flesh of my calf as, with his other hand, he tugged at my shoe. It wouldn't come off. He frowned, eyes dark with concentration, finally jerking it off. I was wearing no stockings. He held my naked foot in his hand, examining it intently, as though he had never seen a female foot before.

"Really, Count Orlov—" I began.

"It is most dainty, the high arch, the pink-tipped toes."

"I think—"

"It is cold, too," he said. "The skin is like ice."

His hand slid slowly down my calf and wrapped around my ankle, and he began to massage my foot, bending it

gently, rubbing his hand over the sole, the heel, bending
the toes back and forth, and the warmth grew and spread,
creeping up my leg. His palm rubbed, his fingers curled,
pressed, squeezed, sending delicious, tingling sensations
throughout my body. The top of his head gleamed rich
golden brown in the candlelight, and his lips were parted,
pink and full and firm. His gray fur coat was sprinkled
with snow that slowly melted in the heat.

"Is warm now?" he inquired.

"Let's try on the boot," I said.

"Yes, I feel sure it fits."

He gripped my calf again and gave my leg a yank,
pulling my foot closer to his chest. It touched the soft gray
fur. The fur tickled. He reached for the boot and bent my
foot and slipped it into the boot. I wriggled my toes, pushed
down as he shoved up, and the boot slipped on as though it
had been custom made. Orlov grunted a little, rocking
back on his heels. I put my foot down, easing it deeper into
the boot. The fur lining seemed to caress my skin. As Orlov
watched, I took off my other shoe, put on the other boot and
stood up, valiantly striving to retain some semblance of
composure.

"I am right," he said. "They fit."

"They fit beautifully," I agreed.

"You are very beautiful. So beautiful."

"Thank you."

"The hair is like copper fire. I long to gather it in my
hands. The eyes are so blue. I long to see them look into
mine with longing. The breasts are so full. I long to
squeeze them tightly."

"You are quite drunk," I told him.

"Me, I can hold my vodka."

"I think you'd better get up."

"Yes, this is a good idea."

He reached for my hand. He tried to pull himself up. He
pulled me onto the floor beside him. He looked amazed. He
shook his head. I got up and got behind him and put my
hands under his arms and heaved and he managed to

stumble up and then he toppled onto the bed. I sighed. He sat up, looking at me with bewildered eyes.

"Are you all right?" I asked.

"I think maybe you are right. I think maybe I am just the tiniest bit foggy. The room is very warm. The walls seem to weave. I rest here for a few minutes."

"I don't think that would be wise."

"Yes, you are the very proper young woman. You do not have the men in your bedroom. This I am always aware of, and I do not make the seduction. I am very considerate. I think of you and I sleep with the whore in Paris, the barmaid in Berlin, the peasant wench at the posthouse. I use the restraint. This is noble of me when I want so much to have you for myself."

The liquor had really gone to his head now, and he had no idea what he was saying. I realized that. Hands propped behind him, he looked up at me with navy blue eyes full of the deepest yearning, his cheeks flushed, his brow moist, and I longed to brush that damp golden brown lock from his brow and run my finger over the full pink curve of his lower lip. It had been so long, so very long since I had felt a man's warmth inside me, and this man was so beautiful, his childlike charm so intriguing, combined with his brute strength and rugged virility.

"I should not say these things," he said mournfully.

"You really shouldn't," I agreed.

"I am drunk, I think. I should not have had the second bottle."

"It was most unwise."

"Now you will be angry with me because I want to pleasure you."

"I am not angry, Count Orlov."

"I have wanted to pleasure you since I first see you in England."

"I know."

"Is very difficult to be so correct when I want this so."

"Can you get to your room?" I asked.

"I think this is impossible."

"I'll go fetch one of the men servants," I told him.

I left the room. I paused in the hall for a moment and closed my eyes and took a deep breath, and then, squaring my shoulders, I went downstairs and found Vladimir sitting at the table with Ivan and two others. They were drinking vodka and eating rice cakes. I told him in a crisp, cool voice that his master was upstairs and needed assistance. Reluctantly, Vladimir got up, gave me a hostile look and followed me. Orlov was snoozing contentedly atop the pile of furs. Vladimir shook him and pulled him to his feet. Orlov protested, surly now, ready for a fight. Vladimir curled Orlov's left arm around his shoulder, curled his right arm around Orlov's waist and led him out of the room.

I closed the door. I could hear them stumbling down the hall and hear Orlov's sullen protests, and finally there was silence. I undressed and put out the candles and climbed into bed shortly thereafter, but I did not close my eyes. I stared at the moonlight streaking the darkness and listened to the crackle of the fire in the silver brazier and it seemed I could still feel his strong hands massaging my foot. It seemed I could still feel those sensations tingling within me, sensations I had not felt in too long a time. I tried to put it out of my mind. I failed.

I got very little sleep that night.

Chapter Nine

THE WHITE-LIVERIED SERVANT WHO CAME into my room the next morning was the same slim, fair-haired youth who had served dinner to Orlov and me at The Wayfarer. On the silver tray he set down on the bed-side table were a crystal goblet full of orange juice, a silver pot of coffee, a porcelain cup, a flaky croissant, a pot of strawberry jam, a platter of sausage and bacon, a linen napkin. He informed me that we would be leaving in an hour and departed as unobtrusively as he had entered. Sunshine blazed into the room, dazzlingly bright as it reflected off the snow. I sat up in bed, yawning, and leisurely consumed the lavish breakfast, dreading yet another day of wearying travel.

Lucie came in as I finished dressing. She had changed into a gown of dark golden velvet and wore her golden brown sable cloak. She looked fresh and full of vitality and enviably young. I felt old after my sleepless night. Adjusting the long sleeves of my blue velvet gown, smoothing the bodice, I sat down to pull on the boots. Lucie arched a brow when she saw them. I told her her uncle had brought them to me, that they had belonged to one of the cossacks.

"Vanya," she said. "He has very small feet."

"You know them all by name?" I inquired.

"Most of them. Vanya is very special. Before my uncle and I left Russia, Vanya was like a big brother to me. He taught me to ride."

"Oh?"

"He was very patient, but very persistent. He looks fierce and savage, and he is, I suppose, when it is necessary, but with me he was as sweet and gentle as a lamb."

"It was certainly kind of him to give up his boots."

"They are very fine boots. I am glad you have them. We should have purchased several pair for you before we started. I did not think of it."

I pulled on my kidskin gloves. Lucie stepped over to the window and began to trace patterns on the moist condensation. I put on the heavy ermine cloak and pulled the hood over my head. Only a few coals smoldered in the brazier now, and the room was cold. There were noises in the hall as a fleet of servants dismantled Lucie's room and carried furs, linens, candelabra and such downstairs.

"It's a lovely day," Lucie said. "The sun is glittering on the snow and ice, and no snow is falling. The sky is blue-white. We will take a short walk while they pack."

"Wonderful," I replied.

She smiled at my lack of enthusiasm. "It will be good for you," she told me. "It will get the blood circulating. It will toughen you up."

"Just what I need," I said, picking up the ermine muff.

I had to admit that it was lovely outside, the sky cloudless, a vast white canopy lightly stained with pale blue. There was a bustle of activity as the troikas were loaded, the horses led around from the stables and put in harness, tents folded up. The cossacks were as boisterous as ever, apparently unaffected by last night's consumption of vodka. Three of them stood out front, hurling their sabres in the air, twirling and swinging them in complicated patterns, the dangerously sharp blades slicing the air with a whistling noise. I gasped as one of them began to swirl his sabre in a circular pattern at knee level, nimbly leaping up and down to avoid having his legs sliced off. He flashed a savage grin at me and continued this insane game with renewed vigor.

"Playful, aren't they?" I said.

"This routine with the sabres they practice for hours on

end," Lucie informed me. "It is an important skill. The sabre is used as—how do you say it in English?—as a mental weapon as well as to slash and kill. A man on a horse charges toward his enemy and the enemy is discomfited. If he is yelling and waving a sabre in the air, the enemy becomes unnerved, disorganized, more vulnerable."

I digested this cheery bit of information as we walked on, boots crunching on the icy rime. My feet were warm for the first time since we had crossed the Russian border, and I was very glad that Vanya had such small, dainty feet. I would have to thank him for giving up his boots, I reflected. Lucie and I moved past the line of troikas, stepping out of the way as servants piled goods inside. Horses stamped. Harness jangled. Although it was extremely cold, our heavy cloaks kept us warm enough, and the air was curiously invigorating.

"You feel better now?" Lucie inquired.

"A little. I didn't sleep much last night."

"Fleas?"

"Cossacks," I said.

"They *were* rather noisy," she agreed, "but I didn't notice. I ate date bars and drank tea and read Mrs. Aphra Behn. I found several fleas in the bed. I summoned a servant and he killed them for me."

"The joys of travel."

We had passed the line of troikas and walked slowly down the icy road, huge mounds of snow on either side. Hearing boots crunching behind us, I turned and was not surprised to see Vladimir and Ivan following us, both heavily armed. Once we were clear of the posthouse, we were in a frozen white world without the least sign of human habitation, great drifts of snow making fantastic shapes, icy crusts catching the sun, throwing back vivid spokes of color like fine crystal.

"It *is* beautiful," I admitted, "but I long to see a sprig of green. All this white could become terribly oppressive."

"This is true. This explains much in the Russian character. The snow, the solitude turns one upon oneself."

"But in the springtime, in summer—"

"One waits for the snow," Lucie said. "One knows it is coming. One lives furiously during the warm months, knowing the snow and ice will soon make cavorting in the hay fields and dancing in the meadows impossible."

"That must be sad."

"It is sad, yes, but when the Russian is happy, he is riotously, joyously happy. There is always an edge of desperation to his happiness, you see. This is why the cossacks ride so hard and yell so loud. This is why the folk dancing is so furious, why the peasants prefer such bright colors."

"Are you glad to be back?" I asked quietly.

Lucie did not answer at once. Her face, surrounded by the sable hood, was pensive, and her violet-blue eyes were thoughtful. She dug her hands deeper into her large muff.

"Russia is in my blood," she said. "It is part of me. It will always be, but I—I have few pleasant memories of my life here. I have seen another world now. I love my country, and—yes, I am glad to see it again, but I do not wish to live here. After I complete my studies in Moscow, I will go back to England, perhaps France."

"And become a brilliantly successful actress," I added.

"You make fun of me?"

"Of course not, darling. I believe you will be. I've listened to you read the plays aloud. I've seen the way you interpret the lines, color them with emotion. One day, I'm sure, you will be as famous as Perdita."

"But she is a great beauty."

"She isn't one half as beautiful as you. The—the features you think of as unattractive, others find exotic and unique."

"This is true?"

"Indubitably."

"This word I do not know."

"It means without question, darling. I think we'd better turn back now. My nose is beginning to freeze."

Lucie smiled at my tone of voice. We started back, Vladimir and Ivan tromping sullenly behind. The troikas

had all been loaded when we reached the posthouse. The
cossacks were climbing into their saddles, swinging themselves up with acrobatic ease. Our driver was on his perch,
heavily bundled in fur, casually gnawing on an onion.
Count Orlov was standing in front of the posthouse with
the caretaker who, coatless, shivered with cold. His wife
stood in the doorway, her stolid body immobile, her face
stamped with grief at the loss of her chickens and pig.
Orlov dropped a few gold coins into the man's hand. The
caretaker stared at it blankly, as though he had never seen
gold before, and perhaps he hadn't. Head drooping, shoulders bent, he mumbled something under his breath. Orlov
turned away in disgust, striding briskly to his horse. Lucie
and I climbed into our troika, and a few moments later we
were on our way.

There was no need to light the candles. With the curtains drawn back, the interior was flooded with brilliant
light. The braziers were filled with hot coals that glowed a
bright cherry red, and the furs were soft and warm. The ice
and snow glittering outside made it all seem cozier. Mile after mile of frozen white slipped past the windows, the
shadow of our vehicle racing along beside us, blue and
gray against the white, growing longer as the sun rose
higher. The warmth, the movement, the monotony had a
drowsying effect on me, and I soon nodded off.

Shouting awakened me. I sat up with a start, disoriented. The troika was still speeding along. Sunlight still
streamed through the windows. Lucie looked at me over
the top of her book, completely unperturbed.

"What is it?" I asked. "What's happening?"

"One of the cossacks just spotted a wolf," she said. "I
saw it two hours ago, loping along, following us. I just
caught a glimpse, of course. They're extremely shrewd,
staying out of sight, waiting for the right opportunity to
pounce."

"My God! Is there any danger?"

Lucie put down her book and smoothed the lap robe over
her knees. "Not with a large party like this," she told me.

"'They generally prey on the lone traveler in an open sleigh. This one follows us in hopes someone will lag behind.''

"They—they attack people?"

"Oh yes," she said casually. "Sometimes, when the winter is very bad, they travel in large packs, and no one is safe on the roads. Several years ago two of my father's guests were killed. He was having a house party and Count Lanskoy decided to take Princess Gerebtsova for a moonlight drive. They were married, you see, but not to each other, and so they slipped away in a sleigh to have some time together. It was a very foolish thing to do. Count Lanskoy knew there were wolves. There had been several reports, yet he took the princess out anyway."

"What happened to them?"

"The wolves attacked, not more than a mile from the estate. They were both torn to pieces, as was the poor horse. There was not much left to identify them by, only a few scraps of clothing, part of a hand with a ring on its finger, many bones, much blood. The snow was red with it."

I shuddered. "How—how hideous."

"It is not uncommon," Lucie said, still in that matter-of-fact voice. "When wolves are abroad, people with sense stay inside. Those foolish enough to expose themselves run a grave risk. When starvation is in its last stages and they are crazed with hunger, wolves have been known to attack small villages."

"I don't think I care to hear the details."

Lucie returned to her book. Shaken by the story, I gazed out the window and tried to rid my mind of the gruesome images. The cossacks were still yelling and racing up and down the line of troikas, several of them waving rifles in the air. I saw a large gray shape darting behind a mound of snow, moving so quickly it was barely more than a blur. I peered intently at the mounds of snow as we sped along, and several minutes later I saw it again. This time I could make out the huge body, as large as a small pony, legs and tail extended as it leaped for protective cover. A cossack flew past the troika, half standing, gripping the flanks of his steed with powerful knees, rifle aimed, eyes on the sight, finger curled around the trigger.

There was a shot. I saw the wolf spinning in the air, saw red streams spurting as it crashed to the snow. The cossack let out a triumphant roar as our troika moved on. Lucie never even looked up from her book. I shuddered again and longed for green and shady English lanes with rhododendrons abuzz with bees. What if the wolf had happened along when Lucie and I were taking our walk? Was that why Vladimir and Ivan had followed so closely? What madness had possessed me to come to this strange, savage country?

It was two hours later when the troika began to slow down, finally sliding to a halt. Whenever the weather permitted, we stopped for the noonday meal, enabling the horses to rest while they munched their bags of oats. The sun was still shining brightly, gilding the snow with a silvery yellow sheen, and as there was no wind, the great stove would probably be hauled out and we would have a hot meal instead of the usual cold sausage rolls, cheese, caviar, and smoked fish. I was a bit reluctant to climb out after Lucie's earlier tale, but she laughed and assured me that the wolf following us had been a lone one and that it was much too early in the season for packs to gather.

"Besides, they'd never attack so large a gathering. They're extremely smart, they prey only on the vulnerable."

"I could really learn to love this country," I said wryly as Vladimir opened the door for me. "Snow storms, wolves, peasants on the rampage—how did I get so lucky?"

"At least you've retained your sense of humor."

"In sheer defense," I told her. "To keep from screaming."

Lucie smiled. "It is an adventure," she reminded me. "You're enjoying it."

"Every bloody minute."

Vladimir helped me out of the troika, none too gently.

He still regarded me with suspicion, considered me an outsider, an intruder, and I had to confess that I had not grown fonder of him. I brushed my blue velvet skirt, wrapped the ermine cloak around me, jammed my hands into the muff. It was not all that cold, certainly not as cold as it had been earlier, and I was glad to have an opportunity to stretch my legs, though I certainly wasn't going to take any pleasant little strolls. When Lucie climbed down, I asked her to point out Vanya. The cossacks had all dismounted and were stomping their boots in the snow and laughing and milling about like a gang of rowdy boys eager for action.

"That one over there," she said. "The one with the wolf."

I hadn't seen the wolf. Vanya had just slung the corpse down from the back of his horse and now stood over it with a long, glittering knife. I had intended to go thank him for the boots, but now I hesitated, not at all certain I wanted to get that close to the horrible thing sprawled on the snow. Lucie saw this and, smiling mischievously, took my hand and led me toward the tall, slender cossack.

"Vanya, this is Miss Danver," she said in Russian. "She wanted to see your wolf."

"Damn you, Lucie," I muttered.

But Lucie had already departed, leaving me standing there alone with Vanya and the creature at our feet.

"Is good wolf, no? You understand Russian?"

"I understand some Russian. Is horrible wolf."

"No!" he protested. "Is a beauty! Big. Almost as big as a man, no? See how beautiful the fur, more silver than gray. I make only one tiny hole with my rifle. I am going to skin it. I will give the skin to you."

"Please don't," I begged.

Vanya grinned. He was at least six feet four and, slender as he was, seemed even taller. His dark face was sharp and lean and fierce, made fiercer by an oriental mustache that drooped down on either side of his wide, thin mouth. His nose had been broken a number of times and was decidedly hooked. Hooded by heavy lids, his black-brown eyes glowed like hot coals, thick, winglike black brows arching above them. It wasn't the sort of face you'd like to encounter in a dark alley, I thought; yet despite this there was a most engaging quality about him. One sensed immediate warmth and friendliness.

"I saw you shoot," I told him.

"You did? I am glad. With one shot I bring him down. I am the best with a rifle, though not so good with the sabre."

"I wanted to thank you for the boots, Vanya."

"This is kind of you. It is not necessary to thank me."

"I feel bad about taking them."

"Is a pleasure for me to know they are keeping warm the feet of so gracious and lovely an English lady."

"You may look like a frightening brute," I said in English, "but actually you're rather sweet."

Vanya frowned. "What does this mean?" he asked.

"It means you are very nice, even if you do have dainty feet."

"So you tease me about these cursed feet, too?"

"I couldn't resist it."

"You I will not hit," he said wearily.

I smiled, liking him a great deal. How different he was from the grim and sullen Vladimir. His tall black leather boots were damp with snow, his loose blue breeches bagging over the tops, and the blue coat was superbly tailored to emphasize broad, bony shoulders and narrow waist, the flaring skirt hemmed with glossy gray fur. He smelled of garlic and sweat and gunpowder, a virile perfume that suited him perfectly.

"You like my horse?" he inquired, indicating the handsome steed with a wave of his hand.

"He's a beautiful animal."

"Strong, too. Fierce. Like me. The best."

"You're extremely modest, Vanya."

"What does this mean?"

"Humble."

"Humble? Me? Vanya is fierce, not humble. A man displeases me, I knock him down. Maybe I break his arm, maybe his neck. This I have done. Men know not to fool with Vanya. You wish to ride this horse?"

"I wouldn't dare."

"You are afraid of him?"

"Definitely."

"I get another horse for you. A mare, strong but gentle. Leo brings this mare along for an extra mount. Leo will not refuse to let me use her. He knows I break his arm, maybe his neck if he refuses."

"I—I appreciate all this, Vanya, but I really don't ride that well. I haven't had much practice, you see, and—"

"This we fix. I give you lessons. In short time you will ride like the wind."

"You are terribly kind," I said.

Vanya scowled. "Do not say this to any of my comrades. They will tease me. I will have to bloody their noses. It grows tiresome."

I smiled and told him it would be our secret. Vanya brandished his long knife.

"You stay," he suggested. "I show you how I skin this wolf."

"I'd rather not. I fear I'm a bit squeamish."

"The blood bothers you?"

"It bothers me a great deal," I confessed.

"Is natural. You are the delicate female. English, too. I skin the wolf and cure the hide and give it to you as a present."

He grinned. It was a delightful grin, broad and boyish. For some reason, I had obviously made a conquest. I felt a rush of gratitude for his friendship and longed to give him a hug. I didn't, of course. I merely smiled again and told him good-bye.

"I get this mare from Leo tonight. Tomorrow we will begin teaching you to ride."

"I shall look foward to it."

"In the meantime, you are not to worry about these fool-ish peasants. Vanya will protect you."

He took hold of the wolf's tail, lifted the body up and grinned even broader when he saw the expression on my face. I could hear him chuckling as I scurried away, put-ting his boots to good use. Lucie had been watching us. She was amused by my hasty withdrawal. I made a face at her from the distance and began to stroll past the troikas, feel-ing a pleasant exhilaration after my encounter with the savage-looking, engaging cossack who was the only mem-ber of Orlov's party who had shown me the least friendli-ness. Few would use the word *adorable* to describe him, but it was the one I felt most suitable.

Two huge stoves had been hauled from the troikas, set up on the side of the road and filled with kindling. The chef shouted shrill orders to his underlings and complained vo-ciferously about using up his precious supplies to feed "twenty more yowling heathens" who were totally incapa-ble of appreciating his culinary skills. It was a sad day in-deed when he left the kitchens of the Empress to join this crazy ménage.

Pots and pans rattled, meat and vegetables were cut up, spices added into simmering broth. The underlings could prepare the stew—"Use more water! Go easy on the meat!" —and he would cook for those who could appreciate him. I smiled at the confusion, smelling the marvelous aroma of baking bread as I passed. Tall trees grew on either side of the road, trunks half-buried in snow, branches encrusted with ice that glittered brightly in the sunlight. It was good to walk, to use my legs, to breathe the crisp, invigorating air after being cooped up in the troika for so long. Would we ever get to St. Petersburg?

Servants hastened about on various assignments. Stout canvas bags were hung over the heads of horses so that they might munch the oats inside. Troika drivers were stamping their feet and drinking hot coffee and gossiping with each other. A crowd had gathered to watch Vanya skin the wolf. I saw Orlov in the distance, immersed in conversation with one of the cossacks. He seemed to be questioning the man, and his broad, handsome face was serious as he listened to the man's replies. His legs were planted wide apart. The gray fur coat was open in front, and he stood with fists on his thighs, the coat bunched back.

He was a majestic figure standing there in the snow, taller than the tallest cossack, his body superbly hewn, radiating power and authority, seeming to draw the sunlight to him. I paused beside one of the supply troikas, looking at him, thinking about last night, wondering how much he remembered. Very little, I hoped. I was prepared to forget the things he had said, the words that had come unbidden to his lips in the haze of alcohol, prepared to forget the sensations that stole through my body as his hands squeezed and caressed and massaged my foot, but there would be a certain strain between us if Count Orlov had a clear memory.

I was attracted to him, strongly attracted. I couldn't deny that. Any woman would be. I was drawn by his warmth, his courtesy and consideration, his jovial good humor and boyish high spirits, and I was drawn by his incredible male beauty and vibrant sexuality. I knew, though, that anything other than friendship between us would be most ill-advised, and after Jeremy I was not prepared to become involved. Orlov was attracted to me, too, strongly attracted. That had been clear from the first night we had dined together in that cozy room with its gleam of yellow satin and glitter of gold, but he knew full well I would not be receptive to any advances and had settled for friendship.

Until last night.

Last night he had been tipsy. Last night he had lost control, and all those submerged emotions had come bubbling to the surface. Sober, if he remembered, he would be horrified at what he had said, what he had done, and I prayed he wouldn't remember. Let it continue as it has been. Let us be comfortable with each other, polite and friendly. I sighed and moved to join Lucie, who was standing beside our troika, swathed in rich golden brown sable.

"Enjoy your walk?" she inquired.

"Very much. I feel better, not so stiff."

"Did you see any wolves?" she teased.

"Just one, and damn you for doing that to me."

"It was quite dead, Marietta."

"It was quite horrible just the same."

Lucie smiled, her eyes full of girlish delight. "You made a very big success with Vanya. He told me he is going to give you the skin after he has cured it. That is quite a great honor."

"I'm overwhelmed," I told her. "I'm also starving."

Both of us looked to where the cossacks were lining up to receive their bowls of stew and hunks of black bread. The chef was still shrieking, refusing to relinquish any of his precious rounds of cheese. The cossacks grumbled and made mock-threatening noises, teasing him unmercifully, but he adamantly refused to give up a single round. Orlov finally intervened and said of course his cossacks could have cheese, could have any of our supplies they wanted, we would all share together, and the chef waved his arms in the air in total exasperation. Someone gave him a bottle of vodka. He took a huge swig and then stalked off to shriek at his underlings.

"Poor chef," Lucie said. "More stomachs to fill really does present a problem. It could be serious if we're unable to replenish our supplies at the next village."

"Will that be a problem?" I asked.

"It shouldn't be," she said casually, "but the next village of any size is two weeks from here, under the best traveling conditions. We could easily run quite low on provisions."

"Cheer me up some more," I said. "Tell me about the blizzards and avalanches."

"We don't have avalanches," she informed me, "but occasionally the roads are blocked by treacherous snow drifts. Travelers have been stranded for days, but we have plenty of men to dig a way through."

"That's comforting."

"You sound discouraged," she teased.

"I've had better days."

Lucie laughed, and, remembering the tormented child, I was glad to see her in so mischievous a mood. We climbed into the troika where a table had been set, linen cloth gleaming, silverware sparkling, silver-rimmed pink Sèvres beautifully arranged. Here, in the middle of a desolate road, surrounded by snow and ice, we were served a marvelous meal—spicy beet soup, potato pancakes with sour cream and caviar, flaky apple tarts sprinkled with brown sugar, strong hot tea. Lucie found nothing at all unusual about any of this, but I was still dumbfounded by the incongruity of it. I had to keep reminding myself that I was traveling with one of the richest men in the world, and only staggering wealth made such things possible.

I took another short stroll while the lunch things were cleared away and the troikas repacked. Eight husky servants lifted the great porcelain stoves back into their vehicle. Dishes were washed, dried, carefully packed away. A servant collected the empty oat bags from around the horses' necks. Drivers oiled harnesses, checked rigging. The bustling activity was wonderfully organized, each man knowing his job, doing it efficiently. Only the cossacks were idle, apparently too important for menial tasks. I strolled past the line, ermine hood over my head, my hands in the muff. Soft, tiny snowflakes began to drift down from the sky, floating lightly like puffs of white crystal.

"I see you are wearing the boots," Count Orlov said.

I turned. He stepped up beside me, shortening his stride to match mine as we continued to walk.

"They're a perfect fit," I told him. "I met Vanya earlier and thanked him for them. I want to thank you again."

"Was nothing," he said amiably. "I—uh—I wasn't sure if I *did* give them to you. I remember getting them from

Vanya, and I *think* I remember starting up to your room, but everything else is hazy. I made it up the stairs?"

"You made it," I said.

"I came to your room?"

"And brought the boots."

Orlov gave me a sheepish grin. "I am so pleased to see my cossacks again I drink much too much vodka. I am feeling happy and aglow as I start up the stairs to your room. I hope I am polite and do not make the fool of myself."

"You were extremely polite," I replied. "You gave me the boots and promptly passed out. I had Vladimir take you to your room."

"This I am ashamed of. You must think me a great booby."

I smiled, vastly relieved. The snowflakes were falling faster now, swirling in the air, pelting our faces like moist, gentle kisses. Our boots crunched on the ice as we passed the supply troika filled with great metal containers full of various meats packed in ice, with bags of apples, grain, flour. Swathed in black furs, the chef stood beside the vehicle with a testy expression, as though he expected someone to steal his valuable provisions. Orlov took my arm as we started back toward the troika I shared with Lucie.

"I am afraid I have the bad news," he said.

"Oh?"

"The next posthouse, where we were to stay tonight, has been burned to the ground. The fire is said to have started by accident, but my cossacks believe it may have been deliberately burned."

"Who—who would want to do such a thing?"

"These peasants," he growled. "Several posthouses have been destroyed by fire lately, too many for it to be the coincidence. They are too cowardly to attack, so they do this to harass. No, no, it is nothing you must worry about," he added hastily, seeing my expression. "Is merely a handful of discontented serfs."

"What shall we do tonight?" I inquired.

"Is no problem. We have the tents, the sleeping plat-

forms, the furs and the stoves. We even have the large tent
for the horses so they will not be exposed to the elements."

"You certainly come prepared," I remarked.

"This one must do when traveling in winter. This is the
reason we bring the extra troikas, to carry all these things
we might need. The traveler who is not prepared can have
serious trouble."

Lucie met us at the troika, her young face radiant. The
cossacks had brought along several extra horses, she explained, and she had decided to ride this afternoon. Orlov
nodded, pleased that she was so enthusiastic. I asked her if
it wouldn't be better to wait until it stopped snowing, and
Lucie made an impatient gesture, looking at me as though
I were an exasperating child. Snow? What was a little
snow? She loved to feel it pelting her cheeks, loved to ride
through the whirling white curtains. As we stood there
one of the cossacks came over leading a muscular chestnut
with beautiful lines. Lucie hitched her skirts up, put her
foot in the stirrup, took hold of the horn and swung herself
up into the saddle in one lithe, graceful movement.

"I will see you later, Marietta," she cried.

She turned the horse around and galloped off to the head
of the line, riding astride with the greatest of ease. No
fancy sidesaddle for this daughter of Russia. She rode like
a man and, I suspected, better than most. Orlov watched
with proud eyes as she rode away, then helped me into the
troika, climbing in himself to see that I was comfortably
settled with lap robe in place, books and chocolates within
reach. He checked the braziers to see that there was plenty
of coals, and he actually tucked the lap robe around my
knees. What good care he took of one, I thought. I couldn't
help appreciating that.

"You will be all right?" he asked.

"I will be fine, Count Orlov. I'm not an invalid, you
know."

"This I realize, but you are not used to these difficult
conditions. I feel guilty, subjecting you to them."

"I'm much tougher than I look," I told him.

"This I do not believe."

He stood up straight, his head almost touching the ceiling, and looked down at me with fond navy blue eyes half-shrouded by heavy lids. Being the helpless female was a novelty to me, a role I'd often longed to play, but it really didn't suit me, I decided. Once, perhaps, I could have clung to some man, depending on his strength, but I had relied on my own for too many years now and the toughness I had referred to was an integral part of me. I was a fighter, a survivor, and though the role might have its attractions, a delicate, dependent female I could never be. Still, it was nice to be pampered.

"You are comfortable?" he asked.

"Wonderfully snug," I assured him.

"I leave you then."

The vehicle rocked slightly a few minutes later as the driver climbed onto his perch, and then there was the jingle of harness, the jangle of bells and we were on our way again, gliding smoothly along through the soft, billowing snow, moving through a frozen, crystalline world of blinding whiteness and rainbow-sheened ice, a world so strange, so alien to any I had ever known before. Snug and warm under layers of fur, I rested my feet on the silver brazier with its belly full of glowing pink coals and gazed through the windows and, unbidden, the pain came.

It was always there, always, but much of the time I was able to hold it at bay. If I had not been able to ignore it, at least I had been able to deny its virulent force. Much of the time. The constant travel, the new sights and new people had helped, true, but they were merely distractions, like an apothecary's powder that, when taken, deadens the agony of a migraine yet does nothing whatsoever to heal. The pain was with me still, as strong, as agonizing as it had been when I first learned of Jeremy Bond's treachery, and when I was tired, when I was alone, when there was no powder, I was its helpless prey. If only I could *forget* him. If only I could *hate* him. If only I didn't still *love* him.

The snow was falling heavily now, thicker and thicker,

the wind whipping it into a swirling furor. I closed my eyes, trying to push back the pain, trying to lock it inside. You mustn't think of him. The son of a bitch isn't worth it. Forget him. Forget him. Put him out of your mind. Jeremy Bond is a thorough scoundrel, charming and ruthless and absolutely unworthy. You never meant anything to him. Not really. The minute you were gone he forgot all about you and found a blonde and sallied off with her. And *your* money. The bastard *robbed* you. Stop tormenting yourself this way.

I enumerated all his faults, and they were manifold. I listed all of the reasons why I should detest him, and it didn't help at all. The fact remained that, without him, I was only half alive. The fact remained that, without him, life seemed a bleak gray expanse without a single ray of sunshine, something to be endured, not enjoyed. How was it possible to enjoy anything if Jeremy wasn't there to share it with me? What pleasure in wearing lovely clothes if Jeremy wasn't there to see them? What joy in seeing new sights, experiencing new things if he was not beside me? What point in going on if . . . if one's very reason for living was gone?

You've got to get over him, I told myself. You've got to. This is madness. You'll never see him again. You must face that. You must go on. I was able to rationalize, I was able to reason with myself, but the pain remained, a searing force that filled the emptiness he had left. All these weeks had gone by, and still it was agonizing. As the troika glided through the snowstorm in this alien land, as bells jangled and horse hooves clopped on the icy road, I stared into the future and it was bleak and gray and I knew I must change that. I knew I must get over him. But how?

The surest way to get over a man was to find another man. I knew that from experience. I had loved Derek Hawke for years. I had given myself to him heart and soul and he had savaged them both, leaving a wreck, a shell of a woman, yet I had gotten over him when Jeremy came into my life. Derek meant nothing to me now. He was a name, a face, a memory that stirred not the slightest emotion inside, no bitterness, no regret. Would I ever feel that way about Jeremy? Would I ever be able to summon his image in my mind without this excruciating anguish? Would another man ever supplant him in my heart?

No. No man was *ever* going to get that close to me again. No man was ever going to have that kind of power over me. I wasn't going to be hurt like this ever again, but . . . must I deny myself the pleasures of male companionship because of fear? Wasn't it possible to take the pleasure without the commitment? Wasn't it possible to savor and enjoy and give of oneself without giving heart and soul as well? I wondered about that as I stared at the swirling white curtains that shrouded the landscape. Like the apothecary's powder, the distractions had helped deaden the agony and I had managed to carry on all this time. I had managed to laugh and smile and maintain a facade and, at times, even convince myself that I was making progress, and then the pain returned and I experienced anew the emptiness, the loss, the desolation.

Perhaps I needed a stronger powder.

Calmly, I considered that. I intended to survive, and if that was what it took, should I deny myself the remedy? The most fascinating man I had ever met was on hand. He wanted me. I was strongly attracted to him. I had no illusions about him, it was true, but when I was with him I did not think of Jeremy Bond. Any woman foolish enough to fall in love with Count Gregory Orlov would be letting herself in for a great deal of grief, but must love enter into it? I was fond of him already, and physically, sexually, he was incredibly alluring. Was Orlov what I needed to end this anguish? Covered with furs, my feet resting on the silver brazier, I stared at the Russian snow and wondered about it. Dare I take the powder?

Dare I take the risk?

Chapter Ten

VLADIMIR PUSHED BACK THE HEAVY FUR COVering the doorway and stepped into the hut, followed by two husky servants. I was fully dressed this time, and I gazed at him coolly as the servants picked up the richly decorated porcelain tub and carried it out, water sloshing but never spilling over the rim. Wearing a heavy fur coat over his uniform, Vladimir made no effort to conceal his hostility as another servant entered to remove towels, soap, sponge, eliminating all signs of my bath. All this extra work, those hostile eyes seemed to say, merely to satisfy an eccentric whim. No one else demanded a bath. Even Lucie was content to rely on the elaborate use of perfumes and cologne.

Although all of the men and servants were staying in tents pitched just outside the village, Lucie, Orlovn and I had each been given a hut, their occupants moving in with neighbors during our brief stay. Circular-shaped, made of mud and wood with a steep, conical roof, my hut had been transformed with carpets spread over the dirt floor, my own fur-covered sleeping platform replacing the shabby cot. Candelabra, tables, a chair, and a full-length mirror completed the luxurious effect, but no amount of luxury could dispel the odor of dirt and onions and livestock. I strongly suspected that a goat and several pigs shared the place with the family who had temporarily moved out. The large silver brazier provided a certain amount of heat, but it was still chilly. The place must be freezing without it, I thought, and I wondered how the peasants survived these dreadful winters.

The servant left. Vladimir and I were alone. He continued to stare at me with an open contempt I chose to ignore.

"When shall we be leaving the village?" I asked in Russian.

Vladimir made no reply, looked as though it would be beneath him to address me.

"I know my Russian is not good," I said, "but I also know you can understand me perfectly. I've no idea why you hold me in such contempt, Vladimir, but I suggest you at least *try* to be civil."

The tall Russian muttered something under his breath, still pretending not to understand me, then turned as yet another servant entered with a large white box tied with gold ribbon. He took the box from the servant, ordered him out of the hut and twisted his wide lips sarcastically.

"He orders me to let him know when you wear the apricot velvet gown," he said. "Is unmanly duty, this, but each day I take note of what you will wear. This morning I see you have taken out the gown. I tell him. He grins like a boy and says it is time to deliver the box."

"I don't understand what you're talking about."

Vladimir tossed the box onto the fur-covered sleeping platform.

"Is something he does in London. A surprise he plans. I leave now. I have important duties to perform."

"You still haven't answered my question, Vladimir. When shall we be leaving the village?"

"They should finish with the provisions by noon. The cook will prepare a lunch. We will leave immediately after. Too long we stay in this filthy village."

"I see. Was it too dreadfully painful, speaking to me?"

"If you wish to tell Count Orlov you are displeased, do so," he said sullenly. "He will relieve me of my duties. He will strip me of my rank. He will do anything to make his English lady happy. You are much more important to him than his loyal, devoted servants."

"You would kill for him, wouldn't you?"

"With my bare hands."

"That kind of loyalty is rare indeed," I said. "The count is very fortunate to have such devoted men."

"We protect him," he growled.

"And you feel you should protect him from me, don't you? I'm no threat, Vladimir, not to you, certainly not to Count Orlov."

"We will see," he said, his eyes as hostile as ever.

He turned and left, slinging aside the smelly fur hanging that covered the doorway. I sighed, frustrated by the exchange but determined not to let it bother me. Vladimir would never become a friend, as Vanya had. I would never be able to win him over, nor did I particularly care to, but I saw no reason to let the antagonism blossom into full enmity. I wouldn't say anything to Count Orlov, of course. It wasn't that important. This whole Russian journey had an aura of unreality about it, and Vladimir's hostility was merely another part of it.

Standing before the full-length mirror propped against the wall, I picked up the gold-handled brush and began to brush my clean hair, gleaming with a rich coppery sheen. The long, soaking bath had been marvelous. It was the second I had had since we arrived at the village three days ago, after two long weeks without being able to bathe at all. Two weeks had passed since the day Vanya killed the wolf, and during all that time we had spent the night in only one posthouse, the others having been destroyed by fire or otherwise made uninhabitable—the destruction quite deliberate, apparently done by rebellious peasants said to be roaming the land. We had seen no sign of them, however, and Orlov minimized the threat, assuring me they would soon be put down. After interminable nights spent sleeping in tents, bundled in fur, the wind howling like bands of demonic spirits, it had been a relief to reach the village, squalid though it was.

I put the brush aside and adjusted the bodice of the deep apricot velvet gown I had chosen to wear. It had long, tight sleeves, a modestly low square-cut neckline and a snug waist, the full skirt belling out over several pale apricot underskirts. Why had Vladimir been waiting for me to wear this particular gown? I had almost forgotten the box. Moving to the sleeping platform with its gold brocade covering and lustrous pile of furs, I undid the gold ribbon and removed the top of the box. Thin tissue paper crinkled as I folded it back.

I didn't actually gasp, but my eyes widened in amazement as I beheld the red fox cloak inside. It was gorgeous, the most gorgeous fur I had ever seen, the thick, glossy pelts a rich red-brown with coppery highlights, almost the identical color of my hair. Lifting it out of the box, I was further amazed to find that it was lined with deep apricot velvet that perfectly matched my gown. How had he managed it? It was a glorious garment, so glorious I couldn't resist putting it on, although I certainly couldn't accept such an expensive gift. Yes, the velvet was the same cloth, it might have come from the same bolt, and the fur was just a shade darker than my hair, deep copper red. I pulled the hood over my head and stepped to the mirror, feeling like a queen in the luxuriant cloak.

There was a loud rap at the side of the door. The fur was pulled back. Count Orlov stepped into the hut, grinning a wide grin, beaming with delight as he saw me wearing his gift.

"You are surprised?" he inquired.

"I—I'm overwhelmed."

"You like?"

"It's incredibly beautiful, but—"

"I have it done in London. Lucie is part of the intrigue. I have the furs already, you see, and when I see your hair I know I must have them made into a garment for you. Lucie slips this apricot velvet gown out of your wardrobe and says this cloth must be used for the lining. Is big problem finding an exact match, but I threaten to strangle the furrier if he does not do so."

"Count Orlov, I—"

"I have it made up, and I keep it for the big surprise. I think you are never going to wear this particular gown. I think maybe you have left it behind. This morning Vladimir tells me you have taken out this gown to wear and I fetch the surprise and smile when I think how happy it will make you."

He chuckled to himself, his dark blue eyes glowing with pleasure. Wearing pale tan leather boots and snug tan breeches, a heavy brown fur coat covering arms and torso, he looked more than ever like a great, friendly bear. His head was uncovered, his tawny gold locks attractively windblown, and his cheeks were flushed. He seemed to exude brute strength and vitality.

"I do not have to strangle the furrier. He does a fine job. I give him much gold."

"I—it's a wonderfully thoughtful gift, Count Orlov, and I don't want you to think I don't appreciate it, but—"

His eyes darkened. The wide mouth curled into a mock-ferocious snarl.

"We do not argue," he ordered. "Me, I am in no mood for it. You give me the—how you say?—the bad time and perhaps I strangle *you*."

"I can't accept it," I said quietly. "It's much too lovely, much too expensive."

"You give me the bad time?"

"I'm afraid I must. I—"

He moved over to me in four brisk strides, hands uncurling from fists, flying in the air like huge moths. He seized my throat, fingers curling firmly at the back of my neck, his two huge thumbs pressing lightly against the soft, vulnerable flesh beneath my larynx. Startled, I tilted my head back, looking up into those mock-fierce eyes. He smiled. The thumbs caressed my flesh with just the slightest pressure, just enough to make me swallow and realize that I was totally helpless, that he could crush the life out of me with the greatest of ease.

"You still wish to argue?" he asked playfully.

"I—I don't know if I dare—"

"You turn down my gift in England. This I accept. This I try to understand. I am disappointed, but I do not insist. Now we are in Russia. Here I am in command. Here I am to be obeyed. I command you to accept this gift I have prepared or else I punish you most severely."

His voice was a husky purr, deep, melodious, undeniably sensual, and his eyes were no longer fierce. They were filled with that dark glow of desire I had dreaded seeing in them. His fingers tightened the merest fraction, and I felt a tremulous thrill as his lips parted, wide and pink, as he ran the tip of his tongue over them and tilted his head to one side and lowered it, covering my lips with his own. He kissed me lightly at first, still holding me by the throat, and then he curled one arm around my shoulders, the other around my waist and kissed me with fervor, crushing me to him.

I did not struggle. To struggle would have been futile. His arms held me with bruising force, so tightly I feared my bones would snap, and as his lips forced my own apart, as his tongue thrust foward, filling my mouth, the thrill I had felt moments earlier grew and spread and splintered into a thousand sweet sensations that rendered me an abject slave. Against my will, against my every instinct, I melted against that hard, muscular body and gave in to the splendor of the man, the moment, the magic his mouth wrought inside me. It had been so long, so long since I had felt this rapturous ache, months and months of denial, and if it was the wrong man it didn't matter at all. A part of me that had been locked up tight within and painfully denied had sprung stunningly to life and I savored the return with a trembling relief.

I was still alive. I was still a woman. I was still responsive, and although I tried to hold back, respond I did, leaning back against those powerful arms, my body pressing against his, leg to leg, thigh to thigh as he continued to torment me with his mouth and tongue, making moaning noises in his throat as he probed and plundered. I could feel his manhood warm and swollen and straining against the layers of cloth that imprisoned it and kept it from the orifice it sought. His lips moved to the side of my throat. I gasped. I caught my breath. I clung to him desperately, my legs weak, my knees unable to support me, and then he clamped his mouth over mine again and I fought to hold on to the senses he had shattered so quickly, so thoroughly.

I pulled back. I shook my head. "No," I whispered hoarsely. "No," and the words seemed to come from some other source because I didn't want him to stop. I didn't want to abandon the splendor. I didn't want to come to my senses and be cool and controlled and in command. I wanted to surrender to these sensations bursting inside with soft explosions I feared would cause me to swoon. I pushed my hands against his chest, struggling in earnest as the delirium increased, as I grew dizzy, full of need every bit as potent as his. He drew his head back, his mouth only inches from my own, those powerful arms still holding me in a bruising grip. I looked up at him with eyes that pleaded with him, pleaded for him to continue, for I hadn't the strength to deny him, nor, now, did I want to.

Orlov frowned. He misunderstood my silent plea.

He released me abruptly. I staggered back a step or two, almost falling, seizing the arm of a chair for support. The cloak spilled from my shoulders, fell to the floor in a luxuriant copper red heap. I didn't even notice. I was breathing heavily, as was he, and both of us were incapable of speech for the moment. The delicious ache, the waves of warm languor that filled my blood began to subside, and I felt cold, terribly cold, as though I had been doused with a bucket of icy water. I caught my breath. I stood up straight, surprised to find my knees working properly. I brushed a wave of hair from my cheek with a hand that trembled visibly. I felt a vast relief, but the relief wasn't nearly as strong as the regret, regret I acknowledged frankly and without a single false illusion.

His cheeks were flushed. His eyes were still dark. His lips were parted and he was still trying to control his breathing as his chest heaved. Why had he stopped? Why in heaven's name had he stopped when every fiber of my being longed so ardently for him to continue, to prolong the plunder and bring it to its completion? The iciness inside turned into a kind of numbness, and it was as though I stood apart, removed, observing the two of us from a great distance. I watched with objectivity as he controlled himself, shoved a damp, tawny lock from his forehead, scowled.

"I forget myself," he said.

"Yes." The voice belonged to someone else.

"I take advantage. I vow not to do this. I vow to wait. I vow to be the gentleman, restrain myself, control my desire for you."

"You mustn't apologize."

"Were it another man who takes advantage of you like this, I would kill him for it. I would make him suffer long and hard. No punishment would be harsh enough."

"It was—it was something that happened. You must not blame yourself."

"The blame is mine. I know you still think of this man in London, and I hope you will forget him. I tell myself you will be ready soon, you will want me as I want you, and I vow to wait. Instead, I seize you like the coarsest ruffian. I take advantage. My punishment will be the shame I feel for using you this way."

"Count Orlov—"

"I ruin everything. I do not blame you if you refuse to speak to me ever again."

"The—the flesh is weak," I said.

It was an absurd thing to say, the tritest of statements, but Orlov nodded in vigorous agreement, scowling anew, his brows knitted together over the bridge of his nose. A part of me saw the humor of the situation, this great bear of a man castigating himself because he had lost control and kissed a woman, but I didn't smile. As the numbness wore off, as I truly came to my senses, I felt the regret and knew that he would be shocked were he to know what I was feeling. I sighed, prepared to overlook the incident, but Orlov was still in the throes of high drama. The Russian character demanded this drama, every incident taking on highly colored shades.

"In another moment I would have lost complete control," he said, horrified.

"I know."

"In another moment I would have shoved you onto the sleeping platform and taken you like the most brutal savage!"

And I longed for you to do just that, I said silently. Orlov stood there in anguish. I thought he might actually wring his hands. He didn't. He emitted a heavy sigh and looked at me with abject eyes.

"You will forgive me?" he asked.

"I'll try," I said.

"I do not know how this happens."

"We all have needs," I said quietly.

"This is true. All men have needs. I have been without a woman for too many weeks. This is all the same no excuse for my conduct. Gregory Orlov is not a ruffian like so many of his countrymen. I do not rape defenseless women, except in battle, and I do not debase those under my protection."

"I don't feel at all debased," I told him.

"This is a tragedy. A tragedy."

"Only if you make it one."

He had regained his composure now. Shifting his weight slightly from one leg to the other, he adjusted the hang of the heavy brown fur coat and swiped at a tumble of errant gold locks that had spilled over his brow. He wore a rather sheepish expression and looked for all the world like an overgrown boy who has just been particularly naughty, but that boy had, moments ago, stirred sensations inside me I had thought dead. The boyish charm he had in such abundance was dangerously deceiving. Here was a man, hard and tough and ruthless, who, for some reason—call it integrity—had pulled back at the last moment. Out of respect for me? Perhaps. I knew full well that, had I been a

serving wench or a peasant lass, he would have plundered
savagely no matter how I might have struggled.

"Did I hurt you?" he asked.

"I may be a little bruised," I admitted. "My mouth feels
swollen."

"This is a tragedy," he repeated, looking crushed again.

"I imagine I'll survive."

My voice was cool, much cooler than I had intended it to
be. Orlov frowned and shifted his weight once more, miserable.

"Now you will hate me," he mourned.

"On the contrary," I said. "Now I will put a bit of salve
on my lips to relieve the sting and I will consider myself
flattered that—that you thought me desirable enough to
kiss. If you want to know the truth, I rather enjoyed the experience."

He arched a brow in surprise, clearly not expecting such
a reply. Serving wenches and whores might enjoy abandoned kisses, but demure English ladies were cool and refined and, if they enjoyed it, never alluded to it. Orlov was
undoubtedly a man of vast experience, but he knew very
little about women. Few men did, come to think of it. I
turned away so that he could not see the small wry smile
on my lips.

"You are not angry?" he asked.

"I'm not angry," I said.

"It is forgiven?"

"It is forgotten," I told him.

"It will not happen again," he assured me.

"I'm sure it won't."

"You will accept my gift?"

"It was wonderfully thoughtful of you to have it made up
for me, and I am touched by the gesture. Yes, Gregory, I
will accept it."

I turned to look at him then, my gaze calm and level.

"You call me 'Gregory.' This is the first time."

"I rather think we're on a first name basis now, don't

you? Or would you prefer me to continue addressing you as 'Count Orlov'?"

He shook his head. He smiled. It was a lovely smile. His moods were as sudden, as changeable, as the play of sunlight and shadow on the surface of a pond. One never knew what to expect or when. I took the brush from the table and, turning to the mirror, began to brush my sadly mussed hair. My lips were indeed swollen, still throbbing from the bruising pressure, but the pain was curiously pleasant. Orlov picked up the gorgeous fur cape and, moving over behind me, draped it over my shoulders. I looked up at his face in the mirror. The smile lingered on his lips, curving tenderly, and his eyes were full now of fond admiration.

"You are a remarkable woman, Marietta. Another woman would be angry with me, would dissolve into tears, but you—" He paused, frowning slightly. "I fear I will never understand your sex," he admitted.

"I seriously doubt you ever will."

The smile returned. He stepped back. I put down the brush and shoved the heavy copper red waves from my temples, then faced him. The coals in the large silver brazier had burned down now and the hut was growing colder. The heavy fur felt wonderful around my shoulders.

"I go now," he said.

"I think that would be best," I agreed.

He strode over to the doorway and lifted the smelly fur flap, then, frowning again, paused, looking at me. Cold swept into the hut through the opening, but he didn't seem to notice. There was something else he wanted to say, and he was trying to find a way to articulate it properly. I waited, shivering, and he finally nodded, the words at his command.

"A while ago I promise it will not happen again," he said. "I wish to amend this statement."

"Oh?"

"It will not happen again until you are ready. I think perhaps this will be soon."

He left then, stepping through the doorway, letting the foul-smelling sheepskin fall back into place. I stood for several moments, staring at the hideous fur, bemused, amazed at my own calm and objectivity. I should have been shaken. I wasn't, nor did I feel the least bit of guilt about those feelings he had stirred so easily. I should have felt guilty had I been committed to another man, but that wasn't the case. There was no other man. Jeremy Bond was out of my life for good, and I was trying my best to exorcise his memory. Why should I deny myself the very thing that might best help me forget him?

Opening my white leather cosmetic case, I took out a small porcelain pot of clear lip balm and carefully rubbed the salve over my bruised and swollen lips, remembering those kisses, their furor, the lusty energy behind them. Orlov was a fiercely passionate man, totally abandoned when in the grip of passion, incredibly exciting, and, yes, I was disappointed that he had pulled back, surprised, too. He respected me. He was not content to use me as he would use a serving wench. That was most admirable. Ruthless brute he might well be, cruel and barely civilized beneath the glamorous facade, but no man had ever shown me such courtesy. No man had been so thoughtful and considerate, so concerned about my comfort and well-being.

Best forget about the incident for the time being, I told myself. I pulled the hood over my head and fastened the cloak securely, reveling in the luxury of the garment. Two weeks ago I had decided that a stronger powder was needed if I was to get over Jeremy Bond, and I knew now that I was ready to take it. The right time would undoubtedly come. Until then I did not intend to dwell on it. Leaving the hut, I pulled the cloak closer as the cold smote me with a physical force.

The village was indeed squalid, a large collection of dilapidated huts like the one I occupied built around a clearing with a frozen pond and rusty pump. A huge mud and wood structure contained grain and provisions for the community, and there was a blacksmith's shed and a community bake house where even now a dozen women toiled over the ovens, turning out loaves of coarse black bread. A number of pens and enclosures held livestock, and the only solid-looking structure was a large wooden house painted with bizarre, brightly colored symbols. This was the domain of the local priest, the most powerful man in the village, a wizened old charlatan who used herbs and spells and played on the dark fears and primordial superstitions of the peasants. Plodding, illiterate, they lived much as they must have lived in the Middle Ages.

Chickens squawked, flapping across the clearing. Pigs squealed. Sullen, stony-eyed peasant men watched me as I crossed over to the hut assigned to Lucie. Though flimsily clad in wooden sabots, loose trousers, ragged cloth coats and caps, they seemed immune to the cold. One man in particular glared at me, a surly brute much taller than his comrades, his head uncovered, his thick, unkempt black hair flopping over his brow. His coarse, not unattractive features seemed to have been hewn from solid granite, and the brown-black eyes that watched my every movement seemed to burn with a curious, fanatical fire. He wore brown boots instead of sabots, and his brown trousers and coat, though shabby, seemed a slightly better quality than those the others wore. A thick leather belt cinched his coat at the waist. A dark maroon woolen scarf was wound around his neck, the ends flapping over his right shoulder.

I slipped on the ice, almost fell. A pig darted past me, sliding over the ice. The tall peasant in brown said something to the man beside him. The man nodded, scowling darkly. I knew they were talking about me, and I felt a tinge of uneasiness, wishing the cossacks and our other men weren't all occupied elsewhere. There was no danger, of course. I realized that, and I realized, too, that it was perfectly natural for these people to resent our sudden arrival in their midst. They existed in almost subhuman conditions, their lives an endless round of back-breaking labor just to stave off starvation, and to see us surrounded by every imaginable luxury must be difficult.

Something really should be done about these conditions, I thought. There was indeed a grave inequality. The Negro slaves in Carolina lived better than these people, and it did not seem right for a select few to have so very much, to live in unparalleled splendor while the majority of their countrymen existed on a level not much higher than the animals of the field. No wonder there was so much resentment and rebellion. Empress Catherine, I knew, was trying to relieve their plight, establishing schools and hospitals, showing a great concern for *all* her people, but reform was a long, slow process, and one lone woman, Empress or no, could not easily change conditions that had been accepted for centuries.

Pushing aside the fur flap covering the doorway, I stepped into the hut assigned to Lucie, wincing at the odor that immediately assailed my nostrils. A goat had definitely shared this hut, possibly two or three, and Lucie had tried to mask the noxious smell by dousing everything with perfume. The combination was extremely unpleasant, but Lucie appeared not to notice, lounging comfortably on her sleeping platform covered with fur, reading a book of plays by the light of half a dozen candles blazing in a golden candelabrum. She glanced up idly as I came in, put the book down and reached for one of the exquisite bonbons arranged on a gold plate beside her.

"I see you finally decided to wear the apricot velvet," she said lazily. "Do you like the cloak?"

"It's beautiful."

"It's perfect with your hair."

"It was very thoughtful of the two of you to have it made up."

Lucie took a bite of chocolate and licked creamy white filling from her finger. "Oh, it was my uncle's idea. I merely suggested the lining. What is wrong with your mouth?"

"It—it's just a little chapped. I thought perhaps you might like to go for a short ride. The men won't be through loading the provisions until after lunch."

"I think not," she replied, reaching for another choco-late. "I know I haven't done anything but loll around for three days, but what a luxury to be *stationary*. We'll be on the move again soon enough."

"It would do you good to get out."

"Undoubtedly," she admitted, "but I'm gloriously warm and comfortable. I relish being lazy. Your mouth wasn't chapped yesterday."

"Not as badly," I said.

"Did my uncle bring you the cloak himself?"

"Vladimir brought it."

"But my uncle came to your hut."

"He did, as a matter of fact."

"I see," she said.

Those worldly violet-blue eyes looked at me with lazy amusement, and I had the feeling she knew exactly what happened, knew full well the reason my mouth was swol-len. Lucie, I reminded myself, was even more experienced than I was with members of the opposite sex, despite her youth. She stretched, leaning against the brocaded cush-ions, a half-smile on her lips. I longed to slap the minx.

"I think I'll go for a ride anyway," I said frostily. "Natasha needs exercise."

"You adore that mare, don't you?"

"She's a delightful creature."

"You spend almost as much time on horseback as you do in the troika. I must admit that you've become an expert rider."

"Vanya's an expert instructor."

"That he is. Enjoy yourself," she drawled. "Shall we have lunch together here—or do you plan to lunch with my uncle?"

"We'll lunch here," I said testily, "and if you don't stop devouring all those chocolates, my dear, you're going to get *fat!*"

Peals of silvery laughter followed me as I left the hut. Lucie could be infuriating! I marched purposefully across the clearing and past the village priest's wooden house

with its bizarre painted symbols, chickens flapping in my
wake, the boots Vanya had donated crunching noisily on
the icy ground. Two hefty, stolid women stepped out of the
bake house as I passed, their heads covered with ragged
kerchiefs, each clutching several loaves of black bread.
They stepped back, lowering their eyes, as though to look
upon me would bring them some kind of curse. Several
men watched me but I didn't see the tall peasant in brown.

Our party's tents were pitched east of the village, the
troikas lined up behind them. All the horses were quartered in an enormous tent, with four grooms assigned to
tend them, and it was toward that tent that I moved. All of
the servants were busily loading the troikas with bags of
grain and beans, potatoes and flour and also the huge
metal barrels that now contained the carcasses of chickens, pigs and goats packed in ice. The animals had been
purchased from the peasants, slaughtered and prepared
for packing, an enormous task which was one of the reasons we had been here three days.

Almost half a day had been spent haggling over the purchase itself. The peasants had been most reluctant to sell
any of their beans, grain and flour, even more reluctant to
part with any of their animals. Tempers had exploded. Angry words had been exchanged. The cossacks had grown
ugly and threatening, sabres flashing in undeniable menace, which made the peasants even more stubborn and adamant in their refusal. There might actually have been
open conflict had the priest not intervened. In his strange
cone-shaped hat and flowing blue robes embroidered with
cabalistic designs, he had taken command, wielding an authority that caused the surly villagers to fall back in stony
silence. With his long gray beard and penetrating black
eyes, he did inspire awe, and it was apparent that he was
much feared. He drove a very shrewd bargain, and Orlov
parted with much more gold than he had planned. Much, if
not the bulk of it, ended up in the priest's strongbox
where he would "safeguard" it for his flock.

The cossacks were lounging in front of their tents as I

passed, sharpening their sabres, playing cards, drinking vodka. I didn't see Vanya, and none of them paid any attention to me. The chef and his crew were already preparing for lunch, firing up the huge porcelain stoves, taking out pots and pans. I stopped to take a crisp red apple and a few lumps of sugar. The chef parted with the sugar with considerable protest, as though it were pure gold. I was tempted to stick my tongue out at the old fusspot, but dignity prevailed. One of his assistants snickered as the chef begrudgingly handed me the sugar. The chef banged him on the head with a copper pot.

I was in a surprisingly lighthearted mood as I continued toward the enormous tent. Despite the cold, it was a glorious day, the sky a pure pearl gray. Silvery sunlight gilded the banks of snow, making it glitter like mica, and the trees in the thin woods surrounding the village were completely encased in ice, looking like strange crystal ornaments in the sun. There was no wind. The air was clean and invigorating, filling me with zest.

The beauty of the day wasn't the only reason for my mood, of course. Instead of perturbing me, the encounter with Orlov had had a surprisingly salutary effect. I was still alive. That part of me I had thought completely atrophied had awakened as his hands gently encircled my throat, had sprung vigorously to life as his lips covered mine. I didn't love him, would never love another man, but my body was still splendidly responsive to the touch of a virile and attractive male. I hadn't thought it possible after Jeremy's treachery. Was I finally getting over him? Was I finally vanquishing the pain? The remedy I had chosen might well prove completely effective.

Lifting the large flap, I stepped into the huge tent where the horses were quartered. It was warm inside, for several braziers were burning, and there was a pungent odor of hay and manure and sweaty flesh, not at all unpleasant. With their own tent to protect them from the elements, with lavish supplies of oats and hay and four grooms to tend them, the horses fared better than most of the peasants, who had not failed to notice this irony.

Natasha whinnied with delight as I approached her. She stamped the ground with her front hooves, executing excited little dance steps, it seemed, throwing her head back in ecstasy. She was a beautiful creature, slender but powerfully built, her dark tan hide rich and glossy, as smooth as silk. Her long mane and tail were a lighter, creamy tan, and her large brown eyes were very expressive, almost soulful. In the short time we had been acquainted we had become extremely attached to one another, although she had been skittish and fretful at first, not at all certain she was going to like this strange person who spoke in a foreign tongue and had hair the color of fire.

"Hello, precious," I said. "Look what I've got."

She whinnied again, nuzzling my neck, gently butting my shoulder. I smiled and stepped back, holding out the sugar in the palm of my hand. Natasha accepted it eagerly, her lips moist and velvety as she daintily scooped it up. I gave her the apple. She crunched it with glee, those eyes watching me all the while with rapt adoration. Finished with the apple, she examined my empty palm, hoping for more.

"You're deplorably spoiled," I scolded. "Want to go for a short jaunt?"

Natasha had mastered English more easily and far more speedily than I had mastered Russian. I still spoke that language haltingly and, often, found it difficult to comprehend fully what was being said. Natasha, however, had picked up English with breezy facility and understood every word I said. She began to prance in place, creamy mane flowing. The horses on either side of her looked askance at this capricious, undignified behavior. Just what you'd expect of a high-strung, flirty young mare like her, they seemed to say. Natasha, I might add, kept herself completely aloof from the magnificent grays, occasionally blowing her lips at them or swishing her tail provocatively as she sauntered past a particularly handsome stallion.

I asked one of the grooms to saddle her up and bring her around front. He hesitated, frowning. A husky lad nearly twenty, he had dark blond hair and intelligent brown eyes, his roughly hewn features rather coarse but not unpleasant. Thinking he hadn't understood me, I repeated my request, enunciating each word carefully. The groom nodded, indicating that he understood, but he still hesitated, the frown making a furrow above the bridge of his nose.

"Is Vanya's mare," he said. His voice was a pained, croaking grunt, as though he spoke but rarely and found the process difficult. "He takes her from Leo."

"I know she's Vanya's horse, but I've been riding her for two weeks. You have seen me ride her."

"This is true, but Vanya, he gives the orders. Is not proper for me to take orders from you. Vanya will be displeased. He will beat me."

"He won't," I said. "I promise."

"You go for a ride?"

"I go for a ride," I said, growing impatient.

"Alone? This is not good. I will be held responsible. Vanya will beat me severely. Maybe he even uses the knout."

"He will, I assure you, if he discovers you've refused to saddle Natasha for me."

The husky lad looked troubled, then sighed heavily, shook his head and began to untie Natasha's lead. I caressed her silken cheek and left, waiting outside the tent for the groom to bring her. He led her out a few minutes later, humble, contrite but still looking troubled. I felt sorry for the lad and gave him a friendly smile as he helped me up onto the saddle. I had a little difficulty arranging my skirts, but there was no sidesaddle available. I would have refused one anyway, preferring to ride astride with boots firmly in the stirrups that had been shortened for me. Natasha whinnied quietly, eager to be off. The groom handed me the reins.

"You will be gone long?" he grunted.

"Not long. I'm just going for a short ride."

"Should have man with you. Should have guard."

"I'm not going far," I told him.

"Is not wise. May not be safe. Me, I shall be held responsible."

"Please don't worry about it. It will be all right."

He stepped back, brow furrowed as he watched me click the reins and gently prod Natasha's flanks with my knees. I rode off, delighted to feel the powerful animal beneath me, delighted to feel the rapport we seemed to share. We moved at a brisk trot, Natasha holding back until I gave her permission to break loose. I decided not to follow the road leading out of the village. Instead, we would saunter through the woods. The trees were spaced wide apart, there was plenty of room, and the ground looked relatively smooth. What pleasure it would be to explore that crystalline wonderland of glittering ice. I turned into the woods. I would just explore the outskirts. I wouldn't go far. I smiled to myself as I thought of the groom's apprehension. The lad meant no harm. He was just being cautious.

I should have listened to him.

Chapter Eleven

NATASHA PRANCED DELICATELY OVER THE ICY, snow-covered ground, disappointed that we were not going to gallop but content to caper about, enjoying the crunching sound her hooves made as we moved under the shimmering, ice-encased branches. The trunks, too, were encased in ice, great drifts of snow piled up around them, and icicles hung from every limb, gleaming, glittering in the sun, shedding multihued, iridescent light. Pale blue-gray shadows spread across the ground, darkening to violet in spots, and the white of the snow was even more blinding in contrast. It was indeed a wonderland, a cold and crystal world of fantastic shapes and deceptive beauty, for it could become treacherous if one were trapped among these gigantic crystal ornaments which no longer resembled trees.

We skirted around the edge of the woods, keeping the village in sight most of the time. It was wonderful to be out, to be moving, to be breathing crisp, invigorating air that made frosty vapor when one exhaled. In boots, the heavy apricot velvet gown and magnificent red fox fur cloak with the hood pulled up, I was quite comfortable, although my nose and cheeks were cold. Beneath the soothing layers of salve my lips still stung a bit, throbbing slightly, constantly reminding me of those fervent, near-frenzied kisses. Not a single bird called out as we moved beneath the trees. Not a single wood creature stirred. I led Natasha around a thick, icy tree trunk, past a row of shrubbery completely iced over and looking like a small, frozen waterfall.

The village was to the north of us now. Wasn't it? I looked back, seeing only ice and snow. The village was no longer in sight, although I could hear clattering noises and rough voices in the distance. The sound was muted, curiously distorted, and I couldn't tell from which direction it came. I turned Natasha to the left, heading toward the sound, I thought, but the sound only grew fainter. There was no cause for alarm, of course, none whatsoever, but the beauty of the woods was beginning to pall now, taking on a sharp, menacing edge, and I was ready to go back.

Which direction?

To the right. Yes, I was heading toward the sound now and in a moment or so I would see the tents and troikas through the trees. Natasha moved jauntily, and I was relieved to see the frozen waterfall again, iridescent in the sunlight, ice gleaming with dim violet-blue sheen. It seemed to have changed shape, longer than it had been, the icy cascade taller. It wasn't the same clump of shrubbery. I felt a tremor of panic as I realized I was lost. I could hear the men working in the distance, I could even smell the smoke of campfires, but I was unquestionably lost, without the least sense of direction.

"Let's go back now, Natasha," I said. "*You* know the way."

She twisted her slender neck, looking over her shoulder at me, and I could have sworn she grinned. I gave her free rein. She was enchanted, capering under the trees, heading east. At least I *thought* it was east. Some people were very clever and could tell you from the sunlight which direction was which from the way the rays were slanting, but the light was distorted and diffused here in the woods, and I wasn't all that clever to begin with. Natasha pranced past another clump of frozen shrubbery, through a small clearing, enjoying herself immensely. Was the noise growing louder? Fainter? It seemed to come from all around now, a muted hum. The mare moved on under more trees.

They grew closer together here, and the shadows were thicker, the light less intense.

"We're heading *away* from the village!" I informed her. "You're no help at all."

I turned her around, trying to control the panic that was beginning to well up inside. There was absolutely no reason to panic, I told myself. If need be I could start yelling and someone would hear me and come and the only damage would be to my pride. What an idiotic idea this had been. I should have listened to the groom, should have had more sense. What if we ran into a *wolf?* God, I had forgotten all about the wolves! I urged Natasha on at a faster clip, and, yes, the noise was indeed louder now and the smell of smoke was quite a bit stronger. Any moment now I would catch a glimpse of the village. Natasha started past yet another clump of shrubbery like crystal fountains spraying.

Something leaped from behind the shrubbery. Natasha squealed, rearing up, front hooves waving. I cried out, losing hold of the reins, grabbing the saddle horn. Something grabbed my arm, jerked. I felt myself tumbling, crashing onto the snow. There was a sharp, slashing noise. Natasha squealed again and began to gallop madly away. All this happened in an instant, so quickly, so unexpectedly that it was several moments before I realized what had happened.

Stunned, shaken, I sat up. I had landed on a small snow bank and the heavy fur cloak had helped cushion my fall. I wasn't really hurt, but for a moment I wasn't able to focus properly. I blinked, still stunned, and then I saw the worn brown leather boots, the loose brown trousers, the skirt of a heavy brown coat, a rough tan hand holding the handle of a riding crop, all of this at eye level. Tilting my head back, I looked up into the face of the peasant who had been staring at me in the village. His black-brown eyes glowed with hostility. The large mouth twisted at one corner in a contemptuous leer.

"Yo—you," I said.

He leered. I tried to get up. He thrust a palm against my shoulder, shoving me back onto the snowbank.

"Stay where you are, whore!"

He had leaped out from behind the shrubbery, had jerked me off Natasha and slashed her buttocks with the riding crop, causing her to gallop away in terror. Though angry, disoriented, it didn't occur to me to be frightened. On my back in the snow, furious, I sat up again and brushed snow from my hair. He slapped the riding crop against the side of his boot, looking down at me as a cat might look at a mouse. I could feel my cheeks burning.

"Are you mad?" I cried.

"Some claim all of us are mad. They claim Pugachev is demented, a raving maniac, all his followers as demented as he. They will see. Soon they'll see just how demented we can be!"

"I suggest you step back and let me up."

"I give the orders now," he growled.

"Orlov will kill you for this."

His mouth curled disdainfully. "The mighty Orlov. He and his brothers are at the head of Pugachev's list. All of them will die soon, most painfully. When I come to this village to enlist recruits I never dream I will be so close to one of them. I long to kill him myself, but the risk is too great. My mission is more important than the personal satisfaction of seeing him die. His day will come soon enough."

"Who are you?" My voice trembled, despite my efforts to control it.

"I am Josef Pulaski. I am with Pugachev from the beginning. I share his grief, I share his anguish, I share his dream of revenge. Pulaski is his best lieutenant. Soon I enlist many recruits to join our cause. Men of this village feel the boot of the aristocrats crushing their faces in the ground. The aristocrats take their pigs, their goats, take their potatoes and grain, leave their storehouse half empty."

"Orlov paid for those provisions," I retorted. "He paid dearly."

"And as the winter grows worse and the food runs out, they will be able to eat the gold? Many people will starve to death while the corrupt shaman sits in his painted house, counting the gold."

"The priest—"

"Is shaman, is bogus priest, makes the people fear him with his chants and false magic. Many, many like him in Russia, fool the poor, take what is theirs. They die, too!"

Pulaski slashed his riding crop viciously against his boot as he envisioned those deaths. His thick, unkempt black hair was long in back, heavy locks flopping across his brow, and his face was pale, the skin stretched taut across his broad cheekbones. The black-brown eyes did indeed burn with a fanatical fire, glowing like dark coals as he contemplated his visions of death and destruction. The man was a zealot, and an icy chill went through me as he directed that burning gaze at me again.

"I see you ride off alone," he told me. "This is great good fortune, I tell myself. I am not able to kill Orlov, too many men around him, but I will rob him of his whore."

"I am not—"

"Get on your knees!" he ordered. "You will kneel before me. Soon all you aristocrats will kneel before us, begging for mercy."

"Go to hell," I said.

His cheeks flushed with rage. His eyes glowed with an even darker fire. He raised the riding crop threateningly, and I merely stared at him, terrified now, determined not to show it. He held the brown leather crop over his head, longing to slash it across my face, but he didn't. Some inner voice prevented him. Caught up in a frenzy of bitter rage against a whole society he believed I represented, he nevertheless controlled himself, lowering the crop, spitting into the snow to show his contempt for me.

"No," he said, "I do not mar Orlov's whore. I do not kill her. I take her back to Pugachev. This is great prize. He will reward me, make me a captain in his army."

"You *are* out of your mind," I whispered.

He chuckled, contemplating the glory my capture would bring. I wasn't going to allow myself to panic. My heart was beating rapidly, banging against my rib cage, and my throat was tight and constricted. The man was mad, and the hatred inside him made him capable of any kind of violence. Cautiously, I flattened my palms against the icy ground, trying to move myself into a position from which I could spring to my feet. He saw what I was trying to do. The chuckling stopped abruptly. His mouth tightened grimly.

"You do not trick Josef Pulaski," he said. "You try to, I knock you unconscious."

"I'll scream. Someone will hear me."

"You scream, I kill you."

Keep him talking, I told myself. You must keep him talking. Time is your only weapon. Someone will miss you. Someone will come looking for you. You must keep him distracted and you must not let him know how frightened you are. This was a sensible plan, but I was beginning to tremble inside and I wasn't sure I could speak with a level voice.

"Or—Orlov will give you much gold for—for returning me safely. I will tell him I—I got lost in the woods. I will tell him you—you found me, and he will give you much gold."

"Gold! We do not want their gold. We care nothing for riches! We want vengeance!"

"I—I can understand that. I'm not an aristocrat. I—I'm not even Russian. I'm English. Surely you can tell that from my voice, my features. I am sympathetic with your cause, truly I am, and—"

"You are Orlov's whore! You wear the finery he gives to you. You ride in his fine troika, eat off his fine golden plates. You are as corrupt as the other whore, the German murderess who sits on the throne and makes false promises. You will pay."

"You can't possibly get away with this. Orlov's men will—"

"Yes, he has might. He has many men. They all do. They have strength, but we have guile. Pugachev trains us. Until our army is large enough we use our guile. We strike unexpectedly, kill and burn and disappear. Me, I am one man alone, but I use my guile."

He smiled a chilling smile and began to unwind the long maroon wool scarf from his neck.

"I tie you up," he said. "I stuff a gag in your mouth. I hide you under the shrubbery so they will not find you and when night comes I steal a horse and come for you. I take you to Pugachev. Is long way off, his secret camp. During our journey there I rape you many times. I use Orlov's whore as he and his kind use our women."

He had finished unwinding the scarf now. He pulled a large white handkerchief from his pocket. My pride would not allow me to beg, but I realized that I must. It would please him. It would give him a perverse satisfaction, and it would give me a few more moments.

"You—you mustn't do this," I pleaded.

"Ah, you beg now. It does you no good, I promise."

"I'm not your enemy. I—I'm just a defenseless woman, helpless, at your mercy. If—if you tie me up and—and leave me hidden out here I will freeze to death."

I was right. He was pleased. His black-brown eyes glowed with a cruel pleasure as he savored his power over me. I was, he thought, a soft, pampered aristocrat, the poor, defenseless woman I claimed to be, but that was far from true. He might take me, might tie me up and leave me to freeze, but he wasn't going to do so without a fight, and I'd done my share of fighting in the past. You've been in worse situations, I told myself, and you're not going to let it all end in the middle of a Russian wasteland.

"Have—have you no mercy?"

"Mercy is for the weak. Pulaski is strong."

"You—you mustn't do this."

His lips twisted into a cruel smile. "It gives me much satisfaction. I enjoy making Orlov's whore suffer."

I couldn't keep him talking much longer. Cautiously, I

lifted my knees and planted my boots firmly in the snow, leaning back on my palms, wearing a pitiful expression. I tensed the muscles of my calves, digging the heels of my boots deeper into the snow.

"After I use this scarf to tie you up, I stuff this handkerchief in your mouth and hide you. I pile snow all around so they do not see."

"I—I'll freeze."

"I do not worry about it."

He moved a step closer, reaching out to take hold of my arm. I seized his wrist with both hands and yanked with all my might, pulling him into the snow beside me, and at the same time I sprang to my feet. Pulaski let out a yell, thrashing in the snow. He seized my ankle, his fingers clutching the pliant leather of my boot with furious strength. I tried to pull free. His grip was too strong. I raised my free foot and stomped, aiming for his most vulnerable spot, missing, kicking his abdomen instead. He let out another agonized yell and let go of my ankle and I ran.

I ran with all the speed I could muster, fleeing in the direction Natasha had gone, hoping, praying it would take me back to the village. My boots crunched, crashed on the icy surface, taking good purchase, holding as I fled through the crystal wonderland that had become a nightmare setting, glittering with evil menace. My hood fell back and the cloak flew open, flowing behind me like bizarre red-brown wings. I slipped, stumbled, fell to my knees. I could hear him yelling. I could hear him charging after me, his footsteps thundering, the sound echoing loudly.

I got to my feet. I continued to run. My heart was hammering. My legs were hurting. My lungs seemed ready to explode. He was coming closer, closer, gaining on me every second, and somehow, through some miracle, I was able to pick up speed, run even faster. I crashed into a clump of shrubbery. Ice crackled, splintering like glass, showering to the ground, and wet icy branches seemed to seize me, clutching my skirt and cloak. I pulled free, panting, and I saw him charging toward me, not twenty yards away. I ran, and my legs burned, every muscle tight, taut, agonizingly painful as I continued to punish them.

Under the trees, ducking to avoid a low-hanging branch, across a clearing, past more frozen shrubbery—I flew, and he was right behind me now and my lungs were going to explode and my heart would explode as well if I didn't stop. I gasped, panting, unable to breathe, my throat dry and tight and constricting. He bellowed, not five yards behind me, and I was truly in a panic now, knowing it was over, knowing I was going to die. My knees collapsed. I fell face foward in the snow, throwing my hands out to break the fall as best I could, sliding over the ice, rolling onto my back.

He stumbled to a halt, his chest heaving violently, his cheeks flushed, his face a frenzied mask of rage. It was hopeless now. He would kill me on the spot. I tried to sit up. I couldn't manage it. Josef Pulaski stood over me, his fists clenched viciously, puffs of cloudy vapor filling the air as he heaved and panted and tried to get his breath. I was panting myself, my lungs on fire, and my head was filled with a deafening pounding noise that grew louder and louder like hoofbeats thundering.

Natasha whinnied in anguish, charging toward us. Pulaski yelled, moving aside as she reared at him. Another horse came tearing toward us, this one with a rider. Vanya yelled, a bloodcurdling yell, and swung his sabre in whirling circles over his head. He jerked the reins. The horse skidded to a halt and the cossack literally leaped from the saddle and raised his sabre and crashed the butt of the hilt against the side of Pulaski's head. Blood splattered as skin broke and bone bruised and the peasant crashed onto the ground with arms and legs flying at crazy angles. I screamed as he thudded down beside me. My throat seemed to split apart. Heavy black clouds smothered me, growing darker, darker, claiming me completely.

Strong arms gathered me up, held me tightly, and I struggled to banish the blackness. I moaned. A tender hand stroked my brow, brushed damp tendrils of hair from my temples. I opened my eyes and peered into a shimmering haze and through the haze I saw the terrible, ferocious face of the man who had saved my life. His teeth were bared, lips flattened back over them. His eyes were murderous. The long oriental mustache and the twisted, broken nose made him look all the more savage.

I moaned again. He touched my cheek with incredible tenderness, caressing the skin lightly.

"Is all right now," he crooned.

"I—"

"Is all right. You not fret."

The voice was wonderfully soft and soothing and I closed my eyes for a moment and rested my head against that hard, bony shoulder and felt myself sinking into a sweet oblivion, and when I opened my eyes again my heart was not pounding and my lungs were no longer afire and I was breathing evenly. Every bone and muscle in my body seemed to be hurting, but I paid no attention to that. The joyous relief inside was like a magical potion that made mere pain irrelevant. Vanya still held me, his face as fierce as ever. Natasha stood a few yards away, whinnying plaintively. Vanya's stallion stood immobile, reins dangling in the snow. Pulaski's body sprawled nearby like a gigantic, limp doll, a dreadful, bloody gash above his right temple.

"Is—is he dead?" I whispered.

"He not dead. He does not get off so easily."

"You—how did you—"

"Natasha, she comes tearing into the camp. She rears and whinnies and whirls around in a frenzied circle. I step out of my tent. She rushes toward me and whirls around some more and cries out. My horse, it is saddled in seconds and I am on it and Natasha is charging out of the camp, leading the way."

"Thank God. Oh—thank God. He was—he was going to—"

"Is your fault," Vanya said, and his voice was no longer

soothing. It was harsh, severe. "This is very foolish thing you do, Marietta. This is insane, makes much trouble."

"I—I just wanted to—"

"Vanya protects you. You are my dear friend. If you were my woman, I would beat you most thoroughly and you would be put on bread and water for a week and you would trudge on foot behind my horse as punishment for this bad thing you have done."

"You're certainly sympathetic," I said.

"Orlov, maybe he beats you. I hope so."

I struggled in his arms. He held me fast.

"Maybe I do not give you wolf's hide after all."

"You may take your wolf's hide and—and—"

"Shove it up my backside?"

"Precisely!"

"Ah, you feel much better now. Is good. Vanya smiles. I worry maybe you badly hurt."

He climbed to his feet and pulled me up and, defiant, I pulled free of his arms and my knees doubled up and I threw my arms around his neck to keep from falling. He folded his arms around me again, holding me loosely, tenderly, and I felt enormous gratitude and affection for this savage cossack who had become my friend. I felt wonderfully safe and secure in his arms, as I might feel in the arms of a swaggering older brother.

Vanya looked over my shoulder as five more horsemen came galloping noisily into the woods, and I turned to see Vladimir, Ivan and three other guards dismounting. Vanya tightened his arms around me. Vladimir looked at us and looked at Josef Pulaski sprawled on the snow and scowled, eyes fierce as he took in the situation and surmised what had happened.

"I know this woman causes trouble!" he thundered. "I know it from the first!"

"You, Vladimir, shut up!" Vanya ordered.

"The minute I see her I know she is trouble for us all!"

"You, Vladimir! You say one more word I knock all your

teeth down your throat and watch you choke as you try to swallow them."

Vladimir longed to continue ranting, but he knew full well Vanya did not make idle threats. He fell into a murderous silence, glaring around as though looking for a head to bash. Pulaski moaned painfully and opened his eyes, blinking, trying to focus. Vladimir stomped over and seized his hair and jerked him to his feet. The peasant gave an agonized yell as Vladimir grabbed his wrist, twisted it brutually and shoved the arm high between his shoulder blades.

"I march him back to the village!" Vladimir roared. "You, Ivan, bring my horse!"

One hand holding Pulaski's hair, jerking his head back, the other holding the twisted wrist high behind his back, he gave the peasant a shove and forced him to walk ahead. Josef Pulaski yelled again as Vladimir gave his wrist another twist, shoving it higher. They moved through the icy trees, Pulaski stumbling, screaming in agony as Vladimir continued to twist and shove.

"He's going to break the man's arm!" I protested.

"Is no matter," Vanya assured me. "Can you ride Natasha?"

"In—give me a few more minutes."

"Is very short ride. Village is just beyond those trees."

"I—I was lost," I said.

"Yes, you are a great ninny. This is a good word? You do the foolish thing and you get into trouble. Is Russia we are in. Is not safe for woman to go for ride alone."

"I detest this bloody country!"

"Is not like your England," he agreed.

The other men had already mounted and were walking their horses toward the village, following Vladimir and Pulaski, who were now almost out of sight. Natasha came over to rub her head against my shoulder. I stroked her cheek, wanting to cry now, too proud to do so. I brushed snow from my cloak, took a deep breath and, moving around, attempted to put my foot into the stirrup and catch

hold of the saddlehorn. I couldn't make it. Vanya shook his
head, caught me around my waist and swung me up into
the saddle as though I were as light as thistledown.

"We go slow," he said. "I walk ahead, lead Natasha behind me."

"I'm perfectly capable of riding her back without your
assistance. I'm not a baby, Vanya!"

"This is a matter of opinion," he told me.

He whistled to his horse, which followed us, and, taking
Natasha's rein, walked slowly under the ice-encrusted
trees. Natasha stepped carefully, as though she knew I
was bruised and sore. Sunlight shimmered, paler now. The
shadows spreading across the snow had deepened to a
violet-gray, and the sky was now the color of pewter. It was
colder. Clouds were gathering. Vanya's horse sauntered
along behind us. Ivan and the others had already disappeared.

I held on to the saddlehorn, badly shaken but not really
hurt. I dreaded seeing Orlov. He would blame me, too, and
rightfully so. I had been totally foolhardy, riding out alone.
We cleared the line of trees. I could see the village up
ahead: the troikas, the tents, the cluster of huts beyond. A
loud rumble of voices reached our ears. The clearing in the
middle of the village was filled with men, all of them
shouting and waving their arms.

"What will happen now?" I asked.

"The peasant will be punished," Vanya said. "This will
cause bad feeling in the village. The other peasants, they
will be angry. Is nothing for you to worry about."

"I'm responsible, Vanya. I feel terrible."

"Do not fret about it," he told me. "Vanya takes care of
you."

"What will they do to him?"

"This I do not know. In the old days his eyes would be
torn out of their sockets and he would be turned loose in
the woods at night for the wolves to find."

"Jesus!"

"If he is lucky, Orlov will merely kill him."

There was a tight feeling in my chest as Vanya led me into the village. No one paid the least attention to us as we stopped in front of the huge gray tent. The servants went on about their tasks with lowered eyes, deliberately avoiding looking at us, and the men packing the clearing were too busy arguing to notice our arrival. Orlov was shouting at one of the peasants, a huge, burly fellow who held a pitchfork menacingly. Vladimir was nearby, his arm locked securely around the throat of Josef Pulaski. Pulaski gagged and gurgled, tugging frantically at the arm crushing his windpipe. Every male in the village seemed to be in the clearing, most of them armed with pitchforks and hoes and hand scythes. All our cossacks and guards were there, too, pistols and sabres at the ready. Harsh, angry voices made an incredible din. A full-scale riot was clearly imminent.

Vanya helped me down from the horse, his face impassive. He appeared not to notice the chaos. The groom who had saddled Natasha for me took the reins of both our horses with trembling hands. His cheeks were chalk white as he led the animals into the tent. Vanya watched him with speculative eyes, and I made him promise the lad would not be punished. It was a promise he gave most reluctantly, and although the groom would not receive a beating, I suspected his life would be miserable for some time to come.

"I take you to your quarters," Vanya said.

"I—Vanya, I can't let this happen. The man didn't—he didn't actually harm me. I must tell them that. I—"

"I am most patient, Marietta. I treat you like the tender child who has been naughty. Because you are Vanya's dear friend, because you do not belong to him, I do not give you the rain of blows, the black eye, and bloody nose you deserve, but if you give me trouble now I will knock you out and carry you to your hut across my shoulder."

"I must—"

His right hand balled into a tight fist. His eyes darkened. I fell silent. He nodded curtly and, slinging a protective arm around my shoulders, led me around the edge of the clearing toward my hut. I was trembling now, barely able to walk. The men continued to shout. A cossack shoved one of the peasants to the ground and planted a boot across his throat when the man tried to get up. A pistol was fired into the air. I stumbled and closed my eyes for a moment, consumed with guilt, in anguish. Vanya tightened his grip on my shoulders, leading me on. Two heavily armed cossacks were guarding the door of my hut. Slinging the sheepskin aside, Vanya led me in.

"Thank God you're alive!" Lucie cried, rushing toward us. "I didn't know *what* happened. When Vladimir led the peasant into the village all hell seemed to break loose."

"I'm all right," I said in a faint voice.

"I hurried out when I heard the noise. My uncle ordered me to go back to my hut. I came here instead. Marietta, I've been frantic!"

Vanya sat me down in the chair. He opened a decanter and poured brandy into a glass and ordered me to drink it. I obeyed. The fiery liquor seemed to set my throat afire, but I scarcely noticed. Lucie seized my hand, squeezing it tightly. Numb with delayed shock, I looked at her as though I had never seen her before.

"Is she—did he—"

"I think not," Vanya replied. "She claims he did not harm her."

"What—"

"She was sprawled on the ground. He was standing over her. He may not have harmed her, but he intended to do so. For this he must pay."

"Marietta, are you—are you really all right? Your face is pale. You look strange. Vanya, give her another glass of brandy. Oh, I should have gone with her! Vladimir and Ivan would have followed us and none of this would have happened!"

"Here, you drink the brandy. One crazy woman Vanya can deal with. Two is impossible even for him."

The roar outside began to subside somewhat, voices lowered, shouting becoming an angry grumble. Lucie stepped to the doorway and held the sheepskin back, peering out, much to Vanya's displeasure. The two cossacks guarding the door didn't look any too pleased either.

"The shaman has condescended to come out," Lucie announced. "The peasants are making a path for him. He's going to speak to my uncle."

Leaving the chair, I joined her in the doorway. Vanya scowled but didn't try to interfere. He hovered behind us, one hand toying with the hilt of his sabre, the other holding a cocked pistol, ready to defend us to the death if necessary.

The wizened old priest in his flowing, embroidered robes and tall cone-shaped hat moved with unquestionable authority. There was something hypnotic about him as though he were indeed imbued with those dark powers the peasants believed him to possess. Gregory Orlov stood with legs spread wide, fists resting on his thighs, his own authority every bit as potent. The shaman nodded, acknowledging him as an equal. He seemed completely unperturbed by the furor that had turned his quiet village nearly into a battleground.

"What is this that upsets my people?" he inquired. Despite his age and physical frailty, his voice was a deep, powerful rumble.

"This man—he follows a female of our party into the woods. He accosts her. My men capture him."

Orlov jerked his head to one side, identifying Pulaski as the individual in question. Still locked in Vladimir's brutal hold, Pulaski wriggled, tried to speak. Vladimir yanked his arm back savagely. The tall peasant made hideous gurgling noises, clutching at the arm that punished him.

"This is true?" the shaman asked. "Let him speak."

Vladimir loosened his hold. Pulaski rasped hoarsely, still unable to speak. Scowling, Vladimir relieved the pressure a bit more, clearly displeased. Pulaski coughed, his face a bright pink.

"Speak up!" the shaman ordered.

"I follow her, yes," Pulaski admitted, his voice a painful rasp but audible now. "I speak to her. I do not harm her. If she says I harm her she lies!"

The priest turned back to Orlov, ignoring the peasant.

"The woman is unharmed?"

"I have not seen her," Orlov replied. "My men say there is no apparent injury. This is unimportant. The man must die."

The peasants grumbled loudly, a few of them shouting. The shaman raised his arm out straight, sweeping his eyes over the crowd, commanding them to be silent. They obeyed. A curious hush fell over the village, broken only by the noises of Pulaski who now struggled mightily to break the powerful hold restraining him. Face utterly impassive, Vladimir drew his arm back with brutal precision. Pulaski grew still, barely conscious now.

"His is a serious offense," the shaman agreed.

"He must die!" Orlov insisted.

The grumbling began again, a menacing rumble far more frightening than the shouting had been. Restless, irate, seething with discontent at a thousand injustices, the peasants were obviously ready to fight for their comrade and, curiously, were not at all intimidated by the fierce cossacks and guardsmen who, though fewer in number, were far superior in strength. Pitchforks and scythes would be no match for the pistols and sabres Orlov's men had been trained to use with deadly efficiency. I had the feeling Pulaski was responsible for this suicidal attitude, that he had been stirring them up to fever pitch for many days, perhaps weeks.

"Silence!" the shaman ordered. "This man is not of our village," he continued in his normal voice, addressing Orlov. "I have not the authority to agree to his death."

"I do not need your authority," Orlov retorted.

The shaman looked around at the men crowding the clearing, the peasants willing to fight to the death, eager to do so, the heavily armed cossacks restless, spoiling for a rousing fight. He hesitated a moment before continuing, and I could almost see his wily mind working as he shaped the words.

"My people are most unhappy, as you see. This man comes to our village, and he makes many friends. He causes trouble, this I admit. He preaches new ideas, sows discontentment. This I do not like, but if I permit you to kill him my people will fight. There will be needless bloodshed. Some of my people will die."

Orlov's belligerent manner left little doubt that there would indeed be bloodshed. He and the shaman both knew that the peasants would be slaughtered, the cossacks suffering few if any injuries. Orlov was growing more impatient by the moment, temper steadily rising, and his men grinned in anticipation of a lusty fray after months of inactivity.

"We've got to stop it," I whispered. "I'm going to—"

Vanya seized my arm just above the elbow, his fingers curling around it in a steely grip that caused me to wince. "You will do nothing," he said. "Vanya hurts you badly if necessary."

"You must let me—"

"Be still!" he commanded.

I obeyed, gnawing my lower lip, trembling at the thought of what was going to happen any moment now. One of the peasants shoved a cossack standing beside him, raised his scythe, yelled. Calmly, without even flinching, the cossack put a bullet between the man's eyes. The peasant fell to the ground, blood and brains splattering. Several of the peasants turned pale. The cossack blew on the barrel of his pistol and calmly reloaded as another frightening silence fell over the crowd. Neither Orlov nor the shaman seemed particularly disturbed by the incident, seemed scarcely to notice, locked as they were in a battle of wills.

A woman began to wail inside one of the huts. The body of the peasant lay crumpled on the ground where it had fallen, those around it deliberately averting their eyes from the grisly sight.

"How many more of your people must die?" Orlov inquired.

"No one else need die," the shaman replied. His voice was not quite as authoritative as it had been. "We are intelligent men, and neither of us wants bloodshed. This is true?"

Orlov stared at him in stony silence.

"We make a compromise," the shaman continued. "I do not permit you to execute this man who comes to my village, but I give you permission to punish him. I allow you to use the knout. My people watch you administer this punishment. It shows them the danger of these new ideas he preaches, makes them adhere to the old ways we both value."

Orlov was still silent, considering. Pulaski was struggling violently in Vladimir's grip, eyes glazed with terror. The knout, I suspected, could be worse than death.

Orlov finally nodded. "I agree," he said. "I use the knout on him myself. Fifty lashes."

The shaman smiled a deprecatory smile, as though they were bartering over a piece of merchandise and Orlov was trying to pull a ruse.

"No man can survive fifty lashes of the knout," he said. "This we both know. Thirty will kill most men. You will administer fifteen lashes."

"Twenty," Orlov retorted.

The wily old priest gave a shrug and spread his palms out to signify defeat at the hands of a superior trader.

"Twenty it is," he agreed.

"Each one will count," Orlov promised.

The peasants were not at all pleased by this compromise, but the death of their comrade had cooled their ardor considerably. Some had already begun to leave the clearing, resuming the blank-eyed, downtrodden mien that was customary. The shaman roared orders to the rest of them, speaking so quickly, so harshly I couldn't understand what he was saying. The cossacks made no effort to hide their disappointment, scowling darkly as they watched the men disperse.

Lucie let the sheepskin fall back across the doorway. Vanya released my arm. I rubbed it vigorously, certain there would be an ugly bruise.

"I am sorry for this," Vanya said quietly. "I do it for your own good. For you to interfere would have been most dangerous. All is well now. This man is punished and we leave the village as planned."

"Are you feeling better, Marietta?" Lucie asked.

"I'm fine," I lied.

The girl seemed completely unaffected by the horror of the scene we had just witnessed, but she was Russian, I told myself, and shattering violence was apparently commonplace in this country, its people immune to it. I had seen a fair amount of violence, too, in my time, but it always left me with this dreadful sick feeling. I moved back over to the chair, shaken, holding on to the back of it to keep from falling.

"It is best if you go back to your quarters now," Vanya told Lucie. "One of the men in front will accompany you and stand guard outside of your door until it is time to leave."

"I should stay with Marietta. She needs—"

"I'll be all right, Lucie," I said in what I hoped was a fairly normal voice. "I—I just want to rest."

The girl left reluctantly, one of the cossacks standing outside the door escorting her across the clearing. Vanya poured another glass of brandy and forced me to drink. It was silent outside. The woman had stopped wailing. There were no voices, no footsteps, no rattle of tools. After a long while I heard the crunch of boots on ice and, a moment later, a heavy pounding noise. They were driving a stake into the ground. Josef Pulaski would be tied to it with his arms over his head. His coat would be ripped off and his naked back exposed and Gregory Orlov himself would wield the treacherous knout, a long-handled whip with a small piece of metal tied into the knot at the tip of the lash.

Vanya seemed to read my thoughts. "Is best not to think of it, Marietta," he said gently. "This man is evil. He stirs the people to rebellion. He and his kind burn the posthouses, cause much trouble."

"He—he mentioned a man named Pugachev."

Vanya nodded. "This man is their leader. He attempts to raise an army to destroy all aristocrats, to take Catherine's throne. Russia is full of such madmen. Pugachev will soon be captured, soon be put down. The Imperial Army is very strong. They soon find his secret camp. You sit now. You rest. Vanya watches over you."

The next hour was almost unbearable as I sat there in the hut, listening to all the horrible sounds coming from the clearing. The pounding noise ceased. There was the crunch of more footsteps, the sound of a struggle, a cry as Pulaski was tied to the stake. The shaman's voice rang out then, commanding his people to come and watch. I wished I were anywhere else, wished I had never stepped foot in this brooding, brutal country of ice and snow and bloodthirsty violence accepted with a shrug. There was a ripping noise as Pulaski's coat was torn away, then silence, silence that seemed to last forever.

"I can't stand it, Vanya. I must—"

He placed his hands on my shoulders, gently holding me down.

"Will soon be over," he told me.

There was a loud snap, a whistling noise as the long leather lash flew through the air, a deadly crack as the knout found its target, followed by a terrible, agonized scream. A collective gasp came from the crowd assembled, forced to watch, and I knew the first lash had brought the longed-for blood. The second lash followed several moments later—Orlov was in no hurry—and the sounds were repeated, the scream even more shattering. My hands gripped the arms of the chair, my knuckles bone white. I was responsible for this torture, this terror. Josef Pulaski had planned to abduct me, do me grievous harm, but no man should have to endure such torture, no matter what his crime. I winced as the lash snapped and whistled and cracked a third time. The scream torn from Pulaski's throat bore no resemblance to human sound.

A long silence followed. Tense, I waited for the snap, the whistle, the crack. Each second that passed seemed an eternity.

"Bring a bucket of water!" Orlov ordered. His voice was harsh, ugly. I hardly recognized it. "Throw it in his face! I want him conscious."

Scurrying noises as his order was obeyed, a loud splash, a groan, another lash, another inhuman scream. On and on it went, one lash following another, the torture cleverly, cruelly prolonged. Three more times Pulaski passed out. Three more times he was revived. When at last the final lash had been administered, he made a low, gurgling sound, half moan, half sob, and that, too, ended abruptly. I heard them sawing the rope that held him to the stake, heard a thud as his body fell to the ground, and then there was a shuffling, crunching noise as the peasants left the clearing.

Time passed. A servant brought a lavish lunch to my hut. I told Vanya to send the man away. I couldn't possibly eat. Later on more servants came to clear out the hut, to remove the carpet, the furs, all the luxurious items that had been provided for my comfort. Vanya led me slowly to the troika Lucie and I shared, and as we crossed the clearing I saw the tall stake that had been driven into the ground, the pieces of rope dangling. The snow around the stake was splattered with brilliant crimson flecks.

Lucie was waiting beside the troika. She told me she was going to ride her horse for the first lap of today's journey, and I was relieved. I didn't relish anyone's company just now. She studied my face for a moment, gave my hand a reassuring squeeze and left. Vanya told me to climb inside. I shook my head. I said I would stand out here for a few minutes, that I wanted to breathe some fresh air. He frowned, looking as though he were afraid I might do myself some harm. I insisted he get on about his business, and he left reluctantly, looking back over his shoulder at me several times before disappearing behind one of the supply troikas.

The sky was a much darker gray now, deep pewter, heavily laden with ponderous clouds that promised more snow. The sunlight was a dull silver, growing duller, and ice and snow no longer glittered but gleamed instead with a silver-gray sheen touched with violet. It was colder. I pulled the red fox fur hood closer to my face, the soft fur caressing my icy cheeks. All around was a bustle of activity as the last items were packed away, the last horse saddled, the last campfire extinguished. Our driver climbed onto his perch, his huge black fur coat with matching cap pulled down over his ears. In a few minutes we would be leaving the village and I would never see it again, but what had happened here would live in my memory forever. I would never be able to forget those horrible sounds or those vivid red specks on the snow.

I saw Gregory Orlov moving down the line of troikas toward me. I didn't want to speak to him. I didn't even know if I could face him. I started to climb into the troika, hesitated, turned back around. I couldn't avoid him. I might as well confront him now and get it over with. His bulky brown fur coat was open in front, revealing the tan velvet tunic beneath, and his head was still uncovered, the tawny golden brown locks damp, dull. His face was slightly moist, too, the cheeks flushed pink, and as he stopped in front of me I could smell sweat and that potent male musk that seemed stronger than ever. His eyes were not angry, not accusing as they looked into mine. They were tender, full of concern.

"You are not hurt?" he asked.

"I'm not hurt."

"Your voice, it is cold."

"I'm sorry."

"Your manner is cold, too. It is because of what happened?"

"I don't care to discuss it, Count Orlov."

"This morning you call me 'Gregory.' "

"I'd as soon forget this morning."

"I see. You are the genteel English lady. You recoil from me because I whip this man, give him much pain. You think Orlov is a savage brute. Is this not so?"

"You—you kept reviving him. You wanted him to suffer as much as possible. You—"

"This is so," he said, his voice sharp now. "It is necessary this man be punished, necessary I give him this pain, set an example for all the others he has influenced, who might decide to follow him. You do not understand these things, Marietta."

"I don't suppose I do."

"I do this for you. I do it for every well-bred woman in Russia who is threatened by Josef Pulaski and his kind. I am sorry if you do not see this. I am sad if you hate me because I must wield the knout myself."

"I don't hate you, Count Orlov."

"Your voice, your manner tell me otherwise."

"I'm sorry. I—I'm terribly upset. I've had a dreadful shock, and I don't—I don't feel like discussing it."

His eyes were tender once more, heavy lids drooping over them. He wanted to comfort and console me. I could see that. He wanted to take my hand and pat it, draw me against his broad chest and stroke the back of my head as he might stroke a disturbed child, but he didn't. I couldn't hate this man. I understood all that he said and understood that, to his way of thinking, he had done what he had to do, but that didn't make the savage cruelty any easier to accept.

"You will feel better later," he said.

"Yes."

"I do not bother you any longer."

"I appreciate your consideration."

He looked pained. He started to turn away. I stopped him.

"Is—" I hesitated, dreading to ask the question. "Is Pulaski going to live?"

Gregory Orlov shrugged. "Maybe he lives. Maybe he dies. Is not important."

He sauntered away. The cossacks began to ride up and down the line and harnesses began to rattle and male voices rang out with hearty glee. I climbed into the troika and closed the door. The driver clicked his reins, and in a moment the long runners began to slide over the ice and we were moving again, leaving the village just as the first gusts of heavy snowflakes swirled from the pewter sky.

Chapter Twelve

LUCIE SIGHED AS WE STEPPED FROM THE POSThouse into the brilliant morning sunlight. Her golden brown hair fell to her shoulders in a gleaming mass, and her lovely young face was petulant. Like me, Lucie was growing weary of this constant travel, and it didn't matter that we were within a week and a half of our destination. She glanced at our troika as though it were a torture chamber and said that she guessed she'd have to endure it, she was far too lazy to ride her horse this morning.

"At least it's not snowing," I said. "It's a gorgeous day."

She gave me a look that implied I was disgustingly ill-informed and walked on to the troika. Despite her mood she was lovely in soft gray fur and a violet brocade gown embroidered with silver flowers. Though not anticipating another long day of travel any more than Lucie was, I felt quite refreshed after a good night's sleep in a wonderfully comfortable bed and the sumptuous breakfast.

After leaving the village twelve days ago, we had found only one posthouse destroyed by fire, the others undamaged, and as we drew nearer St. Petersburg I was delighted to find that the posthouses grew more and more comfortable. The one in which we had just spent the night was as pleasant as a good English inn, fireplaces in every tidy room, a spacious taproom downstairs. The roads were better, too, much wider, smoother, and while before it had seemed we were the only people in the world foolhardy enough to travel across the country in this weather, we now encountered other travelers on occasion.

"You sleep well?" Vanya inquired.

Lost in thought, I hadn't heard him approach. I nodded, smiling.

"And you?" I asked.

Vanya frowned. "Me, I am most foolish. I drink too much vodka. I play cards with Leo, Nikolai, and others. Nikolai cheats. I lose much money. Nikolai loses half of one ear. I slice it off when we fight with knives."

"That's dreadful!"

"Not to worry. Nikolai is very ugly fellow. It makes him prettier."

"You're terrible, Vanya."

"This I know. I saddle Natasha for you this morning?"

"I believe I will ride her," I told him. "Lucie is not the best of company this morning."

"She is young. She is bored. She brightens up when we reach St. Petersburg. I go saddle Natasha for you now."

The ferocious-looking cossack departed, and I looked up at the sky, relieved to see a clear blue-gray vault without a sign of clouds. We had been through two very severe blizzards, the first coming upon us just after we left the village. Our progress had been reduced to a snail's pace, and after the second blizzard, four days later, we had lost half a day while the men wielded shovels and cleared away an enormous snowdrift that made the road impassable. Today, though, was going to be beautiful. Although it was bitterly cold, as usual, there was no wind, and the radiant sunlight seemed to caress my cheeks as I stood there in front of the posthouse.

I was wearing a deep topaz silk gown and a cloak of lustrous golden brown sable Lucie had loaned me. The red fox cloak had been packed away. I doubted I would ever wear it again. The garment had too many unpleasant associations for me, and even now, twelve days later, I shuddered when I thought of the horror of all that had happened.

Hearing someone coming from the posthouse behind me,

I turned. Gregory Orlov paused for a final word with the innkeeper, handed the man a bag of coins and then continued toward me. He wore high black boots, snug navy blue velvet breeches and tunic and a waist-length black fur cape with matching hat, looking superbly handsome, if somewhat strained when he saw me standing beside the path.

He forced a pleasant smile onto his lips. I forced one onto mine, feeling as strained as he. Count Orlov had been as friendly, as considerate as ever since that day in the village, but there was a remoteness in his manner that had not been there before. It was as though an invisible wall had been placed between us. He no longer sought me out, seemed to avoid me, in fact, and when we did speak he was a bit too polite. Both of us were embarrassed now by this unexpected encounter.

"You are ready to leave?" he inquired.

"I'm waiting for Vanya to bring Natasha around."

"I see. You ride again today. It is beautiful day for this. We will make very good time, I think."

His voice was friendly, his manner extremely polite, but the invisible wall was undeniably there, locked in place, preventing both of us from really communicating. Though apparently relaxed, he was clearly eager to move on, and I was finding it desperately hard to think of something to say.

"The posthouse was very comfortable," I finally managed.

"Yes. I'm glad you have a good place to sleep. The journey has been very difficult."

"I—I really haven't minded."

"In five days' time we come to the estate of my friend Count Rostopchin. We stay there a day or so before going on to St. Petersburg. You will enjoy the rest."

"It will be welcome, I'm sure."

"Do not ride the horse too long today," he cautioned. "You do not want to tire yourself."

"I won't," I said.

He gave me a polite nod then and moved on in that long,
brisk stride of his, boots crunching the ice, the short black
cape swinging from his shoulders. I had ambivalent feelings as I watched him depart. I was relieved, for it had indeed been difficult to find anything to say—as much for
him as for me, I suspected—but I felt a curious disappointment as well. I missed that easy warmth, that intimacy,
that sense of my being someone very special to him that he
had conveyed before. Orlov had withdrawn from me, and
though I told myself it was for the best, that it was precisely what I wanted, a subtle discontentment marred
each day.

It was my own fault, of course. I had as much as told him
to let me be when he stopped to speak to me just before we
left the village. I had been cool, withdrawn, and Orlov undoubtedly felt he was obeying my wishes in adopting this
new, remote politeness. We had reached an impasse, it
seemed, and I had no one to blame but myself.

Vanya was walking past the line of troikas, leading a
prancing, saddled Natasha. With Vanya's assistance I
swung up into the saddle. Feet planted firmly in the stirrups, I adjusted my skirts and the hang of my cloak, eager
to start riding.

Signals were given. Orders were shouted. The line of
troikas began to move slowly down the road, gradually
picking up speed. The cossacks yelled lustily and waved
their sabres, filled with their customary high spirits. The
posthouse receded in the distance, growing smaller and
smaller, out of sight now, and the frigid white beauty of
the Russian countryside glistened all around.

Natasha was thrilled when I let her race and romp up
the line, expending all that marvelous energy. Though I
couldn't keep up with the cossacks, nor did I try, I was a
skilled enough rider now to give the capricious creature
free rein without the least fear of my tumbling off- -as I
had done a humiliating number of times when Vanya had
been instructing me. Sitting securely in the saddle with

back straight and my hands loosely clasping the reins, I moved with her, the two of us a single unit.

My hood fell back. My hair flew free. The icy air smote my cheeks and stung my brow, and it was exhilarating as we covered mile after mile and the huge troikas sped along with bells jingling, harnesses jangling, a merry noise splintering the somber silence of this desolate land. An hour went by, two, and though still rowdy, the cossacks settled down to a vigorous gallop, and I forced a disappointed Natasha into a steady, sedate gait. Vanya rode past us and grinned fiercely and swirled his sabre at us, and, from the window of our troika, Lucie glanced out at me with a bored expression.

Count Orlov rode at the head of the line, a handsome centaur on the powerful black steed whose coat gleamed like polished ebony. The horse was larger, more muscular than any of the others, a truly magnificent beast as befitted its rider. A superb horseman, Orlov rode with total authority, dominating the gigantic stallion with casual ease. He seemed as immense, as mysterious, as subtly menacing as the land itself—harsh, cruel, beautiful, and perpetually fascinating.

How did I feel about him? How did I really feel? I had been appalled by his savage cruelty to Pulaski, but I knew in my heart that, from Orlov's viewpoint, the cruelty was completely justified, even necessary, and I knew as well that that cruel streak had always been there. I had sensed it beneath the warmth, the jovial facade. It seemed to be an intergral part of the Russian character, seething beneath the surface, just waiting to be unleashed. They all had it. Even the gentle, teasing, protective Vanya could change into a monster of cruelty when provoked. I had seen it happen. Could I blame Orlov for something that was clearly inherent? The Russian male looked upon such matters as pain and punishment and death with a much harder, more practical eye than his more civilized English counterpart.

Joseph Pulaski would have killed me without a moment's hesitation, had planned to leave me bound and gagged under the frozen shrubbery, perhaps to die. He had planned to take me as a prize to the demented peasant who was his leader, to rape me repeatedly on the journey. He was a vicious troublemaker, stirring other peasants to violent rebellion, was savage, brutal, demented himself. Wasn't his punishment entirely just? And hadn't part of Orlov's harshness been because I myself had been Pulaski's victim? "I do this for you," he had said. "I do it for every well-bred woman in Russia who is threatened by Joseph Pulaski and his kind."

Orlov was right—I didn't understand these matters. With my heritage, my background, my upbringing, I was incapable of seeing them from the viewpoint of those who belonged to this strange country. I had been too hard on him, I told myself. I was responsible for that invisible wall that had come between us, and, as the icy air numbed my cheeks and nose, as I forced Natasha to a slower trot, I finally acknowledged that the invisible wall bothered me a great deal. Far more than I would have liked to admit. I missed the warmth, the tender concern, the attention.

I was attracted to him, strongly attracted. I couldn't deny that. It was, I knew, a purely physical attraction that had been there from the very beginning—first stirring that evening we had dined in the gold and yellow room—and it had steadily grown ever since. Sensibly, I had ignored it, being quite cool and reasonable . . . and then he had kissed me and I had known the full strength of this attraction and the full strength of my need for solace, for reassurance, for a remedy to counteract Jeremy Bond's betrayal and all that it had done. Ready at last to take the powder, to throw all caution to the winds and savor anew the sweet splendor his fierce kisses had stirred inside me, I had drawn back, horrified by his cruelty, and then that damnable wall had come between us.

It's just as well, a cool inner voice told me. You were on the verge of making a very bad mistake, and you're well out of it. Attracted to him you may be, but any relationship with Gregory Orlov could only lead to complications you're not prepared to deal with. In a short time now you'll be in St. Petersburg and three months later you will be on your way back to America and all this will become a distant memory. *Use your head, Marietta.* Leave things as they are. I gripped the reins in my gloved hands, listening to that sensible voice, knowing it spoke without emotion and with wisdom I must heed.

A commotion ahead pulled me out of myself and brought me back to the reality of the moment: the powerful horse beneath me, the cold air numbing my cheeks, the immense white snowbanks and ice-encrusted trees on either side of the wide, level road. Orlov had raised his arm overhead, signaling the party to halt. The cossacks had unsheathed their weapons. Something was obstructing the road ahead, something large and gray and shapeless, a kind of barricade, it seemed. I rode foward slowly, foolishly, too curious for caution, and as I drew nearer I saw that it was a large sleigh overturned in the middle of the road, blankets, bags and mothy-looking furs scattered around it. The horses that had pulled it were nowhere to be seen.

Orlov saw me approaching. His face was thunderous.

"Get back!" he ordered. "Have you lost your mind? It might be an ambush!"

I halted Natasha, but I didn't retreat. Orlov and seven cossacks slowly approached the sleigh, weapons at the ready. There was a groaning noise. A black-gloved hand suddenly appeared on the top side of the sleigh and then a head wearing a thick black wool hat pulled down low over ears and brow. The hat had a frivolous black woolen ball atop it, and the face beneath was lean, attractive and unquestionably English. A pair of fine blue-gray eyes watched the menacing approach with considerable surprise.

"I say, chaps! Easy on!"

The words, in English, had no effect whatsoever on Orlov and his men. They continued toward the sleigh. Its former occupant shrugged and raised his hands in the air to show that he was unarmed. A half-amused, half-dismayed smile curled on a wide mouth with full lower lip. He moved out from behind the sleigh, hands still raised, not at all frightened. There was something jaunty, almost playful in his manner, an undeniable cockiness in the tilt of his head, the curve of that mouth.

"My Russian is rather limited," he said in that language, "but I assure you I shan't attack. Odds are hardly in my favor, are they? Are you chaps always so grim?"

"He's English!" I called. "Put down your weapons."

The men ignored me. Silent, sober, they advanced, completely surrounding the sleigh. The Englishman shrugged, lowered his hands and thrust them into the pockets of his heavy black wool coat. Belted at the waist, it was a fine coat, exquisitely cut by the best English tailor, but it was a trifle shabby. His black leather cavalry boots were deplorably skuffed, and the dark gray English cord breeches that clung tightly to his very long legs were just short of threadbare. A new, very expensive, mustard yellow wool scarf was wrapped snugly around his neck and tucked between the wide lapels of the black coat.

"If you're going to shoot me, shoot," he said chattily. "I've had an absolutely wretched day and that would be a fitting climax."

"You are English?" Orlov asked gruffly.

"I've got the papers to prove it, but, alas, they're in St. Petersburg. Didn't figure I'd need 'em out here."

"What are you doing here?" Orlov demanded.

"Freezing," the man confided. "I left the village of Riganoye bright and early this morning—crack of dawn, actually, wanted to get a good start. I started out with two sturdy but rather lackluster gray stallions pulling my sleigh, incidentally. Seem to have lost 'em."

His Russian, though serviceable, was spoken with a pronounced English accent, and the heavy, cumbersome language was hardly suited to his chatty manner of speech. Orlov frowned, comprehending only half of what the fellow said.

"He is, I think, harmless," he told his men. "We do not kill him."

"Relieved to hear that," the man quipped.

He was quite tall, a good three inches over six feet, and extremely lean, not a spare ounce of flesh on that loose, wiry frame. He couldn't be much over twenty-three or twenty-four, I thought, though some Englishmen kept that youthful aura well into their thirties.

"What is it you call yourself?" Orlov inquired.

"I call myself all sorts of things, depending on the circumstances. My official appellation is Lloyd, Bryan Lloyd, with a *y*. My mother thought an *i* would be altogether too common."

Orlov shook his head, perplexed. "This man, he does not make sense. I do not follow what he says."

"Think you could give me something fiery to drink, preferably your famous vodka? Seems I've been sprawled unconscious in the snow for quite a long time, three or four hours at least. If it hadn't been for this hat I'm wearing, the crack I got over my head would probably 've bashed my skull in."

"Someone cracks you over the head?"

"I was clicking along, minding my own business, humming a jaunty tune if memory serves, when these three frightful-looking ruffians leaped out from behind that snowbank over there. Two of 'em seized the horses. The third gave a mighty yell and pounced on me waving a heavy wooden board. Happened so suddenly I didn't have time to defend myself—and I'm pretty good at that. The board smashed across my head and everything went black and the next thing I knew I was hearing bells—yours."

"When does this happen?"

"Couldn't 've been much later than nine, nine-thirty. I see they left my bags. Guess they figured there wasn't anything worth stealing besides the horses. They didn't get a bargain there, I assure you."

"What do they look like?"

"Sturdy, lackluster, gray, ready to be put out to pasture,

both of 'em. My father wouldn't let me use any of the *good* horses. Said if I was going to be traipsing about the Russian countryside visiting isolated villages no one has ever heard of I bloody well wasn't going to take his thoroughbreds."

"The *men,*" Orlov said patiently. "What do *they* look like?"

"Just got a quick glimpse of 'em," Bryan Lloyd replied. "They were big brutes, shabbily dressed, wooden sabots, thin coats. Looked half-starved to me. Peasants. Obviously on the run. Surprised they didn't steal my coat," he added. "Mighty glad they didn't."

Orlov nodded portentously, as though his worst fears had been confirmed, and then he turned and ordered a general halt for lunch. The tall Englishman perked up considerably at the word *lunch.* Orlov and his men dismounted and went to inspect the sleigh, which, it seemed, was damaged beyond repair. The peasants had apparently pushed it over before running off with the horses.

"Think you might give me a ride to St. Petersburg?" Lloyd asked as the men began to haul the damaged sleigh off the road.

"We do this, yes," Orlov told him. "You are friend, not foe."

I had dismounted now and handed Natasha's reins to one of the servants. Rubbing gloved fingers over my numb cheeks, adjusting my sable hood, I moved purposefully over to Orlov and the Englishman. One of the sleigh's runners was shattered, I noticed, and part of the bottom had been bent. Bryan Lloyd shook his head mournfully as it was pulled over a snowbank. Two grim servants began to gather up his bags, the blanket and mothy-looking furs.

"Take the bags to our troika," I said crisply. "Do whatever you wish with the furs and blankets."

"I say!" Lloyd protested. "I've grown very attached to those blankets!"

"They're falling apart," I said in English. "So are the furs."

"The mother tongue!" he exclaimed. "Can't tell you how good it is to hear it. About the blankets—I travel about on my own, you see. It wouldn't do for me to drive a splashy rig. Too much temptation for bandits. Reason I wear these old clothes. They take me for a poor worker and move on to more promising candidates."

"Your masquerade didn't do you much good this morning," I observed.

"A chap's luck is bound to run out sometime or other. The men were obviously desperate. You're English, aren't you? What in the world are you doing with this party?"

"It's a long story," I replied. "You look pale. You probably have a bad lump on top of your head. I feel sure you're hungry. I'll take care of him," I told Orlov, who had been scrutinizing us both intently, straining to understand what we said. "There's plenty of room in our troika."

"Is so," Orlov said, nodding. "Is your countryman. You find out why he is out here all alone. Me, I cannot make the head or the tails of anything he says."

I smiled to myself and, taking Bryan Lloyd by the arm, led him toward the troika I shared with Lucie. Though jaunty and putting on a good front, he was indeed pale, and his legs were a bit shaky as we walked. I feared he might have a slight concussion. He emitted a low whistle as he took in the splendor of our vehicles.

"I assume the big chap on the black horse must be someone important," he said.

"Count Gregory Orlov," I replied.

Bryan Lloyd arched a brow. "Orlov? So he's come back at last."

"You know of him?"

"Everyone in Russia knows of the mighty Orlov. He's almost a legendary figure. Never thought I'd actually meet him, particularly under circumstances like these. If I might be so bold to ask, what is your connection with the famous count?"

"I'm his niece's paid companion."

That dark, winged brow shot up again. "You? A paid

companion? Thought they were dowdy, self-effacing old ladies in black, always fetching shawls and pouring tea. Never saw one in silks and sable before."

"You have now," I said tartly.

"Hold on," he protested. "I meant no offense. It's just that you happen to be the most gorgeous female I've ever laid eyes on. I find it hard to visualize you fetching shawls, pouring tea, being dowdy and self-effacing."

"I rarely am, Mr. Lloyd."

"I don't even know your name. Would it be highly presumptuous of me to ask?"

"I'm Marietta Danver," I said, "and you are indeed highly presumptuous. Something of a scamp, I suspect."

"Is it that obvious?"

"I've had a lot of experience with scamps," I said dryly.

Bryan Lloyd smiled. It was, of course, a perfectly dazzling smile, warm and engaging, bringing a responsive smile to my own lips. The youth had all the makings of a heartbreaker, and I suspected he had already broken quite a few despite his age. If he were ten years older I would have avoided him like the pox.

"Here we are," I said, opening the door of our troika.

I helped him in. He was much weaker than he thought, shivering a little as he climbed inside and sank onto the cushioned seat opposite Lucie. He was even paler now, his brow moist with cold sweat. He had been going on sheer bravado all this time, and now he looked ready to pass out. I plumped a cushion behind him, spread a fur over his knees, poured a glass of brandy and told him to drink it. Lucie watched all this with cool, incurious eyes, undeniably haughty as she sat across from us. Bryan Lloyd hardly noticed her. He drank the brandy in greedy gulps, growing weaker by the minute.

"How is your head?" I asked.

"Hurts like hell, if you really want to know."

"Here, let me see."

I pulled off his black knit hat with its fluffy black ball. His hair was thick and silky and wavy, a very dark blond. I touched the top of his head. He yowled. There was a large bump, as I had suspected. I told him we were going to have to put ice on it. He made a grimace, looking pathetic and put-upon and extremely young now. I took ice from a silver bucket in one of the cabinets and wrapped it up in a silk scarf and placed it on his head.

"It's going to melt and drip all over me," he complained.

"We'll deal with that when the time comes."

"I say, do you think I might have another glass of that brandy? Finest I've ever drunk."

"You've had enough for the time being. After lunch, if you eat all your food, I might let you have a few more drops."

"Christ, you'd think I was still in the nursery!"

"I suspect you haven't been out of the nursery all that long, Mr. Lloyd. Just how old *are* you?"

"Twenty-nine," he lied.

"Twenty-one," I said.

"Twenty-four," he confessed, "but don't let on."

He seemed to see Lucie for the first time then and gazed at her with considerable interest, the gray-blue eyes full of speculation. Lucie tilted her chin disdainfully and stared out the window, very much the imperious Russian noblewoman, although a bit too young to carry it off with any great aplomb. Bryan Lloyd cut a comical figure as he slouched back against the cushions, bundled in furs, the hastily improvised ice pack lopsided atop his head, but Lucie hadn't failed to note the lean, handsome face with its fine chiseled nose and cheekbones, the cleft chin, the sensual curve of that full lower lip. I introduced them. Lucie nodded curtly. Bryan Lloyd grinned and said he was positively enchanted and then dropped right off to sleep. I suspected the brandy he had drunk so quickly had something to do with it.

"Where did you find *him?*" Lucie inquired.

"In the middle of the road. His sleigh had been turned over, his horses stolen. Didn't you hear the commotion?"

"I didn't pay any attention. I just assumed we were stopping for lunch. What's he doing in *our* troika?"

"Someone had to look after him. As he's my countryman, I took on the job. I fear I'm going to have my hands full."

"He looks like a great big baby," Lucie observed acidly. "Look at those legs. They're as long as a giraffe's."

"Nicely shaped, though."

"A gawky English giraffe! Just how long are we going to have to share our troika with him? All the way to St. Petersburg?"

"You don't have to share it at all," I said sweetly. "If it's going to be an imposition, I'm sure your uncle can make other arrangements for him."

"Oh, I wouldn't want to put anyone *else* out," she replied, a martyr now. "I guess I'll just have to endure it."

I smiled. The minx didn't fool me in the least. She was interested, all right, gawky English giraffe though he might be. The subject of our conversation slept soundly, his lips parted, snorting every now and then. The ice began to melt. He scowled and stirred in his sleep as an icy rivulet trickled down his temple. I removed the ice, replaced it with more, patted his temples and brow dry. He snorted, nestling his cheek against a cushion. Lucie gave an exasperated sigh and immersed herself in a book, or pretended to. Shortly thereafter our lunch arrived, a most lavish repast. Bryan Lloyd's nostrils twitched. He sniffed. He opened one eye. Seeing the food, he sat bolt upright, wide awake.

He had an enormous appetite, plowing into the golden brown roast chicken with relish, devouring a whole stack of potato pancakes, half a pot of caviar, an egg in aspic, several thick slices of tender pork roast as well, finishing things off with a flaky apple pastry sprinkled with cinnamon sugar and a large cup of coffee. Coffee drunk, pastry crumbs brushed away, he handed me the empty cup, grinned and, a moment later, was fast asleep again. Lucie was absolutely appalled, had never been so appalled in all her life, and told me so in no uncertain terms. She had no idea how she was going to endure the company of this childish, ill-mannered English oaf for the next week and a half even if he *did* have hair like thick dark yellow silk and remarkable blue-gray eyes.

"I imagine you'll manage," I said.

"I'm only doing this for you, Marietta. I want you to understand that."

"I understand perfectly," I told her.

Bryan Lloyd slept soundly for the next three and a half hours as we moved on through the frozen countryside, runners gliding smoothly over the ice, bells jingling pleasantly. I changed the ice twice more, noting that the lump seemed to have gone down quite a bit. Beneath the thick yellow hair his scalp was pink and swollen, but I didn't think he had sustained any real damage. Removing the ice at last, I smoothed his hair back and patted the icy moisture from his brow. He sighed heavily and emitted a little moan, nuzzling the silken cushion in blissful contentment. Lucie put down the volume of plays she had been thumbing through.

"He's going to be all right," I remarked. "The swelling's gone down now, and he's not nearly as pale as he was. Look, there's a faint pink flush on his cheeks."

"He's certainly *lean,*" Lucie observed. "I've never cared for excessively lean men."

"He may be lean, but he's very sturdy. Strong as an ox, I'd wager."

"I doubt it," she sniffed.

"Wanna wrestle?" he asked.

He opened his eyes. Lucie and I gave him accusing looks. He grinned.

"How long have you been awake?" I demanded.

"Just a couple of minutes. Speaking of wrestling, I used to be quite good when I was at Oxford. Celebrated for my arm lock and my side head lock. Lethal, both of them. Once I got him in one of those locks, the other chap might as well have given up. Won every match, I did. Won a lot of pocket money on side wagers, too. Always bet on myself. I was class champion, by the by."

"You went to Oxford?" I said.

"Came down with top honors," he confessed. "Poetry, philosophy, a dab of physics. Took my degree in history. Specialized in the Assyrian Empire. Not a bloody lot of *use* to me but an entertaining subject just the same. Know anything about the Assyrians?"

"Not a thing," I told him.

"I'll tell you all about them someday."

"I've no doubt you will. In detail. I've rarely met a young man so reticent," I said with sarcasm.

"Or modest," Lucie added.

"What about some more of that brandy now?"

I poured it for him, enchanted in spite of myself. Bryan Lloyd took the glass, nodded his thanks and settled back against the cushions with a look of lazy bliss in those handsome blue-gray eyes. The errant dark blond wave had tumbled across his brow again. With his unruly, silken hair and his youthful, clean-cut features he looked seventeen, only the full swell of that sensual lower lip bespeaking a more advanced age.

"Can't say I've ever traveled in such style," he remarked, looking around at the luxurious trappings. "All the comforts of home and then some. I'm used to roughing it a bit more—open sleigh, mothy blankets, plodding nags. That's more my style."

"Exactly why *were* you roughing it out here in the middle of nowhere?" I inquired. "Or is it highly presumptuous of me to ask?"

"Can you keep a secret?"

"I've been known to."

"I was on an extremely important diplomatic mission," he confided. "My father is chief adjutant to the British ambassador in St. Petersburg. A very important chap, my father—number-two man at the embassy. The ambassador is preparing a report to send back home on the living conditions of the peasants and all this unrest that's causing such a flap. He needed some firsthand information, told my father to get it for him. Being the sensible fellow he is, and knowing my desire to see something of Russia besides the drawing rooms, he assigned me the task."

"Oh?"

" 'No more of this lounging about, sponging off the old man,' he told me. 'If you're going to stay here you might as well make yourself useful.' So off I went in my open sleigh, visiting sundry villages, asking questions, making a lot of notes."

"Wasn't he afraid you'd get hurt?" Lucie asked.

"I think that was the idea," the youth informed her. "Actually, I have a way with people and I'm more than capable of watching out for myself. I found the peasants quite unmenacing, if somewhat uncommunicative. They shared their food with me, let me sleep in their huts with the goats and pigs, always treated me like an honored—if unwanted—guest. Didn't tell 'em what I was up to, of course, said I was gathering material for a book on Russia."

"They understood that?"

"Most of 'em had no idea what a book was. They considered me an eccentric foreigner with a funny accent and a bewildering curiosity about their ways. I always gave the village priest a nice gift, got him on my side. My sleigh was filled with such gifts when I started out," he added.

Young Bryan Lloyd wasn't quite the irresponsible young rogue he seemed to be on first impression. The handsome blue-gray eyes gleamed with intelligence, and I strongly suspected that the cocky manner and frivolous banter concealed a cool, tough efficiency. He would never have been entrusted with so delicate a mission were that not the case.

"So you're in the diplomatic service?" I said.

"Not actually. As I said, I was just helping my father out. I'd been visiting him for four months, attending all the parties, charming all the ladies, adorning all the drawing rooms. I was getting restless, leaped at the opportunity to do something besides dress up and scintillate."

"And what did you do before you came to Russia?"

"A bit of this, a bit of that." He shoved the heavy blond wave from his brow. "I spent a lot of time in the theater," he said.

Lucie's cool demeanor didn't alter in the least, but her interest was definitely aroused by the word *theater*.

"You're fond of the theater?" I asked.

"Fond is hardly the word I'd use. It's a fascinating world, full of maddening, exasperating, infuriating idiots who should have been drowned at birth but happen to be blessed with special magic. Belong in cages, all of 'em. Instead they swagger about in all their splendor, scattering the magic like gold dust for the benefit of lesser mortals."

"You seem to know a great deal about it," Lucie said coolly.

"Enough to know a man's mad to get involved in that world."

"Oh?"

"Ever hear of a play called *The Complaisant Wives?*" he asked her.

"I'm afraid I haven't."

"Neither have I," I said.

"It was a marvelous play," he informed us, "full of wisdom and sparkling with wit, packed with dramatic conflict. Belongs with Dryden, Congreve, Goldsmith, the best. It opened in London six months ago. The audience threw rotten tomatoes at the stage. The journalists who came to review it actually chased the poor author out of the theater. Brandishing *knives,*" he added.

"What did he do?"

"Only thing he could do—fled the country."

"And came all the way to Russia."

"How did you guess?"

"I'm quick that way," I said. "So you wrote a play?"

"Penned every immortal word, shaped every phrase

with my sweat and blood. People don't appreciate quality in the theater," he said glumly. "They want fireworks and foolery, nothing more. Next time that's what I intend to give 'em."

He gave Lucie a sidelong glance, trying his best to impress this lovely young woman who sat across from him with such regal bearing, but Lucie wasn't about to let herself show the slightest curiosity. Ignoring him, she gazed out at the ice and snow flowing past the window as we sped along. Bryan Lloyd was clearly perplexed. I could tell that he wasn't accustomed to being ignored by youthful members of the opposite sex.

"You plan to write another?" I asked.

"Imagine I'll have to," he said. "Can't let myself be remembered solely as the author of that fiasco. I learned a lot from the experience, made dozens of mistakes, know how to go about it now. I've got several ideas. Imagine I'll set to work with a vengeance as soon as I get back to London."

Lucie was seemingly fascinated by the passing scene, gazing with rapt attention at snowbanks and icy trees. Bryan Lloyd curled his lower lip, frustrated at his inability to arouse her interest. I smiled to myself, amused by the age-old game both were playing. I couldn't resist a bit of deviltry.

"You must know a lot of people in the theater," I said.

"Far too many of 'em. Madmen all."

"Have you ever met Mrs. Robinson?" I asked.

"The Divine Perdita? She was one of the complaisant wives! She wrecked my play, the slut! I was an unknown playwright and the management thought she would draw in the crowds and she condescended to appear in the piece after demanding positively absurd changes in the third act. The play called for *ensemble* acting, everyone holding up his end, working together, and La P. turned it into a one-woman vehicle, hamming all over the place and totally ignoring the rest of the company. Wretched woman! I'd love to strangle her!"

Lucie couldn't resist that. She had to come to the defense of her idol. She turned to look at him, her face beautifully composed, and when she spoke her voice was cool and level.

"I've seen Mrs. Robinson act," she said. "I saw her as Jacintha in *The Suspicious Husband.*"

"Yes, she went into that immediately after *Wives.*"

"I think she's a wonderful actress."

"She's an ambitious little slut who happens to have a nice face and a passable voice and a knack for meeting the right men. Sheridan put her where she is. Quite taken with her, he was, made her his protégée, used his influence to promote her career. She's used him shamelessly, but she's about ready to dump the old boy now. Has her cap set for the Prince of Wales, she does, and I've no doubt she'll eventually snare him."

Lucie didn't believe a word he said. A pale pink flush tinted her cheeks, but she refused to let him see her ruffled. She brushed an imaginary speck of lint from her violet brocade skirt, adjusted her soft gray furs.

"I shouldn't doubt he'd be interested in her," she replied. "Mrs. Robinson is a remarkably beautiful woman."

"You think so?"

"She has an ethereal quality."

"Ethereal!" he scoffed.

"I wouldn't expect you to appreciate it."

"You ought to see her without make up," Lloyd told her. "She looks like a startled poodle. Everything you see on stage is artificial, including her bosom. Even all decked out and bathed in soft light she's not one-tenth as lovely as *you* are. You could probably act her off the stage as well. Almost any woman with a decent voice could, and you've got a wonderful voice, full of color and interesting shadings."

Lucie, of course, was far too sophisticated to respond as he had hoped to this obvious ploy. Coolly ignoring the flattery, she picked up her book and began to read. Bewildered by his lack of success, Bryan Lloyd curled his lower lip again, arched one smooth eyebrow and promptly went back to sleep until the next meal. I smiled, tucking the fur lap robe back around his long legs. Lucie lowered her book and gave me a withering look. Exasperated she might be, but I doubted she would find the rest of our journey quite as tedious and boring.

Chapter Thirteen

STANDING AT THE ELEGANT FRENCH WINDOWS
of my bedroom, I gazed out at Count Vasily Rostopchin's
celebrated gardens, patterned after those Le Notre had
created at Versailles. In full bloom, they must have been
spectacular, but now the carefully terraced flower beds
were covered with snow, the formal walks layered with ice.
Marble fountains were still. Lily ponds were frozen. Magnificent nude statues seemed to shiver on their pedestals,
the bizarrely shaped evergreen topiary shrubs providing
the only touch of color. Light was fading now, violet-gray
shadows spreading over the snow, the pewter sky streaked
with amethyst banners that blurred softly as the pale
silver disk of sun disappeared.

Time to start dressing, I thought, turning away from the
windows. Earlier I had luxuriated in a bath for over an
hour and now wore only a thin petticoat of pale yellow silk,
the half dozen gauzy yellow skirts swaying as I moved over
to the beautiful cream and gold wardrobe where a servant
had hung the clothes I would wear during our brief visit
with Count Rostopchin. Each garment had been carefully
pressed, handled with loving care. I took down the pale yellow silk gown completely overlaid with a deeper yellow
gauze appliquéd with floral patterns in glittering gold
spangles.

I smiled, thinking of our reception when we arrived this
afternoon. Our host had greeted Orlov as he might greet a
long-lost brother. The robust cries, vigorous punches and

bearhugs had brought a particularly fierce wrestling match to mind, with the thin Rostopchin definitely getting the worst of it. In his powdered wig, sky blue satin and frothy cream lace, he looked as fragile as a porcelain doll, and I feared he might break as Orlov pounded his back and caught him in a crushing hug. In another country such hearty physical displays of affection might have elevated eyebrows, but in Russia it was the norm, the more rugged the male, the more demonstrative his manner. Friendship among men was a joyous thing to be celebrated with gusto.

Gusto gave way to courtliness as Count Rostopchin turned to welcome Lucie and me to his home. Restrained, refined, he kissed our hands, the epitome of the gracious French gentleman. Following the example set by Catherine herself, Rostopchin, I discovered, was enamored of everything French. Young Bryan Lloyd had been amused to note Rostopchin's high-heeled shoes with their diamond buckles, his perfumed handkerchief and painted face, had been less amused when Rostopchin greeted him as proper French gentlemen his age greeted young boys. The youth's expression was a sight to behold as the count took him by the shoulders and planted a resounding kiss on each cheek. Lucie had barely been able to restrain a titter.

Remembering Bryan's blush, his silent outrage at this treatment, I smiled again. All dignity, he had explained to the fifty-seven-year-old count that he was not a *petit garcon,* was, in fact, pushing thirty. Rostopchin elevated one plucked brow and said he had taken Bryan for a choirboy. That delighted Lucie. It made Bryan long to murder the foppishly attired but extremely virile Rostopchin, who made matters worse by patting the youth on the head and informing him that the nursery had been made ready for him. Though blessed with a marvelous sense of humor himself, Bryan Lloyd did not appreciate being teased about his ultrayouthful appearance. He had sulked for over an hour, vowing to grow a beard in self-defense.

Count Rostopchin's obsession with things French had caused him to turn the interior of his vast house into a rep-

lica of one of those exquisite mansions outside Paris where
French nobility held court. The cream, gold and shell pink
bedroom assigned to me was a perfect example of the reno-
vation. The pink walls were divided by gilt-framed panels
depicting elegantly clad shepherds disporting with scantily clad shepherdesses in flowery glades while plump nym-
phets and cupids beamed with approval. Painted in soft
pastel shades against a cream background, the panels, by
Boucher, had been originally commissioned by Madame de
Pompadour. The soft blue rugs patterned with dusty pink
flowers and delicate green leaves had been specially
woven for that lady, while the magnificent cream and gold
furniture had belonged to her successor, the voluptuous
Jeanne Du Barry.

Crystal pendants glittered on gilt wall sconces where
candles glowed warmly, and a superb Boucher portrait of
Louison hung over the cream marble mantlepiece, that
young lady as sensuous and scantily clad as any of the
shepherdesses, a garland of flowers her only attire. The
total effect of all this was excessively grand and erotic, and
as I fastened my dress I wondered about the other women
who had occupied these seductive quarters. Twice widowed, with no legitimate heirs, Count Vasily Rostopchin
was, according to Lucie, a notorious womanizer with an in-
satiable appetite for ballet dancers, opera singers and winsome coquettes, devouring them as another man might
devour chocolates. The delightful pastime, though typically French, had become so obsessive and prolific in
Rostopchin's case that even Catherine had expressed her
disapproval, and she was hardly prudish. As a result,
Rostopchin was no longer welcome in St. Petersburg and
spent much of his time in Paris where his appetites were
understood and his lavish generosity greatly appreciated
by its many recipients.

Rostopchin, I knew, had been an ardent supporter of
Catherine's and, like Orlov, instrumental in putting her
on the throne. In the old days, before Orlov's fall, the
silver-haired count had been one of the most important

men at court, fawned upon and feared by all who hoped to win favor. Banished from the court, all his influence gone, the aging Russian nobleman accepted his lot with a good-natured shrug and continued to enjoy himself immensely. Unlike Orlov, he never pined for glories lost. According to Lucie, who had provided all this information, he was far too busy enjoying pleasures of the present to regret what was gone. Despite the difference in their ages, he was Orlov's closest friend and looked upon the younger man as his son. Rostopchin was one of the few people in the world Orlov genuinely respected.

Moving over to the full-length mirror in its ornate gilt frame, I examined myself critically. The gown was truly spectacular, the full puff sleeves falling off the shoulder, the form-fitting bodice cut daringly low. The waist was snug. The skirt spread out in splendor, golden spangles glittering against yellow gauze and silk. My hair was piled on top of my head in a stack of sculpted coppery red waves, three long ringlets dangling in back. I had applied a touch of pink to my lips, a suggestion of blush to my high cheekbones, and my eyelids were lightly brushed with pale brownish mauve shadow. The woman who gazed back at me was unquestionably mature, the sapphire eyes dark, disillusioned, full of sad wisdom, but I had no doubt Count Rostopchin would appreciate my efforts to please him.

A wry, self-mocking smile played on my lips as I picked up one of the elegant crystal bottles of perfume. Who do you think you're fooling? I asked myself. You're not wearing this dress for Rostopchin, you're wearing it for Orlov. The perfume was subtle and seductive, bringing to mind sun-kissed roses and naked flesh. I dabbed it behind my earlobes, between my breasts, applying it a bit more generously than I ordinarily did.

"I think I'll just forget about dinner tonight," Lucie said. "I couldn't possibly go down now."

I turned. She had opened the door so quietly I hadn't heard her. Standing in the doorway, she looked at me with a distinctly peeved expression.

"What do you mean?" I asked. "Are you feeling ill?"

Lucie sauntered on into the room, her satin gown rustling softly.

"I feel positively wretched," she confessed. "I intended to go down and dazzle everyone with my splendor, and now, after seeing you, I realize I'll be merely a shadow to your sun."

"Nonsense," I said.

I replaced the crystal stopper in the perfume bottle, set the bottle aside and sighed. Lucie observed me with critical eyes, her head tilted slightly to one side.

"No one has a *right* to be so gorgeous," she complained. "You look positively magnificent, Marietta."

"You look rather magnificent yourself," I told her.

Lucie frowned, looking touchingly young as she stepped over to the mirror I had just vacated. Her hair was pulled back from her face, cascading down in back in a rich tumble of golden brown waves. The pale tan shadow on her lids made her eyes seem even more exotic, and light pink rouge accentuated her lovely high cheekbones. Her mouth, currently pouting, was a soft shell pink, and the scattering of light, almost invisible, golden tan freckles across the bridge of her nose added a piquant effect.

"I hate this gown," she said. "I don't know why I ever let you persuade me to buy it."

The gown, purchased in London, was light tan satin with pencil-thin brown stripes. The short sleeves were puffed, the neckline modestly low, and a brown velvet sash emphasized her slender waist, the skirt swelling out over the gauzy brown underskirts. It was very English, elegant in its simplicity, and she had never looked lovelier nor so young and vulnerable.

"I should have worn something scarlet," she said.

"The gown is perfect, Lucie."

"I look like a child!"

"You look sweet and demure, exactly the kind of young woman a man like Bryan Lloyd would find interesting."

"Who cares what *he* thinks?"

"Englishmen find innocence far more intriguing than worldliness," I told her. "He won't be able to take his eyes off you."

"I haven't been innocent in years."

"Bryan doesn't know that," I said.

Lucie gave me an exasperated look. I smiled.

"I saw the two of you walking in the gardens earlier, Lucie. You seemed to be very deep in conversation."

"He wanted to see the statues," she replied. "I agreed to show them to him. Hardly a thrill, I assure you. He did nothing but talk, talk, talk the whole time and scarcely glanced at the statues."

"He seemed to be glancing at you quite a lot," I remarked.

Lucie opened one of the bottles of perfume, smelled the fragrance, oblivious to my comment. I knew she wanted to discuss Bryan, but she was too contrary to confess her interest in the lanky blond youth. She dabbed a bit of perfume on the back of her wrist, set the bottle down.

"I wonder if I should wear some jewelry," she said idly.

"At your age jewelry isn't necessary."

"I feel thirty-five."

"You look sixteen."

"So does *he,*" Lucie said, "but he's actually quite mature and terribly intelligent, too. Even profound at times. Don't let that boyish manner fool you."

"It hasn't."

"He's quite serious about his career in the theater, Marietta. He has some marvelous ideas. I shouldn't be surprised if he became a very successful playwright."

"Nor should I."

"He has so much energy, so much zest. Just listening to him exhausts me. His talk *is* fascinating though," she admitted. "He's interested in so many things, has such a wealth of knowledge. Of course, he's terribly boastful."

"I've noticed that."

"He's the best playwright, the best wrestler, the best dancer. Are all Englishmen so egotistical?"

"The majority of them."

"I suppose he is rather attractive," she conceded.

"Rather," I said.

"But much too young."

"Much," I agreed.

"He thinks he's a man of the world, ever so experienced. All the ladies fall in love with him. He has to fight them off with a stick, he says. Have you ever heard anything so ridiculous?"

"Rarely."

"He *has* had experience, though," she said.

"Oh?"

"A woman can always tell."

"You're probably right."

"Do I really look all right, Marietta?"

"You look lovely, Lucie. Are you ready to go downstairs?"

"I want to work on my hair a bit more," she said. "You go on down, and I'll join you in a little while."

A few minutes later I was moving down the graceful curving white staircase with its pale golden carpet. Magnificent crystal chandeliers hung from a high ceiling, shedding radiant light on the hall below. The walls were covered with sky blue silk, divided by magnificent gilt-framed ivory panels painted by Fragonard in soft pastel colors. Stylish ladies swung in flower-garlanded swings, skirts billowing to reveal well-turned ankles and shapely limbs, while handsome cavaliers in plumed hats and satin watched from the ground. Lovely floral rugs of pink, pale blue and lime green were scattered over the highly polished parquet floor, and Boulle tables held bouquets of fresh-cut flowers and a collection of exquisite Sèvres figurines.

I was examining one of the Fragonard panels when Count Vasily Rostopchin stepped into the hall, resplendent in pale rose brocade and frothy beige lace. With his powdered wig, thin, painted face and lascivious eyes, he personified the degenerate French courtier. As is often the case, the frilly, effeminate attire merely served to emphasize his thorny, still potent virility. A licentious old roué he might be, but he was affable and good-humored, and I liked him.

"Ah, Miss Danver," he said in his dry, raspy voice. "Alone, I see, and looking like a goddess. If we hurry, we can dash up to my bedroom and have a quick tumble before any of the others come down."

"I fear it would be much too exhausting for you, Count Rostopchin. All those stairs."

"There's a broom closet in the back hall. One of my favorite places, that closet. If the walls could talk—"

"I'm sure my ears would burn," I said.

"I seriously doubt that," he replied. "The broom closet is out?"

"I'm afraid so, Count Rostopchin, I wouldn't want to wrinkle my gown."

He looked utterly crestfallen, then resigned. He sighed. I smiled, enjoying the light badinage as much as he.

"I suppose I'll have to suffer," he said.

"It seems you must."

"It shan't be easy. You're a delectable piece, Miss Danver."

"I'm pleased you think so."

"As a quick topple seems to be out of the question, perhaps you'll join me for a glass of wine while we wait for the others."

"I'd enjoy that."

He led me into a white and gold drawing room that might have been transported in its entirety from Versailles. Mirrors gleamed in golden frames. Crystal pendants shimmered with diamond brilliance. Another Fragonard, a portrait of Madame de Pompadour, hung over the white marble mantel. I admired it as he poured the wine.

"You like Fragonard?" he inquired, handing me a delicate glass of sparkling amber wine.

"His work is lovely indeed."

"The panels in the hall once graced the apartment of the Marechal Duc de Richelieu, First Gentleman of the Bedchamber. A most appropriate title. Now there's a man who's always enjoyed a succulent piece—still does, even in his eighties. He may be diminutive—not much taller than a twelve year-old—but that's never prevented him from enjoying a multitude of delicious liaisons and dalliances with the world's most beautiful women."

"Indeed?"

"He was Louis XV's closest confident, you know, supplied the King with mistresses. Sampled them all himself first, of course."

"Of course."

"Good friend of mine. Had a devilish time getting the panels from him. The old scamp flatly refused to part with them for any amount of money. I finally won them from him at cards."

"Cheating, no doubt."

"I always do. It's a fine art. Did you happen to notice the Boucher in your bedroom?" he asked.

"The portrait of Louison? It's a splendid work."

"Presented to me by the lady herself," he said proudly. "She was Irish, you know, Louise Murphy of Dublin, a cobbler's daughter who wound up in Paris at the ripe age of eleven and quickly became Boucher's favorite model. Pompadour saw one of the paintings and decided the lass was just the morsel to perk up the King's flagging appetite."

"Oh?"

"She was a clever one, Pompadour, realized Louis was no longer interested in her sexually. Rather than risk having a serious rival, she decided to provide him with nubile girls who would satisfy his appetite and present no threat to her position. Louison was one of those selected. She kept the King happily occupied, eventually had three children by him. It was all quite casual, Louison entertaining a number of other gentlemen during those periods when King Louis didn't require her services."

"I see."

"Delightful girl," he said. "Had a positive penchant for jewels, rubies in particular. I smothered her in 'em. I'd like to smother *you* in 'em."

"I've never cared for rubies," I said.

"Emeralds?"

"Can't abide them," I confessed.

"Diamonds, then. Never met a woman who wouldn't do anything to acquire a strand."

"You just have," I told him.

Count Rostopchin looked crestfallen again and poured himself another glass of wine. I felt wonderfully at ease with the charming old reprobate. The beige lace at his throat and wrists billowed as he crossed the room to stand beside me after pouring his wine. His rose brocade vest and frock coat were superbly cut, embroidered with floral designs in dusty rose silk.

"Gregory has done very well for himself," he remarked, his eyes admiring me.

"I'm Lucie's companion, Count Rostopchin, not her uncle's mistress."

Rostopchin elevated one thin, carefully plucked brow. "It's been a long time since I've seen him, but he can't have changed *that* much."

"He's been very considerate," I said.

"Gregory's always been considerate, but he's never before been in close proximity to a gorgeous creature like you without making a conquest—by fair means or foul. The ladies were generally willing, I might add."

"I'm not surprised."

"It got him into no end of trouble."

"So I've heard."

"Catherine finally had her fill of his infidelities, alas, gave him the gate. I fear he's never gotten over that. All these years he's been traveling about, plotting ways to win her favor again. I happen to know Catherine still thinks of him fondly, but it's much too late. The Ukrainian has firmly enslaved her."

"The Ukrainian?"

"Gregory Aleksandrovich Potemkin, 'Cyclops' as he's known in court circles. Some say he employs black magic to maintain his hold on her—he's always consulting shamans, dashing off to monasteries, going into trances. He's something of a mystic, given to black moods, sudden rages, the occasional vision. The visions somehow always seem to portend something beneficial to himself."

"Why do they call him Cyclops?" I asked.

Rostopchin smiled and took a sip of wine. "He lost one eye a number of years ago," he said. "It's quite ironic, actually. The Ukrainian possessed a marvelous talent for mimicry, and the Orlov brothers brought him to Catherine's attention, thinking he would amuse her. He promptly set about mimicking the Empress herself. The brothers were horrified. The lady was delighted—she found him wonderfully wry and witty. He became a regular visitor at the Hermitage, where Catherine entertained."

"And?"

"And the Orlov brothers grew intensely jealous of the gigantic, ungainly lout who was encroaching on their territory. There was a fight. All five of them set upon him, it's said, beat him soundly. That's when he lost his eye. If anything, the black satin patch he wore afterwards merely improved his appearance. Potemkin has the reputation of being the ugliest man in all of Russia."

"A reputation justly deserved," Bryan Lloyd said, strolling casually into the drawing room.

"Ah, our young English friend!" Rostopchin exclaimed.

He made as though to approach his guest. Lloyd held out a warning hand.

"Kiss my cheeks again and I'll punch you," he promised, "even if you *are* my host."

Rostopchin cackled, vastly amused. Bryan grinned and allowed the count to shake his hand.

"An enchanting boy, this one," Rostopchin declared. "I don't know whether to spank him or give him a glass of wine. Perhaps I'll just send him up to his room with milk and cookies. It's already past his bedtime."

"Keep it up and you're going to find yourself in one of my headlocks. I'm famous for 'em at Oxford."

Rostopchin pounded him on the back and gave him a glass of wine. The men had clearly warmed to each other, badinage aside. Bryan looked particularly appealing in brown leather pumps, white silk hose and snug tan knee breeches, his vest and frock coat of the same tan broadcloth. The latter had rich brown velvet lapels and cuffs. His dark blond hair was neatly brushed, his lean, attractive face aglow with youth and vitality.

"So you've met Potemkin?" his host inquired. "They say he frightens little children. Did you flee in terror?"

"Hardly, although I must confess I wouldn't care to run into him in a dark passage. His face is ravaged, his body bloated. He's enormous, lumbering about like an ungainly bear. Curious thing about it—the women find him absolutely irresistible. There's no accounting for it."

"Women are strange that way," Rostopchin observed.

"The man's a monster of ugliness, and they're swooning left and right from Catherine on down. He's slovenly, lazy, a complete lout in his personal habits, and they pant after him like—uh—like dogs in heat. Must be some kind of magic."

"Women are attracted by other things besides physical appearance," I informed them.

Both men gave me amazed looks. I took another sip of wine.

"Potemkin obviously has other attractions," I continued. "He's said to be quite intelligent. Maybe it's his mind that appeals to them."

"The man does have an incredible mind," Bryan admitted. "Don't know when I've ever encountered such— hypnotic intelligence. Listening to him talk I quite forgot what he looked like. Fellow held me spellbound. He has a voice like velvet, deep and dark yet softly caressing. I have to confess I found him thoroughly fascinating, if a little frightening."

"So he *did* frighten you," Rostopchin said eagerly.

"Made me a bit uneasy," Bryan admitted. "He took a fancy to me, decided to take me under his wing and make me feel welcome. He was friendly and attentive and gracious, all warmth, but I somehow had the feeling he was a cat and I was a mouse and he was amusing himself with me. The man has strange powers—I can't really explain it."

Bryan shrugged and finished the rest of his wine. The neatly brushed blond waves were already beginning to follow their natural bent, one wave tilting toward his brow, soon to slant across it. Most young men his age would have been tongue-tied and intimidated in such opulent surroundings, but Bryan was as relaxed as he would have been in his rooms at Oxford, completely at ease.

"Our young friend moves in exalted circles," Rostopchin remarked, almost as though he were reading my mind.

"My father's a diplomat," Bryan replied. "I grew up meeting the rich and powerful. Something I found out early—they're just like everyone else, only richer, more powerful. I say, mind if I have another glass of wine?"

"Help yourself," his host said.

"Rarely tasted better. French, isn't it?"

"The very best vintage. Carefully imported."

"Thought so," he said. He refilled his glass to the brim. "Anyone else want more?"

"No thank you," I said.

"Drinking is one of the few vices I fail to overindulge in," Rostopchin confided. "Finish the bottle if you like."

"Might do that," Bryan said.

"He's also quite talented," Rostopchin told me. "I have a keen interest in things theatrical, and a friend of mine sent me a copy of his play. I read it only a few weeks ago."

"You *did?*" Bryan called from across the room.

"I was speaking to Miss Danver, child."

"You actually read my play? What did you think of it? Be frank."

"I've always had a fondness for complaisant wives. Yours were most engaging, if a bit too chatty for my taste. Offhand, I'd say it probably read better than it played—too much talk, not enough stage action."

"Everyone's a critic," Bryan moaned.

"Still, an impressive achievement for a lad not yet dry behind the ears. I've no doubt your next play will be a rousing success."

Lucie and her uncle joined us a few minutes later, the latter looking incredibly handsome in pearl gray velvet breeches and frock coat and white satin vest embroidered in black. He gave me a polite nod, seeming not to notice my gold-spangled yellow gown. I felt a sharp pang of disappointment as he engaged Rostopchin in conversation and ignored my presence completely. I drank another glass of wine, damning all men, telling myself I couldn't care less if they all dropped off the face of the earth. Lucie seemed to share my opinion.

"Look at him," she snapped, "drinking like a fish!"

"Bryan does seem to enjoy his wine," I agreed.

"No manners at all! Just waved at me when I came in, then poured himself another glass. And I put this white rose in my hair just to impress him."

"It's lovely," I said.

"I wanted to look innocent."

"You do, dear."

"To hell with him!"

"I know exactly how you feel."

The dining room was done in white and gold with a pale salmon pink ceiling and ivory panels painted with delicate salmon, orange, tan, and brown flowers. A majestic chandelier hung over a table set with magnificent golden cutlery and white and orange Sèvres etched with gold. The meal was served by footmen in white satin knee breeches, salmon frock coats and powdered wigs. The food was as

gorgeous as the setting and marvelously delicious, al
though I had little appetite. The conversation was general,
dominated, of course, by the cocky young Englishman
who, prompted by our host, blithely expressed his opinions
of Russia and all things Russian.

Lucie sat in stony silence, picking at her food, making no
attempt to be social. Her uncle was amiable and relaxed,
delighted to be here with his old friend, but he wasn't enjoying himself nearly as much as he pretended. I saw that
immediately. Despite his easy smile, his good-humored
chuckles and his affable manner, he was preoccupied, giving only part of his attention to the amenities. He glanced
at me every now and then, his navy blue eyes friendly
enough, but the invisible wall was still there.

I might as well have been wearing sackcloth. My sumptuous gown was totally wasted. So was the elaborate coiffure, the tantalizing perfume. I felt like an utter fool, and I
vowed to forget all about Count Gregory Orlov. I would be
cool and polite. I would give him the three months I had
promised to give him, collect my salary, and leave this bizarre, bewildering country as quickly as possible. I toyed
with my fillet of sole, pushing a piece through a pool of rich
creamy wine sauce, longing for the meal to end.

Gracious, garrulous, teasing young Lloyd and urging
him on, Count Rostopchin seemed completely unaware
of the undercurrents affecting the rest of us. He was, I
sensed, a simple, uncomplicated man with a great capacity
for pleasure. Inept at intrigue, free of complex emotions,
he gadded through a gilded world of fashion, frivolity and
fleshly indulgence, a preposterous old scoundrel without a
serious thought in his head, immensely likeable nevertheless. The courts of Europe were filled with his kind. He
turned to me now, smiling a roguish smile.

"More wine, Miss Danver?" he inquired.

"No, thank you," I replied.

"I'll have some more," Bryan said.

"You've had quite enough," our host told him. "One

more glass and you'll undoubtedly start telling us about your next play. Eat your fish like a good little boy."

"There's going to be trouble," Bryan growled. "I must warn you that I have absolutely no compunction about beating up a man old enough to be my grandfather."

"Grandfather! I'm not a day over forty-five. These wretched lines and wrinkles you see marring my handsome visage are the results of riotous living, not encroaching old age. You're an impudent pup, sir!"

"And you're a liar. Forty-five? What a hoot!"

"I may adopt him," Rostopchin confided. "He's a joy."

"He's also drunk," Lucie said sullenly.

Bryan gave her a glowering look and decided to ignore the remark. Orlov chuckled. The footmen removed our plates and brought in the next course. I felt as though I were trapped inside a gilded cage and longed to flee, but I managed to maintain a polite, social composure, almost screaming with relief when the meal was finally over and we adjourned to the enormous library done in pale blue, white, and gold, thousands of leather-bound volumes filling the lacquered white shelves. The men had brandy. Lucie sat down at the pianoforte and began to pick out a plaintive tune. I wandered about examining the wonderful *objets d'art*, still feeling trapped.

"You admire these things?" Orlov inquired.

Perhaps fifteen minutes had passed. Lucie was still at the pianoforte, studying a piece of music. Rostopchin and Bryan were cackling over a folio of pornographic engravings, and I was gazing disconsolately at a Sèvres porcelain of a splendidly attired courtier ardently embracing a plump shepherdess in pink. Immersed in thought, I hadn't been aware of Orlov's approach, and I looked up at him in surprise.

"I—I've always admired fine porcelains," I said. "Count Rostopchin's collection is particularly lovely."

"This is so," he said.

He hadn't the least interest in porcelain, didn't so much

as look at the superbly detailed example I had been gazing at. The dark navy blue eyes with their heavy, drooping lids never left my face. The lids made him look indolent, lazy. I had never realized before just how seductive those eyes were, so dark a blue, blue-black, so attentive, making one feel so . . . so female and fragile. I lowered my gaze, feeling a faint blush tint my cheeks.

"I notice you do not eat much tonight," he said.

"I wasn't hungry," I replied.

But you noticed, I said silently.

"Does this mean you do not feel well?"

"I feel fine," I said.

"The journey is very hard on you. Soon it will be over."

"Yes."

Lucie began to finger the keys again, idly picking out a tune. Across the room, Rostopchin and Bryan had taken down another heavy folio and opened it on a table. The room was so large, the others so distant, that Orlov and I might have been alone. I seemed to be having trouble with my breathing, my bosom rising, straining against its silken prison, my nipples taut and hard as Orlov continued to gaze at me with lazy eyes. Dozens of candles created pools of golden light. The room seemed suddenly very warm, almost overwhelmingly so.

"You are uncomfortable?" he asked.

"Not at all," I lied.

He was standing so close, so close I could feel the warmth of his body and smell his skin and sweat and hair and the scent of velvet. He looked at me, and I couldn't meet those eyes, couldn't look into their depths and read the message there. I looked at his mouth, wide and firm and fleshy, curving full and pink. I remembered the touch of those lips. I tried to forget. I remembered how insistent, how assertive they had been, forcing my own apart so that his tongue could thrust and probe. The wine, I told myself. I had far too much wine. I feel weak. I feel dizzy. The room is so warm.

Bryan said something I couldn't make out. Rostopchin cackled.

"I—I like your friend very much," I said.

"Yes, Vasily is a good friend indeed."

Why was he standing so close? I could . . . I could reach up and touch that broad, flat cheekbone, the skin stretched so tautly across the bone. I longed to do just that. I caught my breath, my nipples rubbing against silk. The sensation was like a subtle caress. Orlov was fully aware of my discomfort, but he did not step back. He was so very large, so solid and muscular, his body exuding brute strength, making me feel small, vulnerable. Damn him for doing this to me, I thought, and I felt a touch of panic as smooth silk softly tormented my expanding nipples.

"He is very fond of you," I remarked.

Did my voice tremble? Why did my throat seem to ache?

"Vasily is the only one of my friends who remains loyal after my fall," Orlov said. "The others, they fade away like shadows, but Vasily remains my friend,"

"He—he certainly admires the French."

"Yes, this is—what do you English call it?—this is his chief eccentricity. The French furniture, the French art, the French clothes—is very tiresome, but it gives him pleasure. Me, I am proud to be Russian and have no patience with this passion for things French."

"I think I will go back up to my room," I said.

"I will escort you."

"That isn't necessary."

"This I will do," he said firmly.

There was no point in my protesting, no point at all. My knees seemed weak, and I was still a bit dizzy as we moved slowly across the room, Orlov close beside me. As we joined them, Bryan and Rostopchin looked up from the book spread open before them on the table. I caught a glimpse of the engravings and quickly averted my eyes. Orlov explained that I was not feeling too well, that he was going to take me up to my room. Rostopchin was concerned. I assured him I was just a little tired.

"A good night's sleep is all I need," I told him.

"You should be comfortable. The bed is very special."

"Du Barry slept in it," I said.

He arched a brow, surprised. "How did you know?"

"I guessed."

I smiled. He kissed my hand. Bryan turned the page. Lucie gave me one of her exasperated looks as Orlov and I left the room. I felt terrible, deserting her like this, but Bryan would eventually tire of the engravings and Rostopchin would leave them alone together and the two young people would undoubtedly circle each other cautiously and continue the game begun the moment they met.

Orlov and I walked down the hall, past the lovely, titillating Fragonard panels that had once belonged to Richelieu—all those billowing petticoats and naked limbs, all that exuberant sexuality in flowery surroundings. The French were obsessed by flesh, it seemed, or . . . perhaps they were simply more honest. Orlov took hold of my arm as we started up the staircase, his fingers curling tightly just above my elbow, squeezing the flesh. My skirts rustled with a silken music, gold spangles shimmering in the candlelight. I felt as though I might faint.

He maintained his grip on my arm when we reached the hallway leading to my bedroom. Neither of us had said a word since leaving the library. I wasn't sure I could speak without betraying the emotions that filled me with a sweet, familiar torment. We reached the door of my bedroom. Orlov released my arm. I turned, polite, cool on the surface, that composure hard won, impossible to maintain much longer. He looked into my eyes, still silent, and his own were twin pools of desire, dark and smoldering beneath drooping lids. His mouth tightened, the lower lip full, taut. The invisible wall was gone, the air between us charged with age-old tension.

Would he make the first move? Should I? I stood poker-stiff, so cool, my chin tilted, looking up at him with frosty composure that utterly belied the sensations stirring within. Orlov frowned, bothered, uncertain, waiting for a signal I was unable to give him. Damn my reserve. Damn my pride. He continued to gaze at me, the frown deepening, and then he stepped back, nodding curtly, and I knew it was not to be. Tonight it was not to be.

"Thank you, Count Orlov," I said politely.

"I hope you will feel better."

"I'm sure I will."

He hesitated, clearly reluctant to leave, tormented himself and either unable or unwilling to make the move both of us wanted him to make. The man celebrated for his sexual conquests was, now, as awkward and inarticulate as an adolescent boy. Why did he hesitate? He wanted me. The snug fit of his velvet breeches left no doubt about that. Why didn't he make the move, and why must I be so frostily composed when I longed to melt against him and assuage the needs consuming me?

"You—you wanted to say something else?" I asked.

He scowled, angry now, though whether with me or with himself I couldn't determine. He took a deep breath, his chest swelling.

"I do not force you," he said brusquely.

He turned and moved briskly down the hall and I went into the pink and cream room with gold gilt gleaming in the candlelight and subtle, erotic art on every side. A fire burned cozily in the fireplace. The satin bedcovers had been turned back. The room was warm, the air perfumed with the sensuous fragrance of cut flowers. The voluptuous Louison seemed to watch me as I removed my spangled silk gown and draped it over a chair. The randy shepherds and coy shepherdesses seemed to taunt me as they cavorted on the gold-framed panels. The French found it so easy, so natural, so gloriously right and uncomplicated.

I do not force you, he had said. Did he think force would be necessary? Was I so very unapproachable? Had my experience with Jeremy made me so aloof and guarded that another man was afraid to reach out to me? I suddenly realized that Orlov wasn't responsible for that invisible wall that had sprung up between us. I had created it myself. Removing the pale yellow petticoat, I put out the candles and, naked, climbed into the bed Du Barry had once used to entertain her royal lover. The bed was very large, too large for one person, and the perfumed silk sheets seemed to caress my flesh. As pale silver moonlight streamed through the windows, I gnawed my lower lip, empty, bereft, with only myself to blame.

Chapter Fourteen

LUCIE LOOKED BORED AND IRRITABLE AS WE strolled slowly down the long white gallery, examining Count Rostopchin's collection of paintings. They were, for the most part, by Boucher, Fragonard, and Watteau, of that flowery, fleshy school he seemed to admire so much. Georgeously framed, lining one wall, they were indeed beautiful, but I didn't care if I never saw another fluttering petticoat, another passionate shepherd, another flowery garland draped across a naked shoulder. Lucie seemed to feel the same way. It was early afternoon now. Both of us had slept late, lingering over breakfast in our rooms, skipping lunch.

"Louison again," Lucie remarked. "Boucher must have painted her hundreds of times. Insipid little thing, isn't she?"

"She's quite pretty."

"Much too plump," Lucie declared. "Look at those vacuous eyes. You can tell she never had a serious thought in her life."

"I don't imagine she had to think all that much."

"Do men really *like* that? Do they really want a plump, curvy little imbecile?"

"I've no idea what men want," I said dryly.

"I thought you were an expert?"

"If I were an expert, my dear, I wouldn't be strolling down a gallery with a sulky young woman."

"There's no need to be bitchy about it."

"You, my dear, do not have a monopoly on bitchiness."

"Let's don't fight," she said. "I did quite enough fighting last night, thank you."

"Oh?"

"With Bryan," she replied.

We paused in front of a majestic, full-length portrait of Louis XIV by Hyacinthe Rigaud. The Sun King stood with one hand on his hip, the other leaning on a golden cane. An ermine-lined, black velvet robe embroidered with gleaming gold *fleurs-de-lis* seemed to engulf him, although his legs were bare, red heels and white silk stockings making him seem a bit more human. The puffy, sensual face was framed by a curly black wig much too large for him.

"Did he use one of his famous holds on you?" I asked.

"He tried," she said. "Rostopchin, the old devil, left us alone shortly after you and my uncle left. Bryan tried to interest me in those wretched engravings. I told him I wasn't interested. He told me I might find them quite educational. Can you imagine?"

"I can imagine."

"The cheek! I played it cool and demure, the proper young maiden. Perdita never gave a better performance. He told me I needed to loosen up. He said I had no idea what I was missing."

"If only he knew."

"That was cruel, Marietta."

"I know, darling. It was unforgivable. I—I'm terribly sorry. I had a very bad night."

"No harm done," she said. "It happens to be true—I've had more experience than that—that callow youth ever dreamed of having, and I felt like a bloody hypocrite, fluttering my lashes, attempting to blush. I was quite convincing, though."

"He retreated?"

"On the contrary, he advanced all the more. You're right—Englishmen *do* find innocence intriguing. I suppose it's their desire to corrupt. Corrupting me was definitely on the agenda last night."

"What did he do?"

"He took my hand. He looked deeply into my eyes and told me there was a world of pleasure he longed to show me. His voice was low, his eyes dark and dreamy. I almost laughed in his face. I figured it would be a serious tactical error."

"Definitely."

"He ran his hand up my arm, took hold of my shoulder, squeezed it gently, terribly sincere. He told me I was the most beautiful creature he had ever seen, told me he'd perish on the spot if he couldn't savor the sweetness of my perfect pink mouth."

"No wonder his play was a failure," I said. "If he used lines like that it's a miracle they didn't stone him."

"I wish they *had.*"

"Not really, dear."

"Not really," she confessed. "He squeezed my shoulder with one hand and touched my throat with the other and parted his lips, all sleepy and seductive, looking like a moon-sick calf. I drew back, timid, confused. He pulled me into his arms and crooned that he would never, never hurt me, and then he kissed me for a very long time."

"How was it?"

"Divine. I don't know that I've ever been kissed so—so thoroughly. He certainly knows what he's doing. I struggled like a kitten. He tightened his arms."

"And then?"

"And then I broke loose and slapped him so hard he went reeling backward and fell flat on his bottom. I felt rather bad about that, but instinct told me it was the right thing to do. He was livid—rightfully so, I suppose. He pulled himself up and glared at me and told me I was a spoiled, silly little simp who hadn't a clue what life was all about."

"And you said?"

"I said I knew what *he* was about, all right. I told him I found his juvenile attempts at seduction insulting to my intelligence. He looked like he wanted to murder me."

"I shouldn't wonder."

"He shouted some more and then stormed out of the room. He's not accustomed to being rejected."

"Apparently not."

"I didn't want to reject him," she admitted. "He may be churlish and a bit too sure of himself, but—he's terribly appealing."

"I agree."

"That cocky, confident manner of his is—is really merely a defense. Beneath it all he's terribly serious and quite insecure."

"He needs a steadying influence," I said.

"Exactly."

We moved down the gallery, eyeing more Bouchers, more Fragonards, more flowery Watteaus. There was a portrait of Madame de Montespan by Mignard, an interesting study of Louis XIV as Mars, a landscape by Boucher blessedly free of cupids and naked nymphs. Lucie seemed thoughtful now, a pensive expression in her violet-blue eyes. In her simple dusty rose frock, with lustrous golden brown waves streaming down her back, she looked every bit as innocent as Bryan Lloyd believed her to be.

"I—I keep thinking about the conversation we had back in London," she said quietly. "You were so—so understanding. You told me I should save myself for the right young man. I—it was very hard, but I promised myself I wouldn't—wouldn't do those things anymore."

"Lucie—"

"These past months, I've learned to respect myself. I've even learned to like myself—at least a little. Having a friend like you has helped. I know I would never have been able to keep my promise if I hadn't had you."

"I've been an awful bitch at times."

"So have I," she said. "Last night I—I almost broke my promise to myself. I've never met anyone like him. I've never *felt* this way about anyone before. It's not just wanting to sleep with him—"

"I know, darling."

"Do you think I could be in love?"

"I think it's highly possible."

"Damn! Wouldn't you know it would be someone utterly impossible. I wish I'd never met him."

"I know that feeling."

"Celibacy may be admirable," she complained, "but it's damned hard on a person."

I wisely refrained from comment. Lucie sighed and tossed her head, lustrous waves swaying. We had reached the end of the gallery and turned back, eventually reaching the main hallway. The house was silent. The men had gone out much earlier. When she saw the magnificent gold and white porcelain clock on one of the tables, Lucie let out a little gasp.

"I must fly!" she exclaimed. "I promised Bryan I'd meet him at the stables at two."

I looked surprised at that. She smiled ruefully.

"He knocked on my door this morning," she told me. "He was very serious and sober and contrite. He asked me to forgive him for his unbecoming conduct last night, said he'd had too much to drink. He vowed he'd be a perfect gentleman if only I'd let him make amends. I was terribly sweet and understanding."

"Of course."

"It's almost two. I have to change. I'll see you later, Marietta."

She hurried down the hall and raced nimbly up the stairs, waves bouncing, dusty rose skirt fluttering wildly. I watched her with a satisfaction not untinged with envy. She was a young girl in love, with all those charming mannerisms such a state imposed, and when I thought of the miserable, self-tormenting creature she had been in England I was amazed at the transformation. If I had had something to do with it, then all these months of hardship and frustration had been worthwhile.

I wandered idly about the great house, encountering no one but an occasional silent footman, and I had the feeling I was adrift in an empty, luxurious ship. I was sad, rest-

less. My cheeks were pale. There were faint gray shadows
beneath my eyes. I selected a book from the library and
tried to concentrate on it, but it was futile. I put the book
aside and resumed my wandering, admiring the splendor
on every side, beginning to find it oppressive. Eventually I
found myself at the entrance to an enormous glass conservatory that had been appended to the east side of the house.

I stepped inside, closing the door behind me. Brilliant afternoon sunlight streamed down through the domed glass
ceiling, gilding the vivid green leaves of hundreds of exotic
trees and plants. There were flowers, too, opulent cream
and mauve orchids speckled with gold, purple bougainvillaea in thick strands, roses of every description. I marveled
that they could be blooming at this time of year, the
ground outside covered with thick white blankets of snow.
The moist, warm air inside was laden with heady fra-
grances, a dozen perfumes mingling, blending to produce a
scent that was almost intoxicating.

The glass walls and ceiling were beaded with moisture.
Moisture dripped from pale green fronds, from large, rub-
bery green-black leaves, from spikes of the richest emerald
and jade. I was amazed to see pineapples growing, to see
palm trees and bizarre shrubs that must have come from
the Orient. Here, too, I knew, Rostopchin was following
the example of Empress Catherine who had had a spectacular domed glass conservatory built on the roof of the
Winter Palace, filling it with shrubs, trees, plants, and
flowers from all over the world. I stroked a satiny green
leaf, fingered a strand of delicate yellow-green ivy, gazed
in wonderment at long green stalks that spouted marvelous bird-shaped flowers of orange and blue. Water dripped,
pattering softly. The moist air seemed to caress my skin.

Turning a corner, I came across a bed of moss, a bank of
ferns. Growing in glazed white pots were a dozen rose
bushes, each in full bloom, the roses a gloriously subtle
shade of pink, rich yet delicately pale, a perfect pink, the
pink of a fragile shell. Pink was furled in tight buds. Velvety petals spread and swelled in full-blown pink roses. I

had never seen such beautiful flowers, the sight of them so poignantly lovely it almost brought tears to my eyes. It was as I was examining these roses that the door to the conservatory opened. I heard footsteps approaching. I turned.

Count Gregory Orlov walked down aisles of greenery toward me.

I wasn't surprised. Not really. I stood there in front of the blaze of pink roses in my simply cut tan silk frock, watching him approach. He had removed his jacket and vest. He wore brown leather knee boots and snug brown breeches and a full-sleeved, loosely fitting shirt of thin beige silk, opened at the throat, the garment bagging where it had been casually tucked into the waistband of his breeches. He paused a few feet away from me, placing his hands on his thighs. He looked at me. He didn't speak, nor did I. A long moment passed.

"I come looking for you," he finally said. "One of the footmen tells me he sees you going toward the conservatory."

"You've been out?" I asked.

"Rostopchin and I leave early this morning. We ride around the estate. He points with pride to the improvements he has made. Me, I am bored. I want only to speak with you. I can think of nothing else."

"Where—where is Count Rostopchin now?"

"He goes to the summerhouse to placate his mistress. She is a Frenchwoman, an actress. She is irate that he banishes her to the summerhouse during the time of our visit. She throws a tantrum. Vasily finds it amusing. Me, I would beat her."

"You would beat a woman?"

"If she deserved it. This Minette, I meet her. She is a skinny, painted shrew, very rude and spiteful. I long to beat her black and blue, but then I am in a very bad mood at the time."

"Oh?"

"I am thinking of you, thinking of all the things I wish to

say. I am impatient to be gone, but Vasily insists we stop so that I can meet his treasure. He does not wish to have her in the house while you and Lucie are here. Vasily is very proper about these matters."

"I see."

"I search the house. I find you at last."

"This is a wondrous place," I said quietly.

"There are things I need to say."

"These roses—look at them, Gregory. The petals are like soft pink velvet. I—they're so beautiful I could cry."

"I do not see them. I see only you."

"Please—"

"Last night I wish to make love to you."

"I—I don't think I care to hear this. Talk is—"

"You shall," he said. His voice was firm. "Last night I see you in the golden gown and my throat aches, my muscles tighten, I am filled with passionate desire. I control myself. I can barely sit at the dinner table. I wish to roar like a madman each time I glance at you."

"Gregory—"

"In the library, I watch you. You look so sad, so lost. It is time, I think. It is time I make her forget about this man she grieves for. It is time I force her to forget. I go over to you. I am polite. You are polite, too, and cold, as cold as ice."

"I—I didn't—"

"You shut up. You listen. I take you upstairs, planning to force you to acknowledge my passion. All this time I wait and wait, so patient, and I tell myself I cannot wait any longer. I must have you. I want you so much I am ready to drive my fist through the wall."

His hands were balled into fists now, and his handsome face was stern, the navy blue eyes dark, determined. His tawny golden brown hair was slightly damp, and his skin was damp, too, moistened by the air. I gazed at him, beautifully calm, all inner turmoil resolved. His thin beige silk shirt clung lightly to his chest, and a tiny rivulet of moisture ran down his temple.

"I wish to tell you this last night as we stand in front of your door," he said.

"Why didn't you?" I asked.

"You are like the block of ice, lovely, aloof."

"If only you knew," I said.

"I leave you. I go out to join my men in the quarters Vasily has provided for them. He has also generously provided women for them, six healthy peasant girls with rosy cheeks and flaxen hair. They giggle and titter and make the eyes. I drink much vodka. I take one of these plump girls and make love with her. I am fierce and strong. I pound and pound until she cries out for me to stop."

I was silent. He scowled.

"I tell you this because it is important you know what I am feeling. I take this girl and use her roughly because I cannot have you. All the time I am thrusting inside her I am seeing you in my mind. I am longing for you to be beneath me."

"I see," I said.

"You are shocked by this?"

"No, Gregory, I'm not shocked."

"You are offended?"

I shook my head. He looked bewildered now, all the vehemence gone, his face glistening with moisture. It seemed to droop wearily, the soft roll of flesh beneath his chin more pronounced. Water dripped all around us with a quiet pattering sound. Leaves rustled in the warm air. Gregory reached up to brush a damp wisp of hair from his brow. I turned to look at the roses again, touching one delicate shell pink petal with the ball of my thumb.

"I should not have told you these things," he said.

His voice sounded strained. I could feel him standing there behind me, his presence so strong it seemed to fill the air with energy. I stroked the rose petal, in command now, in control. I felt that age-old power every woman feels when she knows the game is hers.

"Now I have spoiled things," he told me.

"No, Gregory."

I turned back around. He was ill at ease, shifting his weight from one leg to the other. He was perspiring freely, the thin silk shirt moist, hanging limply now. His eyes were full of misery. Men are so dense, I thought, so slow to comprehend the things women know instinctively. I smiled at him, confusing him all the more, and he frowned.

"You make me crazy," he said roughly. "Never have I known a woman who makes me feel like—like a great, stupid ox."

"I'm sorry."

"I look at you and I want to smash something. This is the only way to release these feelings boiling inside me."

"The only way?"

"If you were a peasant woman or a whore I would know what to do, and I would not hesitate, but you are a fine lady. I fear to offend you. I fear you will think me a brute, a boor."

"Poor Gregory."

"You taunt me?"

"You have far too many fears," I said lightly.

He frowned again, puzzled. "This means?"

"This means no woman likes to be placed on a pedestal for too long. A time comes when she longs to be brought down to earth and made to feel she's flesh and blood. Kindly extend my apologies to Count Rostopchin," I continued. "Tell him I will not be dining downstairs tonight. I prefer to remain in my room."

I left him there, moving slowly, serenely down the dripping green aisles. I left the conservatory without looking back. I fetched a book from the library and took it to my room and read, peaceful and content, and later as the light began to fade, as shadows gathered on the snow, and pink and orange banners melted on the horizon, I found a servant and requested a bath, and I bathed in perfumed water and washed my hair, reveling in the rich lather and the delicious warmth of the water. Bath things removed by two husky footmen, candles glowing, a fire crackling quietly in the fireplace, I dried my hair. Louison seemed to watch from over the mantel, her dark, seductive eyes understanding all, approving.

No elaborate coiffure tonight. I let my hair fall free in a rich tumble of waves. They glistened with a deep red-gold sheen in the candlelight. No spangled gown tonight either. I donned a petticoat of frail, cobweb-colored lace with a form-fitting bodice that half concealed, half revealed the flesh beneath. The full skirts floated like smoke as I moved across the room, and I smiled to myself as I slipped on the gown of pale pearl gray satin printed with tiny sapphire and silver flowers. The cloth was sumptuous, the gown itself simple and elegant in cut with a full skirt that spread in gleaming folds.

I waited. It was dark outside now, moonlight gilding the snow with a silvery sheen, candles creating a warm golden glow inside. It was after eight when I heard the expected knock on the door. I opened it, surprised to see a scowling, disapproving Vladimir instead of one of Count Rostopchin's servants. I stepped aside. Vladimir entered, followed by three other servants who carried a small round table, two gilt chairs, and various other items. I watched silently as the table was set up in a corner, covered with a snowy white cloth, two places set with gorgeous bone china adorned with blue and gold and solid silver cutlery, all under the scowling supervision of Vladimir.

He finally nodded his approval. The other three servants left, returning a few moments later with dishes of food and a silver bucket with a slender bottle nestling in ice. Vladimir continued to scowl as dishes and bucket were placed on the table, and then, giving me a long, fierce look, he jerked his head toward the door, ordering his men out, following them a moment later. Not a word had been spoken. I closed the door behind them, totally unperturbed by Vladimir's hostility. By this time I had long since grown immune to it.

Several minutes passed. Draped in her garland of flowers, naked flesh glowing pink in the candlelight, Louison seemed to wait too, smiling coyly. Du Barry's bed stood in gold and white splendor, the shell pink satin counterpane smooth and inviting. If ever a room was designed with seduction in mind, it was this one. Candles flickered, washing everything with a golden haze. The air was softly perfumed, filled with a subtle, erotic atmosphere. Boucher's shepherds and shepherdesses cavorted on the panels in soft, delicate hues. A delicious anticipation tingled inside me as I waited for him to join me.

He knocked. I opened the door. He smiled, peering at me over an armful of roses, the glorious pink roses I had admired earlier in the conservatory.

"I bring these," he said. "I hope to please you."

"I'm very pleased."

"I cut them myself," he continued. "I carefully remove every thorn. I jab my thumb quite bad, bring blood."

"Poor dear," I said. "Did it hurt?"

"I hardly notice. I suck the blood away and go on cutting. I want to do this job myself. I do not call a servant."

"It was very thoughtful of you."

I led him inside the room. He pushed the door shut behind him. I took the roses from him and placed them carefully on the dressing table.

"You tell me you do not dine downstairs tonight. You say you remain in your room. You must eat, I tell myself. I take the liberty of arranging a light meal."

"How kind."

"I come to join you. You are displeased?"

"What do you think?"

"I think maybe you are glad to see me," he said.

His voice was a deep, husky rasp. His hooded navy blue eyes took in my glistening hair, my naked shoulders and the sumptuous low-cut satin gown. It was hardly the garment one would wear to spend an evening alone in one's room. Orlov had read my subtle invitation correctly, all right, and he had the exultant, confident manner men have when they know a certain conquest is in the offing, sexual energy carefully, impatiently contained, a good-humored glow suffusing from within. He grinned, a wide, lovely grin that perfectly expressed his expectations.

He was wearing supple gray leather knee boots and clinging gray breeches that fit his muscular legs like a second skin. His fine white lawn shirt was as thin as air, bagging slightly at the waist, opened at the throat, the full sleeves gathered at the wrist. Casual, elegant attire, much more appropriate than gold-frogged velvet uniform, I thought. With his rich golden brown hair attractively tousled he looked like an aging choirboy, wonderfully virile and spectacularly handsome, exuding magnetism quite impossible to resist.

"Let me see your thumb," I said.

He held it out. I took it in my hand, examining the narrow cut outlined with tiny clots of dried blood. I stroked it lightly. His huge fingers curled around my hand, clasping it firmly, his thumb gently scratching the inside of my palm. Tantalizing sensations stirred as his fingers uncurled and wrestled with mine, squeezing, pressing, bending. My knuckles cracked as he bent my fingers back clasping them tighter. He grinned again, pink lips stretching wide, dark eyes gleaming.

"I hurt you?" he asked.

"I'm afraid you don't know your own strength."

"I know my strength," he said. "Later on I show you."

"Oh?"

"Me, I have the stamina of ten."

"I've always found boasting unbecoming."

"I do not boast. I speak the facts."

"We'll see," I said, pulling my hand free.

"I am so happy. I want to throw my arms wide and embrace the world. I want to yell until my throat is raw. For months I look forward to this night. For months I dream of it. I think you do not want me. I fear I will frighten you away if I say the things I long to say."

"I—I needed time," I said.

"This I realize. I give you lots of time. I suffer. I scowl. I pound my pillow with my fists because I want you so much, because you are not there beneath me to receive my gift of passion."

The words might have been ludicrous coming from another man, but he was Russian, and florid melodrama was perfectly natural to him. I smiled anyway, turning away from him, moving to stand in front of the fireplace. Gregory looked at me, feasting his eyes, the bulge in his breeches growing more and more pronounced. For all his need, he was in no hurry, nor was I. Both of us knew the tantalizing delights of prolongation. He sauntered lazily toward me and stood in front of me, looking down at my face, my bare shoulders, the swelling curve of my half-exposed bosom.

"Never have I known so beautiful a woman," he crooned huskily. "Never have I wanted so strongly, waited so long."

"You must have known dozens of women."

"Hundreds," he said. "None of them like you."

He took hold of my arms and tilted his head, lips parted. He pulled me toward him and lowered his head and I tilted mine back and his fingers tightened on my arms and our lips met and sweet splendor blossomed inside. After a long, long minute, he drew back, his dark eyes glowing, a smile curling on those lips so recently caressing my own.

"I open the wine now," he said.

He stepped over to the table and grasped the neck of the slender bottle and pulled it out of the ice. Pressing his strong thumbs against the cork, he began to ease it out, grimacing in concentration as he did so. It flew free with a loud pop, shooting across the room. A foamy amber spray fizzed in the air like a miniature geyser. Orlov jumped back, startled. I smiled as he fumbled about and finally filled two fragile crystal glasses, bringing them over and handing one to me.

"I am very clumsy," he admitted.

"But endearing," I said in English.

He did not understand. "This is good?" he asked.

"Very good," I told him.

The wine was ice-cold and deliciously tangy with tiny gold bubbles dancing in the glass. I sipped it slowly. Orlov drank his own, watching me all the while over the rim of the glass. Those hooded, seductive eyes glowed darkly and told me I was the most beautiful, the most desirable woman in the world, the only woman who could make him feel such passion. Although I was much too wise in such matters to believe this silent flattery, it was wonderful to see that look in a man's eyes once again, reassuring to know I still had the ability to cause it.

He finished his wine and smiled a provocative smile, his hair burnished dark gold in the candlelight, his face brushed with shadow, planes and angles pronounced. I held the wineglass with my right hand, and his fingers curled over mine, lifting the glass to my lips. I took another sip, and he continued to guide my hand until the glass was empty.

"Now I feed you," he murmured.

He led me over to the table and, hands on my shoulders, gently pushed me into one of the chairs. He lifted my hair and kissed the back of my neck and I arched my back, my breasts straining against their satin prison. Chuckling softly, Gregory moved around and spread a thin sliver of toast with glistening caviar and sprinkled it lightly with finely diced onion and boiled egg. He stood over me. I opened my mouth, took a bite. He nodded with approval, feeding me the rest of the toast as though I were an invalid and he my tender caretaker.

"Good?" he inquired.

"Delicious."

"Now the specialty," he said.

He lifted a silver lid to reveal a plate of raw oysters on pearly half shells. They gleamed a wet silver-gray with a faint pinkish sheen. I shook my head and told him that raw oysters were not my favorite thing. Orlov ignored me, spearing one with a small silver fork.

"These are special. The chef marinates them in spiced wine. They are love food, make you feel very sensual."

"I'd rather not—"

He curled one hand around my neck and tilted my head back until I gazed at the ceiling. He squeezed lightly, forcing me to open my mouth, and I felt the oyster slipping over my tongue. I bit, swallowed, felt it sliding down my throat. The taste was subtle, exotic, pleasing indeed. He smiled when he saw my expression, spearing another shimmering oyster, feeding it to me, and I felt a glorious ache stirring inside.

"You like?" he crooned.

I nodded, wonderfully indolent, and he placed his hands on my shoulders, looming over me, so large, so magnetic, the thin white lawn shirt belling as he leaned down to cover my mouth with his own. That glorious ache spread inside me as his lips pressed and probed, parting mine, his tongue slipping inside my mouth as easily as the oysters, long and firm, the tip jabbing lightly at the back of my throat. My head seemed to whirl as he straddled me and lowered himself, his buttocks resting heavily on my thighs, his long legs stretching out on either side of the chair. He wrapped one arm around the back of my neck, leaning against me, crushing me, kissing me with a tender fury that went on and on until my senses shredded.

He tightened his legs around my thighs and shifted until he was even closer, his swollen manhood pressing hard against my abdomen through the layers of cloth. The chair creaked, wobbled dangerously, and I feared it would collapse under our weight, but I didn't care, I didn't care at all. His free hand dug into the bodice of my gown, fingers probing beneath the thin lace undergarment to curl tightly around my breast, squeezing so tightly I winced, my nipple swelling against his palm. His mouth held mine captive, smothering moans of ecstasy.

I was spinning, whirling in a delirious void of sensations that exploded inside with shattering force. Never, never had I felt such furious need, and I remembered what he had said about the oysters and knew they must have been doctored with some aphrodisiac and didn't care about that either, didn't care at all. I held on to him, my hands moving over the sculpted muscles of his back, exploring the width of his shoulders, finally catching hold of his hair and tugging violently as his hand squeezed my breast and his kisses continued to torment and the chair tilted dangerously.

He climbed to his feet and took my hand and pulled me out of the chair. My legs were so weak I would have fallen had he not curled his arm around my shoulder, supporting me, guiding me over to the bed. The fury inside me had begun to ebb, changing into a tingling ache, as though my blood had thickened and coursed slowly through my veins like warm honey. When Gregory let go of me I was surprised to find that I could stand. I watched him pull the shell pink counterpane back, revealing the silken sheets, and I seemed to be seeing it through a soft haze, everything faintly blurred. The golden light of candles seemed to melt into mist, and the delicately colored figures on the panels seemed to come alive, dancing in the mist.

Gregory stepped behind me and began to unfasten the tiny invisible hooks that fastened the back of my gown. He did it with practiced skill, his large fingers nimble and sure. He's done this many, many times, a voice whispered in my mind. The bodice loosened, dipping forward, finally falling as he took hold of the sleeves and slipped them down my arms. Sumptuous folds of gleaming pearl gray satin spilled to the floor, the tiny sapphire and silver flowers melting into the cloth. I stepped out of the circle, the cobweb-colored skirts of my petticoat floating on air. Gregory picked up my gown and draped it over a chair and turned and stood with his hands on his hips, gazing at me with lazy eyes, a smile spreading on his lips.

My flesh was visible beneath the frail cloth of my petticoat, as though seen through soft gray smoke, my full breasts lightly veiled, taut pink nipples pressing against the tissue-thin lace. The skirts covered my legs like swirls of smoke. Gregory gazed, savoring the sight as the honey-sweet lethargy spread through me, tingling, tormenting. I would die, I would dissolve if that ache were not soon assuaged, and he knew it. Was that smile faintly mocking? Why had he given me the oysters? Did he think the aphrodisiac was necessary? I closed my eyes for a moment, whirling slowly through the void, and then I stepped out of my shoes and removed the smoky petticoat, tossing it aside, watching it float to the floor.

He did not move. He continued to smile, lazy, in no hurry at all, prolonging that ultimate pleasure in order to relish it more. I raised my arms and stroked the back of my neck, lifting the heavy coppery red waves up, letting them spill through my fingers. Gregory grinned and strolled over to the dressing table and gathered up the pale pink roses and then sauntered toward me. Holding one rose by its long stem, he clutched the rest of them against his chest and, grinning still, began to stroke my body with the velvety soft petals of the single rose, causing sensations I never dreamed possible. The lethargy turned into throbbing agony as the petals gently caressed my throat, my breasts, whipping lightly across my nipples, gliding down my stomach. My knees buckled. He gave me a rough shove. I fell onto the bed, writhing on the ivory silk sheets.

Slowly, with lazy deliberation, he ripped the petals from the roses and pelted me with them. The petals were soft, soft, thin flakes of pink velvet, yet I could feel each one strike my skin. I turned this way and that, moaning, trying to elude that soft shower, and Gregory Orlov chuckled, scattering a final handful over me, tossing the stems aside. Petals spilled over my naked body, slipping beneath me, their perfume filling the air with an intoxicating fragrance. Gregory looked down at me, his erection throbbing painfully against the snug gray cloth encasing it, yet his manner was still indolent and relaxed.

"I make this a night to remember," he promised in a husky purr.

He moved about the room, blowing out the candles one by one, and as the hazy golden light vanished, a silvery mist of moonlight spilled in through the windows, brushing surfaces with a pale sheen, intensifying the blue-gray shadows that filled the corners. I could see him clearly as he sat down to pull off his boots. He set them aside, peeled off his stockings and, barefooted, stood with legs apart, slowly removing the thin white lawn shirt, letting it float to the floor like a soft shred of cloud. Hooking his thumbs inside the waistband of his breeches, he pulled them down, leaning over, stepping out of them, naked now, looking like an animated Roman statue in the misty silver light, but no statue had ever possessed such a manhood. It seemed to stretch and strain toward its goal, throbbing with a life all its own.

He padded slowly through moonlight and shadow and stopped at the side of the bed, proudly displaying his virility. I closed my eyes, unable to endure another moment of this excruciating torment. I felt the mattress sag and felt his knees between mine and I spread my legs and he lowered himself and I cried out as that warm, pulsating tip entered with torturing slowness, a fraction of an inch at a time, stretching me on a rack of pain that seemed to pull my limbs apart and brought pleasure beyond compare. With dazzling expertise and inhuman control he continued to tantalize and torture, shredding my senses, denying his own pleasure in order to prolong mine, still rigid and as strong as steel as I hurtled into a shattering oblivion of ecstasy.

Again he stretched me on that rack and led me to the brink of blissful destruction, and this time, when I had arrived, he allowed himself to participate in my pleasure, sharing it with shuddering glee, and later, during the night, I woke up to find the moonlight gone and darkness like black velvet shrouding the room and felt his hands exploring my body and I stretched, aching, bruised, the ashes of aftermath still warm, filling me with that delicious glow that made my blood tingle. I moved nearer, curling my arms around him, and he shifted positions and pulled me under him and we shared new splendors, a rough and rousing bout this time, the springs creaking loudly, limbs thrashing, my nails clawing his back, his teeth sinking into my shoulder, both of us lost to a wild abandon that knew no bounds.

When I woke up the next time, the room was filled with a soft pinkish light that slanted through the windows in softly diffused rays, gradually melting into gold. I was all alone in Du Barry's bed, and I doubted that that celebrated lady had ever experienced such incredible physical bliss. The man who had provided it was perched on the edge of a chair in his gray breeches, struggling to pull on the supple leather knee boots. He was shirtless, and as he leaned over I saw the broad curve of his naked back, crisscrossed with four thin red trails where my nails had clawed. I sat up against the pillows and pulled the rumpled ivory silk sheet over my breasts, gloriously replete, my hair spilling over my shoulders in a copper red tangle.

I watched as he got one boot on and smoothed the thin leather up over his calf. Golden brown hair spilled over his brow as he leaned forward, the tawny locks damp. His muscular torso was coated with a faint sheen of perspiration. I understood now why Empress Catherine had kept him so long, tolerated so much from him. Gregory Orlov was the consummate master of the art of love, his incredible technique a veritable marvel of expertise. One couldn't take him seriously, of course. He could be very engaging and one could be terribly fond of him, but there was no danger of a deep emotional involvement. What a splendid pet for a woman to enjoy.

He picked up the fine white lawn shirt and stood and, seeing that I was awake, grinned lazily, looking at me with hooded eyes. Misty golden pink light bathed him as he raised the shirt.

"You feel good?" he asked.

"I feel battered."

"Me, I feel very, very happy." He pulled the shirt over his shoulders and adjusted the hang. "This afternoon we leave for St. Petersburg. As soon as we get there I make all the arrangements."

"Arrangements?" I was puzzled.

"For our wedding," he informed me.

Stunned, I stared at him. He tucked the tail of the shirt loosely into the waistband of his breeches. Oh Lord, I thought. Oh Lord. What on earth have I gotten myself into?

BOOK THREE

Chapter Fifteen

I SLOWED NATASHA TO A WALK, IN NO HURRY at all to get back to the Marble Palace, and Vanya caught up, slowing his horse, too, riding along beside me, fierce and savage-looking in his fur cap and cloak. He was heavily armed, as were the two other cossacks who followed. It was a gorgeous, sun-spangled day, much too gorgeous to stay inside, and Vanya had agreed to go for a ride with me, ordering two of his friends to come along for added protection. There was no danger in St. Petersburg, but Vanya insisted on this precaution.

We had ridden to the great harbor at Kronstadt, west of the city, where the powerful Russian navy was headquartered. The river Neva provided a natural outlet to the Baltic Sea, and ships from all over the world sailed into the harbor, bringing exotic goods. I had been amazed at the size and splendor of the place. One of the largest and busiest ports in the world, Kronstadt was like a gigantic doorway giving Russia an opening to Europe and the rest of the world. Peter the Great had planned it that way. In St. Petersburg one did not feel closed in and landlocked. One had the feeling that . . . that escape was possible.

We were on our way back now. It had been a long ride, and I felt pleasantly tired. The ride had done me good. We had arrived in St. Petersburg ten days ago, and they had been ten days of intense emotional strain. It was glorious to be out in the open, bathed in sunlight, breathing fresh, crisp air, with magnificent vistas everywhere. We were passing through Peterhof, and on our left, beyond terraced gardens and amazing fountains, rose the immense white and gold palace of Peter the Great, an incredibly beautiful sight with its long wings and gleaming white marble steps. I sighed as we rode on, still amazed by the splendor. To our right, behind the graceful white marble balustrade, snowy slopes led down to the Neva, an awesome river that flowed like a gigantic blue-gray-green ribbon unfurling in the sunlight. In the distance ahead St. Petersburg spread out like a fairy-tale city, a wondrous place indeed.

It was surely one of the most beautiful cities in the world, I thought, and certainly one of the most fascinating. Built along the riverbank, it was stunning to behold with its majestic buildings and breathtaking white marble palaces, its spacious gardens and squares. The many canals and bridges brought Amsterdam to mind, while the magnificent Nevsky Prospekt with its glittering, elegant shops put any street in Paris to shame. The center of culture and commerce, St. Petersburg far outshone the less-favored Moscow. Moscow was for the masses, St. Petersburg the swank playground of pampered aristocrats who thronged to its theaters and opera houses, danced in its marble halls. The Admiralty dominated the city, along with the Winter Palace, and the hundreds of handsome naval officers were the delight of pretty shopgirls and worldly countesses who were bored with the blue-blooded fare at court. Awash with delicious scandal and political intrigue, the city exuded an aura of robust sophistication.

"I still can't believe that seventy some odd years ago this was all just a swamp," I said.

"It was desolate marshland," Vanya told me. "Peter the Great decides to build a city here on the banks of the Neva. He wants *a window to Europe,* he says. People tell him it is impossible to build a city over a swamp, but nothing is impossible to Peter."

Vanya scowled. I could tell that he had no fondness for that great ruler. He drew his horse closer to Natasha, staring at the city we approached.

"He has thousands of peasants sink a forest of piles, has them fill it in with dirt they have carried in bags and inside their blouses. They work under incredible hardships. Many, many of them die, and their bodies are tossed into the swamp along with the piles and the dirt. There are those who will tell you St. Petersburg is built upon the bones of the workers."

"How—how dreadful," I said.

Vanya shrugged his shoulders as though to imply that this huge loss of human life was totally insignificant, but the look in his eyes said otherwise. I was reminded of the fact that, although he wore Orlov's colors and devoted his life to the service of the aristocracy, Vanya was from the people, as were most of the other cossacks. His grandfather might well have been one of the peasants who died filling in the swamp.

"But Peter has his city," he continued. "Once the swamp is filled he brings his architects and more workers and his dream city materializes. He orders a thousand of the nobility to leave Moscow and build houses here on the banks of the Neva. They have no choice in the matter. They obey. A like number of merchants and shopkeepers are ordered to set up business in the city, and workers skilled in various arts and crafts are shipped here to join them. He names the city St. Petersburg after his patron saint, and the world marvels over the miracle he has wrought."

This was a long speech for Vanya, and I was surprised at his bitterness. He lapsed into moody silence as we rode into the city. I saw it with new eyes now, and as I gazed at the magnificent splendor I couldn't help thinking of those peasants who had died bringing the place into being. The sun continued to splash radiant light over waterways and parks, gilding marble columns, but the depression I had been fighting for days took hold now and turned everything gray.

"You enjoy seeing the harbor?" Vanya asked as we crossed the Nevsky Prospekt.

"It was very impressive."

"Your eyes are sad as you gaze at the ships," he said. "I feel you wish to be on one of them. You are not happy in Russia."

"I—I don't belong here, Vanya."

"Vanya understands. It is not your land, your people. You wish to be in this place you tell me about, this Texas."

"It seems so far away."

"Soon you will be leaving. Vanya will miss you."

"I'll miss you, too," I told him.

We rode on in silence, Natasha prancing restlessly, wanting to race again and not at all happy at the slow canter I imposed upon her. We crossed another bridge, nearing the Marble Palace now, and I felt myself tightening up as I thought about Orlov and the strain between us. I had no idea how I would resolve the situation or, indeed, if it could be resolved, but I firmly refused to marry him. He was as firmly determined that I would and chose to believe I was merely being coy. What woman would turn down the honor of becoming the wife of Count Gregory Orlov? He believed he could wear me down with gifts and calm reasoning. I returned the gifts. I refused to listen to reason. The situation had grown steadily worse since our arrival, and Orlov's patience was wearing dangerously thin.

I tried to relax as we turned into the drive. The Marble Palace stood in its own private park, the trees bare now, silvered with ice, the gardens white with snow, but the palace itself was still one of the wonders of the city. It was large and dignified, a handsome structure, not nearly as ornate as some of the other palaces. The source of wonderment was the exterior walls, which consisted of alternate bands of pink marble from Finland and blue marble from Siberia, the colors soft and harmonious, creating a luxurious, elegant effect of great beauty. Catherine had built it for her lover in 1772, and it was considered a masterpiece of architectural style and grace.

We stopped in front of the majestic portico and Vanya dismounted, helping me alight as the other two cossacks

rode on around to the stables. He told me he would tend to
Natasha, see that she was properly rubbed down. I asked
him to give her an extra portion of oats. I thanked Vanya
again and stood on the marble steps for a few moments,
watching him lead the horses away. A liveried servant
opened the door. I stepped inside, trying to throw off the
dread that gripped me.

I removed my fur cloak and handed it to the servant. I
was wearing a topaz velvet gown with long, tight sleeves
and a low bodice edged with soft brown fur. In one of the
hall mirrors I saw a tall woman with windblown coppery
red hair and unhappy sapphire eyes. The lids were shadowed with pale gray. The face looked thinner, high cheekbones more pronounced. Shoving the unruly waves back, I
sighed and moved on down the hall, praying I wouldn't run
into Gregory.

Even in my present mood I couldn't help but marvel
anew at the incredible beauty of the place. A gift of love
from a still-devoted and appreciative Empress, the Marble
Palace was filled with the richest, most beautiful furnishings money could buy, subdued elegance the theme. The
near-garish splendor of Rostopchin's mansion was missing
here, the spacious rooms exquisitely appointed in tasteful
harmony that dazzled the eye. Precious *objets d'art* stood
out all the more for lack of clutter, each one superbly displayed. One had the impression of warm, pale marble, satiny woods, creamy velvets and delicate gilt, jeweled and
enameled objects gleaming.

There seemed to be an unusual amount of bustle this afternoon. Although the hall was empty and I had seen no
servants besides the one who had carried my cloak away,
the palace seemed to hum with activity, sensed, not seen.
From the distant ballroom came a curious noise, like hammering, I thought, and as I paused, puzzled, I heard scurrying footsteps and caught a glimpse of four servants
moving past an open door in back of the hall, their arms
laden with huge baskets of flowers. I sensed activity in the
kitchen, too. Although it was a long way from the hall, I

seemed to hear the clatter of pans and, softly muted by distance, the shrill cries of the chef, but perhaps I was imagin- 'ing it. I moved on, idly wondering what was afoot.

"You are back, I see," he said.

I had just reached the staircase as he strolled slowly out of one of the reception rooms. He was wearing dark brown velvet breeches and frock coat and a splendid golden brocade vest embroidered in brown. He had gone out visiting earlier, I knew, and his tawny golden brown hair was pulled away from his face and tied at the nape of his neck with a brown velvet ribbon as current fashion decreed. He had rarely looked as handsome as he did now, gazing at me with an idle speculation in those hooded eyes.

"I have been out myself. I come back and ask for you. The servant tells me you have gone for a ride. This I did not know about."

"I wasn't aware I had to ask your permission," I said.

"I assume you have gone shopping with Lucie."

I gazed at him coolly, on the defensive. I had refused to marry him, and, after that night at Count Rostopchin's, had refused to sleep with him again as well, but I had reluctantly agreed to remain in St. Petersburg as Lucie's paid companion for three months as we had originally agreed. Was he accusing me of neglecting my duties?

"Lucie and I have been shopping almost every afternoon. I didn't feel I could take another afternoon in the shops on the Nevsky Prospekt, so I decided to go riding instead. As Vladimir and three of the other guards went with her I didn't feel I was being remiss."

"You misunderstand me," he said.

"Do I?"

"You are cold. There is a snap in your voice."

"I'm sorry. I—I suppose I'm a little tired."

He smiled fondly, and I forced myself to relax. He was going to be congenial, then. There would be no sullen looks, no angry silences. Orlov was accustomed to having his own way and, thwarted, was beginning to show a side of his nature I had only glimpsed before. It was as though we were playing a subtle cat-and-mouse game, and I never knew what he was going to do or say.

"Come," he said. "We will have a glass of wine. It will make you feel better."

"I think not," I said.

"You find me so repulsive you won't even have a glass of wine with me?"

"You know that's not true."

"You avoid me. You are tense when I am near."

"I—I just don't feel like fencing with you today. I've told you over and over again that—that I'm honored by your desire to marry me but that I can't possibly become your wife. You keep—"

"We do not fence today," he told me. "We call a truce, yes? We have a glass of wine and be friends."

I couldn't refuse, not without insulting him, and I reluctantly followed him into the cream and tan drawing room with its delicate gold gilt and light orange velvet upholstery. Gregory poured our wine, and I gazed at the smooth marble walls that should have been cold but, instead, gave the room a surprising warmth. Catherine must have loved him very much to have given him a palace like this, I thought, and I wondered if she would ever acknowledge his presence in the city. Orlov had expected a royal summons from her as soon as we arrived, and after ten days his failure to receive one had darkened his mood even more.

She knew he was here. There was no way she could help knowing. Gregory had gone visiting almost every day, using the spectacular silver and blue carriage pulled by six white horses that was even more elaborate than the one he had used in England, and we had gone to the theater and opera five times, sitting in jewellike boxes that left us exposed to the stares of the rest of the audience, and stare they did. Orlov had insisted I come along with him and Lucie. I had agreed in order to avoid any more unpleasantness, and he had been deliberately attentive to me in public, displaying me as he might display some prized possession. The city, I knew, must already be full of delicious speculation about our relationship, and instinct told me that this was exactly what he wanted.

Gregory handed me a glass of wine. I took it, still a bit stiff and defensive. He smiled again, and again I felt myself the mouse. He had something in mind. He had not asked me in here simply to have a glass of wine.

"Relax, Marietta," he crooned.

"It's not easy with you standing so close."

"I do not eat you," he promised. "I do not even try to persuade you to change your mind about marrying me."

"Oh?"

Gregory looked into my eyes for a moment, and then he sauntered casually over to the pale cream and tan marble fireplace with its superbly carved mantelpiece. He glanced at the gorgeous gold clock sitting atop it, idly examined one of the pair of orange porcelain vases etched with golden leaves. He was deliberating about something. I could see that. I took a sip of wine, waiting. After a few moments he turned, drank his wine, and set the glass aside. When he spoke, his voice was light, carefully controlled.

"I accept your decision," he told me. "At last I accept it. At first I am disappointed, then hurt, and then I decide you are perhaps playing with me and wish to be persuaded. Women enjoy these games."

"Some of them do," I said. "I don't happen to be one of them."

"I am puzzled, too, by your refusal to sleep with me again. That evening at Vasily's you are most responsive. We can discuss this, no? You respond passionately, and I know it is not merely the oysters. I know you enjoy it as much as I do. This is so?"

"You were more than adequate," I replied coldly. "You can rest assured you—haven't lost your skills."

A smile flickered over his lips. "This does not worry me," he said. "I do not imagine for a moment that it is my performance in bed that causes you to turn down my proposal."

This cool display of male arrogance shouldn't have surprised me. I had certainly seen enough of it in my time. I finished my wine, and as I looked at the man standing across the room I realized that I didn't know him at all. The warm, jovial Orlov with his charming speech patterns and engaging mannerisms had been a total fraud, a role he played with consummate skill. Dazzled by his physical presence, immersed in my grief over Jeremy, I had never bothered to look beneath the surface. Although I had often sensed the cold ruthlessness, I had ignored it, and from the first I had underestimated his intelligence.

"I think about it for a long time," he said, "and then I decide you use me. You sleep with me because you think it will make you forget this man who deserts you in London."

I looked at him, and I couldn't deny it. How had I ever considered him a charming simpleton, a sexually magnetic pet? He was as shrewd and perceptive as any man I had ever known.

"It—it isn't something I'm proud of," I said. "I—I never pretended to love you, Gregory. I found you wonderfully attractive and I knew you wanted me and—and, yes, I thought an affair with you would help me forget Jeremy."

He sauntered over to pour himself another glass of wine, and I sensed he was enjoying my discomfort.

"I was mistaken," I continued. "When you started talking about marriage I realized how—how unfair to you I'd been, and I knew I had to pull back at once before it went any further."

"You are very honest," he said. "This I admire."

"I didn't mean to mislead you."

"No harm is done. We have a splendid time together. It is a most memorable night. Rarely have I enjoyed myself more. I am only sorry that we shall not have more such nights."

"That's out of the question."

Another smile flickered, this one faintly mocking. "You no longer find me attractive?"

"I'm no longer willing to deceive myself."

"You still love this Jeremy?"

"I do," I admitted. "It's something I must live with. I hope that time will—will heal these feelings, but I know now another man isn't going to help."

"Not even Orlov?"

"Not even the great Gregory Orlov."

He chuckled, genuinely amused, and that surprised me. The male ego being what it is, it would have been far more natural for him to be offended, and my tone of voice had hardly been pleasant.

"Any other woman would have jumped at the chance to marry Orlov," he informed me.

"That well may be."

"Even if I have the hump back, even if I have the hideous face, she would be more than eager because of my great wealth. She would think of the jewels, the clothes, the fine houses. She would pretend to find me the most appealing man in the world."

"Some women might."

"You do not consider these things at all. The great wealth never enters your mind."

"I'm not interested in your fortune, Gregory."

Orlov nodded. I was very uncomfortable and wished he would come to whatever point he hoped to make. Setting his glass aside, clasping his hands behind his back, he began to pace, deliberately again. Watching him, I was reminded of a lion prowling. Sleek, handsome, he radiated the strength and powerful magnetism of that animal, and, remembering the knout and the bright crimson flecks in the snow, I felt he could be just as savage.

He stopped. He stood facing me, hands resting on his thighs, and as he looked at me his eyes were cool and decidedly calculating.

"I think it is time we—how is it you English say?" He paused, frowning, groping for the right words. "Ah, yes. I think it is time we place the cards down on the table. This is the correct expression?"

"More or less."

"You are honest with me. I am not completely honest with you."

Am I supposed to be surprised at that? I asked silently. I ran a finger around the rim of my empty glass, waiting for him to continue.

"I persuade you to come to Russia with us as Lucie's companion and it is in this capacity that you join us. I agree to pay you a large salary and see that you leave for America three months after we arrive."

"That's right."

"I have another reason for wanting you to come," he said.

"Oh?"

"It is—" He hesitated, rather uncomfortable. "It is important that I arrive in St. Petersburg with a beautiful woman, the most beautiful woman I can find, and the minute I see you I know that you are that woman. I know I must bring you to Russia with me."

"I see."

"You do?" He looked surprised.

"I think so. Sir Harry—Sir Harry tried to warn me. He told me you never do anything without good reason, that the reason is not always the obvious one. He tried his best to persuade me not to come to Russia."

"Sir Harry knows me a long time," he said.

"He suspected you might have an ulterior motive."

"'Ulterior?' This is not a word I would use. I—uh—I use a little deception, I tell a few white lies, but it is not ulterior. All along I plan to pay you well."

"But not for keeping Lucie company."

He smiled a sheepish smile, the naughty little boy again, but I no longer found the pose endearing.

"Is good for Lucie that you come along. This much is true. She needs a companion for the long journey. I see you are very fond of her, and I believe maybe you will come if I use this fondness as a lever. If I tell you the real reason I want you to come, I fear you will refuse."

Two nights ago, in the lobby of the glittering opera

house, we had encountered one Countess Dedotov, a plump, supercilious woman in pink satin and diamonds who had the reputation of being one of the biggest gossips at Catherine's court. Orlov had introduced me as "a close friend," and as he chatted with the fluttery, painted old fool he had casually fondled my arm. I had maintained a cool silence, and, not wishing to embarrass him, I hadn't pulled away. Oh, yes, I knew the reason Orlov wanted me to come to Russia with him.

"Catherine is a very jealous woman, isn't she?" I said.

"This is so."

"Perhaps something of the dog-in-the-manger as well."

"This I do not understand."

"The dog in the manger did not want his bone, but he did not want any other dog to have it. Some women are like that. They have lost interest in a man and no longer want him, but when they see him with another woman they decide to get him back."

"Women are strange this way."

"You—you wanted to use me to make Catherine jealous."

"This I admit."

"You believed that if she saw us together her—her interest in you would be rekindled."

He nodded, relieved that I had guessed, that he had not had to explain it to me. He looked ever so guileless now, smiling a broad smile, that disarming charm in full force.

"Is this so bad of me?" he asked.

"You made love to me," I continued, "and then you asked me to marry you so that—so that our relationship would be all the more convincing. You never intended to marry me, did you?"

"Well—"

"You intended to introduce me as you fiancée and flaunt me about town on your arm and—and—" I was growing angrier by the moment. "And then you intended to discard me like—"

"This is not true!" he protested.

"God *damn* you, Gregory Orlov!"

Blindly, I reached for the vase on the table beside me. I heaved it over my head. I hurled it. Orlov cried out and ducked as it flew past him and hit the wall with a resounding crash and shattered into a thousand glittering gold shards. He looked stunned. I was rather stunned myself.

"That was priceless!" he exclaimed.

"I don't care!"

"It was one of a kind!"

"I don't *care!*"

"Catherine gave it to me!"

"I don't *give* a sod, you son of a bitch! Please try to get that through your thick skull."

Gregory's eyes widened in amazement. "Ladies do not use such language," he said in a shocked voice.

"I'm not a lady! I never have been, and I—I'm getting bloody good and tired of acting like one. I wish I'd had a pistol. I would have blown your bloody head off."

"This 'bloody' is not a nice word at all, I think. In England it has a bad meaning indeed. No?"

"You're bloody right!"

Gregory couldn't control himself any longer. He burst into gales of robust laughter, a rich, hearty sound that made me all the angrier. I glared at him, fuming, and finally all the fight went out of me and he stopped laughing. I was exhausted, but I felt much, much better.

"You really know how to fire a pistol?" he inquired.

"I happen to be a crack shot."

"This I would never have suspected."

"There are a lot of things about me you would never have suspected."

"I see the fire in your eyes. It is most startling. You are very beautiful when you are angry like this. You have the fiery spirit. You might almost be Russian."

"Go to hell," I said wearily.

"I do not intend to discard you after I have won Catherine's favor again, Marietta. This is not my intention at all.

I intend to send you back to America a very wealthy woman. From the first this is my intention."

"I'm tired, Gregory. I'm going up to my room."

"I plan to use you, yes. Is not a major crime. Is not gentlemanly of me to mention it, but you use me, too, in a different way. Me, I am not consumed with fury when I discover it."

You're right, I thought, I'm no better than you are, and I have no one to blame but myself for this whole wretched mess. I should have listened to Sir Harry. I should never have come to Russia, but it's a little late now to cry over milk spilled a long time ago. I looked at the dazzlingly handsome, thoroughly unscrupulous man who stood across from me in his splendid attire, and I could no longer even be angry with him. I left the room, moving wearily toward the sweeping marble staircase.

Orlov followed me. He touched my arm. I turned.

"Now that we have placed these cards down on the table, maybe we can discuss this like the sensible adults."

"I'm afraid I don't feel very sensible at the moment."

"You first agree to stay in St. Petersburg for three months as my niece's companion. I see now that you no longer wish to do this, and I understand it. I am an honorable man. I will give you the salary you have earned, and I will put you on a ship that will eventually take you to America."

"That's very kind of you."

I placed my hand on the cool marble banister, ready to go on up. Orlov put his hand on top of mine, gently restraining me.

"I ask that you consider a new proposition. I ask that you agree to stay for one month only."

"And pretend to be your mistress," I said.

He nodded. "I ask that you continue to appear with me in public and act as hostess at the grand receptions I plan to give. You will wear the gowns I have had specially made for you—the gowns you refused to accept when I give them to you last week—and you will wear the jewels as well and pretend to be very happy in my company."

"I think not, Gregory."

"For this I will pay you, at the end of one month, the equivalent of one hundred thousand English pounds. This is a very large amount of money, Marietta. With it you can go back to this Texas you speak of a rich woman. With it you could probably *buy* this place."

"I probably could," I said dryly.

"You may also keep the gowns and the jewels," he added.

"How generous."

"For this I ask only that you play a role like one of the actresses Lucie admires. For one month only. Is this so difficult to do? It—uh—it will merely be a role. In public you are my gracious, elegant mistress. In private we are just the—how you say?—just the business associates. I do not come to your bedroom unless I am invited."

I made no reply. Orlov removed his hand from mine and stepped back and smiled a winning smile.

"You will consider this?" he asked.

"I'll consider it," I replied.

He looked relieved. "I give my first reception tonight. I send out the special invitations last week. Everyone accepts. They are most eager to see Orlov again and meet the mysterious Englishwoman with the brilliant blue eyes and flaming red hair."

I imagine they are, I thought.

"My guests arrive at ten for the late supper and dancing, and I hope you will be downstairs to greet them with me."

I left him standing at the foot of the stairs and ascended the curving marble staircase and walked down a long corridor and stepped into the lovely, airy sitting room with its pale gold and white walls and golden brown parquet floor partially covered with a luxurious beige rug patterned with tan and gold and pinkish brown floral designs. Sunlight splashed in through windows that looked out over the back gardens, the radiant rays bathing the magnificent furnishings, the exquisite *objets d'art* tastefully scattered about. A fire burned cozily in the white marble fireplace, but the room was still a bit chilly. The Marble Palace might be one of the architectural wonders of St. Petersburg, but it was almost impossible to heat.

Passing through the equally elaborate bedroom, I stepped into the adjoining dressing room. One wall was completely covered by an immense yet delicate white wardrobe with gilt doors that folded back like a screen. It contained all my clothing as well as half a dozen glorious new gowns that had been made for me by Catherine's own dressmaker. How clever he had been, I thought. One of my simple muslin frocks had been "borrowed" in London without my knowledge and shipped off to Russia in a diplomatic pouch along with details of my coloring and specific instructions about the kind of gowns to be created. All during the time we were traveling across Russia a fleet of seamstresses had been working, creating gowns as sumptuous as any Catherine herself owned.

I hadn't worn any of them, of course. I had refused to accept them, yet they hung in the wardrobe nevertheless, putting the gowns Lucille had made to shame. Even in London, months ago, he had been so sure of himself and of me that he had ordered the gowns, spending a small fortune on them. How could I ever have been taken in? And so easily? I had played right into his ever so capable hands, from that very first evening at The Wayfarer right up to that passion-filled night in Du Barry's bed. What a fool I had been. What a monumental fool! Sitting at the dressing table, I picked up the gold-handled brush and began to brush my hair with vigorous, angry strokes, angrier with myself than with Orlov.

How could I have been such a poor judge of character? I fancied I knew something about men, and, to be fair, I had never had any illusions about Orlov, yet that warmth, that charm, that incredible physical allure had blinded me all the same. I winced as a particularly vigorous stroke tugged painfully at the roots of my hair. You were in a very vulnerable state, I told myself. You were distressed and distraught over Jeremy Bond, easy prey for a man like Orlov, but that's still no excuse. At least you didn't fall in *love* with the bastard. At least you had that much sense. I put the brush down and glared at my reflection in the glass. Well, luv, you've gotten yourself into a fine mess this time. So what are you going to do about it?

I was in the sitting room some time later when the door opened and Lucie came in, looking sulky and depressed and thoroughly out of sorts. She wore a lovely pale blue silk frock striped with violet, and her hair spilled loosely down her shoulders in a mass of unruly waves. I was standing in front of one of the windows. She flopped down on the sofa, as undignified as any girl her age when in a histrionic pout.

"Did you enjoy your shopping trip?" I asked.

"It was a crashing bore! There's not anything left in St. Petersburg I care to buy."

"The shopkeepers will be crushed. You've been keeping them all solvent ever since we arrived."

"Must you be bitchy today?"

"I happen to be in an extremely bitchy mood."

"Six days!" she exclaimed, far too absorbed in her own mood to inquire about the reasons for mine. "Six whole days without a single word from him, and I've only seen him *twice* since we got here. He's found someone else. I *know* he has."

"Perhaps he has," I said.

"Marietta! Do you really *believe* that?"

"Of course not."

"You just wanted to taunt me!"

"I'm sure there are a dozen reasons why Bryan hasn't come to see you, Lucie. He's probably extremely busy. He has to prepare that report for his father, and—"

"He's already finished it," she interrupted. "He told me about it the last time I saw him. His father was delighted. So was the ambassador. The report was amazingly thorough and provides invaluable information. The ambassador said that if he had the authority he'd give Bryan a medal."

"I'm not surprised."

"He was probably lying through his teeth about the medal!" she snapped. "Bryan, I mean. Not the ambassador. He's the most arrogant, conceited, infuriating creature I've ever met and I don't know why I even *care*, but— Oh, Marietta, what am I going to *do?*"

The sophistication and world-weary poise she had once affected were entirely gone now, and she was as wretched and confused as any young woman in love. She hated Bryan Lloyd, she wailed miserably, absolutely hated him, and if he didn't want to see her she certainly didn't want to see him and it was just as well because he was impossible, impossible, and she was much too mature for him anyway, she was a grown-up, a woman of experience, and he was a callow *youth*.

I listened to her wail, but I was too concerned with my own dilemma to pay her much mind. After a while her words became mere noise and I gazed at the fire as though in a trance, hardly aware she was in the same room. When I finally became aware of the silence, I looked up to find Lucie studying me with concerned eyes.

"I—I'm sorry," I said. "What were you saying?"

"I haven't said anything for the past five minutes," Lucie informed me. "Something is bothering you, Marietta. You—you look peculiar. Here I've been rattling on like a despicable brat and you—you're worried about something."

"I—" I hesitated, wondering how much I should tell her.

"I'm going to pour you some brandy," she said, getting up from the sofa. "I don't like the way you look."

"I don't want any brandy. Brandy isn't going to help."

"What *is* it, Marietta. What's happened?"

"I—I had a long talk with your uncle this afternoon."

Lucie looked worried now, seriously worried, her violet-blue eyes grave as she took my hand and led me over to the sofa. I sat down and she sat beside me and I looked at her, knowing I couldn't spare her or myself, knowing I must be entirely frank. Slowly, hesitantly, I told her all that had been said this afternoon, all that I had learned, and Lucie toyed with a handful of silk skirt, tugging at the material, crumpling it up nervously, and when I was finally finished she looked down at her lap, her lip trembling.

"I—I didn't know, Marietta. I swear I didn't. I thought—I actually believed it was—it was because of me he wanted you to come. I knew he found you attractive, of course, what—what man wouldn't? I knew you slept together at Count Rostopchin's, but I had no idea he planned to—"

Lucie cut herself short and took a deep breath, trying to compose herself. I was surprised to see that the sun had already gone down. The room was growing dark. I got up and began to light the candles that stood in the beautifully wrought wall sconces. Lucie brushed her skirt. Her expression was cool and controlled when I finished with the candles, but her eyes were inexpressibly sad.

"He's been obsessed with Catherine ever since she sent him away," she told me. "All this time he's been trying to find some way to win her favor back. It's—it's the only thing he can think about. It's ruined his life. I should have known. When he insisted you come with us I should have known it—it wasn't for my sake."

"Lucie—"

I sat down beside her and took her hand. Lucie gave me a bitter smile.

"He used you. He uses everybody. I understand how you feel. I understand why you—you feel you must leave. I'll be—sorry, of course, but I understand."

"I'm very fond of you, Lucie."

"I know. You—you've been wonderful, Marietta. The only friend I've ever had. I'll be sad to see you go, particularly since—since Bryan has lost interest in me, but I—I'll get along somehow. Somehow I always manage to get along."

"Damn!" I said.

I let go of her hand and stood up abruptly. Lucie looked at me, dismayed. I frowned and started out of the room.

"Where—where are you going?" she asked.

"I'm going to find a servant and order a bath. Your uncle is going to hold a grand reception tonight and the guests will be arriving in less than three hours."

Lucie climbed slowly to her feet, and the hope that filled her eyes was heartbreaking to behold.

"You—you mean—"

"I'm going to use my head," I told her. "He's offered me a bloody fortune to play this little charade, and I'd be an idiot to turn him down. I've traveled halfway across the world, and—by God—I might just as well make it worth my while!"

Chapter Sixteen

Count Orlov was delighted that I had finally decided to spend some of his money. When I told him that I needed the right jewelry to go with the gown I intended to wear to the theater Tuesday night, he insisted I go to Maitlev's and buy anything I wanted. Maitlev's was on the Nevsky Prospekt, the richest, most exclusive jeweler in St. Petersburg. Catherine herself frequently bought jewelry there, and all of her court patronized it. Any special purchase made there was soon gossiped about in the marble corridors of the Winter Palace, and Orlov wanted people to know his "mistress" shopped there.

"Buy the necklace, the earrings, the bracelets," he told me. "Diamonds, emeralds—anything you want. Orlov does not care what it costs."

He insisted I take his carriage, and that presented a problem, but I had a private talk with Vanya and found a solution quickly enough. I was slightly nervous as I came downstairs in my sky blue silk gown and a hooded white ermine cloak. Instinct told me that if Orlov knew what I was planning he would be furious, would forbid me to go, and I prayed I could carry it through without his knowing. Having to take the Orlov carriage complicated matters—he wanted me to be seen, of course, and the carriage was highly visible—for there would not only be the driver and the footman to contend with but six outriders as well.

My heart sank when I saw Vladimir waiting for me in

313

the grand hall, and I muttered an expletive I rarely used. He *would* be one of the outriders, I thought. Orlov would naturally send his most trusted guard to accompany his mistress. Wearing the familiar silver-trimmed dark blue livery, the tall fur cap and the short, heavy blue cape trimmed with the same sleek black fur, Vladimir scowled, no happier about his assignment than I was. During the intervening weeks, we had become no friendlier than we had been when he brought the red fox fur to me at the village. The hostility still burned in his eyes as he nodded curtly and led me outside.

The carriage stood waiting on the drive, gleaming like an enormous jewel in the early afternoon sunlight. The white laquer exterior was overlaid with ornate silver filigree, and the blue lacquer doors, framed in silver, bore the Orlov crest in silver and precious gems. The lacquer roof was domed, surmounted by a silver crown, and the vehicle was pulled by six white horses in silver harness, dark blue plumes waving atop their heads. No one would miss us as we drove through the streets of St. Petersburg, as Orlov intended.

Vladimir opened the door for me. I climbed inside and sank back against the dark blue velvet upholstery. I looked out the windows draped with cloth-of-silver curtains, watching the Marble Palace disappear as we drove through the park and turned onto the street.

I had been playing my role for eight days now, playing it to the hilt. Cool, composed, gorgeously gowned, I had greeted Orlov's aristocratic guests that first night with just the right amount of reserve, friendly but not forthcoming. I was a bit aloof with the women, slightly warmer toward the men, flaming their curiosity about me with subtle hints about a colorful past which, in truth, was far more colorful than anything they could imagine. Gregory did not overplay his own role. His pride in me was obvious, and he cast frequent fond looks at me throughout the evening, but he didn't stroke my arm or embrace me. When, toward dawn, the guests began to depart, I linked my arm in his and told them goodbye with a gracious smile.

We had been very visible, going to the theater, to the opera, taking long drives together, entertaining select titled guests at intimate soirées. I was the talk of St. Petersburg, I knew, and speculation about me was the favorite pastime of the gossips. I was a celebrated courtesan, Orlov merely the latest in a long line of fabulously wealthy lovers. I was the runaway wife of an English nobleman, whom I had disgraced with my scandalous affairs. I was a bluestocking from Bath, a seamstress from London, an Englishwoman who had been brought up in Paris and slept with half the men in the court of Louis XV, including the King. I was mysterious, intriguing, a delicious new subject for the gossips to prattle about, and Orlov was delighted. Most of that gossip had surely reached the ears of the Empress, and she was bound to be as curious as everyone else. She would summon us to court before long. Gregory was certain she would. She couldn't resist.

I wasn't at all concerned about Catherine, but I was extremely concerned about Lucie. She had taken to staying in her room these past days, wan, listless, reading book after book, hardly touching the food brought to her. A full two weeks had passed now without word from Bryan, and the girl was sinking into a bleak depression, convinced it was all her fault, that she was unworthy of him, that she was a flawed creature no man would ever want. I tried to talk her out of such ridiculous notions, tried to reason with her, but she was Russian, she was very much in love with a man who had apparently lost all interest in her, and no amount of reasoning could cut through those clouds.

Damn Bryan Lloyd, I thought. Damn all men, for that matter. The young scoundrel could at least have written a note explaining his absence. I was not at all convinced he had lost interest in Lucie. In fact, I was almost certain he was as much in love as she was, and I was determined to find out why he hadn't come to the Marble Palace for two weeks.

The carriage bowled down the glittering Nevsky Prospekt, and people turned to stare at the spectacular sight. Extreme visibility was definitely a handicap this afternoon. Gregory mustn't find out, and I only hoped my carefully planned subterfuge would work. Vladimir was suspicious of me already. Would he insist on following me into Maitlev's? I looked out at the exclusive, elegant shops, and my nervousness returned. The carriage came to a stop. I braced myself as Vladimir opened the door. I couldn't let him see my nervousness. Assuming my coolest, most haughty manner, I took the hand he extended and climbed out, my blue silk skirt swaying.

"I may be quite some time," I informed him. "Come back for me in—oh, an hour and a half."

Vladimir looked at me with hostile eyes. "The carriage waits for you here in front of the shop," he said, curling his lip. "I go in with you."

"That won't be necessary."

"I know my duties."

"I'm sure you do," I replied. I adjusted the folds of the ermine cloak. "Your duties are to accompany me and protect me. I seriously doubt I'll encounter much danger inside Maitlev's."

"All the same—"

"I won't have you coming in with me," I said sharply. "You'll frighten the customers with that scowl of yours. You may stand guard outside the door if you wish, and if any villainous brute with a knife or a gun tries to get past you, you have my permission to break his neck."

He looked as though he would prefer breaking mine, but he made no further effort to follow me. A bell tinkled pleasantly overhead as I opened the door and stepped inside. I found the splendor of the place impressive and just a little intimidating, as it was meant to be. Pale beige silk embossed with gold *fleurs-de-lis* covered the walls. A plush dark gold carpet was spread over the parquet floor, and two stunning crystal chandeliers hung from an ornately molded cream ceiling. All this was mere background for the jewels that shimmered and flashed in the elegant glass cases and on inventive display stands. Diamond and sapphire bracelets dangled from the spreading branches of a white artificial tree. Emerald pendants were suspended from the branches of another. The atmosphere was rarefied, redolent of immense luxury.

Several grandly attired customers browsed leisurely among the cases, including a handsome blond guardsman in gold-trimmed white velvet uniform. He obviously belonged to the middle aged woman with the sharp, painted face and preposterously elaborate coiffure. Guardsmen were quite the thing among ladies of the court, I understood. They were easier to manage than lapdogs and more entertaining. This particular specimen lounged idly against one of the cases as his mistress picked out a silver and gold pocket watch for him. Less dear than a jeweled collar, I thought, aware that I was the object of a number of stares. Everyone knew who I was, it seemed. My reputation preceded me, or was it in hot pursuit?

An attractive young clerk started toward me. He was forcibly restrained by a tall, extremely thin man in brown velvet breeches and frock coat, creamy beige lace spilling from his wrists and throat. Maitlev himself I decided as he smiled obsequiously and hurried over to assist me. His thin gold hair was plastered back over his bony skull. His bright gray eyes seemed to be adding up profits. The fawning smile never left his lips, even when he spoke.

"Miss Danver!" he exclaimed. "This is an honor indeed!"

I nodded coolly, not at all surprised that he knew my name.

"You needn't have bothered coming to the shop," he continued. "I would have been only too pleased to bring a selection of my best pieces to the Marble Palace."

"How kind you are."

"I frequently do that with some of my—uh—more exalted customers," he confided. "How many times have I
carried my cases to the Winter Palace? Our dear Empress
rarely buys from anyone else. I suppose you've come to
pick out something to go with the necklace."

"Necklace?"

"Dear me! Don't tell me I've spoiled a little surprise!
Please, I beg of you, forget I said a word. Count Orlov
would strangle me if he found out I'd been indiscreet."

The man obviously loved to babble about his important
customers and the purchases they made. Half of St.
Petersburg probably already knew about "the little surprise" that Gregory planned for me.

"I've come to buy something for Tuesday night," I said
frostily. "I'll just browse awhile if you don't mind."

"Of course! Of course!"

He didn't actually bow and click his heels, but it seemed
that way. He trailed a few paces behind me as I examined
the contents of the cases with a bored, dissatisfied expression, clearly finding nothing that pleased me. The other
women in the shop continued to watch me with open fascination. Two whispered behind their fans. My new notori-
ety made me rather uncomfortable, but I was being
extremely well paid for it. The handsome blond guardsman gave me a practiced smile and looked at me with eyes
that asked if I were in the market for a new pet. His present owner grabbed his arm, thrust a wad of money at the
clerk and marched her prize out of the shop, convinced I
was about to steal him. Having made a quick inspection of
the cases, I turned to Maitlev in disgust.

"I see nothing here I like," I said tartly.

"But Miss Danver—"

"You obviously keep your best pieces in the back."

"I have a few pieces there, it's true, but—"

"Would you care to show them to me?"

Crushed, he hesitated. I tapped my foot impatiently. He

finally asked me to follow him, explaining unhappily that his choice items were on display and I would be disappointed in the trinkets he kept in back. We walked down a narrow hall, passed a small office and finally stepped into a large, cluttered room that was surprisingly dusty and obviously not open to the public. The jewelry in cases back here, though fabulous, was distinctly inferior to that in front, bracelets and necklaces scattered carelessly on pieces of black velvet.

Maitlev was flustered. "As you can see—" he began.

"Where does that door lead?" I interrupted, pointing.

"It leads into an alleyway," he informed me. "That's why it's bolted. I'm sure if you would let me help you, Miss Danver, we could find something that would—"

"I'm sorry to keep interrupting you, Mr. Maitlev, but—well, I have to let you in on my secret."

"Secret? I don't quite—"

"I asked you to bring me back here for a specific reason. I'm going to ask you to unbolt that door now. I—I have to leave for a short while, and my driver and the men who accompanied me mustn't know."

"You're going to walk down that alley!" He was horrified.

"Mr. Maitlev, I—I'm planning to buy a new frock coat for Count Orlov. It's terribly grand, gold cloth, embroidered with silver and black. He insisted I take his carriage this afternoon, and if I had gone directly to the tailor's one of his men might have mentioned it and—and spoiled my surprise."

"I see," he said glumly.

"The tailor is expecting me. He'll be waiting at the end of the alley. After I inspect the coat and pay for it, I'll come back here. I would like for you to remain in this room until I return so that none of the customers will suspect I'm not examining jewelry. People *do* talk, I've discovered."

Maitlev had the grace to blush. He was very distressed.

"I'm sure *you* won't," I continued sweetly, "because if a

single word of this got out I would have to tell Count Orlov that you spoiled *his* little surprise. I would also have to tell him you were insolent to me and called me a very ugly name."

"Miss Danver!"

"So I'm sure you'll be happy to stay back here until I return and never breathe a word of this."

"Not even under torture," he promised shakily.

"When I return, we'll go out front and I'll make a lavish purchase and everyone will be content. Would you unbolt the door, please?"

He almost stumbled over his own feet getting to the door. He slid the heavy bolt back, fumbled with a key and unlocked a steel lock. I gave him a charming smile as I moved past him into the alley. I thought I heard a sob as he pulled the door shut.

The alley was narrow and dark and very, very dirty, littered with filth and rubbish. The splendor of St. Petersburg did not extend to these dark corners and alleyways, I observed. Like every city, it had its squalid underside. I was startled to see an old woman in ragged brown dress and kerchief digging among the rubbish behind one of the shops. She was as startled as I was, backing against the damp brick wall as though she feared I might attack her. A rat scurried out from under the pile of refuse. I stopped, momentarily forgetting my mission, forgetting everything but that look of terror in the woman's eyes.

"Please—don't—don't be frightened," I said.

My Russian was still not perfect, and I couldn't be sure she understood me. She was flattened against the wall, her frail arms held in front of her as though to ward off a blow. I reached into the inner pocket of the ermine cloak, relieved to find the bag of gold coins I usually carried when I went shopping with Lucie. I pulled it out.

"I—I have some money here. Please take it."

The fear left her eyes then, replaced by blazing contempt and hatred so strong it shook me to the core. She drew herself up, curiously dignified in her rags. I moved toward her, holding out the bag of coins.

"Please," I said.

The dark brown eyes continued to blaze. She moved her mouth, her lips clamped shut. I thought she was going to say something, and I waited expectantly. With a loud, hissing sound she spat at me, the spittle spewing in a stream that barely missed me. Too stunned to react for a moment, I stared at her. She believed I was an aristocrat, and I tried to imagine the years of grief and hardship and brutal oppression that had caused her to hate all aristocrats, even one who offered her relief from some of her pain. I hesitated for another moment, and then I tossed the bag of coins at her feet and moved quickly on down the alley.

I saw Vanya as soon as I came out onto the side street leading off the Nevsky Prospekt. He was standing beside a nondescript brown carriage, worried and impatient. When he saw me, he scowled, hurried toward me and hustled me roughly to the carriage. I was still shaken from my encounter with the old woman as he opened the door and shoved me into the carriage. I removed the ermine cloak and put on the heavy blue wool cloak he handed me, pulling the hood up over my head. Vanya tapped the roof with his fist, and the carriage began to move.

"This driver will not say anything," he told me. "I give him two gold coins. Vanya is very angry with you!"

"Angry? I—"

"You do not tell me you come down the alley. You tell me only that you will slip away from the shop and meet me on this street. The alleys of this city are not safe! It is very foolhardy of you to take this risk."

"I—I met an old woman, Vanya."

He stiffened. "She attempts to harm you?"

"No, but—"

I told him what had happened. Vanya listened with a fierce expression as the carriage turned down another street, rumbled over a bridge. We were passing a park as I finished. Vanya stared out at the ice-encrusted trees, silent, sullen, still angry with me.

"I only wanted to help her," I said.

"Yes, this is because you are not like the other women who go to shops like Maitlev's. These other women, they are not evil, but they do not want to think of the people. They think only of their own pleasure and are blind to the suffering around them."

"The poor woman was starving—"

"Many people starve all over Russia, even in this fine city built upon the bones of the workers."

"You—you sound bitter, Vanya."

"This is so. I see these bad things and I know I can do nothing about them. I know that but for the grace of God Vanya might be one of these people who starve. Vanya is strong. He decides at a very young age he is not going to starve."

"So you became a cossack."

"I leave my village. I join the army. I learn to ride, to shoot and use the sabre. I am ambitious. I go far. Eventually I am able to become one of Count Orlov's men and I have plenty to eat, warm clothes to wear, a warm place to sleep."

"But *you* don't hate all aristocrats."

"Vanya is very loyal, very grateful. He does not waste time on hatred which does no good."

He fell silent again, brooding. He would protect Lucie or me to the death under any circumstances, I knew, but if the peasant rebellion everyone feared actually broke out I felt his sympathies would be with the people, as, indeed, would mine. The encounter with the old woman had merely underlined the flagrant inequalities I had seen in Russia. I tried to put it out of my mind as we passed a spacious square with marble fountains and, a few minutes later, turned into the courtyard of the British embassy.

"I should only be a few minutes," I said, opening the carriage door. "You needn't come in with me, Vanya. We're on British soil now."

"Vanya will wait."

I climbed out and closed the door and pulled the heavy blue wool cloak closer about me, moving quickly across the courtyard and up the flat marble steps. The huge reception hall had marble floor and walls, but there was a snug, cozy atmosphere nevertheless. There were potted plants in profusion, comfortable rugs on the floor, and the furniture, while certainly not shabby, lacked any hint of showy ostentation. A large British flag hung on the wall behind the reception counter. A very slender, rather officious-looking young clerk in brown broadcloth and wire-rimmed spectacles shuffled some papers and stood up.

"May I help you?" he asked.

It was lovely to hear English again, even if it was spoken with a decidedly affected accent.

"I would like to speak to Bryan Lloyd," I said. "I believe he's staying here with his father."

The clerk looked surprised. He hesitated a moment and then asked me to wait, disappearing through one of the doors behind him. The embassy was immense, and one had a feeling of buzzing activity behind those marble walls. The upper floors, I knew, were devoted to living quarters for the staff and British citizens who were visiting or in need of a place to stay until they could leave Russia. Bryan had his own bedroom and sitting room beneath the attics.

After what seemed a very long time, the clerk returned, but Bryan was not with him. The man who came in a few seconds later was as tall, as bony and loose-limbed, and had Bryan's same fine blue-gray eyes. The hair, thick and wavy, was a luxuriant silver-gray, and the lean face was handsomely lined, a serious face full of character. Its expression was solemn and disapproving as he approached me.

Sir Reginald Lloyd wore sober black broadcloth breeches and coat and a deep wine-colored waistcoat. His ruffled

white neckcloth was the finest of linen, slightly crumpled,
I noticed, in need of a good pressing. Sir Reginald had been a
widower for almost nine years. He was in his early fifties
now, a strikingly handsome man, and I imagined there
were any number of women who would snatch him up if
given half a chance.

"Miss Danver," he said.

"You know my name."

"Almost everyone in St. Petersburg knows your name,"
he told me.

His deep baritone was mellifluous, a lovely voice, but not
at all friendly. His eyes were more gray than blue, and
they gazed at me with frosty disapproval. I realized that he
must consider me a cold-blooded adventuress, a totally
amoral courtesan. To a man of Sir Reginald's character,
that kind of woman would be total anathema.

"I wanted to speak to your son," I said.

"I'm afraid Bryan is no longer here."

"He—he's left Russia?"

"I didn't say that, Miss Danver. He's no longer staying
here at the embassy."

"Per—perhaps you could help me," I said.

Sir Reginald glanced at the clerk who, though immersed
in his paperwork, was obviously straining to hear our
every word. He asked me to follow him to his office, and we
moved down several long corridors, finally arriving at the
small, pleasantly littered room where he did his work for
his country. Books and papers were scattered everywhere.
A map of Russia hung behind the large, beautifully varnished mahogany desk. A cup of half-finished tea was on
his desk, I noticed, and a scattering of crumbs indicated
that he had been too busy to leave his office for lunch.

"Won't you sit down, Miss Danver."

"I don't want to take up too much of your time, Sir Reginald. I realize you're an extremely busy man."

"I'm not too busy to discuss my son. Anything that con-
cerns Bryan is of major importance to me."

The rich voice was polite, but barely. He moved behind his desk, but he did not sit down either. We faced each other like highly civilized adversaries, and I didn't know quite how to approach him.

"Bryan has mentioned me to you?" I asked.

"He spoke of you in glowing terms, Miss Danver. Bryan is very young and, I fear, not always the best judge of character."

"You don't share his high opinion of me, do you, Sir Reginald?"

"My opinion of you isn't of the least importance," he replied, "but I must warn you that the embassy shall not stand behind you should your schemes go amiss. We're engaged in delicate diplomatic relations with a difficult and frequently belligerent government, and your kind can do considerable harm to those relations."

"Despite what you may think, Sir Reginald, I am not Count Orlov's mistress. I came to Russia as his niece's paid companion."

"Indeed?"

He didn't believe me. I hadn't really expected him to. I could understand Sir Reginald's disapproval, his frigid, official manner—it was only natural. Nevertheless, I sensed that beneath it was a warm, compassionate man who, overworked and harried, probably shockingly underpaid as well, was completely dedicated to his job. His eyes looked a bit weary now. He ran a hand through the thick silver-gray waves, uncomfortable. Cool disapproval did not come naturally to him, and I could see that this interview was a considerable strain.

"You said that Bryan is no longer staying at the embassy. Is he still in St. Petersburg?"

Sir Reginald nodded. "He's taken a rather squalid set of rooms at one of the student hostels. He needed to be alone for a while, he informed me. My son is a very independent young man."

"Could you give me the address?"

"I could, but I don't know that I shall. I've not always been the perfect father, but I've always tried to keep his best interests in mind. I'm not sure that seeing you would be in his best interests."

"Surely—" I paused. "Surely you don't think I have designs on him?"

"I didn't mean to imply that, Miss Danver," he said wearily, "but you are—uh—Orlov's guest, and seeing anyone connected with Orlov is likely to upset him just now."

I was puzzled. "Upset him?"

"Bryan frequently gives an impression of irresponsible frivolity, but he is actually a very serious young man."

"I'm well aware of that."

"He's also quite sensitive—and deeply caring. After trifling with the affections of any number of foolish young women, he's fallen in love at last, and he's taken her letter very hard."

"Letter?" I said.

"Surely you're aware that Lucie Orlov wrote to him, Miss Danver. She informed him that she no longer wished to see him and requested that he make no further effort to contact her."

"When—when did he receive this letter?"

"Almost two weeks ago, I believe. He had been to visit her at the Marble Palace and returned raving about the girl, how wonderful she was, how beautiful, how bright. A servant delivered her letter the next morning. My son was demolished."

"I'm sure he was," I said. My voice was flat.

"Naturally I would have preferred for him to have fallen in love with an English girl, someone with a similar background, but one can't regulate these matters. The Orlov brothers are—uh—not held in the highest esteem by our government, or by the people of Russia, for that matter, but a seventeen-year-old girl can't be held responsible for the sins of her father and uncles. I was prepared to accept the match."

Someone else wasn't I thought. I felt very, very cold.

"I'll have to confess I felt a twinge of relief when the letter arrived, but it was far outweighed by concern over my boy. His pain is quite genuine, and I would do anything I could to alleviate it. You can see now why I prefer not to give you his address."

"Quite," I said.

"Unless there's something else—" He indicated the papers on his desk, eager to be rid of me.

"I've taken up far too much of your time as it is. Thank you for seeing me."

"I'll show you out."

"You needn't bother, Sir Reginald. I can find my own way."

Sir Reginald insisted. Somehow I managed to maintain a semblance of poise as he led me back to the reception room. I thanked him again, and he nodded politely, wearily, and I stepped outside and Vanya climbed out and opened the door of the carriage for me and we were soon on our way back toward the Nevsky Prospekt.

"It goes well?" Vanya inquired. "You speak to Lucie's young man?"

"He wasn't there," I said, distracted.

Vanya sensed I didn't care to talk about it, and he asked no more questions. Bryan had never seen Lucie's handwriting before. The letter had undoubtedly been written on a piece of her personal stationery, and he would have no way of knowing she hadn't penned it herself. Gregory had never particularly cared for the youth, but neither had he seemed to object to Lucie seeing him. Why had he done it? Why had he deliberately destroyed their happiness? Couldn't he see what it had done to Lucie? Didn't he care?

The carriage stopped on the side street, near the entrance to the alleyway. I changed cloaks again, pulling the ermine hood up over my head. Vanya helped me out of the carriage and led me down the alley, one hand holding my elbow, the other on the hilt of his dagger. His expression

was fierce as he searched the shadows, prepared to plunge
the dagger into the heart of anyone who dared accost me.
The old woman was gone. So was the bag of coins. We
stopped before the back door to Maitlev's, and Vanya
banged on it loudly with his fist and scowled savagely as
Maitlev opened it and peeked out. The poor man almost
fainted when he saw the cossack.

"That will be all, Vanya," I said.

I stepped inside. Maitlev's hands trembled as they
turned the lock and shoved the bolt back into place. I felt
rather sorry for him, and I thanked him graciously for his
cooperation and told him I would be eternally grateful.
Some of his normal color returned, and by the time we returned to the front of the shop he was relatively composed.
Glancing at the clock, I was dismayed to see that well over
an hour had passed since I entered the shop. Vladimir
would be growing more and more suspicious. I plucked a
diamond and sapphire bracelet from one of the artificial
tree limbs.

"I'll take this," I said.

"And earrings to match?" Maitlev inquired.

"Of course."

"We have several lovely pairs over here in this case. Let
me show them to you."

I tried to hide my impatience as Maitlev pulled out a
tray of dazzlingly beautiful earrings, the diamonds flashing brilliantly, the sapphires burning with shimmery blue
fires. The other customers were intrigued and made no effort to conceal their interest as I hastily selected a stunning pair that perfectly matched the bracelet. Maitlev
insisted I try them on. I snapped the bracelet onto my wrist
and, stepping over to a mirror, fastened the earrings onto
my lobes. I didn't ask what they cost. It wasn't important. I
told him I was delighted, told him to send the bill to Count
Orlov and left the shop, still wearing the jewels. I could
hear a buzz of excited chatter as I closed the door behind
me.

Vladimir was leaning against the wall outside, and he gave me a sullen, suspicious look as he straightened up. I stared at him icily, daring him to say anything. He gave me an insolent nod and walked over to his horse. The footman opened the door for me, and I climbed in, adjusting folds of ermine, smoothing down my blue silk skirt.

I stared out the window, but I saw none of the shops, none of the gawking pedestrians. I had not remained in St. Petersburg because of the money, even though that was the reason I gave. In fairness to myself, I knew that the only reason I wasn't now on board a ship leaving Russia was that pained look in Lucie's eyes. I had stayed because of her, because I couldn't bear to leave while she was so miserable. I was extremely fond of her, and I felt a curious responsibility for her. I wasn't going to stand by and let her uncle destroy what was perhaps her one chance for happiness. She and Bryan were young, true, but they were very much in love. Lucie needed someone like him, and I suspected he needed her as well.

I would contact him. There couldn't be too many student hostels in St. Petersburg. I couldn't check them out myself, of course, not without giving myself away, but I could have Vanya do it. He could come and go freely, and he would locate Bryan for me and . . . and somehow I would arrange a secret meeting and tell him what had happened and see that he and Lucie got together again. I would be risking the wrath of her uncle but that wasn't going to deter me. Calmly, I made my plans as the carriage took me back to the Marble Palace.

I did something I rarely did when I returned. After removing the cloak, I sought him out, finally locating him in the spacious study. Orlov was sitting at the rosewood desk, beaming as he studied the creamy white card in his hand. He hadn't heard me come in, and I studied him for a moment, noticing the way a ray of sunlight burnished his tawny hair, noticing the soft, curiously sensual roll of flesh under his chin, noticing the way his loose white silk shirt clung to the musculature of his broad shoulders and back. Oh yes, the allure was as potent as ever, but I was totally immune to it now, and the thought of our making love again was abhorrent to me.

I coughed. He looked up, surprised. He got to his feet, grinning like a boy. He was wearing soft white leather knee boots and clinging white kidskin breeches, the thin white shirt tucked carelessly into the waistband, the full bell sleeves gathered at the wrists, and yes, he did look like a mature Adonis. I was unmoved. I knew what was beneath that radiant facade. I smiled nevertheless, a polite, perfunctory smile.

"You are back!" he exclaimed. "You buy the nice jewelry?"

I held out my wrist, displaying the bracelet. "I bought this, and these earrings as well. I'm afraid they were very expensive."

"This does not matter." He sauntered toward me. "Ah, yes, they are nice jewels. The diamonds have a special sparkle. The sapphires are the color of your eyes."

"Everyone stared," I said, knowing it would please him. "I'm sure half of St. Petersburg will know I was at Maitlev's by this evening. They'll probably know what I bought and how much it cost as well."

"The ladies gossip. This cannot be helped."

"I felt like I was on display the whole time," I told him, "but I managed. Maitlev was very helpful. He's a nice little man."

"I will give him the nice bonus."

"He certainly earned it," I said wryly.

Orlov smiled. He was certainly in a good mood this afternoon. There was a youthful exuberance about him, a new vitality that seemed to charge the air with vibrations. I had the feeling he wanted to seize me in a mighty hug and swing me around in sheer excess of joy.

"You do a very good job in your role," he said. "Orlov is very pleased with you."

"I'm being well paid."

"Every man in St. Petersburg envies me my good fortune. Maybe I give *you* the nice bonus, too."

"That would be lovely."

My lack of enthusiasm was apparent. He tilted his head to one side and peered at me, a slight crease above the bridge of his nose.

"You do not look happy today," he said.

"I'm worried about Lucie, Gregory."

"Lucie? She stays in her room. She broods. This is not unusual. Lucie is always a moody girl."

"She's very upset about Bryan Lloyd," I said.

I wanted to make absolutely certain. His expression altered, the slight frown becoming a scowl.

"This boy is not good for her," he told me.

"He hasn't come to see her in two weeks now, nor has he sent a message or made any effort to communicate with her. She—she's extremely fond of him. I believe she may even be in love with him."

"She will get over this nonsense soon enough," he said.

"You think so?"

"She will meet a fine Russian man with a title and land. Orlov will find him for her. She will become the mistress of a fine estate, and she will forget all about this gawky English boy who has the scattered brains and the empty pockets."

"I see."

Orlov shrugged, as though to rid himself of a trivial subject. "This is not important. I have the great news to tell you."

"Oh?"

He beamed again, the exuberance returning in full force. He bounded over to the desk and picked up the creamy white card he had been studying and waved it in triumph.

"It has happened!" he exclaimed.

I was silent. He waved the card again.

"Tomorrow night there is to be a reception for the Turkish ambassador at the Winter Palace. It is a very important affair. The invitations are delivered by hand! Count Gregory Orlov and Miss Marietta Danver are requested to attend. Catherine can wait no longer. I bait the hook very carefully. She bites at last!"

Chapter Seventeen

ALTHOUGH I WAS NATURALLY CURIOUS, I wasn't at all excited about going to the Winter Palace. I had seen enough aristocratic Russian splendor to last me a lifetime, knowing as I did how the rest of the country lived. Orlov was excited enough for both of us, I thought, touching one of the coppery red waves Monsieur André had so painstakingly arranged. All day long Gregory had been full of excited anticipation. I wondered if Catherine was really as easy to manipulate as he thought. Somehow I doubted it. At any rate, we were going to see her at last and he was confident he would soon be occupying his old apartment at the palace.

I was ready to play my part. The French hairdresser Orlov had summoned had spent over two hours doing my hair, pulling it back sleekly from my face and sculpting the waves in back, leaving a dozen long ringlets to spill down between my shoulder blades. He had affixed a delicate platinum spray over the right side of my head, in front of the waves. It curled from my temple halfway across my crown, the fragile wire tendrils shimmering with two dozen magnificent diamonds. I hadn't the rank to wear a tiara, but I doubted there would be a tiara in the palace more stunning than this superb ornament, which complemented my coiffure and emphasized its artistry.

Monsieur André had wanted to help me with my makeup as well, but I had firmly refused. The Russian ladies I had seen wore far too much, their faces obviously

painted, and I preferred a more natural look. The Frenchman wrung his hands and insisted I would look pale as a
ghost, but as I studied the results in the mirror, I knew I
had made the right choice. I needed no coat of powder, no
crimson rouge, no black satin beauty patches.

Stepping back a few paces, I turned this way and that,
giving the gown a final inspection. The gorgeous light tan
brocade had a rich metallic sheen and was lavishly embroidered with exquisite flowers in orange, brown, bronze, and
thread of gold. It had cost the equivalent of two hundred
English pounds a yard and was the richest, most sumptuous material I had ever seen. The unusually full skirt
swelled over a dozen bronze gauze underskirts, and with
its elbow-length bell sleeves that dropped off the shoulder,
its daringly low-cut heart-shaped bodice and snug waist,
the gown was a masterpiece, no flounces, no ruffles, no gar-
lands of ribbon to distract from the incredibly luxurious
cloth.

Well, Marietta, I told myself, if you're going to make an
Empress jealous you're certainly dressed for it.

Leaving my rooms, I walked down the hall and slowly
descended the curving white staircase, the extremely full
skirts swaying, rustling with a crisp, crackling noise.
Gregory was waiting for me downstairs, and the look in
those deep navy blue eyes told me he was more than
pleased. He looked splendid himself in dark brown brocade
breeches and frock coat and a cream satin waistcoat embroidered with gold and brown floral designs, pale cream
lace dripping from his cuffs and spilling from his throat.

He took my hand, helping me down the last two steps.
The wide pink mouth curved in an appreciative smile.

"Almost perfect," he said.

"Almost?"

He tilted his head and looked at me with a mock frown.
"Something is missing—ah, yes, diamonds. Not enough diamonds."

"The hair ornament is gorgeous, Gregory."

"I think you will like it when I purchase it for you.

Still—come with me. We will see if we can make you perfect."

Still holding my hand, he led me into the drawing room
and over to a table on which sat a long, flat case. He let go
of my hand and looked at the case as though wondering
how it got there. Very playful. Very boyish. He opened the
case, his eyes widening in mock surprise. I watched him
lift the necklace out of its bed of velvet. The diamonds
seemed to drip from his fingers in a glittering cascade that
flashed and sparkled in a shimmering white and gold
blaze. He smiled. He held it out with both hands so that I
could more properly appreciate its spectacular beauty.

"This should do, yes?"

The necklace was like an incredible web of diamonds,
scalloped loops suspended from three interlocked strands.
In the center of each and dangling at the bottom were
amazing pale golden diamonds, the color of topaz but far
more brilliant, each rare pear-shaped pendant larger than
the largest grape, gleaming with fiery white-gold sparks. I
had never seen its like.

"It—it's magnificent," I said in awe.

"It has a most interesting history," he informed me,
shaking the necklace so that the gems flashed and shimmered all the more. "Catherine is most jealous of this
Marie Antoinette of France and wishes to outshine her,
so she has Maitlev commission this necklace. Marie
Antoinette's own jeweler creates it and it is shipped to
Maitlev, but there is a problem."

He moved behind me and lifted the long coppery red
ringlets and fastened the necklace around my throat. It
rested heavily against my skin, the gleaming jewels dripping in fiery loops, the pendants dangling, emphasizing
the full swell of my breasts, which were half-exposed by
the extreme décolletage.

"When the necklace arrives, Catherine's ministers are
screaming and pulling their hair and saying she cannot
possibly afford so fabulously expensive a necklace. She reluctantly agrees to economize and Maitlev is left with the

necklace no one can afford until Orlov returns and buys it for you."

She's going to love me, I thought wryly. If I'm lucky she'll simply behead me.

He stepped back around and, taking my hands, held me at arm's length, admiring me as he might admire a work of art.

"You are the most beautiful woman in Russia this night," he said. "I think you are perhaps the most beautiful woman in the world."

Knowing him as I did, I was still touched, for I could tell that he was completely sincere. I thanked him quietly for the compliment and lowered my eyes demurely, and Gregory squeezed my hands, fetched our fur cloaks, and led me proudly out to the waiting carriage. My skirts were so full that it took some negotiating for me to get through the door. Once we were inside, Gregory had to sit across from me as the magnificent spread of embroidered brocade completely covered one seat. It was a relatively short drive, and both of us were silent, immersed in our own thoughts.

I could sense Gregory's excitement as he helped me out of the carriage, my skirts crackling as I manipulated them. It was a beautiful night with a thousand stars hanging in a soft black sky, and rays of moonlight bathed the Winter Palace. I had an impression of acres and acres of stately white marble columns supporting ornate porticos, the windows beyond aglow with golden light. Guardsmen in white uniforms lined either side of the stairway, holding torches aloft to light our way as we slowly climbed the steps, other couples moving ahead of us, more carriages arriving below. Our wraps were taken from us, and footmen in white satin knee breeches and gold-embroidered white satin frock coats and powdered wigs waited to escort us through a dazzling labyrinth of corridors and public rooms.

Candles blazed, brightly illuminating the palace, and the splendor of it was impossible to absorb. It was like being inside a gigantic jewel box, I thought, each chamber more splendid than the last. We were finally led into a gold and white foyer and handed over to a stony-faced chamberlain whose duty it was to announce us. The huge double doors were opened and the chamberlain moved forward, banging his long staff on the floor.

"Count Gregory Orlov!" he thundered. "Miss Marietta Danver!"

All eyes were upon us as we stood at the top of a shallow flight of marble steps leading into a vast reception room with a sky blue ceiling painted with pink-hued white clouds, the superb oval molding framing it lavish with gold gilt. Half a dozen immense chandeliers shed radiant light, hundreds of crystal pendants glittering, and the creamy white walls were divided by pale pink and sky blue panels framed in gold and overlaid with leafy gilt designs. It was a spectacular setting for the brilliant, bejeweled crowd who stared openly as Gregory tucked my hand into the crook of his arm and led me slowly down the stairs and into their midst.

Gregory beamed, savoring his moment of triumph. I felt numb, as though this were all happening to someone else. Marietta Danver, a former convicted thief and indentured servant who had trekked the Natchez Trace on a mule, who had made a perilous journey through the swamps of the Gulf of Texas pursued by cannibal Indians, now in the Winter Palace, waiting to meet Catherine of Russia—it seemed unreal. I didn't want to be here. I wanted to be in Texas with Em and Randy, people who were real, people who had suffered and survived as I had, who didn't live in a brilliant, artificial world like carefully nurtured greenhouse flowers. I took a deep breath, preparing myself.

There must have been two hundred people in the room, the women gorgeously gowned and bejeweled, the men as splendidly attired, and an inordinate number of the them were strapping, handsome young military types in full-dress uniform. The Turkish ambassador, in colorful native garb, was surrounded by a chattering clique, but Catherine hadn't appeared yet. I knew from Gregory that, except for state occasions, she liked to dispense with ceremony and the boredom of tedious protocol, conducting court affairs with a breezy informality horrifying to certain of her ministers and those of the old regime who felt it unseemly for an Empress to be quite so cavalier.

As Gregory and I moved across the polished parquet floor I could feel the stares and hear the excited whispers exchanged behind fans. I nodded at several people who had dined at the Marble Palace, smiled politely, began to play my role. We were quickly surrounded, for Gregory's appearance here tonight was of tantamount importance in court circles. Was he to be reinstated? Was Potemkin to be supplanted? Would Orlov soon wield his old power and influence? The whole structure of court politics could change overnight, and those whose livelihood depended on the favors of those in favor made certain to cover all bets. Greetings were effusive, compliments lavish, smiles openly fawning.

"Well, Gregory, I never expected to see *you* here again," a tall brunette announced.

Her voice was sarcastic and, amidst all the gushing insincerity, quite refreshing. Rather heavyset, she wore a black velvet gown appliquéd with silver leaves, the full skirt parting in front to reveal a cloth-of-silver underskirt. Well into her forties, she had a round, fleshy face dominated by cynical brown eyes and a sullen scarlet mouth that drooped at the corners. Her heavy eyelids were coated with mauve shadow, and she wore far too much powder, yet she still had a curiously potent sexual allure. One was reminded of a bruised, overripe peach still savory to the bite.

"Ah, Protasova!" Gregory exclaimed. "I thought you would have retired to a nunnery by this time in order to repent of your sins."

"Were I to retire to a religious order, a monastery would be more likely. All those love-starved men."

"You would be the answer to their prayers, Protasova. No doubt about it. I would like you to meet my friend.

Marietta, this is Madame Protasova, chief lady-in-waiting to Empress Catherine. Protasova, Miss Marietta Danver."

The cynical brown eyes swept over me, missing not a detail.

"I've heard a great deal about you," she said.

"And I've heard a great deal about you," I replied, ever so sweetly.

I had indeed. Madame Protasova was known as *l'épreuveuse,* "the tester." According to rumor, her job was to test candidates for Catherine's bed. If the applicant showed sufficient strength, stamina, and invention, a favorable report was passed to the Empress. If not, he was summarily dismissed, all hopes of royal favor extinguished. The opulent, aging brunette looked well suited for her work, I thought bitchily, yet her frankness and refusal to fawn raised my opinion of her considerably.

"You're every bit as beautiful as they claimed you are," she informed me. "I assume that hair is natural. No dye could simulate such a brilliant color."

"It's natural," I said.

"Would that my own were," she retorted. "Living at court is hazardous to hair. Mine turned gray years ago. I'd kill to look like you," she continued, "and if killing would turn the trick I'd lay waste left and right."

"I believe that was a compliment."

"Begrudgingly given," she said dryly. "Well, Gregory, your arrival in St. Petersburg must have been something of a disappointment. No triumphal arches erected to greet you, no gold medal struck by the Imperial mint in your honor. Catherine had all this done in '72," she added, seeing that I was puzzled. "When he returned from a mission in Moscow."

"I treasure that medal," he said.

"One of the less popular issues."

"The arches are still standing."

"In shocking disrepair, I've noticed, and covered with bird droppings."

Gregory scowled, uncomfortable under that cynical

brown gaze. He and Protasova were clearly old adversaries, and he was no match for her. Catherine apparently liked to surround herself with strong, formidable woman, I reflected, remembering Princess Dashkova in London. Having deflated his ego, having spoiled his jovial, expansive mood, Protasova allowed a smile to curl on her scarlet lips.

"Cheer up, Gregory dear," she said in a consoling voice. "I don't expect you to believe it, but I'm actually on your side."

"This I doubt," he retorted.

"You may have been a troublesome lout, but as long as you had enough expensive toys to keep you occupied you were at least manageable and didn't meddle in matters over your head. The current incumbent fancies himself a great statesman and feels he should run the country."

"I rue the day my brothers and I bring this Ukrainian to Catherine's attention," he grumbled.

"As do a number of us, dear. Good luck with your little scheme. It may be obvious, but I hope it works. Charmed to have met you, Miss Danver."

She sauntered away with a soft swish of black velvet and silver skirts and a few moments later was immersed in intimate conversation with one of the handsome guardsmen. Mouth in a petulant curl, Gregory cast resentful looks in her direction, but his good humor soon returned as more old acquaintances came over to welcome him back and tell him how splendid he was looking. He basked in the adulation, delighted in the compliments, convinced they were all sincere, convinced his charm and magnetism were solely responsible for all the fuss.

I smiled politely and listened to the outrageous flattery, wishing I were anywhere else. A gushing old princess in peacock blue taffeta told me I was a vision to behold. I thanked her. A doddering courtier with a dissipated face and lascivious eyes said he would like to pay my rent after Orlov tired of me. I elevated an eyebrow. We had been here for half an hour now, and the evening was already beginning to seem interminable. Catherine hadn't appeared yet, nor had her consort. My attention began to wander, and I glanced around the enormous room, noting the spectacular gowns, the glittering jewels, the animated faces, and had the feeling I was trapped in an exotic aviary with gorgeously plumed birds of prey. And then I saw the tall, lean youth in pale gray velvet and my heart seemed to leap.

He was standing near one of the gilt-embossed blue panels, talking with a woman in amethyst satin and black lace, a mass of long blonde ringlets falling between her shoulder blades and belying the weary middle-aged face. His black leather pumps had silver buckles. His white stockings were of silk. The knee breeches and frock coat were English in cut, and his white satin waistcoat was embroidered with fragile black leaves. The heavy blond hair gleamed, one wave tumbling over his brow, and there were faint gray shadows under the lackluster gray-blue eyes. He looked bored and disconsolate and scarcely listened to the vivacious chatter the woman fired at him.

As though feeling my stare, he glanced up and saw me across the room, but he didn't nod. He merely gazed as though I were a stranger, then gave his attention to the woman with blonde ringlets. I had to speak to him. I had to explain. Orlov took my hand and led me over to another cluster of people, and when I looked again Bryan was no longer standing beside the blue panel. I was certain he hadn't left the reception. Somehow, before the evening was over, I would locate him again and find an opportunity to be alone with him for a few precious minutes, whether Gregory liked it or not. He had looked so pale, so drawn, all that marvelous vitality completely missing.

"—is good to be back," Orlov was saying. "You must come to see us at the Marble Palace."

"I shall eagerly await the invitation," Count Razumovsky replied. "And how do you like Russia, Miss Danver? "

"It's very interesting," I said.

"Court life must be quite different in—"

He cut himself short. A hush fell over the entire assemblage. The double doors at the end of the room opposite the steps had opened and a giant in outlandish finery shambled clumsily into the room, dominating it at once. Though hunched and walking with a stoop, he was easily the tallest man here, taller even than Orlov, and his large, awkward body reminded one of a bear's. His greasy powdered hair was pulled back and tied with a black velvet ribbon at the nape of his neck. His pasty pale face was pockmarked, the lips thick and sensual, the nose too large and crooked. A black satin patch covered his left eye. He was hideously ugly, there was no question about that, yet his magnetism galvanized the whole room.

Gregory Aleksandrovich Potemkin wore scuffed black pumps with bejeweled buckles. His silk stockings were baggy, one of them deplorably snagged, and his rumpled white satin knee breeches looked soiled. His frock coat was golden brocade lavishly embroidered with black and silver and scarlet flowers, and exquisite gold lace spilled from his neck and cuffs. His hands were inordinately large and looked gnarled, a workman's hands, powerful enough to crush a skull as easily as an eggshell. Several diamond and ruby rings flashed on the long fingers. Although the attire was indeed outlandish, he wore it with reckless aplomb. Preposterous Potemkin might appear, even repellent, but it was impossible to take one's eyes off him.

He lumbered forward a few more steps and peered around like a surly bear abruptly awakened from a long sleep. The room was still silent, and the air seemed to vibrate with tension. The royal favorite lurched, blinked, seemed about to fall, and then he straightened into a moderate hunch and toyed with the lace at his throat, looking directly at Gregory. Breaths were drawn in sharply, held. The people standing around us moved back discreetly, silently, and suspense crackled as the two giants faced each other across the long room.

Orlov stood proudly with head held high, an arrogant,

confident smile on his lips. Only moments ago he had been a resplendent sun, shedding the radiance of his presence throughout the room, the center of all attention. None of that radiance had gone, but it had been eclipsed by the curiously sinister magnetism of his successor. If Gregory was like a resplendent sun, Potemkin was like a swollen moon shining in a dark, forbidding sky. I was reminded of a sorceror who kept mere mortals enthralled by dark spells and primordial magic.

Potemkin lumbered slowly toward us, and I, too, was caught in his spell, utterly fascinated, frozen, it seemed, unable to breathe properly. He paused a few feet away from us and shook his shaggy head and then smiled. At least I thought it was a smile. Those thick lips curled and lifted at the corners, though whether in amusement or disdain it was impossible to determine. That one black-brown eye glowed like a dark coal, the brow above it lifting into a high arch.

"Orlov," he said. "I heard you had returned. It is most interesting to see you again."

His voice was surprising, a deep, rich, musical voice that seemed to tenderly caress each word, a voice made for singing. I remembered that he was an accomplished musician and was said to serenade the Empress with love songs he had especially composed for her. I could imagine that voice crooning, caressing, lulling one into a delicious stupor.

He moved forward and curled his huge hands around Gregory's arms and gave him a tug, pulling him against his chest, and then he kissed him resoundingly on each cheek. Powerful and strong as he was, Orlov might have been a slight, delicate boy in that powerful grasp. Potemkin released him and stepped back, pleased with his unexpected gesture. Gregory was dumbfounded, but he quickly regained his composure.

"It has been a long time, no?" Potemkin said. "The last time I see you you give me this." He pointed to the black satin patch covering his left eye. "It makes me more beautiful, I think. The pretty boy becomes an irresistible man."

And, strangely enough, Potemkin had once been a very pretty boy, I knew. The pox, the broken nose, the loss of his eye had destroyed the angelic face, and years of excessive indulgence in all the pleasures had cruelly bloated a body once slim and upright. The physical appearance might have changed, but the sexual allure that had enchanted an Empress was still so strong it seemed to assault one physically.

When Gregory Aleksandrovich Potemkin turned his dark gaze on me, I understood his power over women. My knees grew weak. Warm waves seemed to wash over me, caressing my skin. I seemed to have lost all will, suddenly helpless, an abject slave to that powerful magnetism. Potemkin peered into the innermost depths of a woman's heart, conjuring up forbidden fantasies that left one shaken and utterly exposed. His physical appearance mattered not at all. In the blaze of that raw sexuality he might have been a god.

He smelled of garlic and vodka and potently of sweat, but that powerful body odor was like the headiest of musks, incredibly virile. It took me several moments to compose myself, to shake off that hypnotic spell, but I still wasn't breathing properly.

"I hear about your beautiful friend, Orlov," he said lazily. "I think it would be nice if you introduce me to her."

Breaking his silence, Orlov performed the introductions. Potemkin took my hand, imprisoning it in long, powerful fingers that were rough, lightly callused. Lifting it slowly, he turned my palm up and lowered his head and planted his moist lips in the center of it. They seemed to burn my skin, caressing, sucking it. I repressed a gasp and pulled my hand away, stammering a polite inconsequentiality, praying I wouldn't faint. Potemkin smiled, fully aware of his effect upon me.

"You have not lost your taste in women, Orlov," he said. "This one is a treasure. I think maybe I steal her from you."

"This is not likely, Potemkin."

"We shall see," Potemkin replied. "It is good to have you back in St. Petersburg. Things have been most dull of late. I think maybe now they will liven up considerably."

"Perhaps they will," Gregory said ominously.

Potemkin smiled again, a great, shaggy bear amused by the posturings of a fawning cub, and, indeed, that's what Gregory seemed beside him. Potemkin shook himself and glanced around the room. People had begun to talk and circulate again, but all attention was riveted on the three of us. Gregory had lost some of his confidence now, and he sought to regain it, puffing up his chest, adjusting his expression.

"You come all the way from England, I hear," Potemkin said, turning to Orlov. "Was the journey eventful?"

"I do not know what you mean by *eventful.*"

"You were not attacked by peasants?"

Gregory scowled, shaking his head.

"They grow more and more brazen," Potemkin said. "This Pugachev has a large army, they tell me, and it grows larger every day. Soon he will begin to march, one hears, burning everything in his path."

"The Imperial Army is looking for this man. Is this not so?"

"They have been for months," Potemkin replied. "There have been a few minor skirmishes in the north, but our best officers have yet to locate his secret camp. They have captured two or three of his men and put them to the rack, but all died without revealing the information. They believe he is a saint, the reincarnation of Peter III, come back to avenge his murder. This is what he believes himself."

Orlov shifted uncomfortably. "He is clearly a madman."

"This is so, but you know how superstitious these peasants are. Pugachev tells them the soul of Peter III has entered his body and taken possession of him and they shake their heads in wonderment and take up their pitchforks and scythes to join his army."

Potemkin's one dark, glowing eye closely observed the

effects of these words upon his rival. A smile played on his thick lips as he continued.

"Were Pugachev actually to march, you and your brothers would be in particular danger. Don't you all have estates in the north?"

"This is so. My brothers are still in the country. I visit them soon."

"In the north," Potemkin repeated. "This is where Pugachev is building his army. No doubt our men will squelch him before he even gets started, but your brothers must be uneasy, so exposed there in the north."

"My brothers have their cossacks," Orlov said hotly. "This is not suitable conversation, Potemkin. You will distress the lady."

"This I would never do," he said in mock alarm, turning to me. "Have I distressed you, Miss Danver?"

I shook my head. He was all attentive concern.

"You look a trifle pale. I will devote the rest of the evening to cheering you up. It will be a most enjoyable task."

Gregory started to say something, but before he could shape the words the double doors at the end of the room were opened again and two strikingly handsome guards in white velvet uniforms festooned with gold braid held them back, standing at attention as their Empress stepped through. She stood a moment, beautifully framed, then moved slowly into the room. She lifted her hand, signaling that there was to be no formality tonight, yet everyone bowed and curtsied as she made her slow progress, personally greeting her guests and thanking them for coming. Catherine might be casual and informal, I reflected, but there could be no question that she was Empress of All the Russias. Never had I seen so regal a bearing, so majestic a mien.

She had never been a beautiful woman, and now, in middle age, had added a considerable amount of excess poundage to that stately frame. One would hesitate to call her fat, but she was certainly well padded. Well rounded, too, I observed. Rubenesque. Her powdered hair was pulled back

from her face and arranged in coiled waves, a diamond and
ruby tiara across her crown with matching earrings
dangling from her lobes. Her cheeks were round, her
mouth a plump pink rosebud, her nose a trifle long. Surmounted by dark curving brows, her dark blue eyes glittered with lively intelligence.

A sumptuous diamond and ruby necklace sparkled at
her throat, and her silver brocade gown was embroidered
with delicate ruby red flowers, silver tissue lace edging the
bodice and full puffed sleeves. The scalloped flounces of the
very full skirt parted in front to display the ruby velvet underskirt. Catherine of Russia might not be beautiful, but
she was a striking figure, radiating power and authority
and, yes, great sensuality. Here was a woman born to rule
and born to savor all the pleasures of the flesh. As she drew
nearer, I felt a nervous tremor welling up inside, for I suspected that she was indeed a very jealous and possessive
woman.

She was speaking to a group of people nearby now, only
yards away. Potemkin smiled with secret amusement,
toying idly with the gold tissue lace, watching his mistress
smile at a remark one of her courtiers made. She seemed
totally unaware of our presence, lingering to exchange a
few more remarks with those nearby. Orlov stood tall and
proud, an expectant gleam in his eyes. He had regained all
his confidence and, if possible, looked even more resplendent as the object of his obsession turned and moved majestically toward us, her silver brocade skirt spreading,
diamonds and rubies flashing brilliantly.

As she stopped in front of us, Potemkin nodded with a
studied nonchalance I found both rude and shocking. Gregory made a deep, impressive bow, clicking his heels, and I
curtsied with much rustling of skirts. Catherine's dark
blue eyes sparkled with something that might have been
amusement, but it was impossible to tell. They were wonderfully intelligent eyes, eyes that observed everything
with wry detachment. Her complexion, I noted, was as soft

and smooth as satin, unmarred by the heavy cosmetics ladies of her court used so lavishly.

"It's been a long time, Gregory," she said.

"Much too long, my Catherine."

"You're looking very well. Very handsome too. You haven't lost your looks."

"I am most flattered you think so. You are lovelier than ever."

"Nor have you lost your lying tongue."

"It is true, my Catherine. You are a vision."

"And much heavier than I was last time you saw me."

"This only gives one more to admire."

Catherine smiled a rueful smile and turned her attention to me. Gregory quickly performed an introduction. Those dark, intelligent eyes examined me from head to toe as everyone in the room watched with bated breath. I stood statue still, my cool composure belying the nervous tremors inside. Catherine of Russia intimidated kings and caused nations to quake, and I felt sure my knees might give way at any moment.

"I see we have the same dressmaker," she remarked.

"So it would seem," I replied.

She looked at the necklace. "And the same taste in jewelry," she added wryly. "A gift from Orlov?"

I nodded, and the rueful smile returned to her lips. I thought I detected both understanding and kinship in her eyes, and I sensed instinctively that this woman was not going to be my enemy. *We both know men,* those eyes seemed to say. *We're on to all their little tricks. They're really quite transparent creatures, aren't they, not at all a match for us.* Perhaps I imagined the message, but I saw at once that my relationship with Orlov perturbed her not a jot.

"He has magnificent taste," she said, and I knew she was speaking of me, not the necklace. "It seems you and I have quite a lot in common, Miss Danver. We'll have to get together for a cozy chat one day soon. I'll send a carriage for you."

"I would be most honored."

"You're late," Potemkin said rudely, fixing his mistress with a scathing eye. "The guests wait and wait. They cannot go in to eat until you get here, you know that."

"Paperwork. Reports. I'm never free of them. I wanted to finish signing some documents before—"

"It is no excuse!" he snapped. "If you let me handle these things for you, you would have time to entertain properly."

Catherine looked at him, and, for a brief moment, her face was utterly naked, the face of a woman who was sexually enslaved to a crude, dominating male. The blue eyes were full of silent pleading. The soft pink mouth parted, and she tilted her head back as though to avoid a blow. That look told me all I needed to know about their relationship. The brief moment passed, and the eyes became cool, defiant.

"I'm prepared to put up with a lot from you, dear one," she said, "but I am not yet prepared to turn the government over to you. Gregory, would you do me the honor of escorting me in to dine? You may escort Miss Danver, Potemkin. She will dine at your table. Gregory will dine with the Turkish ambassador and me."

Orlov extended his arm. She gave him a smile and placed her hand inside the muscular curve and he led her away, causing an excited buzz of whispers all over the room. Potemkin laughed a throaty laugh and took my hand roughly, tucking it in his arm.

"I know why she does this," he said pleasantly. "She thinks it will humiliate me, make me look bad in front of all our guests. I know all these little games she plays. She will pay later," he promised.

He led me toward an archway leading into the adjoining room, Catherine and Orlov preceding us, the other guests forming up behind us. The smell of sweat and garlic was overwhelming at such close contact. He pressed his forearm and bicep together, squeezing my hand between them, looking down at me with a gleam in his eye.

"This suits me fine," he said as we strolled. "I have the opportunity to woo you."

"Wooing me would be a complete waste of your time, Count Potemkin."

"You say this. You do not mean it. No woman is able to resist Potemkin's spell. They melt into his arms. You will be no exception. This I assure you."

He laughed again, and I fought to resist his strange power. Dark desires seemed to stir inside me as he helped me into a gilt chair at one of the small tables in the dining *salle*. Catherine was already seated nearby, and the other guests began to assemble at the larger tables below us. Potemkin and I were to dine alone, it seemed, while Orlov and the Empress entertained the guest of honor. Potemkin placed a rough hand on my bare shoulder.

"Do not be afraid, little bird. Potemkin will be very gentle."

He took a chair across from me and smiled, his eye glowing with dark amusement, and I did indeed feel like a small bird trapped by a giant, predatory eagle. Forbidden fantasies seemed to shimmer behind thin veils in my mind, and a curious lethargy seemed to steal over me. I quickly took a sip of wine, remembering Count Rostopchin's talk of mysticism and the black arts. I didn't doubt that Potemkin was well versed in them. How else could I explain the strange enchantment he cast over me? I found him utterly appalling, and yet . . . I took another sip of wine, steeling myself against his charm.

The meal was magnificent, magnificently served by footmen in gold and silver livery. I heard Orlov laughing at the table nearby as I nibbled a piece of truffle. Catherine laughed, too, and she seemed inordinately vivacious. I suspected it was for Potemkin's benefit. The enormous room was filled with bright chatter and laughter, but all attention was focused on the two tables up front. Was history being made? Was Catherine about to oust Potemkin and take back her former lover?

Potemkin dipped a fleshy artichoke leaf into a small bowl of butter, looking at me as he ate it.

"My little English dove. That's what I shall call you. We will find us a cozy nest. How your wings will flutter when Potemkin impales you with his wondrous prick."

I almost dropped my fork. Potemkin laughed his throaty laugh and, throughout the rest of the meal, described in salacious detail exactly what he intended to do to me and how I would respond. His lovely, melodious voice seemed to chant as he employed the crudest, most explicit words, and I tried not to listen to that hypnotic voice, tried not to visualize the things he painted so vividly. When the delectable cream and chocolate gateau was placed in front of me, I could only stare at it with burning cheeks.

"You do not eat much," he observed.

"I'm not hungry."

"Potemkin has a voracious appetite. He longs to devour his little English dove."

"Count Potemkin, you—you are the most obscene, the most appalling man I have ever encountered."

"All of them tell me this in the beginning. Later they beg me for more of my appalling company."

He ate his cake greedily, his eye never leaving my own. After what seemed an eternity, Cathering finally rose, signaling that the meal was over. There would be dancing in the ballroom, and tables had been set for those who preferred to gamble. Potemkin helped me out of my chair. People were starting to follow Catherine and Orlov out of the room. I caught a glimpse of pale gray velvet and sleek blond hair and, smiling ever so politely, asked Potemkin to excuse me. He looked very unhappy as I moved quickly away.

I caught up with Bryan in the corridor leading to the ballroom. He looked at me with dull blue eyes, neither surprised nor pleased when I took him by the arm.

"I need to speak with you," I said.

"I see nothing to prevent you."

"Is—is there someplace where we can get a breath of fresh air? I desperately need it."

"I suppose I could take you into the courtyard."

"Please do."

People stared at us with avid curiosity, and eyebrows were elevated as Bryan led me down a side corridor. Was Orlov's mistress going to seduce the diplomat's son? What delicious speculation there would be. It was wonderful to step outside, to breathe air not oppressed with odors of sweat and stale powder and strong perfumes. The small courtyard was completely enclosed, filled with shadows, pale rays of moonlight illuminating a marble statue, marble benches, softly gilding the leaves. It was chilly, but I welcomed the cold.

"A favorite trysting place," Bryan told me. "Before the evening ends, the shrubbery will be thronging with passionate, panting bodies. Well, Miss Danver, it seems you've finally met the high and mighty of the land."

I noted the formal "Miss Danver" but decided to ignore it. Folding my arms around my waist, I took several deep breaths, trying to clear my mind of Gregory Potemkin and the horrifying spell he seemed to have cast over me.

"You look upset," Bryan said.

"I—I've just had a very unpleasant experience."

"Potemkin? I saw you dining with him."

"He's deplorable."

"And deplorably powerful. Fortunately he's also extremely intelligent and not without political acumen. He hasn't been totally disastrous to the country yet."

"Does—does he really practice the black arts?"

"Some people think so. He's studied with the religious mystics and picked up all the tricks of the shamans, but I doubt he actually lights black candles and draws peculiar hexagons on the floor. He spent several months with Mesmer, and that probably accounts for much of his unnatural power."

"Mesmer?"

"A physician from Vienna who has developed a method

of putting people into trances. It's know as *mesmerism.* The subject is fully conscious yet completely under Mesmer's control. He's the sensation of Europe, and I'm sure Potemkin learned a great deal from him."

I shuddered in the moonlight. Bryan brushed the heavy blond wave from his brow. Shadows stirred around us. Leaves rustled. We could hear faint strains of music coming from the ballroom.

"I don't imagine you asked me out here to talk about Potemkin," he said. "Vanya was skulking around my hostel this afternoon, asking for me. Once he'd discovered I had rooms there, he left abruptly."

"I sent him, Bryan. I—I didn't have an opportunity to speak to him today, but I felt sure he'd locate you. If I hadn't seen you here I would have contacted you somehow."

"I thought not to come, but finally decided it would be better than sulking in my rooms. I suppose this is about Lucie. How is she?"

"Distraught," I said.

"Oh?"

"She didn't send that letter, Bryan. She didn't know anything about it. She's been—she's hardly eaten. She stays in her room. She's convinced you despise her. She's very much in love with you."

Bryan was silent for several long moments. In the moonlight I could see his face. It was grave and young and lined with pain.

"She—didn't send the letter?"

"Her uncle sent it. He wants her to marry a title, an estate."

"She *loves* me?"

"Desperately, and—and I believe you love her, too."

"I shouldn't like to think of life without her," he told me. "I thought she—I believed—"

"I know what you must have thought, what you must have felt."

"I have to see her, Marietta!"

He seized my hands and held them tightly, the old vitality returning in a youthful flood. He told me that he loved her, loved her with all his heart and soul, didn't care about Orlov, didn't care about anyone but Lucie, they weren't too young, not at all, and he was going to have her, by God, nothing would stop him. I let him talk. I listened, and when he finally stopped for breath I began to talk myself, slowly, calmly, outlining my plan.

"Do—do you think it will work?" he asked when I finished. "It sounds a bit risky. I wouldn't want Lucie to be in any—"

"I daresay there is a certain amount of risk involved, but I feel sure Lucie would run twice the risk in order to see you again. I'll make the arrangements, Bryan. Vanya will bring a message to you when I feel it's safe to proceed."

"You trust this chap?"

"Completely."

"I don't know, Marietta. If Orlov were to discover—"

"He won't," I said patiently. "We've been out here far too long, Bryan. You'd better take me to the ballroom now. I have a performance to give."

When we returned I resumed my role and danced with a dozen courtiers. I smiled at their compliments, fended off their advances and watched out for Potemkin, whom I wished to avoid at all costs. I had a glass of champagne with Madame Protasova who told me that Potemkin had vanished with a giddy young lady-in-waiting and that, after leading the first dance and dancing together two more times, Catherine and Orlov seemed to have vanished as well. I shrugged with cool indifference and went to watch the gambling for a while and finally, around four, partook of the buffet set for the guests, eating blintzes, caviar, and scrambled eggs with a dashingly attired blond guardsman who was extremely attentive and hopeful.

"I'm free every afternoon," he told me.

"How nice for you," I replied.

"I often ride in the park. Do you ride?"

"When I can," I said.

"I have a set of rooms in the city. I'd love to show them to you."

"I imagine they're quite popular with the ladies."

He grinned. "Very," he said, "although they rarely see anything but the ceiling."

"Is it a nice ceiling?"

"Divine, I'm told."

I handed him my plate. "Then I suggest you stare at it and think of what you're missing."

"But—"

"I've more interesting things to look at," I said as I turned away.

Catherine appeared near dawn to bid her guests farewell. Standing at the door of the ballroom, she looked as regal and majestic as she had when the evening began. Empress she might be, but Catherine was still the perfect hostess, smiling and exchanging a few words with her guests as they departed. Her dark, intelligent blue eyes were serene. Her powdered hair had a silvery sheen. She was a stunning figure in the silver brocade and ruby red gown.

Orlov located me in the ballroom, hardly able to contain his elation. His lips wore a perpetual smile as we joined the procession leaving the room. When we reached Catherine, he made another deep bow and told her it had been an evening he would treasure forever. The Empress gave him a polite nod and, smiling pleasantly, reminded me of the cozy chat we would have soon. Gregory beamed euphorically as we were led back through the labyrinth of corridors and collected our wraps.

The sun was just coming up as we descended the long flight of wide marble steps to the waiting carriage. The pearl gray sky was tinted with luminous pink and gold streaks, and shadows melted all around us.

"We dance together three times!" Gregory exclaimed. "We play cards together and everyone watches! She takes me to her rooms and tells me to amuse myself while she reads more reports, signs more documents."

I wasn't really surprised. "She *worked?*" I said.

"I know my Catherine," he told me. "She is being coy. She does not wish to seem too eager to take me back."

Everyone would know she had taken him to her rooms. No one would know she had spent all those hours at her desk, least of all Potemkin. Poor Gregory, I thought. How long would it be before he discovered that Catherine had used him just as he had intended to use me? Let him enjoy his illusions, I told myself. They would crumble soon enough.

I had other things to think about.

Chapter Eighteen

OUR APPEARANCE AT THE WINTER PALACE AND
the events of the evening caused a veritable storm of gossip and the wildest speculation. Catherine had taken
Orlov to her bedroom and they had made passionate love
for hours on end. She and Potemkin had had a vicious argument and he was definitely on his way out. During the
course of the evening I had had an interlude with Potemkin, had seduced Bryan Lloyd, and made assignations with
half a dozen guardsmen. Orlov was going to move back
into his old apartments. Potemkin and I were going to
leave Russia together. Gregory and Potemkin were going
to fight a duel. The whole city buzzed with delicious,
improbable rumors. This frivolous, foolish wagging of
tongues seemed to be a major pastime of the court.

It took a stunning, shocking event in real life to divert
the gossips from their latest succulent morsel, and when
news of the Menshikov massacre reached St. Petersburg
two days later, the Orlov–Potemkin rivalry was immediately overshadowed. As horrifying detail after detail was
revealed, a frightened and uncomprehending court could
talk of nothing else. Their rarefied, greenhouse world suddenly seemed all too vulnerable, and their pampered exis-
tence had been threatened. What happened to the
Menshikovs could have happened to any of them, they
knew, and shudders of horror ran through the marble corridors.

Count Alexander Menshikov and his wife Sophia had

been bright stars in Elizabeth's court, brilliant favorites
with their own cliques. Alexander had been a particular
pet of the gouty, depraved old Empress, a virile lover who
helped her forget enroaching senility and the inevitable
loss of power. Sophia was one of Peter III's playmates and
openly scornful of the dull German princess he had married. Nevertheless, after the coup, Catherine had not banished them. Elizabeth and Peter were gone and the dull
German princess sat on the throne, but Menshikov and his
wife, now in their fifties, were still welcome at the Winter
Palace. Some claimed Catherine kept them around to remind her of the old days and the determination that had
enabled her to triumph against all odds. No longer dazzling, yet colorful and popular, the Menshikovs had continued to shine, their viperous wit and vivacity amusing a
tolerant Empress who was far too busy to bear grudges.

Two months ago the Menshikovs had temporarily retired to his estate in the north so that he could recover
from "a slight illness" that, the gossips claimed, was actually syphilis. With them were their three daughters, their
sons-in-law, six grandchildren, their private physician, and
Countess Anna Pastukov, Sophia's widowed sister. A
week and a half ago, while the Menshikovs and entourage
were having a late breakfast, a band of over two hundred
peasants had swarmed the estate, yelling like madmen,
waving pitchforks, scythes and hoes. The household servants were hacked to pieces. Countess Sophia, her sister
and daughters were brutally raped unto death, then dis-
membered. The physician and the three sons-in-law had
been shot, beheaded, the children impaled on pitchforks,
and Count Alexander Menshikov had been dragged outside and crucified as the peasants set fire to the house.

The smoke from burning buildings had brought a troop
of the Imperial Army to the scene several hours later.
Broken, battered, bleeding profusely, Count Menshikov
was still alive on his rough wooden cross and was able to
gasp out details of the massacre before dying in the arms of
the officer in charge. The peasants had disappeared, not a

trace of them to be found, but the army had made horrible reprisals nevertheless, riding into villages, rounding up men, questioning, killing, burning huts. Over five hundred peasants had been slaughtered during the days that followed.

"It will be a long time before these peasants dare strike again," Count Razumovsky declared, sipping a glass of brandy. "Catherine has ordered four more battalions to the north. They will flush out this Pugachev soon enough and bring him to St. Petersburg in chains."

"Were—were the peasants Pugachev's men?" I asked.

"More than likely," Razumovsky replied, "but it was an isolated incident. He hasn't begun his march. None of the neighboring estates were attacked."

"Pugachev has vowed to march to St. Petersburg within the year," Prince Danzimov informed us. "He claims he'll burn everything in his path. Any word from your brothers, Orlov?"

"A message arrives from Alexis this afternoon," Gregory said. "He tells me everything is quiet in our part of the country. This massacre takes place almost a hundred miles west of his estate. My brothers Feodor, Vladimir, and Ivan have had no trouble either."

"Your own estate is near them?" Prince Danzimov asked.

"We are brothers. We have estates close by each other. Is a conclave of Orlovs in the north. Many cossacks."

Countess Razumosky shivered dramatically. We were still at the dining table with our guests, three nights after the reception at the Winter Palace. Countess Razumovsky was a skinny, horse-faced woman with far too much make-up and an elaborate coiffure, her lime green gown festooned with silver lace. Her husband was a stalwart giant in his late fifties, his table manners as deplorable as his onion-scented breath. Prince Danzimov, an attractive bachelor in his thirties, was accompanied by Countess Panin, a sultry-eyed widow with pouting lips. Count Boris

Naryshkin and his wife Natalya completed the party, both of them stout, superior and terribly grand.

"Poor Sophia," Countess Razumovsky said. "She was a dear, dear friend, you know. She begged Peter and me to *visit* them. If his duties at court hadn't been so heavy we might actually have *gone.*"

"Not likely," her husband said. "I couldn't abide either of them. Vicious parasites. Gadflies, without an ounce of substance between them. Still, a horrible way to die. They say Menshikov was forced to watch his wife and daughters being raped, saw his grandchildren impaled."

Countess Razumovsky shivered again. Countess Panin idly examined her diamond and emerald bracelet, finding it difficult to hide her boredom. Footmen stood by discreetly in the grand marble dining room with its frescoed ceiling and glittering chandelier. We had dined magnificently from golden plate. My duties as hostess had never been so difficult.

"The Menshikovs will be avenged," Prince Danzimov remarked. "Finding Pugachev and stamping out this insurrection is Catherine's first priority. There've been peasant rebellions before, of course. This is nothing new."

"They should all be shot," Count Naryshkin said dryly.

His attitude was only too typical of his class, I thought, biting back a retort. I was horrified by the fate of the Menshikovs and felt that the perpetrators must have been frenzied and crazed with a lust for blood, but I knew all too well the conditions that had driven them. Slaughtering hundreds of innocent peasants was not likely to help the situation.

"Catherine is altogether too indulgent," Count Razumovsky observed. "Building schools, hospitals, trying to educate the peasants—it can only give them ideas. These programs for The People are foolhardy and a terrible drain on government."

"Would you have her build more palaces instead?" I inquired.

"Better palaces than schools for peasants," Count

Naryshkin said. "These people have the mentality of oxen. Oxen, at least, serve a useful purpose," he added, sipping his brandy.

"I, for one, will sleep much easier now that she's sent four battalions north," Countess Razumovsky said. "I was simply *distraught* when I first learned the news. I had visions of bloodthirsty peasants rampaging through the halls of the Winter Palace."

"This will never happen," her husband assured her.

I was vastly relieved when, finally, we left the table and adjourned to the drawing room. A fire crackled in the marble fireplace. Dozens of candles burned in elegant sconces. More wine was served. Countess Panin was still bored, a sulky, seductive creature in her low-cut leaf brown velvet gown. She wasn't any happier when Prince Danzimov idly sauntered over to me. I was standing alone, apart from the others.

"You seem preoccupied," he observed.

"I have a lot of things on my mind," I said truthfully.

It was after eleven. Would they never leave? I had made all the arrangements and Bryan was probably skulking around in the gardens at this very moment, waiting for my signal. Prince Danzimov smiled. Tall, with broad shoulders and a lean, muscular build, he had glossy black hair, deep gray eyes, and attractive features, the nose Roman, the mouth full, the jaw strong. He was a bit too polished, a bit too suave and far too conscious of himself.

"I understand," he said.

I gave him a surprised look. "You do?"

"You're concerned about the future."

"I suppose I am."

"Orlov may soon be occupying his old quarters in the Winter Palace. Where does that leave you?"

"You're very perceptive, Prince Danzimov," I said.

"I fancy I understand women."

"I'm sure you do."

He was so very predictable. I knew what he was going to say before he said it, and I played the little game, answering by rote. How surprised he would be if he knew how tedious I found him.

"I'm a very wealthy man," he told me.

"So I've heard."

"Not as wealthy as Orlov, of course, no one is, but I've always managed to keep my women in satisfactory style. They've never been without jewels, expensive gowns, a lavish apartment."

"How pleasant for them."

"I keep them satisfied in other ways, too."

"Oh?"

He smiled. "I could give you references."

"Countess Panin, for example?"

"Sonya and I are merely—consoling each other. Both of us are currently unattached."

"I see."

"I could be very good to you, Miss Danver."

"I'll keep that in mind," I said.

He smiled again, bowed and sauntered across the room to join the other men in their discussion of politics. Countess Razumovsky and Countess Naryshkin were avidly talking about dressmakers, the horror of the Menshikov massacre quite forgotten. Countess Panin looked as though she might expire from boredom at any moment. The ornate silver and blue enamel clock on the mantelpiece continued to tick. It was a very cold night. Bryan was probably freezing. Lucie was undoubtedly biting her nails.

It was another hour before our guests finally departed. Gregory and I bade them goodbye in the magnificent entrance hall, and when they were gone he turned to me with a pleased smile. He looked splendid in his navy blue brocade frock coat and breeches, the sky blue waistcoat embroidered in silver.

"They all believe I will soon have my old power," he informed me. "Razumovsky tells me of these shipping concessions he longs to control. Naryshkin says we need a very strong man in the Treasury. He could manage finances much better than the present comptroller."

"And they think you'll soon be able to get these things for them."

"This is so. They both hint I will find it most profitable."

"I suppose you'll receive a hefty share of the spoils."

"This is how it works," he told me. "Everyone is happy. Everyone is rewarded."

"Prince Danzimov wanted something, too."

"Oh? He does not mention it."

"Me," I said. "As soon as you discard me."

Gregory grinned, not at all bothered. "Danzimov is quite the ladies' man. He does not miss an opportunity. I—uh—cannot blame him for making this advance. You are most beautiful tonight in this bronze velvet gown."

"It's growing late," I said. "I think I'll go on up to my room."

"I will accompany you."

"It isn't necessary, Gregory."

He took my arm and led me toward the sweeping marble staircase. "It gives me pleasure," he said huskily.

"We made an agreement, Gregory."

"Is true. I agree to pay you very generously. I keep my word."

We were moving up the stairs now, his hand grasping my elbow lightly. His palm was warm against my flesh. He smelled of silk and body moisture and that familiar male musk I had once found so heady. I knew very well what he had in mind. Damn, I thought, tonight of all nights he wants to turn seductive again. Do men never think of anything but assuaging that urge?

"I'm not talking about the money," I said as we reached the landing. "We agreed it would be—merely a business arrangement."

He nodded, tightening his grip on my arm, guiding me down the hall. "This is so."

"You agreed not to come to my bedroom unless I invited you."

He chuckled playfully, ever so amiable, convinced the legendary Orlov charm would win him the prize. We reached the door of my room. He let go of my elbow and turned me around so that my back was to the door and I was facing him. Eyes gleamed darkly, full of warmth. The wide pink mouth curved in a provocative smile.

"We make an agreement, yes, but I think you want me as much as I want you," he murmured.

"You're quite mistaken, Gregory."

"It has been a long time since Rostopchin's," he said in his huskiest, most seductive voice. "I think of that night often."

"So do I," I said.

"You do?"

"I wonder how I could have been such a fool."

He frowned. "This is not a nice thing to say, Marietta."

"I'm sorry if you're offended."

"We had a glorious experience that night."

"It was rather glorious," I agreed, "but things are different now."

Candles flickered in wall sconces in the hall. His face was softly brushed with shadow. He moved closer, placing a palm against the door on either side of me, his arms making a prison, his chest almost touching my bosom. I had to tilt my head back to look up into those sensuous eyes.

"You are a very desirable woman," he crooned.

"I'm very tired," I said.

"We make love. I make you feel good."

"I'm afraid not."

"I throb for you. Look."

I looked. He did indeed.

"That's too bad," I said.

"You would leave me in this condition?"

"I have a suggestion, Gregory."

"Yes?"

"Go play with yourself."

My frankness startled him, as I had intended it to do. He looked dismayed, then offended, then extremely angry. I reached behind me, opened the door and, slipping from under his arms, stepped quickly inside and closed the door behind me. "Damn!" he roared. He pounded his fist against the door and then stormed down the hall. I sighed, thinking how peaceful it would be to live in a world without men. No fencing, no feinting, no fighting off unwelcome passes. First Prince Danzimov, then Gregory. Glancing at the clock, I saw that it was already after midnight. Bryan was probably longing to strangle me.

Moving quickly through the bedroom and into the dressing room, I fetched a fur cloak and retraced my steps, cautiously opening the door and peering up and down the hallway. No one in sight, but many of the servants were still up, and Gregory was undoubtedly prowling about downstairs, slamming things around, fuming at my lack of response. It was imperative that no one see me. Not daring to use the main staircase, I hurried down the hall and turned into a narrow side corridor that would eventually lead to the back hall. I felt terribly exposed and vulnerable, and my footsteps rang much too noisily on the uncarpeted floor.

Passing a bank of windows, I saw that it had begun to snow heavily outside. Only a few candles were burning in the back hall, and the walls between those dim yellow pools were washed with shadows that seemed to shift and slide ominously. The hall went on forever, and my heels still rapped with the sound of gunfire. I paused to take off my shoes and moved on much more quietly, shoes in hand. Long moments passed before I finally reached the servants' staircase, a dark black pit, totally unlighted. Gripping the smooth wooden banister for guidance, I cautiously began my descent.

It was freezing cold. Even in my fur cloak I shivered, moving slowly, step by step, my hand sliding along the banister. It was so dark I couldn't see anything, the darkness a palpable thing that seemed to swallow me up, the air black and damp, stroking my face. I couldn't risk a candle. Careful, I warned myself. Be very careful. There's a turn here, and the stairway branches off to the left. You don't want to fall and break your neck. Following the curve of the banister, I turned to the left, and I could see misty yellow light below, a faint haze from candles in the lower hall. Relieved, I took a deep breath and moved down another step, then froze as I heard shrill laughter. My heart seemed to stop beating as the diabolical sound rose, echoing weirdly in the enclosed space.

"—wouldn't dream of it. What kind of girl do you think I am?"

"I know what kind of girl you are. Peter told me all about what went on in your attic room last night."

"He never!"

"He said it was bliss. Come on, Lizzie. Let me sample a bit of that bliss. I'm much stronger than Peter. Much nicer, too."

One of the maids appeared at the foot of the stairs, a plump, buxom creature with curly black hair and rosy cheeks. I had never seen her before, but the servants were trained to do their work silently, invisibly, and except for those who actually waited upon us, remained out of sight. Lizzie was joined by a strapping footman whom I *had* seen before, a blond giant with roguish brown eyes. He curled his arm around her waist, squeezing her tightly. Lizzie laughed again.

"Come on, lass. Give us a kiss."

"I oughtn't!" she protested. "You're a cocky brute, Ivan, much too sure of yourself."

"Give us a sample of bliss."

He swung her around and planted a lusty kiss on her lips and the girl struggled valiantly and lost the battle and giggled when he finally removed his mouth from hers. He plunged a hand into her bodice. She squealed, trying to slap the offending hand. He squeezed her breast, grinning wickedly. Lizzie sighed, melting at last, and Ivan curled an arm around her shoulders and led her up the steps toward me. Panic gripped me. I moved quickly back up to the landing and huddled against the wall and prayed they would be too preoccupied to see me in the darkness.

"I've been looking forward to this," Ivan told her. "I've had my eye on you for a long time."

"Had your eye on Betty, too, didn't you? That isn't all you had on her."

"There's a turn here. Watch your step."

"As if I didn't know these steps by heart. Come up and down 'em ten times a day. Betty told me you're the worst of the lot, rough and randy, ready to pommel a girl till she screams for mercy."

"It isn't mercy they're screaming for," Ivan growled.

"You're awful!"

They moved past me. Lizzie's arm actually brushed my own, but she was much too immersed to notice. I waited several moments, listening to their footsteps climbing the rest of the stairs, and then, shaken, moved nervously down the rest of the steps. The lower hall was deserted, but I could hear noises coming from the kitchen. Dishes rattled. The door was open. I would have to move past it to reach the corridor leading to the west wing. Hesitating for only a moment, I scurried past, relieved when I entered the broad, unlighted corridor.

The worst part was over now. The west wing was unoccupied, the rooms shut up, the furniture covered with dust sheets. My feet were freezing. Moonlight spilled through the uncurtained windows, gilding the walls with silver, intensifying the shadows. I turned and moved down a shallow flight of steps that led to one of the back doors. The matches and candle were still in the niche where I had hidden them. I lighted the candle and waved it in front of the glass panes of the door.

This was all terribly risky, of course, but it was the only way. Lucie and I were always accompanied by Vladimir and several others when we went out shopping, and there was no way she could slip away to meet Bryan without their finding out. Bryan had to come here. I knew she was far too nervous and distraught to traverse these halls herself without detection, so I had arranged to meet him myself and take him to her room. Once he knew the way, he could come on his own late at night when everyone was asleep, and all I would have to do was see that the door was unlocked.

He tapped furiously on the glass. I had been so intent on giving the signal that I had forgotten to unlock it now. I slid the bolt and turned the knob. A gust of snow blew in as he flung open the door, almost knocking me down. The candle blew out. He stamped snow off his boots, absolutely livid.

"I've been waiting for hours!"

"For God's sake, be quiet!" I warned.

"I've been *freezing!*"

"Keep your voice *down!*"

"I'll probably catch my death of cold," he whispered furiously. "I think I already have. Maybe it's *frost*bite! I've been huddling behind that goddamn marble column for at least two hours."

"Will you stop whining!" I hissed. "I didn't know we were to have guests tonight. I didn't know they were going to stay so long. You're supposed to be a bold, intrepid young lover, risking all for the girl he loves, and you sound like a petulant child."

"You're a vicious bitch!"

I had to smile. He saw it in the moonlight, and I thought he was going to strike me. He shivered and brushed the snow from his hair and glared at me, and I placed my hand on his brow.

"You don't have a bit of fever," I told him.

"I'm very sensitive to colds. This is insane, Marietta. We're never going to make it without being caught."

"Not if you keep carrying on like a banshee," I said calmly. "Several of the servants are still up. Gregory is, too. We're going to have to be extremely careful."

"It's dark. I can't see a bloody thing."

"There's plenty of moonlight. Follow me. There are seven steps here. They're low and flat. Be careful."

I moved up the steps. So did Bryan. He made four of them, slipped on the fifth, and went sliding back down,

arms and legs flying at crazy angles, landing with a crash
and a cry I felt sure would bring the whole house down on
us. He sat up, groaning, rubbing his head. I hurried to him
and took his hand, yanking him back to his feet.

"Maybe we'd better just forget the whole thing," I said
acidly. "Maybe you'd better just *leave.*"

"Jesus, Marietta! I didn't do it deliberately. I could have
cracked my skull open. I think maybe I did."

"You're perfectly all right. Here, take my hand again."

Bryan straightened up, his eyes full of silent apology. I
sighed and took his hand and led him on the long journey
up the stairs, down the hall, past my own rooms, past the
staircase to Lucie's sitting room.

A trembling Lucie opened the door immediately. Her
face was chalk white.

I pushed Bryan through the door just ahead of me, then
closed the door and leaned against it, so relieved I could
barely stand. Lucie was wearing a light tan muslin frock
sprigged with pink and brown flowers. Her hair was
brushed, falling to her shoulder blades in a gleaming
mass, a brown velvet bow fastened in back. A fire was
burning vigorously in the fireplace, I noted. Thank good-
ness for that. I heaved another sigh, stood up straight, and
told Bryan to take off his clothes.

"What!" He was horrified.

"Do as I say," I ordered.

"Now just a bloody minute! I came here to see Lucie. I've
heard all that *talk* about you, but—"

"Fetch him a towel, Lucie, and a robe or something he
can wrap up in while his clothes dry. You go stand by the
fire, Bryan. I'll give you exactly twenty seconds to start
disrobing. Hang your clothes over the fire screen."

Dismayed, offended, afraid to disobey, he set his boots
down and took off his coat. In a few moments he was shivering, and Lucie gave him a towel and a long brown silk
robe. She had regained her color. Her eyes were full of wry
amusement as she poured a glass of brandy for him. In a
matter of minutes the anguished girl had been trans-

formed into a poised and lovely woman. Bryan wrapped the robe around him and belted the sash and began to dry his hair with the towel. I slipped on the shoes I had been carrying all this time.

"I'll leave you two alone now," I said quietly. "I'm sure you have quite a lot to talk about."

"Thank you, Marietta," Lucie told me. "Don't worry about anything. I'll see that he gets out."

I returned to my rooms and had a glass of brandy myself, weak from nervous exhaustion. I sat in the large gold velvet chair and stared at the dying fire, sipping the brandy, sad now, a prey to those memories that invariably returned when I was tired, when I was low and alone. Lucie's story was going to have a happy ending, I would do everything in my power to see that it did, but my own had no such conclusion in sight. There was no Prince Charming waiting to take me away, no love-filled future to be shared. I took another sip of brandy and watched the tiny yellow-orange flames leap and lick, growing weaker as the log flaked away.

Where was he now? What was he doing at this very moment? Why couldn't I hate the son of a bitch for what he had done to me? Why couldn't I forget him? I saw the floppy chestnut hair, the vivid blue eyes, the twisted nose and grinning lips and remembered the fights, the fury, the feeling of being gloriously alive. Jeremy Bond had saved my life a number of times, and then he had robbed it of all meaning. Who was he wooing now? Who was he dazzling with that roguish charm? Why, oh why, did I have to remember when I wanted only to forget?

I was amazed to find the brandy glass empty. I got up and poured more and sat back down in the chair. The room was growing chilly, but the fur cloak was still around my shoulders and what did a little chill matter? I remembered and the candles spluttered out and the fire died and moonlight invaded and the memories merged into dreams and he was there with a teasing smile on his lips and a wicked gleam in his eyes and I slapped him and he seized me and I came alive again and joy flooded through me and I knew this was where I belonged, wrapped tightly in his arms, my haven, my Heaven. Jeremy, Jeremy, Jeremy, never let me go. Don't leave. Don't go. Don't vanish again . . . I opened my eyes and saw the pink-gold light of early morning and saw Lucie standing over me, looking at me with inquisitive eyes.

"You never went to bed?" she asked.

"What time is it?" I said groggily.

"It's six-fifteen. The brandy bottle is almost empty, Marietta."

"It couldn't be. I don't drink."

"Apparently you *did,*" she replied.

"Do you have to be so bloody chipper?"

"I—oh, Marietta, I'm so happy I could dance!"

"Do and I'll kill you," I promised.

I got up, feeling stiff and sore and slightly dazed. I would have committed any number of crimes for a cup of coffee. As though reading my mind, Lucie skipped blithely over to the tray she had brought and poured me a cup, and I muttered a sullen thank you as she explained, interminably and in a disgustingly cheerful voice, that she had gone down to the kitchen and found the chef already up and squabbling with an assistant and told him she'd awakened early and charmed him into making coffee for her and brought the tray up herself because she simply *had* to talk to me.

"Not until I've had at least two cups," I warned.

She moved over to a window and held the drape back and more light spilled into the room and I blinked and drank the coffee which was wonderfully hot and strong but really didn't help all that much. Impatient, unable to contain herself, Lucie let the drape fall back into place and started chattering again in that bright, joyous voice and I shook my head and held my hand out in front of me, swallowing the rest of the coffee. She refilled my cup.

"Feeling better?"

"Not really."

"He wants to marry me, Marietta."

"I assumed he would."

"We talked and talked and he looked so engaging in that brown silk robe I just wanted to hug him. I didn't. I was very dignified and proper even though he was naked under the robe. His hair started drying and got all feathery and soft and his clothes dried and started steaming and—and he's writing another play, it's almost finished, he's been working on it at the hostel and it's going to be wonderful, Marietta, a huge success. It was almost five o'clock before he finally put his clothes back on and left."

"Did he—"

"I showed him the way myself. No one saw us. We were very careful. I took him to the back door in the west wing and he left without even kissing me good-bye. He's coming back tonight but we've decided it would be much easier if I slipped down to one of the empty rooms in the west wing and met him there."

The clock struck six-thirty. I cringed and took another gulp of coffee.

"We—we'll have to run away, Marietta," she said, her voice solemn now. "We'll have to leave Russia and get married in London. My uncle would—there is no other way. Bryan is going to book passage for two on the next ship that can get us to England. He's going to drive out to Kronstadt this afternoon to take care of it."

"I see."

"It's the only way. It—it's going to be tricky, but once we're on that ship there's nothing my uncle can do. I'm a little frightened, but we'll work it out. I—I love him, Marietta."

"I know you do, darling."

"He loves me, too."

"Of course he does."

Lucie perched on the arm of a chair, spreading her muslin skirts out, and in the softly diffused light she looked so young, so radiant and lovely, it made my heart ache.

"In the past I—I've done a lot of things I'm not proud of,"

she said in a quiet voice, "but—when I'm with Bryan none of that matters. When I'm with him I'm a different person. I—I feel pure again. That sounds crazy, I know, but when I'm with him I'm the person I was *meant* to be."

"I understand, Lucie."

"I'm not a dewy-eyed girl, Marietta, I haven't been for a long, long time. I know it won't all be sunshine. I know there'll be difficult times. Bryan is temperamental and moody and often childish—he's an artist, you see. He needs me, and—it's glorious to be needed."

I nodded, wanting to cry. Lucie brushed a golden brown wave from her temple and stood up.

"Will—will you help us, Marietta?"

"You know I will, darling."

Lucie gave me a hug and smiled and left the room. My dream had evaporated and Jeremy was gone for good, but I vowed Lucie's dream was going to come true. I would do anything I had to do to see that it did, no matter what the risk. It was too late for me now, my chance had come and gone, but one of us was going to have that happy ending.

Chapter Nineteen

GREGORY WAS GROWING MORE AND MORE impatient as day after day passed and Empress Catherine failed to summon him. After their night of cozy intimacy at the Winter Palace, he had been prepared to move into his old quarters at once, certain the evening had been a complete success. Now, ten days later, ugly doubts were beginning to crack his confident facade. His mood grew progressively more sullen, with frequent outbursts of temper. I had been appalled to see him strike a footman, knocking the poor man to the ground when he failed to perform some minor duty promptly enough to suit the testy Orlov. The relationship between the two of us had deteriorated considerably since my refusal to let him sleep with me again, and I suspected that he was beginning to blame me for Catherine's continuing neglect.

He was puzzled, resentful and, finally, optimistic when a messenger arrived with a royal summons—for me, not Gregory. I was to appear at the Hermitage at four o'clock the next afternoon for "English tea with the Empress." A carriage would be sent for me. After ranting and railing, Orlov was finally able to convince himself that this was a very good omen, that Catherine wanted to break the bad news to me herself and send me packing with, no doubt, a most generous gift. She was very diplomatic about these matters, he informed me, and would naturally want me out of the way before restoring him to his position of glory. I was not to be nervous. She was no dragon. She would be very tactful, very polite, and if I handled myself properly I would probably embark for America an even wealthier woman.

I was extremely nervous as I left in the royal carriage the next afternoon, but not because I was to take tea with the Empress. Lucie had come to my room in the morning, tense and apprehensive. She and Bryan had been meeting in the west wing almost every night and both had been extremely careful and were certain no one had seen them—until last night. As she was slipping down to meet Bryan well after midnight, Lucie had run into Vladimir in the back hall. Flustered, she finally managed to stammer that she had awakened to find herself hungry and was on her way to the kitchen to see if she could get something to eat.

"He—he wanted to know why I had used the servants' stairs, why I carried no candle," she said. "I told him I—I didn't want to disturb anyone. He was very suspicious, Marietta. I—there was nothing I could do but go on into the kitchen and order a light snack sent up to my room on a tray."

Vladimir had escorted her back up to her bedroom and had brought the tray up himself a short while later. It had been two in the morning before she had dared leave her room again, and although she had seen no one she had had a peculiar feeling that someone was watching her, following her to the room in the west wing where Bryan was waiting. It was probably her imagination, she admitted, and there had certainly been no one around when Bryan slipped out at five and she returned to her room, but the encounter with Vladimir had completely unnerved her. She couldn't help but worry. Had he believed her story? Would he report the incident to her uncle? If it had been a footman or one of the other servants she could have carried it off with aplomb, but Vladimir—Vladimir was like a watchdog, savagely suspicious and always on guard.

Vladimir hadn't said anything to Orlov yet, I was sure of that, and I tried to convince myself that he had accepted the girl's story, but I was every bit as worried as Lucie and found it hard to shake the nervous apprehension as the carriage moved smartly along. It was a brilliant day. I gazed out at the elegant parks and majestic marble buildings. Put it out of your mind, Marietta, I told myself. No use worrying about something that hasn't happened yet. Take each thing as it comes. Concentrate on seeing Catherine now. God knows that's going to be strain enough.

I seriously doubted that she intended to send me away with a generous gift to soothe any hard feelings, just as I doubted she had the slightest intention of taking Gregory back. I suspected, instead, that it was pure feminine curiosity that had prompted her to send for me. Catherine was Empress of All the Russias, yes, but she was also very much a woman, and it was only natural that she should be curious about me. I kept remembering that silent message I seemed to have read in her eyes, that sense of female conspiracy against the male, and instinct told me that Catherine saw me not as a rival but as a sister conspirator.

As we drove past the Winter Palace, I smoothed down my skirts and arranged the glossy sable cloak about my shoulders. I had selected a simple light brown silk gown ribbed with deeper brown stripes for the occasion, feeling tea was no time for opulent attire. My hair, just washed, fell to my shoulders in natural coppery red waves, no sculpted coiffure, no diamond ornaments. Catherine would be meeting Marietta Danver today, not Count Orlov's artificial doll.

Through the trees ahead I could see the Hermitage, its columned portico a statement of elegant simplicity. Completed in 1767, it was actually more like a large house than a palace, a small architectural gem that reflected the personality of the woman who had had it built—dignified and majestic but completely unassuming, displaying the European influence far more than the baroque heaviness of the Russian taste. Though perhaps a bit larger, the Hermitage was not unlike any number of fashionable town houses to be found in Paris and other affluent European cities. It was to the Hermitage that Catherine repaired when she wanted to temporarily forget the pressures of her position.

A footman helped me out of the carriage. Another escorted me up the steps, and yet another showed me into the spacious foyer with its high ceiling and very broad staircase rising to the second floor and main rooms. White marble gleamed and lovely works of art vied for one's attention. I gave up my sable cloak and was ushered up the stairs and down a hall to a set of white double doors gilded with gold leaf patterns.

The doors were opened. I was announced. Catherine put down her quill and greeted me with a welcoming smile.

"Miss Danver! I'm so glad you could come."

She was wearing a pink silk gown with rows of pink ruffles on the skirt. The gown was a bit rumpled, the ruffles limp. Her powdered hair was decidedly untidy, the chignon at her nape coming undone, stray wisps touching her temples and brow. There was a smudge of dust on her cheek, and the fingers of her left hand were ink-stained. Her desk was covered with a hodgepodge litter of books and papers and rolled-up documents, and at the moment Catherine of Russia resembled nothing so much as a plump, rather flustered German hausfrau fretting over the household accounts.

I made a deep, formal curtsey. She waved her hand to one side, indicating that we would dispense with formality.

"Give me just a moment," she begged. "I must add a tiny postscript to my letter to Voltaire. Terribly rude of me, but if I don't finish it now—" She smiled apologetically, picked up the quill, and scribbled furiously.

I watched, ill at ease. Sunlight streamed radiantly through half a dozen windows, filling the room with light. It wasn't a large room, but the ceiling was painted a pale salmon pink and lavishly patterned with gold leaf. Magnificent ivory wainscoting, also patterned with gilt, covered half of the walls, the portion above the same shade of salmon as the ceiling. The furniture was elegant, white and gold, with chairs and sofa upholstered in silvery gray velvet. Several lovely vases were abrim with cut flowers, their scent filling the air, and books and papers were scattered everywhere, even stacked haphazardly on the floor. A fire burned pleasantly in the white marble fireplace.

Catherine finished her postscript, stuck the quill in a silver ink pot and stood up, wiping ink from her fingers with a lace handkerchief. Catching sight of herself in the mirror over the fireplace, she hastily dabbed away the smudge of dust on her cheek, then turned to me with another smile.

"You must forgive me, my dear. I'm afraid I lost all track of time—documents to read and sign, letters to answer, reports! Paperwork! I'm perpetually awash in a sea of paper! Being an Empress isn't all roses, I can assure you. There aren't enough hours in the day to take care of all my responsibilities. I should *delegate,* my ministers tell me—meaning I should turn everything over to them—but I prefer to do it myself. That way I can be sure it will be done and done *properly.*"

"I'm sure it must be quite taxing," I said.

My voice was rather stiff. Even rumpled and untidy, she was still Empress, exuding power and authority, and I wasn't certain how to react to her warmth and effusiveness. Aware of this, Catherine smiled, her deep blue eyes both friendly and amused.

"I'm not wearing my crown now, my dear. Relax. This afternoon we are just two women planning to enjoy a nice, long gossip."

"It—it won't be easy," I admitted.

"I intimidate you?"

"A bit."

She smiled again. "I promise not to say 'Off with her head!' Do relax, my dear. Tea will be here in a few minutes. Very English, it shall be. My cook almost went mad learning to make English scones and clotted cream, finding the proper strawberry jam. And watercress! You've no idea how difficult it was to find watercress for sandwiches. All in your honor. I wanted you to feel at home."

"I'm very flattered, Your Majesty."

" 'Ma'am' if you must, 'Catherine' if you will, but for a couple of hours I really would prefer not to be 'Your Majesty.' I'll have to put the crown back on soon enough—a meeting with my ministers this evening. I shall be terribly majestic and intimidating then, I promise, and have them all trembling. It's the only way to keep them in line. There isn't one of them who believes a lowly woman has the ability to rule. We are, you know, the inferior sex."

"So I've heard. It's never been my personal observation."

"I knew it!" she exclaimed merrily. "The moment I saw you I knew you were a kindred soul, an intelligent, strong-willed woman with a mind of her own. You have that strength and independence I so ardently admire."

"You determined all this in one brief meeting?"

"An Empress must learn to assess character promptly—and correctly," she informed me. "I knew at once that you did not love Gregory, that you were very uncomfortable, that you were not overjoyed at the part you were playing in his little intrigue. Gregory, like every other man in my life, shockingly underestimates my intelligence."

"I never believed you would be taken in by it," I said.

"I *am* a jealous woman, alas, frightfully jealous—it's one of the manifold flaws in my wretched character—but only over the man of the moment. Once I've let a man go he can sleep with anything in skirts for all I care. Gregory gave me almost ten years of physical bliss—and ten years of hell. I agonized over his infidelities, I turned quite gray, I finally said 'Enough!' and got him out of my system. It wasn't easy," she added.

There was a knock on the door, and a moment later a servant entered pushing a gilded white trolley laden with a sumptuous array of food. The servant withdrew silently, and Catherine looked at the food with glee. Here was a woman who savored all the pleasures, I reminded myself,

be it a delicious iced cake or a muscular blond guardsman.
The servant had left the trolley in front of a lovely sofa upholstered in soft gray velvet. Catherine asked me to please
be seated. The teapot was an exquisite piece, the creamy
white porcelain etched with delicate green and mauve
flowers, a sculpted purple flower atop the gold-rimmed lid.
Catherine poured tea into matching cups and, noticing my
admiration, gave me a wry smile.

"This china was a royal gift from Denmark," she explained, "especially designed for me in Copenhagen—
there are hundreds of pieces. Notice the flowers."

"They're beautiful," I said.

"They're *wild* flowers! Weeds, to be more precise. Relations between Denmark and Russia were strained at the
time, and the china was actually a subtle insult. Weeds to
you, Catherine. How I laughed! The Royal Copenhagen is
my favorite plate."

She handed me a cup and settled down on the sofa beside
me with much fluttering of limp pink ruffles. The gown
had short, narrow sleeves, and her bare arms were plump
and white and smooth, the flesh of the upper arms sagging
ever so slightly. Reaching for a gold-rimmed plate with a
particularly pretty brown and green weed etched in the
center, she filled it with sandwiches, scones, tiny iced
cakes and bade me to do the same.

"Poor Gregory," she said, picking up a delicate watercress sandwich. "He deserves credit for trying, and I found
his little intrigue quite amusing, much too amusing to
spoil at once. Let him think he still has a chance for a
while. Let him preen and plan."

"He hasn't a prayer, of course," I said.

"Not a prayer," she replied. "I am completely devoted to
my other Gregory—Potemkin. I'm afraid he's my dark obsession, and I'm hopelessly besotted. It's not good, I know,
it's not even healthy, but—ah, the flesh, it's so deliciously,
deplorably weak."

She sighed, thinking no doubt of that weakness, a half-smile on her round pink mouth. I sipped my tea and took a cucumber sandwich.

"He's very accommodating," she continued. "Potemkin makes me feel totally female—and it's not easy for an Empress to feel female, my dear. All day long I rule—at night it's nice to let someone else rule, let someone else be in command."

Catherine ate her watercress sandwich, took a sip of tea, nibbled an iced cake. The fire burned cozily. Sunlight continued to stream through the windows in brilliant rays, making bright pools on the floor. The cut flowers and pleasant array of books and papers gave the room a homey, comfortable air the magnificent wainscotting and elegant furniture couldn't rescind.

"He's terribly trying at times," she said. "He's moody, overbearing and frequently quite brutal, but Potemkin understands me and knows my every need. He will often bring a particularly virile, good-looking young man to my attention. Does my frankness shock you, my dear?"

"Not at all," I replied.

"All Europe considers me a horribly depraved woman —I'm fully aware of my reputation. I don't feel particularly wicked—I suppose it's because I determined a long time ago that I was going to be a survivor and would pay no attention to what people thought. When I arrived in Russia I was a very young girl, full of innocence, full of romantic notions, full of ideals. My mother accompanied me. She was soon sent back to Germany. I was left all alone. My life was completely taken over by Empress Elizabeth, not the most loving woman I've ever known, a tyrannical dragon, in fact, absolutely ruthless."

The Empress paused to refill her tea cup and take another cake. Her blue eyes were cold as she remembered those other days.

"I was forced to marry a man who was little better than a drooling idiot, her precious nephew, Peter, heir to the throne. He was physically incapable of consummating the marriage—he spent his time playing with tin soldiers in bed or beating his cocker spaniels with a riding crop or, later, drilling his real live soldiers until they dropped. I endured—unspeakable mental and physical horror," she said in a cool, level voice. "I was a foreigner, drab and dull, utterly despised, utterly ignored. My sole purpose was to provide yet another heir, and when it seemed that wasn't to be I was despised even more."

I was silent, sensing she rarely spoke of these things, sensing she needed to unburden herself and knowing it is often much easier to talk to a sympathetic stranger than to one's most intimate acquaintance. She sighed and set her teacup aside, gazing at the fire, seeing another place, another time.

"Elizabeth was determined to have another heir and, as I mentioned earlier, she was absolutely ruthless. If her nephew was incapable of siring one, a substitute could be provided. She brought Serge Saltikov to me—he was like a god in my eyes—young and handsome, strong, virile, everything Peter wasn't. I fell hopelessly in love—my first love, my first man. I lost my heart and, incidentally, lost my virginity as well. As soon as I was pregnant, Elizabeth sent him away. He was richly rewarded for the service he had performed, and I was turned over to a pack of doctors who watched me night and day and reported my every movement to Elizabeth. I—I wanted to die. I prayed for death. It seemed the only possible delivery from the misery crushing my soul."

The Empress of All the Russias sighed and toyed with one of the limp pink ruffles on her skirt, silent for several moments, remembering, and finally she turned to me with a bitter smile.

"My prayers were almost answered. My delivery was an extremely difficult one, conducted in public, as is the custom. I was surrounded by gabbling women and bored courtiers and totally incompetent doctors. I was on a mattress, on the floor, in a stuffy, crowded room with closed windows and fetid air. After hours and hours of terrible pain I finally gave birth. Bells peeled joyously throughout the city. Lavish celebrations ensued. My son was bundled up and delivered to Elizabeth at once—I didn't see him again for months. I was left there on the mattress, on the floor, totally alone in that horrible room. I was weak, bleeding, half-dead, but that wasn't important. I had done my job and given the country another heir and was no longer of any value."

The bitter smile flickered on her lips. She took another sip of tea and gazed at the gold rim of the cup without seeing it.

"Hours passed," she continued. "I lay there on the mattress, dying, and the midwife staggered in to give me a glass of water, then staggered out again to drink more vodka and the candles spluttered out and I was in total darkness and something happened to me—I'm not sure I can even explain it. The drab, passive little German princess did die, I believe, and a completely different person took her place. Strength I never knew I had filled me, and as the rays of early morning sunlight stole through the windows I knew I was going to survive."

She fell silent, gazing at the rim of the cup, and a full minute went by before she finally sighed and set the cup down.

"Empress Elizabeth was a doddering, gouty, dyspeptic old woman whose days were already numbered. My husband was a savagely cruel imbecile, utterly incapable of ruling. When I finally rose from that bloodstained mattress I was prepared to do anything I had to do to save my adopted country from the disaster that would ensue if Peter ruled. My son was born in 1754, and eight years were to pass before my opportunity came, but when it came—I was ready, and I was every bit as ruthless as I had to be."

Had she had Peter murdered? Had he been strangled to death by one of the Orlovs, or had he indeed died of colic while held prisoner? I doubted anyone would ever know for sure. As Catherine drank more tea, I thought of the story she had just told me, and I could see the bloodstained mattress and smell the fetid air in that room where Catherine of Russia had supplanted the abused and neglected German princess. I knew that during the following eight years Elizabeth and Peter between them had turned her son completely against her. Catherine had rarely even been allowed to see him, had been allowed no say whatsoever in his upbringing. By the time she took the throne, Grand Duke Paul was a weak, petulant, moody child given to fits of insane temper, sadly resembling the man officially acknowledged as his father.

Now married and in his late twenties, he hated his mother, I knew, blamed her for Peter's death, and was perpetually plotting against her, though far too weak and ineffectual to present any real danger. Grand Duke Paul was kept under firm control and, history repeating itself, she had taken over the training and upbringing of her grandson, Alexander, determined to make him a worthy successor to the throne. With all the grief and disappointment she had known, with all the abuse she had endured in those early days, was it any wonder she had become so strong and autocratic?

Catherine was silent, the blue eyes pensive now, her lips pink and soft. I felt a curious sympathy for her. The Empress of All the Russias was an extremely unhappy woman, I sensed, and I sensed as well that her rampant sexual indulgences were a kind of compensation for that first, lost love. Was Catherine unconsciously seeking to recapture that early bliss she had experienced with the man who had sired her son and broken her heart? I thought it highly possible and found it very sad, for I knew all too well that that first shimmering joy, once lost, can never be recaptured.

Catherine sighed heavily and, shaking off the pensive mood, turned to me with an apologetic smile.

"Heavens!" she exclaimed. "I don't know what came over me. I don't usually talk so—so intimately about myself. Perhaps it was because I feel an unusual kinship with you. I feel you've experienced—many of the same disappointments in life."

"I've had my share of them," I said.

"Now," she said, "about these scones! I must confess I've never actually eaten one. You must show me what to do with the clotted cream and strawberry jam. Does one just pile it on top?"

I nodded, and she prepared a scone and bit into it and declared it magnificent. Finishing it with relish, she licked her fingers and promptly prepared another, piling on the thick, sweet cream and jam.

"Now, dear, turnabout is fair play. You must tell me all about yourself. I've heard all sorts of stories, but I'm sure the truth is much more fascinating!"

"I—I hardly know where to begin."

"Why don't you begin with the first man," she suggested. "I've found the history of a woman's life is usually shaped by the men she has known."

"I—I suppose that's true," I said. "If I hadn't met Sir Robert Mallory, if he hadn't raped me and then falsely accused me of stealing his wife's jewels, I would never—my whole life would have taken a different course."

And as Catherine ate scones and had another cup of tea, I found myself telling her about my life, about Derek Hawke and Jeff Rawlins and Helmut Schnieder, the husband I never spoke of, the man I had tried to blot completely from memory. I told her about Nicholas Lyon and Corrie and Em, about Jeremy Bond and all that had happened between us. I felt a strong rapport with this woman, despite her exalted position, and I found myself sharing intimate details with her as easily as I would have shared them with Em.

"And—and that's how I happen to be in Russia," I concluded.

"What an incredible story!"

"There's a lot I'm not proud of. I should never have agreed to participate in Gregory's plan."

"Nonsense, my dear! You would have been foolish to

turn down all that money. A woman alone must fend for herself as best she can."

Although I had been open about everything else, I hadn't told her about the part Lucie played in my decision to stay, nor had I revealed any of her secrets. I had merely said that I was very fond of the girl and that my fondness for her had been responsible for my coming to Russia in the first place. I poured another cup of tea.

"You're not going to have a scone?" Catherine asked.

"I'd better not," I said.

"Self-control! How I admire it. No wonder you have such a glorious figure. I lost mine years ago—not that I was ever so shapely. How fortunate it is you didn't fall in love with Gregory."

"He's a fascinating man."

"And absolutely phenomenal in bed."

"True," I said.

"Your Jeremy was better?" she inquired.

"I was in love with Jeremy. That makes all the difference."

"You love him still," she said.

"I hope he burns in hell!"

"Of course you do, and quite rightly, but that has nothing to do with still loving him. Rogues—" Catherine smiled and shook her head. "Why do we invariably find them most attractive?"

"God knows."

"Your Jeremy sounds like a particularly dashing specimen. Would you believe I've never had an Englishman?"

"If hard pressed I suppose I could."

Catherine looked at me in surprise, then threw back her head and burst into peals of rich, lusty laughter. I took a sip of tea, surprised at my own audacity.

"Oh, dear, I *do* admire dry wit. Most people would find me far too intimidating to make such a delicious remark. At any rate, it's true—I've never had an Englishman. I understand they take their time."

"Jeremy did," I said.

"Was he the best you've ever had?"

"Unquestionably."

Catherine smiled and, sighing, took the last scone and piled it with clotted cream, adding a generous spoonful of strawberry jam. "Sex is such a stimulating subject. Some women I know claim it's not all it's touted to be. As for me, the worst I ever had was wonderful."

"I suppose it's an acquired taste—like olives."

"And I could never stop until I ate the whole bowlful!"

Both of us laughed, and Catherine stood up. I quickly followed suit. Sunlight shimmered, thinner now.

"Alas," she said, "I must put my crown back on and become the regal, imperious Catherine again. I've enjoyed your visit immensely, my dear. It's rarely I have an opportunity to be—merely another woman."

"That you'll never be," I said.

"Come, I'll walk you to the door. It's highly unorthodox, of course, but the servants have grown quite immune to my shocking lack of formality when I am *at home* with guests."

She opened the double doors and we moved slowly down the hall, side by side. Even in the rumpled pink gown, with her untidy hair and ink-stained fingers, she was still the Empress, wrapped in dignity and projecting an authority no informality could nullify. Footmen stood at attention as we passed, all of them, I noted, extremely tall and attractive. Apparently Catherine liked to keep a supply of olives on hand.

"It's been a memorable afternoon," I said.

"One day you can tell your grandchildren you had tea with Catherine of Russia."

"I doubt there'll be grandchildren," I replied.

"Nonsense. You'll meet another man, my dear. He won't be like your dashing English rogue, but he'll have his own special qualities. At the moment you think you'll never get over this Jeremy, but—one does."

"That's a comforting thought."

"One never forgets, but one does get over them."

I sensed she was speaking of Serge Saltikov, that first love who had come into her life like a god, who had left as soon as his unusual service to Russia had been performed. I sensed, too, that, despite her words, she had never really gotten over him, that the pain, bitterness and disillusion he had caused had colored the rest of her life.

"Men!" she said as we started down the staircase. "I seem destined to fall for absolute rotters."

"I know the feeling well."

"What's wrong with us, my dear?"

"I wish I knew."

Catherine smiled. "If the perfect male came along, he would bore either of us to tears."

"There's no such thing as the perfect male," I replied.

A particularly muscular footman stood at the foot of the stairs, handsome in his snug velvet livery. Catherine touched his arm lightly as we passed. He gave her an almost imperceptible nod.

"At least there are plentiful snacks," she told me. "I've found an olive or two whets my appetite for the main course. You see, I really *am* as wicked as they say I am!"

"Wickedness, like beauty, is in the eye of the beholder."

"You're a born diplomat, my dear."

"I hope I can be diplomatic with Gregory when I get back. He expected you to pay me off and send me packing on the next ship, leaving the field clear."

Catherine smiled a rueful smile as the great doors were opened for us and we stepped into the sunshine.

"Poor Gregory. I'd like to think it was his undying love for me that prompted his plan, but something tells me he had quite a different motive."

"What shall I say to him?"

"Tell him I was merely looking you over," she said. "He's gone to so much trouble, poor dear. I suppose I should let him enjoy himself a while longer. I will invite the two of you for an intimate dinner and cards next week—Thursday night is free. You'll come then."

"I shall look forward to it."

The Empress smiled. "It should be vastly amusing."

"Thank you for a marvelous visit," I said quietly.

"The pleasure was all mine, my dear. I had a splendid time, and I discovered your delicious English scones. More temptation to contend with—I'm sure it will be a losing battle!"

Catherine took my hand and squeezed it. I made a deep curtsey. A footman handed me my fur cloak and escorted me to the waiting carriage. I climbed inside, and during the ride back to the Marble Palace I thought about the remarkable woman who was so complex, so contradictory, so strong and yet so very vulnerable. The Empress of Russia was a woman of many contrasts, and I knew that the warm, amiable hostess of this afternoon no more represented the true Catherine than did the imperious bully of the council table. She was a combination of both, I suspected, a warm and loyal friend, a formidable foe.

Gregory was going to be very disappointed to learn that the Empress hadn't ordered me to leave Russia, but that didn't overly concern me. I would be leaving soon now—the month I had agreed to stay was almost over. The intimate dinner at the Hermitage next Thursday would be my farewell performance. What a relief it would be to leave this country. I wondered if Bryan had been able to book passage for himself and Lucie yet. Before I left Russia I intended to see her safely on the way to England, even if it meant my staying a bit longer.

As the carriage turned into the drive of the Marble Palace I thought about Lucie's encounter with Vladimir last night, and the apprehension I had felt earlier returned. If Gregory found out she had been secretly meeting Bryan in the west wing . . . The carriage stopped in front of the elegant marble portico and a servant opened the door for me. I climbed out. There is no point in anticipating trouble, I told myself.

Something had happened while I was at the Hermitage. I sensed it the moment I entered the front hall. A heavy, ominous atmosphere seemed to hang over the Marble Palace, and the very silence seemed to retain the vibrations of angry shouting. I handed my cloak to a footman, a hollow feeling in the pit of my stomach as I sensed those vibrations stirring in the air. When Gregory stepped into the hall, I knew. As soon as I saw his face I knew Vladimir had spoken to him.

"You were gone a very long time," he said.

"I—I suppose I was."

His face was stern, all hard lines and surfaces, as though it had become a stony mask. He did not bombard me with questions about my visit with Catherine, did not, in fact, say anything for several long moments, still preoccupied with the scene that had taken place during my absence. What had happened? What had he said to her? What had he done? I longed to rush at him and demand answers, but I remained cool and poised, as though I suspected nothing.

"Come into the drawing room," he ordered.

I followed him obediently. My brown silk skirt rustled loudly. Orlov was wearing brown knee boots, wheat-colored breeches, and a loose silky beige shirt. His tawny hair was pulled back and fastened at the nape with a brown velvet ribbon. His navy blue eyes were stony, and there was a dangerous curl at one corner of his mouth. Thin, pale sunlight slanted through the windows in wavering shafts, dusting the room with gold that gradually faded. Shadows stretched over the gleaming parquet floor.

"She offered you money?" he asked.

I shook my head. "It was—a very friendly visit. I think she just wanted to—to size up the competition."

"She continues to bide her time," he said sullenly.

"She plans to invite both of us to an intimate dinner next Thursday night. The official invitation will arrive in a day or so. I—I have the feeling she will make her move then."

"I do not understand why she invites both of us."

"She spoke very highly of you, Gregory."

"She seemed jealous of you?"

"She was very curious about me, wanting to know all

about my past and how I came to meet you. I told her about the accident. I told her you were the most exciting man I had ever met, that I was completely unable to resist your masculine allure."

He stood in a shaft of sunlight with his arms folded across his chest, his hair burnished a dark, dull gold. He seemed hewn from solid granite, and I had a moment of nervous alarm. Did he know that I was involved? Did he know I had helped them? The only other time I had seen him in such a lethal mood was just before he had flogged Joseph Pulaski in the village. Dear God, I thought. Oh, dear God. I had to see Lucie at once.

"I think I'll go on upstairs now, Gregory."

"There's something you need to know."

"Oh?" I spoke the word ever so lightly.

"Lucie has been secretly meeting this Englishman, this Bryan Lloyd."

I was silent, waiting. He scowled angrily.

"She has been slipping down to the west wing late at night and meeting him in a room there. Vladimir finds out about it last night. He discovers her wandering in the hall. She makes a feeble excuse and goes back to her bedroom and later on slips out again. He follows her to the west wing and hears them talking in the room and later watches the Englishman leave the palace."

"I—I see. Is—is that so very awful, Gregory? They're young and—"

He curled his hand into a fist and banged it down on the table beside him. A vase tottered, toppled, fell to the floor with a loud crash. He didn't even notice.

"She admits everything! She defies me! She claims she is going to marry this moneyless youth, this foreigner! She tells me I have no right to plan her life. No right! Her father ignores her. He is embarrassed by her presence in his house. I take pity on her. I give her everything— everything! And this is how she shows her gratitude!"

He continued to thunder and rave, banging the table again, cheeks flushed, eyes flaming with fury, and, finally spent, he took a deep breath and heaved his chest and regained some of the lethal calm. I had never seen him in such a rage before, and it was a frightening sight. He had been . . . unhinged, unbalanced, resembling nothing so much as a madman. I knew my cheeks were pale. Gregory stared at me and took another deep breath.

"I have given orders," he said.

"Orders?" My voice was surprisingly level.

"She is confined to the house. There are to be no more shopping trips, no more excursions. Vladimir will be stationed outside her room each night to see that she does not slip out. My men have been ordered to shoot this Bryan Lloyd on sight if he dares step foot on my property."

I said nothing. I felt icy cold.

"I have taken all her jewels and locked them up in my safe, and she is to have no money. She will be as poor, as moneyless as he until she comes to her senses."

"I suppose you will feed her," I said, "or do you intend to put her on a diet of bread and water?"

Gregory ignored the question. "She will see reason soon enough," he continued. He was calmer now, his voice normal. "She will brood for a while, but she will soon see this is for her own good. She will marry the man I have chosen for her and be grateful to me for looking after her interests."

"You've already chosen the man?"

"I have a talk with him yesterday. We come to an agreement. He asks for an enormous settlement, but me, I am glad to pay it. He has a fine estate and his title is one of the best in Russia."

"Do I know him?"

"Prince Danzimov, who dined with us last week."

"Danzimov!" I was horrified. "The man's a notorious womanizer, Gregory, a completely unprincipled rake without a shred of morality. He asked me to become his mistress in this very room. You can't seriously consider marrying her off to a—a man like that."

"You do not understand these matters," he told me.

"She will be a princess and have much esteem. She will have a place at court and be mistress of a fine country estate. Danzimov is still young and not unpleasing to look at. He is a wealthy man. I have done quite well for her."

"He'll make her utterly miserable."

Orlov gave me a patronizing smile. "Like so many of your countrymen, you are the sentimentalist. You have the foolish notions about love. In Russia we arrange these things sensibly. You are not pleased by my choice, I see, but it is really none of your concern."

"You're quite right about that."

"Now, tell me more about Catherine and this invitation she will send. I was distracted before and didn't give it the proper attention."

"If you don't mind, Gregory, I'd rather go up to my room just now. I'm very tired. We'll discuss my visit at length later."

Gregory nodded and, all charm again, escorted me to the foot of the staircase. The icy coldness still possessed me as I climbed the stairs, and I had never felt such steely resolve. My rooms were to the right of the landing. I turned to the left, moving resolutely down the hall toward Lucie's quarters. I didn't bother to knock. I went straight in, closing the door firmly behind me and turning the lock.

The sunlight was a thin silver now, fading fast, and only a few shimmering rays slanted through the windows. None of the candles had been lighted, and the room was a hazy bower of soft blue-gray shadow with weak bars of silver melting on the floor. I had expected to find Lucie distraught and in tears. She wasn't. She was sitting on the sofa, her hands in her lap, beautifully composed. She looked up at me, but she didn't speak. I supposed she was in a state of shock. I moved toward her, and then I gasped, noticing her face for the first time. Her left cheek was swollen, already turning an ugly mauve, and the skin of her cheekbone was scraped and flecked with dried blood. My knees went weak.

"He did this to you?" I whispered.

"I'm all right, Marietta."

"You must tend to it. Ice. Salve. You must—"

"Don't fuss over me. Please."

"Lucie—"

"I'm not the first woman with a swollen cheek, and I doubt I shall be the last. It doesn't even burn anymore. It feels numb."

Her voice was perfectly level. There was a poignant dignity about her as she sat there on the sofa in her blue muslin dress, her hands folded neatly in her lap. I forced myself to quell the emotions raging inside and fought to regain some semblance of calm.

"He told you, I suppose," she said.

"He told me. He didn't say he had struck you."

"A minor detail," she replied. "He probably considered it too insignificant to mention. I managed to slip out and find Vanya—Vladimir doesn't begin his watchdog duties until nightfall. Vanya took a message to Bryan at the student hostel and—and Bryan won't be coming tonight. I don't want him shot."

I was too tense to sit down. I moved over to stand in front of the fireplace. The fire had not been lighted. The room was growing cold. I shivered, folding my arms around my waist.

"How could he?" I said. "How could he be so brutal and uncaring?"

"You've never really known my uncle, Marietta."

"I'm beginning to realize that."

Lucie lifted one of her slender hands to brush back a loose wave of golden brown hair. "He's very accomplished at showing only that part of his character he wishes an individual to see. He can be tender and warm, as he was with you in the beginning, but he can also be—an entirely different person."

The silver was melting. The shadowy haze thickened, all color fading, yet neither of us moved to light the candles. Lucie sat perfectly still on the sofa, silent for several moments, and then she raised her head, looking up at me. A final shaft of pale silver sunlight fell across the upper portion of her body, and I saw her face clearly. Her eyes had never been so calm, so old.

"My uncle feels responsible for me," she said quietly. "My father never cared for me. He gladly turned me over to his brother and made it quite clear it wouldn't matter if he never saw me again. My uncle took very good care of me. He was very generous, even after he tired of me."

I looked into those calm eyes and realized what she was saying and a wave of horror swept over me. Lucie saw my expression in the dim haze and smiled a bitter smile.

"I never told you," she said. "You never guessed. He was the first, Marietta. I was thirteen years old. I was in the stables on my father's estate. My uncle came upon me there. He shoved me down onto a pile of hay and took me by force. He came to my room that night and took me again, and a few days later my father agreed to let me go away with him. My uncle was the first person who ever paid any kind of attention to me, and I—I suppose I equated that attention with giving my body, so—when my uncle grew tired of me and looked for new diversions, I began to give it freely."

I understood so much now, and in addition to the horror I felt a great sadness that was almost overwhelming. Lucie got up and moved about the room lighting the candles, blossoms of wavering golden light marking her progress.

"And then you came into my life and—and gave me hope that I might become another person," she continued. "I met Bryan, and I actually believed I might find real happiness."

"You shall," I said.

"The ironic thing about it is—we were so close. Last night he informed me that he had finally been able to book passage for us. The ship leaves next Thursday night."

"Thursday night," I said, thinking.

"At ten o'clock. We were to sail from St. Petersburg to Copenhagen, from Copenhagen to Oslo, and then across the North Sea to London. Bryan told me all about it. It was—it was to be a grand adventure. I've never been on a ship before, you see, and—"

"You'll be on that ship, Lucie," I promised.

Lucie shook her head. "There's no possible way," she replied. "My uncle will be watching my every move. Vladimir will be guarding my door. I—please don't build my hopes up again, Marietta. I couldn't stand—I couldn't bear—" And for the first time tears sparkled in her eyes and spilled over her lashes. "I've resigned myself. I haven't the strength to—"

I stepped over to her and took her hands and held them tightly. Lucie lowered her eyes, tears glistening on her discolored cheek.

"Look at me, Lucie," I ordered. My voice was sharp.

She raised her eyes. The expression in them was almost unbearable to behold.

"You're going to leave on that ship at ten o'clock next Thursday night," I told her. "I promise you that, and it's a promise I intend to keep come what may. Do you believe me?"

"But—but how?" she whispered.

I didn't know that yet. "You'll just have to trust me," I said.

Chapter Twenty

TIMING WAS EVERYTHING. I REALIZED THAT. We were due at the Hermitage at eight o'clock. We would leave the Marble Palace at seven-thirty. It was now twenty minutes before seven and my nerves were on edge and I felt I was going to fly into pieces. I knew it was a wild, foolhardy plan that would never, never work and would only bring disaster down upon all of us. My hands trembled as I fastened the hooks of my gown. How could I have ever believed such an incredibly risky plan would work? Gown properly fastened at last, I took a deep breath and closed my eyes for a moment, willing myself to banish the panic inside. You must be calm, Marietta. You *must* be calm. If you can't go through with your part of it, everything will fall apart.

Calm. Serene. Cool. Perfectly natural, as though nothing untoward were afoot. You can do it. You must. I took a deep breath and opened my eyes and gazed at myself in the mirror. Monsieur André had come to do my hair again, and I had wanted to scream the whole time he had fussed and fiddled and plied his trade, chatting incessantly. The rich coppery red waves were artfully arranged atop my head, with three long sausage ringlets draped over my left shoulder, a spray of diamonds and sapphires fastened above them. Monsieur André had clapped his hands with glee upon completing his job, declaring it perfection, a masterpiece of hairdressing. Had there been a pistol in my hand I would have shot him.

My gown was of pale sky blue silk brocade embroidered with tiny, delicate flowers of rich sapphire blue. The short, puffed sleeves were full, the neckline heartshaped, cut extremely low, and the skirt swelled out from the tight waist, spreading over half a dozen stiff sapphire underskirts. The skirts responded noisily to my every movement, rustling, crackling, swishing, as though imbued with a life of their own. It was a sumptuous garment, but I was in no mood to appreciate its beauty.

I picked up the diamond necklace I had worn to the Winter Palace, looking at the glittering stones worth several fortunes. Because of its extreme value Gregory kept it locked up in his safe—along with all the jewels he had taken from Lucie—and a servant had brought it up to me only a few minutes ago. It didn't go with the gown, Lucie's diamond and sapphire necklace would have been much more appropriate, but that wasn't why I had requested it tonight. It was the final touch, my own contribution, and I felt not the slightest compunction about the use I intended to make of it.

Ten minutes before seven. Was I ready? Could I go through with it? I still felt tremors of panic, but they were under control now. My heart was no longer palpitating. My hands were steady. I studied my face in the glass and saw it betrayed none of the emotions trembling inside. My sapphire eyes were serene, the lids lightly shaded with pale gray-blue shadow, and the high cheekbones were skillfully tinted with a suggestion of natural pink. The lips were a deeper pink, no longer trembling at the corners.

I was as ready as I would ever be. I longed for a glass of brandy to fortify my nerves, but I didn't dare have one. Wrapping the necklace in a large white handkerchief, holding the handkerchief at my side, half concealed in the folds of my skirt, I left my rooms and started down the hall. You've done a number of things far riskier than this, I reminded myself. There's nothing to be alarmed about. If you can't handle Vladimir, you might as well give up and retire to a convent.

He was stationed in the hall outside Lucie's room, and he glared at me as I approached, eyes dark and hostile, filled with suspicion. I held my chin at a haughty tilt, gazing at him imperiously, the handkerchief with its fabulously valuable enclosure completely hidden by folds of sky blue silk. He stepped in front of me, blocking my way. He seemed to loom there before me, towering, exuding menace. My knees felt weak. My throat tightened. He scowled, and my courage seemed to ebb.

"What is it you want?" he growled.

"That's none of your bloody business," I said tartly. "Kindly step out of my way."

"I have my orders."

"I believe your orders are to see that Lucie doesn't leave her room at night, not to prevent me from seeing her."

My voice was like the cutting edge of a knife. My eyes gazed at him with demolishing hauteur. Vladimir hesitated a long moment, then reluctantly moved aside. I swept past him and opened the door. My heart was palpitating again as I stepped inside and closed the door behind me. Lucie was seated on the sofa. She leaped to her feet and started to say something. I shook my head and put a finger to my lips. She understood at once.

"I promised to come show you my gown before we leave," I said. "Do you like it?"

"It's beautiful," she replied. Her voice, like mine, was loud enough to be heard in the hallway outside.

"I love the color. I love what Monsieur André did with my hair, too."

"He's wonderful."

"I couldn't decide on a perfume. I want everything to be just right."

"I have several perfumes in my dressing room. Perhaps one of them would suit you."

"I'm tired of the essence of poppy," I said as we moved across the room. "I want something provocative yet—yet subtle."

We passed through the bedroom and on into the dressing

room and I sank onto the dressing stool in a state of almost complete collapse, my skirts protesting with silken hisses and angry crackles. Lucie wrung her hands, ready to collapse herself. Neither of us spoke for several moments, and I was finally able to control my jangling nerves. I sat up straight. Lucie's face was pale, and a vein throbbed at her temple.

"Everything's going to be all right," I told her.

"I—I'm so scared, Marietta."

"There's no need to be. Everything is arranged."

Setting the bulky handkerchief down on the dressing table, I began to examine the bottles of perfume. I felt sure Vladimir had been eavesdropping outside the door, and he would notice if I wasn't wearing perfume when I came out. I intended to be very close to him.

"You saw Bryan today?" Lucie asked.

"Vanya and I went riding this afternoon, and Bryan met us in the park. He has all his instructions. I'm sure the closed carriage is already waiting just beyond the back gate."

"I—I just hope this works."

"It's going to," I said, confident now. "In three hours you'll be on your way to England."

Opening a bottle of perfume, I sniffed the scent and dabbed some behind my earlobes.

"Where's the cloak?" I asked.

"It's hanging in the wardrobe."

"You'd better go ahead and put it on," I said. "Poor Lizzie. I hope she doesn't miss it right away."

The cloak had been a last minute inspiration. Even though they would take the back stairs and avoid the main rooms, Vanya and Lucie could hardly slip out of the house and, passing the barracks, reach the back gate without being seen. If Lucie was wearing one of the maid's cloaks, if she kept the hood pulled well over her head, anyone who might see them would think Vanya was stealing out for an amorous night on the town. I had gone up to Lizzie's attic room this morning and, in the rickety wooden wardrobe, had found two cloaks, one blue and one brown, the latter decidedly shabby. I had lifted it deftly and brought it down to Lucie's room without being seen. Lucie put it on over her muslin frock now. It was much too large, but that was good. It would completely cover her clothes and, pulled forward, the hood would conceal most of her face.

"Before we met Bryan, I went to several shops," I said, touching the back of my wrist with the perfume stopper. "I bought you several dresses, shoes, undergarments, a heavy cloak, everything you'll need on your journey. I had them delivered to Bryan's room, along with a small trunk."

"I was worried about clothes," Lucie confessed.

"We couldn't risk your trying to take anything tonight. It would look too suspicious. I hope you'll approve of my selections. There's a violet-blue velvet I know you'll love."

"How—how did you pay for all these things? You don't carry that much money around with you."

"I billed them to your uncle."

"Wasn't that—risky?"

"By the time he gets the bill I intend to be on a ship myself."

"I—I wish you were going with us tonight, Marietta. I hate to leave you behind. When he—when he discovers I'm gone he's going to be insane with anger. If he suspected you've helped me—"

"He won't," I said. "Vladimir will receive all the blame for neglecting his duty."

"Still—"

"Don't worry about me, darling. I can take care of myself. I've been doing it successfully for quite a few years now."

Replacing the crystal stopper into the top of the perfume bottle, I stood up, sky blue skirts rustling like dry leaves. Lucie's cheeks were still pale, and her lovely violet-blue eyes were full of emotions she tried valiantly to control.

"I—I'm going to miss you so much," she whispered.

"I'll miss you, too, Lucie."

There was so much more she wanted to say, but the emotion was too strong. She wrapped her arms around me and held me close for a moment, trembling, and I found it difficult to control my own emotions. I stroked her hair and, finally, gently, loosened her arms and eased her away. She brushed a tear from her cheek and forced a brave smile onto her lips.

"I'll never forget you," she said.

"And I'll never forget you either, darling, but I'll have the consolation of knowing you're with Bryan."

"I can't believe it's all going to come true."

"Sometimes it does," I said lightly. It was difficult to keep the sadness out of my voice.

"Bryan wants me to go ahead with my plans to become an actress. He's going to help me. He promises to write a play for me as soon as I'm ready. He thinks we should *both* have careers."

"You're going to be wonderfully happy, darling."

"And all because of you."

"I—I have a gift for both of you," I said. "Times aren't always easy for struggling playwrights and aspiring actresses. Sometimes they can be difficult indeed. This should help."

I unwrapped the necklace and held it out to her. The diamonds sparkled with a thousand shimmering fires. Lucie stared at them in amazement, unable to speak for a moment.

"When sold it should bring enough to keep you both very comfortable for quite some time—for the rest of your lives if you're sensible. I suggest you contact Robert Bancroft at the Bank of England and let him handle investments for you."

"Marietta, it—that necklace is worth—"

"I have a rough idea what it's worth," I said tersely.

"My uncle will—"

"Your uncle bought it for me. I'm giving it to you, and I don't intend to argue about it."

"He—"

"Take it, Lucie."

I placed it in her hand, and Lucie looked at me. Another tear slid down her cheek, which was still faintly discolored. She finally slipped the necklace into the pocket of her cloak.

"I'd better leave now. Vladimir will be even more suspicious if I stay any longer."

"Oh, Marietta—"

"We must both be strong, Lucie."

She nodded, wiping away a tear. I fought back my own.

"Vanya is waiting at your end of the hall, hiding behind one of the tall Boulle cabinets. As soon as I lead Vladimir away, Vanya will come for you and lead you downstairs and to the back gate. Bryan will be waiting with a carriage, and Vanya will accompany the two of you to Kronstadt and see you safely off."

"I—I'm going to break down."

"No you're not. Keep the cloak wrapped around you and keep the hood up around your face. Good-bye, Lucie."

She tried to speak. She couldn't. The tears streamed down her cheeks. I gave her a quick hug and left the room. Lucie followed me through the bedroom and paused at the doorway leading into the sitting room, one hand gripping the frame as though for support. I moved on to the hall door, and then, my hand on the knob, I paused and turned, and I shall never forget the sight of her standing there in the doorway, so young, so lovely, on the brink of a whole new life. I blew her a kiss.

"Be happy, darling," I whispered.

And then I opened the door and stepped into the hall and pulled the door shut behind me. Vladimir was standing a few feet away, his arms folded across his chest. I gave him a haughty look and, tilting my chin up, started toward him. Vladimir scowled. I took another step and let out a little cry, pitching forward. His arms flew out instinctively as I toppled against him, and he clutched me, supporting my full weight.

"Oh—oh dear—" I cried.

"What is it?" he growled.

"I—I think I've turned my ankle—"

"If this is some—"

"It hurts. Oh, Lord—"

I winced and made a pained, moaning noise, playing it to the hilt, leaning heavily against him. Vladimir glowered, extremely discomfited, his hands gripping my shoulders. I pulled away from him angrily and attempted to stand and stumbled, falling against him again. He grabbed my upper arms and pulled me up straight.

"You don't have to be so rough!" I snapped.

"You can't walk?"

"I can't even *stand!* Do you actually think I enjoy having your hands on me? Stop squeezing so tightly. You'll bruise my arms!"

He curled his lower lip, dark eyes glowing. He would much prefer bruising my throat, I knew, but he loosened his tight grip. I took a deep breath, wincing again, and then I pulled my arms free and managed to stand on my own for several seconds.

"You are all right now?"

"I think so—"

I started to take a step, wobbled perilously and seized his arm.

"Damn!" I cried.

"It still hurts?"

"It hurts like bloody hell! Tonight of all nights, with the Empress expecting us at the Hermitage in less than an hour. Maybe—maybe it's just a light sprain. You'll have to help me to my room."

"My orders are—"

"I don't give a good goddamn about your orders! And I've had just about enough of your insolence! You'll help me to my room and fetch Court Orlov or I'll see that you're flogged!"

The threat had no effect on him, but my tone of voice did. Despite what he might think of me, I was clearly his superior, and Vladimir was a servant, trained to obey.

Scowling fiercely, extremely unhappy at this turn of events, he curled an arm around my shoulders, and I shifted position, leaning against his side. Slowly, awkwardly, we began to move down the hall. I hopped, halted, hopped again, gasping every now and then.

"Careful! Not so bloody fast!"

Vladimir grunted, supporting most of my weight, and we moved on, passing the elegant Boulle cabinets and the tables laden with priceless porcelain figurines, passing the stairwell. I stumbled, clung to him, made him stop for a moment while I caught my breath, and Vanya, I knew, was creeping down the hall behind us toward Lucie's door. Perhaps he had reached it and the two of them were already scurrying off in the opposite direction, Lucie wrapped up in the shabby brown cloak.

I dared not look back. Vladimir and I continued our erratic progress toward my door, and it was so clumsy and uncomfortable I was afraid I might turn my ankle for real, hopping as I was in high-heeled shoes. A full ten minutes must have passed before we finally reached the door to my sitting room, but I couldn't be sure that was enough time. I had to delay him a while longer. He opened the door and helped me inside and I hopped over to the large chair and tumbled into it with noisy crackling of silk.

"I need a stool," I told him. "There's one over there by the fireplace. Get it for me."

Vladimir gave me a murderous look, but he brought the stool over and set it in front of the chair. Slowly, wincing all the while, I lifted my injured ankle onto it and gnawed my lower lip as the pain swept over me. Mrs. Robinson would turn green with envy if she could see *this* performance, I thought. I emitted a weary sigh. Vladimir stood over me, scowling.

"Anything else?" he asked insolently.

"I'd better massage it," I said. "There's a small bottle of alcohol on my dressing table. Bring it to me."

He hesitated. I stared up at him with icy hauteur, silently defying him to disobey. He muttered something under his breath and stalked into the bedroom and on into the dressing room beyond. He spent a good three or four minutes looking for the bottle of alcohol which, actually, was in one of the bottom drawers. He brought it in, handed it to me, and I had difficulty opening it. The cap was screwed on much too tightly. Two bright spots burned on his broad cheekbones as I handed him the bottle and told him to open it.

"Thank you," I said, taking the bottle back. "And now if you would be kind enough to bring me a handkerchief, I'll be quite finished with you. My handkerchiefs are in the middle drawer of the wardrobe."

It took him several more minutes to find a handkerchief and bring it to me, and I knew I shouldn't press my luck any further. I thanked him with icy politeness and told him to find Count Orlov and ask him to come up to my room. Vladimir left, closing the door behind him much too forcefully. I leaned back against the velvety softness of the chair, absolutely spent yet still plagued with nervous tension. Would someone see them crossing the yard and stop them, challenge them? Would there be a hue and cry? Would they make it? I closed my eyes, praying they were even now in the carriage and on their way to Kronstadt.

The clock over the mantel ticked slowly. One minute, two, three. In the interests of verisimilitude I lifted my skirts and rubbed alcohol over my left ankle and then set the bottle aside. Six minutes went by, seven, eight. The house was very quiet. No angry shouts in the distance. They must have made it. They must be on their way. The ship sailed at ten, and by the time Gregory and I returned from the Hermitage they would be long gone, sailing out into the Baltic. Five more minutes passed and I heard footsteps in the hall and braced myself as Count Orlov opened the door and stepped inside, his eyes full of concern.

"Something is wrong?" he inquired.

"I just turned my ankle," I said. "I massaged it and rubbed it with alcohol. I think it's all right now."

He frowned and, before I could stop him, moved over and

kneeled down and lifted my skirts back. Fortunately I had
rubbed the ankle vigorously with alcohol and it was still a
bright pink. Gregory examined it carefully and said it
looked slightly swollen. So much for observation, I
thought. He asked me if it hurt and I said not any longer
and he stood up and helped me to my feet. I took several
cautious steps, limping just a little. I told him I thought it
would be all right, and he looked extremely relieved.

"This had me worried," he said.

Gregory Orlov had never been more handsome, more
dazzling than he was tonight in his richest attire. His navy
blue leather pumps had diamond-studded buckles, and his
stockings were of the finest white silk. His navy blue satin
knee breeches and frock coat were superbly cut to accentuate his physique, his coat was adorned with a row of large
diamond-studded buttons. His waistcoat was silver brocade lavishly embroidered with blue- and silver-thread
flowers, and the lace flowing at his throat and wrists was a
frothy silver tissue. Oh yes, he was dazzling. How could so
much virile beauty be combined with such evil?

This was a man who could take great satisfaction, and
probably a perverse pleasure as well, in flogging a peasant
to the point of death, a man who could brutally rape his
young niece and use her as his whore with no remorse, a
man given to maniacal rages and acts of casual cruelty
performed without thought. How warm he could be, how
tender and engaging, this a carefully calculated façade to
conceal his total amorality. I shuddered to think how I had
fallen under his spell, and it was all I could do to look at
him now without revealing the loathing he inspired.

"You can walk all right?" he asked.

"I'll have to move a bit slowly, but—it's fine now."

The necklace, I thought. He's going to notice I'm not
wearing the necklace and ask me why and ask me where it
is. Dear God, what will I tell him? I glanced at the clock. It
was seven-thirty, time for us to depart. Lucie and Bryan
were well on their way to Kronstadt. I told Gregory I
would like to freshen up a bit before we left and he nodded

and I went into the dressing room and applied a touch more pink to my lips and stared at my face in the mirror. I wanted to flee the house myself. I wanted to get as far away from Gregory Orlov as possible, but I knew I had to keep playing the game until it was finished. I couldn't back away now.

I went back to the sitting room and told him I was ready and he took my arm and we went downstairs, moving very slowly because of my ankle. Gregory helped me into a sumptuous white mink cloak when we reached the foyer, slinging a sleek waist-length black sable cape around his own shoulders, and in a few minutes we were in the carriage and on our way and he still hadn't asked me about the necklace, too preoccupied with his forthcoming triumph to notice the omission.

It was a lovely night, calm and clear, the sky a smooth, cloudless black hung with dimly twinkling stars and bathed in moonlight. Pale, silvery rays floated through the carriage windows, and in the hazy half-light I looked at the man sitting across from me. He seemed to be sculpted in black and white, the face pale, brushed with shadow. Brow and eyes were barely visible, but a slanting ray softly illuminated his lower face. A thoughtful smile idled on the full, splendidly shaped mouth, and as I gazed at it I suddenly knew that this powerful Russian nobleman was not merely amoral and cruel. He was completely unbalanced, driven by an obsession that had carried him far from the shores of sanity. Madness took many forms. Gregory Orlov had been tottering on the edge for many years, ruthless, erratic, given to bouts of gleeful, boyish elation and alternate bouts of fury.

"You are very quiet," he said.

"I'm rather tired, Gregory."

"Tonight will be the great triumph."

"I hope so."

"You are happy for me?"

"Of course," I lied.

"You do not sound happy. You sound most sad."

"I agreed to stay a month," I said. "And that month is almost over. I will be leaving Russia soon."

"And this makes you sad. You do not wish to leave your new friends."

"I will miss Lucie."

"You will not miss Orlov?" he inquired.

"You've been very generous, Gregory."

He chuckled quietly, and in the semidarkness, in the close confines of the gently rocking carriage there was something chilling about the sound. I experienced a moment of stark fear as I realized my own vulnerability, and I drew back against the cushion, my skirts rippling, rustling. Gregory leaned forward, his whole face illuminated now, brushed with pale silver, eyes gleaming darkly. The handsome features seemed stamped with a subtle menace. Was I imagining it? I had been under a great strain. Were my nerves getting the best of me?

"You do not have to leave," he said. "After I am back in power I could do even more for you."

"Catherine would love that."

"I can handle Catherine. I still want you, Marietta."

"Tomorrow I will go to Kronstadt and see about booking passage," I told him.

Gregory smiled and leaned back, completely in shadow now, only his large hands visible in the moonlight, resting lightly on his knees. When he spoke, his voice seemed strangely disembodied.

"We will see," he said.

I didn't like the sound of those three words. The carriage continued to rock gently, the wheels spinning with a whirring noise, horse hooves clopping with a monotonous rhythm. You're tense, I told myself. You're reading things into his words. Relax. You're got a very long evening to get through, and it isn't going to be easy. Lucie will soon be safe, out of his reach, and that's all that matters at the moment. The carriage bowled around a curve, and moonlight spilled over my side of the carriage, leaving Gregory in

shadow. I could feel him staring at me, as though in speculation, and the vague uneasiness persisted.

Although it was a short drive, it seemed to take us forever to reach the Hermitage. Gregory climbed out and
helped me alight, and a footman holding a flaming torch
led us up the steps. We surrendered our wraps to another
footman and followed a third to a drawing room on the
ground floor. The Hermitage was ablaze with candlelight,
crystal glittering, marble gleaming, a warm, cozy atmosphere prevailing despite the splendor.

A number of people were chattering and drinking wine
in the drawing room as we were shown in. Empress Catherine hurried forward to greet us, a welcoming smile on
her lips. She wore a magnificent gown of pale gray watered
silk, the skirt adorned with scallops of pale gray lace and
small pink velvet rosebuds. I curtseyed. Gregory made a
very impressive bow and, taking her hand, lifted it to his
lips. Catherine's deep blue eyes sparkled with amusement
as she told us how pleased she was that we could come.

"We are honored, my Catherine," Orlov crooned.

"You're looking unusually splendid tonight, Gregory."

He smiled, preening, and, eyes still amused, Catherine
patted him lightly on the cheek and then took me away to
introduce me to her other guests. I had already met Madame Protasova, the sultry, overripe brunette known as
"the tester." She was particularly voluptuous in a low-cut
gown of crushed purple velvet, diamonds and amethysts at
her throat, her lids coated with mauve shadow. She was accompanied by a tall, spectacularly handsome youth in military uniform. He had thick blond waves and innocent blue
eyes and seemed terribly ill at ease. I doubted he was a day
over twenty.

"And this is Peter," Catherine said fondly. "He has just
recently become an officer. He grew up in the country and
finds St. Petersburg somewhat overwhelming."

"Peter is going to go far," Protasova purred. "He's aptly
named."

The youth blushed as prettily as a girl. Protasova

laughed. Catherine saw another guest arriving and begged her chief lady-in-waiting to look after me while she went to greet the newcomer.

"That's Prince Dmitri Golitsyn who's just arrived," Protasova informed me. "He's our ambassador to France, on leave from his post in Paris. Golitsyn helps Catherine select works of art—he's always shipping huge crates to the Winter Palace. He also keeps her informed on the doings of Voltaire and Diderot."

Prince Golitsyn was tall and lean with distinguished features and silver-gray hair. In his late fifties, he had the carriage and confidence of a much younger man.

"The giggling blonde in pink who is drinking her third glass of champagne is Countess Anna Zavadovsky, who is all of nineteen and Catherine's newest lady-in-waiting," Protasova continued. "She has the intellect of a rabbit and the personality of a poodle, but for some reason Catherine finds her amusing. The thin, dour, middle-aged man in steel gray frock coat and blue waistcoat is her husband, who keeps an eagle eye on his young wife and wishes she weren't quite so popular."

Count Zavadovsky did indeed look dour and disapproving, frowning darkly as his wife took yet another glass of champagne and smiled winsomely at the footman who served it. She was a pretty thing with her bouncy silver-blonde ringlets and guileless blue eyes. Her lovely figure was splendidly displayed in the pink gown with its full gathered skirt, snug bodice and plunging neckline that left over half her ample bosom exposed. Young Peter cast a sly, admiring look at the latter. Protasova slapped his wrist and ordered him to go fetch me a glass of champagne.

"He's full of potential," she said wearily, "but he still has a lot to learn."

"I'm sure you'll soon have him trained."

"Depend on it. The old frump in the preposterous brown wig and outlandish mauve taffeta is Madame Koshelev. She's sixty and widowed and a dreadful bore, but Catherine loves to have her when there's to be cards. Koshelev's a wizard at the card table, makes a small fortune at gambling, and no one's ever caught her cheating."

"She looks like someone's sweet old grandmother," I observed.

"She turns into a killer when she has a pack of cards in her hands. Try not to play against her tonight."

Peter returned with my champagne and gave me a shy smile, his eyes roaming down to my décolletage. Protasova sighed and slapped his wrist again.

"I don't think he ever saw a woman until he got to St. Petersburg," she told me.

Gregory was talking intently with Catherine, who listened to him with a distracted smile. Protasova took me over and introduced me to the ambassador to France, then hurried back to nab Peter, who was moving toward Countess Zavadovsky. Prince Golitsyn was a charming, cultured man, as dignified in manner as he was in appearance. He asked me if I was interested in art and told me about the magnificent collection of Girardon bronzes he had recently acquired for the Empress.

Catherine came over to inquire if I was enjoying myself, a warm and gracious hostess putting her guests at ease. Gregory had been cornered by Madame Koshelev and looked miserable as she gabbled amiably. Anna Zavadovsky was casting coy, flirtatious looks at Protasova's handsome young trainee, and Protasova kept a firm grip on his arm and looked as though she would like to murder them both. Count Zavadovsky looked as though he would like to help her do it.

Half an hour passed and I discussed art with Catherine and Prince Golitsyn and said I would love to see the paintings in the gallery here in the Hermitage. I finished my glass of champagne and refused a second and the Empress moved on to chat with her other guests and I found myself listening to Madame Koshelev talk interminably about her accomplished nephew and her bright grandnephews and her adorable grandniece who was only two and a half but already a clever little charmer.

Lucie and Bryan would be at Kronstadt now. They would probably have already boarded the ship which—I glanced at the clock—which would be leaving in an hour. Madame Koshelev's mauve gown smelled of camphor and her brown wig was slightly askew and her mouth kept moving, moving, moving, spilling out fond anecdotes. "We will see," Gregory had said. "We will see." *What did he mean?* What was I doing here? What on earth was I doing standing in this room, listening to this woman, when I wanted to run, wanted to scream? Protasova rescued me from Madame Koshelev and said I really should have more champagne and I agreed and took it gratefully.

Catherine and Gregory were having another talk across the room. He was smiling and she looked like a patient adult indulging a tedious child, but he didn't see that, of course. He thought she was fascinated. Count Zavadovsky had cornered his wife and was berating her in a low, furious voice and Protasova had strolled over to talk with Prince Golitsyn and young Peter was standing in front of me and casting sly glances down at my bosom and telling me he really preferred younger women, women nearer his own age. He said I was very mature and experienced and all but he bet I wasn't much older than he was, and I told him he was very sweet and charming and very good-looking but completely out of his league.

Twenty minutes ticked by. Only twenty? It seemed several hours since I had last glanced at the clock. What were we waiting for? Why hadn't we gone in to dine yet? Would the evening never end? Peter had moved away and Madame Koshelev had trapped *him* and Catherine was chatting pleasantly with the Zavadovskys and Count Orlov strolled over to me looking very pleased with himself and I thought of what he had done to Lucie and what he had done to the peasant Josef Pulaski and it took great effort to keep from shuddering.

"It goes very well," he said happily. "Catherine and I have a talk together. We speak of old times."

"That's wonderful," I replied.

"She remembers. Her eyes grow all misty as I remind her of days gone by and special joys we share. I think before the night is over she tells me she wants me to come back to her."

"Perhaps she will."

"I notice you are not wearing the diamond necklace," he said.

"I—" What was I going to tell him?

"You have me send it up to you this evening, yes?"

"It didn't go with my gown. I decided not to wear it."

"You do not have it returned to me."

"I left it on my dressing table."

"This is a very valuable piece of jewelry. It should have been put back into the safe."

"I suppose it was—careless of me, but I had other things on my mind at the time, Gregory."

"This is so," he replied. "You realize what an important evening this is for me. You wish—"

There was a stamping, snorting noise in the hall outside. The set of double doors leading into the room were hurled open and Gregory Aleksandrovich Potemkin lumbered in with all the grace of a wounded water buffalo, stunning the assemblage and completely paralyzing conversation. His pasty, pockmarked face was as hideous as I remembered, the black patch covering his left eye, a leering smile on the thick, sensual lips. His greasy locks were coated with stale powder, fastened at the nape with a piece of ribbon, and he was wearing a loose flowing garment of dark red brocade heavily embroidered with black and scarlet patterns. With its long, full sleeves and high neck it resembled some bizarre monk's habit and, soiled and rumpled, looked as though he had been wearing it for several days.

"I arrive at last!" he announced. "Now we can have the good time!"

Gregory had stiffened, tense with repressed fury. He had clearly not expected his rival to appear tonight. Catherine moved forward to greet her lover, her gray watered silk skirts swaying, gray lace fluttering beneath the clusters of pink velvet rosebuds. She took his hands. Potemkin gave her a sullen look and pulled free, gazing past her at the guests. When he saw Gregory and me he grinned and, pushing Catherine aside, shambled over to us. He had been drinking heavily. He smelled of liquor and sweat and garlic and grease.

"I am so happy you can make it!" he roared, pounding Gregory on the back. "Is very amusing to see you here tonight, Orlov. It will be an interesting evening."

Gregory was too livid to reply. Potemkin's grin broadened as he turned to fasten that dark, glowing eye on me.

"You bring the beauteous Miss Danver, I see. For this I forgive you everything. How are you, my beauty?"

"I've had better days."

"She enchants me!"

I tried to hide my repulsion, and I tried to deny the strange, perverse allure of the man. It was as though some dark power were drawing me to him, pulling at me, awakening urges inside I wasn't even aware of. The room seemed to waver, fading away, vanishing into mist, and there was just this man and these urges. The eye glowed, black-brown, burning with a message only I could read, and the lips curled into a mocking smile. A part of me stood back objectively and saw the pockmarked face and smelled the garlic and sweat and recoiled, perfectly aware of what was happening, but another part was drawn to him as surely as steel is drawn to magnetic rock. Potemkin chuckled and turned away, and the spell was broken.

I felt a bit dizzy. Colors were brighter, voices louder, the room filled with a new energy as Potemkin lumbered around in his bizarre red brocade robe, greeting the other guests. Prince Golitsyn nodded curtly, making no effort to conceal his dislike. Young Peter was awed, blushing when Potemkin laughed and tickled him playfully under the chin. Madame Koshelev gave him a warm, grandmotherly smile, and Countess Zavadovsky giggled nervously and looked as though she might swoon. Catherine watched him with proud, worshipful eyes, a pensive smile on her soft pink mouth. She loved him. She loved him with a slavish devotion that was her greatest weakness, her greatest glory.

"This man!" Gregory growled. "We will come to blows. It is inevitable. Maybe I even kill him."

"You mustn't let him rile you," I said, fully recovered.

"This is so. You are right. He wants to make me lose control so that he can laugh and sneer."

Protasova strolled over to join us. "You look a bit pale, Gregory," she said. "Are you all right?"

"Me, I am fine. *I* am not out of my head with drink."

"Potemkin does like the fruit of the vine," she remarked.

"The man is a disgrace!"

"I quite agree, but as long as the Empress is enthralled the rest of us will just have to endure."

Another fifteen minutes passed before a servant announced that dinner was ready to be served. Catherine came over and asked Gregory if he would escort her to the dining room. He beamed, bad mood forgotten as he gave her his arm. Potemkin staggered out with a giggling, enchanted Countess Zavadovsky hanging on to his arm, and her husband was forced to lead out Madame Koshelev who would undoubtedly tell him all about her grandnephews. Prince Golitsyn offered his arm to me, and Protasova followed behind us with Peter. Skirts rustled noisily and voices rose as we progressed down a long hall to the dining room. Potemkin roared with laughter up ahead, stumbling along with clumping feet.

The dining room was intimate, elegant, aglow with candlelight, the elongated table set with the finest crystal, china, and silver. There was a silver engraved place card at each setting. Gregory helped Catherine into her seat at one end of the table, and Prince Golitsyn helped me into mine. He was to be seated across from me. Anna Zavadovsky was giggling. Madame Koshelev couldn't locate her place. People were moving about. A rough, heavy hand rested on my shoulder. Garlic and liquor assailed my nostrils as Potemkin leaned down, his lips almost brushing my ear.

"I think tonight I fuck you," he tenderly murmured.

Chapter Twenty-One

IT SEEMED THE MEAL WOULD NEVER END.
After murmuring those words in my ear Potemkin had
taken his place at the end of the table opposite Catherine
and devoted his attention to Anna Zavadovsky, who sat on
his left, and young Peter, seated opposite her. Not once
during that interminable meal did he so much as glance at
me. He ate noisily, lustily, tearing his capon apart with his
hands, keeping up a steady flow of outrageous comments
that sent Zavadovsky into fits of nervous giggling and
brought repeated blushes to the cheeks of the handsome
young officer. Count Zavadovsky was not at all pleased.
Prince Golitsyn was disgusted. At the other end of the
table Catherine charmed Gregory and amused Protasova.
Happily unaware of the tense undercurrents around her,
Madame Koshelev consumed her food with silent efficiency, as though it had been some time since she'd had a
decent meal.

Course followed course, each more elaborate than the
one before. I barely touched my food. A magnificent custard was brought in, surrounded by macaroons and covered with hot apricot sauce. Potemkin roared with glee,
declaring it his favorite dessert. Countess Zavadovsky
squealed and bucked in her chair as Potemkin pinched her
under the table. Her husband turned ashen. Potemkin
roared with laughter and began to spoon custard into the
girl's mouth. Peter's cheeks burned a delicate shell pink.
Madame Koshelev swiftly devoured her custard, ate her

macaroons and, seeing that I hadn't touched mine, silently inquired if she might have it. I passed it over to her, wondering how much longer I could sit without screaming.

The meal was finally over. We adjourned to the drawing room where liqueurs were served. Count Zavadovsky monopolized his wife, keeping her away from Potemkin. Potemkin, several new grease stains on his outlandish red robe, had decided to torment Peter for a while and, one arm hooked heavily around the youth's shoulders, he regaled him with accounts of some of the more perverse sexual practices among the Turks. Peter looked as though he wished he had never left the country as his tormentor went into ever more explicit detail. I refused a liqueur and attempted to make light social conversation with Prince Golitsyn.

Catherine was talking with Gregory across the room, and they made a lovely couple, I thought objectively. His virile splendor complemented her mellow middle-aged glow, made her seem almost beautiful. He leaned forward, speaking to her in a low, husky voice, the charm visibly employed, and she opened up a silver lace fan and fluttered it and smiled, toying with him. She happened to glance up and see me looking at them. Her eyes twinkled as she gave me a conspiratorial nod.

"—must come to Paris one day soon," Prince Golitsyn was saying. "I'll show you some real treasures. The statuary in the gardens at Versailles is as splendid as any I've ever seen, and as for painting—"

I listened to every word he said and made all the appropriate replies but it was impossible to concentrate. Potemkin's melodious voice kept rumbling in the background, talking about buttocks now, talking about lard and how to apply it in order to facilitate a certain sexual act. With the exception of his miserably squirming victim, everyone else ignored the voice and those words, rarely heard in polite circles. Madame Koshelev and Protasova were discussing various maneuvers at the card table and Koshelev was confiding that confidence was the secret. Catherine looked over Gregory's shoulder at Potemkin and shook her head fondly. Her lover was "being naughty" again, her eyes seemed to say.

Liqueurs finished at last, Catherine announced that it might be interesting to play a few hands of cards. Madame Koshelev nodded enthusiastically, no doubt contemplating her winnings, and, his arm curled loosely around young Peter's throat, Potemkin roared that he intended to "show this young pup a few new tricks." The young pup blushed furiously and made a futile attempt to pull away from his overpowering new mentor. Anna Zavadovsky was pouting as her husband took the liqueur glass from her hand. Protasova sighed and said she had a feeling tonight was going to cost her.

"You look a bit tired, my dear," Catherine said to me as we strolled into an adjoining room where card tables had been set up.

"I have a slight headache," I replied.

"You hardly touched your food."

I was surprised. "You noticed?"

"There's very little I don't notice, my dear. It's a habit I developed a number of years ago. People don't *notice* me noticing, but I do."

Empress Catherine smiled, toying with her silver lace fan. I wondered if she had noticed Potemkin leaning over my chair, murmuring into my ear. I wondered if she suspected what he had said.

"You enjoy cards?" she asked.

"Ordinarily I do, but—I wonder if I might excuse myself tonight. I would much prefer to see the gallery. I've heard so much about your collection from Prince Golitsyn. He says there is none comparable in all Europe."

"And well he might. He was responsible for helping me acquire most of the best pieces. Of course you may skip the cards, my dear. I'll have one of the footmen show you to the gallery."

"It won't leave someone without a partner?"

"Actually, it will simplify things. Potemkin is going to

coach Peter, and that will leave exactly eight of us to play. There will be coffee and refreshments after cards."

I told her I would be back to watch them play as soon as I had seen all of the paintings, and Catherine told me to enjoy myself and directed a footman to take me to the gallery. Madame Koshelev was rubbing her hands with glee as I left. Still holding on to Peter, Potemkin was telling him he had to be sharp, had to be crafty, had to show no mercy. It was with relief that I followed the footman out of the room and down the hallway and past the wide marble staircase into the east wing.

It was very rude of me, I knew, leaving the others, and probably a shocking breach of protocol as well, but I simply had to be alone for a while, away from the people, the noise, the tension. The footman led me around a corner and down a short flight of steps and asked if I would require anything more. I shook my head and thanked him, and he bowed and departed, leaving me alone in the magnificent gallery. Dozens of paintings in ornate golden frames lined the pale cream walls, each a masterpiece of its kind, aglow with vibrant color, but I scarcely glanced at them.

It was after eleven. Their ship would already have cleared the harbor by now, I thought. Lucie and Bryan were sailing toward that happy ending, beyond Gregory's reach. The future awaited them, golden with promise, and I felt sure both would realize their full potentials. Lucie would become an actress. Bryan would write her plays. Together they would share a rich and fulfilling life, with none of the financial woes that so often cast a bleakness over youthful aspirations. Gregory would be furious when he discovered the diamond necklace was gone. I would pretend to be shocked myself. I would blame myself for being so careless, leaving it there on the dressing table for anyone to steal. He would interrogate all the servants and make a huge uproar, but its disappearance would remain a mystery.

I felt a touch of apprehension as I thought about his inevitable rage, and I felt even more as I recalled his enigmatic behavior in the carriage. Did he intend to go back on his word? Did he intend to attempt to keep me in Russia? Our "agreement" would mean nothing to Orlov. Breaking it would give him not a moment's pause. Gregory Orlov was a dangerous man. I knew that, but I had dealt with dangerous men before, quite a few of them. I wasn't afraid of him. I told myself that, and I tried very hard to convince myself it was true. He had great wealth, great power, and he was utterly ruthless, but I had a few resources of my own, honed sharp by years of struggle.

Tomorrow I would have Vanya take me to Kronstadt and I would book passage on the very next ship to Copenhagen, and once in Copenhagen I would make other arrangements, wait for a ship that would eventually get me to America. If Orlov refused to give me the money he had promised, I would simply open his safe in the dead of night and take it. Almost eight years ago I had been convicted of theft and was transported to America, when I had never stolen a thing in my life. Since that time I had become as accomplished at picking locks and opening safes as the most skillful footpad in London. Life was full of irony, I reflected. One acquired a number of useful skills when it became a matter of survival.

My skirts rustled as I moved slowly down the gallery, surrounded by some of the finest paintings in the world. Lost in thought, I failed to appreciate their beauty, hardly saw the glowing colors and wonderful images captured on canvas. Somewhere a clock struck, the chimes softly reverberating in the silence. Eleven-thirty. I had been here almost half an hour. They were undoubtedly having a marvelous time in the card room, Madame Koshelev raking in her winnings and nibbling the chocolates I had seen in silver dishes on the tables, Gregory beaming at Catherine and reveling in what he considered his triumph, Potemkin tormenting young Peter and telling him how to play his hand. What luxury it was to be alone, with only

the paintings and the silence and the bright glow of candlelight.

I paused in front of a large Nicolas Lancret canvas depicting a young man and his maiden embracing in a grassy
woodland clearing. The colors were soft, subdued, trees a
misty green and brown, grass a pale greenish tan, flesh
tones glowing warmly. The girl was wearing a blue dress
and her glossy hair spilled between her shoulder blades in
a tumble of loose waves. The man was tall and lean and
had rich chestnut hair that flopped over his brow as he
bent to cover her lips with his own. Lancret's style suggested Watteau, though without the frills and flowery gar-
lands. His was simpler, cleaner, evoking a poignantly
romantic mood.

I gazed at the painting and emotions stirred and soon I
was seeing another grassy clearing, another couple. I had
been wearing a blue dress that night, too, and his rich
chestnut hair had flopped over his brow just as in the
painting, and his lips had parted, covering mine, and his
arms had enfolded me, and the stars had blazed overhead
in the Texas sky as he lowered me to the pile of rustling
hay. The splendor of that night lived again in memory,
every detail remembered, mourned. Splendor lost, splendor gone, never to be savored again. Jeremy lost, Jeremy
gone, leaving me alone in a world without meaning.

Tears I refused to shed welled up inside. I turned away
from the painting, desolate, determined to overcome. I had
lived for twenty-four years without being aware of his exis-
tence, and I could bloody well live the rest of my life without him. If . . . if I were only half-alive, at least I would be
free of the constant emotional turmoil Jeremy Bond in-
flicted. The memories would fade, and, God willing, one
day I would be able to think of him without this stabbing
pain in my breast. I took a deep breath and turned and
stared in shocked silence at Gregory Potemkin.

"You are thinking of me?" he inquired.

How had he come down the gallery without my hearing
him? How had he been able to creep up on me, so silent? It

was almost as though he had simply materialized here before me.

"I think perhaps you are lonely," he crooned.

"How—how did—"

"I grow tired of coaching young Peter. He picks the game up quickly. He even wins a hand from the wily Madame Koshelev. He does not need me. I think perhaps the lovely Miss Danver needs me much more."

"I prefer to be alone," I said coldly.

"This is not so. Just now you are thinking how sad it is to be alone, to have no man to make love to you."

He seemed to loom before me, enormous, filling the hallway with his presence, his powerful aura that charged the air with energy. His huge, rough hands lightly caressed his thighs as that one dark eye peered at me, looked into my soul, saw all my secrets. A gently mocking smile curled on those fleshy lips. The man was a wreck, a ruin, his face pitted with pockmarks, yet a curious attractiveness remained once one : . . once one got beyond the initial ugliness. It had to do with strength, not beauty, fascination, not features. I felt that pull. I fought it.

He gestured toward the Lancret canvas, raising his arm, pointing, and the sleeve of his embroidered red brocade robe fluttered, flowed on air. The mocking smile widened.

"You look at this painting. It reminds you of other times. It makes you feel empty inside. You have very strong needs. For a long time you deny them and they build up, demand release, relief."

His voice was low, melodious, soothing the senses like soft music, music more important than words. I hardly heard the words. I heard the melody, and it filled me with warmth, soothing, comforting, caressing. He moved nearer, the smile so gentle, so . . . so understanding, the dark eye gleaming with compassion.

"Potemkin will help you," he murmured. "He will release those emotions welling up inside you. He will unlock secret sensations and make you feel the new ecstasy, ecstasy beyond your wildest dreams."

"No," I said.

"You fight. It is foolish to fight."

"No," I repeated.

"You want me," he murmured.

"No," I whispered.

"You want these hands to stroke every inch of your body and explore every soft secret. You want the weight of this body to crush you and imprison you. You want to be impaled on my prick."

I shook my head. He smiled, nodding.

"You want me. You need me."

He understood so much, and he sympathized, he wanted to help. He smiled tenderly, tenderly, moving nearer, and I seemed to be swallowed up, seemed to lose all will, drawn to him, lonely, longing to yield completely to his power. Strength and stony self-control melted, and a wonderful weakness stole through me. How pleasant to let someone else command, control. I was so tired, so tired, too tired to struggle.

"Ah, yes, it is what you want. Say it. Say you want me."

I parted my lips, but the words refused to come. That other Marietta refused to say them. She stood back, looking on, fully aware of what was happening and utterly horrified, resisting the pull, fighting it, fighting it still. She struggled against the weakness, the longing, the lethargy that lulled senses into stupor.

"I find you—totally repulsive," I said.

He chuckled softly, a lovely sound.

"You repel me."

"You say this, but it is not true. You know it is not true. You want me to take you. You want to yield. You will submit to me. Ah, yes, you will submit. Submit."

The dark eye gleamed with a diabolical glow, black-brown flames smoldering, compelling me to obey. Look away, the other Marietta told me. *You must look away.* You will not let him do this to you. The bright candlelight began to grow dim, melting into mist. The paintings disappeared and there was nothing but this giant looming before me in his bizarre red robe, the most fascinating, the most marvelous man alive.

"You feel a warmth burning inside you," he said. "It's stealing through your blood, warming you, wonderful. Feel it."

"I feel."

"Your skin is tingling. Feel it tingle."

"Yes."

"It is wonderful, this tingling. You have never felt anything like it before."

"Never," I whispered.

"You are filled with yearning. You yearn to make love to me. You yearn to receive me, enclose me with your flesh, take me deeper, deeper, this is so, say it is so."

"It is so."

He smiled and it was a wonderful smile and never, never had I wanted anything as I wanted this man who was a god, glorious, and the other Marietta was no longer there and I was drifting, dreaming, all reserve, all restraint melting away. I could feel it melting, turning into warmth that flowed through my veins like thick, sweet honey. He slowly raised one large hand and it floated gracefully, caressing the air, and then it landed softly on my shoulder and the fingers spread out and squeezed my bare flesh like rough tentacles curling, uncurling, and a thousand sensations exploded inside as his hand moved up to curl around the back of my neck.

He chuckled, reveling in his power over me, and I knew that, knew he was a monster of depravity employing black arts on me, but that didn't matter at all. The spell was too strong and knowledge was meaningless. The lethargy possessed me completely now as his hand tightened on the back of my neck, drawing me nearer until my face was buried in folds of red brocade. He turned me around, holding me at his side, one arm wrapping around my waist, and we were moving, floating through the mist. I was powerless, absolutely without will, an abject slave to sensation. He guided me along and we turned and moved down a

narrow corridor and then another and he unlocked a door
and led me into an incredible womblike room.

Candles glowed, bathing the dull red walls with pale
golden shadows. A red carpet covered the floor, dull brick
red, like the walls, and there was an enormous scarlet velvet sofa, deep and plush and inviting with piles of scarlet
pillows, a sofa designed not for sitting but for love. Heavy
scarlet velvet drapes covered the windows, and low ebony
tables held dark gold candelabra and an amazing collection of small, erotic Italian bronzes, mythological figures
by Bologna, wrestling, writhing, entwining, copulating in
an astonishing variety of positions. Leafy dark green
plants with tight, waxy white buds grew in dark red urns,
scenting the air with a strong, sweet smell.

He closed the door and chuckled and we were alone in
the small red room. My limbs felt limp and the hot honey
coursed slowly through my veins and my head was spinning. This was not real. This was not happening. This was
a bizarre, erotic dream and I was trapped in it as though
trapped in a silken web and he was the spider, a great, glorious spider, ready to claim me, and struggle was useless
because the silken strands bound me securely, and though
I could move I could never break free. Potemkin held my
elbow in a firm grip, the rough, callused fingers squeezing skin and flesh, and without that support I would have
crumpled, for my legs were no longer working. Nothing
was working. Nothing was real. It was a dream . . . a
nightmare, yes, a nightmare, and I must wake up. I must
not let the spider spring.

He was not golden. He was not glorious. He was evil,
evil, and I must free myself of these silken bonds. Golden
shadows leaped nimbly on the dull red walls, and the walls
seemed to close in on me and I had trouble breathing. I
was going to suffocate. My bosom heaved. My breath
caught in my throat. Panic began to set in, vibrating inside me, a wild thing beating furiously and pounding
against my rib cage. I gasped, unable to breathe at all now.

"Relax," that lovely voice crooned, sweet, soothing mu-

sic that lulled gently and drove the panic away. "You are
not afraid. You want this to happen as much as I do. Relax.
You are not afraid."

I took a deep breath, another, and panic was gone, and I
was not afraid any longer but I was still in the middle of a
dream. Golden shadows flickered over the bronzes, too,
and the small, exquisite figures seemed to come to life
there on the tables, performing their various acts in the
wavering gold light, moving in and out and up and down
and to and fro, rolling and writhing as I watched in
horrified fascination. The giant in red brocade grinned and
told me that this was what we would do, pointing, and this,
pointing again, and this as well, and I was not afraid, no, I
wanted it to happen as much as he did, yes, but it wasn't
real, it was a dream, and I would never do those things
with him when I was awake because he was evil, evil, a
great crimson spider ready to spring.

"No," I said.

"Do not resist. You will not resist. You will enjoy."

"No."

"Look at me. Do not turn away. Look at me."

"I must—"

"You must obey. You will obey."

I must obey. I would obey. It was only a dream. It was
not real at all. Marietta was far, far away, safe, in suspen-
sion, and this was not happening to her, it was happening
to someone else. He led me over to the sofa and released his
grip on my elbow and I spilled onto the sofa and sank into
scarlet, nestling on soft pillows, looking up through half-
lowered lids as he stood over me smiling a satisfied smile,
awesome and beautiful, all powerful, savoring the ecstasy
soon to be his, mine, too. There was no fear, no, I was drifting again, floating in a golden haze, warm and lethargic
and wonderfully weak, waiting for this god to do with me
as he would.

He leaned over me, catching my wrists in his hands,
twisting them slightly as he spread my arms wide. My
bosom rose and my right breast popped out of its prison of

sky blue silk and stood full and firm and milky white and
tipped with a tight, throbbing pink nipple that grew
harder, tighter as he gazed down at it. "Ah," he exclaimed,
and he released my wrists and kneeled down and wrapped
his arms around my waist, pulling me forward, his mouth
opening, covering the nipple, sucking vigorously. I arched
my back, reeling as the honey warmth exploded into flame,
and fire swept through me, magic fire that brought pleasure, not pain, and it must be put out before it consumed
me completely. Potemkin raised his head and looked at the
swollen nipple and curled one huge hand around the
breast and squeezed tightly, kneading the flesh, and I
moaned, knowing I was going to die.

His fingers squeezed tighter and he was chuckling
again, a merciless executioner deliberately toying with his
victim, prolonging the torture, delaying the death. I threw
my head back and stared at the dull red ceiling and saw
the painting there, fleshy figures encoiled, coupling on
clouds, bathed in pink-gold light, and the rough fingers
continued to squeeze and the magic fire continued to
course through my veins and I floated, floated on clouds
like those above, and soon our figures would encoil and
couple and it would be . . . it would be wrong. He was making me do this, making me, and I despised him, he was repulsive, I must break free before . . . before something
terrible took place.

The Marietta who was safe and suspended far, far away
stirred and struggled to reclaim herself, to break the spell
that held her captive. She caught hold of his greasy hair
and tugged viciously, jerking his head back, and he cried
out and struck her across the face as she tried to get up
from the sofa. He stood up and scowled, weaving to and fro,
and then he lunged, falling atop me, pinioning me to the
sofa beneath his great weight, and it was me now, free at
last, free of those silken strands, that spell, furiously fighting the hideous creature whose swollen manhood poked
and prodded like a stiff, steely rod through layers of cloth
even as his huge hands sought to remove those silken bar-

riers, as I heaved and pushed and tried to throw him off me. He was too strong, too large, too heavy, and I saw it was futile, but I wasn't going to let it happen. I wasn't. I clamped my legs together, pushing at his chest as his lips sought mine.

"That will be quite enough," Catherine said sharply.

Potemkin froze at the sound of that cold, imperious voice, and I looked over his shoulder and saw her standing there in the doorway regal and composed and as hard as stone. He climbed off of me and smoothed his rumpled red brocade robe and looked at her with a sheepish smile. I sat up and shoved my right breast back into my bodice, filled with humiliation as the Empress of All the Russias gazed icily at the two of us.

"You win at cards?" Potemkin inquired.

"At cards, yes."

"The game is over?"

"Would that it were."

"This means nothing. I just amuse myself."

"Our guests have adjourned to the drawing room for coffee and refreshments, Gregory," she said. "I think it might be wise if you joined them."

Still smiling that sheepish smile, he nodded and sauntered toward the door. Catherine stepped aside to let him move past. Stunned, still weak, I climbed to my feet and adjusted the bodice of my gown. I felt as though I had finally broken surface after being underwater and almost drowning. Standing in the doorway again, Catherine watched Potemkin start down the hall and then turned to look at me. Her features were beautifully composed, betraying no emotion at all.

"Are you all right?" she asked.

I nodded. I could feel the spots of color burning on my cheeks. Her voice was cool. So were her eyes.

"I—I didn't—"

"You needn't explain, my dear."

"He—"

"I'm fully aware of what happened. It has happened before. I know you are not to blame, Miss Danver."

Each word was like a chip of ice. She knew I was not to blame, but she had seen her lover atop me, attempting to enter, and she had seen me struggling beneath him with my breast exposed. That sight was engraved on her mind, and she could never look at me again without seeing it reenacted. As a woman, I understood. It would have been the same with me.

"Did he hurt you?" she asked.

I shook my head. "I'm just—a little weak."

"Will you be able to join the others? For the sake of appearances?"

"I think so. In—in a few minutes."

I smoothed down my skirts, shamed, striving to regain at least a modicum of composure. Catherine stood very still, cool and impervious, waiting, and after a while I was able to hold myself straight and meet her gaze with dignity. That silent rapport still existed between us, each attuned to the other's mind, but a gulf separated us now. Intimacy was no longer possible.

"You will want to tidy up," she said.

"Yes," I replied.

"There is a powder room for guests beyond the main hall. I will show you the way."

"I would appreciate it."

Candlelight flickered over the bronzes and the red walls and the figures on the ceiling as I followed her out of the room. We moved silently down the corridor and turned and moved past the gallery with the vibrantly colored paintings hanging in their ornate gold frames, and an eternity seemed to have passed since I stood staring at the Lancret. Eventually, we reached the main hall and Catherine led me past the wide marble staircase to a gilt white door beyond.

"You'll find everything you need inside," she said.

"Thank you."

"I'll return to my other guests now."

"I'll join you shortly."

Catherine hesitated, a slight frown marring that mask of composure. "I am very sorry this happened, Miss Danver."

"I am, too."

"Gregory is easily tempted. Ordinarily he is more discreet. I imagine you are wondering why I tolerate it."

"You love him," I said.

"And I cope, as any woman must. I've found the best way to deal with these matters is to remove the temptation."

"I understand."

"I thought you would. I'll speak to Orlov before you leave tonight."

"You won't tell him what happened—"

"Of course not."

She gave me a polite nod, turned and left, her head held high, her back straight, the skirt of her gray watered silk gown belling as she moved away. I felt that I had lost a friend, and somehow this was more distressing than what had happened with Potemkin. I stepped into the powder room and found a splendid array of cosmetics and perfumes, a silver brush and comb, all the accouterments a fashionable woman might need, including a silver box of patches. I stared at myself in the mirror and made the necessary repairs, calm now, almost numb, and a few minutes later I started back toward the drawing room.

None of this mattered, I told myself. Lucie was safe, on her way to England now, and I would be leaving Russia myself in just a few days and all this would become mere memory. A year from now, in the clear, clean spaces of Texas with its grassy plains and arching blue skies, Catherine and Potemkin and Orlov would be insubstantial shades, Russia a distant land with no reality as I strolled under the cottonwood trees and smelled the sage. This perspective was an invisible shield, protecting me from emotional turmoil as I stepped into the drawing room.

Potemkin was teasing young Peter again and paid not

the slightest attention when I entered the room. Madame Koshelev was counting her winnings and eating a dish of ice cream. Gregory was talking with Protasova, lording it over her now that he believed himself back in power. Protasova wore an expression of patient boredom. Catherine was chatting with the Zavadovskys. She looked up and smiled at me and motioned to a footman to attend to my needs, the perfect hostess looking out for her guests. I turned down coffee and ice cream but accepted a glass of light wine. Prince Golitsyn asked me if I had enjoyed seeing the paintings, and I managed to fake an appreciation I had been too distracted to feel.

Half an hour passed and, protected by my shield, I managed to present a polite social facade. Catherine was gracious and charming, acting her part superbly, and no one suspected the heartache she must be feeling. Potemkin roared and rollicked, transferring his attention from Peter to Anna Zavadovsky, who tittered nervously. Madame Koshelev dropped off to sleep in her chair, brown wig askew, and, after a tactful signal from Catherine, Protasova announced that it was past Peter's bedtime. Catherine said it had been a lovely evening and thanked us all for coming.

She accompanied us to the main hall and chatted pleasantly as we were handed our wraps. Potemkin had disappeared. Protasova had already taken Peter away. Standing near the door, looking very regal, Catherine told the Zavadovskys goodbye and smiled as Prince Golitsyn led a drowsy, befuddled Madame Koshelev out to her rented carriage. Gregory helped me into my white mink cloak and whirled the sleek black sable around his shoulders, very dashing, very confident. Catherine acknowledged my curtsey with a polite nod.

"Good-bye, Miss Danver," she said.

Her voice was cool. I returned the nod.

"I wonder if you would stay a moment longer, Gregory," she said. "I would like a word with you."

"Of course, my Catherine."

"Stefan will show Miss Danver to the carriage."

The footman took my arm and led me down the steps to the drive where another footman stood with torch held high. The Orlov carriage circled around. I was helped inside. It had started to snow lightly, large white flakes swirling lazily in the night. I settled back against the velvet upholstery and wrapped the cloak around me, prepared for a long wait, but only a few minutes passed before Gregory came down the steps. He moved slowly, haltingly, like a man in a daze, and in the pale orange glow of the torch he looked completely stunned.

The carriage door was opened for him and Gregory climbed inside and sat down across from me, silent, hardly aware of where he was. He looked at me as though he had never seen me before in his life, then turned to stare out at the night as the carriage began to move. He sat very still, one large hand gripping the edge of the seat so tightly the velvet upholstery ripped. Horse hooves tapped on the pavement with a steady clop clop. The carriage rocked gently. Moonlight wavered through the windows, and in the misty silver haze the man sitting across from me looked ten years older. His face seemed to sag. His eyes were dark with dismay. The dream he had cherished for such a long time had been utterly, irrevocably destroyed.

"I do not understand," he said after a while. His voice was hoarse. "I do not understand."

I made no reply. He was not speaking to me.

" 'I think St. Petersburg is beginning to tire you,' she tells me. 'I think you will be happier in the country. I expect you to leave tomorrow.' She tells me this. She gives me no explanation."

"I'm sorry, Gregory."

" 'You will be happier in the country,' she tells me. This is a direct order. I am banished to my country estate in the north until she lifts the ban. I do not understand."

There was nothing I could say, and he would not have heard anyway. He kept repeating himself in a hoarse, hollow voice, and when we finally reached the Marble Palace and the carriage stopped he raised his head and looked at me as though to inquire where we were.

I climbed out. Gregory followed me. We went inside and a servant took our cloaks and carried them away and Gregory looked around at the elegant foyer, seeing only his own despair. In the bright glow of candlelight his face looked even worse, the color of damp putty, the full mouth twitching at one corner. His hair looked a duller gold. All energy and vitality seemed to have been drained out of him, and that powerful magnetism that gave him such a radiant glow was completely missing now.

"I think I will go on upstairs," I said.

He turned, really looking at me for the first time.

"No," he said.

"I'm very tired, Gregory, and—"

"You will stay with me. We will have a drink."

He might have been speaking in his sleep, yet his voice was firm. I knew it would be a mistake to agitate him in any way, and I meekly followed him into the drawing room, watching as he poured peppered vodka into a glass.

"Will you have one?" he asked.

"No, thank you."

He swallowed the vodka and stared across the room, and color began to return to his face. His mouth tightened. I could sense the fury slowly mounting inside him, and I felt a vague tremor of alarm. I knew full well that Gregory Orlov was unbalanced, and at this point anything might push him over the edge. He had sustained a great shock, and when he found out that Lucie was gone . . . I felt suddenly chilled.

"She refused to give me an explanation. 'Why do you do this, my Catherine?' I ask her, and she looks at me with eyes like blue ice and tells me that the Empress of Russia does not have to explain herself. She tells this to me!"

He scowled, splashing more vodka into his glass. The shock had worn off now, and bright spots of color burned hotly on cheeks that had been ashen only minutes ago. I must leave tonight. I realized that now. I mustn't be here when he discovered Lucie was gone. I would slip back downstairs after he went to sleep and I would open the safe and take the money he owed me and . . . and, yes, I would go to the British embassy. Bryan's father didn't like me, didn't approve of me, but he wouldn't deny me sanctuary for . . . for a day or so. Orlov had to leave St. Petersburg, and when he was gone I could book passage and . . .

"What do you know about this?" he asked.

I looked up. He was studying me with hard, shrewd eyes.

"I—I don't know what you mean," I said.

His glass was empty again. He refilled it a second time and gulped the vodka with a jerking motion of head and hand.

"You know something. I can tell this. It is written on your face."

"That—that's ridiculous, Gregory."

"You go to see her at the Hermitage. The two of you talk, conspire against me. You laugh at me."

"You're imagining things—"

"All this time you know she is not going to take me back. She tells you to humor me."

There was a strange tremor in his voice, and his eyes, now, seemed to burn with maniacal light. The mighty Count Orlov couldn't accept blame for his failure, his ego wouldn't permit that. He had to blame someone else, and in casting about he had accidentally stumbled upon some truths, and . . . and I had to remain very, very calm. He set his empty glass aside, rage simmering, smoldering, threatening to erupt.

"You know that's not true, Gregory," I said.

"You are against me. You are all against me. I was going to have my apartment in the Winter Palace again and I was going to have power and I was going to have glory as I did before and there would be triumphal arches erected for me as they were before and another medal cast in my honor and everyone in Russia would know Orlov was back where he was meant to be. Catherine wanted me back, I know she did, and you—you undermine me!"

"Gregory—"

"It is true!"

His eyes were blazing, and my blood turned cold for I knew he was no longer rational. I knew he had finally lost that precarious mental balance and toppled over the edge. He pressed his lips together and took several deep breaths. The fury that raged inside him was controlled, held in check, and a lethal calm possessed him now. It was far more disturbing than his rage would have been. He took a step toward me, stopped, stared at the doorway.

"What do you want?" he asked harshly.

Vladimir stepped into the room. I felt the color leave my cheeks.

"Lucie is gone," Vladimir said.

"Lucie is gone?" Orlov did not seem to understand. "Lucie is in her room. Lucie would not leave me."

"She left hours ago," Vladimir told him. "This one"—he jerked his head at me—"she tricks me. She pretends to have a bad ankle. She leads me away from my post."

"Lucie is gone?" He spoke the words as a child might, slowly, without comprehension.

"I go back to my post after you leave with this woman. I knock on the door after a while and there is no answer. I think she is sulking. I wait. I knock again. I go inside and she is not there."

"Lucie is not gone," Orlov said. He shook his head.

"We search the palace. We search the grounds. She is nowhere to be found. One of the men remembers seeing Vanya leave the grounds with a maidservant. All the maidservants are accounted for. None of them left the palace tonight. One of them says her cloak has been stolen."

Orlov looked at Vladimir and looked at me. He clenched and unclenched his hands. My heart was palpitating. There was no way out. There was no escape. I was trapped between a madman and a savage who hated me with a vengeance. Vladimir curled his lip, glaring at me.

"This one helps her. She and Vanya. Vanya returns and I order the men to seize him. He puts up a fight. He wounds two of the men. He is badly wounded himself, but he gets away."

Count Gregory Orlov continued to clench and unclench his hands and finally curled them into tight fists. He looked at me thoughtfully, as though wondering how I came to be standing in his drawing room.

"Vanya gets away," Vladimir said. "This one does not."

"This is so," Orlov replied.

"From the first I know she is going to make trouble. What are we going to do with her?"

"This I will have to think about," Orlov said.

Panic swept over me like a tidal wave and receded just as quickly, leaving me dazed for a moment, and then a strange calm possessed me and I faced both of them defiantly, too proud to cringe, too proud to cry, and determined to show no fear.

"Lucie is gone," Orlov said. "You helped her."

"I helped her," I said.

"Where is she?"

"She's beyond your reach now."

"Where is she?" he repeated.

"If—if you must know, she's on a ship. It left Kronstadt at ten. She's safe. Thank God she's safe. She's going to marry Bryan. You'll never be able to touch her again."

"Your ankle was not hurt."

"I faked it."

"You—you tricked me."

"I did what I had to do."

"You—the necklace—" he said suddenly, and his eyes grew wide with disbelief. "You do not wear the necklace. You—"

"I gave it to her. She was entitled to it. She—she told me everything. Lucie told me how you raped her, how you—your own niece! Yes, I tricked you, and I'm glad. I'm glad!"

Count Orlov stared at me in shocked disbelief, and the bright spots of color began to burn on his cheeks again. He tightened his fists. The rage he had held in check was beginning to overflow, beginning to consume him. He shook

his head from side to side and then threw it back and let
out a roar and I stared in horror as he charged, one arm
swinging back, swinging forward, the huge fist flying
through the air like the ball of a mace.

It crashed against my cheek and lights exploded inside
my head and a thousand hot sharp spears stabbed as I
stumbled, fell, hurtling into a spinning oblivion of blackness. I whirled in blackness, burning, falling faster, faster,
and it grew darker and I heard a moaning noise like an animal whimpering and it was far, far away. Blackness swallowed me, smothered me, and then it turned to dark purple
and then gray and the pain was worse than ever and
strange silver-orange lights were spinning before my eyes
and I was groping through layers of thick fog and there
were voices, distant, distorted.

"—do with her now?"

"—leave tomorrow—take her along—will decide later
what punishment is fitting for what she has done to me—"

Silver-orange lights whirled and spun and the fog lifted
and the pain was a shrieking, shattering thing that
stormed across my brain in violent flashes. Between those
blinding flashes I saw a woman in sky blue silk sprawling
on the floor, two gigantic men looming over her like immense tree trunks in a glittering forest of crystal and gilt
and marble. The forest began to spin and colors began to
blur and pain seared and blackness swallowed me again,
pulling me into welcome oblivion.

BOOK FOUR

Chapter Twenty-Two

THE SILENCE IN THE NORTH WAS A TANGIBLE presence, hovering just beyond vision, holding its breath. The air was still, and when a bird cried out in the woods surrounding Count Orlov's estate, the sound was magnified, echoing loudly, finally fading, the silence even more ominous after that shrill intrusion. Though the trees were encased in ice and the ground covered with snow, it wasn't that cold as I strolled restlessly over the grounds. The sky was a translucent white, blurry with pearl gray streaks, and there were pale amethyst shadows on the snow. In the distance the house crouched squat and ugly, a long, low two-story structure of dark gray stone with a dull greenish gray slate roof, leaded windows like glazed reptilian eyes watching me.

The front door opened. A tall figure in dark blue livery and black fur hat stepped out. Although he was too far away from me to discern features, I knew it was Vladimir. He never let me out of his sight for too long, was forever checking on me, watching grimly, waiting for me to make a foolish move. We were isolated here in the bleak north country. This was the end of the earth, it seemed, and I had been given complete freedom ever since we had arrived two and a half weeks ago. What could I do? Where could I go? Were I insane enough to attempt flight, they reasoned, I would freeze to death in the woods—if I weren't torn to pieces by the starving wolves whose chilling howls could be heard every night.

The bruise on my cheekbone had faded now to a faint mauve shadow that was barely discernible. I had been unconscious for hours, awakening to find myself in a moving carriage. The journey from St. Petersburg had taken three long days. Although I was a prisoner, my carriage zealously guarded by Vladimir and another of Orlov's men, I had been treated with cold politeness, all of my needs tended to promptly. Upon arrival here, I had been shown to my quarters and given free reign of the property. The servants treated me like an unwanted but privileged guest, mystified by my presence and even more mystified by the conduct of their master—who had gone quite mad.

Count Gregory Orlov spent almost every waking hour downstairs in the great, gloomy drawing room in the front of the house, just off the great, gloomy hallway with its dark staircase winding up to the second floor. In front of a roaring fire, surrounded by shadows and delusions, he drank bottle after bottle of vodka and rambled to himself and to the shadows, yelling loudly at times, at times sobbing pathetically. Vladimir tended to him as he might tend to an infant, taking him food which remained largely uneaten, supplying him with bottles, taking him upstairs to bed when he finally lapsed into a drunken stupor. Orlov had moments of lucidity, but they were rare. Most of the time he had no idea where he was, what was real or what was a figment of his haunted brain.

He had not touched me since that dreadful night at the Marble Palace when he discovered Lucie had gone. He had not once spoken with me. He would decide upon a punishment fitting for what I had done to him, he had informed Vladimir, but had plunged into the abyss of madness and, except for those few rare moments, was not even aware of my presence. Vladimir was waiting for instructions, waiting patiently for Orlov to tell him what to do with me. In the meantime I wandered about the dark, brooding house with its ponderous furniture and threadbare rugs—there was no elegance here, no opulent display of wealth, the place was a bleak and neglected mausoleum. More often, I wandered about the grounds as I did now, plotting the escape they deemed impossible.

Vladimir watched me from the distance as I walked over the snow in my topaz velvet gown and dark brown fur cloak. Surprisingly enough, all of my things had been packed and brought along, so I was able to dress warmly. Ignoring the distant sentinel, I strolled slowly, my heels crunching on the hard snow, and after a while he went back into the house. How long would it be before Count Orlov had a brief lucid spell, remembered his grievances against me, and told Vladimir to kill me or . . . or worse? His twisted, perverted mind might well devise some horrible torture, some hideous fate that would make death seem a welcome relief. I knew that, and I did not intend to wait around.

A woman alone, without transportation, would have no chance of surviving in this country, that was quite true, but I did not intend to be alone, nor on foot. During these past two and a half weeks I had made allies, and I had made several plans. If Mitya and Grushenka were able to do their parts, the three of us might well be leaving tonight. Casually, taking my time in case Vladimir might be watching from one of the windows, I strolled back toward the house and then, without apparent purpose, circled around it toward the back. I passed the barracks with the cobbled yard in front where Orlov's cossacks warmed themselves by fires and consumed vodka. They paid no attention as I wandered on past the other outbuildings, finally reaching the stables.

An overpowering smell of mud, manure and horseflesh assailed my nostrils as I stepped into the stables. Horses neighed, stamping in their stalls, impatient for their ration of oats. The rough flagstone floor was littered with damp hay. The ceiling was low, and it was dark and shadowy inside, only a few rays of sunlight stealing through cracks in the rough wooden walls. How I missed Natasha. She had been left in the stables in St. Petersburg, along with several more horses. Did she miss me and Vanya?

And Vanya . . . where was he? He had fled into the night, badly wounded. How bad had his wounds been? Was he all right? I would probably never know, and that saddened me.

Passing the stalls, I came to the enormous room where oats and harnesses and various supplies were kept, an open hayloft above. A shaft of sunlight fell across the huge pile of hay beneath the loft, leaving the rest of the room deep in shadow, a black and gray cave. I smelled rotting leather, rust, dried sweat. Chickens squawked, running loose. Hay sprinkled down from the loft, and then a huge heap came tumbling down. The prongs of a pitchfork glittered above. There was a rustling noise, movment, a loud grunt, then another heap of hay fell onto the pile below.

"Mitya?" I called quietly.

A heavy rope came swinging down from the rafters like a vine, and a moment later the tall, husky groom came shimmying down out of the gloom. I saw a pair of muddy boots emerge into the shaft of sunlight, then long legs in worn brown cord breeches, a powerful torso covered with a coarse, soiled white shirt, then a head capped with thick, unruly brown hair. The rope swung to and fro, flying wildly as Mitya dropped to the ground. He brushed hay from his broad shoulders and rested his hands on his thighs, glaring at me with a sullen expression.

"I wait for you," he said gruffly. "I send the other two grooms away to soap the saddles so they will not be here when you come, and I wait for you. I begin to think you are not coming."

"I couldn't just leave the house and come directly to the stables. Vladimir is always watching me. I had to stroll about and—and more or less wander to the stables to see the horses. He knows I love horses. He won't think anything amiss. We have to be discreet, Mitya."

"What does this word mean—this 'discreet?' "

"It means careful."

He nodded sternly. "Yes, it is important to be careful. I am very careful last night when I slip away and go to the village to see Aloyosha Fyodorovich. No one sees me leave. No one sees me come back."

"Did—is he going to help us?"

"He is very cautious. Where does this rough stableboy who smells of manure get all these gold pieces, he wants to know. He is most suspicious. He does not want trouble brought upon his house."

"What did you tell him?"

"I tell him a very grand lady pays me to help her and gives me these gold pieces to buy a sleigh and horse. I tell him you are running away to meet your lover and this he understands, but he wants to know more. I tell him I will deal with him or I will go to Alexy Petrovna in the next village and deal with *him* and Alexy Petrovna will pocket all this gold. Aloyosha Fyodorovich agrees to help us then."

"He will provide the horse and sleigh?"

Mitya nodded again. "It will be waiting for us in the clearing just beyond the east woods. I give him half of the gold pieces and tell him he will have the rest when we reach the clearing and find he has brought the horse and sleigh. He is said to be an honest man, but it is better to trust no one when there is gold involved."

Obtaining transportation had been my first concern. There was absolutely no way we could steal one of the troikas or sleighs or carriages here and harness the horses without alerting the cossacks and guards. Mitya had informed me that a horse and sleigh might be obtained from a man he knew of in the village, but it would cost much money. Getting the money had been simple, as Orlov kept a safe here.

"You did well, Mitya," I said.

Mitya scowled. He was only nineteen years old, but he looked much older with his sullen mouth and broad, flat cheekbones and humped nose. Brown eyes glared at the world with a hostile glow beneath arching brows. They grew tender only when he looked at Grushenka. When he was with Grushenka the animosity disappeared and this harsh, surly youth became gentle and playful. They were in love and their future held no promise, he a stableboy, she a maid in the big house, but that was changed now. The gold I had deftly stolen from the safe two nights ago would not only pay for the horse and sleigh, it would enable Mitya and Grushenka to make a new start once we safely reached St. Petersburg.

Chickens squawked, pecking at the hay. A door opened in the other part of the stables. Mitya cocked his head.

"You must leave," he said gruffly.

"Tonight, then?" I asked.

"Tonight, after everyone has gone to sleep. I will meet you and Grushenka outside the kitchen door. You must steal a gun."

"A gun?"

"This we must have. This I cannot buy. The wolves," he said.

"I—I see."

"You steal the gold easily enough," he told me. "It should not be difficult for you to steal this gun. Ammunition, too. You know about this?"

His brusque, surly manner was both rude and irritating. Mitya vehemently detested all aristocrats, the oppressors of his kind, and he considered me one of them. He didn't trust me, wasn't at all sure this wasn't all some kind of elaborate trap. Had it not been for Grushenka, he would never have agreed to help.

"I know that a gun is virtually useless without ammunition," I replied, somewhat tensely.

He scowled at me and nodded impatiently toward the door as clumping footsteps approached. I opened the creaking wooden door and stepped out into the sunshine as the other two grooms joined Mitya beneath the hayloft. Pigs were squealing in one of the pens nearby. Two of the cossacks were arguing loudly. I strolled past their campfires, ignored. The cobbled yard was littered with the shards of broken bottles. Bored, restless, the cossacks were resentful of this sudden relocation to the somber north country and uneasy about their master's peculiar conduct.

They were unhappy about their accommodations as well. The flimsy wooden barracks were falling apart and freezing cold. The food was abominable. Orlov's elegant, temperamental chef had flatly refused to go to the north, and the slovenly cook who occupied the kitchens here produced wretched meals that could barely be called edible.

Entering the house through one of the back doors, I passed through a dusty hallway filled with rotting saddles and crumbling boxes and discarded furniture, and then I proceeded up the narrow passageway that ran alongside the main staircase and led into the enormous front hall. I paused, listening to the unnerving chanting noise coming from the drawing room. His voice low and rumbling, Gregory seemed to be repeating some woeful litany broken by sobs. I shuddered, folding my arms around my waist.

The drawing room door opened. Vladimir stepped into the hall. I caught a glimpse of Orlov sprawled out in the large leather chair in front of the blazing fire, his arms and legs hanging limp, lifeless. His face was haggard, pale, dark mauve shadows under haunted eyes. Vladimir closed the door and looked at me in the glow of the cheap wax candles that filled the air with a noxious smell. You are responsible for this, his dark eyes told me. You will pay. I stood my ground, defiant, meeting that glaring accusation with haughty composure, and he finally curled his lip savagely and moved on to fetch another bottle of vodka.

A gun. I had to steal a gun. There was a whole shed full of rifles, ammunition, and powder in back, attached to the barracks, but there was no possible way I could break into it. As disorganized and undisciplined as they were, the cossacks kept a guard posted in front of the armory, and several of them were invariably underfoot. There must be a gun somewhere in the house, I reasoned, but where? Hearing footsteps on the stairs, I turned. Grushenka came down, glancing nervously toward the drawing room.

"The—the count is in a very bad way, isn't he?" she said.

"I'm afraid so, Grushenka."

The girl crossed herself. "We are very afraid, all of us.

The priest in the village says a demon has possessed Count Orlov. He says the demon is angry and may fly out and possess us too if we are not faithful. Old Mathilda hasn't slept a wink since the demon appeared. She does not wash the linens as she is supposed to do. She spends all her time in the basement room praying in front of her painted wooden icon."

Vladimir came back into the hall with a new bottle of vodka. He glared at us before going back into the drawing room. Grushenka crossed herself again as he closed the door behind him.

"That one, he has a demon inside him, too."

"I must talk to you, Grushenka. Come, let's go into the back hall."

"Did—did you speak to Mitya?" she asked.

I nodded. "We will be leaving tonight."

Grushenka wrung her hands, extremely apprehensive as we walked back to the dusty hallway with its litter. Tall and slim, with enormous gray eyes and thick wheat-colored hair worn in a long braid that fell heavily between her shoulder blades, Grushenka was seventeen years old, a shy, sweet-natured girl who could neither read nor write. I had sensed at once that she might be a possible ally, but it had taken me days to win her over. When finally I learned of her love for Mitya and their dreams of a future together, I had promised to help her make those dreams come true if she and Mitya would help me get back to St. Petersburg.

She had been reluctant at first, but I had finally won her trust, and she had brought Mitya around.

"I—I am so afraid," she said now, glancing around the room.

"There's nothing to be afraid of," I lied.

"They will come after us."

"Undoubtedly," I replied, "but if we leave tonight we will have at least ten hours' head start before they discover we've gone. We'll avoid all the main roads, and when we reach St. Petersburg we'll go directly to the British embassy."

"St. Petersburg is so far away. I—I've never been farther than the village."

"Mitya will be with you, Grushenka. You'll have many gold pieces. You'll be able to begin a whole new life."

"This—this does not seem possible," she said quietly. "I still cannot believe it. All my life I must work very hard for others, get up before dawn, take out the slops, take orders and abuse. It is the same for Mitya. He must bow and obey and work from dawn to dusk for others, and we are the lucky ones. At least we do not starve like many from my village who do not work at the big houses."

"It will be different in St. Petersburg," I promised. "Mitya will be able to open his own livery stable and work for himself. You will be married, live in nice rooms."

"It is a dream," she said.

"And it will come true if—if we're very careful."

Grushenka nodded and drew herself up. In her wooden sabots, her voluminous blue skirt and white blouse, a white apron printed with red and orange tulips tied around her waist, she looked very young and endearing, but there was determination in her manner now. Her gray eyes were resolute.

"I—I am not afraid any longer," she said. "I will do anything I must to see this happen. If there is danger, I will face it."

"There well may be danger," I admitted, "and that's why we must have a gun. You must help me find one."

"But I—"

"You've worked here in the house for several years, haven't you?"

"Since I am seven years old," she replied. "The house is kept open all the time the count is not in residence. I am one of the servants who keep it clean."

"You must have been in every room in the house at one time or another," I said. "Think, Grushenka. Did you ever see a gun?"

The girl frowned, concentrating, and then she looked up at me. "I remember one time, Count Alexis, he comes to his brother's house to get some papers he needs to have. He unlocks the small office behind the library. I go into the library to dust, and I see inside."

"There was a gun?"

"A whole rack of guns behind the desk," she told me. "The Orlov brothers, they are great hunters, and this is where the count keeps his equipment. There are powder horns, too, I think, and wooden boxes with ammunition."

"Marvelous!" I exclaimed.

"The office is always kept securely locked. None of the servants are allowed to go inside. The door is very heavy. We cannot possibly—"

"Take me there," I said.

The girl led me back to the front hall and into the large, musty library with its dark wooden panels, dull red carpet, and towering shelves full of dusty, mildewed volumes that had probably never been read. The big gray marble fireplace was empty. No candles were burning. The room was in shadow, but a shaft of dim sunlight slanting through the worn velvet drapes provided enough light for me to see the large oak door to the left of the fireplace. Stepping over to it, I saw that the lock was formidable indeed, a heavy iron contraption that required a heavy iron key. Could I open it?

"You see," Grushenka said. "It would take an axe to—"

"Go stand watch just outside the library door," I told her. "If anyone approaches, cough."

Grushenka gave me a bewildered look, but she didn't argue. Removing a pin from my hair, I stuck it through the keyhole and saw at once that it wasn't going to be strong enough to get the job done. Removing a second pin, I twisted the two of them together and tried again, pressing, probing, prying gently until the end of my makeshift pick made contact, met resistance. Kneeling down, I pushed carefully. The pins slipped. I muttered a curse under my breath and repeated the process. Easy now, I told myself, easy. Push hard but push gently. You can do it. Three full minutes passed before I finally heard that reassuring click. I was definitely losing my touch.

The office was extremely small, the air so fetid and dusty I could hardly breathe. I smelled yellowing paper and rat droppings and dirt and, yes, a distinct scent of fresh oil. The office might not have been properly cleaned for years, but the rifles in the rack behind the large oak desk had been taken out and cleaned just recently. Who was responsible? Vladimir? Unlocking the rack was child's play after the door. It took less than forty seconds for me to unfasten the padlock and remove the long steel bar that held the rifles in place. Selecting the best, I took it out, propped the butt against my shoulder, aimed it, getting the feel. Yes, this would do nicely.

How long had it been since I had handled a rifle? Well over a year ago. We had been huddling behind a barricade of fallen tree trunks on the edge of a river on the Gulf of Texas and the Karankawa Indians were attacking and Em and Corrie and I were loading rifle after rifle as Jeremy and Chris and Randolph fired, and I had fired, too, and Em had clubbed an Indian with one of her stolen silver candlesticks and . . . I placed the rifle on top of the desk, deliberately banishing the memory. There was no time to think of the past now. The next few hours, the next few days were what mattered.

Three powder horns hung from pegs on the wall. I took one down. The powder was dry. I placed it beside the rifle and opened one of the battered wooden boxes on the floor. It contained bags of shot. I removed two of them. Mitya was going to be extremely pleased. He'd be even more pleased when he discovered I was an expert marksman. If only I had a pistol as well . . . I don't know what prompted me to open the desk drawer, but there it was, resting atop a stack of ancient ledgers, a long, English-made pistol newly cleaned and oiled.

I took it out, testing its weight in my hand. It wasn't loaded. I remedied that with cool efficiency, then slipped the loaded pistol into the inside pocket of my cloak. The pistol was easy enough to conceal, but what was I going to do with the rifle and powder horn and bags of shot? I couldn't blithely carry them up to my room. I would hide them, yes. I would hide them in the library, then fetch them tonight when we were slipping out of the house. Carrying them into the library, I looked around for a likely spot, finally depositing them behind a chair in a shadowy corner of the room.

A door opened. Grushenka coughed. Footsteps crossed the hall. The office door was still standing wide open. Momentary panic gripped me. I froze as Vladimir asked Grushenka what she was doing, why she was standing there. If he came into the library now and saw the office door open he would . . . I flew silently across the room and closed the door and locked it, then, blindly, grabbed a book from one of the shelves.

"—is she?" Vladimir was asking.

"I do not know. I see her here in the hall and she asks me if I have seen the book she was reading. I go back to the pantry, then I remember I have left my dust rag—oh, here she is."

I strolled casually out of the library, apparently lost in thought and surprised to see them standing there. Grushenka was visibly nervous, hands twisting the skirt of her apron. Vladimir gave me a dark, suspicious look.

"I found the book, Grushenka," I said idly. "I left it in the library."

"What is this book?" Vladimir growled.

"Essai sur l'histoire générale et sur les moeurs et l'esprit des nations," I replied. "Voltaire. Volume three. Fascinating material. I'll let you have it when I've finished."

He scowled at my mockery. The huge old clock in the hall struck four, the gongs sounding loudly. Grushenka scurried away, disappearing down the hall. I gave Vladimir a cool, haughty look, sauntered past him and moved toward the staircase. I could feel him watching me as I ascended, the pistol hanging heavily in the inner pocket of my cloak. It was with relief that I turned on the landing, finally moving out of his sight. The windows were uncurtained in the hallway upstairs, silvery white sunlight filtering through the dusty panes, making shimmery pools on the worn blue rug.

My bedroom was large and comfortable, with pale cream walls and sturdy but attractive golden oak furniture. A lavender satin counterpane covered the bed, a matching canopy with lace panels arching above, and a dark purple rug covered most of the hardwood floor. I set the book down on a table beside a collection of blue and white porcelain eggs etched with gold, removed the pistol from the pocket and tossed the cloak over a chair upholstered in dark blue brocade. A fire burned in the cream marble fireplace, but the room was still cold. A prison, however pleasant.

Thrusting the pistol out of sight under one of the bed pillows, I stepped over to a window and, pushing aside the drape, leaned against the side of the frame, gazing pensively at snow-covered lawns and the mass of icy trees beyond. The amethyst shadows stretched across the snow were longer now, deepening to amethyst-gray, and the sky was darker, too, more pearl gray than white. The window looked west, and in the distance, on the horizon, a dark gray plume spiraled to touch the sky. Smoke? Resting my head back against the wooden frame, I thought of all that had happened these past months since the accident, and it seemed incredible that I should be here in this bleak, frozen land, the prisoner of a madman.

I thought of the journey ahead, frankly acknowledging the hazards it entailed, and I wondered if we would make it. I wondered if it was right for me to expose Mitya and Grushenka to such danger. They would be richly rewarded, yes, and my journey to America would be well financed, but . . . what if we didn't make it? The odds were not good, I realized that. Vladimir and others would be in fierce pursuit as soon as Orlov discovered I was missing, and then there were the wolves . . . I thought of those bloodcurdling howls I had heard night after night since we arrived, and I remembered the horror stories Lucie had told me that morning Vanya had killed the wolf.

Frowning, I moved resolutely away from the window. I couldn't start having reservations now. I had come too far. I had a pistol, a rifle, plenty of ammunition, and I was a crack shot. We were going to reach St. Petersburg, and Mitya and Grushenka were going to have a chance to live like human beings, and I was going to leave this wretched country at last!

Leaving my bedroom, I found a servant and ordered more wood placed on the fire and ordered a hot bath prepared. It was an unusual request for this time of day, but it might well be the last bath I would have for some time. Thirty minutes later the fire was roaring and I was soaking in the tub before it. Grushenka came in with an extra towel, placing it on the stool beside the tub.

"I—I slipped out to the stables to see Mitya," she said. "I told him about the gun. He was most relieved."

"I imagine he was."

"He is still doubtful about this, but—but I told him to take heart. It is a chance we take, but if we do not take this chance we live the rest of our lives without hope. It is very sad to live without hope, this I know."

"We're going to make it, Grushenka."

She nodded confidently. "And I, too, have made a contribution. I steal into the pantry and fill a cloth bag with food—apples, loaves of bread, a round of cheese, some dried meat. This you do not think about. I carry it out to the stables, and Mitya hides it."

I squeezed out my sponge. "I hadn't thought about food," I confessed.

"It is taken care of now," she said, very pleased with herself.

"You will need a warm cloak, Grushenka. Take that one over there. Carry it to your room. If anyone asks what you're doing with it tell them I ordered you to mend a tear in the lining."

Grushenka stared at the cloak I had tossed over the

chair when I came into the room earlier. "But—but these
are real sables," she said in a hushed voice. "I could not
possibly—"

"The cloak belongs to you now," I told her. "Take it and
go, Grushenka. I'll see you downstairs later."

She gathered the rich golden brown cloak into her arms
with a reverent expression, her lower lip trembling. Tears
sparkled in her enormous gray eyes. She stroked the fur
and turned to me and started to speak, but she could not.
She merely shook her head and, after a moment, silently
left the room.

After I had dried myself thoroughly and pinned my hair
up, I slipped into a heavy gray silk petticoat with six full
skirts, a luxurious garment certainly not designed for
traveling but sturdier—and warmer—than the other gauze
or lace undergarments in my wardrobe. Reaching under
the bed, I pulled out the thick cloth bag I had sewn to a
long sash, intending to tie the sash around my waist. The
golden coins tinkled noisily as I lifted the bag, and I shoved
it back under the bed, deciding it would be better to wait
until later to conceal it under my clothes. I didn't want
Vladimir or anyone else to hear a mysterious tinkling
noise beneath my skirts and grow suspicious.

The safe had been frightfully easy to open, even in the
dark, and I had been delighted to find the gold coins piled
in a box. I had scarcely made a dent in the pile, taking only
what I could carry in my pockets, but the cloth bag contained a small fortune nevertheless, more than enough to
set up Mitya and Grushenka in St. Petersburg and take
care of my own needs. I was becoming quite an accomplished thief, I reflected, but I felt no remorse about stealing from Count Gregory Orlov. The box had contained
enough gold to feed and clothe a whole village for several
years, and he would never even miss what I had taken.

Holding back the doors of the heavy golden oak wardrobe, I examined the garments inside. Gorgeous, lavish
gowns, none of them suitable for riding over a frozen
wasteland in an open sleigh. After much deliberation I re-

moved the garnet velvet from its hanger. The cloth was heavy, the thickest, finest velvet made, a rich, glowing garnet. The gown had long, tight sleeves, a modestly low square-cut neckline, and a very full skirt. It would be warmer than any of the silks, brocades or satins, I decided, slipping it over my head and putting my arms through the sleeves. Fastening the hooks, adjusting the bodice, I smoothed the skirt over the gray silk underskirts and then turned to the mirror above the dressing table.

I saw myself with my hair pinned up, with a faintly discolored cheekbone, but after a moment the image shimmered and changed and I saw another Marietta, hair spilling to her shoulders in coppery red profusion, standing patiently as Madame Lucille clucked and clicked her tongue and scurried about sticking pins in the hem, bright scraps of cloth and ribbon littering the floor of her fitting room in New Orleans. Lucille had made the gown for me in that sultry, indolent city I knew so well. She had assured me that the color was just right, complementing the color of my hair, the cloth too warm for New Orleans, yes, but perfect for the brisk climate of England. Earrings dangling, hair piled atop her head like an untidy gray nest, she had informed me that Derek Hawke would be dazzled, though why I should want to travel all the way to England to marry *him* when Jeremy Bond was madly in love with me was quite beyond her comprehension.

The garnet velvet had crossed the Atlantic with me— and Jeremy—and it had been in the trunk on top of the carriage when I had left him in London to go to Hawkehouse and when Ogilvy and I began that return trip and I had urged him to go faster, faster, faster still . . . The gown had come all the way to Russia in a troika, had been transported from St. Petersburg to this brooding, somber north country. Standing in that fitting room in New Orleans while Lucille pinned up the hem, I had been absolutely confident about the future. I would go to England, I would marry Derek Hawke, and I would live happily ever after . . . and here I was wearing the gown, planning to escape a madman who, at any moment, might tell his henchman to murder me.

The watery silver blur shimmered, solidified, and I was looking into the glass again, seeing the pinned hair, the drawn face, the eyes full of ruthless determination. I removed the pins from my hair and brushed the thick waves until they fell into a lustrous tumble. Sitting down on the edge of the bed, I pulled on a pair of dark gray leather boots that reached to mid-calf. They had pointed toes and high heels and were lined with fur, elegant but very sturdy boots much like the ones Vanya had given to me on the road. I took down the heavy, dark silver-gray mink cloak with its generous hood and gray satin lining, draping it over the chair, placing a pair of soft gray leather gloves on top of the glossy folds.

Everything ready now, all preparations made, nothing to do but wait, and that wasn't going to be easy. I moved back over to the window. The feathery spiral I had seen on the horizon was darker now, definitely smoke, I determined. What could be burning? Restless, nerves beginning to grow taut, I decided to go downstairs and see about dinner. Carelessly cooked, indifferently served, meals were hardly a high point of my day, but I intended to have a solid meal tonight even if I had to cook it myself.

As I started down the stairs I heard a confusion out front, horses stamping on the drive, voices yelling loudly, footsteps pounding. I paused on the landing, curious, and then the front door banged open and two gloriously handsome gods burst into the hall, both tall and stalwart and glowing with vitality. I had never seen either of them before, but I recognized them at once as they stamped snow from their boots and shook their broad shoulders and filled the air with crackling energy that was almost visible. Both had been here at the house twice before, on the day after we arrived and two or three days ago, but I hadn't seen them on either occasion.

The taller of the two had golden brown hair and a short, neatly trimmed beard and flashing navy blue eyes. He was attired in dark brown velvet breeches and frock coat and a gold-embroidered brown brocade waistcoat, a rich brown fur cape slung around his shoulders. In his mid-forties, he had the vigor of a much younger man and the mannerisms of a hearty rake who loved wine, women, and war with exuberant relish. This was Count Alexis Orlov, Lucie's father, almost as magnetic as his brother Gregory had been, in a much earthier, more primitive way.

His brother Feodor was leaner, not quite so tall, with dark yellow blond hair and lively brown eyes beneath drooping lids and arching brows. Although the coloring was different, the build slighter, Feodor more closely resembled Gregory feature by feature. In blue velvet and short black fur cape, he exuded the Orlov magnetism, but there was a total lack of refinement, a crude, brutal aura that proclaimed him a tough, a bully, a man who used his fists instead of his head and took pleasure in punishing those weaker than he.

"Gregory!" Alexis roared.

"We waste time!" Feodor protested. "We should already be on our way after these butchers!"

"We need Gregory's help. If we're to exterminate them we need a stronger force."

"I have fifteen men, you have twenty. Gregory won't help us. He's gone off his head, you know that as well as I do!"

"Shut your mouth, Feodor! Gregory's having a bad period, we all do, it's the family curse, but he's not balmy. He's merely depressed and drinking too much. Come out, Gregory! Your brothers are here!"

"The peasants will get away!"

"Control yourself, Feodor. You'll be able to spill your share of blood soon enough. We'll catch up with them and you can kill to your heart's content."

"We waste time!" Feodor repeated. "They are on the run already and instead of charging after them we come here to reason with a madman!"

"Our brother is not mad!"

"You're an idiot yourself, Alexis!"

Alexis doubled up his fist and banged Feodor on the side of the head and Feodor crashed against the wall and stumbled against a table and a large vase tumbled off and shattered on the floor. Eyes flaming dangerously, Feodor let out an enraged roar and charged his brother with fists flying and Alexis nimbly sidestepped and threw an arm out and caught Feodor around the throat and slung him around in front of him, holding him securely as Feodor squirmed and flailed his arms about, trying to break free.

"Gregory!" Alexis called. "Come see your brothers!"

Feodor gurgled, his face bright pink. Alexis relaxed his hold and patted his brother affectionately on top of the head, which infuriated Feodor all the more. The drawing room door opened, and Gregory came staggering out, his face a sickly gray, moist with sweat. His hair was moist, too, clinging to his skull like a wet, tawny cap. He stared at his brothers, blinking, the haunted eyes gradually filling with recognition.

"Alex—Alexis. Fe—Feodor. You come to see me. You come to see your poor, unhappy brother. You are not the shadows, this I know. You are standing in my hall."

"See, Feodor," Alexis said. "He is drunk; but he knows who we are. Are you all right, Gregory?"

"Why are you strangling our brother Feodor?" Gregory asked.

Alexis chuckled, releasing his brother. Feodor coughed and spluttered, a furious look in his eyes, but he made no further attempt to strike back.

"Our little brother gets too big for his breeches," Alexis explained amiably. "I have to discipline him, as when we are boys. Always he must be kept in line with a blow on the head."

"This is so," Gregory agreed.

Feodor glared at his siblings with burning resentment. Alexis punched him playfully on the shoulder.

"We have come for your help, Gregory," he said. "It is most urgent. We need your men, all of them."

"You need my men?" He spoke the words slowly, as though trying to determine what each meant.

"The peasants are on the rampage again. Pugachev's men. Early this afternoon a mob of them attack the Vasilchikov estate, twenty miles to the west. They butchered the men, raped and killed all the women, set fire to the house, yelling like demons. One of the manservants managed to steal a horse and rode to my place."

"Pugachev," Gregory said.

"The Imperial Army is nowhere in the vicinity. We're going to ride after these butchers ourselves, exterminate them once and for all. We need your men to ride with us."

"Pugachev," Gregory repeated. "Yes, I remember this name. He makes my Catherine very upset."

"He's raving!" Feodor exclaimed. "His men won't take orders from anyone except him! I told you we were wasting our—"

"You wish another blow on the head!"

"Look at him! He's—"

"Yes," Gregory said, his eyes lighting up with excitement. "Yes, it is the answer! I will take my men and ride after this peasant who makes all the trouble! I will capture him and take him to her in chains, and then my Catherine will be grateful—she will see—she will—"

His voice broke, and he nodded, unable to contain his excitement. Standing in the shadows of the landing, looking down, I saw that wild gleam in his eyes as the obsession gripped him anew. Most of the pallor had left his ravaged face. Damp tawny locks were splayed across his brow. In his high gray leather boots, his soiled gray velvet breeches and the loosely fitting white lawn shirt damp with perspiration, Count Gregory Orlov was an utter ruin, all grandeur gone, and he bore very little resemblance to that magnificent, golden creature I had first seen in England.

"Yes!" he cried. "This is what I will do! My Catherine will lavish me with honors again! New triumphal arches will be erected in my name! I will shine with glory!"

Gregory turned and staggered back into the drawing

room, and loud noises poured through the open door. A piece of furniture was knocked down, falling to the floor with a bang. Glass shattered. He cursed, an enraged roar. His boots stomped heavily as he stumbled about. Something metal clattered on the stone hearth, and he roared again. Alexis and Feodor exchanged looks, Alexis tolerant, not at all perturbed by his brother's peculiar conduct, Feodor consumed with impatience. After a few moments, Gregory burst back into the hall with a black fur cloak slung around his shoulders, waving the sabre that had been hanging over the mantel. Feodor ducked. Alexis beamed with approval and pounded Gregory on the back.

"All the time I know you will help us!" he declared.

"Come!" Gregory cried. "We get my men! We ride after this monster who threatens my Catherine!"

He whirled the sabre in the air. Feodor threw open the front door. The Orlov brothers charged out of the house.

Chapter Twenty-Three

UTTER PANDEMONIUM PREVAILED DURING the next hour as horses were saddled, rifles distributed, equipment fetched, campfires put out, cossacks yelling with demonic glee. Staggering, waving his sabre on high, Gregory Orlov was in the middle of things, shouting demented directions, urging his men to hurry, hurry. Calmly, first things first, I went to the kitchen and sliced beef and bread and ate it with a wedge of cheese and a glass of milk. I found Grushenka and insisted she eat, too, and afterwards we stood at the hall window upstairs, watching the frantic activity below.

"They're all leaving," she said. "I don't understand."

"There's been another massacre, Grushenka. The Orlovs are going after the peasants who committed it."

"Those—those dreadful people. One of them comes to the village several months ago, tries to enlist the men, get them to join Pugachev's band. The men of our village run him out, want no part of the trouble he brings."

"You know about Pugachev?" I asked.

The girl nodded. "Everyone in these parts knows about Pugachev. Some say he is a saint. Others say he is a devil. He is going to free Russia of tyranny, he claims, and this he does by burning and killing, not—not just the aristocrats but our own people as well, the servants who work in the houses and any peasant who defies him or disagrees with his methods. He brings nightmares into our lives."

In the courtyard below Mitya and the other two grooms

were leading the horses out. The horses neighed and reared, alarmed by the noise and confusion. A cossack leaped onto his steed, shouting lustily, tumbling to the cobbles as the horse bucked. Most of the men had been drinking vodka all day and were as drunk as Orlov, waving their sabres wildly. Several fired pistols into the air, and one began to fire at the chickens, who scattered about the yard in a frenzied panic. It was a crazy, disorganized pageant of frantic activity, but eventually all the cossacks were armed and mounted, some weaving perilously in the saddle, others clutching their horse's necks for support, and Vladimir appeared to help Gregory mount, speaking to him in a low, inaudible voice.

Both men glanced up toward the house, Gregory impatient, Vladimir intense. Vladimir said something else and Gregory muttered an indifferent reply and swung into his saddle with surprising agility. Vladimir nodded and stepped back, looking toward the house again. Feodor and Alexis walked their horses over to stand beside Gregory's. Gregory shouted an order, waved his sabre in the air, and the procession charged toward the drive, hooves thundering on the cobbles. A moment later Vladimir stood alone in the deserted yard with its litter of broken glass and the blackened ruins of campfires. The thunder of hoofbeats could be heard in front, growing fainter and fainter as the sound receded, and finally a brooding silence prevailed once more, broken only by the cluck of chickens.

"He—he left that Vladimir behind," Grushenka said, worried.

"Probably three or four others as well," I told her, "but that still lessens the odds against our being caught. Don't worry, Grushenka. It will be much easier now with Orlov and the cossacks gone."

"I'm growing nervous again," she confessed. "I—I have this strange feeling something is going to happen."

"You're just apprehensive. In only a few hours we'll be in the sleigh, on our way to St. Petersburg. You go on downstairs now and—go on about your business as though nothing were afoot."

"Mitya—he said he would meet us outside the kitchen door at ten."

"And we'll be there," I said.

Grushenka left me, and I gazed out at the courtyard for a few more minutes. Vladimir had disappeared. The chickens had stopped clucking and strutted about idly, pecking at the food scraps they found among the cobbles. The house was unnervingly still. I felt as though I were on a vast, deserted ship becalmed in the middle of a motionless sea. I was every bit as apprehensive as Grushenka had been, far more apprehensive than I cared to admit to myself. With Orlov gone, Vladimir would be keeping a much closer watch over me, that I was sure of. Instead of making our escape easier, Orlov's departure with his brothers and the cossacks only made things worse. Vladimir would very likely station himself in the hall outside my bedroom door. Well, I told myself, you'll simply have to deal with it. You're not going to lose your courage now.

Time seemed to hang suspended. Ten o'clock seemed an eternity away. Going back to my bedroom, I fetched the book and took it back down to the library and checked to make sure the rifle and powder horn and bags of ammunition were still behind the chair. The room was full of deep purple-black shadows now, the smell of old leather and dust stronger than ever. The house was so still, the silence so ominous. My nerves were on edge. I almost expected someone to leap out from the shadows and seize me. A board creaked, as though the deserted ship were settling on the still water. How was I going to endure this agony of waiting? With each passing minute my courage, my resolve seemed to grow weaker.

I longed for a brandy, decided I didn't dare have even one. I couldn't afford to dull my senses. Leaving the library, I wandered restlessly about downstairs, not actually wringing my hands but showing every other symptom of taut nerves. I encountered no one. The servants were all occupied elsewhere, silent. My garnet velvet skirt rustled with the sound of whispers as I moved slowly about the empty corridors. Where was Vladimir? Had he come back inside? What had he said to Orlov? What had Orlov replied? Why had they both looked up at the house? I felt sure they had been talking about me. The house was cold. I shivered, scolding myself for this attack of nerves, and finally I went back upstairs and moved down the hall and looked out over the front.

The sun was going down. The dark gray sky was streaked with golden orange banners, and the blinding white snow was burnished with orange light, as though the world were aflame. The light gradually faded, banners blurring to a misty pink, darkening to gray, the sky slowly turning purple-gray. How desolate the land looked, how bleak, the leafless, ice-encased trees like skeletal phantoms in the distance, frozen immobile by the cold. What a horrible, horrible country this was, seething with violence and unrest. As the last light disappeared, as the purple sky melted to black, I heard a wolf howling in the woods. It was a bloodcurdling sound, all the more chilling in the stillness.

Three days and nights it would take us . . . perhaps more. Vulnerable, exposed in an open sleigh, in a country alive with starving wolves and bloodthirsty peasants who . . . who butchered and burned. There might well be a blizzard, snow turning to sleet, sleet turning the world into a silver-gray fury of blinding, battering chaos. What were our chances of safely reaching St. Petersburg? Slim indeed, I told myself, and then I frowned and straightened my shoulders and turned away from the window.

All right, Marietta, you've had your little spell. Now, by God, you're going to pull yourself together and show some spunk. You've been in far worse situations than this and you always came through. Stop it at once.

A footman was lighting the cheap wax candles in the hall as I went back to my bedroom. He was the first human being I had seen in—I glanced at the huge clock near the staircase—in an hour and forty-five minutes. It had been that long since I sent Grushenka back downstairs, since Gregory and his brothers and the drunken, disorganized band of cossacks charged off to join Alexis's and Feodor's men to pursue the peasants. How much blood would be spilled during the next day or so? How many innocent men would die? What was it about this dreadful country that turned men into savages with a lust for blood?

I went into my bedroom and closed the door. The tub had been taken away. The bedcovers had been turned back. Nerves still taut, I sat down in the chair near the fire and gazed at the flames and listened to the monotonous ticking of the clock on the mantelpiece. Where was Vladimir? He must be inside the house somewhere, but I hadn't seen him. Was he, even now, stationed in the hall outside my bedroom, standing guard? I mustn't think about that now. I must close my eyes and relax . . . relax. In less than a week, if I were fortunate, I would be on a ship on my way to America. I would see Em again and Randy and I would see those wide, sun-swept plains and the cottonwood trees and the endless blue skies that turned to dark velvet at night and blazed with stars. How they had blazed that night that Jeremy took me into his arms and . . . He was there. He was smiling that crooked, teasing smile. I clung to him.

I awoke with a start. Grushenka was shaking me. Her gray eyes were full of alarm. For an instant I was still in Texas, still in Jeremy's arms, and he was telling me everything would be all right, and then the dream shattered and I saw that the fire had burned down and that the clock showed ten minutes after ten and I couldn't believe that I had actually fallen asleep. Grushenka stepped back, clutching nervously at the dark sable cloak wrapped around her shoulders. I stood up and brushed the folds of my garnet velvet skirt, still rather dazed. Grushenka bit her lip.

"I—I waited for you downstairs. I waited and waited and when you didn't come I—"

"I fell asleep, Grushenka. I was so tense and nervous I

knew I had to relax, and—oh my God! Did anyone see you come up to my room?"

Grushenka shook her head. "Everyone—all the servants, they—they're in their rooms, terrified. Mathilda is on her knees, praying fervently. They are afraid Pugachev's men will attack the house and burn it now that Count Orlov and his cossacks have gone."

"Nonsense," I said. "There's no way Pugachev's men could know the house is unprotected."

"Pugachev has spies everywhere. He knows everything that happens, almost before it *does* happen. I—I'm frightened myself," she confessed. "We must leave quickly."

I was already kneeling down, pulling the bag of coins out from under the bed. "Have you seen Vladimir?" I asked over my shoulder.

"Not since we saw him down in the courtyard. Maybe he's in his room, too. I stepped outside and spoke to Mitya before I came up to your room. He told me there are three other guards posted outside. One of them is already dead drunk and sprawling on the steps of the barracks. The other two are wandering around with rifles at the ready, looking for peasants."

"So we just have two guards to worry about—and Vladimir."

Reaching up under my petticoats, I tied the sash securely around my waist. The bag of coins sewn to it rested heavily against my left thigh. I picked up the soft gray gloves and began to pull them on. Grushenka was very upset, casting apprehensive looks toward the window.

"Do—did you hear something?" she whispered.

"Just the log crackling in the fireplace."

"It—it sounded like—like shouting. In the distance."

I stretched my fingers and smoothed the gloves up over my wrists. "You're imagining things, Grushenka."

"I'm just so—so frightened. I've had this peculiar feeling all day—the village priest calls it the second sight. I'm very sensitive, and I *feel* things. Before something happens

I seem to—to know. The day Dmitri was gored to death by a bull I—I kept seeing a field and seeing blood and—"

She cut herself short, her cheeks pale, her gray eyes enormous and full of apprehension. Illiterate, raised in a land of dark superstitions and even darker religious mysticism practiced by charlatan priests who thrived on the ignorance of their flock, it was not surprising that a high-strung girl should be a prey to such feelings, genuine or not. I took her hands and squeezed them.

"It's going to be all right," I told her.

"I know. I'm just—"

"You're just nervous. So am I."

"I'll feel much better when we—when we get out of this house."

"I'll be ready in a moment."

Picking up the dark silver-gray mink cloak, I draped it over my shoulders and fastened it at my throat, and then, reaching under the pillow, I pulled out the pistol. Grushenka stared at it with wide eyes, as though it were some animate thing that might bite or snap. Holding it at my side, half-hidden by the folds of my skirt, I moved over to the bedroom door and opened it. The candles had burned down to half their length, ridged with streaks of melted wax. Wavering yellow-orange light leaped and licked at the walls, the darkness between all the gloomier. No one was in sight.

"You have to leave all your lovely clothes," Grushenka said, glancing at the wardrobe.

"Clothes can be replaced," I replied. "Come."

Grushenka followed me into the hall, keeping behind me as we crept silently toward the stairwell. My own nerves were taut again, my heart beating rapidly. I fully expected Vladimir to step out of a shadowy doorway and block our way. We would use the back stairs, of course. It would be madness to use the main staircase . . . I paused. Damn! The rifle. I had forgotten it. I would have to go down to the library and collect the rifle and ammunition and powder horn. Why hadn't I had the sense to sneak them to the back hall earlier, when I was wandering through the empty house?

"What—what is it?" Grushenka whispered.

"I have to go down to the library," I said.

"But—"

"The rifle. The powder horn. The ammunition."

"I—I was so nervous I forgot about that."

"So did I. You go on down the back stairs, Grushenka. I'll meet you and Mitya in a very few minutes."

"I'll go with you. You'll need someone to help carry—"

"This cloak has large inside pockets. I won't have any trouble. We're wasting time, Grushenka. Go on. Wait for me outside the kitchen door."

The girl hesitated, extremely worried, and then she scurried silently down the hall and turned in the direction of the back stairs. I hesitated for a moment, too, standing at the top of the stairs, not at all relishing crossing that great expanse of hall downstairs with all the candles burning, being so exposed and vulnerable. It couldn't be helped. I took a deep breath, then started down. The third step from the top creaked loudly. It sounded like a gunshot in the stillness. I flattened myself against the wall, thankful the stairwell itself was shrouded in shadow. I waited. Nothing happened. I took another deep breath and moved on down to the landing.

The great, gloomy hall was bathed in murky yellow-orange light as candles spluttered in their holders. Furniture threw long shadows across the hardwood floor with its worn Persian runner. The huge clock in its ornate wooden case tick-tock, tick-tocked, the brass pendulum swinging slowly to and fro, the monotonous noise only accentuating the ominous silence. The house seemed to be waiting for me to make one more move, seemed to be listening. I moved down one step, then another, repressing an urge to scream. *Where the hell was Vladimir?*

I moved down one more step. He came out from behind the giant clock and stood looking up at me.

My heart leaped. I seemed to freeze. The dark black-brown eyes glowed with hostility and . . . and something else. His lips twisted into a sardonic, mocking smile. In his black boots and dark blue velvet livery, with the fur-trimmed blue cape around his shoulders, he was a terrifying sight, gigantic, as tall as a tree, it seemed, that powerful physique solid muscle. His head was uncovered, the thick blond hair gleaming dark yellow in the candlelight. Shadows lightly brushed the lower part of that fierce, not unattractive face. The eyes glowed, dark hot coals, glowing, gleaming. The sardonic smile was utterly chilling.

"You go somewhere?" he asked. His voice was much too polite.

"I—I came down to fetch another book from the library."

"In your cloak?"

"The house is extremely cold—or hadn't you noticed."

"I think you lie," he said.

"I don't give a good goddamn what you think."

Don't let him see that you're frightened. Play it haughty. Don't, for Christ's sake, let him suspect you're scared to death and can hardly keep from swooning.

"The haughty lady," he said. His voice was ugly now. "Always so cold, so imperious. You put Vladimir in his place, you believe. You remind him he is dirt beneath your feet."

"If the shoe fits," I retorted.

He scowled darkly. "What does this mean?"

"It's an English expression," I said coldly. "I'm afraid I haven't the time to explain it now."

"You are in a hurry to fetch this book."

"That's right."

"You lie. You trick me once. You make the fool of me. This won't happen tonight. Tonight I put you in *your* place."

"Oh?" I was blithely unconcerned. "And just where is my place?"

"On your back, like the whore you are."

I stared at him in horror, my blood icy as I recognized

what else burned in those hostile eyes. He moved nearer the foot of the stairs, standing in a pool of candlelight, and I saw the enormous bulge in the fork of his breeches and knew what he planned to do. My knees wobbled, threatening to fold up beneath me.

"Don't—don't come any closer," I warned.

"I take you right here in the hall, on the floor, with all of the candles burning. I take you with all my force, pounding hard, thrusting deep, laughing as you squirm and squeal beneath me. You probably enjoy this kind of punishment. You probably beg for more."

My throat went dry. I tried to speak. I couldn't.

"I wait a long time for this," he told me. "The first time I see you I know I will someday have you. You are in your bath in the English inn, and I pull you up out of the water and dry you off and later on I must take the barmaid by force in the upstairs broom closet. She squeals and squirms against the wall as I thrust. I cover her mouth with my hand. I force her because I cannot have you. After I am spent I take her throat in my hands and squeeze a little and I tell her if she reports this to anyone I come back and choke her to death. She keeps her mouth shut, and I take her several more times before we finally leave the inn."

"You—you're unspeakably vile," I whispered.

"She is a whore, like you. She grows to love that broom closet."

He moved a step nearer. The bulge was throbbing, straining against dark blue velvet. His eyes were glittering with brutal desire, black-brown flames snapping. His mouth lifted at one corner in another mocking smile as he savored his power, my helplessness. I was gripping something in my hand, gripping it so tightly my palm and fingers hurt. The pistol. I had actually forgotten I had it. My hand was at my side, the pistol concealed by the swell of my skirts.

"Stay back," I said.

"You are afraid."

"Not at all."

"Your voice shakes."

"Stay back, Vladimir. I'm warning you."

He laughed, a deep, rumbling laugh that reverberated in the stillness. I gripped the pistol tightly, a deadly calm possessing me now. I looked at him standing there near the foot of the stairs and knew without question he wasn't going to lay a hand on me. The laughter faded away, the silence heavier than before, and I, too, thought I heard distant shouting, a faint, barely audible sound that might have been the wind. Vladimir smiled, his eyes relishing every detail of my person, his erection swelling even more.

"When Count Orlov starts to leave, I ask him about you. 'What about the woman?' I ask. 'What shall I do with her?' 'Do anything you like with her,' he tells me. 'She's yours now.' He gives me his whore."

"I belong to no one," I said.

"You belong to me. I use you like I used the barmaid. I give it to you rough. I make you pay for all your disdain and haughty airs. I make you cook for me and lick my boots and spread your legs, and when I feel like it I beat you thoroughly. When my friends return, I share you with them. I laugh as I watch them take you, one right after the other. In Russia we know what to do with women like you. We know how to treat them."

"Chivalry is dead, it seems."

"What is this 'chivalry'?"

"Something you couldn't begin to comprehend."

I wondered what caused a man to become so twisted, so full of hatred and violence. Vladimir had hated me vehemently from the moment he first laid eyes on me, had longed to hurt and humiliate me. Why? Was it because I represented something he knew he could never hope to attain? Was it because he secretly hated serving another man, hated his master and, not daring to express this hatred, channeled it toward someone he could hate openly—a foreigner, a lowly woman, a whore in velvet who treated him coldly and made him feel his inferior position all the more keenly? Whatever the reason, the hatred was there, burning in his eyes along with the lust, and it was a frightening thing to behold.

"Now you pay," he said.

He moved slowly to the bottom of the stairs and placed his large hand on the smooth wooden railing.

"Don't take another step," I said coldly.

"And if I do?"

"Don't," I said.

He grinned. "You will hurt me?"

"I will kill you," I said.

"This is very funny. This is a big jest."

"It's no jest, Vladimir. It's a promise."

"I laugh."

"You won't, I assure you."

"No more talk. Now I take."

He moved up one step, another, then another, slowly, relishing his power over me, savoring the sensations inside, a great, malicious cat slowly stalking a mouse, taunting his prey. I stood very still, not at all alarmed, held fast by a steely resolve. I told him to stop. He chuckled, eyes glittering. He moved up another step, just four steps below me now, and he lifted his foot to move up another and I raised the pistol from under the folds of velvet and cocked it and aimed it between his eyes.

Color drained from his face. He opened his mouth to say something. The words never came. He tried to grab at the gun and I squeezed the trigger and his forehead seemed to explode into a mass of redness. The impact threw him against the railing and the wood creaked and then his body flopped over to the other side and crashed against the wall and crumpled and tumbled haphazardly downstairs, arms and legs flailing crazily. It landed on the floor in a twisted heap, a dark red pool forming beneath his head. The barrel of the pistol was smoking still, tiny spirals of smoke curling in the air. I blew on it and lowered it and stared at the corpse below as echoes of the deafening gunshot reverberated throughout the house.

Perhaps a minute and a half passed before the front door

burst open and one of the guards came tearing in with rifle raised. His face was ashen, and it turned even grayer when he spied the twisted corpse and the pool of blood. A towering brute with rough-hewn features, deep-set blue eyes and thick black hair, he wore the Orlov livery and short fur-trimmed cape and had apparently lost the black fur hat in his haste to reach the house. I had seen him several times, but I couldn't recall his name. Holding the rifle firmly, he came nearer the corpse, staring at it in dismay, and then he looked up and saw me standing on the staircase.

"What happened?" he cried.

"I shot him," I said.

"You shot Vladimir?"

"He intended to rape me. I warned him I would kill him. He didn't listen."

The guard's face slowly suffused with color, the blue eyes snapping with anger. "Vladimir was my friend!"

"I'm sorry about that."

"This afternoon, after the others leave, he comes out, we have vodka together, he tells me what he plans to do with you. Orlov gives you to him and he says he will share. Now he is dead!"

"Very," I said.

"You murder my friend!"

He stared at me with blazing eyes, gripping the rifle tightly, and after a moment an idea dawned on him and I could almost see the thoughts shaping in his none-too-bright mind. Orlov had given me to Vladimir and Vladimir had intended to share. As Vladimir was dead, why not take me for himself? Sensual speculation replaced the anger in his eyes. He grinned a wide grin, extremely pleased with his good fortune. My pistol was useless until it was reloaded. He knew that. He put the rifle down, leaning it against the wall, looking at me with merry greed.

"This is very interesting," he said.

"Don't even think about it," I told him.

"You can't shoot me. You have already fired."

"I can bash your brains out with the butt of the pistol."

"I like this. I like a spirited woman. We have many good times fighting together."

Over his shoulder, beyond the hallway, I saw Mitya step in through the front door, which the guard had left open. My expression didn't change. Slowly, silently, he crept toward the guard. I looked at the man with eyes that were suddenly appreciative of his masculine charms. A provocative smile shaped on my lips. He was surprised by this sudden change in my attitude.

"You like the idea, yes?"

"I might. I—I never cared for Vladimir, but you—you look quite appetizing."

"The women always like me. Once a very great lady in St. Petersburg, a princess, she *pays* me to make love to her."

"There's no accounting for tastes," I said. "Come—come a little closer. Let me get a good look at my new protector."

"I protect you good. Vladimir, he has disdain for all females. He never likes them, always takes them by force. Me, I stroke them and pet them and make them pant and purr before I stick it in."

"A true gentleman," I said.

He came nearer, almost stumbling over the corpse he had completely forgotten. Mitya reached silently for the rifle left leaning against the wall, took hold of the barrel with both hands, raised it. The guard grinned at me, stepping closer. Mitya swung the rifle back in a high arc and the heavy butt came smashing down on top of the guard's head and there was a horrible noise like a melon splitting in two. His mouth flew open. His eyes glazed instantly. His knees gave way and he fell heavily, landing half atop the corpse.

"Is—is he dead?" I asked shakily.

"Probably," Mitya said. "We must hurry. They come."

"Who—what are you—"

He pointed toward the open door. Through it, far in the distance, I could see bright orange fireflies dancing in the woods facing the house. They swayed and swirled, moving closer, and I could hear the shouting clearly now, raucous cries that chilled the blood. The fireflies were torches. Pugachev's peasants were on their way to the house, would be clearing the woods any moment now, and then they would be swarming over the lawns. I was stunned, momentarily unable to move a muscle. Mitya scowled and leaped up the steps and took my wrist and dragged me roughly down into the hall.

"The other rifle—it's in the library—" I exclaimed. "The powder horn and bags of shot. We must—"

"Lead the way! Quickly!"

I flew into the library with Mitya close behind. No candles were lighted, and the room was a dark cave. I stumbled against a table, cursed aloud, groping my way toward the corner where I had left the rifle behind the large chair. The shouting outside grew louder, closer. They must have cleared the trees. Jesus! Where was the chair? I fell to my knees and my head bumped against the arm of the chair and I uttered a cry of relief and reached behind the chair and grasped the rifle, handing it to Mitya.

"The powder horn—I can't find—"

"Hurry!"

"Here it is. I've got it. Can you take the bags of shot? No, you've got both the rifles. I can manage—"

I slipped the pistol and the powder horn into the roomy pockets inside the cloak and, gripping a bag of shot in each hand, climbed to my feet. Mitya was already on his way out of the room. I stumbled after him. Reaching the hall, I foolishly peered out the door and saw men in the distance, racing toward the house, waving torches, waving pitchforks, waving scythes. They must be able to see us in the lighted hall as well. From the basement came the sounds of a woman shrieking in terror. Old Mathilda, probably. Her prayers weren't going to help much now.

"Grushenka!" I cried.

"She's waiting in back. We can't go out the front door. I've never been inside the house. You must lead the way!"

"Follow me!"

Gripping the shot bags tightly, I dashed down the hall, past the corpses, past the staircase, my cloak flapping, the money bag banging against my thigh. The house was filled with screams and cries of alarm now as the servants began to scatter and race through the rooms. A terrified maid darted past us, heading for the front hall, splitting the air with her screams when she spotted the corpses. I led Mitya through the dusty back hall with its clutter of discarded furniture and boxes and on into the kitchen with its huge iron stove. The slovenly cook was huddled against the wall, clutching a skillet, her face the color of dough.

"Run!" I cried. "You must leave at once!"

She shook her head, muttering gibberish. Mitya threw open the back door. Standing in the shadows beside the steps, Grushenka gave a cry of relief as we hurried out. The moon was high in a cloudless black sky, and the bright moonlight washed the yard with silver, mottling the inky black buildings with silver and pewter gray. Mitya led the way across the cobbles, past the barracks, past the pens, around the stables. The peasants had almost reached the house now. Their shouting was a demonic din, sounds from hell itself, and the cries and shrieks of terror from within the house added to the horror.

We paused for a moment in back of the stables, standing against the wall, in the shadows. Before us lay a vast expanse of snowy ground, dazzling in the moonlight, coated a pale silver-blue, the woods beyond at least four or five hundred yards away. Until we reached the shelter of those trees we would be clearly exposed in the brilliant light. My heart was pounding. My lungs felt as though they were ready to burst. Grushenka was gasping for breath, an expression of stark terror on her face. We could hear glass shattering, wood splintering. In moments they would be tearing around to the back and swarming all over. None of us relished the thought of racing across that brilliant expanse of ground, but we couldn't stay here.

"We must go," I said.

"I—I don't think I can make—" Grushenka began.

"You must!" Mitya cried.

"Mitya, I—"

"Come! We have no time to lose!"

We dashed out of the protective shadows and started across the ground and were immediately bathed in bright silver. It was as light as day here on the snow, with no shadows to relieve the glare. Our footsteps crunched noisily as we ran, and I stumbled several times, certain I was going to fly facedown and skid across the hard-packed snow slippery as ice. Grushenka had the food bag slung across her back and she dropped it and it burst open, cheese, bread, apples, and meat scattering in every direction. She cried out, stopped, began to gather things up. Mitya slung one of the rifles over his back by its strap and seized the girl's wrist, propelling her forward, yelling that there was no time. We raced on, pursued by demons, it seemed, for the cries echoed weirdly, reverberating all around.

On and on we ran, the trees two hundred yards away a haven of darkness and shadow in this blazing silver hell. My foot turned the wrong way, lost purchase. I fell to my knees, dropping both bags of ammunition. One skidded twenty feet away, spewing shot like hard black marbles over the snow. I grabbed the other and got to my feet and lurched on ahead, my ankle smarting. A hundred yards. Seventy-five. Behind us the wild fury of noise rose in volume. Were they pursuing us? I dared not look back. I was going to collapse any moment now. My lungs were going to explode. My heart was going to burst open. I couldn't run any longer. I couldn't! Fifty yards left now. Only fifty. I had to make it. Madly, blindly, I pushed on, and the blazing light vanished and shadows enveloped me and I leaned against the trunk of a tree, panting furiously.

I closed my eyes, and for several moments I knew nothing but agonizing pain as my lungs burned and my heart continued to pound and my breath came in furious gasps. My throat felt raw, as though the skin had been lacerated.

My mouth was dry. My bosom heaved, and my legs seemed to be on fire. I whirled in darkness, it seemed, only half-conscious but still aware of the torture, and eventually my heart stopped battering against my rib cage and beat more slowly and I caught my breath and opened my eyes. Grushenka was sobbing. Mitya was holding her tightly in his arms, telling her not to look.

I looked.

Through the trunks of the trees, beyond the vast expanse of silvered snow, I saw the great house, dark against the brightness, like some little girl's doll house from this distance, the outbuildings even smaller, and I saw the flickering orange lights blazing in the windows and saw the tongues of flame reaching out to lick the walls. I saw the tiny figures dancing and leaping like imps in the glare, dozens of them, dozens and dozens, waving their makeshift weapons as their frenzy increased. The stables and barracks were already sheathed in vivid flame, burning rapidly, roofs collapsing, flames shooting higher.

I saw a slender female figure running across the snow, saw three men pursuing her, pouncing on her as she fell, one grabbing her arms, another grabbing her feet, the third falling atop her, and I saw a footman fleeing and saw tiny imps chase him and saw one of them swing a shovel, hitting his head, knocking him down. The others had shovels too, and they began to stab at him and he was literally hacked to pieces, decapitated. One of the imps held up a tiny dripping ball and waved it and I realized it was a head and shuddered and turned away, clinging to the trunk of the tree.

"I do not think they see us," Mitya said. "They would have come after us if they had. I see you fall. Are you all right?"

"I didn't hurt myself. Grushenka?"

Her face was buried against his chest, his right arm still wrapped around her. She was trembling violently.

"She will be all right, too. This rifle you give me, it is loaded?"

"The one you took from the guard is, of course, but there wasn't time for me to load the other one."

"We do this now," he said grimly.

He handed the rifle to me, and I realized he had never loaded one before, had no idea how to go about it. I took out the powder horn and opened the bag of shot. Although the woods were thick and full of deep shadow, rays of moonlight sifting through the canopy of bare limbs mottled the ground with patches of silver, and there was plenty of light for him to see me as I loaded the rifle. He watched carefully, memorizing each step, nodding curtly when I handed it back to him. I loaded the pistol as well, then put the powder horn and the bag of shot inside the pockets of my cloak, keeping the pistol in my left hand, ready to fire.

"How far is the clearing you mentioned?" I asked.

"Not far. Half a mile perhaps."

"I just hope your man is there with the horse and sleigh."

"He will be," Mitya assured me. "He very much wants the rest of the gold I carry here in my pocket."

Grushenka straightened up and moved away from the shelter of Mitya's arm. Her face was still pale, her cheeks tear-stained, but she made a valiant effort to pull herself together, made an effort not to listen to the horrible shouting and the sound of crackling flames that carried clearly across the night. Wrapping the cloak more closely around her, she apologized for dropping the bag of food.

"It couldn't be helped," I said.

"Now we will have nothing to eat. Now—"

"We worry about that later," Mitya said curtly. "Now we get to the clearing as soon as possible."

We started through the labyrinth of trees, Mitya leading the way, Grushenka and I following close behind. We moved through alternate patches of shadowy darkness and gleaming moonlight, frequently ducking to avoid low-hanging ice-encrusted branches, and the hideous noise gradually grew dimmer as we moved deeper into the woods. Looking back through the maze of tree trunks, I could see a vivid orange glow, like sunset, and finally that disappeared and there was nothing but the blue-gray sheen on the snow and silvery rays of moonlight penetrating the gloom, intensifying the darkness. Our footsteps crunched loudly on the snow, the sounds magnified in the stillness of the woods and echoing strangely, as though we were being followed.

I prayed Mitya knew where he was going. I was already hopelessly lost and had no idea in which direction we were moving. One rifle slung over his back, the other held awkwardly in front of him, he forged ahead confidently, eyes and ears alert for any unusual sound or movement. I knew he was looking for wolves. I tried not to think about wolves. Please, God, spare us that, I prayed. Tomorrow I can face them, but not tonight. Grushenka was nervous about them as well, tripping along closely behind Mitya, casting apprehensive glances into the shadows. I gripped the pistol tightly, having no confidence at all in Mitya's ability to use the rifle. I started with alarm as something gray and furry darted out in front of us. My finger tightened on the trigger, but it was only a hare. My nerves weren't going to take too much more of this. If and when we ever got to St. Petersburg I would probably be certifiably mad.

An icy branch lashed my temple and knocked the hood away from my head. My hand felt frozen as I reached up to pull the hood in place. I was devastatingly cold, even bundled up as I was. Mitya had only a shabby cloth coat, a filthy sheepskin cap pulled down over his brow. Were we to stop moving, we would surely freeze to death. Thank God I had given Grushenka the sable cloak. I should have stolen one of Gregory's cloaks for Mitya. Perhaps there would be blankets on the sleigh. If there *was* a sleigh. I knew it was only my imagination, but it seemed to me we had been trekking through these woods for hours. My cheeks and nose felt like solid ice.

"We are almost there," Mitya said.

"Thank God," I whispered.

"Yes, the sleigh is there. I can see it."

Grushenka sobbed with relief and crossed herself. Up ahead, through thick columns of icy trunks, I could see a brilliant patch of snow, brushed a silvery blue by moonlight, and, yes, there was the sleigh, a small, dilapidated vehicle on wide wooden runners, the horse stamping restlessly in the snow. Dilapidated or not, it was the most beautiful sight I had ever seen, the horse a magnificent beast even though its back was sagging and its legs frightfully wobbly. We hurried forward, stepping into the clearing a moment or so later.

It wasn't a large clearing, perhaps thirty yards in circumference, a rough pathway barely wide enough for sleigh and horse leading into it, leading out on the opposite side. Mitya started toward the sleigh. Grushenka grabbed his arm, her face reflecting her alarm. Mitya frowned and tried to pull away, and then he felt it, too. Something was wrong. Something was definitely wrong. It was in the atmosphere, hanging over the clearing like an invisible pall. The horse whinnied nervously, stamping in the snow, and the sleigh skidded a little on the icy surface. I felt the evil. It was almost tangible. It was all around. The hair on the back of my neck seemed to bristle. My blood ran cold.

"Where—where is Aloyosha Fyodorovich?" Mitya asked, puzzled. "He brings the horse and sleigh like he promises. He would not leave before collecting the rest of the gold."

The horse whinnied again and took a few steps, dragging the sleigh forward a couple of feet, and we saw the body then. Grushenka tried to restrain him, but Mitya tore loose from her grip and went over to investigate. I followed him. I wished I hadn't. Aloyosha Fyodorovich had been hacked to pieces, like the footman. The severed limbs still poured blood out onto the snow. I gasped, turning my head away, afraid I was going to retch. Mitya shook convulsively and stepped back. A moment passed, perhaps two, and then Grushenka screamed as the peasants came leaping out from behind the trees on the opposite side of the clearing.

I raised the pistol. I fired. One of them tumbled over backward, falling to the ground. Mitya swung the rifle up and tried to fire. A pitchfork sailed through the air, the sharp prongs going through his throat. He grabbed the handle of the pitchfork and made a horrible gurgling noise and staggered back, falling over, already dead before he hit the snow. Grushenka screamed again, tried to reach him. Four men grabbed her and threw her to the ground, tearing greedily at her clothing. Rough hands seized me. I smashed the butt of the pistol into a face, blood splattering as a nose broke. An arm flew around my throat. I was pulled violently back against the side of the sleigh, and half a dozen hands began to pull at my skirts.

"No!" a voice thundered. It was laced with steely authority. "Not her!"

The horse reared, whinnying wildly. Grushenka screamed one more time before a hand clamped over her mouth. The men pulling at my skirts fell back. The man holding my throat released me. Josef Pulaski moved slowly toward me, his hands on his thighs, his sheepskin coat flaring open. He had survived the flogging after all. A triumphant smile curled on his lips as he stopped two yards in front of me, and in the brilliant moonlight I could see the cruel satisfaction in his eyes as he studied me.

"We meet again," he said.

"You—"

"Have your pleasure with the other one," he told his men, "then kill her. This one we save for something special."

Chapter Twenty-Four

WE HAD BEEN WALKING FOREVER, IT SEEMED, trudging steadily over the hardened snow, stopping only to drink water from the canteens and eat the food Pulaski had appropriated from one of the villages we passed. There were eleven men in the party, the youngest in his late teens, the oldest in his mid-fifties, all of them sullen, silent and consumed by a burning hatred of the ruling class, which had brought them together in the first place. We were on our way to Pugachev's secret camp, this much I knew, although not a one of them had spoken a word to me. The main body, those who had attacked and burned Orlov's house, were apparently two or three hours behind us, traveling in small groups to avoid arousing too much suspicion.

A day and a half had gone by since the nightmare erupted. After the men had finished with Grushenka, after her broken, bleeding body had finally been abandoned, Pulaski had ordered the men to move and we had begun our journey, moving through the woods, along the narrow road, finally, around three in the morning, reaching an abandoned hovel where we had remained until daybreak. I had been bound securely, a gag stuffed into my mouth, and Pulaski had shoved me into the corner. All of them slept, packed tightly in the one-room hovel, snoring loudly, and after a while sheer exhaustion had enabled me to sleep as well. Pulaski had untied me as the first pink light of dawn slanted through the cracks in the walls.

He shoved a canteen at me, allowed me to take a few sips, and then he had fastened the noose around my neck again and took the end of the long rope and led me outside, forcing me to walk ten or twelve paces behind him. The noose was not tight, not unless I stumbled, not unless I failed to keep pace. Then it tightened painfully, and I would have strangled to death had I not regained balance or quickened my step. Pulaski never even bothered to glance back. He just kept walking, holding the end of the rope securely. He had not spoken to me either, not once. I was a pariah, beneath his notice, led along behind him like a calf being led to slaughter. We had walked all day, stopping at the village where he and his men had brutally commandeered food from the already starving peasants, trudging on then to spend the night in yet another deserted hovel.

It was perhaps five in the afternoon of the second day, and I walked briskly, the rope cutting brutally into my throat whenever I failed to keep in step. Why did I bother? Why didn't I simply drop in my tracks and let it all end? I had no doubt Pulaski would simply keep on moving and drag my body along behind him. I had considered it. After witnessing the horror in the clearing, after seeing what they had done to Grushenka, I had had no desire to go on living, or at least I thought not. Somehow, though, despite the shock, despite the horror, a spark inside me refused to stop burning, even though all my senses were numbed, and I couldn't do it. I kept on walking behind him, grabbing at the rope when I stumbled to relieve that terrible pressure biting into my throat, coughing, gasping, quickening my step to put an end to the pain.

Once, shortly before noon, horsemen had been heard approaching from the distance. The men had scattered quickly into the woods for cover, Pulaski seizing my wrist and dragging me along roughly, clamping his large hand over my mouth as soon as we reached shelter, almost smothering me. The hoofbeats grew louder and harnesses jangled merrily and a few moments later I could see the riders through the frozen branches of the shrub we crouched behind. They all wore the handsome uniform of the Imperial Army, and there were perhaps twenty men in all, no doubt a reconnaissance group looking for signs of Pugachev's secret camp. Pulaski's hand tightened brutally over my mouth, forcing my head back against his shoulder. The soldiers passed on by, and shortly thereafter we were on our way again. So at least part of Catherine's army was in the vicinity, I thought. They were probably scattered over a hundred-mile area, searching and interrogating or killing any peasants they found suspicious.

The Orlov brothers and their men were undoubtedly doing the same, wreaking destruction in their wake. Several hours had passed between the time they rode off and the time the peasants hit the house. By that time Gregory and the others had been at least twenty miles away, riding east in pursuit of the peasants who had slyly backtracked, keeping to the woods to avoid being seen. Although none of my captors had addressed a word to me, I had learned from listening to their rough remarks to each other that Pulaski had known earlier that Aloyosha Fyodorovich was planning to provide a horse and sleigh for "a lady," and he and his small group of men had detached themselves from the main body, had followed the man to the clearing and killed him only minutes before we arrived.

The sun was bright, sparkling on the snow and ice, transforming the trees into iridescent crystal wonders, and the sky was a pale gray-white with just a faint suggestion of indigo. It wasn't nearly as cold as it had been two nights ago when I had been trekking through the moonlit woods with Mitya and Grushenka. In my boots, heavy silk underskirts, velvet gown, and mink cloak, I was comfortable, as far as the weather was concerned. The money bag still slapped heavily against my left thigh—because of their weight, the coins didn't jingle as I had feared they would. My captors hadn't discovered my small fortune, nor had they discovered the powder horn and bag of shot inside the pockets of my cloak. The pistol, of course, had been knocked out of my hand as soon as I had broken the nose of one of my attackers with the butt. The man was still in pain, his nose swollen and inflamed, but, stoically, he trudged along without complaint.

Walking briskly ten paces behind Pulaski, the noose lightly encircling my neck, I tried to tell myself that I had been fortunate. I had not been killed. I had not been raped. I had not been molested in any way after Pulaski issued his orders. I was to be saved for "something special," and although I realized I might soon wish fervently that I *had* been killed there in the clearing, that spark inside me burned on, the instinct for survival fanning it, preventing me from giving up and allowing myself to be strangled by the noose. I wasn't going to give up. I couldn't. My situation might look hopeless, but as long as there was breath left in me I would hold on tight . . . and hope.

Escape, of course, was currently out of the question. Even if I were able to break free from my captors and elude them, I would be alone in the middle of a frozen wilderness, without food, without a chance of survival. Perhaps when we reached the camp I would be able to steal a horse and a rifle and some food, improbable though that seemed. You're still alive, Marietta, a voice deep inside told me. You're going to keep right on walking and keep right on praying and somehow you're going to pull through.

Pulaski raised his arm in the air, signaling it was time to stop again. I crumpled gratefully to the ground, sitting on the hard-packed snow. Pulaski distributed the canteens and hunks of cheese and strips of dried beef, and after all the men had been provided for, he came over to where I was sitting and tossed a thin strip of meat and a piece of cheese into my lap and handed me a canteen, allowing me to take only a few sips before he jerked it away from me. He stood a few feet away, watching me with disgust as I greedily devoured the cheese and gnawed the tough dried meat.

Hands resting on his thighs, he twisted his lips contemptuously. Look at the great lady now, those fanatical blackbrown eyes seemed to say. Thick, unkempt black hair slanted across his forehead, and the thin face was even paler than it had been the first time I saw him, skin stretched tautly across broad, flat cheekbones. His back must be a solid mass of ugly pink scars, I thought, remembering the whistling sound of the lash, the flecks of blood I had seen on the snow after he had been cut down. Turning, he stalked away to speak to one of his men, leaving the end of the rope on the ground.

I finished the cheese and dried beef, still hungry, thirsty as well. How long would it be before we reached the camp? It must be nearing six now. The sun was already low in the west, long shadows stretching across the snow. Exhausted, my feet and ankles throbbing, I savored this brief respite from walking, but all too soon Pulaski grabbed the end of the rope again and gave it a brutal tug, forcing me to clamber to my feet.

We resumed our march, the shadows growing longer across the narrow road, the sky turning a deeper gray. Perhaps half an hour passed, and then Pulaski gave a signal and we turned off the road and started through the woods to our right, moving through that sparkling crystal wonderland that gradually took on a pinkish orange glitter as the sun began to sink. The ground seemed to slope upward, and there was a multitude of frozen bushes, some of them towering ten feet high, gleaming brilliantly. Shadows spread thickly as we moved deeper into the woods. The pinkish orange light faded, growing dimmer and dimmer. The air seemed to thicken, tinted a hazy violet-blue by twilight.

We had been moving through the woods fifteen minutes or so when the sound of voices reached us from the distance, coming from the direction of the road. Pulaski halted, cocking his head, alert. The other men gripped their weapons tightly, and then, after a few moments, Pulaski said something I couldn't understand and everyone relaxed. The trees were widely spaced in this section, large open areas between the thick, icy trunks, and soon we could see the band of peasants approaching us, a noisy, boisterous group brandishing their crude weapons gaily and, from the looks of it, unsteady on their feet. Pulaski's men greeted them lustily, three or four rushing back to meet their comrades. Moments later we were surrounded by the throng.

There were perhaps twenty-five of them, a rowdy, filthy, dishevelled mob who stank of liquor and sweat and garlic. One of them was waving a distinct brass poker surmounted by a small brass eagle with wings spread wide, a poker I had last seen standing on the hearth in Orlov's library. This, then, was part of the mob who had attacked the house. They were all quite curious about me, asking who I was, what I was doing here, why I hadn't been killed. Pulaski gripped the end of the rope firmly, scowling, warning the newcomers to keep away from me.

"She is Orlov's woman!" he thundered. "I take her to Pugachev. Do not touch her!"

"Look at her!" one of the newcomers cried in a coarse, rumbling voice. "I want her!"

He staggered over to Pulaski, prepared to argue. Tall and slender, wearing high black boots, snug black breeches and a bulky sheepskin coat that had been dyed black, he looked a touch less disreputable than the others, although his cheeks were streaked with mud and the wide black sheepskin hat pulled down over his brow shadowed his eyes. He pounded Pulaski on the back affectionately and called him comrade and said comrades were supposed to share. He tried to grab the end of the rope. Pulaski gave him a terrific shove that sent him reeling back. He slammed into a wall of bodies, yelled a curse and then grinned good-naturedly and slung an arm around the neck of one of his friends and began to bellow an indecent Russian ballad.

"Anyone else tries to touch her, I will kill!" Pulaski declared. "Is it clear?"

"Who put him in charge?" the peasant in black sheep-skin cried.

"Quiet, Nikki!" his friend warned. "Here, have the rest of this vodka."

Arm still hooked around his friend's neck, the peasant called Nikki took the greasy bottle and tilted it to his lips, gulping down the remaining vodka. Lurching unsteadily, half strangling his comrade, he hurled the emptied bottle into the woods and roared that he needed some ass.

"They'll be plenty of whores at the camp, Nikki, and a good-looking devil like you can have your pick."

"I wanted *that* whore," Nikki wailed, on the verge of tears now. "I never get anything I want. My soul is bleak. I think maybe I slit my throat and bleed on the earth of Mother Russia."

"If you don't shut your mouth, Pulaski'll slit it for you."

Nikki began to sob and his friend led him to the back of the crowd and we moved on, noisily now, everyone but Pulaski talking merrily; several of the men finishing bottles of vodka which, I learned, they had taken from the basement of a house they had burned this afternoon. Night was falling fast, and torches were lighted, shedding a bizarre dark orange glow over the motley crowd trekking through the woods. Led by Nikki, the men began to sing loudly, drunkenly. Pulaski marched sternly, jerking the rope, disgusted by the high spirits and playful antics of the newcomers. Serious, intense, a zealot with a burning mission, he had no patience with such frivolity.

Another hour and a half passed, perhaps longer, and the woods grew thicker, the frozen shrubs higher, and we turned, following a frozen river to the south. Ahead, through the trees and dense shrubbery, I could see camp-fires burning on the other side of the river, tiny yellow-orange flowers blossoming in the night. There must have been fifty at least, and as we drew nearer I could see crude huts and tents in the flickering glow. A shot was fired. A guard challenged us. Pulaski identified himself and we were allowed to pass. Horses neighed and whinnied and

moved about restlessly as we trudged past a large enclosure, and I saw half a dozen sturdy sleighs lined up in
front of it, some piled high with blankets.

Moments later we entered the camp itself, a huge,
sprawling collection of tents and hastily assembled huts
covering several acres of ground, more or less arranged in
a vast circle. A crude barricade of logs had been thrown up
around the entire area, camouflaged by frozen shrubbery
that had been cut and propped against the outer sides. Hidden as it was in the depths of the woods, the camp would be
almost impossible to locate during daylight hours, and
none of Catherine's army were likely to be gallivanting
about these woods at night. Hundreds of peasants were
milling noisily about the camp, most of them clutching
earthen bottles, gulping heartily. They yelled obscene
greetings as we passed, weaving drunkenly in front of the
campfires. Pulaski held on to the rope and ignored the
cries, shoving several men out of his way, provoking both
laughter and ire.

There were pigpens, chicken coops, cows, a storage
house where sacks of grain and corn and beans were
stored. Everyone was drunk, it seemed. I wondered where
they got their vodka here in the middle of nowhere, and
that question was answered as we passed an enormous
still, the vats bubbling vigorously even at this hour.
Pugachev was wise enough to realize he couldn't control so
vast a mob without providing them with vodka, the manna
of the masses, and with women, who were in great evi-
dence, slatternly, slovenly, hefty creatures with greasy
hair, painted faces and tattered, garish clothing, some of
them so drunk they could barely stand. They railed at me
in hoarse, hostile voices, resenting my looks, my clothes,
longing to tear me to pieces.

"This one burns!" a harridan shouted.

"First she services the men, *then* she burns!" another
yelled.

"Aristocratic bitch! Our Little Father makes her pay!"

"Death to the noble harlot!"

The women were far more terrifying than the men, who seemed very amused by their shouting and obscene gestures. Belligerent as they were, none of the women dared to approach me. Pulaski's men, Nikki, and a few of the others formed a tight guard, marching on either side of me, their weapons and menacing expressions restraining anyone who might come too close.

As we neared the center of the camp, I saw an enormous wooden stake thirty or forty feet high, obviously hewn from the trunk of a single tree. At the top, a sturdy wooden arm twelve feet long branched out to the left, making it resemble a gigantic, inverted L. I wondered what its purpose could possibly be. A gallows? It seemed much too high for that, but it was sinister nevertheless, a forbidding sight that caused me to shudder. Beyond it, fifty yards away, two wooden cages stood, each approximately six feet square. One of them was empty, the other occupied by a gaunt-faced, silver-haired man in soiled, gold-trimmed green velvet who clung listlessly to the wooden bars and looked more dead than alive.

Fifty yards on the other side of the stake, and dominating the whole camp, stood a magnificent scarlet-and-silver-striped tent, as large as a small house. It had a high peaked roof, and surmounting the peak, like some bizarre weather vane, reared a large Imperial Eagle of solid gold. Another eagle, wings spread wide, was embroidered in golden thread directly above the door flap of the tent. Two men in handsome uniform guarded the door, one on either side. The uniforms were almost identical to those worn by Catherine's private guard, although considerably more ornate. These symbols of Imperial tyranny here in the middle of the rebel camp? I found it odd, and then I recalled that Pugachev was supposed to be the reincarnation of Peter III, the "Little Father" of the people who had come back to free them from "the German woman," the daughter of the "Evil One," who had had him murdered because he wanted freedom for all his subjects.

Pulaski led me over toward the tent and, stopping about

ten yards in front of it, let go of the rope and told the men to watch me. He stepped over to the door and identified himself to the guards. One of them stepped inside, returning a moment later to show him in. I loosened the noose and lifted it over my head, tossing it aside defiantly. Pride would not allow me to show the fear I felt, and I was determined to be brave. I stared at the men around me with cool hauteur, my chin held high. Several of them hurried away to join their friends and drink vodka and roust the whores, leaving only Nikki and three other men to guard me. The former kept his head low, the wide brim of his black sheepskin hat hiding most of his mud-streaked face. He was still unsteady on his feet, weaving to and fro.

Three women moved purposefully toward me, gaudy creatures in gypsy attire, skirts vivid splashes of color, fake golden earrings swaying from their lobes. The leader was a tough-looking specimen with abundant raven hair piled high on top of her head. Her scarlet mouth twisted contemptuously, her emerald eyes alight with hatred. The men guarding me grinned and made no effort to prevent the women from approaching me. One of them chuckled and told his companion it was going to be fun watching Tamara deal with me. Nikki nodded vigorously and almost fell down.

"I am Tamara!" the leader announced, swishing her purple skirts. "And I want that cloak!"

I knew I had to stand firm. I knew I couldn't let her get the best of me or the whole pack of them would descend.

"It belongs to me," I said coldly. "Go earn your own."

"Slut! You dare defy Tamara?"

I ignored her. She circled me slowly, her shoulders rolling, hips swaying, the bangle bracelets clattering. I didn't move, my expression icily composed. The woman stopped in front of me and placed her hands on her hips and made a clacking noise with her tongue, and then, smirking at her two hefty companions, she made a grab for my cloak. Her fingers never touched it. I balled my hand into a tight fist and slammed it into her jaw with all my might, sending her crashing to the ground. She sprawled there, groaning. The men roared with laughter, yelling taunts at the fallen gypsy. Tamara got up on her knees and shook her head to clear it and then scrambled toward me with nails extended. I kicked her on the side of the head. Hard.

"This one has much spirit!" one of the men cried as the other two women dragged their unconscious leader away. "Me, I would love to have her fighting in a pile of hay!"

"Me, too!" Nikki exclaimed. "I would break her spirit and ride her until I was saddle sore! Would you like that, woman?"

"Go fuck yourself," I told him.

Nikki slammed a hand against his heart and reeled backward in a parody of shock. "Did you hear her?" he yelled hoarsely. "Did you hear what she said? A lady, and she uses such a word! What is happening to our country? What is Mother Russia coming to? This I cannot believe!"

The others hooted loudly, and Nikki lost his balance and fell on his backside, his black sheepskin coat flying open to reveal the white lawn shirt beneath. He thrashed about, the brim of his sheepskin hat slipping down over his twisted nose. Every group has a clown, and Nikki played his role to the hilt. I paid no attention to his antics, looking across the clearing to the two wooden cages. The prisoner in velvet was kneeling on the floor of his cage, still clinging listlessly to the wooden bars. Two mangy-looking dogs snarled at him, and a woman with a long stick was poking him through the bars. He didn't even seem to notice the vicious jabs.

The man was clearly an aristocrat, probably captured on one of the raids. I wondered how long he had been here and what they planned to do with him. It wasn't going to be anything pleasant, of that I was certain. What was the purpose of that horrible stake that towered so high, the wooden arm extending at the top? In the bright orange glare of the blazing campfires it was like some giant, malevolent symbol of doom. I lowered my eyes, trying to hold back the panic that threatened to overcome me. I could put

on a proud, brave front, I could show spirit and defend myself against the loathsome Tamara, but inside I was
stricken with terror. How long before it overcame me completely?

Throughout the camp there were drunken cries and raucous laughter and the sounds of brawling and fornication.
It was like some gigantic, open-air institution for madmen,
like Bedlam in London, only here they weren't kept in
chains. Here they ran free, hooting and hollering, fighting
and fornicating in the open, onlookers cheering and
shouting lewd comments as a man mounted a whore on the
ground in front of a fire. I had great sympathy for the peasants I had seen on my journey through Russia and
ardently believed something should be done to alleviate
the suffering and starvation, but . . . but these crazed,
drunken creatures were like animals.

Nikki had recovered himself and stood quietly nearby,
his head lowered, a drunken grin on his wide lips. The
other men were impatient with their duties and eager to
join the obscene festivity all around. Tamara had recovered, and she stood in front of a filthy hut, staring at me
with murderous emerald eyes, muttering curses under her
breath. Pulaski came out of the tent, spoke to one of the
guards and then, taking my arm roughly, dragged me to
the silken flap and lifted it and shoved me inside, following
close behind.

Candles blazed brightly in half a dozen pure gold candelabra, shedding a rich golden glow over the cluttered but
dazzlingly sumptuous interior. Exquisite rugs, piled two
or three deep, covered every inch of the floor, and wonderful tapestries agleam with gold and silver thread hung on
the walls, some overlapping. Fires burned in ornate silver
braziers, filling the tent with warmth, and a heady, sicken-
ingly sweet perfume wafted through the air. Priceless
pieces of furniture were jumbled together, every available
surface piled high with glittering art objects of every description, each a treasure. Still more were stacked carelessly on the floor in tottering heaps.

Two guards in uniforms like those worn by the men outside stood at attention, one on either side of an immense throne so covered with gilt it appeared to be carved of solid gold. The man sitting on the throne was solidly built, with massive chest and shoulders, the fingers of his right hand curling around the shaft of a bejeweled scepter crowned by a ruby the size of an egg. He had broad, peasant features, a neatly trimmed black beard and the most remarkable brown eyes I had ever seen. Large and luminous, they glowed with a fervor not known by normal men, beautiful eyes, hypnotic. The eyes of a saint, I thought, or of a completely demented religious fanatic. The "Little Father" wore a gold-embroidered caftan and a high-peaked gold cap with a wide brim of golden mink. The peak of the cap was encrusted with precious gems, and more gems flashed on his thick fingers and on the heavy pendant dangling from his neck.

"Kneel before your Czar!" Pulaski ordered, giving me a brutal shove.

I stumbled forward on the thick rugs, but I didn't fall, nor did I drop to my knees. Pulaski made a threatening noise and started to shove me again, but Pugachev lifted the scepter and shook his head, and then he motioned for Pulaski to leave the tent. Emelyan Pugachev stared at me, the luminous brown eyes full of speculation that was anything but saintly. Although I knew full well he was a rank impostor, a shrewd, conniving charlatan who played upon the ignorance and superstition of the masses, I had to admit that there was a certain majesty about the man, an authority that, if not regal, was still extremely powerful.

As he stared at me, the guards on either side of the throne as immobile as statues, I thought of all I had heard about him during my months in Russia. A simple soldier who had served in the Seven Years' War and in the war with Turkey, he had deserted, been caught, escaped, posing as an Old Believer monk and later claiming he was Peter III, miraculously reappearing to right the wrongs done to his subjects by the German woman. In need of a savior, the people had chosen to overlook the fact that, during his lifetime, Peter had been a drooling idiot celebrated for his brutality and callously indifferent to the plight of the masses. In death he had become a legendary hero, the martyred champion of the plebeian cause, struck down because of his devotion to the poor, and although Pugachev bore not the least resemblance to the tall, narrow-shouldered Czar, thousands were prepared to believe his outlandish claims.

He had quickly gathered a nondescript army around him, escaped serfs, disgruntled cossacks, rebellious factory workers, peasants by the hundreds who believed he had come to save them. A gifted orator, he had fanned their grievances into a blazing fury, and the army had laid waste to the Volga region, burning and killing, committing atrocities that boggled the mind. In the beginning, Catherine's government had paid little attention to the rebellion—the Volga was so remote, and peasants were always revolting. A few regiments had been sent to deal with them, but it seemed nothing could stop the advance of the insurgents. With their "Little Father" in the lead, they hacked a bloody path across the country, moving ever nearer St. Petersburg, and what had at first been a distant nuisance had become a serious threat. Pugachev had vowed to occupy St. Petersburg by the end of the year, and he was now only a few days' march from the city.

"It is a pleasure to meet you at last," he said.

Unlike Peter III, who had barely comprehended the basics of the Russian language and spoke German most of the time, Pugachev spoke his native tongue perfectly. His voice was deep and rich, a voice that could be very persuasive.

"I have been looking forward to this for some time," he continued. "I must say, you are even more beautiful than I was led to believe."

"I am a British citizen. I demand to be released at once and permitted to return to St. Petersburg."

Pugachev ignored my words. "I have always been fond of

red hair," he said. "I have never seen any as fine as yours.
You have a noble air as well. Yes, you would sit nicely on a
throne."

"I demand—"

"You are hardly in a position to make demands, Miss
Danver. At any rate, I am not interested in them. I have
spared your life for a special reason, and that is why you
are here."

I made no reply, and Pugachev continued to caress the
gleaming red ruby, a thoughtful smile on his lips. Although his words were firm, his manner was neither harsh
nor threatening. It was, instead, almost conciliatory, as
though he hoped to win me over through polite consideration.

"I have received many reports about you," he said, "and
my interest was piqued from the beginning."

"Indeed?"

"I wanted you. At first, my motives were admittedly
base. I wanted merely to revenge myself against Count
Orlov, who was responsible for my murder in my previous
incarnation." He spoke this last without the slightest
change of inflection. "Later, when I learned that you were
in disfavor with the German usurper and that Orlov had
brought you to his estate against your will, I began to
think along different lines."

"How could you possibly know—"

"I have men everywhere, Miss Danver, as every great
leader must. I know of your unfortunate encounter with
Potemkin in the celebrated red room, and I know of Orlov's
subsequent treatment of you."

I was astonished, and, seeing it in my eyes, he allowed
himself a brief, deprecatory smile. Like everyone else, I
had assumed that the man was insane, but I was beginning to change my opinion. Emelyn Pugachev was formidably intelligent and remarkably articulate, and I
suspected he was well organized as well, the chaos outside
notwithstanding. He had skillfully manipulated thousands of men—not for any mystical or political reasons, I

would bet, but for personal gain—and so far he had been phenomenally successful. Oh yes, Pugachev knew exactly what he was doing. His luminous, saintlike eyes, his persuasive voice, his remarkable acting ability had all been used most effectively.

"To continue," he said, "it would have been sweet revenge to steal Orlov's woman and degrade her, make her my whore, but how much sweeter, now, to honor her. What delicious irony to make the woman the German has banished my Czarina and place her on a throne beside me in the Winter Palace."

I was too dumbfounded to reply. I merely stared at him, and as the moments passed his glowing brown eyes began to show signs of impatience. Pugachev frowned, his mouth tightening.

"You do not care for the idea, Miss Danver?"

"Do—do you actually believe you're going to reach St. Petersburg, remove Catherine from the throne? Half the Imperial Army is scouting the area for you at this very moment—"

"With a notable lack of success, you will have observed. Over the past weeks I've launched random attacks in this area, primarily to throw them off guard, striking first here, then there, fifty or a hundred miles away. They have galloped all over the country in confusion, as I planned, never coming anywhere near this camp."

"They'll find it eventually," I said.

"Eventually will be too late," Pugachev informed me. "We have marched a long way, hundreds and hundreds of miles, gathering recruits in every village and town, and my lieutenants have been busily recruiting even more men. From all over Russia they cry for justice and take up arms. After our succesful march from the Volga, I established the camp here and have remained for many weeks—waiting."

"For—for the other men to join you," I said. "You don't have nearly enough men here for a successful march on St. Petersburg."

"You're quite perceptive, Miss Danver. Within the next ten days three separate groups will be joining us from different areas of the country. We will number in the thousands, a mighty army, and St. Petersburg will be mine before the month is over."

The deep, beautifully modulated voice was totally without emotion. He was merely stating fact, and it was with horror that I realized he was very likely to succeed with his plan. Catherine did indeed have almost half the Imperial Army here in the north, looking for Pugachev, but they were broken up into regiments scattered all over the area, galloping about in confusion as he had pointed out. Once Pugachev began his march with his thousands of men, he could make a clean sweep to St. Petersburg before Catherine's men could regroup and organize. The man enthroned before me in such barbaric splendor might well be the next Czar of Russia . . . and he wanted me to be his Czarina.

It was absolutely incredible. I could only stare at him with a combination of repulsion and dismay. Gems flashing in the candlelight, his gold caftan gleaming, Pugachev fondled the scepter and looked at me, the saintly brown eyes full of calm speculation.

"It would, of course, be better, more appropriate, to chose a woman of the people to reign beside me, but the peasant mentality is a curious thing. The Russian peasant has an unshakable belief in his own inferiority, and he demands exceptional qualities in those before whom he grovels."

"He would not grovel before Emelyn Pugachev," I said, "but if he believed the man was Czar Peter III, miraculously restored to life—"

He allowed the faintest of smiles to flicker briefly on his lips. "You are a very intelligent woman, Miss Danver, and beautiful. You are clearly a superior individual, and you are also a foreigner, a definite asset. Were I to select as my Czarina one of the hated Russian aristocrats, I would encounter as much resistance as I would were I to present them with a woman of the people, humble and therefore unworthy of their worship."

"I see."

"I am offering you a crown," he said.

"Just like that."

"On the contrary," he replied. "I've given it a great deal of consideration, ever since I first began to hear about the lovely Englishwoman who, though living with Orlov, had a curious sympathy for the people and who, on more than one occasion, spoke up in their defense."

I didn't bother to ask how he knew that.

"We will be married in St. Petersburg," he said, "with all the attendant pomp. The people will love it."

I shook my head. He frowned.

"You do not wish to be my Czarina?"

"That's putting it mildly indeed."

His frown deepened. The saintly brown eyes hardened, filling with anger, but when he spoke his voice was perfectly controlled.

"The alternative, I assure you, will be most unpleasant."

"I'd rather die," I said.

Pugachev hesitated for a moment, and then he nodded curtly. "Very well. Fetch Pulaski," he told one of the guards who had remained immobile all this time.

The guard left, soon returning with Pulaski. Pulaski bowed low. Pugachev made an impatient gesture, in no mood for obeisance.

"Your prize has decided she would rather die than be honored," he said. "Take her to the cage."

"We burn her?" Pulaski asked hopefully.

"Not tonight. Tonight we will burn Mirovich and let her watch. Perhaps she will change her mind. If not, she will provide the entertainment tomorrow evening."

Pulaski nodded and, taking hold of my wrist, dragged me roughly from the tent and across the clearing. The nightmare maelstrom of noise was worse than ever. Several vicious fights had broken out, onlookers shouting and hooting as eyes were gouged and noses bloodied. The whores cavorted lewdly, displaying their wares with raucous glee, and vodka flowed like water. Everyone in the camp was roaring drunk, it seemed, staggering, lurching in front of blazing campfires. Nikki and three or four others followed after us, cheering as Pulaski dragged me past the towering stake and over to the empty wooden cage beyond.

The cage was crudely constructed of thick wooden sticks lashed together with strips of rawhide, forming widely spaced bars on all four sides and on top. The sticks forming the floor were lashed closely together, like a raft. Pulaski unfastened the door and shoved me inside. I stumbled, falling painfully to my knees. Pulaski fastened the door, knotting the rawhide tightly, and then he stood back, gloating as I kneeled on the rough floor.

"She burns?" one of the peasants asked.

"Tomorrow night," Pulaski retorted.

"Such a waste!" Nikki declared. "Me, I could think of better things to do with her."

"So could I!" another cried.

"The bitch burns!" Pulaski growled.

They moved away and I climbed to my feet and caught hold of the bars and stared out at the brawling chaos of drunken humanity. Bathed by the flickering dark orange light of the campfires that sent demonic shadows leaping over the ground, it was like hell itself and Satan sat enthroned inside his silken tent, plotting yet more horror and bloodshed in order to achieve his goal. I was trapped in the middle of hell and there was no hope of escape and I realized it was all going to end here, for never, never would I agree to go along with Pugachev's proposal, not even to save my own life. I could only pray it would end quickly and that my courage would not entirely desert me before the final horror.

The man in the next cage still hung listlessly on to the bars. He hadn't once looked in my direction, just gazed vacantly out at the huge stake in the middle of the camp, as

though he knew what it was for, as though he were waiting. Beyond it, I saw Tamara speaking to her two cronies.
They nodded, looking at me, then laughed gleefully as
Tamara picked up a long stick and started purposefully toward my cage. The stick had a very sharp point. As she
neared the stake, Nikki stumbled drunkenly toward her
and grabbed her in a passionate embrace. She struggled viciously, pulling away, and Nikki grinned wickedly as he
knocked the stick out of her hand and seized her again,
kissing her with exuberant gusto. Tamara kicked and
clawed and Nikki finally let her go and gave her a disgusted look and then cracked her across the jaw, slung her
across his shoulder and carried her away as his friends
cheered.

"Nikki knows how to treat them!" one cried. "Tamara's
going to get it tonight! Several times if I know my man!"

Apparently the jaunty peasant in black sheepskin coat
and cap hadn't nearly the stamina his friend believed him
to have, for I saw him crossing the camp not too long afterward with a bulky bundle in his arms. Nikki disappeared
into the darkness beyond the campfires, and shortly thereafter Pugachev came out of his tent and spoke to the
guards. They summoned Pulaski and several others, and
there was a brief conference in front of the tent. The noisy
mob abandoned their other pursuits to watch with
drunken expectancy as Pulaski and the others marched toward the cages, one of them carrying a great coil of very
thick rope. I watched in horror as they came nearer,
nearer.

The man in the cage next to mine finally came to life. He
screamed in terror. He screamed as they gathered around
his cage and lifted it up and carried it across the clearing
and set it under the stake, as they tied one end of the rope
to the top of the cage and hurled the other up over the projecting arm high above. They caught the free end of the
rope and pulled and the cage rose slowly into the air,
higher, higher, the man inside it still screaming and
thrashing about, causing it to sway precariously. When

the cage was some twenty feet in the air they tied the rope
securely and began to pile wood directly beneath the cage.

Dear God. No. No. I clung to the bars so tightly my
knuckles were bone white. The mob was cheering now as
more and more wood was heaped onto the pile, but the
shrieks of the man inside the cage rose sharply over the tu-
mult. Pugachev was still standing in front of his tent,
splendid in the gold caftan, the gems on the crown of his
mink-brimmed hat glittering in the light. He gave a signal.
A torch was lighted and applied to the pile of wood. Flames
began to crackle, slowly at first, tiny yellow-blue tongues
that licked at the logs, growing stronger, larger, turning
bright orange, devouring the logs, leaping high into the
air, higher still, blazing brightly, almost touching the bottom of the cage, and I sobbed and desperately wanted to
look away but I seemed to be paralyzed and couldn't turn
my head, couldn't even shut my eyes to shut out the horror.

He was being roasted alive. He flailed and thrashed and
finally grabbed the top of the cage and hoisted himself up
and clung there with his hands and knees as the flames
licked the bottom of the cage and the wood caught and began to burn. Thin orange flames slithered up the sides of
the cage like lascivious orange tongues and the bottom
burned briskly, charred pieces dropping down. The man
screamed and clung to the top of the cage as a huge flame
shot up and touched him and his clothes caught and then
his hair. He shrieked one last time and released his hold
and went plummeting down into the blazing inferno,
sparks shooting in every direction as he landed on the
crackling fire. The mob yelled in a frenzy of delight as his
body flopped in the fire, grew still, began to char.

Pugachev nodded and looked very pleased with himself
and stepped back inside his gorgeous silken tent. The
crowd began to disperse now that the entertainment was
over, and my hands seemed to be frozen to the bars of the
cage. I pried them loose and closed my eyes at last and
sank to the floor of the cage, overcome with shock and hor-

ror. Huge black wings seemed to flutter around the edges of my mind, obliterating all thought, all feeling. I must have swooned, must have been unconscious for quite some time, for when, moaning, I opened my eyes, the campfires were smoldering heaps, some black, some glowing pale pink, and the camp was quiet, flooded now with silvery moonlight. A peasant with a rifle marched back and forth in front of my cage, shivering with cold, for it was freezing now and snow had begun to fall from the ashy gray-black sky.

I climbed slowly to my feet and folded my arms around my waist, shivering myself despite the heavy cloak, the layers of clothing. Perhaps . . . perhaps I would freeze to death. Perhaps I would simply grow numb from the cold, then fall asleep, then freeze. What a blessing that would be, What a blessing. I didn't have the courage to face the stake. I knew that. I would scream. Please God, I prayed, let me freeze to death out here in the open. Perhaps if I took off the cloak it would happen sooner. I wanted to take it off, my hands even reached up to unfasten it, but I couldn't do it. I moved around in the narrow confines of the cage as snowflakes swirled, coming down faster now, and my peasant guard cursed the cold under his breath and continued to pace, never once so much as glancing at me.

I stopped, peering across the clearing. The ground was coated with silver, spread with shadows, and the huts and tents were inky black shapes looming all around. There was movement in the shadows beyond the stake. Someone was stealthily approaching, cautiously darting from shadow to shadow. I could make out a tall figure with . . . yes, with a bulky sheepskin coat and a wide-brimmed sheepskin cap. The peasant Nikki scooted across a patch of moonlight, ducked into the shadows again. I watched, fascinated, knowing full well what he had in mind. A nice rousing rape, and then he would put me back inside the cage and no one would be the wiser. What did he intend to do about the guard? Bribe him? Overpower him? He came closer, closer, and then he slipped on the icy ground, his boots crunching loudly as he clumsily regained his balance.

The guard whirled around, rifle raised. Nikki grinned and hailed him and moved over to join him, very chummy. The guard muttered something I failed to catch, and Nikki slapped him on the back and pointed to me. The guard turned, peering through the bars. Nikki whipped out a knife, whipped his hand around, clamping it over the guard's mouth. The blade flashed in the moonlight as the peasant in sheepskin drove it savagely into the guard's back. The guard shuddered convulsively and made a horrible gurgling sound muffled by the hand, and then he went limp, dropping to the ground as Nikki released his grip. Calm as could be, he bent down, wiped the blade on the man's coat and then straightened up, looking at me with a self-congratulatory grin.

He had pushed the brim of his cap up over his forehead and rubbed the dirt off his face and I saw it fully for the first time in the bright moonlight: the strong, cleft chin, the merry mouth, the twisted nose, the vivid blue eyes full of concentration as he sawed at the rawhide fastening the door of the cage. I was hallucinating. I must be. That face, that beloved face had haunted me for all these months, and now I was transposing it over the face of a crude peasant lout come to rape me. I shook my head, blinking. He thrust the knife back into the waistband of his breeches and yanked open the door.

"I say, lass," he observed chattily, "you do get yourself into some of the damndest messes."

Chapter Twenty-Five

STUNNED, I STARED AT HIM, UNABLE TO MOVE, and Jeremy frowned and took hold of my arm and pulled me roughly from the cage, almost tripping over the body of the guard he had just stabbed. He warned me to be very, very quiet, then led me quickly into the shadows and past huts and tents from whence came loud, drunken snores. I was dreaming all this, I knew. It must be a dream, yet I felt the cold, icy air on my face and felt the slap of the money bag on my thigh and felt his fingers holding my arm in a steely grip as we fled through the shadows, passing more tents and huts and the blackened ruins of campfires. The snow fell in soft, feathery swirls, pelting us gently. Our footsteps seemed terribly loud in the silence.

He pulled me against the wall of a hut and pulled me against him and cupped his hand lightly over my mouth as someone groaned and coughed and stepped out of a tent nearby. He curled an arm around my waist, holding me close, and I rested my head on that shoulder covered in soft sheepskin and felt his warmth and felt his strength, felt, too, the tension in his body as one of the peasants stepped into the moonlight and staggered over to a pile of charred wood and proceeded to relieve himself. Finished, he turned and stared into the shadows where we stood and my heart began to pound. Jeremy tightened his hand over my mouth.

"Take it easy," he whispered into my ear. "He can't see us."

The peasant yawned, shook his head, and staggered back into the tent. Jeremy held me for a moment longer, his lips still brushing the lobe of my ear, and I reveled in his nearness, in that strong, muscular arm pinioning me to him, in the musky, masculine smell of his body. Still not convinced this wasn't all an amazing dream, I sighed as he removed his hand from my mouth and felt loss when the arm uncurled from around my waist. One of the mangy dogs barked across the camp as we moved on, dashing from shadow to shadow and avoiding the treacherous moonlight whenever possible.

He led me past the last line of huts and over to an opening in the log barricade, and then we were outside the camp and could hear the horses moving restlessly in the cold. We paused for a moment and I caught my breath and looked at him, the handsome, rakish face all silver and shadow in the moonlight. His full mouth curled into a grin, and I knew then it was all real, knew I wasn't imagining it in some kind of delirium.

"It—it's really you," I said.

"It's really me."

"I can't—I can't believe it. How—"

"It's a long story, lass, and we're a little pressed for time."

"You came—all this way."

"I did indeed."

"Just—just to find me."

"When love commands, the heart obeys. I had no choice, lass. I'd have traveled twice as far if necessary."

"I thought—"

"I've a pretty good idea what you thought."

"The blonde—"

"Later," he said.

"You've got a hell of a lot of explaining to do," I said sharply.

"Ah, that dulcet tone. How I've missed it. I haven't had a really satisfying row since we were together in England. I must say, Marietta, your gratitude is overwhelming.

Here I risk life and limb in order to rescue you from a terrible fate, and—"

"You haven't changed a bit!"

"Nor, thank God, have you."

"Oh, Jeremy—"

He pulled me into his arms and held me close, held me tight, rocking me gently as the snow swirled around us and the wind blew and the horses stamped, and I sobbed and his arms tightened even more and he ordered me to hold on. We weren't out of danger yet, and if there was one thing he didn't particularly need at the moment it was a woman falling apart. I clung to him and fought back the multitude of emotions and, finally, raised my head and looked into his loving eyes, and a wonderful feeling filled my being. It was like awakening from a terrible dream to find myself in a snug, familiar room.

"I'm not going to fall apart," I promised.

"Of course not. You're the bravest lass I know."

"Stop calling me lass! You know I've always hated it."

He smiled in the moonlight. "I beg your pardon, milady."

"Go to hell, you bastard. You could have let me *know* it was you. You just let me go right on thinking you were—"

"Afraid you'd give the show away," he told me. "Quite a performance I gave back there, wasn't it? Simply a matter of getting into the spirit of things."

"You were outrageous."

"But convincing," he insisted.

"I didn't know you spoke Russian."

"I managed to pick up a few phrases here and there—"Kill the aristocrats." "Rape the women." "Pass the salt." We'll talk later. At the moment we have to get ourselves out of here, and there are two more guards to deal with."

"What did you do with Tamara?" I inquired.

"She's resting quite comfortably with a gag stuffed down her throat, trussed up like a hog with several lengths of rawhide. Couldn't let her use that pointed stick on you."

"I saw you carrying a bundle—"

"Provisions. I managed to appropriate us a horse and sleigh. It's waiting beyond that grove of trees, on the frozen river. We'll have to pass the enclosure and the horses are restless tonight. Stay close behind me. Try to make as little noise as possible."

Slowly, cautiously, we moved past the line of frozen shrubs that concealed the barricade of logs, the shadows here thick, moonlight gilding the snow beyond. The horses stirred nervously as we approached their enclosure, and Jeremy stopped as we heard footsteps pacing in the darkness. I stood behind him, feeling safe, feeling secure, not at all frightened now that he was here. He stood very still, so tall and lean, the bulky black sheepskin coat and preposterous hat making him look quite burly. Snow continued to pelt us and it was freezing cold, but I didn't even notice the discomfort. Jeremy was here. It was incredible, it was improbable, but Jeremy was actually here. I could reach up and touch him.

"I'm going after him," he whispered. "Stay here. Stay quiet."

"Don't leave me," I pleaded. "Don't—"

"Shhhh. I'll be back in a couple of minutes."

He crept away in the shadows, moving toward the sound of pacing, and I folded my arms around my waist and gnawed my lower lip, shivering, feeling afraid now, feeling bereft and exposed and vulnerable without Jeremy here to give me courage. For a few moments I could see his dark form creeping through the lighter darkness of the shadows, and then it merged, disappeared, and panic grew inside me. A miracle had happened and somehow he had materialized here in the middle of this Russian wilderness, but . . . what if something happened to him now? I couldn't endure that. Now that we were together again I simply couldn't go on living if anything happened to him. I heard the guard pacing in the darkness, footsteps heavy on the crusty snow, and then he halted and there was an ominous silence broken only by the restless stamping of the horses.

It seemed to last forever. I stood there in the darkness under the icy branches, shivering, and the fear that gripped me like a giant invisible hand was not for me but for Jeremy. Why had the guard halted? A minute went by, another, another, and the invisible hand squeezed tighter and tighter. I knew I couldn't take much more. The tension was too much. I was going to scream. The silence stretched on interminably, and then I heard a soft, shuffling noise and a loud grunt followed by the sound of someone gagging, gurgling, gulping for breath. It lasted several seconds, and then there came a dull thud as a body dropped onto the ground. Jeremy. Oh dear God, was it Jeremy? I couldn't take it any longer. I hurried through the shadows toward the spot that the noises had come from. I slipped on the snow, fell to my knees.

He reached down and took hold of my arms and pulled me to my feet. I struggled viciously, fighting him, and his fingers squeezed my arms so tightly I cried out. He shook me. I kicked him on the shin as hard as I could. He continued to shake me, harder now, so hard I thought my neck would snap.

"What's the *matter* with you?" he demanded.

He let go of me. I slapped him across the face. The sound of palm smacking cheek rang out like a gunshot. Jeremy stumbled back, knees wobbling, almost losing his balance. Beneath the glove my palm burned as though it had been passed through flame.

"Jesus!" he cried.

"Don't you ever do that again!" I exclaimed, and my voice trembled. "Don't you *ever* leave me alone again, not even for a minute. I don't care *what* the circumstances!"

"Keep your *voice* down!"

"I'll kill you. I swear it!"

"You damn near did," he told me.

And then, much to my humiliation, I started sobbing and the tears started to stream down my cheeks. He tried to put his arms around me, and I shoved him away angrily. He emitted an exasperated sigh and rubbed his cheek and waited patiently for me to compose myself. I took a deep breath. I dried my cheeks and took another deep breath and then sighed myself, adjusting the hood of my cloak, looking at him with a cool, dignified expression.

"All finished?" he inquired.

"I don't intend to apologize," I said coldly.

"I don't expect you to. My cheek feels like it's on fire. You pack quite a punch, lass."

"I meant what I said, Jeremy. Don't ever leave me alone again."

"Wouldn't dream of it," he replied. "Sure you're all right now?"

"I'm sure. What happened with the guard?"

"I managed to slip up on him from behind, slung my arm around his neck. He was too stunned to fight, just kept trying to pull my arm away, relieve the pressure. Sturdy chap. Took me a good two minutes to kill him. Think you're up to moving on now?"

I nodded, and Jeremy took my hand and led me through the darkness, past the enclosure where the horses stirred restlessly. My eyes had grown accustomed to the dark now, and I could see that one of the sleighs was missing. I could also see the body of the guard sprawled out on the snow, his head twisted to one side at a peculiar angle. I shuddered, and we hurried along in the swirling snow and crossed a patch of brilliant moonlight and headed for the trees. A few moments later we were moving under the icy branches, and through the trunks of the trees I could glimpse the river ahead, gleaming like a wide silver ribbon in the moonlight.

"I thought we'd follow the river for a while rather than risk taking one of the roads," he said.

"Is it safe?" I asked.

"Safe as houses. Frozen solid, I'd wager. Ice must be three or four feet thick, couldn't possibly break."

The sleigh on the edge of the river was small and dilapidated with wide wooden runners. The horse was tethered to a tree trunk, a blanket secured over its back and hindquarters for warmth. It stood patiently in blinders, idly tapping one hoof on the ice. The sleigh was piled high with mothy fur rugs and blankets, and there were two bulky cloth bags filled with the food Jeremy had stolen. He helped me up onto the seat and lovingly arranged the blankets over my knees. The odor they gave off assaulted my nostrils, but under the circumstances it was the finest perfume.

Jeremy untethered the horse, coiled the rope and tossed it on the floor of the sleigh, then climbed in beside me. The sleigh rocked a little under his weight. He shifted the bags of food around, picked up a rifle, pulled the blankets over his legs and put a mothy fur rug over our knees. His black sheepskin coat smelled as bad as the blankets, and I could smell sweat, too, and leather. He was close beside me, his leg touching mine.

"We have a small problem," he said, reaching for the reins.

"Oh?"

"I was able to steal three rifles, and I took a pistol from the guard back there—he wasn't carrying a rifle. All four weapons are loaded, but I wasn't able to get any powder or extra ammunition. There wasn't time for me to locate the armory."

"No problem," I said.

I reached into the pockets of my cloak and pulled out the powder horn and the bag of shot. Jeremy stared at them in amazement. He took the bag of shot, opened it, examined the bullets, shook his head.

"Got any other little surprises on you?"

"Only a bag of gold."

"Incredible!"

"I believe in being prepared," I said smugly.

"There's no one like you, love—I've always said so. Want to tell me how you just happen to have gunshot and powder in your pockets?"

"It's a long story," I said, "and we're a little pressed for time."

"I may throttle you. I may not be able to restrain myself."

He clicked the reins and the horse began to clop along over the ice, windblown dirt and twigs making the surface less slippery and easily maneuverable. The wide wooden runners slid along nicely. The sleigh swayed gently. I leaned back against the cushion, pulling the blankets closer, warm, snug, in paradise with Jeremy beside me, no dream, his body warming mine, his strong hands holding the reins, his face in profile lean and handsome. He turned to look at me, and that familiar, mischievous smile played on his lips and I could feel fresh tears welling in my eyes. We were together again, at last, through some miracle, and we were already spatting as of old and it was glorious, glorious. He saw the tears glistening in my eyes and held the reins with his right hand and tenderly brushed them from my lashes with his left.

"It's going to be all right," he said, a husky catch in his voice.

"I know," I whispered.

"You're a very brave lass."

"And stubborn and testy and often shrewish."

"That, too," he agreed. "I think I love you."

"I suppose that's why you left London with a blonde and took all my money with you."

"I can explain that."

"It had better be good," I told him.

He smiled again, and then the moon went behind a cloud and the bright silver light vanished and a shroud of blue-black darkness fell all around us, the banks on either side darker still, inky black. The horse's hoofs made a loud, monotonous clop-clop on the ice, and the wooden runners made a skimming, sandy sound, magnified by the darkness and the silence of the night. I was thinking now of the second guard, and Jeremy was too. I could sense the tension in his long, lean body as he gripped the reins. I placed my hand on his arm and felt the taut muscle beneath the sleeve.

"He—he's up ahead, isn't he?" I said quietly.

"Stationed on the bank. He'll be able to hear us, of course, but if this darkness holds he won't be able to see us. We'll be all right."

"I'll take the reins, Jeremy. You take the rifle, just—just in case."

"Can't risk using the rifle, love. In this silence a shot would be deafening. They'd hear it all the way back at the camp—some of them would wake up, drunk as they are, find the cage empty, find the guard I stabbed. No, we can't use the rifle, can't let him use his either."

"So—"

"We'll do the best we can," he said lightly. "Once we're past the guard we'll be able to make good time. Pugachev will send men after us in the morning, of course, as soon as it's discovered you're gone, but with several hours' head start we'll be in fine shape."

Although his voice was deliberately light and reassuring, I could tell he was worried. I was worried myself, but he wasn't going to know it. He didn't need a cringing, frightened female at his side, he needed someone calm and composed and supportive, and that's what I intended to be. Jeremy sighed, trying to control the tension, and I sat up straight, my feet resting on the butt of one of the rifles. The horse clopped on through the blue-black darkness, the sleigh rocking gently from side to side. The surface of the river was a dark pewter gray, spread with murky shadows, and the snow continued to fall in soft swirls.

"Halt!" a voice cried. "Who goes there!"

We heard crunching footsteps on the bank, and then, as though on command, the moon came out from behind the clouds and radiant silver light poured over the scene and we saw him standing there not thirty feet away, a hulking brute heavily bundled up against the cold, a rifle aimed directly at us. He was at least six feet seven, his face fierce, menacing. Jeremy pulled on the reins, bringing the horse to a halt, and, in harsh, rumbling Russian, identified himself as Pulaski.

"Pulaski?"

"Pugachev sends me after supplies. I am not able to leave until after it grows dark. Many soldiers not far from here, he reports."

Jeremy kept his head tilted down, the wide brim of his hat concealing his features. I leaned against him, the fur hood hiding most of my face. Scowling, the guard moved off the bank and took a few steps toward the sleigh, the rifle pointing at us, the butt propped against his shoulder, one finger curled around the trigger.

"Who is the woman?" he roared.

"It is a long journey. I bring my whore along for company. I have vodka, too. Come, I will give you a bottle. You are out here in the cold all night. The vodka will warm your blood."

"You do not sound like Josef!" the guard rumbled.

"Is your imagination, comrade. Come, I share my vodka with you. I even share my whore."

The guard hesitated a moment, still suspicious, and then, rifle held firmly at the ready, he moved cautiously toward the sleigh. My heart was pounding. I held my breath. Jeremy braced his feet firmly on the floor of the sleigh and tightened his leg muscles, ready to spring. His hand slipped under his sheepskin coat and gripped the hilt of the knife, slowly pulling it out. The guard advanced slowly, and Jeremy waited until he was almost upon us, then he sprang out of the sleigh and knocked the rifle out of the guard's arms. It clattered noisily on the ice, skittering several feet away.

Stunned, the burly Goliath staggered for a moment, recovering himself as Jeremy drove the knife toward his heart. He grabbed Jeremy's wrist, twisting it viciously, and they struggled for a moment, grappling like two clumsy dancers, then Jeremy whipped his left leg behind the guard's right leg and shoved mightily and the guard toppled over backward, Jeremy crashing down on top of him, dropping the knife. They rolled on the ice, grunting, pounding, thrashing, and the horse neighed, stamping nervously on the ice.

The guard was on top of Jeremy now, so much larger, so much heavier, and Jeremy squirmed and bucked like a crazed bronco, trying to throw him off, and somehow he managed to slam his knee up into the guard's groin and roll aside, throwing himself on the guard's back, slinging an arm around his throat, but the man was too large, too powerful, and he easily tore free of the stranglehold and slung Jeremy aside and pounced on top of him again, his huge fingers curling around Jeremy's throat, squeezing mercilessly. Paralyzed with shock, I saw that Jeremy was growing weaker, weaker. Teeth bared, dark eyes glittering in the moonlight, the guard squeezed as Jeremy gripped his wrists, trying to tear the hands away from his throat.

Something snapped inside me and I was startled to find myself on the ice, reaching for the rifle that had skittered away when the guard dropped it. You can't shoot him, a voice shrilled inside my head, they'll hear the shot, and I saw Mitya grabbing the rifle by the barrel as I stood on the stairs and I took hold of the barrel and slipped on the ice and almost fell. I stumbled over to the men and swung the rifle back over my shoulder and swung the butt down with all my strength, and my arms jarred painfully as it made contact with the guard's skull, thumping loudly. The butt splintered, broke into pieces, and the guard threw his arms up and slumped forward, covering Jeremy's face with his chest.

There was a moment of dreadful silence, the night still all around, moonlight gilding the ice with silver, horse motionless, casting a long black shadow over the silvered ice. I knew Jeremy was dead and I knew I couldn't go on living without him, there was no point, no purpose, without Jeremy life would have no meaning, and then I heard a groan. Grunting, he heaved and managed to shove the guard off him and sat up, looking at me with dazed eyes. He had lost his hat. A heavy chestnut wave fell across his forehead like a huge inverted comma, the point just above his right eye. He sighed, leaning back on his palms. I was still gripping the barrel of the rifle. I tossed it aside. Jeremy climbed to his feet and staggered, grabbing the side of the sleigh for support.

"Jesus," he croaked hoarsely.

"Are you all right?"

He nodded, wave flopping, and I dug among the blankets and found one of the canteens and handed it to him. He opened it and took several gulps as I gathered up his hat and his knife. The guard was still motionless, a gigantic heap sprawling there in the moonlight. Jeremy screwed the top back onto the canteen and took the knife and thrust it in his waistband and pushed the wave back and squashed the fluffy black sheepskin hat over his head.

"Do—do you think he'll be all right?" I asked foolishly, pointing to the guard.

"Not in this world, love. Maybe in the next."

"He's—dead?"

"You bashed his skull in."

"I—I didn't even know what I was doing. I just—he was choking you to death, and—you're certain he's dead?"

"Quite certain."

"Well, then, I—I suppose we might as well be on our way."

Jeremy shook his head, a grin beginning to form on his lips. "You know, you're pretty handy to have around."

"I try to hold up my end," I said primly.

"Why didn't you just shoot him?"

"They would have heard the shot—remember?"

I climbed back into the sleigh and adjusted the folds of my garnet velvet skirt and adjusted the cloak and pulled the blankets up over my knees. Jeremy sighed heavily and massaged his throat for a moment and then climbed in beside me, covering his own legs, spreading the fur rug over us. I could feel a delayed reaction beginning to set in, and I had to fight hard to keep from shaking all over. Jeremy picked up the reins and clicked them, and we were on our way again, swaying, gliding over the ice, the horse clopping along at a brisker pace than before.

It had stopped snowing. The sky was a deep purple-black filled with ashy gray clouds brushed with silver. The moonlight was brighter than ever, liquid silver bathing the ice and snow. Neither of us spoke for a long time. Jeremy coughed now and then and rubbed his sore throat. We followed the frozen river for several miles, and then we turned into a crude road that wound through the woods, so narrow there was barely enough room for the sleigh, and this eventually led to the main road.

"It should be safe to use this tonight," Jeremy said. "Tomorrow we will have to use the back roads."

"I wonder what time it is."

"Two-thirty, three—somewhere around there."

"I'm hungry," I said. "Starving, in fact. I'd love a big bowl of steaming hot soup and a couple of pork chops and a baked potato dripping with fresh butter."

"Afraid you'll have to settle for what's in the bag," he told me. "Hardly gourmet fare, but the best I could do on short notice."

A thin covering of clouds floated across the moon and the silver faded into a pale pewter, the night dark gray spread with blue-black shadows. I pulled open the bag and rummaged through it and finally removed a chunk of bread and a long, tough link of sausage. The bread was coarse and grainy but had a wonderful flavor, and, though tough, the sausage was delicious.

"You might hand me an apple," Jeremy said.

I did so. He took a noisy bite. The horse was moving at a steady clip as though enjoying the exercise, and the wide wooden runners skimmed smoothly over the hard-packed snow. It was snug and warm under the layers of cover, our bodies close, and the cold air stroking our faces was invigorating and refreshing. Jeremy finished the apple and tossed the core aside. I chewed the sausage and tore off another piece of bread.

"We're no longer pressed for time," I observed.

"That's true."

"You have quite a lot of explaining to do."

"Guess I do," he admitted.

"Why don't we start with London—and the blonde."

"Her name is Laura. She's twenty-four years old, unmarried and extremely devoted to her brother Stephen, Lord Bramley, a charming, irresponsible rapscallion with whom I attended Oxford. Stephen was like a brother to me in the old days, helped me out of many a scrape. Only natural I should agree to help *him* out when, three days after you left, his lovely sister called on me at The White Hart and begged me to rush to his aid."

"How lovely?"

"Very. Hair like pale yellow gold, eyes as blue as morning glories, complexion like cream, and a body like—well, a very nice body indeed. I remembered her as a scrawny brat with pigtails and freckles, slipping clammy frogs into my bed when I visited Stephen at Bramley Hall. I always longed to thrash the little hellion. Fifteen years can make a lot of difference."

"Go on."

"Brother Stephen had jaunted off to Scotland and got himself engaged to a rather shrewish but extremely wealthy heiress—father's a wool magnate, owns a dozen factories. Dreadful chap, ruddy cheeks, ginger whiskers, fierce eyes and a voice like thunder. Anyway, though direly in need of money, Stephen decided he'd best abandon the testy heiress and her even testier papa and four hulking brothers—I forgot to tell you about the brothers."

"I suppose you'll eventually come to the point," I said patiently.

"Stephen bade the querulous Fiona farewell and started packing and before he'd folded his shirts two burly constables burst into his room and he was arrested for breach of promise and found himself clapped into the darkest, dankest cell in Edinburgh. Papa had filed a complaint, hired a slew of tricky advocates."

"So you and Laura went to Edinburgh to extricate him," I said, "and you took my money with you."

"I had to borrow it, love. I had to use it to hire a slew of even trickier advocates. It took almost two months of legal hassle and quite a chunk of the money, but Stephen was finally a free man. The first thing he did when he got back to England was sell a third of his land and return the money I'd used for bribes, legal fees, and the settlement awarded the sweet Fiona."

"What about Laura?" I asked.

"She's currently trying to reform her brother. Laura's a strong believer in reform—all kinds of reform. Prints up pamphlets about the evils of demon gin and distributes them in person in all the grub shops in London. Works for the church. Runs a home for fallen women. If there's one thing I can't abide it's a self-righteous woman—" Jeremy sighed and shook his head. "And with a body like that—such a waste."

"I think you're lying!" I snapped.

"Would *I* lie?"

"You certainly would! What about the money?"

"It's in a bank in New Orleans. I had it transferred there before I left for Russia. In your name, love."

I was surprised. "New Orleans?"

"I figured we'd be heading there eventually. On our way to Texas."

I didn't say anything for a while. I finished the bread and sausage, and then I took several swallows of water from one of the canteens. His explanation was convincing enough—it would be like Jeremy to drop everything in order to rush to the aid of a friend—but I didn't believe a word he said about Laura. He asked for another apple. I handed him one. He took a big bite and yelled and started crying. I'd handed him a raw onion by mistake. He accused me of doing it deliberately. I protested my innocence. He brushed tears from his smarting eyes and grumpily took the apple I offered, examining it carefully before biting into it.

"I fully expected you to be waiting for me at The White Hart when I finally got back to London," he told me.

"Why—why would you have expected that?"

"I knew you'd never stay with Derek Hawke, Marietta. I knew you were in love with me, knew it was only a matter of time before you realized that, saw what was in your own heart. I was prepared to wait."

"You—were?"

"I was prepared to give you a week. If you hadn't returned by then I intended to go fetch you, drag you back to London by your hair if I had to, and then Laura appeared on my doorstep—" He gripped the reins tightly as we hit a bump and the sleigh skidded.

"And you went off to Scotland," I finished for him.

"Had no idea I'd be gone quite so long. I left a letter for you at The White Hart."

"You—" I could hardly get the words out. "You left a letter?"

"Explaining everything. Asking you to wait."

"I—never—I never received it."

Jeremy nodded curtly, his mouth tight. "I know. Mrs. Patterson wasn't at the desk when I went downstairs, neither was her husband. I gave the letter to his cloddish nephew. He was lounging behind the desk, filling in for a few minutes while his uncle was in the yard. I asked him to tell his uncle to see that you got it as soon as you returned."

"Oh, Jeremy—"

"When I got back to The White Hart I found out that you had indeed been there, asking for me, but no one knew anything about the letter. After much searching, it was found stuck between the pages of an old ledger. If Patterson's nephew hadn't already gone back to the country I would have killed him with my bare hands."

"If I had gotten that letter, I—" I hesitated, scarcely able to speak. "I would never have come to Russia. None—none of this would ever have happened."

"Life does play its little tricks on us," he said grimly.

I stared straight ahead, watching the horse's head nod up and down as he clipped along, watching the pewter ribbon of road unrolling before us, ice encrusted limbs hanging overhead. If Jeremy had handed the letter to Mrs. Patterson, to her husband, even to the maid Tibby, I would never have left London. I would have waited there for him, impatient, filled with my love, and instead of fleeing through the night in the Russian wilderness we would be in Texas now. The irony of it was like a sharp pain in my heart. All that suffering, all that grief, all because a cloddish lout thrust the letter between the pages of a ledger instead of giving it to his uncle.

"I was distraught," Jeremy said. "I was almost out of my mind. I had no idea where you were, had no idea what had happened to you. I went to all the shipping offices, all the coach houses, trying to find out if you had left the city and, if so, where you had gone. I hired a coach and went down to see Hawke. I questioned him. I learned nothing. I met his wife and saw their infant son."

"So—so they have a son," I said. "Derek has Hawkehouse and the heir he wanted. I hope he's happy."

I meant it. Jeremy gave a short, bitter laugh.

"He's never going to be happy," he told me. "He lost the one thing in the world he really wanted. He has the house, the heir, a lovely and charming wife, but he doesn't have you."

I didn't say anything. Jeremy tightened his grip on the reins, his profile stony.

"He's still in love with you, Marietta. He'll never be able to forgive himself for not marrying you when he had the chance."

"That's—too bad," I said.

"You don't care?"

"I would like for him to be happy, but—Derek is the past, Jeremy. I wasted an awful lot of years over him, but I came out of it, and I learned the true meaning of love when—when you came into my life."

"Hawke no longer matters to you?"

"No one matters to me but you, Jeremy, and if you expect any more confessions of tender regard you're bloody well going to be disappointed. You know damn well how I feel about you."

Jeremy grinned. "Yes, I guess I do."

"So you saw Derek and learned nothing of my whereabouts. I assume you went back to London."

"And placed notices in all the papers, offering a reward for any information about you. I took myself down to Bow Street and used some of my connections there and had half a dozen runners scouring the city for any trace of you. Like I said, I was almost out of my mind, and then, three weeks later, I had a caller—Sir Harry Lyman. He'd been at his club and just happened to pick up a paper, just happened to see the notice I'd placed in it. He came to see me immediately, and I learned about your accident and learned you'd come to Russia with Count Gregory Orlov and his niece."

"Thank God for Sir Harry," I said.

"It seemed to take forever to get to Russia," he continued. "I came by ship—everyone advised me against an overland journey this time of year. Spent the whole journey fretting and fuming and studying Russian—a chap on board, minor Russian diplomat, gave me lessons. He also told me a hell of a lot about the man you left England with."

"Oh?"

"Were you his mistress?"

"I was paid companion to his niece."

"Did you sleep with him?"

"Go on with your story, Jeremy."

"*Did* you?"

I refused to answer and Jeremy looked very cross and finally, seeing he would get no more out of me, clicked the reins angrily and accidentally gave them a severe jerk and the horse reared in panic and the sleigh skidded wildly to a stop and blankets and bags and canteens tumbled out onto the icy surface of the road. So did Jeremy, landing quite ungracefully on his backside and cracking the back of his head as he fell over.

"God *damn!*" he cried.

"That was beautiful," I said calmly. "Would you like to do it again? I didn't get a really good look the first time."

"Shut *up*, Marietta. I feel dazed. I feel dizzy. Christ, I think I've hurt myself."

"I imagine you'll survive," I said.

I climbed out of the sleigh and went around to calm the horse, stroking its neck gently, speaking to it in a soothing voice. Jeremy climbed shakily to his feet and began to sling blankets back into the sleigh. The moon came out again, its rays not as bright as before, and everything turned pale silver and soft silver-gray, shadows deep amethyst with only a faint suggestion of black. Jeremy brought a large cloth bag around to where I stood, thrusting it at me with considerable hostility.

"Since you're so bloody concerned about the bloody horse you might just as well give it some oats while you're at it."

"You brought oats for the horse? Jeremy, how sweet of you to remember. Here, sweetheart, have some oats—that's right, eat them out of my hand. I imagine you're starved, poor darling."

Jeremy stomped about, tossing more things back into the sleigh, cursing again when he dropped the food bag and food scattered over the ground and he had to gather it up. I dipped my hand into the bag, bringing out more oats, and the horse nibbled them greedily, its lips moist against my palm. It was lovely here, the night so still, the moonlight gleaming, and I felt curiously serene as I fed the horse, as the man I loved grumbled about his minor exertions.

"That's enough, sweetheart," I said. "You'll get more in the morning. Everything back in the sleigh?" I called.

"No thanks to you!" he snapped. "You might have given me a hand, Marietta! My backside hurts something awful. Feels like someone paddled it with a solid oak beam."

"You're such a baby. Want me to kiss it and make it well?"

"Keep it up, just keep it up!"

"It's wonderful, isn't it?" I said.

"What is?"

I put the feed bag back into the sleigh. "This. Us. Just like the old days. I may be out of my mind, but—oh, Jeremy, I do love you so."

"You do?"

"With all your quirks, all your foibles."

"What quirks? *What* foibles?"

I moved over to him and reached up and touched his lean cheek and he pretended to be very cool and aloof and I smiled and stood up on my tiptoes and brushed that wide mouth with my lips and he gathered me to him and kissed me fervently and held me so tightly I felt my ribs might crack, and I gloried in it. After a long time he released me and ran a hand across his brow and said this was hardly the time or place and I said that was a pity and he grinned a wicked grin and said we *did* have plenty of blankets on hand and I told him it was a charming thought but we'd better wait until we also had a roof over our heads.

"You always were a stick," he said. "No spirit of adventure, no mad impulses, no damn fun."

"I know."

"All that time we were traveling through Texas you remained depressingly perpendicular."

"Not *all* the time," I reminded him.

"Yeah, once, and then you got mad at me and went right back to your damnable celibacy. *Did* you sleep with Orlov?"

"Of course not."

"You sure?" he asked.

"Would *I* lie?"

Jeremy gave me an exasperated look and helped me back into the sleigh and clambered in beside me and arranged blankets and rug and we were soon skimming along over the icy road again, the horse frisky after the oats. I moved over, nestling against him, and Jeremy curled an arm around my shoulders, keeping a tight grip on the reins with his right hand. We had been through a nightmare and we were alone in the cold, in the middle of the Russian wasteland, but we were together, and I had rarely felt such bliss.

"What happened when you got to St. Petersburg?" I asked.

"I went straight to the British embassy. I spoke to Sir Reginald Lloyd. He told me that Orlov had left for his estate in the north some two weeks before, apparently taking you with him. I got a horse and came after you. I heard an incredible din as I rode through the woods near the house. I smelled the smoke, and in a few more minutes I saw the flames. I abandoned my horse and crept through the woods, and—Jesus, love, I almost went insane. The peasants were jumping and yelling and waving pitchforks and the house was aflame and I thought you might still be inside it, thought they might have killed you."

"What did you do then?" I asked.

"I crept closer and one of the peasants came staggering by, wearing this coat, this hat, waving a bottle of vodka. I took him out with no trouble and removed my own coat and hat and put on his and joined the melee, yelling like a banshee, waving a scythe I picked up. I grabbed one of the peasants, said I wanted the woman, the redhaired woman, and he told me Pulaski had you and intended to take you back to Pugachev's camp, so I kept on shouting 'Down with tyranny' and became part of the mob, became Nikki the buffoon, making several friends during the next two days as we headed back to camp."

"None of them suspected you?"

"The mob was composed of men from a dozen different villages. Everyone just assumed I came from a different village. When we finally caught up with Pulaski and I saw you with that rope around your neck—" Jeremy hesitated, shaking his head grimly. "It took all the control I had not to start swinging then and there."

"But you stayed in character," I said.

"And did a bloody fine job of it, too," he added. "Maybe I *should* have gone on the stage. I have the gift, no doubt about it."

"It's something you can always fall back on," I said dryly.

"Don't imagine there'll be much call for it in Texas."

"Texas—" I whispered. "Will—will we really get there, Jeremy?"

"Count on it, love," he told me. "Why don't you close your eyes for a while now, try to get some sleep."

"I couldn't sleep," I replied. "There's no possible way."

And five minutes later my eyelids grew heavy and I pulled the blankets up and snuggled against him and felt warm and safe and secure. Jeremy curled his arm tighter around my shoulders, and his warmth, his strength became part of a blissful dream as I drifted off to the soft, scraping noise of wood on ice and the steady clop-clop of the horse. The dream captivated me, melted into lovely fragments, faded away, and I slept a long time, and later, much later, something evil, something frightening pierced the layers of slumber and I shivered and moaned. It came again, a sound, and I sat up, alert, gripped with terror. It was daylight now. Jeremy turned to look at me and gave me a warm, reassuring smile.

"Have a nice sleep?" he inquired.

"Some—something woke me up—a noise."

"Nothing to worry about," he said casually. "It was just a wolf."

"Oh, my God—"

I had forgotten about the wolves.

Chapter Twenty-Six

JEREMY SCOFFED AT MY ALARM AND PATIENTLY
explained to me that wolves were shy, harmless creatures
that presented absolutely no threat. I told him I didn't
know what kind of wolves he had encountered in the past
but Russian wolves were unique unto themselves and did
indeed present a most definite threat. He smiled at my
charming, typically female naivete and, while not actually
patting me on the head, managed to infuriate me with his
insufferable, typically male attitude of superiority. I had a
big, strong man with me, his manner implied, and there
was nothing to worry about.

"I happen to know a little more about this than you do,"
I said sharply. "I've been in Russia longer. They *do* attack
people."

I told him some of the stories I'd heard, and Jeremy listened and smiled again and said Russians thrived on high
drama and loved to exaggerate and, besides, both of us
were excellent shots, had three rifles, a pistol, and plenty
of ammunition.

"Relax, Marietta."

"I find that rather difficult when we're being pursued by
a pack of starving, bloodthirsty wolves!"

"One lone wolf," Jeremy said, "and he was probably
scared by the sound of the sleigh, probably turned tail and
hurried back to his den as fast as he could. It isn't *like* you
to fall to pieces like this, love."

"I'm not falling to pieces!"

"You could have fooled me."

"Go to hell! I just happen to be extremely frightened of wolves."

"Nary a wolf in sight," he said.

He was right, and a good twenty minutes had passed since the howling had awakened me. I was probably over-reacting, but I still resented his smug attitude and his infuriating calm. I rubbed my eyes and gazed at the drab day. The sky was a solemn gray, filled with heavy clouds of even darker gray. The few rays of sunlight that managed to filter through were thin and white, dim, and the usually blinding white snow was tinged gray, too, dull and depressing and bleak. It was extremely cold.

"It looks like it's going to snow again," I said miserably.

"Does indeed," he replied.

"I'd give half my gold for a cup of hot coffee."

"Wouldn't mind a cup myself. You hungry?"

"I could use a plate of scambled eggs and some crisp bacon," I replied. "Some hot muffins and orange marmelade would be nice, too, even some kippered herring."

" 'Fraid you'll have to settle for less, love."

Jeremy pulled on the reins, bringing the horse to a halt. He got out of the sleigh and stretched and yawned sleepily, then pulled the bag of oats out and patted the horse on the back and tied the bag around its neck. I sat under the blankets, still apprehensive, keeping a sharp eye out for the wolves. Jeremy stretched again, throwing his arms wide, leaning back. His sheepskin coat flapped open, and I saw the fine white lawn shirt beneath. Sometime during the night he had tied a bright red scarf around his neck, and it gave him a rakish, piratical look. The wide, mobile mouth, the slightly twisted nose, the vivid blue eyes added to that impression, as did the pistol and the knife thrust into the waistband of his snug black breeches.

"I'll be back in a minute," he said.

"Where are you going? Jeremy, are you out of—"

"Nature calls, love."

I had five minutes of stark terror, sitting there in the sleigh with one of the rifles gripped firmly in my hands, and when he sauntered back onto the road I whirled it around, pointing at his chest. He let out a frenzied yell, jumping at least three feet. I calmly put the rifle down and began to remove food from the bags: bread, sausage, cheese, apples. Still shaken, Jeremy gave me a severe, heated lecture about firearms and safety to which I paid not the slightest attention.

The horse munched blissfully on the oats, and we ate our extremely unconventional breakfast. I borrowed the pistol from Jeremy and took a short walk myself, returning a few minutes later to find him curled up under the blankets fast asleep, the black sheepskin hat tilted down over his eyes, his mouth open. Poor darling. Filled with love, I smiled, and then I removed the bag of oats from around the horse's neck and climbed into the sleigh, nudging him over a little. He made an angry, snorting noise, flopping heavily against me as soon as I had pulled the blankets up around my legs. I gathered the reins up and clicked them. Jeremy sank down farther and farther as we started off, finally settling his head in my lap.

The pistol at my side, I held the reins firmly and clicked them occasionally, prompting the horse to trot even faster. We sped through the gray morning. Jeremy moaned now and then and made puffing noises in his sleep, changing positions, wrapping his arms around my legs, his head still resting heavily in my lap. I felt wonderfully maternal, for there was so much of the little boy in this extremely virile man. I stroked his cheek. He snorted irritably. He had so many engaging, endearing quirks. How could I ever have believed I loved anyone else? Now that I had him back, I never intended to let him out of my sight again. How I loved him. How I longed to prove that love with every fiber of my body and soul.

The morning wore on and the sky grew darker still and the shadows spread pale violet across the grayish white snow. My arms began to ache a bit from holding the reins so long. Although it was impossible to tell from the light, I reasoned it must be almost noon. Jeremy had been sleeping four or five hours. I sighed, shifting my position on the seat. The light grew dimmer. The clouds were threatening. I braced myself, determined to let Jeremy sleep for as long as possible. Perhaps another hour and a half passed before I caught a glimpse of the gray shadow bounding through the trees on my right. It was the merest glimpse, so brief I couldn't be sure I had actually seen it, but my blood ran cold nevertheless.

You're not going to panic, I told myself. You're not going to wake Jeremy up. You're going to be very, very calm. It probably wasn't a wolf at all. It was probably just a shadow. My hands were trembling as I gripped the reins, and my legs were trembling, too. I pressed my boots down hard on the floor of the sleigh, trying to steady my legs. Cold waves seemed to wash over me. You must get hold of yourself, I scolded.

I clicked the reins, urging the horse to go faster still, and another fifteen minutes or so passed and I kept watching the woods to my right, and I saw only crusty mounds of grayish white snow and thick tree trunks and pale violet shadows. Jeremy groaned again in his sleep, burrowing his head in my lap, and I began to relax, began to believe I had imagined it all, and then I glimpsed it again. There could be no mistake this time. The wolf leaped from behind a mound of snow and darted behind another mound, disappearing, but not before I saw the long, emaciated body covered with gray fur, the glowing greenish eyes, the lolling tongue. It had been following us all this time, perhaps since early morning, keeping just out of sight, patient, waiting.

Too frightened to think coherently, I clicked the reins frantically, and the horse picked up even more speed and the wide wooden runners spewed crusty showers of snow on either side of the sleigh, and the sleigh rocked and skidded and the wolf kept up, in plain sight now, leaping, loping, edging closer to the road. Although wearing blinders and thankfully unable to see the wolf, the horse sensed my panic and galloped even faster and I saw that I was going to lose control and turn us over if I didn't slow down.

What to do? What to do? In my panic, strange as it may seem, it didn't occur to me to wake Jeremy. We sped down the icy road, thick woods on either side, and my arms felt like they were being pulled out of their sockets and I felt a stabbing pain in my back and knew I couldn't keep up this speed a minute longer. My foot touched the butt of one of the rifles. I knew then what I had to do, it was the only solution. I pulled gently on the reins, slowing the horse down, and from somewhere deep inside I miraculously found some semblance of calm that formed a barrier against the shrieking panic still alive inside.

I slowed the horse down more, even more, and the wolf slowed down, too, moving along at a lazy gait, head turned toward the road, watching with dark greenish eyes, curious, cautious yet utterly brazen. Now, I told myself. I let go of the reins and the horse continued to trot slowly down the road. I reached down to grab the rifle, knocking Jeremy's head out of my lap. The wolf growled, the long body tensing, preparing to leap. Jeremy tumbled to the floor of the sleigh, waking with a start as I swung the rifle into position and saw the wolf leaping, saw it sailing toward me like a gigantic gray arrow.

I pulled the trigger. The impact of the blast knocked me back against the seat, the butt of the rifle kicking painfully against my shoulder. The explosion was deafening, and through the thick puff of smoke I saw the wolf hang suspended in mid air for a second, saw its chest splattering red and slimy pink as the force sent it hurtling backward, crashing to the ground at the edge of the road.

The horse reared, coming to an abrupt halt, and the sleigh skidded violently. I dropped the rifle, trembling all over. Jeremy climbed up off the floor of the sleigh, his face chalky white, his blue eyes full of shock and, it seemed, twice their normal size.

"Jesus Christ!" he yelled.

"I shot it," I said.

"What the hell is going on!"

I pointed. He was standing in the sleigh now, and he turned and looked at the shattered gray heap at the side of the road and saw the crimson pools on the snow and sat down abruptly. Beads of perspiration began to break out on his brow. After a moment he reached down and picked up a canteen, looked at it, put it down, picked up another. Unfastening the top, he took a great gulp, tossing his head back, and then he wiped his mouth and handed the canteen to me.

"Here, you'd better have a swallow."

I gave him a grateful nod and raised the canteen to my lips. I expected water, of course, and as the raw vodka burned the insides of my mouth and scalded my vocal cords and set my chest afire I coughed and spluttered, eyes smarting with tears. Jeremy took the canteen from me and screwed the top on and set it down while I continued to burn and blink the watery tears from my eyes.

"Why—in—hell—didn't you—*wake me up!*" He enunciated the first five words slowly, carefully, ending in a roar.

I couldn't speak. My vocal cords were still on fire. I waved my hand in front of my open mouth, as though to cool the fire, and Jeremy glared at me with blazing blue eyes that were positively murderous. The sleigh shook as the horse pranced skittishly in place.

"You—you're scaring the horse," I whispered hoarsely.

"I could *strangle* you, Marietta! Of all the goddamn foolish, idiotic, imbecilic—letting me sleep when—"

He couldn't go on. His voice started to tremble and he cut himself off and wiped the perspiration from his brow and sat there with a face still several shades whiter than normal. I opened a canteen of water—making bloody certain it *was* water—and took a long swallow and sighed with relief as the burning ceased. Jeremy still looked like a man in shock.

"I—I didn't think about it," I said.

"You—didn't—think—about—it."

He was being very, very patient, and I was beginning to grow just a bit weary of it.

"You were asleep and I saw the wolf, only at first I wasn't sure it *was* a wolf and I didn't see any sense waking you up and then when I saw it again I was so frightened I forgot all about you and drove faster and faster. The wolf kept up with the sleigh and moved closer to the road and I knew it was going to attack and then I placed my foot on the rifle and remembered we *had* the rifles so I just slowed down and shot it."

"You just shot it," he said.

"I'm an excellent shot. You know that."

"What if you'd missed?"

"I didn't, did I?"

"Goddamn, Marietta—"

"Listen, you son of a bitch, I happen to love you with all my heart and soul, but there are times when I'd gladly slap you silly—particularly when you assume that patient, superior air. I am not, nor have I ever been, a weak, defenseless female who turns into jelly at the first sign of danger, and you had better be damned glad I'm not!"

"I am. I am!"

"Do you feel less a man because *I* shot the wolf?"

"I'm *glad* you shot the goddamn wolf!"

"All right, then."

"All right!"

"We're both a little upset," I said.

"Life would have been so much simpler if I'd married Janette Henderson when I was twenty-six years old. She was rich and she was reasonably attractive and her father wanted to take me into the business—he was a coal king in Newcastle, a whole fleet of barges—but no, I wanted adventure, I wanted to live, and, by God, I *did.*"

"You never told me about Janette Henderson."

"So I lived, carefree, independent, one adventure right after the other, and then I had the poor judgment to go to the Colonies and the wretched luck to wind up in New Orleans and just happened to be passing through the old market and you just happened to be there at the same time and I saw you and that was it and I haven't had a single moment's peace since."

"I didn't ask you to fall in love with me. If memory serves, I did everything in my power to discourage you."

"If only you'd been able to," he said grumpily.

"You don't mean that, Jeremy."

"I've aged ten years since that day in New Orleans."

"It doesn't show," I told him. "If anything, you're even better looking. I love you in that black sheepskin coat and hat. You look wonderfully rugged and virile. That red scarf adds a nice touch, too."

"Don't humor me. I'm still upset."

"I know, darling, but it looks like it's going to start snowing any minute now and I think we'd better be on—what—what's that noise?"

"What noise?"

"Behind us. It sounds like—"

Jeremy raised up and turned around and looked behind us and then he told me to hand him one of the rifles. His voice was very, very calm, frighteningly calm, and I turned around too and saw the four enormous wolves slinking toward us on the road behind, not fifty yards away. They moved stealthily, bodies low to the ground, their huge paws thumping softly on the hard-packed snow. That thumping was the noise I had heard.

"They—they often travel in packs," I said in a tight voice. "The wolf I shot was prob—probably the leader."

"Hand me the rifle, Marietta. Then pick up the reins and go. Not too fast."

I gave him the rifle and placed the other two on the seat beside him, and Jeremy got up on his knees, leaning against the seat for support, resting one elbow on the back of the sleigh as he took careful aim. I picked up the reins and clicked them and we began to move, and although my heart was beating rapidly a hard tight core of calm inside kept me steady. The panic was there, too, a live thing inside, shrill and shrieking, but it was contained. Jeremy was depending on me and both our lives depended on our staying calm. I was not going to let him down.

I held the reins firmly, jiggling them, encouraging the horse to move at a steady trot. Not too fast. Not too fast. He had to be able to fire properly and he couldn't afford to miss. I turned my head and looked back and saw that the wolves were no longer ambling behind, they were running now, pursuing us with swift, loose-limbed gaits. One was ahead of the others, gaining on us by the second, eyes glittering bright as it bared sharp fangs and began snarling. Jeremy fired. The lead wolf turned a somersault, spinning in air, scarlet spraying the snow, then hit the ground with a heavy thump.

I turned my attention back to the horse as Jeremy threw the rifle down and grabbed another, positioning himself carefully. Moments passed, and he didn't fire. I glanced back to see that the remaining three wolves had paused to examine the bleeding gray corpse. They began to howl hideously and then deserted the limp body and raced after us again, moving even faster than before in a series of bounding leaps. The sleigh swayed, rocking, and I devoted all my attention to driving. Bloodcurdling howls split the air behind us, and the horse began to panic, racing faster and faster despite my efforts to control him. As the second shot exploded he broke into a mad run, tearing down the road, hoofs pounding, kicking up crusty splinters of snow.

"Slow down!" Jeremy shouted.

"I'm trying!"

"We're going to turn over!"

The ice-encrusted trees seemed to fly past us on either side in a blur of shiny silver-gray and the road was like a huge pale pewter ribbon being ripped out from under us as the sleigh bounced and swayed and skidded wildly. I held the reins tightly, the thin leather curled around my fingers, cutting off circulation, and, half standing, I pulled with a steady motion, afraid to jerk on the reins, afraid the horse would rear. All of my efforts seemed to be futile and the horse sped along down the road and the wooden runners scraped noisily and sprayed snow.

"Jeremy! I—I can't control him!"

"You must! I can't aim properly at this speed!"

"The wolves—"

"They're still coming!"

"Are they—"

"They're twenty yards behind us!"

I redoubled my efforts, praying fervently, pulling firmly, steadily, fingers numb now, my arms burning with pain, my spinal cord feeling as though it might snap. I stumbled, crashing onto my knees on the floor of the sleigh, and I reared back and somehow managed to regain my seat and still hold on to the reins. Jeremy held the third rifle, trying to take aim, and the wolves howled, racing behind us. I closed my eyes and pulled even harder, and a spear seemed to pierce my back and my arms seemed to pull out of their sockets but the pain was unimportant, slowing the horse down was all that mattered.

"Pull, Marietta! Pull!"

"I'm pulling!"

The horse finally responded to the pressure of the bit in its mouth and slowed down and the sleigh stopped swaying and Jeremy was able to take aim. He pulled the trigger but there was no deafening explosion, only a loud click, for the rifle was the one I had fired earlier and there had been no time to reload it and both of us had forgotten that in the excitement. I didn't panic but momentarily lost my senses and let go of the reins and grabbed the pistol at my side and thrust it up to Jeremy. He shouted at me and I tried to grab the reins but they sailed in the air and slashed the horse across the neck and he reared and the sleigh skidded noisily to the left, almost overturning, crashing into the mound of snow at the side of the road.

Jeremy stood up on shaky legs, gripping the pistol, and I saw the furious streak of gray lightning sail through the air, almost upon us, and Jeremy fired the pistol and fell out of the sleigh as the wolf slammed against his body. The wolf was still alive, howling in pain, thrashing, and Jeremy pulled his knife out and slashed and blood gushed and my hands were shaking violently as I grabbed the powder horn and the bag of shot. The last wolf was crouching low, snarling, preparing to spring, and the horse was neighing and trying desperately to break out of its harness as I seized one of the rifles and fumbled with it, trying to get it loaded.

Jeremy had shoved the dead wolf aside and was on his knees on the ice and gripping the bloody knife in his hand. The wolf crouched even lower, exposing horrible fangs, slobbering, eyes burning, and then it sprang into the air as I leaped to my feet and swung the loaded rifle around and pulled the trigger all in one motion, hitting the beast right between the eyes. It fell crashing to the ground and landed approximately two feet from where Jeremy was still kneeling. He stared at it and then turned to look at me standing in the sleigh with tendrils of smoke still curling from the barrel of the rifle. The horse had stopped thrashing about and stood making pathetic whinnying noises. Jeremy shook his head. His face was white. Mine must have been even whiter.

"Nice work," he said shakily.

"I—I didn't think I was going to get it loaded in time."

He wiped the blade of his knife on the fur of the nearest wolf and climbed to his feet and then retrieved the pistol he had dropped when he tumbled out of the sleigh.

"Are—Jeremy, are you all right?"

"Probably bruised as hell. No injuries."

"I've never been so frightened in—"

"Neither have I, love. I don't mind admitting it."

He thrust the pistol into his waistband and retrieved the hat which he had also lost in the fall. I noticed that his hands shook too as he pulled it back over his head. He sauntered over to stroke the horse and calm it down, murmuring soft, reassuring words into its ear, and I put the rifle down and had a moment of dizziness and stubbornly refused to faint. I climbed out of the sleigh, averting my eyes from the bloody corpses on the road. I still felt light-headed, and my knees threatened to buckle. As small tremors swept through me I bit my lower lip, determined not to give way to them, particularly as I had bragged only a short while ago about being so bloody brave and intrepid and not turning into jelly at the first sign of danger.

"Is—is the horse all right?" I asked.

"Still frightened. He'll calm down in a few minutes."

"Good," I said.

And then the blackness swept over me all at once and I felt myself swaying and when I opened my eyes Jeremy was sitting on the snow and his arms were supporting me, holding me against his chest, and my legs were sprawled out, skirts all atangle. He looked concerned, then relieved when he saw my lashes fluttering. I rested my head on his shoulder for a moment as another wave of weakness washed over me. His left arm tightened around me. He stroked my hair with his right hand.

"I—"

"Don't try to talk, love. Just rest for a moment."

"I didn't faint," I murmured.

"No?"

"Just—I haven't had enough to eat and I was weak and—I didn't actually faint. My knees were shaky and—silly, helpless women faint and I'm—"

"You're so blooming brave," he said, "so blooming stub-born and scrappy. I almost fainted myself when I saw you keel over. I barely caught you in time, lost my balance, landed smack on my backside again. It's taken quite a beating of late."

"And it's such a lovely backside—so flat and firm."

"I'm glad you like it. At the moment it's growing numb with cold. Do you think you can stand now?"

I nodded, extremely optimistic, and Jeremy climbed up and pulled me up and held me as my knees wobbled. He helped me back into the sleigh, then gave me a drink of water from one of the canteens, and I began to feel better. The color returned to my cheeks with a warm flush and my head cleared and I felt extremely foolish as he peered at me with tender concern. Foolish, yes, but wonderful as well, as I saw the love in those expressive blue eyes.

"I—I guess I'm not as tough as I thought I was," I said.

"You'll do until something better comes along," he told me, "and the chances of that happening are slim indeed. I really think you ought to have a swallow of vodka, love."

"No, thank you!"

Jeremy smiled and brushed a damp tendril of hair from my temple. "I'm going to give the horse the rest of the water in this canteen, feed it some more oats. We'll rest for a bit before we get started again."

He poured water into his palm and let the horse lap it up, and then, after more oats, presented it with a long orange carrot he'd pulled from one of the food bags. I asked him why he'd brought carrots and he told me that he'd stolen into one of the cook houses in camp with the two cloth bags and simply grabbed everything in sight: carrots, potatoes, apples, onions, cheese, sausage links, dried beef, bread, two chickens.

"Chickens?" I said.

"Cleaned and gutted and frozen solid, love. Still frozen—haven't had a chance to thaw in this weather. I thought we might have an opportunity to cook them over a fire."

"Next time," I said, "steal coffee."

"You're getting grumpy again. Must be feeling better."

"Much better. How's your backside?"

"Flat and firm," he said. "I have it on the best authority. We'd better get started, love, and we'd better get off this main road. There's a back road that runs parallel to it half a mile or so to the west. I'm sure we have nothing to worry about, but there's no sense taking chances."

He was referring to the peasants. Pugachev would most certainly have sent a band of them after us.

"They—they're behind us, aren't they?"

"They undoubtedly left first thing this morning," he said casually, "but we drove all night, made good time, have several hours' head start. They're not going to catch up with us, love."

His voice was confident, his manner unperturbed, but I wondered if he wasn't just trying to keep me from worrying. Before we started off he carefully reloaded all three rifles and the pistol, handing the letter to me, saying I might like to keep it at my side. A few moments later, snugly bundled under the blankets and fur rug, we set off again through the bleak gray afternoon. I was still sore from my exertions with the reins, still shaken from our encounter with the wolves, but I felt strangely serene nevertheless. After the wolves, anything else would seem mild, and with Jeremy at my side I felt I could easily face any danger.

I linked my arm through his, resting my head against his shoulder. It began to snow lightly.

"I—I should never have left you in London, Jeremy," I said quietly. "I don't know if—if I'll ever be able to forgive myself for leaving you in order to—to go to Derek."

"It was something you had to do, Marietta. That's why I let you leave. As long as you *thought* you loved another man, things would never be right between us."

"You were certain I'd come back?"

"Positive."

"I was such a fool—such a fool."

"You were merely confused, love."

"I think I loved you from the very beginning," I told him. "I just didn't know it, and—and when I finally saw what was in my own heart and realized that you were—you were everything to me, I could hardly contain my joy. I kept urging Ogilvy to drive faster, faster so we could reach London that night, and that was when we had the accident."

"The driver was killed, wasn't he?"

I nodded. "And I would probably have died, too, if Orlov hadn't come along when he did. He took me to the inn and fetched a doctor and—and he and Lucie took care of me.

When I was finally well enough to go on to London you weren't there, and—"

And as the snow floated down in soft, lazy flakes I told him how I came to be in Russia, told him everything that had happened, omitting only that night at Count Rostopchin's when I had finally succumbed to Orlov. I told him about Lucie and Bryan, about Catherine and Potemkin and the bargain I had made with Orlov and the part I had played in Lucie's elopement, and the snow was coming down much heavier when I finally reached the part about Orlov's frenzy and his abducting me, bringing me to his country estate.

"He went completely out of his mind, Jeremy. He did nothing but sit in the drawing room, drinking, talking to himself, and then his brothers came and they all went charging off and—"

I told him about Mitya and Grushenka, and my voice began to shake as I told him about my shooting Vladimir on the stairs, about our flight through the woods and what had happened in the clearing. Jeremy was silent, sober, saying nothing for a long time, and then, in a very serious voice, he promised me that we would never be separated again. It was snowing hard now, coming down in fluffy sheets of whirling flakes. Another half an hour must have passed before Jeremy finally turned down the narrow side road that led through the woods. The road was rough and uneven, icy tree limbs hanging low. I was relieved when we reached the back road which, while not much wider, was considerably smoother.

Another hour went by, and with each minute the snow grew thicker, icier, the flakes stinging our cheeks now like tiny insect bites, and I began to remember stories of Russian blizzards and travelers trapped in them and freezing to death. Jeremy was worried, too, though he tried his best not to show it. He gripped the reins, tense, leaning forward on the seat, his mouth tight. I shivered under the blankets. It had turned much colder. A strong wind had come up. My throat was tight as Jeremy urged the horse to plod on through what was fast turning into one of the dreaded blizzards I had heard about.

"We've got to find a place to stop," he said grimly.

"I—I know."

"Lots of hunters in these parts. There's certain to be a hut or a shed or something. Keep your eyes open."

Another thirty minutes passed, and the snow was so bad now the horse could barely move, staggering along as the wind blew and the icy snow stung. Visibility was almost nil, the world a swirling chaos of spinning white, sleet mixing with the snow now, needle sharp. I peered through the pelting curtains, hardly able to see the trees, and I almost missed the hut set back fifty feet from the road. I pulled Jeremy's arm and pointed. He squinted and nodded, looking vastly relieved as he tugged on the reins and turned up the pathway through the trees.

The hut was low and square and made of rough logs, with a sturdy roof and, surprisingly enough, thick glass windows. The logs were coated with ice, giving them a silvery brown sheen, and an enclosed shed was attached to the hut in back. We stopped in front as snow turned to sleet and pelted down in a battering fury. Jeremy leaped out and started unfastening the harness and ordered me to get inside at once. I grabbed the food bags, the pistol, and one of the canteens and, head lowered to avoid the treacherous sleet, hurried toward the door and threw it open, relieved to find it unlocked. I put everything down and ran back out to fetch more items from the sleigh, grabbing up blankets, a rifle and two more canteens, carrying them inside as Jeremy led the horse around the side of the hut.

The sleet was banging against the windows like hail. I found an old oil lamp on a wooden shelf nailed to the wall and lighted it with one of the matches I found in a box beside it. As the circle of light spread, I saw the crude stone fireplace with a large iron pot suspended over it, a pile of wood on the hearth. There was a cot, a wooden chair, an ancient wooden chest painted with stylized orange and blue birds and yellow tulips, now sadly faded, and a shaggy bearskin rug was spread out in front of the fireplace. The bear must have been enormous, I thought, judging from the size of the rug. By the time Jeremy came in with the rest of the things, I had a fire started in the fireplace, and I was examining the chest, delighted to find that it contained four wooden bowls and battered tin spoons and a tiny dish of salt.

Jeremy put the blankets and rifles down and bolted the door, looking thoroughly exhausted. The wind was howling. I was fearful the sleet would break the glass windows.

"It's—rather cozy," I said. "Obviously built by a relatively prosperous hunter or perhaps a bailiff from one of the big estates. We were lucky to find it."

"Lucky indeed," he said wearily. "I was beginning to worry, love. We'd never have made another hour in this storm. I put the horse in the shed, gave him the rest of the oats and spread the fur rug over him. He'll be fine. The floor of the shed is covered with hay."

The fire was blazing now, filling the hut with lovely warmth, and the water I had emptied into the old iron pot was beginning to bubble. I tossed the frozen chickens into it and asked Jeremy for his knife. He handed it to me, a sleepy look in his eyes, and a few minutes later he was curled up on the pile of blankets, fast asleep as I peeled potatoes and carrots and sliced them and tossed them into the pot along with chopped onions. Jeremy was tangled up in the blankets and snorting in his sleep when, two hours later, I gently nudged him with the toe of my boot. He sat up with a start, blinking, looking quite belligerent.

"What! What is it? What's wrong?"

"Nothing's wrong, darling. I just thought you might enjoy a nice bowl of hot stew."

"Stew?" He seemed amazed. "You made stew?"

"I had all the ingredients—even salt. It's delicious. I've sampled it already. Rich, thick broth, lots of chicken and vegetables."

Jeremy rubbed his eyes. "You're a wonder, love. Hot

stew in the middle of the Russian wilderness, in the middle of a blizzard."

"The blizzard's over. It stopped sleeting over an hour ago. It's snowing lightly now. Poor darling, you were so exhausted you dropped right off to sleep."

I had placed more wood on the fire, and the room was extremely warm. I had removed the gray mink cloak some time before, and Jeremy shrugged out of his sheepskin coat. The hat had fallen off in his sleep, and his thick chestnut hair was all atumble. His shirt was moist with perspiration, clinging to his skin. The vivid red scarf tied around his neck was limp. He was still groggy, looking about the room as though not absolutely certain where he was.

"I checked on the horse," I said. "The windowsills outside were covered with icicles. I broke them off and brought them in and melted them, and then I carried water out to the horse. He's cozy as can be. I also refilled all the canteens," I added.

"As I said, you're a wonder—and gorgeous with your hair spilling about your shoulders, in that velvet gown."

"My hair must be a mess, and the gown's quite the worse for wear—it's dreadfully soiled and the hem's torn and—"

"You've never been more beautiful than you are at this moment, love, and I'm beginning to feel extremely amorous."

"You'd better eat," I said. "You need to build up your strength."

"Yes, guess I do. I've got a feelin' I'm going to need *all* my strength."

I smiled and handed him a bowl of stew, a spoon, and a hunk of bread. He ate with gusto, finishing the first bowl before I'd hardly started mine, taking a second bowl, then a third, declaring it sheer ambrosia, the most delicious stew he ever hoped to eat. I told him there was a little left and said he might as well finish it off. He did so readily and then sat nibbling on a piece of cheese as I set bowls, spoons, and pot aside. He watched me with lazy, seductive eyes, looking for all the world like an indolent, rather scruffy pasha as he sat there on the pile of blankets, nibbling the cheese.

"About that gown—" he drawled.

"Yes?"

"I think you'd better take it off. It's warm in here, much too warm for a heavy velvet gown. I'm planning to take off a few things myself."

"It *is* a bit warm," I agreed, playing the game.

He tugged at the red scarf around his neck, planning to whip it off with debonair aplomb, frowning as he fumbled with the knot. I smiled and then sat down on the chair and removed my boots, flexing my naked feet, massaging them for a moment. Jeremy finally got the scarf off and flung it aside and got to his feet. He spread the blankets out over the bearskin rug, one on top of the other, making a deep pallet in front of the fire. He spread my fur cloak over the blankets and stood back, admiring his handiwork.

"Always wanted to make love on silver-gray mink," he remarked.

"It's a lovely idea," I said.

I stood up and lifted my skirts, reaching under them to unfasten the sash that held the money bag in place. Golden coins tinkled as I placed the bag on the chair. Jeremy watched with one brow cocked.

"You should-a let me do that," he drawled.

"I'm sure you would have enjoyed it."

"A lot," he assured me.

"But you're no good at knots, darling."

"I'm good at other things."

"Oh?"

He sauntered over to me and took me into his arms and gave me a long, lazy kiss, his lips lingering over mine as his arms drew me closer still. I put my hand on the back of his neck and stroked it and then ran my fingers through the rich chestnut waves. He made a moaning noise deep in his throat, swinging me around in his arms. I placed my hands on his shoulders and clung to him as the lazy kiss went on and on and I became a prey to those delicious sensations that had never been so sweet. He raised his head and looked into my eyes, his own a deep, deep blue filled with urgent love. I lifted my hand and caressed his cheek and ran the ball of my thumb along the full pink curve of his lower lip. He opened his mouth, took my thumb between his teeth, gently biting down on soft flesh. Honeysweet warmth spread through me, and the back of my knees began to ache. He took my whole thumb into his mouth and sucked on it, and after a few moments I pulled it free and brushed his lips with mine, tenderly expressing the love that trembled inside me.

"I've waited a long, long time for this," he murmured, pulling back and resting his hands on my shoulders.

"So have I," I whispered.

"I've thought about it, dreamed about it."

"And I as well."

He caressed my throat, his thumb exploring the softness. My breasts swelled, nipples hardening, pushing against the silk bodice of my petticoat. Jeremy drew me back to him and reached behind me and began to unfasten the hooks of my gown, and I pressed my thighs against his and felt the hard, swollen proof of his need throbbing beneath its prison of cloth. He fumbled with the hooks and I shook my head and smiled and reached around to undo them myself. I slipped my arms out of the long sleeves and lifted the gown over my head. Dark garnet velvet rustled softly as I let the gown slip to the floor.

Leaving him but a moment, I stepped over to put out the oil lamp, my gray silk skirts billowing like frail petals, making soft music. Shadows filled the room, walls coated a deep blue-gray, soon shimmering with brilliant orange and gold reflections from the fire. Jeremy sat down on the edge of the chair and struggled to get his boots off. I smiled and knelt and clasped heel and toe and pulled, easing off first one, then the other. I stood and stroked the back of his head as he pulled off his stockings. His thick chestnut waves were soft and pliant, silken to the touch. I ran my fingers through them and gently massaged his scalp. He got up and pulled the tail of his shirt out of the waistband and lifted it over his head and let it float to the floor like a frail white ghost in the semidarkness.

Wearing only his breeches, he turned to me, and I placed my fingers under the waistband and slowly began to pull downward. Jeremy moved his hips, assisting me, and I knelt and continued to tug and heavy black cloth slid down over muscular thighs and calves. Jeremy stepped out of the breeches, kicking them aside. He caught hold of my wrists and pulled me up and cradled me in his arms and nuzzled my neck and gently nibbled at my earlobe. I ran my hands over the smooth skin of his back and felt the strong musculature beneath. Each sensation that swept through me was sweeter, stronger than the one before. The firelight flickered and orange-gold patterns shimmered on the shadowy walls and radiance shimmered inside me as Jeremy unfastened my petticoat and lowered the bodice and caressed my breasts, fingers lightly stroking the swelling flesh, palms massaging the taut nipples with a gentle, circular motion. I felt a shock wave of delirious ecstasy as he circled my waist with his arms and bent his head down and covered each breast with fervent kisses. Arching my back and closing my eyes, I reeled in a sea of shattering sensation.

Jeremy caught hold of the petticoat and pushed soft silk down my body, and layers of skirt billowed like gray petals again, fluttering and unfurling as he shoved them to the floor. His hands slid down my legs, firm, strong hands that had the feel of warm, smooth leather, and when I had stepped out of the circle of silk and shoved it aside with my foot, his hands moved back up my calves and clutched my knees and traveled slowly up my thighs, squeezing gently, leisurely exploring every inch of flesh. And when, shuddering, I could take no more torment and swayed, knees buckling, he caught me and held me to him and lifted my hair and kissed the side of my neck, supporting me as I went limp against him. Murmuring tender words, he lifted me up in his arms and carried me over to the pallet and carefully lowered me onto the incredibly soft mink.

Firelight washed over me, warming my skin as I stretched and writhed on the fur, but another warmth glowed inside me as Jeremy stood there with hands resting on his thighs, lazily admiring me with eyes full of smoldering emotion that need not be expressed in words. I raised up and curled my arms around his legs and rested my head against his thighs, and he caught his fingers in my hair and tugged gently, tilting my head back, and I looked up at the glory of him and he smiled and kneeled down and covered my mouth with his, pushing me back onto the fur, climbing atop me, pinioning me with his weight. His tongue slowly slipped into my mouth, the tip making soft jabs, and I wriggled beneath him and wrapped my arms around his back and spread my legs and wrapped them around his, lifting my body up, up in that splendid search that would end in ecstasy.

He placed a palm on either side of me and raised himself up until he could look into my eyes, and I gazed up at that beloved face and saw the smile spread on that wide mouth and saw the love glowing in those vivid blue eyes, love reflected in my own, and that love bound us, a wondrous magic that augmented each sensation and made each touch twice as tormenting. He smiled and, still gazing into my eyes, told me without words all those things I already knew, and I was breathless, enraptured. He parted his lips. His tongue flicked out, the firm pink tip touching the side of his cheek as, tightening his buttocks, he lifted and lowered and made his entry, and as the first sweet shock shuddered through every fiber of my being I cried out, raising, reaching for more.

Slowly, slowly, flesh filled, flesh clasped, flesh caressed flesh, demanding, pressing, probing deep, deeper, deeper still, and a glorious radiance suffused me, shredding senses with its glory. The beauty was beyond endurance, beyond belief, a shimmering, shattering thing that lifted us both into a realm of sheer enchantment rarely reached.

Still we were not there, still we scaled the peak of ecstasy, climbing higher, yet higher, together, as one, the summit soon in sight. I tightened my legs around him and ran my hands over his strong back and finally caught my fingers in his thick chestnut waves and tugged them as he thrust and strained in jubilant quest. We reached the top at last, stunned and shaken, and, breathless, hung suspended for an instant of soul-shredding bliss. His teeth sank into my shoulder and I cried out again as, together, we plummeted into an abyss of joyous oblivion.

Chapter Twenty-Seven

Radiant sunlight gave the snow a brilliant white dazzle and touched the ice with a translucent rainbow glitter. The sky was a pale blue vault, clear and lovely. Never had there been a more beautiful morning, I thought, and never had I welcomed a new day with greater joy. There was a crisp, invigorating chill in the air, but it wasn't nearly as cold as it had been. I had come outside without my cloak, for Jeremy was still asleep inside, using it for cover. Gazing up at the gorgeous blue sky, I folded my arms around my waist as though to embrace the joy that filled me like a glorious tonic. I had come to feed and water the horse and, that accomplished, couldn't help but linger a few moments to savor the dazzle of the day.

A bird celebrated the sunlight from a tree limb nearby, its song a throaty warble embellished with trills, and as I stood in front of the hut a rabbit darted across the snow. I smiled, for no reason, for every reason, for the languorous ache in my bones and blood, for the teeth marks on my shoulder beginning to bruise, for the ashes of aftermath still glowing warmly within. We had made love a second time on the fur, before the fire, rousing and energetic, and much later, as white flakes floated in the brightness beyond, as pale moonlight turned the walls of our haven a soft silver, as logs glowed a rosy pink, turning to ash, he woke and reached for me and we made love yet again, leisurely, lazily, with tender expression that swelled to splen-

554

dor. The smile curved on my lips as I remembered, rejoicing anew.

I breathed the crisp air and sunlight stroked my cheeks and I realized that I had never been as happy as I was at this moment. Happiness, so elusive, so ephemeral, was mine at last, and it was as though I had been in a stupor before, half-awake, half-alive, incomplete. And so I smiled, folding my arms closer around my waist, listening to the bird's silvery song, complete and completely happy. Jeremy was inside, Jeremy my love, and life had sparkle, was now full of splendid promise. A gentle morning breeze ruffled my coppery red locks, blowing wispy skeins across my cheeks. Snow glistened, gilded with sunlight. I had never dreamed that love, true love, could bring such elation, such jubilation.

I had loved Derek Hawke, yes, but that love had been a dark, brooding obsession, fraught with shadow and doubt, a constant torment tearing me asunder. There had been turmoil and tension and tears, never this joy, never this celebration in the soul. I had loved him, yes, but that love had died in the darkness of its own futility, supplanted by the vitality and exuberant splendor of emotions Jeremy had stirred from the very first. Obsessed by that darker love I had fought the new, denied it until, in the carriage, on my way back to London, it had burst upon me like a shining revelation . . . and then fate had intervened.

An accident, a misplaced letter had almost robbed us of our future together, but, miraculously, we had been given a second chance. The happiness I now celebrated was all the more blessed for having almost been denied. As I gazed at the beauty of the morning I knew I was the most fortunate woman alive. All the grief I had endured was but a small price to pay for the joy I now cherished in my heart. I brushed the silky skeins of hair from my cheek and listened as the last notes of birdsong rose in the air.

Inside, sunshine poured through the windows, filling the room with radiant light. I had put more wood on the fire, and it now crackled heartily, flames a lively orange.

Jeremy was still asleep on the pile of blankets, on his back, one arm thrown over his eyes. The gray mink cloak was twisted around his legs, barely covering him, and his bare chest rose and fell with his steady breathing. His mouth was open, and he groaned as I crossed the room and took up his knife and began to slice bread and cheese.

I toasted the bread over the fire, using a long, thin stick I had brought in earlier, and when it was nicely browned on both sides I placed the cheese on top and held the bread high up over the flames until the cheese melted. It was not a splendid breakfast, but it was the best I could do under the circumstances. When the toast was ready, I nudged Jeremy awake and he sat up with a start and glared at me through a mass of waves that had fallen across his brow. He scowled and lay back on his side and pulled the cloak up over his shoulder. Smiling, I jerked the cloak off him and he sat up again and told me in no uncertain terms just what he thought of bothersome females who wouldn't allow a chap to get some much needed sleep.

"You've been sleeping for hours," I informed him.

"Hunh?"

"It's a gorgeous day, Jeremy."

"Just a few more minutes' sleep," he begged. "I can hardly keep my eyes open."

"Here, have some toast."

"Who wants food?" he snarled.

He took a piece of toast and examined it with disdain and then proceeded to eat all four pieces I'd prepared, and then, while I ate an apple, he gnawed a piece of dried beef, hair still spilling over his brow as he sat with knees propped up, quite naked in front of the roaring fire. I finished my apple. He had two more pieces of beef and then, finally full, gazed at me with that smoky, seductive look in his eyes.

"I'd love a cup of coffee," I said wistfully.

"I can think of something I'd love a whole lot more."

"Oh?"

"Come here, why don't you?"

"Really, Jeremy—"

"Did I dream last night? Did it actually happen?"

"It happened," I said. "You were magnificent."

"That was just the beginning," he said. "I was exhausted, worn to a frazzle, but now that I'm all rested and bursting with energy—"

"You'd better get dressed, darling. It's late."

He gazed at the bright sunlight and frowned and reluctantly agreed that amorous dalliance would have to wait. He got up and stretched and kissed me lightly on the tip of my nose, then began to pull on his snug black breeches. I shook out the mink cloak and held it to my cheek for a moment, then put it on and carried the blankets out to the sleigh. The bird was warbling again, merry notes rising in silvery peels. When I went back inside Jeremy had put on his stockings and was pulling on his boots.

"Wonder what time it is," he said idly.

"Well after ten, I should think."

"Jesus! You shouldn't have let me sleep so long, love."

"You needed it," I replied.

"What time did *you* get up?"

"A couple of hours ago. I washed all the things we used last night—I want to leave everything just as we found it— and then I brought some more wood in from the stack by the shed and built the fire and went back out to feed and water the horse."

Jeremy shook his head. "Such industry, so early in the morning! You're amazing."

"I'm glad you appreciate me."

"Oh, I appreciate you, love. I plan to spend the rest of my life appreciating you."

He stood up and pulled on his shirt and tucked the tail into the waistband of his breeches and tied the red scarf around his neck. His hair still tumbled over his brow in untidy locks. I went over to him and smoothed them back, and he curled his arms around my waist and grinned and looked lovingly into my eyes. Without words, we expressed all that was in our hearts, and I knew Jeremy loved me every bit as much as I loved him. Several moments went by before I finally pulled away.

"You'd better bring the horse around and harness him up," I told Jeremy. "I'll bring the rest of the things out."

"Sure hate to leave this place," he drawled.

"So do I, darling, but we've dallied long enough."

He sighed in mock exasperation, pulled the black sheep-skin hat down over his head and put on the bulky coat. I carried the food bags out and put them in the sleigh and returned for the rifles. The horse had a jaunty, energetic gait as Jeremy led him around, chatting to him as though to an old friend. I brought out the last rifle, the pistol, powder horn, and bag of shot, and then I went back inside and put out the fire and straightened up, checking to make sure everything was as we found it. We owed a great debt to the unknown owner of this place. I silently blessed him as I stepped outside and closed the door.

"Ready to go?" Jeremy inquired.

I nodded, and he helped me into the sleigh and climbed up beside me. We were soon on our way, the horse prancing nimbly down the narrow pathway without any encouragement. As we turned onto the road I cast a final look at the squat log hut that had been our haven. I knew I would never forget it, would never forget the rapture we had shared there. Jeremy reached for my hand and squeezed it.

"I feel the same way, love."

"We're so very lucky," I said quietly.

"That we are."

We drove on through the morning, the pale blue sky arching above as clear and smooth as silk, the trees on either side of the road glittering like crystal. The sleet had frozen, forming a shiny white crust. The beauty was stark and icy, rather forbidding, and the silence, broken only by the sound of horse hoofs and skimming wooden runners, was awesome. Jeremy and I might have been the only two people on earth as we covered mile after mile of this beautiful, frozen world without seeing a single sign of human habitation. An hour passed and then another, and the sameness of the scenery began to grow oppressive. I gazed at the icy limbs, longing for a sight of green.

"Texas is going to seem like paradise after this," I said after a while. "I don't care if I never see snow and ice again."

"I understand Russia's quite lovely in springtime and summer—fields of golden wheat, the forest all shady and green, wild poppies blooming under the hedges."

"I don't think I care to wait around to see it."

Jeremy grinned. "Neither do I. By the time spring arrives we should already be in New Orleans, making preparations for our trek on to Texas."

"I—I miss Em dreadfully," I said.

"Want to know something? I think I do, too. Never knew a lass with such a smart mouth, so much sass. Randy has my sympathy."

"He's lucky to have her—even if she does lead him a merry chase. It's going to be so nice to be among friends." My voice was pensive. "It's going to be even nicer having a place of our own, settling down at last."

"Never thought I was the kind of chap to settle down," he replied. "Uh, before I met you," he added hastily.

"Oh?"

"I figure settling down with you will provide all the excitement and adventure one man can handle."

"Is that supposed to be a compliment?" I inquired.

Jeremy grinned. "Take it as you will, love. Life with you is never going to be dull."

"Not as dull as it would have been if you'd married Janette Henderson," I told him.

He looked puzzled. "Who?"

"The coal king's daughter. Newcastle. All that wealth and not unattractive."

"Oh," he said. "Her. Not a patch on you, love. Come to think of it, I never met a woman who *was.*"

He looked at me and grinned his engaging grin, and I maintained a diplomatic silence, fully aware of the vast number of women he had known, attracting them in droves since early youth. Faithless he may have been in the past, but he wouldn't have an opportunity in the future. I intended to see that he had no *desire* to roam. Living with a rogue like Jeremy Bond was not going to be easy, but those quirks and idiosyncrasies were what made him so appealing, so stimulating and exciting. Thinking of that future, I sighed, nestling against his broad shoulder, and, later, I was surprised to open my eyes and find that we had stopped moving. I sat up, still a bit groggy.

"I must have fallen asleep," I said.

"Sure did, love. Slept at least two hours. Thought I'd give the horse a rest, find something to eat. There's not much left in the bags."

"I know."

"A couple of pieces of dried beef—we're out of sausage—half a loaf of bread, a wedge of cheese. Lots of apples and carrots, though. We're going to have to give those to the horse—we're also out of oats."

"What will we do?" I asked.

Jeremy wasn't at all perturbed. "We'll eat what we have, love. I figure there's a village about ten miles or so ahead—I studied several maps of this part of the country before I headed north. Perhaps we'll be able to replenish our supplies there. If not, we'll improvise. I saw lots of rabbits while you were sleeping away. Roasted rabbit's almost as tasty as chicken."

My leg muscles felt cramped, my body stiff, and it was good to get out of the sleigh. I could hear a dozen tiny bones popping as I threw my shoulders back and stretched my arms. Jeremy pulled a bunch of carrots out of the food bag and fed them to the horse as I walked up and down, restoring circulation, crusty snow crunching under my heels. The horse munched noisily, delighted with its lunch. After devouring all the carrots and two apples, it lapped water from Jeremy's palm, then whinnied with pleasure as he stroked its neck and told it what a good boy it was. I thought about Natasha, sad as I remembered her winsome ways.

I ate bread and cheese, letting Jeremy finish the dried beef, insisting I didn't want any. He ate with his customary gusto, lounging against the sleigh with the smelly sheepskin coat flapping open, the hat at a jaunty tilt. I had an apple and gave Jeremy the last chunk of bread. He was so casual, so confident, as though we were picnicking on an English lane instead of finishing the last of our food on a desolate Russian road. I kept glancing back up the road we had traversed, unnerved by the silence and solitude.

"Looking for wolves?" Jeremy asked.

"I—I was just thinking about the men Pugachev must have sent after us," I replied. "I can't help—worrying just a little."

Jeremy reached for an apple. "No need to worry, Marietta," he told me. "If, between us, we can demolish a pack of howling wolves, a handful of inept peasants would be child's play."

"I—suppose you're right."

"I feel safe as houses with a crack shot like you at my side," he added jauntily. "Chap doesn't have to fret when he's got the best there is backing him up."

"Thanks," I said, "but you don't have to humor me."

He took a bite of apple, chewed it and grinned, looking at me with mischievous blue eyes. "Most of the women I've known were a marvel with embroidery and needlepoint, a whiz at watercolors, could play a pretty tune on the harpsichord. You're the first one I've met who can put a bullet between a man's eyes at fifty paces."

"I had to learn to shoot," I said defensively. "It might not be a particularly feminine accomplishment, but it's been a hell of a lot more valuable to me than needlepoint or embroidery."

"How are you at watercolors?"

"Awful, I imagine. I've never attempted one."

"Well, at least you can cook," he said. "I guess I'll keep you."

He tossed the apple core aside, grinned again and adjusted the slant of his hat. I wanted to slap him and I wanted to smile. Instead, I climbed into the sleigh with cool dignity and arranged the blankets over my knees as he swung up beside me. He gathered up the reins, gave them a smart snap and curled his arm around my shoulders as we glided down the road again with the horse moving at a brisk clip. An hour went by, the road straight and white, monotonous, horse hooves clopping, runners sliding smoothly over the icy surface.

"I thought you said there was a village," I said.

"There is. I promise."

"Ten miles or so, you said. Surely we've come that far already."

"Trust me, love."

I observed wryly that most of the trouble in my life had been caused by my trusting men. Jeremy chuckled, exuding jaunty confidence, but as another half hour passed and there was still no sign of human habitation he began to lose some of his aplomb. The pale blue sky and radiant sunlight that had enchanted me this morning seemed to taunt me now, and I longed for some clouds to dim the blinding sparkle. Snug beside him, our bodies close and warm under the blankets, I tormented myself with visions of elaborate meals, savory meats dripping with juice, steaming vegetables, lavish desserts.

"There!" Jeremy exclaimed, pointing.

"I don't see anything."

"A spiral of smoke. The village must be just beyond that curve in the road."

"I still don't see—"

"It's plain as day. I told you we'd find a village, love."

Jeremy slowed the horse down as, five minutes later, we approached the small village in a clearing to the left of the road. The woods surrounding it had been cleared, and twenty or so brownish gray dwellings stood bleakly under the sun, conical roofs crudely thatched, shaggy, discolored sheepskin hanging over doorways. A slightly more sturdy

hut with odd symbols painted over the doorway obviously
housed the village shaman, and there was a larger building that served as storage hut and community cookhouse.
The dwellings formed a circle around a clearing where a
feeble fire burned. Half a dozen children in shabby clothes
huddled around the fire, roasting potatoes on the ends of
long sticks. The village, in the middle of nowhere, had a
desolate, defeated air, like a pile of cinders long burned
out.

"And in St. Petersburg they dine in marble halls," I said
as we drew up near the fire.

"The peasants have a just cause," Jeremy agreed, "but
Pugachev's way isn't the answer. The Empress is trying to
make reforms, I understand, but I imagine it's a long, slow
process."

"Too slow to help these poor people."

The children had run away as we pulled up, their half-
roasted potatoes abandoned in the fire. The village appeared to be deserted then, an uncanny silence prevailing
as Jeremy and I sat in the sleigh in the middle of the clearing, surrounded by the ash-colored huts. Slowly, door flaps
began to lift, faces began to appear, dull eyes staring out at
us. I heard a goat bleating from within one of the huts. The
sound was quickly silenced. The filthy sheepskin flap
hanging over the shaman's door lifted, and a very old man
in a very shabby purple robe stepped out. He had long gray
tresses and a flowing gray beard. His ancient face was
seamed, emaciated, his eyes large and black and filled
with apprehension as he gazed at us. He made no effort to
approach the sleigh, just stood there in front of his hut,
clearly distressed by our arrival.

Several moments passed, and then a tall, gaunt-faced
woman with a knot of black hair fastened at the nape of
her neck stepped outside, clutching a tattered gray shawl
about her. Her blue dress was faded and worn yet her manner was curiously regal. A little girl with stringy flaxen
hair peeked out at us from behind her legs, blue eyes wide
as she stared at us. Others began to appear, hesitant, ner-

vous, until, in a matter of moments, the entire village had come out to examine us with that same apprehension I had seen in the shaman's eyes. No one spoke. No one moved. They stood like mutes, like zombies. There were very few young men among them, mostly women, children, and old men, although one brawny fellow who looked like a blacksmith stood with his arm curled tightly around the shoulders of a thin blonde woman.

"Not exactly friendly," Jeremy remarked. "Not hostile, either. They seem to be afraid of us."

"I—I noticed."

"The old chap in the purple robe seems to be their leader. I'll have a word with him. You stay in the sleigh, Marietta, and—uh—keep the pistol handy, just in case."

Jeremy climbed out of the sleigh and strolled casually over to the shaman, who shook his head and backed away a few paces, indicating that he had nothing to say. Jeremy greeted him amiably and began to question him in a quiet voice. The man who looked like a blacksmith mumbled something to the thin blonde and marched over to join Jeremy and the shaman. The old men followed him until soon the entire male populace stood in front of the shaman's hut. Although their manner was more timorous than threatening, I rested my fingers lightly on the pistol, ready to spring to Jeremy's defense if the need arose. The men began to speak in low, nervous voices. I couldn't distinguish the words from where I sat, but from their expressions and gestures I sensed they were imploring Jeremy to leave the village at once.

The women stood in front of their respective huts, mute, staring at me. A little boy darted from behind his mother's skirts, dashed over to the fire and snatched up the stick that held his potato. He gave me a quick grin before scurrying back to safety. The tall, gaunt-faced woman in tattered gray shawl and worn blue dress frowned, nodded her head decisively and said something to the woman beside her. Her neighbor looked horrified, attempting to restrain her as the woman started toward the sleigh. She moved in a purposeful stride, shawl wrapped close, head held high.

Stopping beside the sleigh, she gazed at me with level brown eyes. Her black hair was streaked with gray, and, though gaunt and lined, her face had strength and a unique kind of beauty.

"I am Johanna," she told me. "The others, they are afraid to speak with you. I am not afraid. You would like tea?"

"I—I would be most grateful," I replied.

"Come. We will go inside my house."

I hesitated a moment, glancing toward the shaman's hut. Jeremy was explaining to the men that we merely wanted to replenish our supplies, that we meant no harm. Confident he was in no danger, I got out of the sleigh, slipping the pistol into the pocket of my cloak. Johanna led the way to her hut as the other women watched in horror, whispering among themselves. She lifted the sheepskin flap and motioned for me to step inside.

An oil lamp burned weakly, shedding a pale yellow light that washed the windowless walls. There was a cot, a chest, two chairs. A tarnished bronze samovar was bubbling, and the goat I had heard bleating earlier stirred nervously, tied to a stake driven into the straw-littered dirt floor. Two pigs and a number of chickens also occupied the place, the former snoozing peacefully, the latter idly pecking in the straw. The little girl with the flaxen hair and wide blue eyes sat contentedly in a corner, stroking a doll made from a corncob. Johanna spoke to her brusquely, and the child laid down her doll, got to her feet, and scurried out of the hut.

"My daughter Kyra," Johanna said. "Please, do sit down."

"Thank you very much."

"I am most fortunate. I own a samovar. I am able to buy tea the last time the trader comes to our village in his gypsy caravan." She poured tea into a thick brown cup and handed it to me. "I am sorry I have no sugar to offer. This I cannot buy. The tea is strong enough?"

"It's wonderful, Johanna. You are very kind."

Johanna scowled, dismissing such a preposterous assumption.

"I know who you are," she said. "You are the English woman, the one with hair the color of flame. Just four hours ago they are here, this Pulaski and seven others, looking for you."

I could feel the color drain from my cheeks. "They—they were here?" I clutched the cup to keep my hands from trembling.

"They search. They question us. They make threats. If we help you, they say, our village will be burned."

"That—that's why the others were afraid," I said.

"They are afraid, yes, but I, Johanna, am not afraid. My husband Ivan, he was the head man in our village, second only to the shaman in authority. Months ago, this man Pulaski comes to recruit for Pugachev. My husband defies him and—and he is killed."

"I—I'm sorry, Johanna."

"The young men of our village, they go with Pulaski. My son Peter, he is only seventeen. He—he goes, too, travels to the Volga, and two months later he is killed in battle."

She stood staring at the bare brown wall, seeing something else in her mind, and the hands at her sides were curled into tight fists.

"One kind of tyranny has been replaced by another," she said. "This I tell my people, but they are like the sheep. Pugachev is a very evil man, I tell them. They are afraid to cross him."

She turned to look at me, her face hard, her eyes determined. "This is why I help you. I hear this man you are with tell our shaman you need food. I, Johanna, will give it to you, half my portion for the month."

"But then—then you and your daughter—"

"We do not go without. I am fortunate. I have the chickens for eggs, the goat for milk. I barter. I trade tea for bread and meat. If necessary I slaughter one of my pigs."

"I have gold, Johanna. You must let me give you—"

"Gold? What use is it to me? You have blankets in your sleigh, I see. If—if it is your desire, you may give me one of them so that my Kyra will not shiver so at night."

"You shall have two of them."

Johanna nodded curtly and told me to finish my tea. When we left the hut a few minutes later, Jeremy was standing by the sleigh, looking extremely discouraged. The villagers stood silently, watching him as though he were some kind of pariah. The shaman was muttering an incantation, his arms waving in the air. Johanna moved with a stern, defiant mien, showing her people that she, at least, was not a sheep, shaming them for their cowardice. The women whispered nervously, the men looked unhappy indeed, but no one tried to stop her when she took our two food bags and carried them into the cookhouse.

"What happened, Marietta?" Jeremy asked. "The men were adamant, refused to give me so much as a crumb, said we must leave the village immediately. How did you convince her to help us?"

As we stood there beside the sleigh, waiting for Johanna to return, I told him all that she had said, and Jeremy listened with a grim expression, drumming the fingers of his left hand on the back of the sleigh.

"They must have guessed we'd take the back road," he told me. "They must have taken shelter during the blizzard, then, as soon as it was over, traveled the rest of the night."

"They—they would have passed right by our hut."

"Before dawn, obviously. Wouldn't have seen it in the dark and in the snow."

"If—if they had—"

"They didn't," he said tersely. "Here comes our friend."

Johanna came toward the sleigh carrying our two bags and a third, smaller bag of rough brown sack filled with oats for the horse. Jeremy took the bags from her and put

them on the floor of the sleigh. I folded two blankets and
handed them to her. Johanna held them against her
breast, her eyes still hard and defiant as the villagers
stared in silent disapproval.

"You must not take this road," she told us. "It is the one
they took. When they do not find you, they will turn back,
and you would run right into them. You must cut through
the woods and return to the main road."

"We can get through the woods with the sleigh?" Jeremy asked.

"A mile or so back down the road, there is a pathway.
You probably did not notice it before. Turn there. The path
should be wide enough for your sleigh. It twists and winds
through the woods but will eventually take you to the
main road."

"I—I don't know how to thank you, Johanna," I said
quietly. "If you hadn't come to our aid—"

"It is a pleasure for me to defy this Pulaski and the demon he serves," she replied. "Go in safety."

Jeremy and I climbed into the sleigh. He arranged the
three remaining blankets and the rug over our knees and
gathered up the reins. We circled around the fire and
turned back onto the road. When I looked back, Johanna
was still standing near the fire, alone in the center of the
clearing, her head held high, her back straight, arms
folded around the blankets more precious to her than gold.
A mere peasant she was, unlettered and living with livestock in a stinking hut, yet one of the most remarkable
women I had ever met. For me, Johanna would always rep-
resent the true spirit of Russia.

We soon located the path she had told us about and
turned into the woods. The pathway was rough, winding
between tree trunks, but we were able to navigate by driving slowly and carefully. Frozen branches hung low, so low
Jeremy had to push them aside, but eventually the pathway grew wider, more like a road. I was depressed, and,
sensing it, Jeremy reached over and squeezed my hand.

"I don't think we have anything to worry about,

Marietta. Once they realize they passed us during the night, once they turn back, we'll already be miles ahead of them on the main road."

"I—I wasn't thinking about that. I was thinking about Johanna."

"We'd have been in a sad plight without her," Jeremy said.

"She lost her husband, her son—all because of Pugachev. How many women have been widowed because of him? How many have lost their sons? It's hard to believe that one man can cause so much grief."

"Pugachev's a man with a mission. He's not concerned with human life."

"Everyone believes he's a madman," I said, "but he isn't, Jeremy. He knows exactly what he's doing. He may adorn himself in barbaric splendor and carry a scepter and pretend he's the reincarnation of Peter III, but every move he makes is carefully calculated."

"I reckon so. The man's a military genius. He's managed to launch one of the most successful campaigns in recent history almost single-handedly, and all the might of the Imperial Army hasn't been able to put him down. They've underestimated him from the first."

"He plans to take St. Petersburg before the month is out."

"Not much likelihood of that. He hasn't nearly enough men, and as soon as we get to St. Petersburg I intend to give the army a detailed map showing them exactly how to reach his secret camp."

"He has more men joining him," I said, "three different groups, thousands of men."

Jeremy was silent for a moment, concentrating on the reins, the road, a deep crease between his brows. I could see that my last words had disturbed him. When he spoke, his voice was casual, much too casual.

"How do you know this, Marietta?"

"He told me—when I was in his tent."

"I see. Uh—what else did he tell you?"

"He told me they'd be joining him within the next ten days. That's why he's remained in one place so long—he's been waiting for the others. He's had his men strike at random all over this part of the country, first in one spot, then another, fifty miles away, deliberately confusing the army. Catherine's men are scattered about in small battalions, searching for his camp. When the others join him, Pugachev will have a mighty force—"

"And before the Imperial Army can regroup, he'll march on the capital," Jeremy said. "I told you the man was a military genius."

Jeremy manipulated the reins, guiding the horse between icy tree trunks, and when the pathway straightened out, he turned to me, his expression grave. I felt a terrible foreboding.

"You realize what this means, don't you?" he asked. His voice was level. "You realize how important this information is?"

"I—I didn't before, not really. I—yes, I suppose I do."

He said nothing more. It was with a sinking heart that I realized that the fate of thousands, of the entire country, might rest on this information we had, that delivering it to the proper authorities was much more important than our individual safety. I knew Jeremy, knew the kind of man he was, and the sense of foreboding grew as we continued to drive through the icy woods. And only this morning I had been filled with such joy, celebrating the happiness that . . . that might now be taken from me. Perhaps I was wrong. Perhaps he would wait until we reached St. Petersburg to notify the government and not become personally involved. It was a small hope. I clung to it as the silence continued, as Jeremy frowned, immersed in thought.

After what seemed an eternity, we reached the main road and turned onto it, leaving the woods behind. Jeremy urged the horse to trot faster, clicking the reins smartly. He still didn't speak, was still immersed in thought. He might have been alone in the sleigh, seemed to have forgotten me completely. I understood, but that didn't make it any easier. We sped along, and I stared at ice and snow, disturbed, depressed, trying to control the emotional storm growing inside. I wasn't going to give way. I was going to accept whatever came. I wasn't going to cry and . . . and make it even more difficult for him.

I have no idea how much time passed before I felt him tense and saw his strong, capable hands tugging on the reins, guiding the horse to the side of the road. Perhaps sixty yards ahead of us, the road made a wide curve, disappearing beyond the trees. Jeremy's face was hard as he stopped the sleigh and picked up one of the rifles.

"What—Jeremy, what is it?"

"Get out of the sleigh," he ordered. "Get behind it. Here, take this rifle."

"But—"

"Do as I say, Marietta!"

I climbed out of the sleigh and took the rifle, and as he joined me behind the sleigh with the other two rifles, I heard the horses, hooves pounding on the road, beyond the curve, the riders still out of sight. They must have cut through the woods themselves, I thought. Instead of turning around and heading back toward Johanna's village, Pulaski and the others had decided to cut through the woods and search for us on the main road. Jeremy didn't have to tell me what to do. Gripping the rifle firmly, aiming it at the spot where the road curved abruptly, I waited, curiously calm, curiously resigned.

"There are only eight of them," he said. "They won't be expecting anything like this. I love you, Marietta."

"I—I love you, too."

The pounding of horse hooves grew louder, louder, much too loud for only eight riders, I thought. It sounded like a whole battalion. Beside me, his body poised, his blue eyes full of lethal determination, Jeremy waited, finger curled on the trigger of his rifle, shot bag and powder horn at hand. The black sheepskin coat hanging open, the red scarf flaring, hat pulled low over his brow, he was in perfect control. Tightening my finger on the trigger, staring down the length of the barrel, waiting, I wondered if these were the last moments we would ever spend together. I prayed silently as horse hooves thundered, and then the first riders came around the curve and charged toward us.

"Thank God," I whispered. "Oh, thank God—"

I put down my rifle and started to tremble, and Jeremy put his down too and curled his arm around my shoulders as more and more soldiers came around the curve, black boots shining, white breeches snug, scarlet tunics vivid in the sunlight, gold epaulettes shimmering. Orders were barked out in a rough voice and the whole platoon halted. Soldiers dismounted rapidly, rushing toward us with sabres drawn. In moments we were completely surrounded, blades glittering, faces hostile, dark with suspicion. Our rifles were seized. We were bombarded with questions. Confusion prevailed as harsh voices babbled, as sabres waved threateningly, slicing the air around us. It was only natural they be so hostile, I told myself—they round a curve and find two people crouched behind a sleigh, rifles aimed at them—but what if they didn't accept our story? Catherine's army wasn't noted for its compassion.

They seemed ready to cut us to ribbons.

Amidst the chaos and confusion, Jeremy tried his best to explain who we were, why we were here, but his voice was drowned out by the babble and his Russian really wasn't up to it. He kept making horrendous errors, kept forgetting words. They were going to kill us! I stared at the belligerent faces. I shook my head. The hood fell back, uncovering my hair, and one voice rose louder than the others, laced with harsh authority. The soldiers fell back. The man who had shouted the order stepped forward, and his face seemed vaguely familiar. He was very tall, very stern, with silver-gray hair and steel gray eyes and lean, hawklike features.

"Miss Danver," he said. "Captain Khitrov. I dined at the Marble Palace six weeks ago with you and Count Orlov."

"Cap—Captain Khitrov—yes, yes, I remember now. You were with Countess Golovkin. I—I'm so glad to see you. Your men—"

"You can imagine our dismay when we came round the bend and saw the two of you aiming rifles at us. I apologize for the misunderstanding. I didn't recognize you until I saw your hair."

"We—we thought you were peasants. We've been—"

I cut myself short, too distraught, too relieved to go on. Captain Khitrov was all courtesy and suggested I sit down in the sleigh and ordered one of his men to bring some brandy and Jeremy helped me into the sleigh and began to talk with Captain Khitrov in a low voice, leading him away so that I wouldn't overhear. A soldier handed me a small crystal glass with a golden rim and I sipped the exquisite brandy as horses whinnied and soldiers milled about and Jeremy and Khitrov stood talking across the road, their faces grim indeed. Several long minutes passed. I finished my brandy. Khitrov nodded his head in agreement to something Jeremy had said and then went to speak to his men. Jeremy came over to the sleigh then, and I knew. Before he spoke, I knew, and a bright world vanished for me, a dream died.

"You're going with them," I said.

"I must, love. I'm the only one who knows where the camp is. Khitrov is sending men off to contact the various battalions scattered about. They will all assemble at a designated place, and then we'll hit Pugachev's camp and find out about the other three groups and head them off."

"I see," I said. My voice sounded strangely hollow.

"He's dispatching a group to round up Pulaski and his men immediately. Ten of his best soldiers are going to take you on to St. Petersburg, to the British embassy. You'll be perfectly safe."

"And you? Will you be perfectly safe? There'll be battles and bloodshed and—oh, Jeremy."

"It's something I have to do, Marietta. You know that."

"Yes, I know. I understand."

"Time is of the essence. We can't afford to lose a single day."

"I understand, Jeremy."

He took both my hands and held them tight and looked into my eyes, and I held back the tears and put on a brave face and felt my heart breaking.

"Soon," he promised. "Soon it will all be over."

I nodded, and there was much activity as men rode off on their various missions and others assembled. Jeremy and Khirov conferred again and Jeremy came back to kiss me goodbye and then swung himself up onto a horse Khirov provided. An amiable, strapping soldier climbed into the sleigh beside me and took up the reins and nine horsemen assembled around us as he pulled into the middle of the road, their saddlebags heavy with provisions. Jeremy nodded at me as we started down the road, toward the curve.

Goodbye, my darling, I said silently. I didn't look back. There was no point. The dream was over.

Chapter Twenty-Eight

VANYA HAD COME TO VISIT ME SEVERAL TIMES
during the past three and a half weeks, and I was sad as I
realized this would be his last visit, that tomorrow he
would be leaving for Moscow where he would join the personal guard of a nobleman. His new job would be much like
the old, but Count Solveytchik was in his sixties and
known for his conservatism and compassion, as unlike
Orlov as a man could be. I was glad Vanya had found employment that pleased him, glad, too, that his shoulder
wound was finally completely healed and he no longer had
his arm in a sling. We stood in the courtyard of the British
embassy now, the day so bright and sunny I had come out
without a cloak, wearing one of the simple frocks I had
bought soon after I arrived. Snow and ice were beginning
to melt everywhere. Spring was definitely in the air.

Natasha whinnied, arching her neck, looking at me with
large, luminous eyes full of affection. I curled my arms
around her neck and rested my cheek against her silky
skin. Three nights ago, as soon as his arm was out of the
sling, Vanya had slipped into the Orlov stables in the dead
of night, stealing the mare he felt rightfully belonged to
him, and Natasha would be going along to Moscow with
him. I was relieved to know she would have a gentle, loving master and receive gentle, loving care. I hugged her,
rubbing her cheek with mine, and Natasha let out another
ecstatic whinny, tapping one hoof on the pavement.

"She will miss you," Vanya said.

"And I will miss her—and you, Vanya."

The cossack scowled, looking quite savage in his scuffed black boots, baggy brown trousers and belted brown jacket with full skirt hemmed with gray fur. A wide-brimmed gray fur hat slanted atop his head, and a long sabre dangled from his belt. His fierce demeanor couldn't quite conceal the unmanly emotions inside. Scowl he might, but his eyes were perilously tender as I squeezed his hand. He had been badly wounded the night he helped Lucie elope with Bryan, but friends had taken him in, had fetched a doctor and tended to him during the following weeks. When he learned Orlov had taken me to his estate in the north, Vanya had been full of anxiety and had planned to come for me as soon as it was physically possible. Hearing I had returned to St. Petersburg and was safely domiciled at the British embassy, he had been vastly relieved, making the first of many visits.

"They have been good to you here?" he asked gruffly, implying he was ready to lay waste with his sabre were that not the case.

"Sir Reginald has been very kind—so have most of the others. Some of the wives still consider me a bold, reckless adventuress and look the other way when I pass them in the foyer, but I'm quite used to that sort of thing. I fear I've never been quite respectable as far as the good ladies are concerned."

"Vanya will scare them with his sabre!"

I smiled, amused at the vision of Vanya running through the halls of the embassy with half a dozen pompous, officious wives shrieking ahead of him, taffeta skirts flying. My lengthy visits in the courtyard with "that barbarous ruffian" caused their tongues to clatter all the more. I would have enjoyed taking him upstairs to my humble but comfortable rooms on the third floor, but Vanya had refused to come inside the embassy, deeming it "unseemly." He was far more concerned about my reputation than I.

"Oh," I said, "I meant to tell you earlier—Sir Reginald

received a letter from Bryan this morning. It arrived in the diplomatic pouch. Bryan has almost finished his new play. Lucie is studying acting with a marvelous coach who is thrilled with the progress she's making. They've just purchased a small town house in London."

"This is good to hear," Vanya said. "The necklace you give them makes it possible for them to live most comfortably."

"I'm very happy for them," I said pensively.

Vanya scrutinized me with fierce brown eyes. "And you?" he asked. "It is going to end happily for you, too? Pugachev has been captured and taken to Moscow in a steel cage. His followers have been routed. Most of the soldiers have returned to St. Petersburg. The Englishman—he comes with them?"

"He returned to St. Petersburg three days ago," I replied, "but—I haven't seen him."

I gazed across the sun-washed courtyard. The huge wrought-iron gates stood open. A carriage came through and pulled up in front of the embassy steps. Two women climbed out, chatting busily, their arms laden with packages after a shopping spree on the Nevsky Prospekt. Vanya frowned as the carriage drove away.

"He does not come to see you? Something is wrong?"

"It seems his presence is required at the Winter Palace for—for some kind of military talks. He sent word to me as soon as he arrived, but his note wasn't very specific. That was three days ago. I—I haven't heard from him since."

"This is quite understandable," Vanya told me. "He plays a very important part in capturing Pugachev. It is natural the government would wish to confer with him. He will come to you as soon as he can. Of this I am certain."

"I suppose you're right. It's just—just been difficult. I'm not terribly good at waiting."

"It will all turn out well," he said. His voice was gentle and reassuring. "Your man will come to you and you will leave Russia and go to this land you are eager to see again.

Vanya will think of you often when he is in Moscow, serving Count Solveytchik. I have something for you."

He opened the saddle bag and pulled out a pair of beige leather boots lined with soft beige fur, almost identical to the pair he had "loaned" me months ago on the road to St. Petersburg. Brusquely, he handed them to me.

"I bring you these. I know you lose the other pair. You wear them in Texas sometime and think of Vanya."

"I—oh, Vanya, I think I may cry."

"You wear the boots. You think of Vanya back in Russia. If you wish, you might one day write a letter to let me know how you are. You could send it care of Count Solveytchik in Moscow. He would see that I get it."

"I will, Vanya. I promise."

"I am almost glad I have the small, dainty feet," he said gruffly. "They bring us together. I must go now. I must pack and make preparations to leave. Be happy, Marietta."

He scowled and looked very fierce, and then he folded me to him in a tight, rib-cracking hug, released me, and swung nimbly up into the saddle. Natasha whinnied again. I gave her a final pat and fought back the tears as the gentle cossack who had befriended me rode smartly out of the courtyard. Holding the beautiful boots, I let the tears trickle down my cheeks, and several minutes went by before I was composed enough to go back inside.

Lady Clark, Lady Jamison, Mrs. Brown and two other highly respectable wives were talking in the large reception hall with its comfortable furniture, flowered rugs and profusion of potted plants. They fell silent as I moved past on my way to the staircase, all of them staring, mentally recoiling at having such a notorious creature in their midst. I heard a buzz of malicious whispering as I started up the staircase, but I paid it no mind. Grateful for the service I had done his son, Sir Reginald had been kindness itself to me, as had the Ambassador, and I had been given the small but comfortable rooms Bryan had occupied when he was staying at the embassy.

Climbing the second flight of stairs that led up to the third floor, I went down the hall and into my sitting room, closing the door behind me. The pale blue wallpaper was faded, the pink and blue rugs were shabby, and the small white marble fireplace was streaked gray with soot, but sunlight slanted through the windows and the room had a pleasant atmosphere. I set the boots down, stepping over to the window to gaze out at the city. Past rooftops, past trees, I could see the Winter Palace in the distance, majestically silhouetted against the light blue sky. How long would he be there? Couldn't he have stolen time from his important conferences to come see me just once? Were they keeping him occupied all night as well? I had been distraught, angry, resentful, tearful, sad, going through a whole bevy of conflicting emotions when I received his message, and now I felt utterly weary.

The weeks of waiting for word had been sheer hell. Not knowing whether he was alive or dead, not knowing what was happening had been a perpetual torment, followed by incredible relief when word finally arrived that Jeremy was alive, that Pugachev had been captured, the peasants put to rout, the rebellion finally, completely crushed. Pugachev had indeed been carried to Moscow in a steel cage, and, in a generous display of clemency, Catherine had ordered that he be mercifully executed at once without undergoing any of the horrible tortures her predecessors would have made him endure. It was over now . . . and I was still alone.

Sighing heavily, I turned away from the window and sat down in the shabby, overstuffed blue chair and tried to read the novel one of the friendlier embassy wives had loaned me. *The Vicar of Wakefield* was delightful and Oliver Goldsmith a most engaging writer, but I found it impossible to concentrate this afternoon. Setting the book aside, I watched dust motes whirl lazily in the bars of sunlight, watched the pools of light spreading across the floor, and half an hour later I heard the footsteps pounding in the hall. The door flew open, banging back against the wall. I leaped up with a start. Jeremy grinned at me and strode into the room, exuding energy and robust vitality that seemed to crackle in the air about him.

He was wearing white leather boots, snug white breeches and a form, fitting white tunic festooned with gold braid, gold epaulettes shimmering at his shoulders. He looked marvelously, outrageously handsome in the uniform which I recognized as that of Catherine's most renowned regiment. A long sabre dangled at his side, its scabbard of beaten gold. Grinning broadly, he turned around slowly so that I might fully appreciate his splendor.

"What do you think?" he inquired.

"I think it's about time!" I snapped. "Three whole days and not a single word. I've been worried sick!"

"The uniform, Marietta. What do you think of it? I'm a captain! Catherine wanted to make me a count, too, but I told her I wouldn't have much use for the title in Texas."

"Where have you *been* all this time?"

"At the palace. Very important conferences. Had to tell 'em everything I knew, had to sit through a lot of dreary claptrap, hold boring powwows with a lot of prissy generals. Seems I'm a hero. Seems my ideas on military defenses and such mean a lot. Thought I'd never get away. Actually, I have to go back right away."

"Go back!"

"Just for three or four hours, love, then I'll come back and get you. I'm to receive a medal tonight. There's to be a reception at the palace, and Catherine insisted I bring you."

"Catherine?"

"The Empress is very grateful to you. The whole country's grateful to you. If you hadn't talked to Pugachev and gotten that information from him, he might be sitting on the throne this very minute."

"A reception? At the Winter Palace? I couldn't possibly go."

"You've got to, love."

"In this?" I inquired, indicating my simple blue frock. "This happens to be the nicest thing I bought. It's hardly suitable for a reception at the Winter Palace."

"Catherine thought about that," he told me.

"Catherine?"

He was bandying that name about a bit too freely to suit me.

"I told her you'd lost all your clothes, and she ordered her dressmaker to make something for you—woman's been driving her poor staff crazy for the past two days, I understand, but the gown's finished. Should be delivered any minute now."

"Wonderful," I said dryly.

"She's also sending over a hairdresser, some Frenchman."

"Not Monsieur André?"

"Believe that *was* the name."

"Oh God," I groaned.

"I must say, love—you're not very enthusiastic about all this."

"That's putting it mildly."

"Don't you want to see me receive my medal?"

"I don't give a *damn* about your medal! I don't see you for almost a month and I sit here in this room wringing my hands, worrying myself sick, wondering if you're dead or alive and going through *hell* and then you come back and send me a cryptic note and three more days go by and I start wringing my hands again and—"

"There's no need to get excited, Marietta."

"—and then you come swaggering in wearing that utterly preposterous uniform and start babbling about being the Savior of Russia and—and it's "Catherine this" and "Catherine that" and you expect me to—to start leaping about like a trained poodle and get ready for a grand reception at the Winter Palace and wear a gown I haven't laid eyes on and—you can go straight to hell, Mister Bond, and you can go to your bloody reception alone!"

"Feel better now?" he asked casually.

"I certainly do!"

"You wouldn't miss it for the world," he said.

"You're damned right I wouldn't."

"We're leaving Russia first thing tomorrow morning," he told me. "Ship's sailing at dawn, in fact. All the arrangements have been made. There won't be time to come back here after the reception, so you'll have to pack and have everything ready—a servant will stop by the embassy and pick up our trunks, deliver them to the ship."

"Anything else?" I inquired.

"Guess that's about it, love. Oh yes—" He snapped his fingers, suddenly remembering something. "Damn. I must have left 'em in the carriage. Be right back."

He dashed out of the room and I tapped my foot impatiently, and a few minutes later he came tearing back in with cheeks flushed pink and vivid blue eyes flashing and rich chestnut wave spilling untidily over his brow. He grinned at me and held out a long, large jeweler's box covered in midnight blue velvet, a silver clasp fastening it shut.

"*Your* medal," he said. "Actually, it's not a medal, but Catherine felt you deserved a reward for the part you played in Pugachev's capture and so she had a chap named Maitlev trot some of his wares over to the palace and she selected a few trinkets she thought you'd fancy."

"But I couldn't—"

"Open the bloody box, Marietta."

I opened the box. The blaze of diamonds nestling on dark blue velvet was blinding. There was a magnificent necklace with tiers of diamond pendants suspending from looped diamond strands, a pair of diamond pendant earrings, eighteen silver hairpins studded with immense diamonds. The gems shimmered with a thousand brilliant fires, vibrantly aglow. I stared at them, amazed, and then I closed the box and set it aside.

"You have to accept them," Jeremy told me. "You earned them, Marietta, and to refuse them would be a personal insult to the Empress, an insult to all Russia."

"I don't intend to insult anyone," I told him. "I may often act a fool, but I'm not a complete idiot."

Jeremy grinned, relieved, then glanced at the clock, said he had to dash, said he'd pick me up at eight and made a hasty departure, the sabre clattering as he darted out. I frowned and stepped back over to the window and a few moments later saw him cross the courtyard and climb into a sumptuous white carriage trimmed with gold, a gold Imperial Eagle on the door. The driver snapped the reins and the four white horses trotted through the gates, long white ostrich plumes waving from the gold bands about their heads. It seemed Jeremy had done quite well for himself these past three days, I mused, and then I realized the bastard hadn't even kissed me. It was a good thing we were leaving in the morning, lest all this attention turn his head completely.

Sighing, I went into the bedroom and began to pack, using the trunk I had purchased when I returned to St. Petersburg. I carefully folded my gray mink cloak—I had taken it to a furrier on the Nevsky Prospekt who had cleaned it and restored it to its former glory. The garnet velvet gown had been cleaned and mended as well. I put it in beside the cloak and then put in the clothes I had recently bought and the boots Vanya had given me. The improvised money belt with its treasure of gold coins was already safely tucked away in a tiny secret compartment.

I had scarcely finished packing when two footmen in royal livery arrived laden with elegant cream and gold boxes containing my gown, petticoat, stockings, and shoes. I had them place the boxes on the bed, thanked them politely and, when they had gone, went to make arrangements for a bath. I bathed leisurely, using an entire bar of soap, washed my hair thoroughly and toweled it dry. I was at my dressing table, wearing the exquisite pale champagne petticoat with its gauzy layers of skirt, when Monsieur André arrived with brushes, combs, tongs, pots, jars, pins, and an inexhaustible fund of gossip with which he regaled me during the next hour as he worked with my hair.

I was ready to scream when he finally stepped back, waved his hands dramatically and told me he had surpassed himself.

He had indeed worked wonders, arranging the coppery red waves in a beautifully sculpted pile atop my head, leaving a few long, full ringlets to dangle between my shoulder blades. He had affixed all eighteen of the new hairpins, and eighteen diamonds glittered, scattered at random about the coiffure with a stunning effect. Monsieur André had brought cosmetics as well, and he fussed and fidgeted as I applied my usual subtle makeup. Disappointed I wouldn't let him use any of the beauty marks or heavy powder on my face, he insisted on selecting my perfume himself. I was satisfied with the delicate yet exotic teak and tiger lily fragrance he chose and, as a reward, permitted him to help me into the gown.

Although it was created in just two days, the gown was as magnificent as any of those Orlov had ordered for me, perhaps even finer. Made of pale, creamy champagne brocade embroidered with tiny bronze and gold flowers, it had narrow, off-the-shoulder puffed sleeves and a low-cut bodice that accentuated my breasts and slender waist. The extremely full skirt parted in two puffed scallop panels in front to reveal an underskirt of row upon row of cream lace ruffles. The fit was perfect, the brocade rich and luxuriant, the lace exquisite. Monsieur André went into raptures of delight, and I thought he might actually expire when I put on the diamond earrings and the fabulous diamond necklace.

"Oh, to be there tonight!" he cried. "To see them react when you enter the room! The women will all want to kill you, of course, and their husbands and lovers will want to bed you then and there."

"It could be a very interesting evening," I said.

"Never, never have I seen anything more gorgeous! My coiffure is a masterpiece, and so is the gown. You *could* use a spot more makeup—a black satin beauty mark on one of those glorious high cheekbones would be perfection. Even without it you're a veritable vision!"

"Thank you, Monsieur André."

He lifted the last garment out of its box, an elegant cloak of cream brocade bordered and lined with champagne-colored mink. Draping it carefully around my shoulders, fastening it, Monsieur André told me it was the crowning touch—that pale mink, that rich cream brocade, he had never seen a finer cloak. Impatient but polite, I thanked him for his help, and he reluctantly gathered up his paraphernalia and left, blowing me a kiss as he went out the door. I looked at myself in the mirror and admitted that I did indeed look rather nice, and then I stepped into the sitting room to wait for Jeremy, eager to see his reaction to my splendor.

There was none.

"You all packed?" he inquired when he arrived a short while later.

"My trunk is in the bedroom," I replied, fuming.

"A footman will be here to collect it in a couple of hours."

"Fine," I said frostily.

"By the way," he said, "you look absolutely stunning."

"I'm surprised you noticed."

"I noticed," he said, grinning. "Look, I have a suggestion. Why don't we forget about this bloody reception? Why don't I just remove those stupendously beautiful clothes you're wearing and make mad, passionate love to you for the next eight hours?"

"It's an idea," I said. "What about your medal?"

"Who needs it?"

He knew how to rile me, the rogue, and he loved to tease, and I shook my head, amused, exasperated, elated. Jeremy grinned and gazed at me and when I saw the bulge in his snug white breeches I suspected that his suggestion hadn't been made entirely in jest. I smiled and touched his lean cheek and told him the Empress would be terribly distressed if we didn't show up and he said "Who cares?" and I said self-control was an admirable trait and he sighed and said I was no damn fun and I felt absolutely glorious.

He led me downstairs, looking resplendent himself in his uniform and the short white military cape lined with cloth of gold. Lady Clark, Lady Jamison, Mrs. Brown and the others were gathered in the reception hall, buzzing about the royal carriage at the door and the dashingly handsome man who had gone upstairs a few minutes earlier. When they saw the same man come back down with me on his arm, they fell silent, gaping unashamedly at my gown, my cloak, the dazzling array of diamonds. I longed to emulate Monsieur André and blow them a kiss, but dignity prevailed and I gave them a cool nod instead, savoring my triumph as Jeremy led me out to the carriage.

It was a lovely night, the sky a deep, velvety black spangled with stars that seemed to twinkle on and off. St. Petersburg was bathed in moonlight as we drove toward the palace, all soft silver and shadow, and the beauty of the city had never been more apparent. Jeremy sat across from me, my skirts much too wide to enable him to sit beside me, and in the pale light coming through the windows I saw his lazy smile and the love in his eyes and felt his pride, his joy. What had I done to deserve a man like this? Was it really possible to be so happy?

"Grand carriage, isn't it?" he said. "A bit more comfortable than that open sleigh we shared."

"Considerably more comfortable."

"By the way, love, Johanna is coming to St. Petersburg."

"Johanna?" I was startled.

"I told the Empress about her, and Catherine's giving her a small house, giving her a pension, and her daughter will be enrolled in a very good school here in the city."

"That—that's wonderful," I said.

"Catherine's investigating the possibility of helping all the women widowed by the rebellion. Her ministers are tearing their hair out, complaining about costs, but she pointed out that it would be considerably less expensive than the new Palace of Justice currently in the planning stage."

"She truly does have the interest of all her people at heart."

"Yes," he agreed. "She's a remarkable woman."

"Just how well did you get to know her?" I asked, suspicious.

"Oh, we chatted a couple of times. She was present at a couple of meetings."

"I see," I said.

"Here we are," he observed. Was that relief in his voice?

The carriage stopped in front of the Winter Palace, and a footman opened the door for us. Jeremy alighted and turned to help me down. My skirts made a silky sound, rustling quietly. Handsomely liveried footmen holding torches lined the wide marble steps. Jeremy took my hand and led me up the steps. A footman took my cloak inside, Jeremy refusing to surrender the short, dashing cape. He was confident, almost cocky as we followed a footman along the marble halls, not at all awed by the magnificent splendor, as at ease here as he would have been on the open plain. And when the chamberlain announced us and we entered the reception hall filled with glittering, gorgeously attired people, he might have been entering a tavern filled with old drinking mates.

"Quite a mob," he remarked. "I'm the guest of honor, by the way."

"How nice for you," I said dryly.

He smiled and nodded amiably at first one person, then another, and I observed that he seemed to have made quite a number of acquaintances during the past three days. I began to suspect that he hadn't spent nearly as much time in conferences as he had implied, and I began to fume silently when I saw how obsequious everyone was toward him. Their attitude toward me was considerably more ambivalent. I was here, yes, and on the arm of the hero of the day, but after the Potemkin–red room incident which, of course, was altogether too delicious to remain secret in this beehive of gossips, I had been *persona non grata* at court. Should they acknowledge my presence by more than a cool nod? Should they speak to me? They kept their distance until, finally, The Tester sauntered over to us, looking particularly sultry and opulent in a black velvet gown with scarlet panels, a small fortune in diamonds and rubies adorning her throat and wrists.

"It's lovely to see you again, darling," Protasova said. "Let me steal you away from this gorgeous man for a few minutes. I'm dying to talk and you look like you could use a glass of champagne.".

"I certainly could."

As Protasova led me across the room, the others relaxed visibly. If the Empress's chief lady-in-waiting sought me out, I must be *grata* again. Dozens of smiles flashed at me as Protasova motioned to a footman and plucked two glasses from the tray he brought over. An amazingly handsome young lieutenant with dark bronze hair and moody blue eyes joined us, his tight-fitting uniform obviously tailored to accentuate his lean, athletic build. Protasova gave a weary sigh and told him to go wash behind his ears.

"They get younger all the time," she said, "and I, alas, begin to feel older and older. Not that I don't still enjoy my work," she added.

"A new testee?" I inquired. "What happened to young Peter?"

"He failed the test," she replied. "In fact, he ran off with Countess Zavadovsky, she of the frilly pink gown and high-pitched giggles. It caused a minor scandal but no great loss."

I took a sip of my champagne, glancing across the room. Jeremy was surrounded by people, quite the center of attention and savoring every minute of it. Less than enchanted, I finished the champagne and set the glass aside, a flush tinting my cheeks.

"Your Mr. Bond *has* caused quite a sensation," Protasova remarked, observing my ire, "but he'll be all yours tomorrow, darling."

"If he lives," I snapped.

Protasova laughed huskily. "Incidentally," she said, "Potemkin departed for Moscow this morning."

"I'm relieved to hear it."

"His departure ten hours before your reappearance at court was no coincidence, believe me. The Empress has forgiven him, but she's taking no chances. I suppose you've heard about Orlov," she added.

"I—I'm afraid I haven't."

"Terribly sad," Protasova said, shaking her head. "It seems he went berserk when he and his brothers were out pursuing the peasants, started raving and slashing at everyone with his sabre. They had to restrain him—he was bound hand and foot, in fact. His brother Alexis is taking care of him. Gregory's at Alexis's house, and one hears they had to remove all the furniture from his room and pad the walls to keep him from doing harm to himself."

"I'm very sorry," I said quietly.

"Two doctors are in constant attendance, and his chances of recovery are still in doubt. They've been giving him drugs to calm him down—at least he no longer believes he's the Imperial Eagle."

Several people came over to speak to me then, and I was forced to put on a polite social front. The information about Gregory didn't surprise me, nor did it distress me. I was pleased to know he was being cared for, of course, but his fate no longer concerned me. I chatted and answered inane questions and said yes, Mr. Bond was indeed a hero, and when the hero himself eventually came over to lead me away I gave him a look that should have turned him to stone.

"Something wrong?" he inquired.

"We'll discuss it later," I promised.

"Quite a place, this," he said. "I've never seen so many crystal chandeliers, so much pink marble and gold leaf, but you know what?"

"What?"

"I'd rather be in our hut in the wilderness, in front of the fire. What about you?"

I didn't deign to answer, and Jeremy grinned his endearing grin and gave my arm a squeeze. Everyone was looking at us, so I didn't slap his face, nor did I kick his shin. I longed to do both. He knew I was aggravated and knew the reason why and seemed to find it amusing, which didn't help his cause one bit. I saw the way the women were looking at him, not a one of them who didn't long to steal him away from me. He was aware of those looks, too, and he swaggered even more in his outlandish uniform and gold-lined cape.

A hush fell over the crowd as the gilded white double doors at the end of the room opened and two handsome guards in full uniform stepped through, holding the doors back as the Empress of All the Russias made her dramatic, belated entrance. Catherine paused in the doorway for a moment, glancing about the room with dark, thoughtful eyes. She was sumptuously attired in a pink velvet gown appliquéd with silver flowers, the wide skirt parting in front to display the cloth-of-silver underskirt. Her powdered hair was wonderfully arranged in a high pompadour and ringlets, à la Marie Antoinette, a stunning diamond clasp holding one white and two pale pink plumes in place, and diamonds shimmered at her ears and throat as well. The short, rather dumpy woman with round cheeks, long nose and plump pink mouth had never looked more majestic, those dark eyes rather pensive tonight.

When she saw Jeremy and me, Catherine smiled warmly and started toward us, casually acknowledging the bows and curtseys along the way. Jeremy executed a deep, perfect bow when she reached us, and I curtseyed, brocade rustling softly. Catherine nodded and, momentarily ignoring Jeremy, took my hands in hers, squeezing them gently.

"It's nice to see you again, my dear," she said. "I'm very pleased you could come."

"I'm honored to be here, Your Majesty."

"You look radiant," she told me. "I see the gown was ready in time. It's most becoming."

"I want to thank you for it, for the diamonds as well. It is so—very kind and generous of you."

"A small token of our appreciation," Catherine replied. "I didn't want you to leave Russia without a little memento. I see my selection was appropriate—the diamonds enhance your remarkable beauty, my dear."

Her manner was friendly, her eyes full of warmth, but that kinship I had felt when we had tea at the Hermitage was missing. Though he was away, Potemkin was still between us. She smiled and turned to Jeremy and said he looked very striking in his uniform and asked if he found this reception tedious and dull, man of action that he was. Ever the gallant, Jeremy replied that no reception arranged by Her Majesty could possibly be dull, that her gracious presence would immediately enliven any function, tedious or no. Catherine's response to all this charm was purely female. She beamed, looked ready to melt with pleasure. He had a way with women. Indeed he did.

Catherine moved on to greet her other guests, and the English ambassador and his wife came over to talk with us. The ambassador informed Jeremy that, singlehandedly, he had improved diplomatic relations between Russia and England tenfold, that England owed him a huge debt of gratitude. Jeremy said it was nothing at all. Sir Reginald Lloyd joined us a little later and told me that he was to take me in to dinner tonight and considered it an honor. This was news to me, but I smiled and said *I* was honored to be going in with such a handsome and distinguished gentleman.

Jeremy, of course, went in with Catherine when we adjourned to the large gold and ivory and pale pink dining room with its painted ceiling and shimmering chandeliers. She held on to his arm, smiling as he told an amusing anecdote. They occupied a table with the British ambassador and his wife and two court officials, while I dined at the next table with Sir Reginald, Protasova and six others. I tried my best to enjoy the meal, talking about Lucie and Bryan with Sir Reginald, listening to Protasova's witty and deliciously risqué accounts of court intrigue, primarily amorous, but it seemed interminable nevertheless.

Jeremy was having a marvelous time, holding everyone at his table spellbound with accounts of his rowdy adventures in America—I caught a few words now and then. Catherine was clearly enchanted, as vivacious as a girl as she smiled and nodded and encouraged him to tell more. I shouldn't be irritated, I told myself. He was entitled to his hour in the sun. He was indeed a hero, and he had proved his love for me a thousand times over. Still, I toyed with my food and drank far too much wine, longing to leave. Sensing my mood, Sir Reginald told me again what a boon Jeremy had been for English diplomatic relations with Russia and added that his ideas on military defense had pleased and stimulated Catherine's generals. So he *had* spent a great deal of time with them after all, I thought, ashamed at myself for entertaining suspicions.

As Protasova had observed, he would be all mine tomorrow, and when after dinner the formal ceremony was held and Catherine presented him with his medal, I was filled with pride and found it difficult to hold back my tears. He was grave and dignified, standing at attention as the Empress placed the ribbon around his neck, and his words of thanks were brief. He had done no more than any Englishman would have done, he said, and while he was quite grateful to the Empress and to Russia, he felt the medal really belonged to Miss Marietta Danver, whose heroism far outweighed his own and who was responsible for his being in Russia in the first place.

Almost as large as a saucer and oval in shape, the medal hanging around his neck on a dark blue velvet ribbon was completely covered with jewels, the Imperial Eagle in diamonds against a red and blue background, one side rubies, the other sapphires, mounted on and framed in silver. It had been created by the court jeweler especially for Jeremy and must have cost a fortune. Catherine took his hand and smiled and said her country would be eternally grateful to him, and then one of her generals said a few words and the English ambassador spoke and all the while Jeremy stood there tall and solemn and wonderfully handsome, looking every inch the hero.

And afterward, when everyone crowded around him to express their congratulations, he nimbly eluded them and came over to where I was standing. Smiling a tender smile, love in his eyes, he took my hands in his and told me the medal really did belong to me and he intended to hang it around my neck immediately. To keep from dissolving into tears and making a complete fool of myself I tartly informed him that it was much too garish for my taste and would clash with my gown. He said I could be an awful bitch at times and I said he was right and he grinned and gave me a tight, affectionate hug right there in front of everyone.

"Let's leave, love," he said. "I can hardly wait to get you all to myself."

"We can't leave until the Empress does, it would be a shocking breach of protocol. Besides, you're the guest of honor."

"Protocol be damned. Come."

He led me over to Catherine and she smiled warmly and said she hoped the medal would always remind him of his sojourn in Russia and added that she was still sorry he hadn't let her make him a count. Jeremy told her that the medal would remind him not only of Russia but of its gracious and beautiful Empress as well, and the compliment made her glow. Lowering her heavy lids, she gave him a seductive look, tapped his arm playfully, and told him he was absolutely outrageous and it was a good thing he was leaving Russia at once, lest she lose her heart completely.

"You have a prize here, my dear," she said, turning to me. "Hold on to him."

"I intend to," I said.

"I realize it's a shocking breach of protocol," Jeremy began, "but, as you know, we have a ship to board and—" He let the sentence dangle, smiling an apologetic smile.

"It's a long drive to Kronstadt," Catherine said, "and, it's after three. You must leave at once, of course."

And, breaching protocol herself, Catherine left her other guests and accompanied us back to the front entrance, the perfect hostess, Empress or no. A footman brought my cloak. Another hurried out to see that our carriage was brought round. Jeremy slipped the gorgeous mink-lined cream brocade around my shoulders, and the three of us chatted lightly until the footman returned. Catherine gave Jeremy her hand. He lifted it to his lips and told her he would always remember her many kindnesses. Catherine smiled and wished him well and then turned to me, her dark blue eyes full of warmth and, I thought, rather sad.

"I shall think of you fondly, my dear," she told me. "Be happy in your new life."

I made a deep curtsey, and we took our leave, moving down the wide white marble steps by the light of the torches still held aloft by the footmen stationed on either side. Jeremy helped me into the elegant gold and white carriage and, a few moments later, we were on our way, both of us weary and lost in thought. We passed the outskirts of the city and had almost reached Peterhof before Jeremy sighed deeply and said it had been quite an evening, hadn't it. I agreed and told him he had been a credit to his country.

"Hated every minute of it," he confided. "All of those people flocking around me, babbling in French. I just wanted to be with you, love, wanted to take those diamonds out of your hair and take that incredibly lovely gown off your body and let you know how much I've missed you these past weeks."

"You missed me?" I inquired.

"Every single minute," he swore.

I didn't necessarily believe him, but it was sweet of him to say so just the same. Gazing at him sitting across from me in the soft haze of moonlight, a crooked grin on his lips,

I felt a delicious, amorous glow spreading inside and thought how pleasant it was going to be to have him take the diamonds out of my hair and the gown off my body.

The moonlight had faded when we reached Kronstadt, the sky a light pearl gray with a faint suggestion of gold in the east. Despite the early hour the magnificent harbor was bustling with activity, cargo being loaded and unloaded by the light of lanterns that glowed like pale fireflies, dozens of men rushing purposefully about, sailors from the naval base hurrying to their ship for early morning maneuvers. Our ship was an impressive vessel, sails unfurling as crew scurried about in the riggings. The captain himself led us up the gangplank, told us our trunks were on board and said he was most honored to be carrying such distinguished passengers. Catherine had made all the arrangements for our journey, I recalled, so it wasn't surprising he was so attentive and polite.

Even so, I was amazed at our quarters. Both bedroom and stateroom were commodious, the walls paneled in ivory white with gold leaf patterns, lovely carpets spread over the rich teakwood floors. Candles glowed softly in glass globes dripping crystal pendants. A bottle of champagne nestled in ice in a silver bucket on a table in the stateroom. Beside it stood two tall crystal glasses, and there was also a large silver dish of caviar and a silver tray piled high with thin slivers of toast, chopped boiled eggs and onion and an assortment of tempting delicacies. Stepping over to the bedroom door, I gazed at the large, lovely bed with its pale golden satin counterpane and soft mink spread of the same pale hue.

Jeremy came up behind me and curled an arm around my waist, looking over my shoulder at the bed. I could feel his warmth and strength as he pulled me close, resting his cheek against mine.

"Perfect accommodations," he murmured, looking at the bed. "This ship's taking us all the way to New Orleans, incidentally."

That surprised me. I had naturally assumed we would be changing ships at least twice.

"Catherine arranged it," he said. "She wanted to be sure we would travel in style. We'll be stopping in Copenhagen and picking up more passengers in Marseilles, but it was all arranged for our convenience. She's an extremely thoughtful woman."

"She certainly is," I said.

Oh, yes. Catherine was thoughtful and Catherine was considerate. Catherine had gone to an incredible amount of trouble and expense. Catherine had done this, done that—and the two of them had been extremely chummy tonight, so very relaxed in each other's company. I could feel my temper rising, feel a flush coloring my cheeks. He rubbed his cheek against mine, his arm tightening around my waist.

"Catherine's very generous," I remarked.

"It's her nature," he said.

I pulled away from him and whirled around. *"Too* bloody generous," I informed him.

His vivid blue eyes were utterly guileless. "Whatever do you mean?" he asked.

"She's *al*ways generous to the men she fancies. You slept with her, didn't you? Don't you dare lie to me!"

He hesitated for a moment and then decided he had best come clean. "Why do you think she gave me the medal?"

"You bastard!"

"I did it for England, love."

"You son of a bitch!"

"I couldn't *help* it, Marietta," he protested. "When the Empress of Russia invites a chap to pop into bed with her, he can hardly tell her he's got a headache. It was a question of National Honor."

I glared at him and he looked at me with beseeching eyes and I shoved him out of the way and stormed past him and out of the cabin, surprised to find I wasn't nearly as angry as I pretended to be. I went up on deck and heard the sails crackling overhead and felt the gentle rocking motion and realized that we were already under way. I moved over to the railing and rested my hands on the smooth teakwood. The sun was up. The sky was a soft white. Silvery reflections shimmered on the blue-gray water. The majestic harbor of Kronstadt grew smaller and smaller, ships and white marble buildings looking like playthings in the distance.

A cool breeze stroked my bare arms, and I sighed, wrapping the cloak closer, the pale champagne mink collar touching my cheek. Of course he had slept with her. He could hardly have done otherwise, and I really couldn't blame Catherine, either. He was a fascinating, devilishly handsome man, and Catherine of Russia was not to be judged like other women. I was wearing a fortune in diamonds she had given to me, and I wondered if that wasn't perhaps her way of making amends to me for her little indiscretion. No, it was impossible to be angry with her—or with Jeremy either, for that matter. He was a complete rogue, but I had always known it, and that was one of the reasons I loved him.

"Feeling better?" he inquired.

I turned. Lost in thought, I hadn't heard him approaching. He had taken off his uniform and now he was wearing tall black boots and black breeches and a white lawn shirt and—yes, the same black sheepskin coat and hat, thoroughly cleaned and refurbished. The red scarf was tied around his neck. A smile was on his lips. How could one possibly resist him? I gave him a cool look and turned back around to gaze at the receding harbor.

"I'm sorry, love," he said.

"And well you should be."

"It'll never happen again," he promised.

"You're bloody right it won't! You won't have the opportunity."

"I'm forgiven?"

"I'm not sure," I said.

He moved behind me and wrapped both his arms around my waist and drew me up against him and kissed the side of my neck and kissed my earlobe and I relaxed, making no effort to pull away. His arms held me close. Kronstadt was a mere speck on the horizon now, shrouded in mist. I sighed, glad to be seeing the last of Russia.

"There's champagne below," he murmured.

"I know."

"Caviar, too. It'd be a shame to let it go to waste."

"A shame," I agreed.

"There's a glorious bed as well," he added. "Never seen a bed quite so inviting."

He took hold of my arms and turned me around and I looked into his eyes. They were a dark, smoldering blue now, and I felt that marvelous glow beginning to spread through me again, a delicious languor in my limbs. I reached up to caress his lean cheek with my fingertips.

"We have a long journey ahead of us, love," he purred huskily. "Weeks and weeks. What are we going to *do* with all that time?"

"I imagine we'll think of something," I said.